Praise for Stephen Leather's bestsellers . . .

"Stephen Leather should be nestling in your bookshelves alongside Frederick Forsyth and Jack Higgins . . . authentic . . . tersely written . . . exciting stuff with plenty of heart palpitating action gingered up by mystery and intrigue . . . Leather is an intelligent thriller writer" *Daily Mail* (The Tunnel Rats)

"Very complicated. Fun"
Daily Telegraph (Hungry Ghost)

"Masterful plotting . . . rapid-fire prose"
Sunday Express (The Double Tap)

"The book has all the ingredients for a successful blockbuster" *Sunday Telegraph* (The Vets)

Also by Stephen Leather

Pay Off
The Fireman
The Vets
Hungry Ghost
The Long Shot
The Birthday Girl
The Double Tap
The Solitary Man
The Bombmaker

The Chinaman
The Tunnel Rats

Stephen Leather

CORONET BOOKS
Hodder & Stoughton

About the Author

Stephen Leather was a journalist for more than ten years on newspapers such as *The Times* and the *Daily Mail* in London and the *South China Morning Post* in Hong Kong. Before that he was employed as a biochemist for ICI, shovelled limestone in a quarry, worked as a baker, a petrol pump attendant, a barman, and worked for the Inland Revenue. He began writing full-time in 1992. His bestsellers have been translated into more than ten languages. He has also written for television shows such as The Bill, London's Burning and The Knock.

THE CHINAMAN

For Nuala

They made an odd couple as they walked together through the store, the girl and the old woman. The girl was beautiful, quite, quite beautiful. Her sleek black hair hung dead straight down to the middle of her back and it rippled like an oily tide as she wandered through the racks of dresses and blouses. She was tall and slim and wore tight green cord trousers and cowboy boots and a brown leather bomber jacket with the collar turned up. She moved like a model, smoothly and controlled, as if used to being watched. The men that followed her with their eyes had no way of knowing where she came from other than that she was Oriental. She could have been Thai or Chinese or Korean but whatever she was, she was beautiful and that was all they cared about. Her cheekbones were high and well defined and her skin was the colour of milky tea and her eyes were wide and oval and she had a mouth that seemed to be in a perpetual pout. Every now and then something would catch her eye and she would take a dress or a blouse off its rack and hold it up and then shrug, not satisfied, before replacing it. Her hands were long and elegant and the nails were carefully painted with deep red varnish.

By the girl's side walked a gnarled old woman, a head shorter and an age older. Her face was wrinkled and pock-marked like chamois leather that had been left for too long in the sun. Her hair was grey and dull and cropped close to her head and her eyes were blank and uninterested in what was going on around her. When the girl asked her opinion on an item of clothing she would barely look at it before shaking her head and then she'd drop her gaze and concentrate on the floor. She wore a thick cloth coat and a faded scarf and she kept her hands thrust deep into her pockets despite the warmth of the store.

It was a Saturday in January and the weather outside was bitterly cold, piles of dirty slush squashed up against the kerb and wisps of white vapour feathering from the mouths of passers-by. The girl looked over the top of a rack of imitation fur coats topped with a sign that promised thirty per cent off, and through the streaked window. She shivered and didn't know why. She'd lived in London for as long as she could remember, and unlike her mother she was well used to the British climate. It was as if someone had walked over her grave, or the grave of her ancestors.

She took one of the coats and held it against herself. A middle-aged man in a fawn trench coat waiting outside the changing rooms with a carrier bag full of packages looked at her and smiled and nodded his approval. She ignored him and studied the coat. The old woman snorted and walked off. The girl looked at the price tag but even with the sale discount she realised she couldn't afford it.

She looked through the large glass window again at the bustling crowds fighting to get into the department store across the road. She wanted to join them and go hunting for bargains but she could see that the old woman was tired and impatient to go home and they had an hour's travelling ahead of them. She put the coat back on the rack.

A large black and red motorcycle threaded its way through the traffic and parked on the double yellow lines in front of the main entrance to the store. It was brand new and gleaming apart from the tyres which were crusted with ice. On the back carrier box was the name of a courier firm. She watched the rider dismount like a cowboy getting off a horse. He was dressed in black leather with a white wrap-around helmet and a tinted visor. There was a walkie-talkie in a leather case hanging from a belt around his waist and a black receiver clipped to his left shoulder. The rider switched on his hazard warning lights and the amber flashing was reflected on the wet road. He looked up and down the pavement as if checking for traffic wardens and then turned his back on the bike and crossed the road towards the boutique. He stepped to one side to let a trio of giggling schoolgirls leave the shop and then came in. As he passed the girl he looked at her, up and down, and she turned to watch him go, his leathers squeaking with every step. The rider was empty handed so the girl assumed he was there to collect something, but he continued to move through the shoppers, passed the pay counter and then he pushed open the doors at the other side of the shop and went out into the street.

The girl frowned and turned back to the window. The bike's lights were still flashing. Her frown deepened and at that moment the twenty-five pounds of Semtex explosive in the back carrier box exploded in a flash of blinding white light, blowing in the window and striking her with thousands of glass daggers. At the last moment she tried to turn towards her mother, to shield her, but they died together in the hail of glass.

The Press Association news desk received the call as the first ambulance arrived at the department store, blue light flashing and siren whining. The reporter who took the call later told the police that the voice was Irish and had given a codeword that the police identified as genuine; the tip-off was not a hoax. The voice was that of a man, he couldn't tell if he was young or old, and the caller said that a bomb had just gone off in Knightsbridge and that the Provisional Irish Republican Army claimed responsibility for it. The reporter hadn't recorded the call, he was new on the job and no one had told him that he was supposed to. The line went dead and he took his notebook over to the news editor who told him to check with the police that there had indeed been an explosion and three minutes later the story went out over the wires as a flash – IRA BOMB EXPLODES OUTSIDE LONDON STORE – AT LEAST FIVE DEAD.

By the time it appeared on the screen of the news editor of the *Sunday World* he'd already had a phone call from a member of the public keen to earn a tip-off fee. He'd assigned two reporters to start phoning the police and their Sinn Fein contacts and was trying to track down their Belfast stringers.

It was 5.30 p.m., the crossing over point when the day shift began to drift off to the pub and the night reporters were arriving. The picture desk had sent two freelances and a staffer to the scene, but Knightsbridge was at least half an hour's drive away from the paper's Docklands offices.

More information was trickling over the wires on PA and Reuters and the death toll kept climbing with each snatch of copy.

"Jesus, now they're saying twelve dead," said Jon Simpson, the news editor. Behind him stood the chief sub and the editor, reading over his shoulder.

"Splash?" said the chief sub, knowing the answer would be yes. The front page lead at the afternoon conference had been a sixties pop star's drug problem.

"We'll have to pull our fingers out if we're going to make the first edition," said the editor. "We'll take the whole of page one, two and three, let me see the pics first. Hold the MP story until next week and hack back the food safety feature. Hang on, no, drop it altogether. And we'll save the splash until next week as well, it's exclusive." The chief sub scurried back to his terminal to redraw his page plans, shouting to the picture editor to send over everything he had.

"You've got two hours until the first edition, Jon. Get everybody on it." The editor wandered over to the picture desk while Simpson picked up the phone.

"Where's Woody?" Simpson yelled at his deputy who was busy scrolling through the PA wire.

"Where do you think?" he shouted back, raising his eyebrows.

"Drunken pig," said Simpson and rang the King's Head, a short stagger away from the office.

As the phone trilled behind the bar, Ian Wood was downing his second double Bells and trying to look down the front of the barmaid's blouse. She saw what he was up to and flicked her towel at him and laughed. "Don't let Sandy catch you doing that," she scolded and he grinned.

"Your husband's too good a guv'nor to go slapping the customers around," he said, finishing his whisky.

"Another?" she said as she picked up the phone. She listened and then mouthed silently "Are you in?"

"Who's asking?" he mouthed back.

4

"The office," she replied, and he realised they looked like a couple of goldfish gasping for breath. He nodded and took the phone off her. She picked his glass up and refilled it.

"Woody, are you on for a double shift?" asked Simpson.

Woody looked at the double measure of whisky in his glass and licked his lips but hesitated for only a second before he told Simpson he'd do it. Woody was a freelance and he needed the money. If he'd been staff he'd have told the news editor where to get off, but it had been a long time since anyone had given Ian Wood a staff job.

"What's up?" he asked.

"IRA bomb. A big one. Knightsbridge."

"Christ. How many dead?"

"They're saying twelve now, no make that thirteen, but they're still counting. Get out there and get the colour. Link up with the monkeys while you're there, they'll need their captions written." Woody heard Simpson call out for the names of the photographers. "Dave Wilkins is the staffer, find him," he said.

"I'm on my way," said Woody and hung up.

He took the glass off the bar and swallowed it down in one.

"You off, Woody?" said the barmaid, surprised.

"Duty calls, darling," he said. "Can you cash me a cheque?"

"Fifty?" she asked.

"Fifty is magic. You're a life-saver. If ever that husband of yours . . ."

She waved him away and counted out the notes as Woody handed over the cheque.

"See you later," he said, and walked down the dimly lit corridor and out of the pub door into the street. He turned right and walked the short distance to The Highway and hailed a cab heading towards the City.

The driver looked over his shoulder when Woody told him where he wanted to go. "We'll never get near the place, mate," he said. "There's a bomb gone off."

"Yeah I know," said Woody. "I'm a reporter."

"OK," said the cabbie and sped off down the road. "Which paper d'yer work for then?"

"*Sunday World*," replied Woody.

"Yeah?" said the cabbie. "What happened? Page Three girl killed was she?" His deep-throated laughter echoed around the cab.

They hit unmoving traffic long before they reached Knightsbridge and though the cabbie tried to find a way through the side-streets they were soon helplessly locked in.

"Best I can do," said the driver apologetically, his professional pride wounded.

"No sweat," said Woody, getting out. He handed a ten-pound note through the window. "I'll walk from here. Call it a tenner and give me a receipt, please."

"Clamping down on expenses, are they?"

"Yeah, tell me about it."

The cabbie signed a receipt and handed it to Woody. Then as an afterthought he ripped off a few blank receipts from his pad. "Here," he said, "fill these in yourself."

"You're a prince," said Woody, and put them gratefully into his raincoat pocket.

He began to jog slowly towards the sound of sirens, his feet slapping on the wet pavement and his raincoat flapping behind him. Despite the cold he soon worked up a sweat. Ian Wood was not a fit man. He was slightly overweight but that wasn't the problem, he was out of condition because he never took any exercise, hadn't since his schooldays.

The police had cordoned off the area around the store and a burly sergeant blocked his way when he tried to duck under the barrier. He fished out his yellow plastic Metropolitan Police Press card and after the copper had scrutinised it he was waved through.

It was a scene from hell. Wrecked cars were strewn across the road, still smoking and hissing. There was an assortment of emergency vehicles, all with their doors open, radios crackling and lights flashing. There were two fire engines though their hoses were still in place, unused. There had obviously been a number of small fires burning but the firemen had used extinguishers to put them out. There were half a dozen ambulances, and as Woody walked towards the police top brass one of them pulled away and its siren kicked into life.

Something squelched under Woody's shoe and he looked down. He was standing on a hand. It was a small girl's hand, the skin white and unlined, the nails bitten to the quick. The hand was attached to a forearm but that was all, it ended in a ragged, bloody mess at the point where there should have been an elbow. Woody's stomach heaved and he pulled his foot away with a jerk, a look of horror on his face.

He backed away and bumped into a policeman wearing dark-blue overalls, black Wellington boots and thick, black rubber gloves that covered most of his arms. The policeman picked up the dismembered arm and dropped it into a plastic bag he was carrying. As he straightened up, Woody saw that the man's face was covered with a white surgical mask and then he saw the blonde wavy hair and realised it wasn't a man at all, but a woman in her twenties. There were tears streaming down her face. She turned away from him, walked a few steps and bent down again. This time she picked up a shoe with a shattered bone sticking out of a green sock. Woody shuddered. There were dozens of policemen dressed in the same overalls and following the girl's grisly example. Woody realised with a jolt why the body count hadn't been finalised. It was at least an hour since the bomb had gone off and they were still picking up the pieces. Ambulancemen were ferrying bodies on stretchers at the run, some of the victims moaning or screaming, others still, their faces covered with blankets. The policemen in their blood-spotted overalls worked at a slower pace, knowing that it was more important to be thorough than fast. They were not in the business of saving lives, simply collecting evidence.

Woody looked around, surveying the damage. All the windows of the store had been blown in, as had those in the shops opposite, and the stonework was pitted and blackened. Lying half on and half off the pavement was the twisted frame of a motorcycle, the back a mass of scorched and melted metal. It was being examined by two middle-aged men in white overalls.

Shocked shoppers and staff were still filing out of the store, urged on by uniformed constables in yellow reflective jackets, as an inspector shouted through a megaphone that there could be another bomb in the vicinity and would the crowds please keep back. Woody knew that he was just saying that to keep the ghouls away. Two bombs would have meant double the risk for the bombers planting the devices, and the IRA never bothered using two devices against civilian targets, only against the security forces in Northern Ireland. Besides, if there was any chance of a second device they'd keep the ambulancemen back while the Bomb Disposal Squad gave the place a thorough going over.

There were a handful of sniffer dogs and their handlers checking the street, and Woody could see more dogs inside the store, noses down and tails wagging, happy to be working. One of the dogs in the street, a long-haired Retriever, lunged forward and seized something in its jaws. Its handler yelled and kicked its flanks and the dog dropped whatever it had been holding. It was an arm. The handler yanked his dog away, cursing. The dog cowered, all the time keeping its eyes on the prize.

Woody went over to the Chief Superintendent and two inspectors who were surrounded by a pack of reporters and photographers. He recognised many of the faces and he knew that all the tabloids and heavies would be represented. If not, some news editor would be getting his backside soundly kicked. The older hacks were taking shorthand notes in small notebooks while the younger ones thrust mini tape-recorders in front of the police. Behind the pack were two television crews trying in vain to get a clear shot. He heard the click-whirr of a motor-drive and he turned to see Dave Wilkins aiming his Nikon at a torso lying in the gutter.

"They won't use it," Woody told him. "Too gory."

"So?" said the photographer.

Woody listened to the Chief Superintendent explaining what he thought had happened. A bomb in the back of a motorcycle, no warning, the streets crowded and the stores packed. No idea yet how many had been killed. Fifteen at least. Yes, almost certainly linked to the recent wave of London bombings, four so far. Correction, five including this one. Yes, the IRA had claimed responsibility.

"And that, gentlemen," he said with the wave of a gloved

hand, "is all that I can tell you right now. Would you please all move back behind the barriers and let my men get on with their work. We'll be having a full press conference at the Yard later tonight." He politely pushed his way through the journalists, and they moved aside to let him go, knowing that the officer had said all he was going to say. There was no point in antagonising him. Besides, they all had their own police contacts who would be a hell of a lot more forthcoming.

Woody went over to the shops facing the department store, noting down the names on the signs. His feet crunched on broken glass and he stepped to one side to let two ambulancemen with a stretcher out of a boutique. They were carrying a girl, her leather jacket and green cords shredded and ripped and dripping with blood. He knew she was a girl because of her long black hair. There was nothing left of her face, just strips of flesh hanging off white bone. Woody felt his stomach heave again. He'd been at accident scenes before, far too many to remember, but he'd never seen such carnage. The area reeked of death, of blood and burning and scorched meat. He fought to keep his emotions under control, knowing that he had work to do. It was harder for the reporters he thought bitterly. The monkeys had it easy. They looked at everything through the camera lens and that insulated them from the reality of it. But reporters had to be there and experience it before they could write about it, they had to open themselves to the horror, the grief and the pain. Sometimes it was almost too much to bear. Almost.

He stood by one of the ambulances and got some snatched quotes from a couple of harassed stretcher-bearers and then he followed a woman in a fur coat that he'd seen leaving the store, ducked under the barrier and caught up with her. Her eyewitness account was harrowing and she had no qualms about giving her name and address. Her eyes were glassy and Woody knew she was in a state of shock and he held her arm gently as he spoke to her and then gestured over at Wilkins, standing to one side so that he could get a head-and-shoulders shot of her.

"Got all you want?" Woody asked the photographer.

"Yeah," said Wilkins. "I'll head back and leave the free-lancers to get the rest. You coming?"

"No, I'll ring the story in, it'll save time. I'll see you back there."

Woody half-heartedly looked for a call box, but knew that he stood little chance in Knightsbridge. He walked to a small Italian bistro and went inside.

"Can I use the phone?" he asked a waiter. The waiter began to protest in fractured English so Woody took out his wallet and gave him ten pounds. The protests evaporated and he was soon through to the office and dictating to a copytaker straight from his notebook. Twenty-five paragraphs, and he knew it was good stuff. When he'd finished he asked the copytaker to transfer him to the news desk and he checked that everything was OK with Simpson.

"Got it here, Woody," he said. "Great read."

"OK, I'm going back to see what else I can get. I'll call you." He hung up before Simpson could order him back to base. On the way out he got a receipt from the waiter.

There was a pub down the road and Woody gratefully walked up to the bar and ordered a double Bells. It was only when the whisky slopped around the tumbler that he realised how badly his hands were shaking.

The intercom buzzed, catching them all by surprise, even though they were waiting for him. There were three of them in the flat, drinking tea and watching television. They were casually dressed – baggy pullovers, faded jeans and grubby training shoes – and looked like sociology students stuck with nothing to do between lectures. One of the men was smoking and on the floor beside his easy chair was a circular crystal ashtray overflowing with cigarette butts. He leant over and stubbed out the one in his hand, pushed himself up and walked into the hall. On the wall by the door was a telephone with a small black and white television screen; he pressed a square plastic button and it flickered into life.

"Welcome back," he said to the figure waiting down below and pressed a second button, the one that opened the entrance door four floors below. As he waited for him to come up in the lift he went back into the lounge. "It's him," he said, but they knew it would be because no one else knew they were there and if they did they wouldn't be coming in through the front door but through the window with stun grenades and machine guns.

There was an American comedy show on the television and canned laughter filled the room. Through the floor-to-ceiling sliding windows at the end of the lounge the man saw a tug struggle along the Thames, hauling an ungainly barge behind it.

He went back into the hall and opened the door as the lift jolted to a halt. The man who stepped out of the lift was in his early twenties, wearing grey flannel trousers and a blue blazer over a white polo neck sweater. He had dark-brown curly hair and black eyes and was grinning widely. "Did you see it?" he asked eagerly, before the other man even had a chance to close the door. He punched the air with his fist. "Did you bloody well see it?"

"Calm down, O'Reilly," said the man who'd let him in.

O'Reilly turned towards him, his cheeks flaring red. "Calm down?" he said. "Christ, man, you should have been there. You should have seen me. It was fan-bloody-tastic." He turned back to look at the television set. "Has it been on yet? How many did we get?"

"Fifteen so far," said the man sitting on the leather Chesterfield directly opposite the pseudo-antique video cabinet on which the television stood. "You did well, O'Reilly." He was the oldest of the group but even he had barely turned thirty. Although he had the broadest Irish accent he had Nordic blond hair and piercing blue eyes and fair skin. His name was also far removed from his Irish origins but Denis Fisher was Belfast-born and he'd killed many times for the Cause. "What about the helmet and the leathers?" he asked O'Reilly.

"In the boot of the car. Just like you said. It was so easy."

"Not easy," said Fisher. "Well planned."

"Whatever," said O'Reilly. "I deserve a drink." He went into the white-and-blue-tiled kitchen and opened the fridge. "Anyone else want anything?" he called, but they all declined. O'Reilly took out a cold can of Carlsberg and opened it as he walked back into the lounge. He pulled one of the wooden chairs out from under the oval dining-table and sat astride it, resting his forearms on its back.

"What next?" he asked, grinning.

"Yes," said the man who'd opened the door and who was now sitting on a flowery print sofa by a tall wooden bookcase. His name was McCormick. "What do we do next?"

Fisher smiled. "You're so bloody impatient," he laughed. He turned to look at the occupant of the chair by the window, the one they called The Bombmaker. "That depends on what MacDermott here comes up with." The Bombmaker grinned.

The comedy show was interrupted for a news flash and a sombre man with movie-star looks reported that sixteen people had died in a bomb explosion and that the Provisional IRA had claimed responsibility. They then cut to a reporter in a white raincoat standing under a streetlamp in Knightsbridge, who said that police now believed that the bomb had been in the back carrier of a motorcycle and that it had been detonated by a timing device.

O'Reilly punched the air again, and The Bombmaker's grin widened.

The police car drove slowly down Clapham Road. Constable Simon Edgington's left hand was aching from the constant gear changing and he cursed the bumper-to-bumper traffic under his breath. It wasn't even worth switching the siren on because there wasn't enough room for the cars and buses to pull to the side.

"It's getting worse," he groaned.

"Sorry?" said his partner, a blonde WPC called Susan Griffin who had joined the Met on the graduate entry scheme. One of the high-flyers, a sergeant had told Edgington, closely followed by a warning not to try anything on because she'd reported the last constable whose hand had accidentally slipped on to her thigh during a hasty gear change.

"The traffic," he said. "We're going to be all night at this rate."

She looked down at the sheaf of papers on her black clipboard. "This is the last one," she said. "Chinese or something. God, I don't think I can pronounce their names. Noog-yen Guan Fong and Noog-yen Coy Trin. Does that sound right?" The names on the sheet were written as Nguyen Xuan Phoung and Nguyen Kieu Trinh.

He laughed. "Sounds like a disease," he said.

She gave him a frosty look. "It's not really a laughing matter is it, Simon?"

Edgington flushed. Griffin was a year younger than him but she acted as if she already had her sergeant's stripes. But his embarrassment came from the fact that he knew she was right, it wasn't the sort of thing to joke about. He wanted to tell her that he was just nervous, that he was trying to relieve the tension that was knotting up his stomach, and that he'd never thought when he signed up three years earlier that he'd have to knock on the doors of complete strangers and tell them that their nearest and dearest had been scattered all over Knightsbridge by a terrorist bomb. He wanted to explain but knew he'd sound like a wimp so he concentrated on driving.

They'd been given three addresses, all south of the river. The first had been a middle-aged couple in Lambeth, a schoolteacher and his wife. Their teenage son had been in the passenger seat of an old Mini that had been fifty feet or so from the motorcycle when the bomb had gone off. Several pieces of wire that had been wrapped around the explosive had burst through the windscreen and torn his face and throat apart. The couple had already seen a report of the bombing on the evening news and before Griffin had spoken the wife's legs had given way and her husband had had to help her to a chair in their cramped kitchen. Edgington had been quite happy to let his partner do the talking, he didn't think that he could have kept his voice steady. He'd joined the police to catch criminals, not to act as some kind of messenger of death. And she'd done it so bloody well, sat them both down, made them cups of sweet tea, phoned their daughter and arranged for her to come round and look after them. She'd sat with them on the sofa until the girl came and then left them to their grief. All the time Edgington had stood by the kitchen door, feeling useless, but Griffin hadn't mentioned it when they got back into the car.

The next call had been at a small flat in Stockwell. No relatives this time, but a boyfriend who burst into tears and hugged the WPC when she told him what had happened. They were going to get married, he'd sobbed. She was pregnant, he said. She held him until the tears stopped and sat him down and asked him if there was anyone she could call, a friend or a relative. Did she suffer, he asked. No, she lied. The sergeant had told them that the girl had died screaming on the pavement with both her legs blown off. "No, she didn't suffer," she said without hesitation.

He wiped his eyes with the back of his hand and she gave him a handkerchief while Edgington telephoned the boy's mother. She said she'd be around in fifteen minutes and Edgington and Griffin decided that he'd be OK on his own until then. They left him hunched over a mug of tea which he clasped tightly between his hands.

"It's coming up on the left," she said.

The traffic crept along and eventually they reached the turning.

"Number 62," she said before he asked.

He drove slowly, counting off the numbers. "Are you sure?" he asked.

She checked the computer print-out on the clipboard and nodded. "That's what it says here."

He stopped the car and they both looked at number 62. It was a Chinese take-away, with a huge window on which were printed gold and black Chinese letters and above it a sign that said "Double Happiness Take-Away". Through the window they could see two customers waiting in front of a chest-high counter.

"That's it," she said, opening her car door. Edgington

caught up with her as she reached the entrance and followed her in.

Behind the counter was an old Oriental man shouting through a serving hatch in a language neither of them could understand. He turned and placed two white plastic carrier bags full of cartons of Chinese food in front of one of the customers and took his money. There was a loud scream from the kitchen and the man stuck his head back through the hatch and shouted and waved his arm.

He came back to the counter and smiled up at Edgington and Griffin.

"What I get you?" he asked. He was a small man, his shoulders barely above the counter. His face was wrinkled but the skin wasn't slack, his cheekbones were clearly defined and there were no loose folds under the chin. It was hard to tell exactly how old he was, he could have been in his forties and had a rough life, or he could have been a well-preserved sixty-year-old. Griffin noticed how sad his eyes were. They were eyes that had seen a lot of suffering, she decided.

"Are you Mr Noog-yen?" she said, and he nodded quickly but corrected her pronunciation, saying his name as "New-yen". The single customer left at the counter stood openly watching and listening to the conversation. Edgington stared at him until the man's gaze faltered and he studied the menu pinned to the wall.

"Is there somewhere we can talk?" Griffin asked the old man.

"I very busy," he replied. "No staff. You come back later, maybe?" There was a thud from the hatch and he went over and picked up another carrier bag. He handed it to the customer. "Come again," he said.

"I'm afraid we have bad news for you," said Griffin. She looked at the clipboard again. God, she thought, how do you pronounce these names? "Mr Nguyen, do you know a Xuan Phoung or Kieu Trinh?" Both names started with Nguyen so she'd guessed that that was the family name and that everything that came after it were their given names.

The man frowned. Another customer came in and stood behind Edgington. Griffin tried pronouncing the names again but still nothing registered so she showed him the computer print-out and pointed to the two names.

He nodded, his eyes wary. "My wife," he said. "And my daughter."

"I'm afraid there has been an accident," said the WPC. "Is there somewhere we can talk?"

The man waved his hands impatiently. "What has happened?" he insisted.

"Mr Nguyen, please, it would be much better for you if we could sit down somewhere."

"No staff," he said. "My wife not in kitchen, so much work to do. What has happened?" He spoke each word carefully, as if stringing a sentence together was an effort, and he had a vaguely American accent. But he seemed to have no trouble in understanding what she was saying.

"Mr Nguyen, your wife and daughter are dead. I'm very sorry."

He looked stunned. His mouth dropped and his hands slid off the counter and down to his sides. He started to say something and then stopped and shook his head. Edgington turned to the customer and found himself apologising, but for the life of him he didn't know why. He felt his cheeks redden.

"Do you understand, Mr Nguyen?" asked Griffin.

"What happened?" said the old man.

"Is there somewhere we can talk?" she asked again. She didn't want to explain about the bomb while she was standing in a Chinese take-away.

"We can go back of shop," he said. He shouted through the hatch and as he opened a white-painted door a balding Oriental with sleeves rolled up around his elbows and a grease-stained apron came barrelling out. He ignored Nguyen and glared at the customer. "What you want?" he barked.

Nguyen led them down a tiled hallway, up a flight of wooden stairs and through a beaded curtain. Beyond was a small room with heavy brocade wallpaper and a faded red patterned carpet. The furniture was dark rosewood, a square table with carved feet and four straight-backed chairs with no cushions. On one wall was a small red and gold shrine in front of which a joss stick was smouldering, filling the air with sickly sweet perfume.

In a corner by a small window was a semi-circular table on which stood a group of framed photographs of Nguyen with an old woman and a young girl. Edgington walked over to the table and studied the pictures as Griffin sat down with the old man. Most of the pictures were of the girl, she was obviously the focus of the family. In the most recent photographs she looked to be in her mid-teens and she was absolutely gorgeous, long black hair and flawless features. She could have been a model. There were pictures of her in a school uniform and even in those she looked sexy. The old woman was obviously her mother, but there was little or no physical resemblance. The girl was tall and straight and the woman was small and stooped. The girl's skin was smooth and fresh and the woman's dark and wrinkled. The girl had eyes that were bright and sparkling while the woman's appeared lifeless. As he studied the photographs he heard Griffin explaining about the bomb. Edgington did the calculations in his head – if she'd had the child when she was twenty she'd be under forty, and even if she'd given birth at thirty the woman couldn't be much older than forty-eight and yet she looked much older. In one of the photographs, the biggest of the collection, the girl was sitting in a chair, her parents behind her. Nguyen was smiling proudly and had a protective hand on her shoulder. They looked more like her grandparents. Something else struck him. There were no pictures of her as a baby or a toddler. In none of the photographs was she any younger than seven or eight. Curious.

"Please," said the old man behind him and Edgington turned round to see him holding out his hands. "Please, the picture."

Edgington took over the big framed photograph and handed it to him. He didn't speak, he didn't know what to say.

The old man cradled the frame in his arms and then hugged it to his chest. There were no tears and he made no sound, but the intensity of his grief was painful to watch.

"Who did this to my family?" he asked eventually.

"The IRA," said Edgington. They were the first words he'd spoken in the room and his voice sounded thick with emotion. He cleared his throat and Griffin looked up, surprised that he'd spoken. "The IRA have claimed responsibility," he said.

"IRA," said Nguyen, saying each letter slowly as if hearing them for the first time. "What is IRA?"

Edgington looked at Griffin and she raised her eyebrows. Was he serious? He sat down next to the old man.

"Terrorists," he said quietly.

"What do they want, these terrorists?"

Edgington was stumped for an answer and he looked helplessly at Griffin. She shook her head, knowing that what the old man needed was sympathy and a sedative, not a political discussion. The man turned to her. "What do they want?" he asked her.

"They want British troops out of Ireland," she said reluctantly.

"How does killing my family do that?" he asked.

She shrugged. "Is there someone I can get to come and take care of you?" she asked. "Do any of your family live nearby?"

"I have no family," he said quietly. "Now I have no family. I am alone. These IRA, will you catch them?"

"Yes," she said, looking him in the eye.

"And will they be punished?"

"Yes," she repeated. Lying was coming easily to her today.

"Good," said the old man. He nodded as if satisfied.

The second edition was coming off the presses when Woody finally got back to the office. He slumped in his chair still wearing his raincoat. He'd spilled something down the front of it and when he dropped his head on his chest he could smell whisky. "What a waste," he mumbled.

The reporter at the desk next to his leant round a potted plant and said: "Simpson is after your arse, Woody." There was more than a hint of sadistic pleasure in his voice as he passed on the bad news. Like Woody he was a freelance and each time a freelance was shafted there was more work to go round for everyone else.

"Thanks," said Woody, determined not to show how worried he was. He needed the work, God he needed the work, and he'd been banned from most of the London papers over the last twelve months or so. He was finding it harder and harder to get through a shift without drinking, and that didn't go down well in the new high-tech world of modern newspapers. In the old days, the days when reporters looked like reporters and they worked on typewriters that sounded like typewriters, then the Street was full of characters – men and women who could take their drink and whose work was better for it, and who would be fondly forgiven if they were found late in the evening, flat on their backs under their desks. The news editors then would call for the office car and have them sent home. If they were really badly behaved then perhaps a just punishment would be handed out, a nasty door-stepping job in the pouring rain or a night-time road accident in the middle of nowhere, character-building rather than malicious. Not these days. These days most of the journalists seemed to be straight out of university with weak chins, earnest eyes and stockbroker voices. Few of them could even manage shorthand, Woody thought bitterly, and it was a common sight in the newsroom to see them plugged into tape-recorders transcribing their tapes and breathing through their mouths. Woody remembered the purgatory he'd gone through to get his own spidery shorthand up to the required one hundred words per minute, and the rest of the shit he'd had to go through before he got to Fleet Street. Now the papers were all staffed by kids, kids who if you managed to drag them bodily into a bar would drink nothing stronger than bubbly water. Ian Wood was forty-two years old but at that moment he felt he was going on eighty.

"Woody!" screamed a voice from the far end of the room. "Where the hell have you been?"

The question was rhetorical, Woody realised, because it was swiftly followed by a torrent of abuse. He heaved himself out of the chair and ambled over to the source of the noise, hoping that if he got close it'd cut down the decibels and reduce the embarrassment factor. Simpson was sitting back in his reclining chair with his expensively shod feet on the desk. The news editor spent twice as much on a pair of shoes as the paper paid its freelances for an eight-hour shift. They were well polished and gleamed under the overhead fluorescent lights and Woody looked down involuntarily at his own soaking wet, brown Hush Puppies. Woody began to explain but Simpson cut him off and told him that he should have been back hours ago and that he was to get the hell out of the building and not to bother coming back, that he'd got pissed on the job once too often and that there would be no more shifts for him on the paper. Woody could feel that he was being watched by everyone in the newsroom, and he could tell without looking around that more than half the voyeurs were grinning and enjoying his discomfort. His face reddened. He knew there was nothing he could do, he'd have to wait until Simpson had calmed down, maybe some time after Hell had frozen over, but he couldn't face the walk to the door, not with everyone staring at him. He opened his mouth to speak but Simpson waved him away and turned his back on him.

Woody stood there swaying for a few seconds and then with every ounce of control he could muster he slowly walked across the newsroom, his head held high and his eyes fixed on the purple door that led to the stairs and the street and the pub. There was only one thing he wanted, other than a double Bells, and that was to get out of the room with what little dignity he had left intact. He almost made it. He didn't notice the overflowing wastepaper bin and he crashed over it and sprawled against the door. He pushed the door but it wouldn't budge so he pushed harder and then he saw the sign that said "Pull" and cruel laughter billowed around him as he eventually staggered out into the corridor.

He headed for the sanctuary of the King's Head but realised that there would be other reporters there, probably knocking back Perrier with the way his luck was going, so instead he walked to the Coach and Horses. They wouldn't cash cheques for him there, not since the bank had bounced one, but at least he wouldn't be laughed at.

It started to rain so he put up the collar of his coat and hunched his shoulders and he stuck close to the wall until he reached the pub. It was fairly busy with closing time fast approaching, but Woody knew that the landlord paid little attention to the licensing laws and that it would be many hours before the last customer left. He took off his coat and shook it before hanging it up by the fruit machine.

"Evening, Woody," said the barman, a teenager whose name Woody couldn't remember. "Usual?"

Woody nodded and the barman poured a double Bells. A woman sitting on a stool looked at the Bells bottle and then up at Woody. She shuddered. "You should try a real whisky," she said. She was sitting next to a man in a brown leather jacket and they both had glasses of amber fluid in front of them. Woody reached for his glass and toasted them.

"This will do me fine," he said, and drained it in one.

"Now I'll have one of whatever they're having, and one each for them, too," Woody said, mentally calculating how much he had in his wallet. They were drinking a ten-year-old malt the name of which Woody didn't recognise but it was smooth and mellow and warmed his chest. He fell into amiable conversation with the couple, talking about the weather, about Docklands, about the Government, anything but what he'd seen that evening.

They asked him what he did and he told them he was a journalist. Her name was Maggie and his was Ross, he sold fax machines and she worked for an insurance company.

As the level of whisky in the bottle dropped Woody began opening himself up to them, about how unhappy he was in his job and his plans for a new life in Los Angeles. An old pal of his had gone out to LA a couple of years ago and had set up an agency specialising in showbiz features and oddball stories for the tabloids, and he'd been pestering Woody to go out and join him.

"You know, I think I will go," Woody said, and they nodded in agreement and Maggie bought a round. Some time later the man slapped Woody on the back and said he had to go.

He kissed Maggie on the cheek, a brotherly peck Woody noticed, and left. Woody was surprised as he'd assumed they were married or lovers, but Maggie laughed and said no, just friends. He slid on to the stool vacated by Ross, even though he generally preferred to stand while drinking. He was quite taken by Maggie. She had shoulder-length red hair and grey eyes, and the freckles of a teenager even though she must have been in her early thirties. She spoke with a faint Scottish burr and laughed a lot and told jokes dirtier than even Woody thought was proper.

"Are you serious about LA?" she asked, and Woody said he was. She told him that she had a friend living there, and that if he did go she'd put him in touch. She asked for his telephone number and he gave it to her. Eventually she said she had to go. Woody offered to walk her home but she thanked him and said no, she only lived around the corner. Woody shrugged and said goodbye, wondering how she'd react to a brotherly peck on the cheek from him but deciding against it. After she went he finished his whisky and left the pub in search of a black cab. Ten minutes later he was back for his raincoat. It wasn't his night.

Sergeant Fletcher's heart sank when he saw The Chinaman walking slowly up to his desk. He kept his eyes down on his paperwork and wished with all his heart that he'd go away. Nguyen Ngoc Minh coughed quietly. Sergeant Fletcher ignored him. Nguyen coughed again, louder this time. The policeman knew he could put it off no longer. He looked up and feigned surprise.

"Mr Nguyen," he said. "How can I help you?" His fingers tensed around his ballpoint pen.

"Sergeant Fletcher. Is there news about the bomb?" said Nguyen slowly. He stood in front of the desk, his head bowed and his fingers clasped together below his stomach. He was wearing the same clothes he'd worn on his four previous visits to the police station, brown woollen trousers, a blue and green work shirt and a thick quilted coat with a hood. His dark-brown boots were scuffed and worn and if Sergeant Fletcher hadn't known better he might have assumed that the man was a down-and-out looking for a warm cell for the night.

The policeman shook his head slowly. "I am afraid not, Mr Nguyen. But we are doing everything we can, believe me."

The look in The Chinaman's eyes suggested that he did not believe the sergeant, but he smiled nevertheless, his face wrinkling into deep crevices. It was an ingratiating smile, an eager-to-please look that for some reason made the sergeant immediately feel guilty.

"Do you know who exploded the bomb?" Nguyen asked.

"As it says in the papers, the IRA has claimed responsibility."

"And do they know who in the IRA is responsible?"

"No, Mr Nguyen, they do not." Sergeant Fletcher fought to keep himself from snapping at The Chinaman, but it was hard, bloody hard, because every time he came and stood in front of the desk he asked the same questions with the same inane grin on his face. He realised that the man must be devastated, losing his wife and his daughter, and God knows Fletcher wanted to help, but there was nothing he could do. Nothing.

"How long will it be, Sergeant Fletcher?" Nguyen asked quietly.

The policeman shook his head sadly. "I wish I knew," he said.

"The lady policeman who came to see me last week said that the men would be caught."

"I am sure they will be."

"She said that they will be punished."

The silly cow. Fletcher wished she'd kept her mouth shut and not raised The Chinaman's hopes. He made a mental note to find out who she was and give her a piece of his mind.

"I am sure that when they are caught they will be punished, Mr Nguyen," agreed Sergeant Fletcher.

Nguyen began wringing his hands as if washing them. "When will that be, Sergeant Fletcher?" The smiled widened, the lips stretched tight across his yellowing teeth.

It was a nervous smile, Fletcher realised. The policeman put his palms down on the desk. "I do not know. I simply do not know."

"I know you and your men are doing their best. I know they want to catch the men who killed my family. But I wonder . . ." He left the sentence unfinished, his eyes fixed on Fletcher's face.

"Yes?" said the sergeant.

"I wonder if there were any other policemen on the case. How do you say, specialists? Policemen who hunt the IRA. The terrorists."

Fletcher suddenly felt the sky open and the sun beam down. He saw a way of getting The Chinaman off his back once and for all.

"There are such policemen, Mr Nguyen. They are called the Anti-Terrorist Branch."

"Where do I find the Anti-Terrorist Branch?"

Fletcher found himself grinning. "Mr Nguyen, stay right where you are. I'll go and write down their address and telephone number for you."

Elliott Jephcott drove the white Rover off the main road and into the small cobbled mews. He switched off the radio and looked at his watch. It had just turned 8.30 a.m. and he didn't have to be in court until 11.00 a.m. He had plenty of time. He checked his hair in the driving mirror and then reached into the glove compartment for his breath-freshener aerosol and gave his mouth two minty squirts. He put the aerosol back and as he did he saw that a streetsweeper was watching him while he attacked the cobbles with a long-handled brush. Jephcott blushed like a schoolboy caught with a dirty magazine and was immediately angry with himself. A High Court Judge feeling guilty under the scrutiny of a roadsweeper in a filthy donkey jacket? Ridiculous, he thought. He locked the car and walked to the door of Erica's cottage. It opened just as he was reaching for the brass knocker.

"I heard the car," she said. She looked ravishing, her blonde hair carefully arranged so that she gave the impression that she'd just got out of bed. She moved to the side to let him in and he smelt her perfume. It was the one he'd bought her last month and he was pleased that she'd worn it for him. She was wearing a purple blouse with a high collar and pockets over each breast, and a purple, green and pink flower-patterned skirt that reached halfway down her calves, and around her waist was a purple leather belt. On her left wrist was a thick gold bracelet and around her left ankle was a thin gold chain. He'd bought her the jewellery, too. And the Alfa Romeo outside. That had been a twenty-first birthday present. She was worth it, God she was worth it.

She closed the door and stood behind him, helping him to remove his jacket. She took it and put it on a hanger before putting it away in a cupboard by the front door.

"What time do you have to go?" she asked. He knew that she wasn't nagging, not the way his wife did when she asked the same question, she just wanted to know how much time they had together so that she could plan accordingly. He turned and smiled and slipped his arm around her waist.

"Not long enough," he said and kissed her.

She opened her lips as their mouths met and he felt her soft tongue and heard her moan. She took him by the hand and led him upstairs. "Let's not waste any of it," she said.

Outside in the mews, the roadsweeper worked carefully, pushing the litter and dust into small, neat piles before using his shovel to scoop it into the plastic bag on his cart. He whistled quietly as he worked, his breath forming white clouds in the cold morning air. The collar of his donkey jacket was turned up and he was wearing thick, woollen gloves. On his head was a blue bobble hat that had seen better days. He stood up and surveyed the area he'd cleaned and nodded to himself. He clipped the shovel to the side of his cart and moved it further down the mews, stopping next to the Rover. Out of the corner of his eye he saw the upstairs curtains being closed.

He began to sweep around the car, slowly and conscientiously, still whistling. He moved between the cart and the car

25

and knelt down to unclip the shovel. As he did he took a metal box, about the size of a box of chocolates, from the rear of the cart and in a smooth motion slipped it up under the wheel-arch of the driver's side of the Rover. There were two large magnets on the box and they latched on to the metal of the car through the underseal and its coating of mud. There was a small chrome switch on one side of the box and he clicked it on as he pulled his hand away.

Inside the box were two batteries, a black plastic alarm clock with a digital display, a small aluminium tube, a tangle of different coloured wires and five pounds of pale-brown Semtex explosive in which was embedded a detonator. As the roadsweeper unclipped his shovel and carefully swept up a cigarette packet and a pile of dust, the clock began ticking off the seconds. The man was in no hurry. The clock was set for five minutes, but even when the time was up the bomb would not explode. The clock merely completed the circuit for the second switch, a mercury tilt-switch which acted as a motion sensor. The design prevented the device going off accidentally. It was one of The Bombmaker's favourite bombs, and one of the simplest. There were no booby traps because it was a small bomb and if it was discovered the bomb disposal experts would dump it into an armoured chest and take it away rather than try to deal with it on the spot.

The streetsweeper left the mews just as the five minutes were up. He left his cart a quarter of a mile away, along with the hat, the donkey jacket and the gloves. Fisher had planned everything down to the last detail. O'Reilly kept on walking until he saw a black cab. He hailed it and took it to Victoria Station where he waited for half an hour before catching another cab back to Wapping.

The front door of the mews cottage in Chelsea opened at the same time as the cab turned into Wapping High Street.

Erica's hair still looked as if she had just got out of bed, but this time her lipstick had gone and as Jephcott kissed her he smelt her sex rather than her perfume. Her classy clothes had gone, too, and in their place she wore a white silk dressing-gown. Something else that he'd bought for her.

"Tomorrow?" she breathed, her body tight against his.

"No, my love, I'm afraid not," Jephcott replied. "I'll call you." Over her shoulder he looked at his watch. Plenty of time. He kissed her again and then pulled himself away. She closed the door behind him with a final goodbye, and he adjusted his tie as he went to the car. He unlocked the door to the Rover and got in. He looked at himself in the driving mirror and smoothed down his hair before using the breath-freshener again. The Rover started first time and as he edged it forward the bomb went off, blasting through the wheel-arch and taking off both of his legs in a burst of fire and exploding metal.

Detective Chief Inspector Richard Bromley was filling his briar pipe from a weathered leather pouch when the phone on his desk rang.

"It's the front desk, sir. He's here again."

Bromley groaned. "Tell him I'm busy."

"I've done that, sir. He says he'll wait."

"Tell him I'll call him when there's any news."

"I've done that, sir."

Bromley groaned again. He'd had the same conversation more than a dozen times over the past three weeks but he always hoped that it would end differently, that Nguyen Ngoc Minh would just give up and go home. It had started with phone calls to the general enquiry office, but somewhere along the line somebody had told him that Bromley was handling the case. Nguyen began telephoning him twice a day, once at nine o'clock prompt and again at five o'clock, asking for Detective Chief Inspector Bromley, always polite and deferential. When he first spoke to Nguyen, Bromley felt sorry for him and when he asked how the investigation was going he did his best to sound optimistic. That was his mistake, he realised, he should never have raised the man's hopes. Nguyen explained what had happened to his wife and daughter, quietly and seemingly without emotion, and he told

Bromley that the men responsible must be caught. Bromley had agreed and said that they were doing everything they could. Nguyen had thanked him and asked that Bromley call him when the men had been caught. He'd said "apprehended" but had pronounced each syllable separately as if reading the word for the first time. Five seconds after replacing the receiver, the inspector had forgotten all about the man with the strange name and the awkward English. Until the next day when he rang again. He was just as polite, always calling him "Detective Chief Inspector Bromley" and never raising his voice. He simply repeated the questions once more. Was there any news? Did they know who had set off the bomb? Were the police about to catch the men? When? He listened to Bromley's replies, which were less optimistic this time, told him how important it was that the men were found, thanked him, and rang off. He rang again the following day. And the day after. Bromley stopped taking his calls and forgot about him.

Three days after the last call he was told that there was someone waiting for him at reception. It wasn't unusual for people to arrive at New Scotland Yard with information that might be useful for the Anti-Terrorist Branch, but he was surprised that the man had asked for him by name because most of his informers wouldn't have wanted to have been seen within a mile of the building. It was Nguyen. Bromley told the man on reception to send the old man away, but he had simply sat down on one of the hard grey sofas and waited. He'd waited until the main offices had closed and then he'd left, only to return the following day. He'd maintained his vigil for more than a week, never making a fuss or doing anything that would justify ejecting him from the premises. He just waited. Bromley had been impressed by the man's stubbornness, but he was also hugely irritated by it. Several times he'd had to walk through reception while he was there and he'd glanced at the slightly built Oriental sitting with his hands in his lap, head lowered like a monk at prayer. Once he'd looked up as Bromley passed and he'd bitten down hard on the stem of his pipe and quickly averted his eyes, but too late to keep the guilt from his face. The old man had called out his name but Bromley didn't look back as he headed for the sanctuary of the lift.

Bromley tamped down the tobacco with his thumb. It wasn't that he was afraid of talking to Nguyen, it was just that there was nothing to tell him. There had been six bombs in all, a total of thirty-two people dead, and the IRA had claimed responsibility for each explosion and assassination. The bombs had been of different types, though Semtex was always used. They were pretty sure it was the work of one IRA active service unit and that they were based in London for most of the time, but other than that, nothing. They were no closer now than they were when the bombing campaign had started ten weeks earlier. Bromley had told Nguyen that during one of the first telephone calls. Maybe what the old man needed was counselling, or a psychiatrist. Bromley held the phone between his shoulder and his ear while he lit the pipe and puffed it until the tobacco glowed. The pipe, and the tobacco, had been a birthday present from Chris, his fifteen-year-old son, paid for from the money he'd saved working on his paper round.

"She was only sixteen," Nguyen had said of his daughter. Bromley wondered how he would feel if Chris had been killed. His stomach went cold at the thought of it and he heard himself tell the man on the desk that he'd come down and speak to Nguyen.

"You'll come down, sir?" repeated the man, not believing what he'd heard. Bromley hung up without replying.

Nguyen was standing by the reception desk and he stepped forward to meet Bromley as the lift doors opened.

"Detective Chief Inspector Bromley, it is good of you to see me," he said slowly and bowed his head. No mention of the countless times that the policeman had refused to even acknowledge his existence. Bromley felt a rush of guilt. He asked the man behind the desk if there was an interview room free and he was told there was. Bromley took Nguyen through a pair of double white doors and along a corridor to a small square room containing a table and two orange plastic seats. He motioned Nguyen to the seat nearest the door but the old man waited until Bromley was seated before he sat down.

Bromley drew on his pipe and studied him through a cloud of smoke.

Nguyen was smiling earnestly like an eager-to-please servant. His clothes were clean but scruffy, as if they'd been slept in, and his hair was lank and uncombed. The hands clasped on the table were wrinkled but the nails were neatly clipped. After twenty years as a policeman Bromley had acquired the knack of summing people up at a glance but he had no idea where to start with Nguyen. Maybe it was because he was Oriental. Certain points were obvious. Nguyen was not a rich man, but he had the look of a man who was used to hard work and responsibility. There was suffering too, but you didn't have to be Sherlock Holmes to work that out, Bromley knew. His English was reasonably good, though he had to make an effort to choose his words carefully, and there was something vaguely American about his accent. He seemed honest and straightforward and he looked Bromley in the eye as he waited for him to speak.

Bromley took the stem of the pipe from his mouth and ran his left hand through his short-cropped beard. "Mr Nguyen, you must realise that we are doing everything we can to find the people who killed your wife and daughter. Everything that can be done, is being done, you must believe me when I tell you that. There is no point in you coming here every day. If there is something to tell you, we will telephone you or we will write to you. Do you understand?"

The old man nodded twice, and his smile widened. Several of his back teeth were missing, and one of his canines was badly chipped. "I understand, Detective Chief Inspector Bromley," he said slowly.

Bromley continued with the speech he'd rehearsed in his mind while travelling down in the lift. "The men are members of the IRA, we think they are living in London, probably moving from place to place, perhaps living in bedsitters or cheap boarding houses. They will be using false names and they will be experts at blending into the background. What I am trying to say to you, Mr Nguyen, is that it will be very difficult to find them. Do you understand?"

Nguyen nodded again.

"In fact, it might well be that we never find them. That is a possibility that you must come to terms with. Sometimes the IRA will mount a bombing campaign and then the political climate changes and the bombing stops. If that were to happen, we might never catch the men. But at least the killing will stop. Do you understand?"

Nguyen nodded. "No," he said quietly. "That cannot be so."

"It is so," said Bromley.

"It is not something I can accept, Detective Chief Inspector Bromley," the old man said, still smiling as if he was afraid to offend the policeman. "You must catch these men."

"If it is possible, we will, Mr Nguyen. That I can promise. But if it is impossible . . ." He shrugged and put his pipe back into his mouth.

"These men in London. They are doing this because they are told to, yes?"

"We believe they are members of the IRA, yes."

"But this IRA is not a secret organisation. You know who is in it, you know where they are."

"Yes," said Bromley doubtfully, not sure where the man was heading.

"Then why cannot you arrest someone else who you know is in the IRA and make them tell you who is doing the killing?"

Bromley smiled ruefully, knowing that there were a good many men in the Royal Ulster Constabulary and even his own squad who would be more than happy to do just that, to pick them up off the streets and take them to an underground cell and attach electrodes to their private parts and squeeze every bit of information out of them. And there were others who'd welcome a shoot-to-kill policy, official or unofficial, so that they could blow them away without bothering about the niceties of evidence and procedure and witnesses.

"That is not how we do things in this country," said Bromley.

"What I do not understand is why the Government allows this IRA to be," said Nguyen.

"To be what?" said Bromley, frowning.

"To exist, to be," Nguyen said. "Why does the Government not arrest everybody who is in the IRA. Lock them up. Then there will be no more killing. And perhaps then you find who murdered my family."

Bromley held his hands up in surrender. "Life is not so simple, Mr Nguyen. It is a question of politics, not policing. You should speak to your MP."

"MP?" said Nguyen, his brow creased.

"Member of Parliament," explained the policeman. "Perhaps he can help you."

Bromley got to his feet. "Mr Nguyen, there is nothing else I can tell you, I am afraid. I don't want to offend you, but you must not keep coming here. I am very sorry about what happened to your family, but your coming here is not helping. It makes it more difficult for us. Do you understand?"

Nguyen pushed back his chair slowly and stood in front of Bromley, still smiling. "I understand, Detective Chief Inspector Bromley. And I thank you for talking to me." He held out his hand and Bromley shook it. The small, wrinkled hand was surprisingly strong, as if there were steel rods under the old skin. Nguyen turned and walked out, leaving Bromley alone with his pipe.

Tempers were flaring on the football pitch. It wasn't that there was anything at stake other than the game itself, it was just that the army team hated to lose and they were two goals down with less than ten minutes to go before half-time. Their opponents, the local police team, had the edge when it came to skill and finesse but the army boys had the aggression. The referee looked at his watch and missed the sharp elbow jab in the ribs that sent the police sweeper sprawling but he heard the cop swear and he blew hard on his whistle. The crowd jeered as the referee fumbled in the pocket of his shorts for his notebook.

There were two groups of supporters, one on each side of the pitch. The police supporters, mainly loyal girlfriends and bored wives, stood with their backs to Woolwich Common, facing Stadium Road. The army supporters, mostly soldiers with nothing else to do on a Saturday morning, were ranged along the other side. O'Reilly was standing with the police wives as he studied the referee through the lens of his Pentax. The man's cheeks were flushed red as he spluttered at the policeman who was waving his arms and protesting his innocence. He moved the lens to the left and the Queen Elizabeth Military Hospital came into focus and then he saw the road sign. Shrapnel Close. He smiled at the irony of it.

The referee blew his whistle to restart the game as O'Reilly walked slowly along the sideline, stopping every now and again to take photographs. Over his shoulder was a black camera bag. Close to the corner flag was a stack of sports bags and towels and two polythene bags full of quartered oranges. The crowd roared as a big, beefy, army striker sent the ball ripping into the net, and as his team-mates rushed to congratulate him O'Reilly dropped his camera bag down among the sports bags. He walked back to the line and took more photographs before checking his watch. Three minutes to go. A red Renault drove down Repository Road and into Stadium Road and came to a halt at the junction with Shrapnel Close. O'Reilly knew that he'd attract attention to himself if he walked behind the goalmouth while the game was on, so he stayed where he was until the referee's whistle blasted out and brought the first half to a close. The players ran across the pitch to where the bags were as O'Reilly walked over to the car. McCormick opened the passenger door for him and he got in. They both looked over at the footballers, clustered around the now-opened polythene bags and helping themselves to pieces of orange.

"Now?" said McCormick, licking his lips nervously.

"No, Fisher said we wait until we're on Shooters Hill Road," replied O'Reilly.

"Let's go then." McCormick put the car in gear and drove to the main junction and indicated before he turned. He pulled the car to the side some fifty yards down the road. O'Reilly nodded and opened the glove compartment and took out a small walkie-talkie. It was an Icom IC2 transceiver, a hand-held model. There was another in the camera bag, though it had been modified. The Bombmaker had attached a relay switch to the loudspeaker circuit which was connected to a second circuit, containing a 1.5 volt battery and a gunpowder detonator. The detonator was embedded in twenty-five pounds of Semtex explosive, around which was wrapped a cluster of three-inch nails. There was no timing device because the bomb would be detonated at a safe distance by the transceiver in O'Reilly's hand. And there were no booby traps because they weren't sure when he'd be able to put the bag down.

O'Reilly saw the avaricious look in McCormick's eye, the pleading of a dog begging for a bone. He handed it over. McCormick handled it reverently like a holy icon.

"Are you sure?" he asked.

"Go for it," said O'Reilly.

McCormick switched the control switch to "send" and held the transceiver to his mouth. "Bang," he said, and they saw the flash of light followed quickly by the thud of the explosion and felt the tremor through the car seats.

"Come on, let's go," said O'Reilly.

They were driving along the A102 heading for the Blackwall Tunnel by the time the first white-coated doctor reached the blood-soaked pitch.

Sir John Brownlow was getting irritable, so Ellen brewed him a fresh cup of coffee and placed it on the desk in front of him. He smiled his thanks and she could read his discomfort in his eyes. Ellen Howard had been the MP's personal assistant for almost three years and she'd reached the stage where she could pretty much judge what he was thinking by the look on his face. Today he was wearing his professional, caring mask but she could tell that he was far from happy. He hated the regular constituency surgeries where the punters queued up to present him with their problems and to ask him to put their lives in order. The ones at the local party office weren't so bad because they were mainly an opportunity of pressing the flesh with the party faithful, it was when he had to go out and about that he suffered. Ellen knew what the problem was, though she would never dare tell the MP to his face. It was that Sir John simply did not care about the man in the street, and he sympathised even less with their trials and tribulations. But he was all too well aware of how narrow his majority had been at the last election, and he had resigned himself to the fact that being seen helping his constituents with their problems was a vote-catcher. Holding the surgery in a local citizens advice centre eased some of the pain as it meant he could usually pass them on to someone else. Teflon Time, he called it. The trick was to make sure that nothing stuck and that the punters went away thinking that their MP had done his best and was worth supporting.

The middle-aged woman sitting opposite him in a thick tweed coat and a fake fur hat had bought her council house by mortgaging herself to the hilt. Her son had helped out with the payments until they'd had a row and he'd left home. Now the building society was threatening to evict her. If she sold the house would Sir John be able to get her into another council house? The MP smiled benignly and told her that there were people at the centre who would help her negotiate with the building society and have the payments frozen or reduced. He motioned at Ellen and introduced her to the woman and then stood up to shake her hand, patting her on the back as he ushered her to the door. Ellen took her down the corridor into another room and left her with one of the advisers there. Teflon Time strikes again, she thought. There were half a dozen people sitting on a line of chairs in the corridor outside the office commandeered by the MP. There was an old couple, a young man in jeans and a motorcycle jacket who looked like he might be troublesome, two house-wives, and a Chinese man in a blue duffel coat. He was muttering something, reading from a small piece of paper in his hands and repeating something to himself over and over again. As she walked past him it sounded as if he said "elected representative".

"Next please," she said, and the old man stood up and

helped his wife to her feet. Sir John greeted them with his hand outstretched and a caring smile on his face.

Ellen sat behind her own desk, to the left of Sir John's and at right angles to it, and watched and learned. She had hopes of one day following him into the House of Commons. Her degree was in political science and she'd been chairman of her university's student union, but what she needed now was hard, political experience. Sir John Brownlow was providing that, even if it meant that she had to tolerate the occasional wandering hand on her buttocks or suggestive remark, but so far she'd been able to fend off his passes without offending him. Besides, he'd stopped being quite so chauvinistic once she'd become a good friend and confidante of his wife and taken his two teenage daughters to the cinema a few times. Ellen knew what she wanted, and how she wanted to get it, and what she didn't want was to get her ticket to the House by lying on her back with the Honourable Member between her legs.

He spent half an hour with the old couple, and then Ellen took them out and called for whoever was next. The Oriental man looked around, saw that everyone was looking at him, and got to his feet. "I think it is my turn," he said quietly.

She asked his name and then he followed her into the office. Sir John was already in position to shake hands and Ellen saw his jaw tighten when he saw Nguyen, but only for a second. Then the teeth flashed and the eyes crinkled into the face that smiled down from the posters at election time. Sir John was nothing if not professional.

"Mr Nguyen," she said by way of introduction. The MP shook the man's hand firmly and he waited until Nguyen was seated before going back behind the desk.

"How can I help you, Mr Nguyen?" he said, steepling his well-manicured hands under his square chin.

In a low, quiet voice, Nguyen told him what had happened to his wife and daughter, about the bomb, and the conversations he had had with the police and the Anti-Terrorist Branch. "My family died more than three months ago," he said. "And still the men responsible have not been caught."

Sir John nodded understandingly. "But what is it that you want me to do?"

"I wrote to you many times, Sir John. Many times."

The MP gave Ellen a sideways look and she nodded quickly. Yes, she remembered his letters now. Carefully handwritten, every word in capital letters. She had drafted sympathetic replies promising nothing and Sir John had signed them without reading them.

"I asked you to help bring the men to justice," Nguyen continued. "Detective Chief Inspector Bromley said that the capture of the men was a political matter."

"Detective Chief Inspector Bromley?"

"He is a policeman who catches terrorists. But he told me that he could not force the men in the IRA to tell him who killed my family."

"That is probably true, I am afraid," said Sir John. "There are many people who probably feel that the police and the army should have stronger powers, but we are, when all is said and done, a democracy. We cannot torture people or imprison them simply because they do not give us the information we seek." He looked concerned, but to Ellen he sounded pompous and uncaring.

"But could not the Government change the law so that such things could be done? So that the police could force others in the IRA to tell what they know?"

"In theory yes, but it would not happen. I am afraid you must allow the police to do their job, Mr Nguyen. I am sure that they are doing their best."

Nguyen smiled nervously. "What I would like, Sir John, is for you to change the law."

Sir John snorted. "Come, come, Mr Nguyen. What makes you think I can do that?"

"Because you are my . . ." The old man seemed to stumble on the words before finishing the sentence. "My elected representative." He seemed to take pride in the fact that he had remembered the words. "You are my MP. I wish you to change the law so that the killers of my family can be brought to justice."

"You have a strange idea of the powers of an MP, Mr

Nguyen. I cannot change laws just because you think justice has not been done."

Nguyen hung his head and said something quietly.

"I'm sorry?" said Sir John, leaning forward to listen.

Nguyen looked up. There were tears in his eyes and Ellen's heart went out to him.

"What am I to do?" he asked the MP. "My family is dead. What am I to do?"

Sir John leant back in his chair and folded his arms across his chest. Ellen recognised his defensive position. There was nothing he or anyone else could do. The IRA was an insurmountable problem. Even if they were to catch the men behind the latest series of bombings, it would not stop, another active service unit would come to life. The killings would never stop, not until the British pulled out of Northern Ireland. And there was little likelihood of that happening.

"How long have you been in this country, Mr Nguyen?" Sir John asked.

"I have been a British citizen since 1982. Very long time." He reached into his duffel coat pocket and took out a passport, the old type, dark-blue with the gold crest on the front. He held it out to the MP but he seemed reluctant to take it and kept his arms folded. Nguyen put it back in his pocket.

"From Hong Kong?" Sir John asked. Ellen realised then why he was so defensive. He had been one of the most outspoken critics of the Government's offer of passports to the colony's middle classes.

"Do you not have family back in Hong Kong? Can you not go back there?"

The old man looked surprised. "Hong Kong? Why I go back there?"

Sir John appeared equally confused. "That's where you came from," he said. "Surely you still have family there?"

"I not Hong Kong Chinese," Nguyen explained. "I am Vietnamese. From Vietnam."

Realisation dawned on the MP's face and he sighed audibly. He was, Ellen knew, even more vehemently against Vietnamese boat people being offered sanctuary in Britain. God, the number of times she'd listened to him address meetings on the difference between political and economic refugees and how Britain couldn't offer homes to everyone in the world who wanted a better standard of living.

"North or south?" asked Sir John.

Nguyen smiled. "Today there is no north or south. Only Vietnam."

"When you escaped," the MP pressed. "Where were you from then?"

Nguyen shrugged. "Both," he said. "North and south."

"And why did you come to England?"

"Because I could not live in Vietnam. Because the Communists persecuted me and my family. I helped the Americans in the war. When the Americans go they put me in prison. So we escaped. To Britain."

"Why Britain?"

"Because here we can be free."

The MP nodded. "But do you not see, Mr Nguyen? The reason that you can be free in this country and not your own is because we have laws for everybody here. Nobody is above the law. But equally nobody is denied its protection. That is what makes democracy work. That is why you wanted to come here in the first place, to be free. You cannot now ask for the laws to be changed, to take away the rights of others."

"Even if they have killed my family?"

"You must allow the police to do their job. You must have faith in our system, Mr Nguyen." He put his hands on the desk top and pushed himself up. Nguyen tilted his head up and for the first time it gave him a more confident, vaguely arrogant look. Then he stood up and he became once more the stooped old man, alone in the world. Sir John patted him on the back as he guided him through the doorway and into the corridor and then he slipped back into the office.

"Christ, Ellen, these people. They come over here, we give them homes, we give them money, and still they want more. If they don't like this country the way it is, why don't they just get the hell out and go back to where they came from?"

"He's still in shock, poor man," said Ellen. "His whole family was wiped out. Think how he must feel."

"That was four months ago, Ellen. And there have been

what, two or three bombs since then. And how many other victims? Yet you don't hear their relatives demanding that we pull in IRA members off the street and pull out their fingernails."

"He wasn't actually saying that, Sir John. He was . . ."

The MP snorted angrily. "Bullshit! That's exactly what he wanted. And can you imagine what the Press would do if they even thought we were considering something like that? They'd scream 'Big Brother' and 'Violation of Human Rights' and you know they would. Remember Gibraltar? They don't think about the people whose lives were saved when the SAS stopped the car bomb from being detonated. All they remember is the IRA being shot while they were on the ground. Remember the uproar over the *Belgrano*?"

Ellen didn't argue. She knew full well that there was no point in taking sides against her boss. She was there to learn from him, not to antagonise him. She smiled and brushed a loose strand of hair off her face. "I'll get the next one in for you," she said sweetly while wondering how such a racist could ever get elected. There was so much she still had to learn, she realised.

Jon Simpson took the call from the uniformed security guard at reception. "There's a chap down here wants to speak to a reporter," he said gruffly.

"What about?" asked Simpson.

"Dunno," said the guard.

"Do me a favour and ask him, will you?" sighed Simpson. The security guards weren't paid for brain power, just for bulk, but there were times when Simpson wished they were a mite brighter. There was a pause before the guard's laconic voice returned.

"Says it's about the bombs."

Simpson felt the hairs on the back of his neck stand up. The IRA bombing campaign had been going on for more than four months and the police seemed to be no nearer catching the bombers. Maybe the punter downstairs held the key, it was amazing the number of times that they came to the paper rather than going straight to the police. Or perhaps it wasn't so surprising – the paper paid handsomely for information. The news editor looked around the newsroom to see who was free and his eyes settled on Woody who was reading the *Daily Star* and picking his teeth with a plastic paper-clip. It had taken Woody weeks of plaintive phone calls before Simpson had allowed him to start shifting again and only after he'd promised not to drink on the job. Not to excess, anyway. Expecting Woody not to drink at all was asking the impossible. And he was a bloody good journalist.

"Woody!" he yelled.

Woody's head jerked up and he came over immediately, pen and notebook in hand. He was still at the eager-to-please stage. "There's a punter downstairs. Something about the bombs. See what he's got, will you?"

Woody nodded and headed for the lift. The man waiting downstairs was Oriental, wearing a blue duffel coat with black toggles, faded jeans and dirty training shoes. He was carrying a plastic carrier bag and was wiping his nose with a grubby handkerchief. He snorted into it and then shoved it into his coat pocket before stretching his arm out to shake hands. Woody pretended not to notice the gesture and herded the old man towards a group of low-backed sofas in the far corner of the reception area. Carrier bags were always a bad sign, he thought, as he watched the man settle into a sofa next to a large, spreading tree with weeping leaves. Punters who arrived at newspaper offices with carrier bags often produced strange things from them. During his twenty years as a journalist Woody had just about seen everything. There were the paranoids who thought they were being followed and who would produce lists of numbers of cars that were pursuing them, or taxis, or descriptions of people who had appeared in their dreams, or lists of MPs who were in fact aliens operating from a base on the far side of the moon. There were the punters who felt they'd had a raw deal from one of the big international companies and had photocopies of correspondence going back ten years to prove it. There were the nutters who claimed to have written Oscar-winning film scripts only to have their ideas stolen by a famous Hollywood director, and they'd open their plastic bags to show their own versions. Sometimes they were written in crayon. Not a good sign.

"How can I help you?" asked Woody, his heart heavy.

"My name is Nguyen Ngoc Minh," the man said, and Woody scribbled in his notebook, just a random motion because he didn't reckon there was going to be a story in this and he didn't want to go through the hassle of asking the guy to spell his name.

The old man thrust his hand into the carrier bag and took out a colour photograph and handed it to Woody. It was a family portrait of the man, an old woman and a pretty young girl. Woody raised his eyebrows inquisitively.

"My wife," said Nguyen. "My wife and my daughter. They were killed this year."

"I'm sorry to hear that," said Woody, his pen scratching on the notebook. He wasn't using shorthand, he just wanted to be seen to be doing something so that he didn't have to look the man in the eye. The brown eyes were like magnets that threatened to pull him into the old man's soul and several times Woody had found himself having to drag himself back. They were sorrowful eyes, those of a dog that had been kicked many times but which still hoped one day to have its loyalty rewarded.

"They were killed by IRA bombers in January," continued Nguyen. He delved into the bag once more and pulled out a sheaf of newspaper cuttings and spread them out on the low table in front of Woody. Among them he saw the *Sunday World* front-page story on the Knightsbridge bombing and the pictures they'd used inside. Strapped along the bottom was a list of the reporters and photographers who'd worked on the story. The intro and a good deal of the copy was Woody's but his name wasn't there, Simpson had insisted that it stay off. Another punishment.

"I remember," he said.

"There have been many bombs since," said Nguyen, and he pointed to the various cuttings. The judge blown up outside the house of his mistress, the bomb at Bank Tube station, the police van that had been hit in Fulham, the Woolwich football bombing. Good stories, thought Woody. He waited for the old man to continue.

Nguyen told him about the visit by the police, of their promise that the men would be caught. He told him about what he'd later been told at the police station, and by the Anti-Terrorist Branch and finally of his conversation with his MP, Sir John Brownlow. "They all tell me the same thing," he said. "They tell me to wait. To let the police do their job."

Woody nodded, not sure what to say. He'd stopped writing in the notebook and studied the cuttings while the old man talked.

"I want to do something," Nguyen said. "I want to offer money for the names of the men who did the bombs. A reward."

Woody looked up. "I don't think the newspaper would be prepared to offer a reward," he said. Too true, he thought. A right bloody can of worms that would open up. It was OK to offer money for the return of a stolen baby, or to pay some amateur model for details of her affair with a trendy businessman or a minor pop star, but he could imagine the response to a request for a reward in the hunt for IRA killers. Put the paper right in the firing line, that would.

Nguyen waved his hands and shook his head.

"No, no, you not understand," he said. "Reward not from newspaper. From me. I have money." He picked up the carrier bag by the bottom and tipped the rest of its contents on the table. It was money, bundles and bundles of it, neatly sorted into five-, ten- and twenty-pound notes, each stack held together with thick rubber bands. Woody ran his hands through the pile and picked up one of the bundles and flicked the notes. They looked real enough.

Nguyen read his thoughts. "They are real," he said. "There is eleven thousand pounds here. It is all the money I have."

Woody saw the guard staring at the money open-mouthed and so he began to scoop it back into the plastic bag. The old man helped him.

"You shouldn't be carrying so much cash around with you," whispered Woody. "Why isn't this in the bank?"

Nguyen shrugged. "I not trust bank. Many people have money in bank when Americans leave Vietnam. They would not give money back. They steal. I take care of my own money. This all I have. I want paper to use it as reward. Can do?"

Woody pushed the bag across the table. "I'm sorry, no. My paper wouldn't do that sort of thing. And I don't think that any newspaper would."

The old man looked pained by what he'd been told and Woody felt as if he'd just slapped him across the face. He stood up and waited until Nguyen did the same, the bag of money held tightly in his left hand. He offered the right hand to Woody and this time he took it and shook it. He felt intensely sorry for the old man, sorry for what he'd been through and sorry that there was nothing that could be done for him. He heard himself say: "Look, why don't you give me your phone number and if I can think of anything I'll call you?"

Nguyen smiled gratefully and told Woody the number, repeating it slowly and checking as he wrote it down. Woody didn't know why but he had a sudden urge to help the old man, to make some sort of gesture to show that he really did care and wasn't just making polite noises. He wrote down his home number on another sheet of paper and ripped it from the notebook. "Take this," he said. "Call me if . . ." He didn't know how to finish the sentence, because he knew there was nothing tangible he could offer. Nguyen bowed his head and thanked Woody and then left. Woody watched him walk down the road, a small man in a duffel coat with eleven thousand pounds in a plastic bag. "And I thought I'd seen everything," he said to himself.

O'Reilly walked up the steps to the main entrance of the police station and turned round so that he could push open the door with his shoulder. He was using both hands to carry a large cardboard box. The box was new and the lettering on it said that it contained a Japanese video recorder. A housewife with a crying child in a pushchair held the door open for him and he smiled boyishly at her.

He took the box over to the enquiries desk and placed it in front of an overweight uniformed constable who looked at him with bored eyes.

"How can I help you, sir?" the policeman asked unenthusiastically.

"I found this in my back garden this morning," said O'Reilly, nodding at the box. "It's a video recorder."

"You surprise me," said the policeman. He opened the flaps at the top of the box and looked inside. He saw a black video recorder, still in its polythene wrapping. There was a blank guarantee card and an instruction booklet.

"You've no idea where it came from?" the officer asked, and O'Reilly shook his head.

"It looks new," said O'Reilly. "I thought of keeping it but my wife said no, it might belong to someone, and besides, you know, there might be a reward or something. So she said take it to the police, you know, and so here I am." O'Reilly smiled like an idiot. He was wearing horn-rimmed glasses with thick lenses, a flat cap and a sheepskin jacket. That was all the disguise he needed because even if they ever connected the delivery of the video recorder with the explosion, all the guy would remember would be the hat and the glasses. People's memories were generally lousy when it came to describing faces, even with the latest computerised photofit systems.

"Very public-spirited of you, sir," said the policeman. "Now, can you give me your name and address?"

O'Reilly gave him a false name and an address in nearby Battersea and explained again how he'd found the video recorder while the policeman carefully wrote it all down.

"Right, sir, that's all. We'll be in touch if it isn't claimed," he said, and O'Reilly thanked him and left. He passed the housewife outside, kneeling by her child and wiping its face with a paper handkerchief. She looked up at him and smiled and he winked at her. "Lovely kid," he said.

45

The policeman lifted the box, grunting as he did so, and carried it out of the office and down a white-tiled corridor to a windowless storage room. He found a space for it on one of the grey metal shelves, next to a set of fly-fishing tackle and a bundle of umbrellas. The room was full of abandoned or forgotten belongings, all waiting to be taken to one of the city's lost property storage centres. The policeman walked back to the reception desk and forgot all about the video recorder and the man who'd delivered it.

The bomb was similar in design to the one they'd used outside the Knightsbridge department store. The Bombmaker had stripped out most of the workings of the video recorder and replaced it with twenty pounds of Semtex explosive. There were no nuts and bolts in this bomb because the aim was to demolish a building rather than mutilate crowds of people but it used a similar detonator and timer. There were two anti-handling devices, though, just in case it didn't go off for any reason. Any attempt to open the casing would set it off, and it was also primed to explode if it was connected to the mains, just in case any light-fingered copper decided to pop it into his car and take it home. The Bombmaker did not have a very high opinion of the police, be they in Belfast or London.

O'Reilly delivered the bomb at four o'clock and it was set to explode an hour later, just as the shifts were changing at the station. He was back in the Wapping flat well before the timer clicked on and completed the circuit which detonated the bomb in a flash of light. The force of the explosion blew out the front and the back walls of the police station and the two floors above it collapsed down, trapping and killing dozens of men and women in an avalanche of masonry and timber and choking dust.

Woody was reading the morning papers when the telephone rang. As usual he'd started going through the tabloids first, and on the desk in front of him he'd opened the *Sun* and the

Daily Mirror. Both had used pictures of the aftermath of the police-station bombing. The *Sun* had the better photographs but the *Mirror* had the edge when it came to eye-witness accounts. He reached for *Today* as he answered the phone.

"Mr Wood?" asked a voice that Woody didn't recognise.

"Yes?"

"It is Nguyen Ngoc Minh. I came to your office three days ago."

"I remember," said Woody. The Chinaman. He flicked through *Today*. Same pictures as the *Sun*, more or less. Plus a line drawing of the inside of a booby-trapped bomb, a Blue Peter do-it-yourself guide for amateurs to follow. And here's one I exploded earlier, thought Woody with a wry smile. "How can I help you?"

"You have seen the newspapers today?"

"The bombing?"

"These people must be stopped, Mr Wood." Woody was only half listening to the man, he had a sickening feeling that he knew where the conversation was heading. Would the paper offer the reward? Would the paper put pressure on the police? The army? The Government? Woody didn't want to be rude to the old man but he wasn't prepared to be used as the paper's agony aunt. Not on a freelance's pay, anyway. He thought of giving The Chinaman the phone number for *Today*. He began turning the pages looking for the number.

"Mr Wood?"

"Yes?"

"You said that you would help me."

"Well . . ." said Woody, about to back-pedal while he hunted frantically for *Today*'s telephone number.

"I want to speak to somebody at the IRA. Do you know anybody that would talk to me?"

Woody stopped turning the pages of the newspaper.

"What are you thinking of doing?" he asked suspiciously, scenting a possible story.

"I want to talk to somebody in the IRA, that is all."

"I don't think they'll help you, I really don't. And it might backfire."

"Backfire? I do not understand."

"They are dangerous men, if they thought you were a threat to them, or even just a nuisance, there's a good chance they'd hurt you."

"All I want to do is to talk to them."

Woody sighed. "OK, for a start you don't want to talk to the IRA. You'd be better off trying Sinn Fein, that's the political wing of the organisation. The Sinn Fein spokesmen are well-known."

"Could you give me some names, and tell me where I might find them?"

Woody looked at the photographs of smashed brickwork, broken glass and misshapen metal. What the hell, he thought. Why not?

"I'll have to call you back, give me your number."

"I gave you before."

"I know, but I'm using a different notebook now."

Nguyen read out the figures slowly, and Woody promised to ring him back later in the day. He was about to go over to the cuttings library but had second thoughts and instead decided to call one of the paper's Belfast stringers. Might as well get it from the horse's mouth. For a change the stringer, Pat Quigley, was helpful, sober and in his office, a hell of an unusual combination and Woody took full advantage of it. He gave Woody three names, potted biographies, where they lived, and contact phone numbers, and told him a foul joke involving two nuns and a bar of soap from which Woody deduced that the man wasn't a Catholic.

When Woody called The Chinaman back the phone was answered with a guttural "Double Happiness Take-Away".

"This is Ian Wood," he said, suddenly realising he couldn't remember The Chinaman's name. He had just written "Chinaman" in his notebook.

"Double Happiness Take-Away," the voice repeated.

Woody cursed under his breath, then he heard another voice and the sound of the phone being transferred.

"Mr Wood?" said Nguyen.

"I have the information you wanted," Woody said. He read the notes from his notebook, spelling out the names and repeating the numbers several times until he was sure The Chinaman had got them down correctly.

"Thank you, Mr Wood. I not bother you again." The phone went dead before Woody had the chance to ask The Chinaman for his name. There could be a story in this somewhere. "Heartbroken Father Pleads With IRA Killers". "Bomb Mission Of Tragic Dad". That sort of thing. Good Sunday-paper stuff. Woody was about to ring back when there was a shout from the far end of the office.

"Woody! Call for you. What extension are you on?"

"4553," he yelled back, and waited until the call was put through.

"Woody?" said a girl's voice, soft and with a Scottish burr.

"Yeah, speaking," he answered, groping for a pen.

"It's Maggie." Maggie? His mind raced, frantically trying to put a face to the name and the voice. "How are you?" she asked.

"Me? I'm fine, fine." He closed his eyes and began banging the palm of his hand against his forehead as if trying to jolt his memory.

"You do remember?" she asked, sounding hurt.

"Of course I do." He began flicking through the images in his head, searching for a Maggie.

"The Coach and Horses," she prompted.

Maggie! The girl with red hair and grey eyes and the earthy sense of humour. He remembered how much he'd enjoyed being with her, though for the life of him he couldn't recall what they'd talked about, other than the fact that she'd told him a couple of fairly risqué jokes. Would she appreciate the one about the nuns and the soap? Probably not.

"Of course I remember, how are you?" He tried to recall the name of her partner. Todd? Rob? Ross? It bobbed away on the outer fringes of his memory, just out of reach. Most of that evening was a blank, though he vaguely remembered putting away the best part of a bottle of a very civilised malt whisky. Had he kissed her? He couldn't remember. There was something else as well, something sad, very, very sad. Woody's eyes glanced at the photographs in the *Sun* and it all flooded back as if a dam had burst. It had been the day of the big bombing in Knightsbridge. He'd locked away the sickening images of that day, the pictures that had been too horrific to use in the paper, the twisted bodies, the severed limbs, the blood, the Retriever with its jaws clamped on its gory prize. He didn't want to think about that day, but Maggie had been part of it and recalling her brought everything back into focus. He breathed deeply, trying to clear his head.

"I'm fine, too. Isn't it a lovely day?"

"Is it? We've no way of knowing, here. All the blinds are down so that we can use the terminals." That's what management claimed, but Woody reckoned it was just to stop them looking out of the windows and daydreaming.

"Well, take it from me, the sun is shining and the birds are singing. I was wondering if you fancied going out for a drink again one day this week."

"Sure, that'd be great. What about tomorrow night?"

She agreed, and they arranged to meet at the same pub.

"Woody, are you OK?" she asked. "You sound a bit distant."

"Yeah, somebody walked over my grave, that's all. Nothing to worry about. I'll be fine by tomorrow."

When she'd gone Woody put his head in his hands and closed his eyes, but he couldn't block out the images of death and destruction. He needed a drink. Badly.

The function room had been booked in the name of the Belfast Overseas Investors Club but the dozen men sitting at the long mahogany table had little interest in investment. The man standing at the head of the table in a green tweed jacket and black woollen trousers could have passed as a mildly eccentric provincial stockbroker with his greying hair and slightly flushed cheeks. He was in his fifties and looked like a rugby player gone to seed, which is exactly what Liam Hennessy was. But after playing for his country he'd gone on to become a political adviser to Sinn Fein. Married with two children, Liam Hennessy was one of the most powerful men in the Republican movement.

The eleven listening to him were all high-ranking Provisional IRA officials and they had all been called to the hotel in Belfast at short notice. On the table in front of them were jugs of iced water and upturned glasses, but none had been touched. Each man also had a notepad in a red leather folder and a ballpoint pen.

Hennessy stood with his arms folded across his chest and spoke in a soft Irish brogue. He first thanked them for coming, though a summons from Liam Hennessy was not something that any of them could ignore. The group met regularly, always in different venues and under different names so that the security forces wouldn't be able to eavesdrop, usually to discuss financing or strategy or matters of discipline, but today's gathering was special. They had all seen the television reports of the south London police-station bombing and the pictures of ambulancemen and firemen hauling the rubble away with their bare hands, and they had heard that the IRA had claimed responsibility.

To Hennessy's left was a large flat-screen television on a matte black stand, and underneath it was a video recorder. He took a videocassette off the table and slotted it into the recorder. The screen flickered and then there were shots of the Kensington bombing recorded from the BBC news. It was followed by a report of the Woolwich bombing, the explosion in Bank Tube station and the crop of car bombs that had killed or injured judges, police and army officers. Then the screen dissolved into black and white static and Hennessy bent down and switched the machine off.

"This must stop," said Hennessy quietly. He was not a man who needed to raise his voice or bang his fist on the table to make his anger felt. "Never in the history of the Cause have we been closer to getting a political solution. Look at South Africa. The Government there is now talking to the ANC and that would have been unthinkable a few years ago. The ANC's acts of terrorism go way beyond anything the IRA has ever done. With the Americans withdrawing their troops from Europe and the opening up of Eastern Europe, this

Government is finding it harder and harder to justify its armed presence in Northern Ireland. This Government is getting tired, politically and economically, and it is through the ballot-box and by lobbying in Westminster that this war will be won."

There were grumblings from several of the men at the table and Hennessy held up his hand to silence them. "I am not saying that we give up the struggle, nor that we release the pressure here. What I am saying is that it does us no good at all to take the conflict to the mainland. We have tried in the past and the backlash, both political and from the public, has done us more harm than good. That is why what is happening in England now is so detrimental to our cause."

A few of the men nodded in agreement, but Hennessy could see that others were still not convinced.

"We cannot succeed in our political struggle by using violence in English cities. It must stop. Which brings us to our second problem. Who in God's name is behind this bombing campaign?" He looked at the men around the table but was met with a wall of shaking heads. Over the previous four months Hennessy or one of his associates from the upper echelons of Sinn Fein had met with all of the top IRA organisers in Belfast and in Dublin in an attempt to identify the team behind the bombings. When they'd first been told that the terror campaign was an unsanctioned one they had been astonished – most had assumed that it had been ordered on a "need to know" basis. It was inconceivable, they thought, that a campaign of such ferocity and technical sophistication could be masterminded from outside the organisation. The bombs were all variations of IRA designs and explosives, and whenever the bombers claimed responsibility they always gave the current identifying codeword, but as far as Hennessy could determine they were most definitely not acting under IRA authority. Unless one of the men around the table had been lying.

He studied their faces, most of them in their fifties and sixties, hard men whose eyes looked back at him levelly. Most of them had killed, and the few who hadn't had arranged or ordered assassinations, yet to the outsider they would have looked no more sinister than a group of pigeon fanciers gathered to discuss their annual show.

"After an extensive investigation, we have come to the conclusion that we are dealing with a rogue group, a group that we are sure must have been within the organisation until recently, who are now operating on their own," said Hennessy. He saw one or two frowns. "The fact that they know the codewords, even after they are changed, suggests that they still have connections, and high level connections at that. And the type of explosive devices would indicate that they are IRA trained. It could even be that they passed through one of the Libyan training schools."

One of the older members of the group, white-haired and with rosy cheeks from years on the hills around his farm, cracked his knuckles under the table to catch Hennessy's attention. "If what you say is true, Liam, then it should not be too hard to pin these people down."

Hennessy nodded. "In theory that's so, Patrick. But it will require a hell of a lot of legwork. We are going to have to speak to everyone within the organisation who has bomb-making skills, to find out where they are and if they have been out of the country. Or if they have instructed anyone else. And it cannot be one man, so we'll also be looking for any other IRA members who are unaccounted for. In short, gentlemen, we will have to interview every single member of the organisation."

Patrick Sewell leant back in his chair and cracked his knuckles again. "That could cause some resentment, Liam, especially when many of our younger people are actually in favour of what has been happening. The bombing campaign has its supporters, you know. And it wasn't all that many years ago that you yourself weren't averse to taking the struggle over the water."

Hennessy leant forward and placed his hands flat on the highly polished table. "I'm all too well aware that there are hotheads within the movement who would prefer to see us blowing up police stations in London, but they must learn to understand that there is a time for violence and a time for negotiation," he said.

Sewell grinned. "And if they don't agree?"

"Then, Patrick, you are free to blow their fucking kneecaps off, sure enough."

Hennessy grinned and so did Sewell and the group burst into deep-throated laughter. The two men were best of friends and they went back a long way. A hell of a long way. They both had a powdery dry sense of humour and took great pleasure in winding each other up.

Hennessy waited for the laughter to die away before continuing. "There is a second line of enquiry which we must pursue," he said. "Whoever is behind the bombing campaign appears to have a ready source of explosives and bomb-making equipment. I want every single stockpile of arms checked, both here and on the mainland. And I don't mean that we just check that they are there, I mean every item must be verified. Verified and then re-hidden. It could be that they have access to more than one of our stockpiles and have taken a small amount from each place. You see what I mean? A few pounds of Semtex from here, a detonator there, a transmitter from somewhere else. Hoping that we wouldn't notice."

A thin, angular man with tinted glasses and slicked-back greying hair caught Hennessy's eye with a wave of his hand. His name was Hugh McGrath, and his main job within the organisation was to liaise with the Libyans, providers of much of the organisation's money and equipment.

"Liam, you can't be serious. The whole point of these stockpiles is that they remain untouched until we need them. Disturbing them unnecessarily risks drawing attention to them," he said.

Hennessy took his hands off the table and stood upright. He could understand his concern, McGrath had personally supervised the importation of much of the IRA's ordnance and was all too well aware of what it had cost, in terms of hard cash and lives lost.

"We'll be careful, Hugh. We'll be damned careful. But I think that a thorough examination of all our stockpiles will give us our best indication of who is behind the bombing campaign. I agree it's a risk, but it is a calculated one. It's a risk we must take, right enough."

"If you say so," said McGrath, but Hennessy could tell from his tone that he wasn't convinced. He made a mental note to massage his ego after the meeting.

"What I need from you all is a full list of all your ordnance stocks. And I mean every single one, authorised and non-authorised. I know that we all like to have a little something tucked away for a rainy day, but the list must be comprehensive. And alongside the contents of each stockpile I want the names of all the people who know its location."

There were a few heavy sighs from his audience.

"A list like that will be a very dangerous thing, Liam. In the wrong hands it could be fatal," said Sewell.

"I know that. There will be only one copy, and I will have it. I will arrange for the stockpiles to be checked, and I will arrange for different teams to do the checking. Only I will know all the locations. And the men I get to visit the stockpiles will not be told why. If all goes to plan I will eventually know which have been tampered with, and then by cross-referencing the names I should be able to identify the common links. Now, if you don't object, I suggest we compile the list as best we can. Any omissions can be made good later, but only directly to me."

The men reached for their pens as Hennessy sat down again. He waited until the men had finished writing. It took several minutes until the last man replaced his ballpoint pen on the table. Hennessy asked for the written sheets to be passed to him and he placed them in a neat pile and then carefully folded it three ways and slipped the sheets into his inside pocket. He then asked them to tear off the top half dozen sheets from the pads and he gathered them together and screwed them up before dropping them into a wastepaper basket. He used a silver cigarette lighter to set the papers alight. He realised it looked a bit theatrical, but at least it proved that he was serious about secrecy.

At the end of the room was a table covered with a starched white linen cloth, and on it were bottles of spirits and a selection of mixers, an ice bucket and a row of crystal glasses. Hennessy personally poured drinks for the men in the room, never once having to ask what they wanted. They stood in two groups, drinking and talking, mainly about horse-racing and football, there being an unwritten rule that business was discussed only at the table. Hennessy was the first to leave, shaking them all by the hand as he went.

Outside the room he was joined by his two bodyguards, Jim Kavanagh and Christy Murphy, big-shouldered men with watchful eyes. Even here, on home territory, they were constantly alert. Kavanagh led the way, six paces ahead of Hennessy, while Murphy walked one pace behind, covering his back. Kavanagh pressed the button for the lift, checked it when it arrived, and then he and Murphy stood to one side to allow Hennessy in. They then stood together between the door and their boss. The three men moved smoothly as if their actions were well choreographed, and in a way they were because they had been together for more than a decade and had been through the actions many thousands of times. Murphy and Kavanagh knew without looking where Hennessy was and in which direction he was moving, where the danger points were and where they had to stand to get in between their boss and any attackers. Twice they had saved Hennessy's life, and both bore their scars with pride – Murphy's left shoulder was a mass of tangled scar tissue where a soft-nosed bullet had ripped away a chunk of flesh but thankfully had missed the bone, and Kavanagh's legs still bore the burn marks of a badly placed car bomb that had exploded as he was about to pick up his boss.

Hennessy's car, a black Jaguar, was waiting outside the hotel with his regular driver, a small, intense man called Jimmy McMahon, at the wheel. Hennessy stood patiently while his bodyguards checked the pavements and then the three men quickly moved to the car.

They drove through the Belfast traffic, and McMahon's skilful touch on the wheel had them back at Hennessy's office in Donegall Square within five minutes. Only when Hennessy was safely behind his desk did Murphy and Kavanagh relax. They sat on two large, green sofas in the legal firm's reception area until they were needed again. Hennessy's secretary, a buxom redhead, put cups of coffee down in front of them before knocking twice on Hennessy's door and entering before he had the chance to respond. Like Murphy and Kavanagh, she knew her boss well. He was sitting in a high-backed leather chair, his eyes closed in thought. In front of him on his well-ordered desk was a file of outgoing letters awaiting his signature. Hennessy opened his eyes and smiled.

"I'm getting to them, Beth."

She raised her eyebrows. "We'll miss the post, Liam, sure enough we will," she admonished like a schoolteacher scolding a naughty pupil. She was a good fifteen years younger than Hennessy, but she knew there were times when the lawyer needed a good push to get things done. And she always used his first name, unless there were clients around.

Hennessy sighed and took a gold fountain pen from his inside pocket.

"You're a hard taskmaster, Beth, that you are." She stood in front of the desk, her arms folded across her ample bosom, as Hennessy scanned each letter and signed his name. When he'd finished he scooped them up with a flourish and rewarded him with a smile. She was hellish pretty, thought Hennessy, as he did at least a dozen times a day. If he was younger, and single, and if she wasn't the proud mother of twins, and if he hadn't been married to a woman who made his heart ache. God, there were so many "ifs" that it was laughable. He smiled and her lime-green eyes twinkled as if reading his thoughts.

"Anything else?" he asked, replacing the top on his pen.

"Mr Armytage would like you to call him about his case, and you have a four o'clock appointment with Mr Kershaw. And there's a man trying to get hold of you."

"A man?"

"A foreigner. Calling from London." She saw Hennessy smile and she held up her hand. "No, I don't mean he was a foreigner just because he was phoning from England. He sounded foreign, Oriental. Chinese, maybe."

"And what did he want, this Chinaman?"

"He wouldn't say. Said he had to speak to you. If he calls again, do you want to speak to him?"

"I don't see why not. Right, can you get me Tom Armytage's file? He must be getting nervous about tomorrow."

Beth nodded and left his office. Hennessy watched her hips swing as she went, then caught sight of his wife's smiling face in the brass frame on the right-hand corner of his desk, her arms around their two teenage children. Hennessy grinned at the picture. "I was only looking, darling Mary, only looking. You know that."

The phone on the desk rang, making him jump. It was Beth, telling him that The Chinaman was calling again.

"Put him on," said Hennessy, his curiosity aroused.

Nguyen introduced himself and explained what he wanted, speaking softly and slowly, sometimes so quietly that Hennessy had to ask him to repeat himself. When Hennessy finally realised what the caller was requesting he was stunned, unable to believe that the man could be so naïve.

"What on earth makes you think that I know the men who killed your wife and daughter?"

Nguyen was insistent. Polite but insistent. There was a rustle of paper on the line as if he was reading something. "Because you are a political adviser to Sinn Fein, the political wing of the IRA." The phrase came out so confidently and smoothly that the contrast with his earlier carefully controlled speech and ungainly vocabulary convinced Hennessy that The Chinaman had indeed read it, from a newspaper cutting perhaps.

"I do offer advice to politicians, that is true. But I condemn, as do they, violent acts against innocent members of the public, both in England and here in Northern Ireland." Hennessy realised he had shifted into the standard speech he gave journalists or visiting MPs, the words slipping off his tongue as easily as The Chinaman's when he was reading from the cutting. "You have the wrong man."

"If that is so, Mr Hennessy, could you tell me who in the IRA would tell me?"

Hennessy marvelled at the man's stupidity. "Offhand, I can think of no one who would be in a position to help you. And I would add that the sort of men you are talking about are not the sort who would take kindly to being approached with such accusations." Hennessy kept the threat veiled, aware as always of the possibility that the security forces had his lines tapped. "I suggest that you speak to the police, I am sure they are doing their best to identify the men responsible. But I can assure you that I do not know."

Nguyen fell silent for a while. Hennessy was just about to hang up when he spoke again. "I am afraid I do not believe you, Mr Hennessy. You are their adviser. You know who they are."

Hennessy snorted angrily. "I have already explained, I advise politicians, not terrorists. There is a world of difference."

"I think that IRA politics and IRA terrorism are different ends of the same snake," said Nguyen. "It does not matter which end you seize, you still have the snake."

This, thought Hennessy, was like talking to a fortune cookie. "Using your analogy, I would suggest that it makes a great deal of difference which end you attack," he replied. "One end will fight back." Hennessy felt pleased at the turn of phrase. It had given him the same sort of buzz that he got in court demolishing his opponent's legal arguments.

Nguyen was not deterred. "I have chosen, Mr Hennessy. You will tell me who is responsible."

Hennessy's temper flared. "You are wasting my time. Goodbye." He cut the connection and then buzzed Beth on the intercom.

"Yes Liam?"

"If The Chinaman rings again just tell him I'm unavailable. I don't want to speak to him again. Ever."

Nguyen knelt down in front of the red-painted wooden shrine and lit a stick of incense with an old Zippo lighter. He snapped the top of the metal lighter back in place and then held it with both palms pressed together. He rubbed his hands slowly, caressing the smooth metal. The sweet-smelling smoke curled upwards, drifting in the air, and he breathed it in. He opened his hands and looked at the lighter. On one side there was an insignia etched into the metal. There was a short-handled dagger, superimposed on a badge the shape of the blade of a spear, and across the dagger were three bolts of lightning. Above the badge was a banner containing the word "Airborne". Nguyen had had the lighter for many years, but it had never let him down. His wife had carried it out of Vietnam and had proudly presented it to him when they were reunited in a refugee camp in Hong Kong. She had never let him down, either.

He slipped the lighter back in his pocket and sat back on his heels, his eyes closed and his hands together in prayer as he emptied his mind of everything save his wife and three dead daughters. When his first two daughters had died he had been powerless to help and by the time he was in a position to do anything the men responsible were hundreds of miles away. He'd thirsted for revenge then, he'd wanted to tear the men apart with his bare hands, but there was nothing he could do. It had been a long time since the two young girls had suffered, all those years ago in the South China Sea. He remembered how he'd had to watch. How they'd screamed and begged him to help, and how something inside him had died. The urge for revenge had never died, in fact if anything it was stronger now than it had ever been, though it was tempered by the knowledge that he had done everything he could. But this time he would not allow the deaths of Xuan Phoung and Kieu Trinh to pass unresolved into memories. He would not allow the men responsible to escape unpunished. He swore to himself he would not. On the souls of his family he swore it. He didn't move for almost an hour and when he opened his eyes again they were moist, though no tears rolled down his cheeks. He slowly stood up, his joints clicking and cracking as he stretched his legs. He had decided what he was going to do, but he knew there would be a thousand details that he still had to work out, so he took a pencil and one of his daughter's unused exercise-books from a drawer in the kitchen and sat down at the dining-table and began writing.

* * *

It was dark, so dark that the man could see the car's headlights from more than a mile away, carving tunnels of light through the blackness. He lay down in the grass and waited for it to pass. It was two o'clock in the morning so cars were few and far between along the road connecting the A4008 with the A409 near Bushey Heath, just south-west of the M1. The man was lying face down on farmland, his nose close to the dew-damp soil, listening to the engine noise grow louder and then fade away. He got to his feet, picked up the spade and the metal detector by his side and walked towards a small brook that cut through the fields. He had memorised the location and if he was unlucky enough to be caught he'd say that he was just a treasure hunter out looking for buried coins, but getting caught was the last thing on his mind. He heard the trickling water before he reached the bank of the brook, and turned left and followed its meandering path to a small copse. He pushed his way through waist-high bushes until he came to the base of a towering beech tree. One of its roots, as thick as a man's thigh, crawled along the peaty ground for six feet or so before plunging into the earth, and it was midway along its length where the man began to dig. He was well-built and used to physical exercise, and though he was breathing heavily after half an hour he had dug a hole four feet deep and three feet across. He began to take more care then, and before long the spade clunked into something that sounded vaguely metallic. He bent down and pulled up a long thin package, wrapped in polythene. He laid it on the ground next to the tree and unwrapped it. Under the polythene was a sack, tied at one end with a piece of wire. He undid it and pulled the sack down.

Inside were three Armalite rifles and two handguns, along with several boxes of cartridges. There was a plastic-wrapped package labelled Semtex and a polythene bag containing detonators. The man slowly counted them. His eyes were used to the darkness and he could see enough to identify the contents. He had already memorised the list he'd been shown, the list of what the cache should contain, and he mentally crossed them off one at a time. Eventually, satisfied that nothing was missing, he packed up the munitions and put them back in the hole. He replaced the soil and then stamped up and down to flatten the earth before kneeling down and gently smoothing it over. He walked some distance away from the beech tree and gathered twigs and small branches and placed them haphazardly over the freshly dug soil. It would fool most casual observers and in a day or so it would have blended in perfectly with its surroundings. There was little chance of it being discovered. That's why the hiding place had been chosen in the first place.

Nguyen came out of Charing Cross Tube station and walked to the Strand. He found the shop he wanted and stood looking through the window. It was packed with camping equipment, everything from compasses to water-bottles, a huge range of knives, racks of anoraks, sleeping-bags, dehydrated food in silver-foil packets, first-aid kits, crossbows and a range of martial arts equipment. It was all so different during the war, Nguyen thought. So very different. Equipment then was what you could beg or borrow, or take from a fallen comrade or steal from an enemy. And to think that now you could simply walk into a shop and buy it. If they had been able to get hold of equipment like this thirty years ago, then perhaps none of this would have happened and he and his family would be together in a free Vietnam. He shook his head, trying to disperse the thoughts, knowing that there was no point in dwelling on the past.

He walked into the shop and looked through the racks. A young man tried on an army-type pullover with reinforced patches on the shoulders and elbows as his blonde girlfriend looked on admiringly. A skinhead in a shiny green bomber jacket weighed a small throwing knife in his hand and then ran a finger along the blade. A father and son examined a two-man tent as an elderly shop assistant rolled it out along the floor for them. Nobody gave Nguyen a second look.

He picked a camouflage jacket from a rack and looked at it. It was made of nylon and he heard it rustle even as he held it up. Useless, he thought. You'd hear it hundreds of yards away. And the fasteners were made from the Velcro material that made a ripping noise every time you used it. It was for show, like the knife the skinhead was testing. Pretty to look at, but useless in the field. Just by looking at it Nguyen could tell that the knife had no weight, it would bounce off any live target. He took down another jacket, similar colour scheme of dark and light greens, reminiscent of the tiger-striped fatigues he used to wear in the jungle, made from a soft cotton material that probably wasn't waterproof but which looked warm. He tried it on and the sleeves were about six inches too long, even over his jacket. He looked at the label. Medium it said. European medium, obviously, because Nguyen was not small for a Vietnamese.

"Can I help you, sir?" said a young assistant.

Nguyen held up his arms. "Small size?" he asked, and the youngster smiled and helped him get it off. He flicked through the racks and pulled out a smaller size, pressed it up against Nguyen's shoulders, nodded, and asked him to try it on. It fitted.

"Trousers. Same style," said Nguyen, and the youngster found a pair of trousers made from the same soft material.

"Anything else, sir?" he said, and Nguyen nodded enthusiastically.

"Oh yes, yes," he said. "Many things."

He picked up a pair of binoculars, powerful and covered with thick, green rubber, and asked the assistant if it was OK to try them. The boy said yes, but went with him to the door and waited while Nguyen scanned up and down the crowded street.

"I will take these," said Nguyen, handing them to the boy. He walked back into the shop. So many things to buy. "Bottles," he said.

"Bottles?" queried the boy.

"Water-bottles," said Nguyen, pointing to a canteen, khaki-coloured with a green strap. It looked big enough to hold a quart. "Two of those. No, three."

The boy piled up the purchases by a cash register, sensing that the customer was going to be here for some time. On the wall behind the cash register were a number of replica guns and rifles, dull metal and polished wood. They looked so real, Nguyen marvelled. How could such things be on sale in England? he wondered. Some of the guns he recognised, a Colt .45, a Ruger .22, an M9 9-millimetre semi-automatic. Suddenly he stopped, his heart pounding. It couldn't be, could it? His eyes widened and he walked over to stand in front of an AK-47, a Kalashnikov automatic rifle, perfect in every detail with even its curved ammunition magazine in place. He reached up to touch it, to remind himself how it felt. At the last moment, just before his fingers touched the cold metal, he pulled back his hand and shook his head to clear away the memories.

"Compass," he said, and the assistant took him over to a glass-topped counter. On a shelf underneath were a selection of compasses and map-reading equipment. Nguyen pointed at several and the boy took them out for him to examine. Nguyen chose one. "Knife," he said.

There were so many knives, more than he had ever seen in any one place. There were penknives with all sorts of gadgets attached – nail files, spanners, scissors, bottle-openers. There were throwing knives, useless ones like the skinhead had been playing with, but also serious, properly balanced heavy knives that could kill from twenty yards in the right hands. Nguyen held a pair of the heavy knives, feeling their balance and knowing they were perfect.

"Can try?" he asked the assistant.

"Try?"

Nguyen showed him the knives. "Can I throw?"

"Here?" said the boy. "No, no. God, no." He looked confused.

"Never mind," said Nguyen, putting them on top of the camouflage trousers. There was a big selection of survival knives, big sharp blades, serrated on one side, with hollow handles containing a small compass, a short length of fishing line and a few cheap fishing hooks. Nguyen snorted as he looked at them. Joke knives, not what he was looking for. He was looking for a strong blade, one that he could sharpen until it would cut paper like a razor, with a groove in the blade so that the blood could flow out as it was thrust into a body. No groove and the suction effect would make withdrawing the knife that much harder. The tip of the knife had to be angled, too, so that it could ease the ribs apart and allow the killing thrust to the heart. And the handle had to be heavy enough and sturdy enough so that the blade was kept steady as it was used. A knife was important, your life could so easily depend on it. The choice of scabbard was vital too, the action had to be smooth and silent when the blade was withdrawn and the straps had to be strong and hard-wearing. Nguyen spent a lot of time examining the knives in stock before deciding. The one he eventually selected was expensive, one of the most expensive in the shop, but it was the best. He also took a small Swiss army knife, for its tools rather than its blades.

What else? He looked up and down the shop. There was so much he could use. A tent. A sleeping-bag. A small stove. A lightweight blanket made from foil. A folding axe. A rucksack. A first-aid kit. Nguyen was tempted, but at the same time a part of him knew that equipment was often a trap. It slowed you down, you spent more time and effort carrying it and looking after it than you did fighting. He remembered how he used to go into the jungle in fatigues and sandals, with a water-bottle, a few pounds of cooked rice in a cloth tube tied around his waist and nothing else but his rifle and ammunition. He and his comrades travelled light and covered ground quickly and silently. How they laughed at the ungainly Americans, sweating like pigs under the weight of their huge rucksacks. You could hear them coming for miles as they hacked and tripped their way through the undergrowth. So many were killed before they even had a chance to open their precious backpacks, but they never learned.

"Anything else?" asked the assistant, jarring Nguyen's thoughts.

He walked over to a rack of walking boots but decided against buying a pair. The ones he had back at his house would be better because they wouldn't need breaking in. "I want a small rucksack," he said. The assistant showed him a big, blue nylon backpack on an aluminium frame with padded straps and Nguyen said it was too big and that the colour was wrong. "Too bright," he said. He pointed to a small dark-green rucksack, the sort that children might use to carry their school-books. It had no frame and when Nguyen tried it on it lay flat against his back. He adjusted the straps and walked up and down the shop. It felt comfortable and made next to no noise. He removed it and handed it to the assistant. "This one is good," said Nguyen.

The assistant placed all Nguyen's purchases in a large plastic carrier bag, totalling them up on the cash register as he did. Nguyen paid in cash. As he waited for his change he looked wistfully at the AK-47 replica. So many memories, he thought.

On the way to the Tube station he walked past a photographer's shop with shelves full of cameras and lenses. He went in and asked if they sold flash-bulbs.

"Flash-bulbs?" said the man behind the counter. "Don't get much call for those these days. They all have built in flashes now." He frowned and rubbed his chin. "I've got some somewhere, I saw them a couple of weeks ago. What sort of camera are they for?"

Nguyen shrugged. "Any sort. But not the square ones, the ones they use in the little cameras. I want the single bulbs."

"Yeah, I know the sort you mean. Hang on, let me check out back." He disappeared through a door and Nguyen heard boxes being moved and drawers opening and closing.

"You're in luck," he called. "How many do you want?"

"A dozen," Nguyen shouted back.

The man returned with two packets and handed them to Nguyen. "I can't guarantee they'll still work, mind," he said. "They're old stock and I don't know how long they've been there."

Nguyen examined them carefully and then nodded. "They will be perfect," he said. He paid in cash, put the packets into his carrier bag and left the shop.

* * *

"We need more explosive," The Bombmaker said. Fisher ran his fingers through his hair and sighed. He stretched his legs out and lay back in the leather sofa.

"How much do we have left?" he asked.

"A couple of kilos, no more. We've plenty of detonators, though."

Fisher smiled. "Fat lot of good they'll be to us without the stuff that goes bang," he said. "I'll get us more, don't you worry."

McCormick came into the lounge from the kitchen and put down four mugs of coffee on the table by the side of the sofa. O'Reilly got up from his easy chair and took one of them. He walked over to the french windows and looked over the Thames as he drank.

"Isn't it about time we moved?" asked McCormick.

"Why move?" said Fisher.

"In case they track us down. We've been here for months, sure enough. Normal procedure is to keep moving, never stay in one place for too long."

Fisher shook his head. "No, that's exactly what they'd expect us to do. They'll be checking all the small hotels and bed and breakfast places. A group like us moving around will stick out like a sore thumb. And after the Knightsbridge bombing every landlady in Britain is on the lookout for Irishmen. How long do you think it would take until we were rumbled?"

"I suppose you're right," said McCormick reluctantly. "It's just . . ."

"Look," interrupted Fisher, "we've had this flat rented for almost a year. It's on a long-term lease, paid direct from a dummy company bank account. As far as the landlord is concerned, it's rented to a stockbroking firm who use it for visiting executives from the States. This place is perfect."

O'Reilly tapped on the window. "And if the SAS knock on the front door, we can leg it over the balcony and down the Thames," he said.

"If the SAS find out we're here, we won't be going anywhere," said McCormick. "Bastards."

"Nobody is going to find out where we are," said Fisher. "Nobody. So long as we stay right where we are. Our more immediate problem is to get hold of some more Semtex."

O'Reilly turned away from the window, sipping his coffee. He took the mug from his lips and smiled. "You want me to get it?"

Fisher nodded. "Tonight. I'll come with you."

"I can do it."

"I know. But this one is hard to find. You'll need me there."

McCormick coughed. He took a handkerchief from the back pocket of his jeans and sneezed into it. "I'm going down with a cold," he said, but nobody registered any sympathy. He inspected the contents of the handkerchief and put it back into his pocket. "And when we've got the stuff, then what?" he asked.

Fisher's eyes sparkled and he looked over at The Bombmaker. "Something big," he said. "Something very, very big."

Nguyen took the Tube back to Clapham and stored his purchases in the shed at the back of the yard behind his shop. It was a big metal garage but the main door had long ago been boarded up and now it contained three big chest freezers full of frozen meat and vegetables, sacks of rice and bottles of soy sauce. There was also a long wooden bench and racks of tools along one wall. Nguyen placed his carrier bag on the bench, padlocked the door and then went through the shop to his van which was parked outside. He drove to a large do-it-yourself store in south London and spent more than an hour filling a large trolley. He bought sections of plastic drain-pipe, insulation tape, three large bags of fertilizer, a soldering iron and several packs of solder, and other tools that he knew he'd need which he didn't already have in his shed. He paid in cash, and on the way back he stopped at a large filling station. He filled the tank and bought two large plastic bottles of antifreeze, three cans of Shell motor oil and half a dozen cans of white spray paint to match the colour of his van, and a can of black paint.

Pham was washing bean sprouts in the kitchen sink and he grunted a greeting as Nguyen walked by. Pham had agreed to buy the restaurant and had already paid Nguyen in cash. The bank had agreed to transfer the mortgage on the property to him and after a long but good-hearted argument over the value of the kitchen equipment and the food in the fridges Nguyen had agreed to accept thirty thousand pounds. Nguyen didn't ask where Pham had got the money from, but he had relatives in Manchester who had probably helped out. He was planning to switch to Vietnamese cooking, though Nguyen doubted that it would be a success, so far away from the West End. He and his wife had decided when they first moved to London that they were more likely to make money if they kept to a Chinese menu, even though they personally found the cuisine bland and boring. Still, it was up to Pham now. Nguyen had promised to be out by the end of the week but he knew that Pham was keen for him to go as soon as possible so that he could move into the flat upstairs.

After putting the rest of his purchases away in the garage, Nguyen sat at his table and crossed off the list everything he'd already bought. There were three items left: two kinds of acid and glycerine. He knew how to make the acid he needed from other quite innocuous and easily available materials. It was messy, but possible, but there was no need because this was England not Vietnam and here there were firms where you could buy chemicals, no questions asked. He took a well-thumbed copy of Yellow Pages and looked up Chemical Manufacturers and Suppliers. After three calls he had found one firm who would supply him with concentrated acids (for etchings, he'd said) and he arranged to collect a gallon of glycerine from another firm. Nguyen thought it prudent not to buy all three from the same supplier.

*   *   *

Fisher stopped the car and switched off the engine and the lights, allowing the darkness to envelop them like a shroud. He and O'Reilly waited until their eyes became used to the blackness, listening to the clicking noises from the engine as it cooled. They were parked at the end of a lonely lane not far from Bexley station, half an hour's drive south-east of central London. Both men were dressed in dark pullovers, jeans and black shoes, outfits that wouldn't stick out at night but which didn't obviously mark them out as burglars. If they were unlucky enough to come across the police then they'd just pretend they were a couple of queers looking for a bit of privacy. That had been Fisher's idea, and O'Reilly hadn't been exactly bowled over by it.

"Look, I promise not to kiss you," Fisher had joked.

O'Reilly had laughed nervously.

"Not on the mouth, anyway . . ." O'Reilly had winced and Fisher knew he'd hit a nerve so he let the joke drop. He mentally filed O'Reilly's over-reaction for future reference, a possible weak point. Fisher did that with everybody he came into contact with, memorising their strengths and weaknesses and the buttons that had to be pressed to get the desired responses.

"Are you right?" he asked O'Reilly.

O'Reilly nodded. They got out of the car and Fisher led the way, climbing silently over a stone wall and walking across the dew-laden grass. O'Reilly's foot knocked against something hard that crunched and rolled, and then he heard a rustling noise behind him, something small scampering through the grass and making snuffling sounds. Hedgehogs, he realised. There were dozens of them, rolling into tight, spiked balls whenever they sensed the two men.

They reached another wall, this one taller than the first, and they had to scramble over. It surrounded a graveyard, close-clipped grass and gravelled paths, the gravestones a mixture of old stone crosses, chipped and weather-worn, and new, clean-cut marble. To their left was a grey stone church with a steeple. In the distance a vixen barked, and her call sparked off a cacophony of howls from dogs in the nearby housing estate. The two men dropped down into a crouch, their backs against the wall, while Fisher got his bearings.

He pointed towards a white concrete angel with spreading wings. "This way," he said, and took O'Reilly along the grass verge, past the angel and between two waist-high tombs, the sort vampires might lie in to sleep away the daylight hours, safe from sunlight. They walked through the drooping branches of a willow and then Fisher headed over to five tombstones lined up in front of the boundary wall like a stud poker hand. He kicked the one in the centre.

"There it is," he said. "Help me get it up."

They knelt down together, scraping away the soil to slip their hands underneath the stone and then they pushed it up, grunting with the strain until it came off the ground with a wet, slurping sound. They stood the stone upright and then leant it against the wall. The smell of damp, stale earth filled O'Reilly's nostrils and made him want to gag. Fisher scraped away the soil like a dog looking for a bone. Less than a foot down his fingers touched plastic and he pulled up a polythene-covered parcel which he handed to O'Reilly. There were two other bundles, one of which was obviously a rifle, but Fisher ignored them. All they needed this time was Semtex. They unwrapped the parcel and took out half the packages of explosive, six in all. They took three apiece, rewrapped the rest and put them back in the shallow hole before pushing the damp soil back and replacing the gravestone. They checked the surroundings to make sure that they were still alone in the graveyard, and then they left as silently as they'd arrived.

Nguyen drove his Renault van down the alley behind the shop, the early morning sun glinting off the bonnet. He'd already opened the two wooden gates that led to the shop's back yard where they usually unpacked deliveries and transferred the food into the freezers in the garage. He parked the van and switched off the engine. He had put on a pair of old overalls after he'd bathed that morning, and he pulled on a pair of plastic gloves. The van was white, three years old and mechanically sound. It had always been parked outside because the garage was used for storage, so it was rusting a little, and it had taken a few knocks from other cars. The name of the restaurant and the telephone number had been drawn in black paint on both sides. Nguyen had painted each letter himself, slowly and carefully, it had taken him hours, but it was the work of minutes to spray over them with a can of white spray paint. He sprayed the paint thinly so that it wouldn't run and he waited thirty minutes before giving it a second coat, and then a third to make sure that the lettering was completely covered.

While the third coat dried he transferred the tool box, bottles and bags from the garage, methodically crossing the contents off the list in his exercise-book so that he was sure he hadn't forgotten anything. It was all there, the acids, the bags of fertilizer, the bottles of antifreeze and cans of oil. He'd forgotten nothing. When he'd finished he used a screwdriver to prise the lid off the can of black paint and, resting a brand new artist's brush against a piece of garden cane, painted on a new set of letters and numbers. As he worked he suddenly felt as if he was being watched and he turned and looked at the upstairs window. A curtain twitched. It could have been Pham wondering what he was up to, or it could have been the wind. Nguyen stared up at the window but saw nothing so he returned to the painting.

When the final letter was in place he stood back and admired his handiwork. It was good. Almost as good as before, even though it had taken him about half as long. "Green Landscape Gardeners" it said, along with a London telephone number he'd taken from the Yellow Pages. The white paintwork around the lettering looked whiter than the rest of the van, but driving through the city streets would soon fix that up. The hairs on the back of his neck stood on end and he whirled around, but this time the curtains weren't moving and there was still no one there.

He went into the house through the back door and up the

stairs. His suitcase was already packed. He picked it up and was on the way to the door when he had a sudden urge to kneel and pray before the shrine. He got down on his knees and used his Zippo to light a stick of incense. He closed his eyes and breathed in the perfume and tried to empty his mind, to steel himself for the trials to come.

The incense filled his lungs. It was the same rich scent that always reminded him of his parents' farm, the room where he'd been born so many years ago. When was it? Could it really have been so long ago? Could it really have been 1943? Where had the years gone, how had they slipped by so easily? He could still picture every inch of the small family farm, close to the Gulf of Tonkin in North Vietnam.

Nguyen shuddered and opened his eyes. They were moist and he wiped them with the back of his hand. It was time to go.

He carried the bag downstairs, not bothering to say goodbye to Pham. He put the case in the back of the van, locked the doors and drove the van out of the yard. He headed north, towards Stranraer in Scotland and the ferry to Northern Ireland. Before he left London he stopped at a garden centre and loaded up the van with bags of peat and more fertilizer, a selection of bedding plants, and a spade and a fork.

It was a long, tiring drive to Stranraer, but Nguyen knew there was no real alternative. He needed the equipment and supplies in the van, so flying was out of the question. He had thought he'd be able to take a ferry from Liverpool direct to Belfast, but he'd discovered that the route had been cancelled some months earlier. The only car ferries now operating seemed to be from Stranraer to Larne in County Antrim, north of Belfast, or from Holyhead in Anglesey across to Dun Laoghaire, near Dublin in the South. Either route would mean hours behind the wheel, but he had reservations about driving through Southern Ireland and across the border. Better, he thought, to go direct to Northern Ireland and not worry about Customs or passports. He drove through the night and slept in the van during the morning before catching the ferry.

When he arrived at Larne he saw two men in a Ford Granada being taken to one side and their car searched by four men in bottle-green uniforms while a Labrador retriever sniffed around and wagged its tail, but he wasn't even given a second look. He knew why, it was nothing more than racism working in his favour. He was Oriental and the fighting in Ireland was between Caucasians.

He drove the van from the ferry terminal south to Belfast city centre. It was late evening and he had to find somewhere to stay. He stopped at a filling station and filled up with petrol and then bought a street map. He asked the teenage girl if she knew where there were any guest-houses but he couldn't understand her when she replied. He asked again and this time she spoke more slowly, as if he were a child, but the accent was so strange he couldn't follow what she was saying. He smiled and paid for the petrol and the map and left, none the wiser. He was starting to realise that he was, after all, in a different country.

There were other reminders. The police wore green uniforms and drove around in heavily fortified blue-grey Land-Rovers with metal screens protecting the sides. And there were soldiers everywhere wearing camouflage uniforms and helmets and carrying automatic rifles at the ready, barrels aimed at the ground. The army used green Land-Rovers, open at the top so that the men in the back were exposed but able to react quickly. It made good sense, Nguyen thought.

He drove by what he thought was a prison until he saw a sign that said it was a police station. He was so surprised that he stopped to look at it. He had never in his life seen such a thing, not even in Saigon. Thick metal mesh fences surrounded the building which had what appeared to be a gun turret on one corner. The top of the fence was a tangle of barbed wire and all the windows were firmly shuttered. It was a fortress. He had been considering asking a police-man to suggest a place to stay, but from the look of it the police in Northern Ireland were not geared up for handling general enquiries from the public. They were in a state of siege.

There were posts at each corner of the building, and on the top were surveillance cameras covering all the approaches.

There was a metallic rap against the passenger window of the van and Nguyen jumped. An unsmiling face under a peaked cap glared at him. He knocked on the door again with the barrel of his handgun. Nguyen leant over and wound down the window.

"Can I be of help to you, sir?" the policeman asked. Another officer appeared on the driver's side of the van. In the rear-view mirror he saw two more.

Nguyen smiled and waved the map at them. "I need somewhere to stay tonight. Do you know anywhere?"

The officer was already relaxing. He slid his gun back into his holster.

"Give me the map," he said. Nguyen switched on the small reading light and the policeman jabbed a finger in the bottom left-hand corner. "See this road here, Wellington Park?"

Nguyen nodded.

"There are a few places there, quite cheap." He handed the map back to Nguyen. "You'd best be on your way. And in future don't hang around in front of police stations in a van. We're a touch sensitive about that sort of thing. Understand?"

"I am sorry," said Nguyen. "Thank you for your help."

The policemen grouped together and watched him go, four stout figures in dark-green bullet-proof jackets.

Nguyen followed the map until he reached Wellington Park. He drove slowly down the road, looking left and right. He soon saw a guest-house but it had a sign in the window saying "No Vacancies". Further down the road there was another house with a sign saying "Vacancies" and Nguyen stopped the van in front of it.

It was dark now and the van appeared yellow under the streetlights. Nguyen pressed the doorbell and waited. The front door was wooden with two vertical strips of dimpled, frosted glass. Through the glass he saw a light come on and a figure ripple towards him. The door opened to reveal an overweight elderly woman with close-cropped grey hair and horn-rimmed spectacles. She was wearing a blue and white diamond-patterned dress and a plain white apron and was drying her hands on a red tea-towel.

"Do you have a room?" Nguyen asked her.

She looked him up and down and then scrutinised the van over his shoulder, screwing up her eyes to read the lettering.

"How long would you be wanting it for?" she asked.

Nguyen had difficulty understanding her accent but she spoke slowly enough for him to get the drift.

"Two nights, that is all. A room with a bath."

The old woman sucked her teeth and shook her head. "No baths in the rooms, but I do have one with a shower and a toilet. And a small wash-basin. It's right at the top of the house, very cosy."

Nguyen said he'd take it and the woman seemed doubtful, but then he pulled his wallet from his jacket and offered to pay her cash, in advance, and she smiled and ushered him inside. On the way up the stairs she introduced herself as Mrs McAllister as the notes disappeared behind the apron. He told her his name and she tried to repeat it, but gave up. The room was small with a single bed, an old wooden wardrobe, a dressing-table with an oval mirror, and a bedside table with a brass lamp with a pink lampshade. There was an ornate crucifix above the bed and to the left of the dressing-table was a black-framed photograph of John F. Kennedy. The ceiling sloped down to a window overlooking the street. Opposite the window was a door leading to a tiny bathroom with a tiled floor, a shower cubicle, a wash-basin with a cylindrical gas heater on the wall above it, and a low toilet with a black plastic seat. It was perfect.

The two pirates stood by the bar, tapping their feet to the driving beat of a pop song that Woody only vaguely recognised as they sipped orange juice from tall glasses. One of the pirates was middle-aged with a greying beard and a black patch over one eye, the other was younger with curly blond hair and flushed cheeks, but they wore matching outfits, baggy white shirts, red scarves around their necks, tight black breeches, white socks and shiny black shoes with big brassy buckles.

"Pirates?" said Maggie as she followed Woody to the bar.

"Yeah, they're with the pirate ships," said Woody, squeezing in between two stockbroker types and trying to catch the attention of the young barmaid.

"They would be," said Maggie, still mystified.

Woody pointed over her head, towards the large windows at the far end of the bar. "Pirate ships," he explained. "They're a tourist attraction. A sort of cross between Madame Tussaud's and the Cutty Sark. Those guys are sort of tour guides, cross their palms with silver and they'll take you below decks and tell you blood-curdling tales of life on the salty sea." The barmaid finally saw his plaintive look and came over. She gave him a beaming smile which faded a little when she saw that he was with a girl. Woody tended to attract barmaids, but was never sure why. He was still good-looking, he knew that, though he had allowed himself to go a bit recently. It was his eyes, an old girlfriend had told him. "Your eyes make me go weak at the knees, they're hot. Really hot," she'd said. Woody reckoned it wasn't anything to do with his looks, though. He thought it had more to do with the way he made them laugh. Sometimes he laughed them into bed before they realised what was happening. Woody winked at the barmaid, ordered drinks and carried them over to an empty table, close by the window so that Maggie could look at the sailing ships.

"They're not real, are they?" she asked, sitting down.

"I don't think so, they were built to pull in the punters to Tobacco Dock."

He raised his glass to her and she smiled. He was glad he'd taken her to Henry's Bar in Tobacco Dock because at least they could sit in comfort. Standing at the bar was essential when you were with the lads, but Maggie demanded a higher standard of comfort. No, that wasn't right, she didn't demand it. She deserved it.

"What are you thinking?" she asked.

"Just thinking how pretty you look," he said.

"Why thank you kind sir," she laughed. "You look exhausted."

"Yeah, I'm not sleeping well. It's the heat."

She frowned. "It's not that hot at the moment," she said.

Woody laughed. "No, it's my place. I've a bedsit in a house with about a dozen others, and mine is right next to the only bathroom. The landlord has fitted a hot-water tank as big as a Saturn rocket and my room is always in the high eighties. I have to have the window open even in winter."

Maggie smiled and shook her head. "Why don't you move, you daft sod?"

Woody shrugged. "It's cheap."

"You're not short of money, are you?"

Woody was immediately embarrassed because the answer was yes, he was bloody short of money. Always was. And always would be unless he got a staff job. The shifts weren't coming as often as they used to, he was overdrawn at the bank, yet he still had to stand his round at the pub while he brown-nosed his way back into the good books of the guys on the news desk. "No, it's convenient, that's all." Sure, if you fancied an hour on the bus to get into work.

"So is LA still an option?" she asked.

"Sure. Sure it is."

They drank and sat for a while looking at each other in silence. Woody spoke first.

"Now it's my turn to ask what you're thinking about."

Maggie pulled a face. "I was actually wondering why you didn't get a better job, why you waste your time on a comic like the *Sunday World*."

He sighed deeply, and explained that he didn't even have a job with the *Sunday World*, that he was only a freelance, dependent on shifts, and that even that didn't pay particularly well, not since the print and journalists unions had been broken along with the dockers and the miners and any other groups that had once been able to withhold their labour. She listened patiently and then reached over and touched his shoulder, a friendly nudge that showed she understood. Maybe even cared. She asked him why he couldn't get a staff job. At first he didn't want to tell her, but she pressed, pointing out that he was obviously bright, she'd begun reading his stuff and she could tell that it was good, so what had happened? She wormed it out of him eventually, his time on one of the broadsheets, the investigation into high-level corruption within a north of England police force, the drive home along the motorway, the blue flashing light in his rear mirror, the two surly traffic cops and the discovery of two hundred grams of cocaine under the passenger seat of his office car.

"They framed you?" she asked, wide-eyed.

"Yeah. I managed to avoid being sent down, but I lost the job and for a few years I couldn't get any sort of work. The papers didn't trust me, partly because of the drug thing, but I know for a fact that the cops were putting the word around, too. I stuck with it, though, went to work in the West Country for a while, and then some of the nationals began taking my copy again and now at least I've got my foot in the door. I'm lucky to have that, I guess."

"Jesus, Woody, that's terrible. That's appalling."

"That's life, Maggie."

She forced a smile. "I suppose the *Sunday World* isn't that bad," she said sympathetically. "Do they let you travel much?"

"Oh sure, we get around. There are always lots of freebies to be had."

"And do you get political stuff to do?"

"Sure. That's one of the good things about working on a Sunday paper. They have small staffs so there isn't too much specialisation. I mean, I have to do a lot of showbiz crap and weird stuff, but we get to help out with the big ones too."

"What are you working on at the moment?" she asked.

Woody coughed.

"Pardon?" she asked.

Woody looked shamefaced. "Vampire cats," he said. Maggie collapsed into hysterics.

The man approaching the churchyard was short but power-fully built and even in the dark it was obvious he was not a man to get into a fight with, not by choice anyway. He was wearing a brown leather jacket, scuffed and cracked with age, and dark-brown corduroy trousers. He carried a small sack, tied at the end with a short length of rope, and in one of the pockets of his jacket there was a flashlight and half a dozen metal snares. He'd done a fair bit of poaching in his youth, but he wasn't looking for rabbits, the snares were just cover in case he was discovered. In the back pocket of his trousers was a short-handled knife with a wicked blade which he was quite prepared to use if anyone saw through the poacher's disguise.

Somewhere in the dark he heard a hedgehog snuffle then squeal and he stopped and listened but heard nothing other than the night sounds of the English countryside and an airliner rumbling high overhead, red and green lights flashing.

He swung easily over the wall and landed silently in freshly dug soil. He was standing within inches of a new grave, a gaping black rectangular hole that seemed bottomless. He breathed a sigh of relief, if he'd vaulted the wall just a couple of feet to the right he'd have pitched headlong into it and broken a leg, or worse. The luck of the Irish, he thought with a smile. He stepped off the mound of earth and used the sack to smooth away his footprints before moving on. He skirted around the church and headed for the five tombstones.

He knelt down and lifted the stone that covered the stock-pile, pushing hard with his legs. He carefully leant it against the wall and then stood still, counting off sixty seconds in his head as he listened for anything out of the ordinary, because there was no way a poacher would be able to explain what he was doing lifting a gravestone, especially a gravestone that concealed IRA explosives. Still nothing, even the hedgehogs had fallen silent.

He dug into the earth with his hands and pulled out three polythene-covered packages, working quickly but carefully. If he was surprised to see half of the Semtex explosive missing, his face showed no sign of it. He rewrapped the parcels, replaced the soil and dropped the stone back over the hiding place. He brushed the dirt from his hands, checked that the surrounding area was clean and then walked down the gravel path and out of the churchyard.

Beth McKinstry was on the telephone when Nguyen walked into the office. He stood in front of her desk and waited. He was wearing his only suit, a grey one that was starting to go shiny at the elbows. He had on a white shirt and a blue V-necked pullover with three white skiers across the front. He was holding a white carrier bag in both hands, clasping it to his chest like a baby. Murphy was sitting on the sofa reading a magazine and massaging his aching shoulder. He'd looked up when Nguyen entered, but immediately dismissed him as any sort of potential threat and carried on reading.

Beth watched Nguyen as she talked, frowning slightly. He smiled and nodded at her and she looked down. She didn't look up again until she'd finished the call. As she replaced the phone Kavanagh came out of Hennessy's office and quietly closed the door behind him. He barely glanced at Nguyen before sitting down next to Murphy.

"Yes?" said Beth.

"Please, I would like to speak with Mr Liam Hennessy."

"And your name is?" she said.

"Nguyen Ngoc Minh," he answered.

"Can I tell him what it is about?" She couldn't even attempt to repeat his name.

"It is very difficult to explain," he told her.

She reached for the intercom button but stopped halfway. "Are you the man who phoned last week?" she asked.

"I phoned many times," said Nguyen.

Beth took her hand away from the intercom. "I'm afraid Mr Hennessy is very busy. He won't be able to see you."

"I must see him," Nguyen repeated.

"He's busy!" insisted Beth, raising her voice. Her cheeks flushed red.

Murphy and Kavanagh glanced up. The secretary was

good-natured to a fault and rarely lost her temper. Nguyen said nothing, he just smiled.

"If you leave your number I'll call you to arrange an appointment once I have spoken with Mr Hennessy," she said.

Still Nguyen said nothing.

"You must go!" she said. Murphy and Kavanagh got to their feet and walked over to Nguyen.

"Best you do as the lady says," said Murphy quietly.

Nguyen looked at Murphy and the Irishman could see there was no trace of fear in his eyes. "I must see him," he said quietly.

Kavanagh put his hand on Nguyen's shoulder. "What's the crack?" he asked Beth.

"He's been ringing up at all hours asking to see Liam. He won't take no for an answer."

"Yez heard the lady, Mr Hennessy doesn't want to see yez," said Kavanagh, gripping Nguyen's shoulder and pulling him away from the desk. For a second Nguyen was off balance and he clutched the carrier bag tightly as if afraid that it might fall.

"What have you got there?" said Murphy, for the first time regarding the man as a possible threat. It wasn't likely that the Loyalists would use a Chinaman to attack Hennessy, he thought, but these days you never could tell. He reached for the bag.

"My shopping," said Nguyen.

"Let's see," said Kavanagh. "Let's see what yez got there." At first it looked as if Nguyen would resist, but then the tension in his wiry body eased and he handed the bag to Kavanagh. Kavanagh opened it. It contained two bottles of lemonade, a loaf of bread, a can of Heinz baked beans and a brown paper bag full of new potatoes. Seeing that he was satisfied with the inspection, Nguyen held out his hands for the bag, but Kavanagh kept it away from him.

"Pat him down," he said to Murphy. Murphy moved behind Nguyen and ran his hands expertly up and down his body, checking everywhere that a weapon could be concealed. There was a Swiss Army knife in one of the side pockets of the suit, but other than that there was nothing remotely suspicious – a small roll of Sellotape, a box of matches, some string, a set of keys, a pack of cigarettes and a wallet. The normal sort of pocket junk that anyone might have on them. "He's OK," he said to Kavanagh, who handed back the carrier bag.

"Go," he said. "Before we make yez go."

Nguyen shook his head. Kavanagh and Murphy roughly seized an arm each and were preparing to frog-march him out, when the door to Hennessy's office opened. Hennessy's face creased into a puzzled frown when he saw what was going on.

"It's the man who's been phoning," said Beth, before he could speak.

"Ah . . . The Chinaman," said Hennessy, walking across to Beth's desk. "You're a long way from home."

Nguyen held the carrier bag tightly to his chest. "You would not talk to me on the telephone," he said.

"Out," said Murphy, but Hennessy held up his hand.

"No, if he's come all this way I might as well talk to him, boys."

"Yer man's got a knife," said Kavanagh.

"A knife?"

"A Swiss Army knife."

"Well take it off him. Look at him, for God's sake. How much damage can he do with two strapping fellows like yourselves around? Jesus, Mary and Joseph, let the man be."

Kavanagh took the knife from Nguyen and Murphy took the carrier bag.

"You can pick them up on your way out," said Beth as Hennessy led Nguyen into his private office. He waved him to a hard-backed leather seat in front of his desk while he closed the door behind them.

Nguyen sat with his hands folded in his lap while Hennessy sat down behind the desk and leant forward, his arms folded across the wide blotter which took up most of its surface. "Let me tell you right from the start, you are wasting your time." Hennessy said each word clearly and slowly as if addressing a particularly thick-skulled juror because he wasn't sure how good The Chinaman's command of English was. "I realise you are upset and angry, and I understand how you must want revenge for what has happened to your family, but there is nothing I can do to help you. And you must know that it is very dangerous for you to be in Belfast asking about such things." He pressed the tips of his fingers against his temples as if trying to suppress a headache and studied Nguyen. "It is very dangerous," he repeated.

Nguyen nodded thoughtfully. "I do understand. But if you do not know who the men are, you can surely find out. I want you to find out for me."

Hennessy shook his head, amazed at the man's audacity, or stupidity. Nguyen took the pack of cigarettes and the matches from his pocket.

"Can I smoke?" he asked Hennessy. Hennessy nodded and Nguyen held out the pack to him, offering him one. The lawyer refused and watched as Nguyen lit a cigarette and inhaled deeply. Hennessy noticed how steady The Chinaman's hands were, as steady as the unblinking brown eyes that seemed to look through his skull as easily as they penetrated the wreathes of smoke.

"You will change your mind," said Nguyen, and it was a statement, not a question.

"No," said Hennessy.

Nguyen smiled, and it was the smile of a man who has the sure and certain knowledge that he is right. He stood up and bowed once to Hennessy and then left the office. Murphy and Kavanagh were waiting for him outside, and they gave him his carrier bag and the penknife. He thanked them politely and turned to Beth and thanked her as well.

"Can I use your toilet?" he asked, and she told him there was one in the corridor outside. She pointed at the large sheet of glass at the entrance to the reception and through it he saw the door with "Gentlemen" on it. He thanked them all again and left the office, closing the door quietly behind him. The washroom was small with whitewashed walls and a black tiled floor. There was a wash-basin, a urinal and a toilet in a cubicle. There was a mirror screwed to the wall above the basin and by the door was a paper-towel dispenser and below it a large steel wastepaper bin.

Nguyen entered the cubicle, shut the door and locked it. There was a black plastic lid on the toilet and he closed it and then sat down, placing the carrier bag gently on the floor. He took one of the bottles out and held it between his knees. It contained the antifreeze. He took out the second bottle, the one containing concentrated sulphuric acid. He used the Sellotape to bind the bottles together, wrapping it round and round until he was certain they were secure. He took out the length of string and tied it around the necks of the bottles, making quite sure there was no way it could slip. Individually the bottles of liquid were inert, but together they were very dangerous. He put the bottles on the floor and draped the string over his left leg. He took the box of matches out of his pocket and slid the string through it. He pulled the string to check that it was safely tied and then put his hands under the bottoms of the bottles and stood up slowly. The cistern was high up on the wall and Nguyen stood on the toilet seat to attach the string to the lever which operated the flushing system. When he was sure it was secure he carefully removed his hands. The bottles turned slowly in the air above the tiled floor. He unscrewed the caps from the bottles and slipped them into his pocket. Then he pulled the filter off the cigarette and stuck the frayed end into the matchbox so that the burning tip was about three-quarters of an inch beyond the match heads. Nguyen stepped down, picked up the carrier bag and left the cubicle. He used the penknife to slide the lock closed so that it showed "Engaged".

As he left the toilet he smiled a goodbye to Beth. There was no rush, it would take at least two minutes for the cigarette to burn down far enough to set the matches alight. He walked slowly down the stairs and into Donegall Square. Overhead a helicopter hovered high in the air like a bird of prey searching for a victim.

The intercom on Beth's desk buzzed and Hennessy's voice summoned her into the office. From their sofas, Kavanagh and Murphy watched her hips swing as she walked to the door.

"I would," said Murphy, whispering because he knew what a tongue-lashing he'd get if she heard him.

"Who wouldn't?" replied Kavanagh. "But her old man'd focking kill ye."

Hennessy was standing by his window watching Nguyen walk down the road, swinging his carrier bag full of shopping.

"I'm sorry, Liam," she said, before he could speak. "He caught me by surprise. Next time I won't let him disturb you."

"That's all right, Beth. Just tell Murphy and Kavanagh to take care of it if he turns up again." Nguyen stepped off the pavement, crossed the road and disappeared into a side street. Hennessy turned his back on the window. "I think that man is going to be trouble," he said.

"Don't be silly, Liam," she said as if admonishing a child. "What can a man like him do?"

The sound of the explosion made them both flinch, Beth putting her hands to her face and Hennessy ducking away from the window. Through the open door they saw Kavanagh and Murphy dive to the ground. "Keep down!" Murphy yelled at them.

"What's going on?" Hennessy shouted. They didn't answer. They were as confused as he was.

Beth was already on the floor, crouched by the side of the door. Hennessy went over to her and put his arms around her.

Murphy and Kavanagh were crawling over the carpet to check out the corridor. Kavanagh nudged open the door. The corridor was empty, then a pale-faced young man in a three-piece suit nervously appeared from an office further along.

"Mother of God, what happened?" said the young man.

Kavanagh got to his feet. Smoke was billowing out of the Gents, acrid-smelling and burning as he inhaled. He coughed and his eyes watered as he gingerly pushed open the door to the toilet. Fumes billowed out and the sprinklers in the corridor hissed into life and he ducked back into the office. In the distance he heard a police siren, and then another. He told Murphy to guard the door while he went back to Hennessy's office and helped him and Beth to their feet.

Beth flopped on to a chair and Hennessy went over to his drinks cabinet and poured two Irish whiskies. He didn't offer one to Kavanagh, who was teetotal. Beth gulped hers down and Hennessy followed her example.

Before long, half a dozen green-uniformed RUC officers in bullet-proof vests came tearing down the corridor. A bull-necked sergeant ordered them to stay where they were and left a constable to keep an eye on them. The area round the toilet was cordoned off and then two men in dark-blue over-alls carrying big black cases went in. The phone on Beth's desk rang, startling them all, and she asked the constable if it was OK to answer it. He nodded, his face blank. The men in the RUC had no love for Hennessy and his associates and Hennessy knew that the constable would probably have preferred them all to have been plastered over the walls by the explosion rather than sitting at the desk and drinking whiskey. While Beth was talking on the phone a CID officer in a sheepskin jacket arrived. He flashed his card to Hennessy and introduced himself as Inspector Greig. Behind him stood a young plain-clothes sergeant, a tall, gangly youth with a small, toothbrush moustache. He had the same couldn't-give-a-shit look as the uniformed constable.

"It seems as if you've had a wee bit of bother, Mr Hennessy," said Greig. "Unless it was one of your own boys being a tad careless."

Hennessy shrugged. "These things happen," he said. "Can I offer you a whiskey, Inspector?"

Greig refused, as Hennessy knew he would. "I suppose it's a waste of time asking if you have any idea who might have done this?" said Greig, smiling through tight lips.

Kavanagh laughed sharply but Hennessy threw him a with-ering look. It was bad enough having the RUC in the office, but if they antagonised them they'd end up being hauled in for questioning and Hennessy didn't want the inconvenience or the publicity.

"Anyway, you'd better take care in future, Mr Hennessy."

"What do you mean?"

"It looks to have been more of a warning than anything else. According to our forensic boys it was a home-made device, in fact device is hardly the right word. They reckon it was a couple of bottles of chemicals that did the damage."

Murphy remembered the bottles in The Chinaman's carrier bag but said nothing.

"An accident?" said Hennessy.

Greig smiled thinly again. "I hardly think they tied themselves to the toilet cistern," he said. "No, it was a simple chemical bomb, the sort we used to make as kids. Sulphuric acid and ethylene glycol. Antifreeze to you and me. Tie a bottle of each together and drop on to a hard surface. Bang! Did you never do that when you were a kid, Mr Hennessy? Great crack." He could see by the look on the lawyer's face that the answer was no. Greig shrugged. "I suppose we went to different schools, eh? Anyway, it would make a big enough explosion to wreck the room, and you wouldn't be laughing if you were in there, but it never stood a chance of damaging the building. It wasn't what you'd call a serious bomb, if you get my drift. Which makes me think that perhaps it was a warning. I don't suppose there's any point in asking if you've got any enemies, is there Mr Hennessy?" Greig was enjoying the Sinn Fein adviser's obvious discomfort.

"I'll certainly keep you informed if anyone comes to mind, Inspector," Hennessy replied.

"I won't hold my breath."

"Probably best," said Hennessy.

"Can I show you out, Inspector?" asked Beth, sensing that underneath the banter her boss was beginning to lose his temper.

Greig hesitated as if loath to let Hennessy off the hook, but then he nodded and followed her out of the office. His sergeant looked hard at Murphy and Kavanagh as he went out, but the two men returned his gaze with easy smiles. They were long past the stage of fearing the police, the army, or anyone else who tried to impose their authority. Greig went into the toilet to speak to the forensic team again. The sergeant turned to speak to Beth but she closed the door firmly in his face.

Hennessy watched her from the door of his office and, satisfied that she wasn't in shock, gently closed the door.

Kavanagh and Murphy tensed, fearing the sharp edge of Hennessy's tongue a thousand times more than hard looks from under-age detectives, but his anger wasn't directed at them.

"I want that Chinaman found," he said with barely suppressed fury. "I want him found and brought to me."

The phone rang and Hennessy picked it up.

"Liam, it's him!" said Beth. She knew that Hennessy had said he wouldn't take any more calls from him, but she was smart enough to know that the situation was now different.

"Put him on please, Beth. Are you OK?"

"I'm fine, Liam. Really." The line clicked and Hennessy waited for The Chinaman to speak.

"Mr Hennessy?" said Nguyen, not sure if he had been put through.

"What do you want?" said Hennessy.

"Mr Hennessy, you know what I want. I telephoned to see if you had changed your mind."

"Why would I have changed my mind?" said Hennessy quietly.

"You know why," said Nguyen.

Hennessy took a deep breath. "I think that perhaps it would be a good idea if we spoke about this again. It might be we can come to an arrangement. Come back and we'll talk."

Nguyen laughed without humour. "I think not," he said. "You will not see me again, Mr Hennessy. But you will be hearing from me."

"It will take a lot more than a loud noise in my toilet to change my mind."

"So be it," said Nguyen, and hung up.

"The bastard," spat Hennessy. "Who the hell does he think he is, threatening me like that?" He slammed down the phone and glared at the two men by his desk.

"Get his description to the boys," he said. "I want him found."

"It might be an idea if yez left Belfast for a few days, just in case," suggested Kavanagh.

"Are you telling me that you can't protect me in my own city?" said Hennessy.

"I'm not saying that, but it would be easier if we went down to yez farm. That's all."

"No," said Hennessy. "He is not driving me out of my own city, he's not going to make me run like a scared dog. Just put the word out."

He waved them away impatiently and flopped down into his chair. He took a mouthful of whiskey, and then another. He knew he shouldn't have lost his temper, but the bombing had shaken him badly. It made him acutely aware of his own mortality, that his own threescore years and ten wasn't all that far away, and the fact that a vindictive Chinaman with a bottle of antifreeze could steal away the years he had left made him very angry. And afraid. The supercilious detective had said it had been a warning. Very well, he would regard it as just that.

Nguyen didn't drive straight back to the guest-house. Once he'd collected his van from the car park off Gloucester Street he headed north along Victoria Street and then cut westwards across the city along Divis Street, past grim blocks of flats, to where it turned into Falls Road. It wasn't that he was worried about being followed, because he knew he was long gone from Donegall Square before the bottles crashed on to the floor. It wasn't that he enjoyed driving, either. He'd always found sitting behind the steering wheel stressful and he'd been looking forward to the day when his daughter would pass her driving test so that she could do all the restaurant deliveries for him. He drove around to get a feel of the city and its people, and at the back of his mind lurked the thought that by understanding the people of Belfast he might be able to understand why the IRA had killed his family. The city centre was prosperous, shiny fronted shops and clean pavements. The cars in the streets were mainly new and well cared for and there were few signs of a city in the throes of sectarian violence. "Belfast Says No" said a banner Nguyen had seen hanging under the green dome of City Hall in Donegall Square, but he didn't know what the city was saying "no" to.

There was a strong police and army presence, with some streets sealed off with metal railings manned by armed policemen and turnstiles to allow pedestrians through one at a time, but there was no air of tension, none that Nguyen could detect, anyway. He had a large-scale map of Belfast and its surroundings spread over the passenger seat, and as he stopped at a red traffic light he scanned it, trying to pronounce the strange names: Knocknagoney, Ballyhackamore, Cregagh, Skegoneill, Ligoniel, Ballynafeigh.

A horn sounded and he realised the light had turned green. He missed first gear and went into third by mistake and the van stalled. The horn blared out again and it was joined by others until he got the engine started-again and pulled away jerkily.

He drove along the Falls Road, the Royal Victoria Hospital on his left, and the city changed character. It took on a brooding, menacing air. He saw burnt-out cars down side roads, rusting hulks that had obviously been there for months, like the skeletons of long-dead animals. There were children everywhere, in push-chairs, playing football on the pavements, walking with their parents, standing on street corners, loitering outside pubs, children with worn clothes and unkempt hair and runny noses. He drove by red-brick houses that had been gutted and never repaired, derelict wrecks like rotting stumps in a mouthful of bad teeth. There were splashes of colour among the drab greyness – extravagant murals on the gable ends of the terraces, paintings of masked men with machine guns, elaborate crosses, memorials to hunger strikers who had died in prison, and the tricolour, the Irish flag. There were slogans too, many of which Nguyen didn't understand, but there were some he could read: "Support The Provisionals", "Troops Out", "Ireland for the Irish". He drove by a pub, windows protected with thick wire mesh. There were two men standing either side of a black wooden door with their hands in their pockets and they scrutinised the van with hostile eyes. Lookouts, Nguyen decided. He would have to be more careful where he showed himself. The city centre had lulled him into a false sense of security. Out here, in the Catholic working-class areas, he could feel the mistrust in the air like the cloying damp of a morning mist. The men saw that Nguyen was Oriental and immediately lost interest in him.

The road curved gently and on his right Nguyen saw a huge graveyard which stretched as far as he could see, and then another cemetery on his left as he followed Glen Road and then turned left at a roundabout and headed south-east on Kennedy Way through the district shown on the map as Andersonstown. He slowed down to look at two depressing rows of flats, precast greying concrete with dirty windows and badly painted frames. The muddy verge of trampled grass that surrounded the blocks was littered with empty crisp packets, tattered pages of abandoned tabloid newspapers, stale fish and chip wrappers and broken bottles, the flotsam and jetsam of inner city life. Nguyen was unable to understand why the people who lived there did not take better care of their surroundings. How could they tolerate such squalor, he thought. Living in poverty was one thing, but that was no excuse for behaving like animals. He shook his head sadly.

He drove towards a place called Malone and the surroundings improved, the depressing neglect giving way to well-kept gardens and freshly painted houses, and then he indicated left on to Malone Road, heading back to the city centre. Just before he reached the city's Botanic Gardens he turned left into Wellington Park, musing over what he had seen. The people who lived in the depressed areas had little to lose, he realised. If his enemy came from the rubbish-strewn slums and the neglected high-rise monstrosities, then surely prison would hold no fear for them. Children reared there would be tough, uncaring, loyal to their own and aggressive against intruders. Their poverty would bind them like iron chains. He wouldn't be taking on one man, he would be going against the whole of the IRA. He switched off the engine and stared out with unseeing eyes. It had to be done, whatever the cost. He had no choice. He owed it to his wife, and to his daughters.

*　　　*　　　*

Liam Hennessy stood in his garden and looked up at the rocky outcrop they called Napoleon's Nose. Not that it looked like a nose, or any other part of Napoleon's anatomy. Jackie, his red setter, loped out of the house and over the lawn towards him. He bent down and ruffled her ears and let her lick his hands.

He walked around the lawn with his dog, checking the trees and plants. He was a keen gardener but his law practice and political activities left him little time to attend to the half acre or so that surrounded his four-bedroomed red-brick house in Antrim Road. He employed part-time a retired gardener who had formerly helped to tend the city's Botanic Gardens, but he insisted on checking his progress every morning. He knelt down and examined a heather-covered rockery and Jackie ran up and licked his cheek with her sloppy tongue. He pushed her away and laughed.

"She wants a walk," said his wife. He turned and straightened up, brushing his knees.

"You could creep up on the devil himself, Mary," he laughed. She handed him a mug of tea.

"Your dog wants a walk," she repeated. Mary Hennessy looked a good deal less than her forty-six years, tall and slim with dark brown, lightly curled hair in a pageboy cut. Hennessy looked at her appreciatively as he took the mug. She didn't look like a woman who had two teenage children. Her skin was smooth and lightly tanned and the few wrinkles she had made her look all the more beautiful. She still turned the heads of men half her age and she knew it. There were times when he was so afraid of losing her that his stomach churned.

"Our dog," he corrected.

She nodded at the setter as it sat at his feet looking up at him with undisguised love. "Just look at her," she said.

"I can remember when there was a look not unlike that in your own fair eyes," he teased, and she laughed. The phone rang and she ran across the lawn to the house. She runs, for God's sake, thought Hennessy, she runs like an excited child and she laughs out loud. He tried to remember when he'd last laughed out loud. He couldn't recall exactly when it was

93

but it was after hearing Ian Paisley being interviewed on television and it wasn't a gentle, lilting laugh like Mary's, it was sarcastic and biting.

"Jackie," he said, "I am getting old."

The red setter looked up at him and woofed as if agreeing and he reached down and patted her on the head.

"There's no time for a walk, old girl. The car will be here any moment, sure enough."

Jim Kavanagh and Christy Murphy were at Hennessy's side all day and most of the evening, but during the night they went home to sleep and their places were taken by two men from a pool of about a dozen trusted volunteers who stayed outside his house in whatever car they were using. Jimmy McMahon took the black Jaguar to his own house in north Belfast and brought Kavanagh and Murphy with him first thing in the morning. Hennessy looked at his watch. They were late.

Mary appeared at the back door and waved to him. "It's Christy," she shouted.

Jackie's ears pricked up and she romped towards her in the mistaken belief that she was being called in for some titbit. Hennessy walked after her, cursing under his breath and taking care not to spill his tea. The Jaguar had only just come out of the garage after a very expensive service and he hoped it hadn't been in an accident.

Mary handed the phone to him. Murphy sounded short of breath. "The bastards tried to kill us," he said.

"What are you talking about?" asked Hennessy.

"The bastards tried to blow us up."

"Calm down, Christy," Hennessy soothed. "Just tell me what happened."

He heard Murphy take a deep breath before speaking. "We went to get the Jaguar out of Jimmy's garage. He got into the driving seat and was just about to start up the sodding thing when we saw it. Holy Mary, mother of God, if we hadn't spotted it we'd all have been . . ."

"What happened?" interrupted Hennessy impatiently.

"They used a flash-bulb and a couple of wires."

"A flash-bulb?"

"A flash-bulb, and it had been covered in some sort of red powder. It was a home-made detonator, as soon as the ignition key was turned it would have exploded the petrol in the tank."

"OK, Christy. Where are you now?"

"We're all in Jimmy's house."

There was a muttering in the background and the sound of a bottle clinking against a glass. The boys were having a wee snort to calm their nerves, and Hennessy didn't blame them. They'd had two narrow escapes in as many days.

"Listen, this is what you do. Have you removed it?"

"Sure enough, we pulled it out of the tank, but it's still connected."

"Leave it just as it is. Call Willie O'Hara and get him to look at it, he knows what he's doing. And get him to check out the whole car, from top to bottom. As soon as he's given it the all clear, you and Jim come on over. And Christy?"

"Yeah?"

"Take it easy."

He replaced the receiver. The mug of tea was still in his left hand, untouched. He sipped it, a deep frown on his forehead.

"Something wrong?" asked his wife.

He nodded. "Somebody has just tried to blow up the car."

Mary's eyes widened and her mouth opened. He hadn't told her about the explosion at the office because he hadn't wanted to worry her, but he took her into the kitchen and sat her down at the pine breakfast table and told her that there had been two attempts on his life, albeit half-hearted ones.

There was a scratching noise at the door and Hennessy walked over to let in the dog. She scuttled beneath the table and Hennessy realised then how vulnerable he was. He went down the hall, opened the front door and waved over the two men sitting in a blue Ford Escort to the left of the driveway. He told them to be extra careful and sent one of them to stand guard by the back door until Murphy and Kavanagh arrived.

He returned to the kitchen and flashed his wife a smile as he sat down.

"Who do you think is behind this? The Ulster Defence Association?"

Hennessy shrugged and looked down at his mug of tea. A brownish scum was beginning to form on the surface and he poked it with his finger.

"There was some clever dick inspector at the office who said it might be a warning."

"A warning?"

Hennessy looked up and was pleased to see the concern in her eyes. "The bomb in the office wasn't really a bomb, it was a home-made affair that was limited in terms of the damage it could do. And from the sound of it the job they tried to do on the car today was pretty amateurish, too. I mean, they must be pretty stupid not to realise that the first thing we do every morning is to check out the car."

"But why would anyone want to warn you, Liam? The UDA don't normally bother issuing warnings, do they?"

She was right, of course. In recent years there had been an unspoken agreement between the various political groupings not to assassinate the top echelons, an understanding that the leaders had to be able to talk with their opposite numbers without the constant fear of a shotgun blast through the letter-box or a pistol to the back of the neck. The Brighton bombing had shown that no one was safe, not even the Prime Minister, and the whole world had seen a President take a bullet from a lone gunman. The Paisleys and the Adamses and the Hennessys wouldn't last a week if they ever declared open season on each other, but as it was they could move fairly safely through the city. They still kept their bodyguards and trusted the opposition about as much as they trusted the British Government, but the bad old days when a bodyguard had to take a bullet in the shoulder to protect Hennessy were long gone. But if the truce was now over, there'd be no warning, they'd just cut him down with a hail of bullets as he got out of his car. They wouldn't mess around with do-it-yourself bombs. No, this couldn't be political. But if it wasn't political, what was it?

He stood up and put his hand gently under Mary's chin, tilting her head upwards. "There was a man came round to the office yesterday, a Chinaman. His wife and daughter were killed in one of the London bombings. He thinks I'm responsible."

"He came all the way to Belfast to see you?"

"He wants me to tell him who's behind the bombing campaign. I sent him packing and a few minutes later our toilet exploded. Now this."

She shook her head away from his hand. "Why haven't you told the police this?"

"We're not sure it's him. And anyway, it's the sort of thing we can handle ourselves."

"Liam!" she said angrily. "You're playing with our lives here!"

"If it is him we'll soon stop him, don't worry. He's Chinese, he won't be difficult to spot in Belfast."

"I hope you're right," she said. The look of concern had gone now, and it had been replaced by something else, something that seemed to Hennessy to be uncomfortably like contempt. It was a look that his wife was giving him more and more often these days, he thought with a heavy heart. He couldn't seem to do anything right. He decided not to try to win her around, knowing that he was sure to fail.

"I'll be in the study until Jim and Christy get here," he said as he walked out of the kitchen. Jackie rushed out from under the table, her claws clicking against the tiles, and loyally followed him out.

He went into his study and closed the door. Jackie went to her wicker basket by the side of the french window which led on to the small patio and she settled into it with a deep and mournful sigh as if offering sympathy for the rough treatment he was getting from Mary. He knew that she would prefer him to take a tougher line with the Protestant extremists, and on more than one occasion she'd urged him to mount an all-out offensive against the UDA. It was so strange, he thought, the way that he himself had mellowed over the years and she had become more and more committed to an armed struggle. The more he tried to persuade her that the only

97

solution was a negotiated one, the more she seemed to turn away from him, physically and emotionally. But he knew that he was right, that his way was the only way forward. Anything else would only end in bloodshed. Knowing that he was right didn't make him feel any better.

There was a safe set into the wall behind a framed hunting print over a cast-iron fireplace; Hennessy opened it and took out a brown A4 manila envelope. He flicked the open end with a thumbnail as he walked over to the desk. Inside was a sheaf of papers, each a report on an individual arms cache. There were fifteen in all, and he was expecting a further six by nightfall. He spread the sheets out on the desk and examined them. Three of the caches had been interfered with. In all, fifteen kilograms of Semtex had been taken, along with a dozen detonators, two mercury tilt switches, two handguns and a small amount of ammunition. Everything else necessary for the construction of bombs – wires, timing devices, transmitters – could be bought from High Street stores. Hennessy was sure that the maverick IRA team had been stealing from the organisation's munition dumps and he was equally certain that they were being helped by somebody inside the organisation. The trouble was that there was no pattern, no connection between the three dumps. They were the responsibility of three different IRA cells. He grunted and gathered up the papers. Jackie lifted her head and watched him put the sheets back into the envelope.

"Maybe the remaining inspections will supply the answer," he said to her and she chuffed in agreement.

Hennessy heard a car arrive outside and footsteps crunching on the gravelled drive before the doorbell rang. He waited to see if Mary would answer it, but he wasn't surprised when she didn't. He went and opened the door to let in Kavanagh and Murphy and a small sharp-faced man with a straggly moustache and grey, watery eyes, Willie O'Hara. Jimmy McMahon stayed outside in the Jaguar, reluctant to let it out of his sight. Willie was wearing his normal baggy grey suit, the trousers held up by a greasy brown belt, and he was carrying a paper bag. Hennessy took the three men into the study. "Was the car clear?" he asked O'Hara.

"Other than this?" answered the little man, holding up the bag. "Yeah, this was all, but it would've been more than enough." He reached in his hand and took out a coil of black wire and held it out to Hennessy. "Crude, but it would've done the job."

There were two pieces of wire, each about ten-foot long, and both had been soldered to the flash-bulb.

Hennessy pointed to the red powder which covered the flash-bulb. "What's this?" he asked.

O'Hara's eyes shone. "Ground up match-heads," he said. "Mainly potassium chlorate. Just to add an extra kick. Probably wouldn't have been necessary, but it's a nice touch."

"How does it work?"

"Whoever it was had prised open the fuel cap and left the flash-bulb dangling just inside the tank, in the fumes above the petrol. You turn the key and up she goes."

"Guaranteed?"

O'Hara frowned, wondering what Hennessy was getting at. "Pretty certain. I mean, it's not the sort of gadget we'd use because there's always an outside chance that the bulb might fall into the petrol in which case it wouldn't ignite it. And it's also pretty easy to spot."

"A warning?"

O'Hara nodded eagerly. "Yeah, that's exactly what I was thinking. Is somebody giving you trouble?"

"I've an idea who it might be, yes. Willie, thanks for your help." Hennessy shook him by the hand and showed him out, telling Jimmy to drive O'Hara wherever he wanted to go.

Back in the study he sat behind his desk and told Kavanagh and Murphy to make themselves comfortable. He offered them tea or coffee but they declined. He didn't offer them anything stronger because even under stress Kavanagh didn't touch alcohol and he could already smell whiskey on Murphy's breath and they'd all need clear heads.

"I'm coming round to thinking that maybe you were right about what you said yesterday, Jim," Hennessy said to Kavanagh.

"About going to the farm?"

Hennessy nodded. "I think it's best. The weekend's

coming up, and I can just as easily run things from there, for a short time at least. Mary and I will go tonight, Jimmy and Christy can come with us and we'll take another couple of lads with us just to be on the safe side."

"Ye want me to stay here?" asked Kavanagh.

"I want you to organise a search for this Chinaman. He shouldn't be that hard to find, not in Belfast. There can't be that many Chinese here, and this one's a stranger, from London. He's got to be staying somewhere."

"No problem," said Kavanagh.

"And I'm bringing Sean Morrison back."

Both Kavanagh and Murphy smiled. They knew Morrison well and had worked together on many occasions.

"He's still in New York?" asked Murphy. Morrison had left Belfast more than two years earlier.

"Yeah, he's liaising with the various Noraid groups in North America." Morrison had told Hennessy he wanted to get out of Belfast for a while and his request had come at a time when fund-raising in the United States had been going through a rough patch. Morrison had made a difference, not the least because his broad Belfast accent and typical Irish good looks went down so well with the Americans. He looked just like they expected an IRA activist should, tall, broad-shouldered, with curly black hair and piercing blue eyes. He spoke well and with conviction about the aims of the organisation and the Noraid groups had used him to full advantage. Morrison had also been a great help in arranging for forged passports and visas for IRA members who wanted to get in and out of the United States without being identified, and had recently begun to form links with arms suppliers. He had been a godsend. But right now Hennessy needed someone he could trust, and he trusted Morrison with his life.

He told Kavanagh to start the hunt for The Chinaman right away, and asked Murphy to step up security arrangements around the house. He waited until he was alone before picking up the phone and calling New York.

Morrison answered on the third ring, his voice thick with sleep.

"Good morning, Sean. What time is it in the Big Apple?"

Morrison groaned. "Almost five o'clock," he said. "What's wrong, Liam?"

"I need you back here, Sean."

"When?"

"Today."

Morrison groaned again. "You don't ask much, do you?" He didn't ask why because he knew the security forces weren't averse to tapping Hennessy's phone, legally or otherwise.

"I'd like you to come straight here, to my house," Hennessy continued. "'I'll explain everything when you arrive. How long do you think it'll take you?"

"Ten hours or so, Liam, a lot depends on the timing of the direct flights." His voice was clearer now. "I'll call you if there are any problems."

Hennessy thanked him and replaced the receiver. He picked up the wires and flash-bulb that Willie had left on his desk and toyed with them, deep in thought.

Nguyen drove the Renault to a Chinese take-away and bought six portions of plain boiled rice, three of roast pork and three of roast chicken. He told the Hong Kong Chinese behind the counter that he didn't want any sauce or anything, just meat. The food came in the same foil containers with white cardboard lids that he'd used in his own shop in Clapham. He asked for a carrier bag, put the food in the back of the van and then drove to a pub in the countryside to buy ice. The landlord of the first place he tried said he didn't have enough for his own use, never mind to sell to someone who wasn't even a regular. The man behind the bar at the second pub was more sympathetic to Nguyen's story of a wife with an arthritic leg which the doctor said would be helped if she lay with it in an ice bath. He sold him three carrier bags full of ice-cubes shovelled from a large clanking ice-machine for a nominal sum and Nguyen drove back to the guest-house as quickly as he dared. He parked the van, put the packs of ice and one of the bags of fertilizer into two holdalls and carried them inside. Mrs McAllister was dusting the hall and she smiled when she saw him. "Lovely day, isn't it?" she said.

He smiled, nodded and slipped by her. He put the fertilizer on the bathroom floor, dropped the ice into the bottom of the shower and listened at the door until he heard the landlady go into the kitchen. He slipped downstairs and refilled the holdalls. He carried them back up the stairs, walking softly on the balls of his feet close to the wall so that he made the minimum of noise. The less he saw of the landlady and the other guests, the better.

He entered his room and slid back the brass bolt before placing the bag on the bedcover and unzipping it. He unpacked the bag carefully, first removing the two glass bottles of concentrated acids, which he took one at a time into the bathroom and put on the floor by the shower.

He tore open the plastic bags and tipped most of the ice into the shower and then fetched a box of salt and sprinkled it over the cubes before pushing the bottles of acid into the freezing mixture.

While it cooled he emptied the holdall on to the bed. There was the bottle of glycerine, a can of motor oil, several boxes of matches, a tube of glue, a jumble of plastic piping, plastic-coated wire, a box of baking soda, a pair of washing-up gloves, a thermometer, a Pyrex measuring jug, two large Pyrex saucepans and a Teflon-covered stirrer. He took what he needed into the bathroom and switched on the light so that the ventilator would start working. The acid fumes would be painful if he inhaled them.

Nguyen had worked with explosives a lot during the war. Whenever possible the Vietcong had bought explosives or used equipment captured from the Americans, but supplies weren't always easy to get and they were quite capable of manufacturing their own blasting gelatine, TNT, plastic or nitroglycerine. Most of the raw materials for explosives could be bought quite legally, though in the later years of the war there were restrictions on the sale of electric timing devices. Not that it mattered, though, because clockwork alarm clocks were just as good.

It took almost half an hour before Nguyen had completed the complex and dangerous series of chemical reations that left him with an oily white substance forming a milky layer at the bottom of the measuring jug.

Nguyen settled back on the cold floor and sighed. His jaw ached and he realised he must have been grinding his teeth with the tension. He was starting to get a headache, a piercing pain behind his eyes that could be a result of the stress or more likely the effect of the fumes. He got to his feet, his knees cracking as he straightened up and walked unsteadily into the bedroom. He opened the window wide and then sat on the edge of the bed, breathing deeply to clear his head.

When he felt a little better he took the bag of fertilizer into the bathroom and tore it open. He spread out one of the empty plastic bags that had contained the ice and scooped handfuls of fertilizer on to it. it was important to get the ratio of motor oil, nitroglycerine and fertilizer right. He added the oil to the fertilizer first, kneading it like dough until it had been absorbed and then carefully poured out the nitroglycerine a little at a time, placing it back in the shower between pourings. The nitroglycerine could be used as an explosive on its own but it was dangerously unstable and would explode if knocked or dropped or if it got too hot. Once it had been mixed with the fertilizer and oil it would be quite inert until detonated but would be almost as effective.

Nguyen worked slowly and methodically and it took him the best part of an hour until all the nitroglycerine had been worked into the mixture and he had a dark-brown gooey paste on the plastic bag. He stripped off the gloves and laid them on the floor and went back into the bedroom. The headache was worse. He looked at his watch. It was six o'clock. He had plenty of time, so he lay down on the bed and rested.

He woke with a start two hours later when the landlady knocked on the door. "Would you care for a cup of tea, Mr Minh?" she called.

Nguyen thanked her but said no and she went back down the stairs. He sat up and rubbed his eyes. The curtains were blowing into the room and the sky was darkening outside. He slid off the bed and turned on the light. There was a lamp on the dressing-table and he put it on the floor, under the window, and pulled out its plug from the mains. He spread a newspaper on the shiny wooden surface and then took the soldering iron, solder, flash-bulbs and wire and put them on the newspaper. He plugged in the iron and while he waited for it to heat up he used the Swiss Army knife to cut twelve sections of wire, each about eighteen inches long, and then stripped a short section of plastic from the end of each piece. He soldered a wire to the bottom of each of the flash-bulbs, and another to the side. He used a battery to test one, touching the ends of the wires to the two terminals. It burst into white light and hissed as it melted. He tossed it on to the bed.

In Vietnam they'd had a plentiful supply of blasting caps, but they were hard to get hold of in peacetime. Not that it mattered, because the home-made explosive was sensitive enough to be detonated by a flash-bulb. Nguyen had decided he would make extra sure. He opened two boxes of matches and emptied them on to the newspaper. He stripped off the red heads until he had a pile of several dozen and then he crushed them with the blade of his knife, one at a time. Occasionally one would burst into flames as he worked and he'd use the blade to extinguish the fire. When he'd finished he had a neat pile of red powder. He smeared glue over the bulbs and then rolled them in the powder until they were completely covered. He left them to dry on the newspaper while he prepared the plastic piping. It was the sort used as drainpipes in cheap housing. He'd cut each piece with a hacksaw so that they were about a foot long. He sealed up one end of each pipe with strips of insulation tape and then took them into the bathroom. He put his gloves back on and half filled each pipe with the explosive mixture, then went back for six of the detonators. He held the wires in his left hand as he carefully eased the sticky mixture around the detonators, two for each pipe, and pressed it down. When he'd filled all three he sealed the ends closed with tape with just the wires protruding. They looked childish and inelegant, but Nguyen knew how deadly and effective they were. Properly planted in a road, they could destroy a car and leave a crater more than six feet across. All that was needed to set them off was to pass an electric current through the wires.

He wrapped them in newspaper and put them into the holdall. He placed the tools on top and zipped up the bag. Everything else he put into a black rubbish bag. He tied the top and lifted it, but realised immediately the thin plastic was in danger of tearing, so he slid it inside a second bag, and then a third, before twisting the open ends together and fastening them with tape.

It was almost ten o'clock. He lay down on the bed and looked for a while at the picture of the former American president. He closed his eyes, knowing that his internal alarm clock would wake him at dawn, but sleep eluded him at first. The face of the man who had first committed the US military to suppressing the Communists in the North floated in front of him and brought with it a flood of memories. He tried to push them away but they were persistent and eventually he surrendered to them.

Nguyen's father was a fanatical Communist but also appreciated the value of money and when Nguyen was nine years old he sent him to live with a cousin in Hanoi, almost 250 miles to the north of their village. The cousin ran a small garage in a back street and there Nguyen learnt how to service cars and each week he sent back half of his meagre wages to his father. In the evenings he went to a night school run by a local Catholic priest where he was taught to read and write and to question the Communist views he had picked up from his father.

He turned eleven on the day that Vietnam won its battle for independence and the French pulled out and he was in the street cheering with his friends when Ho Chi Minh returned to Hanoi. There was no peace, not even when the last French soldier left Vietnam. The struggle then became a struggle between North and South. Nguyen was eighteen when the first American soldier died in Vietnam, working in an armaments factory which manufactured grenade launchers. The factory was in a ramshackle hut in a Hanoi suburb containing little more than rows of metal tables, a brick forge with bellows powered by a bicycle and a lathe run by a rusting Citroën engine that had been fixed to a heavy wooden frame. He spent four years in the factory during which time he married Xuan Phoung and she bore him two children, both girls. They were three good years, the work he did seemed distant from the fighting going on in the south and though the hours were long and the work hard they lived in a small flat in a pretty part of Hanoi and there were occasional supplies of fresh vegetables sent up from his father's farm.

It all changed in 1967 by which time US bombs were regularly falling on Hanoi. Nguyen was drafted into the North Vietnamese Army. There were no arguments, and it didn't matter that he had a young wife and two babies. It would have been earlier if he hadn't been helping the war effort in Hanoi, but now they said his skills were needed down south. After two weeks basic training Nguyen was sent into action as a sapper. Before he left Hanoi he arranged for his family to leave Hanoi and stay at his father's farm. It was a lot closer to the fighting than Hanoi, but he knew that the bombing could only get worse and that in the city there would be no one to take care of them.

Nguyen and his fellow sappers were taken to within twenty miles of Saigon, to an area the Americans called The Iron Triangle, where they spent six months helping to build and equip a network of tunnels that housed hundreds of NVA and Vietcong soldiers. Deep underground were hospitals, training schools, supply stores and munitions factories. For weeks on end he never saw the sunlight. Nguyen was then put to work manufacturing home-made mines from captured US 105-millimetre howitzer shells of which the NVA had an abundant supply. The cash-rich Americans were notoriously careless with their equipment and there were crates upon crates of the shells for Nguyen and his team to work on.

One day when he was supervising a new batch of the mines a VC officer came to watch and began talking to him. The officer had been a mechanic many years before and it turned out that he'd originally worked in a garage in Hanoi not far from where Nguyen learnt his trade. The man complimented Nguyen on his work and after watching for a while longer he went away. The following day Nguyen was called to his commanding officer and told that he was being transferred to a Vietcong guerrilla unit. He'd asked what sort of unit and the officer had shrugged and said that it didn't matter. Nguyen didn't press it because he knew there was no point. He wasn't surprised when he was told that he was ordered to report to the VC officer who'd been watching him earlier. That was when Nguyen had been taught to fight. And to kill.

Nguyen was told that he'd be working in a team of three, setting booby traps on trails used by the American forces. He was given a black uniform to replace his grey NVA fatigues, but he was told he was to keep his AK-47 rifle. And that was that. Nguyen spent almost a year living in fear, creeping out of the tunnels at night, planting mines, setting trip wires and doing everything possible to terrorise the Americans. He became expert at moving silently through the jungle and quickly learned to camouflage himself so effectively that he was almost invisible from a few feet away, even during daylight.

Nguyen himself gave little thought to the politics involved: he was happy to fight for his country and, besides, if he had ever expressed any reservations about what he was doing he would have more than likely been shot in the back of the head. But that all changed one night in the summer of 1968 while he was in temporary attachment to a VC training camp close to Chap Le. The camp was only thirty miles away from Dong Hoi and Nguyen was hoping to be granted leave so that he could visit his family on his father's farm, when word reached him that his father had died. When he officially applied for leave it was refused, with no explanation. He went anyway, borrowing a battered Vespa scooter and driving through the night. When he arrived at the farm he was greeted by his tearful wife and children, and he learnt the full story.

A truckload of Vietcong soldiers had arrived at the farm three days earlier and demanded that they provide them with food and supplies. They helped themselves to rice from the storage sheds and half a dozen chickens. One of them untethered a bleating goat and began pulling it towards the truck. Xuan Phoung had protested that she needed the milk for her children, but one of the soldiers pushed her away and when she tried to take the goat back hit her in the stomach with the butt of his rifle. Nguyen's father went to pick her up and the soldier turned on him, hitting him on the head. The soldiers dragged him to the truck, along with the goat, and drove off. They took him to a nearby hamlet and tied him to a stake and called out all the villagers to watch. They accused him of being a bad Communist and of conspiring against the National Liberation Front and then they slowly disembowelled him as the crowd cheered.

The old man was still dying as Xuan Phoung arrived on foot at the village, and she cut him down and cradled his head in her lap. The VC had left by then and one of the braver villagers helped bury him. No funeral, because that would antagonise the Vietcong and there would be more killings.

Xuan Phoung took Nguyen to the unmarked grave and stood with him in silence as tears ran down his cheeks. He made his mind up then, as he stood by the wet soil, and later that night he took his wife and two children, precariously balanced on the scooter as they headed south. As they got closer to the area controlled by the South Vietnamese forces he took them into the jungle, travelling by night and hiding from all patrols, US, NVA and VC, until he reached a South Vietnamese camp near Hue, on the banks of the Perfume River.

There he gave himself up to the ARVN, the Army of South Vietnam, and applied to join Chieu Hoi, the "Appeal to Return" programme. He'd read about Chieu Hoi in the jungle after a low-flying helicopter had thrown out handfuls of propaganda leaflets. The VCs kept them and used them for lighting fires and as toilet paper.

His wife and children were resettled in a safe village south of Saigon while Nguyen was sent to a rehabilitation camp. He wasn't there long. He'd never had any great love for Communism and the ARVN realised how useful Nguyen would be. When he crossed over he hadn't thought that he'd be fighting for the South, he'd had some vague hope that they'd simply allow him to go back to what he enjoyed doing, working in a garage somewhere and spending the nights with his wife and daughters. He was wrong. The ARVN didn't threaten to put a bullet in his head, but they didn't have to. The South was infiltrated with VC soldiers and agents and if Nguyen and his family weren't kept in a safe village they'd be killed within weeks. Their survival depended on the goodwill of the Government of South Vietnam. And the price exacted for that goodwill was for Nguyen to serve them in the best way he could.

Once he'd satisfied them that he wasn't a VC agent he was sent to the Recondo School, run by the 5th Special Forces Group at one end of Nha Trang airfield, near Saigon. The Recondo School was where the US army trained the men who made up the Long Range Reconnaissance Patrols – or Lurps to the men who served in them. The Lurps operated in six-man teams deep in enemy territory as the eyes and ears of the army, and often as its assassins.

It soon became obvious to the instructors that there was nothing Nguyen could learn from them. Within two days he was teaching them about VC booby traps and camouflage techniques and then the top brass got to hear about his talents and inside a month he found himself seconded to a Lurp unit on the edge of the Iron Triangle.

Time and time again, Nguyen was sent into enemy territory, along the same trails that he'd travelled when he was a VC. He knew many of the hiding places and the supply dumps and the secret trails, and he had a sixth sense for spotting the VC trip-wires and traps.

Nguyen was allowed regular visits to his wife and daughters, and as he drew regular US army pay, life was good fighting for the Americans, until it became obvious that the NVA were going to overrun the South. Nguyen began to worry about what would happen if the Americans pulled out, but he was always assured that he would be taken care of and that his family would be given sanctuary in the United States. He'd believed them.

Nguyen tossed fitfully on the bed, sweat beading on his forehead. His breath came in ragged gasps as he relived in his mind what had happened to his wife and his three daughters, how they'd died and how he'd been powerless to help.

Mary Hennessy was sitting alone in the lounge watching television when the doorbell rang. She got to her feet and smoothed down her dress before going into the hall, but Murphy had got to the front door ahead of her. There were four suitcases by the door, mainly clothes that she wanted to take with her to the farm. Liam had said they were only going for the weekend, but she could see that he was holding something back, and realised that he'd been badly shocked by the two bombing attempts and that they'd probably end up staying on the farm until it had been sorted out.

It was ten o'clock already, but Liam had said he was waiting to see someone before they left and it was a desire to see who the mysterious visitor was rather than a sense of politeness that had taken her to the hall. He was hidden by the door, all she could see was a sleeved arm shaking hands with Murphy, but then she heard his spoken greeting and she gasped, her hand flying involuntarily up to her mouth. The door opened wider and he stepped inside. Morrison was holding a blue holdall in his left hand and he bent down to put it on the floor by her suitcases and it was only as he straightened up that he saw her. He smiled and his eyes widened.

"Mary," he said, in a voice that could have meant a hundred things. He seemed unsure how he should greet her, stepping forward as if to kiss her on the cheek but then holding himself back and offering her his hand instead. Was that because Murphy was watching them, or because he knew Liam was nearby, or was it something else? It had been two years since she had seen Sean Morrison and she couldn't read him as easily as she used to. His hand felt strong and dry and she pressed her fingers into his palm, holding him a little longer than was necessary. He squeezed her gently and he seemed reluctant to take his hand away. That's what she told herself, anyway. She was immediately glad that she'd worn her blue silk dress which showed her figure off, especially around her waist. She wanted to look good for him. He looked wonderful, his hair was longer than when she'd last seen him but otherwise he hadn't changed: smiling blue eyes, his mouth which always seemed ready to break into a grin, and a body that could have belonged to a dancer.

"It's good to see you again, Sean," she said. "How's New York?"

"Hectic," he said. "A lot different to Belfast, I can tell you."

"You're here to see Liam?"

He nodded. "Yeah, is he in the study?"

She wanted to keep him in the hall, to talk with him and find out why he was back, but she knew that she'd already spent too long looking at him, any longer and Murphy would suspect there was something going on. Mary smiled to herself. He'd be wrong, of course. There was nothing going on between her and Sean. There hadn't been for two years, but she could tell from his touch that the electricity was still there between them.

"He's waiting for you," she said. "Perhaps I'll see you later." She held his gaze for a couple of seconds and then turned and went back into the lounge. She poured herself a brandy and held the balloon glass between both hands and breathed in its rich bouquet. "Welcome back, Sean Morrison," she said quietly to herself, smiling.

In the study, Morrison shook Hennessy's hand and sank down into one of the chairs in front of the desk. "The boys seem nervous," said Morrison, and Hennessy explained briefly what had happened, the phone calls from London, the visit from The Chinaman, the explosion in his office and the attempt to blow up the car. Morrison listened without comment, but when Hennessy had finished he was frowning, not sure what was wanted from him.

"You've brought me back to deal with this Chinaman?" he asked.

Hennessy shook his head. "No, no, we'll take care of him. No, Sean, I need your help to stop this bombing campaign on the mainland." He told Morrison about his fears of a rogue IRA unit, and the missing ordnance.

"That explains a lot," said Morrison. "At first the bombings were good news in the States, donations poured in, but some of the recent stuff has produced a real backlash. The Tube bombing especially. The Irish Americans are keen to support us, but massacres like that . . . I've got to tell you, Liam, I'm bloody pleased to hear you hadn't sanctioned it. How can I help?"

Hennessy spoke to Morrison for another quarter of an hour and then the younger man left for the airport to catch the last shuttle to Heathrow.

Mary Hennessy looked up when her husband entered the lounge and tried to hide her disappointment when she saw that he was alone.

"It's been a long time since Sean Morrison was in Belfast," she said. Hennessy went over to the drinks cabinet and poured himself a double measure of whiskey.

"I need his help," he said.

"With The Chinaman?"

Hennessy swirled the whiskey in his glass and shook his head. "Something else. I need someone I can trust, somebody without an axe to grind, and he's been away for almost two years now. He's, how can I put it, untainted. Yes, that's the word I'm looking for. Untainted."

"So he'll be coming to the farm with us?" she asked.

"No, I need him to go to London." He saw from her face that she didn't understand and he smiled down at her. "I need his help to get to the bottom of the bombings. Despite everything that's happened, that's the more important issue at the moment."

Mary's eyes narrowed. "You've got a plan?"

"Something like that." He finished his drink and put the empty glass down on the cabinet. "Are you all packed?"

She said she was, and they went together to the car where Jimmy McMahon opened the door for them and put the luggage in the boot. They sat together in the back while Murphy slid into the front seat. Jackie squeezed under Hennessy's legs and woofed quietly to herself. A red Ford Sierra with three young men waited at the entrance to the drive, its engine running. Four other heavily built men got into a dark-brown Range Rover and followed the Jaguar out into the road. They drove in convoy, the Sierra first, then the Jaguar, and the Range Rover bringing up the rear, down the Antrim Road, through the city centre and on to the A1, the main road south.

Nguyen was jolted awake by a distant siren. He lay for a while on his back staring up at the ceiling and trying to calm his breathing. He was soaking wet, drenched with sweat as he always was when he came out of the nightmare. The visions were always the same: the small boat drifting in the South China Sea. His daughters screaming for help. The helplessness. The anger.

He focused on what he had to do, driving all other thoughts from his troubled mind and gradually his breathing steadied. He sat up slowly and looked around the room as if seeing it for the first time. He checked his watch. It was six o'clock in the morning. Time to go.

The ice in the shower had melted away and Nguyen stepped in and washed himself all over. He didn't use any soap or shampoo because he didn't want any lingering smell of perfume. He towelled himself dry and put on a pair of loose jeans, a faded grey sweatshirt and an old pair of black sneakers before packing the rest of his stuff in his suitcase. He checked the room carefully to make sure he'd forgotten nothing and then he looped the holdall and its deadly contents around his neck and carried the case and the black plastic bag of rubbish down the stairs. He took out his key and left it and a ten-pound note by the telephone and then slipped the catch on the front door and gently eased it closed behind him. He took the rubbish bag down the side of the house and put it in the bin. The case he put in the back of the van, the holdall he slid under the passenger seat. The van started first time and he drove slowly down Wellington Park and turned left into Lisburn Road, the A1. On the seat next to him lay several large-scale maps that he'd bought from a newsagent in the city centre. Ian Wood had told him that Hennessy had a farm between a town called Castlewellan and a place called Haltown in County Down, about forty miles south of Belfast. He hadn't been able to say exactly where, but Nguyen didn't expect to have any problem finding it. The van identified him as a landscape gardener, he'd just drive around claiming to have mislaid Hennessy's address and eventually he'd find someone to point out the right farm.

Sean Morrison had booked into the Strand Palace Hotel late on Friday night so he waited until Saturday morning before calling the offices of the Anti-Terrorist Branch and asking for Detective Chief Inspector Bromley. He wasn't surprised to be told that he wasn't in, because it was Saturday, after all. He asked the duty officer if Bromley was at home or away on holiday and was told that he'd be in the office on Monday.

"Can you get a message to him for me?" Morrison asked.

The duty officer was crisp and efficient, not the least because of Morrison's Irish accent, and he confirmed that he could pass on a message to Bromley.

"Tell him Sean Morrison wants to speak to him."

"Can you give me your number, please, sir?" asked the officer. Nice try, thought Morrison. Either the guy was naïve in the extreme or he had a very dry sense of humour.

"Just tell him Sean Morrison needs to talk to him urgently. I'll call back at noon. Tell him to either be in the office or to have you give me a number where I can reach him. Got that?"

"Yes, sir." Morrison cut the line.

Morrison's next phone call was to Liam Hennessy but a woman's voice answered. "Mary?" he asked.

"Sean? Where are you?"

"London," he said. He wasn't sure what to say to her. Two years was a long time.

"Do you want to speak to Liam?" she asked, and he realised from the edge to her voice that her husband was in the room with her. He immediately felt relieved, as if Hennessy's presence solved the problem of which way the conversation would go.

"Yes," he said.

Morrison heard the phone being handed over and then he heard Hennessy's voice. "Everything OK?" said Hennessy.

"Everything is fine. I was just calling to let you know where I am. I've booked into the Strand Palace . . ." Hennessy interrupted him, telling him to wait while he got a pen and paper. "OK, go ahead," he said.

"I'm at the Strand Palace Hotel," said Morrison, and he dictated the number to Hennessy, who repeated it back to him before hanging up.

Jim Kavanagh had press-ganged a dozen IRA men to help him with the search for The Chinaman, most of them teenagers, but their lack of experience didn't matter because most of their enquiries were done over the phone. They'd moved into Hennessy's office in Donegall Square, the air still acrid from the explosion. Kavanagh divided them into six pairs and distributed copies of the city's Yellow Pages and tourist guides he'd obtained from the Tourist Information Centre in the High Street. The Chinaman had arrived from London, which meant that, unless he had friends or relatives in the city, he'd have to have booked into a hotel or guest-house. He distributed the telephone numbers of all the places where a visitor might stay among the teams, one member to make the phone calls, the other to keep a record. There were more than enough telephones to go round. He hoped they'd be lucky because if not the next stage would be to visit every Chinese family in Belfast and that could take a hell of a long time.

Kavanagh made himself a cup of coffee and settled down on the sofa in the reception area. He was preparing himself for a long wait when a gangly red-haired youth burst into the room, breathing heavily.

"I think we've got it!" he said.

His partner, a head shorter with shoulder-length brown hair, came running after him waving a notebook. "A guesthouse in Wellington Park. The landlady is a Mrs McAllister, she says there was an Oriental man staying with her for two nights."

"Is he still there?" asked Kavanagh, getting to his feet.

"She said he left this morning."

"Damn his eyes!" cursed Kavanagh. He called over two men, bigger and harder than the teenage helpers, Roy O'Donnell and Tommy O'Donoghue. He went with them to collect his car and they drove to Wellington Park.

Mrs McAllister showed them into her lounge, a fussy room with a statue of the Virgin Mary in one corner, dozens of small crystal animals on the mantelpiece and lace squares on the backs of the easy chairs. She was a Catholic, a good Catholic, and whereas she didn't have much sympathy for the IRA she knew better than to obstruct them. Kavanagh asked her to describe her former guest and she did her best but found it difficult: not very tall, black hair, brown eyes, rough skin. She was able to give a better description of his clothes and Kavanagh knew she was talking about the same man that he'd seen in Hennessy's office.

"How did he get here?" he asked.

"He had a van, a white van. It was some sort of delivery van, I think, with writing on the side."

"Can ye remember what it said?"

She shook her head. "I'm sorry, son, I can't."

"Not to worry, Mrs McAllister. Can ye show me his room?"

She took him upstairs leaving O'Donnell and O'Donoghue sitting uncomfortably in the lounge. "You keep a very tidy house, Mrs McAllister," soothed Kavanagh as she led him to the bedroom door. She waited outside while Kavanagh checked the room. There was nothing under the bed or in the cupboard drawers. He went into the bathroom but it too was spotless and smelt strongly of pine.

"Yez'll have already tidied up the room, then?" he asked the landlady.

"Aye, son. I dusted and ran the Hoover over the carpet this morning. He was very clean, though, you'd have hardly known the room had been slept in. Except for the bathroom, there was a funny smell in there. Like vinegar or something. I had to spray air freshener around."

"Vinegar?"

"Something like that, a terrible bitter smell."

Kavanagh looked around the gleaming bathroom, not sure what he expected to find.

"I don't suppose he left anything behind, did he Mrs McAllister?"

"No, nothing. He even made the bed before he left. He went early this morning, before I was up. He'd paid the bill in advance, even left me a tip." She was burning with curiosity but knew it was pointless to ask what it was he'd done. If they wanted her to know they'd have told her.

"And ye've no idea where he went? He didn't ask for directions or anything?"

The landlady shook her head. "I barely spoke to him."

Kavanagh tut-tutted to himself, not sure what to do next. The van was a possibility, but a white delivery van with writing on the side wasn't much to go on. Still, it would probably have English plates which would make it a bit easier to find. "OK, Mrs McAllister, thanks for your help. I'm sorry we disturbed yez."

They went back downstairs. O'Donnell and O'Donoghue were already waiting in the hall, expectant looks on their faces. Mrs McAllister opened the door for them and watched them go down the path. She suddenly remembered something and called after Kavanagh. "Oh, son! You might want to check the dustbin round the back. When I was emptying the Hoover I saw he'd left some rubbish there, in a black bag."

Kavanagh's hopes soared and he practically ran down the path to where two dustbins were standing. The first one he looked in contained nothing but kitchen refuse, but in the second, under a layer of carpet fluff and dust, he found a black plastic bag, knotted at the top and sealed with insulation tape. He pulled it out, ignoring the cloud of dust that billowed over his trousers. He opened the bag and looked inside and frowned.

O'Donnell appeared at his shoulder. "Anything?" he said.

"I think so," said Kavanagh. "I want O'Hara to see this."

Kavanagh put the bag into the boot of the car and the three men drove to O'Hara's house, a two-up, two-down terrace in Springfield Road. He was in the kitchen eating bacon and eggs when they were shown in by his wife. His sharp eyes fixed on the bag by Kavanagh's side.

"What have ye got there, Jim?" he asked, wiping a piece of bread across the plate and popping it into his mouth.

"I'm hoping yer'll tell me, Willie. When yez finished your breakfast, that is."

O'Hara took the hint, putting his knife and fork together on the remains of his meal. His wife took the plate and put it in the oven to keep warm and then left the room, knowing that it was IRA business and that the men would want to be left alone. O'Hara wiped his greasy hands on his grey trousers and cleared the rest of the table, a stainless steel cruet set, a bottle of Heinz ketchup and the morning paper.

Kavanagh lifted the bag on to the table and O'Hara gingerly opened it. He took the contents out one at a time: the empty bag of fertilizer, the Pyrex pans, the measuring jug, sections of piping, a burnt-out flash-bulb, empty bottles, empty matchboxes, pieces of cut wire. He inspected each item closely before eagerly moving on to the next one like a schoolboy going through his presents at Christmas, hoping that each one would be better than the last. When the black bag was finally empty and all its contents lined up beside it, O'Hara looked at Kavanagh, a wicked grin on his weaselly face.

"This is from the wee bugger that tried to blow up Liam's car, isn't it?" he asked.

Kavanagh wasn't impressed by the small man's insight – the flash-bulb was obviously the same type that they'd found in the Jaguar's petrol tank. "He left it behind when he checked out of a guest-house this morning. What do yez make of it?"

O'Hara waved his hand at the ragbag collection of items. "This is trouble, right enough," he said. "Big trouble."

Morrison checked his watch for the hundredth time and called the Anti-Terrorist Branch. This time Bromley was there. "I'm sorry to drag you in on a Saturday," said Morrison.

"I'm always happy to speak to public-spirited citizens, Mr Morrison," said Bromley with more than a hint of sarcasm. "The last FBI report that passed over my desk had you alive and well and living in New York. What brings you back to these fair shores?"

"I need to see you," answered Morrison.

"Not thinking of changing sides and working alongside the forces of law and order, are we?"

"Let's just say that I want to make you an offer you won't be able to refuse."

"In what context?" asked Bromley, suddenly serious.

"Not over the phone. I have to meet you."

Bromley snorted. "In a dark alley, I suppose. Come off it, Morrison, why the hell should I put myself at risk? Haven't you been reading the papers in New York? The IRA has declared open season on us here. If you want to speak to me you can come here."

"And how long do you think I'd last if I was seen going into your office, Bromley? I'm not after a bullet in my mouth."

"I suppose that's a Mexican stand-off, then," said Bromley.

"Not necessarily. You can choose the venue, so long as you go alone. Somewhere with lots of people where you'll feel safe and where I can blend into a crowd. Somewhere noisy so I know we won't be recorded."

"When?"

"This afternoon."

Bromley considered the offer for a few seconds. "I can't today. It'll have to be tomorrow. In Trafalgar Square. Be close to Nelson's column at four o'clock."

"Make sure you come alone," said Morrison. "Don't put me under any pressure. I'm not wanted for anything, and I won't be carrying. I just want to talk."

"So you said."

"One other thing – I don't know what you look like. How will I recognise you?"

"Don't worry, Mr Morrison. I've seen enough photographs of you, I'll introduce myself."

"That's maybe so, but don't creep up on me. I startle easily."

"Understood. Until four tomorrow, then."

Morrison hung up. Nothing to do now but wait. He switched on the television and rang down to room service to order a club sandwich and coffee.

Hennessy was walking across Three Acre Pasture with Jackie at his heels when he heard the shrill whistle, two piercing blasts that made the dog jump. He shaded his eyes with his hands and saw Murphy standing by the kitchen door waving his arm high above his head. When Murphy realised he'd caught his attention, he made a miming action with his hand, holding it clenched to his ear. The phone.

It took him a brisk five minutes to get back to the farmhouse, by which time Murphy had gone back inside the cool, oak-beamed kitchen. He held the receiver out to Hennessy, who was slightly out of breath. It was Kavanagh. He described the visit to the guest-house and what they'd found in the dustbin.

"And what did O'Hara say?" Hennessy asked.

"Nitroglycerine," said Kavanagh. "The Chinaman made nitroglycerine in the bathroom. Willie reckons he mixed it with weedkiller and packed it into plastic pipes and is planning to use flash-bulb detonators, the sort of thing he stuck in the petrol tank of the Jag."

"How much damage could they do?"

"Judging by the stuff he left behind, Willie says he could have made three or four devices, each big enough to blow up a car. It's hard to say because a lot depends on the purity of the nitro he made, but Willie says the guy seems to know what he's doing."

Hennessy felt a cold chill run up his spine because the sort of bombs Kavanagh was talking about didn't sound like warnings. It looked as if The Chinaman was raising the stakes. "What are your plans now, Jim?" he asked.

"I reckon the van's the best bet. The landlady said he's driving a white delivery van with black writing on the side. I'll have our lads scour the city. It shouldn't be too hard to find, a Chinaman in a white van with English plates. We'll get him, Liam. Don't ye worry." Kavanagh tried to sound as optimistic as possible because he could sense how worried his boss was.

"OK, keep at it, Jim. And let me know as soon as you get anything."

"Will do," said Kavanagh.

Mary came into the kitchen as he replaced the receiver and asked him if he wanted a coffee. He declined and said he'd prefer something a little stronger. She sniffed, a noise that was loaded with disapproval. She was wearing tight Levi jeans, cowboy boots and a floppy pink pullover that he'd last seen their daughter wearing. He took a bottle of whiskey down from the Welsh dresser and poured himself a double measure.

"I'm driving down to the village to get some bread," said Mary. "Do you want anything?"

He sat down in an old rocking chair and rocked backwards and forwards, nursing the whiskey. "I'm fine," he said.

She turned to look at him, standing with her hands on her hips. "I don't think you should be moping like this, Liam."

"I'm not moping, I'm thinking. And you're acting like my mother."

"And you, Liam Hennessy, are behaving like my grandfather. Now pull yourself together and stop feeling sorry for yourself." She turned on her heels and banged the kitchen door behind her. He heard the car start up and drive off and wondered what it was that was upsetting her so much.

When he first met Mary all those years ago her temper and unpredictability were among her attractions. She was stimulating, she was fun, and there was never a dull moment with her. She'd quietened down after the birth of their children but now that they were at university she seemed to be behaving more and more like she did when she was in her early twenties. Some days she was so gentle and loving that she took his breath away and yet on others she was so cold that he felt sure she was about to leave him. Sexually, too, she had him in a state of constant confusion. When they'd first married they seemed to spend all their time in bed, and it was hardly surprising that they'd had two children so quickly. He'd wanted more children but she'd said that two was enough though even then sex had been good and regular, albeit more calculated and careful. It had been when the children were in their teens, at school, that she had seemed to withdraw from him. She even went through a period when she'd slept in one of the spare bedrooms, claiming that she was having trouble getting to sleep. When he did approach her she would be friendly but insistent: she didn't want to be touched. Eventually she moved back into the main bedroom. He never found out why, but even when she slept in his bed she only occasionally allowed him to make love to her and when she did it was usually quick and unenthusiastic.

Sometimes, though, she would be totally different, she'd wait until he'd switched off the light and climbed into the bed and then she'd reach for him and it would be like it was in the old days, she'd hang on to him tight, biting his shoulder, making him lie on his back as she rode him on top. Those were the worst nights, because she'd close her eyes as she gasped and groaned and he knew deep inside that she was thinking about someone else, that he was being used, but while it was happening he didn't care because her love-making was so energetic and sensual that he wanted to die. Only afterwards, when she flopped down on to the sheets and rolled away from him to curl up with her own thoughts, only then did the revulsion set in. He would lie awake with tears in his eyes, filled with self-loathing, and promise himself that next time she reached for him in the dark he'd refuse her and tell her that he wanted her to make love to him, not to use him as part of whatever fantasy she was enjoying. But he never did refuse her.

Hennessy was genuinely confused by the way she acted in bed, because in every other respect she was a perfect wife and mother. She ran the house like a dream, their children were good-looking, intelligent and well-balanced, she took an interest in his work and his politics, she laughed at his jokes, she entertained their friends, she seemed to thrive in his company. Everyone who knew them said they were the perfect couple, and when they were with friends of their own age he took a particular pride in her apparent youth and vitality. She was stunning, and while her women friends had put on weight and had their hair permed and started to dress like their mothers, she had kept her figure, so much so that she would still go without a bra if the dress warranted it. Over the years Hennessy had tried to talk himself into accepting his wife as she was, to convince himself that the lack of sex was a small price to pay to have her in his life. Sometimes he believed it. He rocked himself backwards and forwards in the chair. The motion was reassuring and he closed his eyes.

The drive from Belfast to the B8 between Castlewellan and Haltown took a little over ninety minutes, but it took another three hours for Nguyen to locate Hennessy's farm. The two towns were about ten miles apart and there were many farms nestled among the patchwork of fields and hills. Eventually a bearded giant of a man in a tractor sent him in the general direction, to the north of the B8, away from the border, and some time later he came across a postman in a battered old van who pointed at a collection of weathered stone buildings and modern barns.

Nguyen spent some time examining his large-scale map of the area. He circled the spot where the farm was. To the east was the Tollymore Forest Park, and to the south-east was a rocky ridge called the Mourne Mountains. Due south was a place called Warrenpoint, which rang a bell in Nguyen's subconscious. He couldn't remember exactly what it was, but he knew something bad had happened there in the past, an explosion or a massacre. The name had cropped up in a news programme on television, he was sure of that much. He'd regularly watched television news with his daughter as a way of helping her to improve her English.

There was a wooded hill a mile or so behind the farm and according to the map he'd be able to get close to it if he took the road to the village of Rathfriland. He started the van and drove to within half a mile of the hill. He parked in a layby, slung the binoculars around his neck, took his compass from the glove compartment, pocketed the map and walked briskly up the hill, following a stony track that zig-zagged through the lush grass. The track was obviously used by a shepherd to round up his flock. There were dog droppings in several places and boot-prints of a man who walked with a stick and all around were sheep and young lambs.

He reached the top of the hill and lay down in the grass, surveying the farmland and its buildings far below through the powerful binoculars. The farmhouse was an L-shaped building, stone with a steep, grey slate roof. Nguyen was looking at it from the rear, he could see the back door leading off the kitchen. The main part of the house was two-storeys high but the shorter section of the L was one-storey and seemed to be made up of outbuildings, the windows streaked with dirt. There was a square tarmac courtyard in the angle of the L where there were several cars parked: a Range Rover, a Jaguar, two Land-Rovers and a Ford Sierra. Nguyen recognised the Jaguar and smiled. He hadn't expected Hennessy to be there. It was an added bonus. Bordering the courtyard, directly opposite the outbuildings, was another single-storey building and behind it was a grass paddock. In the paddock two horses stood nose to nose. At right angles to the stables was a two-storey cottage built in the same solid style as the main house which Nguyen guessed was the farm manager's home.

In front of the cottage was what looked to be a vegetable garden, with tidy rows of cabbages and other green vegetables, and beyond it a small orchard of mature fruit trees. A gravel driveway led from the courtyard, between the farmhouse and the stables, and curved around the front. The fourth side of the courtyard was bordered by two open-sided barns, one full of bales of hay, the other stacked high with sacks at one end, the rest of the space being used as a shelter for farm equipment. Behind the barns were three gleaming white towering silos, like rockets awaiting lift-off.

The driveway led to a single-track road which wound between the fields, linking up with several farms before disappearing to the north where, according to the map, it linked up with the B7. There were passing places every few hundred yards and hedgerows both sides. The fields were mainly devoted to the raising of cattle and sheep but there were crops, too; several of the patchwork squares were yellow with rape-seed and there were green plants growing in a field behind the barns that could have been potatoes or turnips. The area undulated like a down quilt that had been thrown untidily on to a bed and the places that were steep or inaccessible had been left wooded.

Nguyen laid the map on the grass and took his bearings with the compass. With a pencil he drew several routes to Hennessy's farm, from the B180, the B8, the B25 and the B7, following the contours through woodland wherever possible or alongside hedgerows and ditches where there was no tree cover. There was a stream trickling through Hennessy's land, too small to be shown on the map, and with great care Nguyen traced its route as a thin pencil line. He also carefully drew a sketch map of the farm buildings, showing their positions relative to each other, and made a sketch drawing of the farmhouse, including the drainpipes. The soil-pipe was next to the middle of five upstairs windows and the glass was frosted and there was a circular ventilator fan in the right-hand corner so Nguyen marked it as the bathroom. In the distance a twin-rotor helicopter, a Chinook, flew close to the ground, heading towards border country. He waited until it had passed out of sight before walking back down the hill.

His first priority now was to find somewhere to hide the van, because he'd soon be spotted if he kept driving around in the vicinity of the farm. There were very few vehicles around and most of the ones he came across were tractors or army Land-Rovers. Farmers and soldiers both gave him curious looks but neither seemed to regard him as a threat. He could see, though, that they read the signs on the side of his van and he knew that an Oriental landscape gardener would not be easily forgotten. He dismissed the idea of leaving the Renault in one of the nearby villages or towns because being so near the border any strange parked vehicle was bound to attract attention. He needed a place a good distance from the farm, but close enough that he could get to and fro within a few hours. Five or six miles or so would be about right, and ideally with a route that offered some cover from the army patrols and the helicopters which occasionally buzzed overhead. Looking at the map, it seemed as if Tollymore Forest Park offered the best prospects. He drove east along the B8 and then turned left on to the B180 which cut the woods neatly in half on the way to the village of Maghera. He eased the van along the road looking left and right for places to turn off and spotted several possibilities. When he emerged from the forest he clunked the gears through a three-point turn and headed back towards Haltown. He ignored the first three tracks as being too obvious from the road. The first path he'd identified as being suitable went deep into the trees but the Land-Rover tracks in the mud were too fresh and there were too many of them, suggesting that it was used regularly by foresters or possibly by the army. He turned the van round and drove back to the main road. The second track was more what he'd hoped for, a single pathway that was overgrown by ferns and brambles. He drove the van far enough into the trees so that he couldn't be seen from the road and then got out of the car and checked the ground and the overhanging vegetation. The tyre prints in the dried mud were old and flaking and there were fresh green shoots growing through them. The ferns that had encroached on to the track were unbroken and there were no smears of dirt or grease. No one had driven a vehicle down the path for at least a week, and probably much longer, and there were no footprints, none that were human, anyway. He saw where foxes had crossed the path, and rabbits, but that was all.

Satisfied, he got back into the van and slowly drove it down the track, gripping the steering wheel tightly as it jerked like a wild thing. When he'd gone a hundred yards or so further, he turned off the track and guided the van carefully between the trees. When he was sure that anyone driving down the track would not be able to see the van he switched off the engine.

Nguyen spent an hour going back along the route to the path, covering over his tracks as best he could. It wouldn't fool anyone who was searching for him, but a casual observer would be unlikely to spot where he had driven off the track. He gathered armfuls of ferns and dead wood from the forest floor and spread them across the roof of the van. He'd seen enough helicopters flying overhead to know that there was a risk of being spotted from above, albeit a slim one. He picked up handfuls of damp soil and rubbed them over the sides of the van, and the front and back, transforming the white paintwork into muddy smears, and then took more branches and draped them all around it.

He looked at his watch. There were hours to go before dusk so he climbed into the driver's seat and took a portion of rice and another of pork from the take-away carrier bag. He ate slowly, chewing each mouthful thoroughly before swallowing, not tasting or enjoying the food but knowing that it would provide the energy he needed. When he'd finished he settled back in the seat and tried to sleep, saving his strength for the night ahead. In the distance he heard the whup-whup of a single-rotor helicopter, flying low and fast. He slipped into sleep.

The air was filled with the throbbing of helicopters. It was 1975. Nguyen was with his wife and daughters running through the crowded streets of Saigon, sweating from fear and the heat. The roads were packed tight with panicking faces, young and old, families and individuals, all heading towards the US Embassy and the helicopters. Almost everybody was carrying something, a suitcase, a big wicker bag, a bicycle loaded with clothes or electrical appliances. Children barely big enough to walk were clasping bags to their chests, old women were bent double and gasping for breath as they hurried along with bags attached to both ends of bamboo poles. Nguyen had told his wife to pack one bag for the four of them and he carried it while she held the two children. She was crying as they trotted down the street and the faces of the children were drawn and frightened. Nguyen appeared cold and impassive but inside his mind was racing.

He and his family had moved into Saigon because it wasn't safe for them in the country any more. The NVA was walking all over the ARVN and by February Nguyen heard whispers that a helicopter evacuation of Saigon was being planned. Hue fell on March 24 and less than a week later the NVA overran Da Nang and the South Vietnamese were struggling to hold a defensive line north of Saigon. The Defense Attaché Office put together a list of seven thousand or so people it reckoned should be evacuated as the ARVN fought a last-ditch battle at Xuan Loc, just thirty miles east of Saigon. The noise of exploding rockets kept Nguyen's children awake at night. Nguyen went to see his commanding officer and was told that if Saigon fell he would be evacuated along with the American forces.

On April 28 he was told to prepare for evacuation the following day. The NVA attacked Tan Son Nhut airfield on the northern edge of Saigon, preventing commercial aircraft from flying out with evacuees. The plan now was for helicopters to ferry the US forces and their supporters out to ships waiting offshore. Nguyen, along with thousands of other Vietnamese who had served the US forces, was told to wait at home where he would be picked up by a specially marked bus. They waited, but the buses never arrived. Nguyen phoned the US embassy every fifteen minutes but was always given the same answer. Wait. He heard helicopters flying in the direction of the embassy and he waited. He heard the rumble of guns at Bien Hoa and still he waited. When he heard the crackle of small-arms fire he grabbed his wife and children and ran into the street. It was almost 9.30 p.m. and the streetlights were on.

Nguyen dropped the bag in the street and took one of the

girls from his wife, scooping her off her feet and letting her sit with her legs around his neck. She giggled and played with his hair. His wife picked up the other girl. Time was running out. There were fewer helicopters hovering over the embassy. The roads were packed with cars, trucks, bicycles and pedestrians, and everyone seemed to be heading towards the embassy. The crowds were moving faster now, and they had to be careful not to trip over abandoned luggage as they pushed down Thong Nhat Avenue. In the distance they could see the squarish block of whitewashed cement that was the American embassy. More helicopters flew overhead. The crowds were so thick that Nguyen and his family couldn't get any closer than fifty yards or so to the nine-foot wall that surrounded the embassy. The top of the wall was wreathed in barbed wire and protected by Marines with machine guns. The only way in was through the gate, and that was only opened when refugees could produce the correct paperwork and identifying codeword. Nguyen's daughters were crying. Midnight passed and with it came an end to the distant thudding explosions at the airport and still the helicopters came and left after picking up the lucky ones from the landing pads on top of the embassy building. Dawn broke and they had made almost no progress, the solid mass of anxious humanity locked solid. Nguyen's wife almost collapsed from exhaustion but was held up by the pressure of the people around her until he managed to slip his arm around her waist and support her. She looked at him with pleading in her eyes but there was nothing he could do. The papers that guaranteed sanctuary were in his breast pocket but they were useless unless he could get to the embassy gates. It was hopeless. The crowd roared and screamed and Nguyen looked up to see a helicopter lift off from the roof and head out towards the sea where the Seventh Fleet waited. The chopper was alone in the sky and Nguyen realised it was the last one. There were no more guards around the wall, none on the embassy roof. The Americans had gone. Xuan Phoung cried softly. The crowds dispersed quickly, knowing that the T-54 tanks of the North Vietnamese Army would soon arrive. The streets were littered with abandoned ARVN uniforms and equipment.

Nguyen took his family back to their small flat and helped Xuan Phoung put the exhausted children to bed. He held her tightly and kissed her, and she led him by the hand to their tiny bedroom and he made love to her, urgently and with more passion than he'd shown in a long time. It was the night that Kieu Trinh was conceived.

Nguyen jerked awake, his face drenched with sweat. It was dark outside and he sat for a while, forcing himself to relax. He filled his mind with images of the Buddhist shrine at his home – his former home, he reminded himself. He climbed over the back of the seats into the rear of the van and placed the three pipe bombs into the rucksack. He also packed the filled water-bottles and the remainder of the take-away food, along with six coils of plastic-coated wire, two clockwork alarm clocks and a few tools that he reckoned he would need. The batteries which he planned to use to detonate the bombs were zipped into the pockets of the camouflage jacket so that there could be no possibility of them accidentally going off. He also packed the binoculars and the map.

He stripped off all his clothes except for his underpants and socks and then slipped on the camouflage trousers and jacket. He pulled on a pair of thick wool socks and his old, comfortable boots. He rolled up the right leg of his pants and tied the scabbard of one of the throwing knives to his calf. The other knife he tied to one of the straps of the rucksack so that it hung upside down, the handle lowermost where it was accessible in an emergency. He did the same with the big hunting knife.

When he'd finished his preparations he climbed into the front of the van and left by the driver's door. He kept his eyes firmly closed while he opened and shut the door because he didn't want the internal light ruining his night vision. There was no point in locking the door because if the van was discovered it would all be over anyway, but he buried the keys near the roots of a tree he'd be sure to recognise later.

He covered the door with tree branches and stood for a minute taking a bearing from his compass. There was a thin sliver of moon in the cloudless sky and enough starlight to see by. He headed west through the trees, parallel to the B180. He moved at a brisk pace but even so the constant weaving to and fro to avoid trees meant that it took the best part of two hours to cover three miles and emerge from the forest. He kept going due west for another two and a half miles, travelling across fields, sticking close to hedgerows wherever possible, until he reached the B8. After crossing it he took another bearing from the compass and began walking north-west. He changed direction twice to avoid farms and several times he dropped to the ground when helicopters buzzed overhead. Eventually he reached Hennessy's farm. Behind the buildings loomed the empty blackness of the hill which he'd climbed the previous day.

He lay in the sweet-smelling grass for a full thirty minutes before he was satisfied that everyone inside was asleep, then he began to crawl silently towards the farmhouse. He didn't want to risk crossing the road leading to the farm, even in the near-darkness, so he circled around the stables and the manager's cottage and behind the barns until he arrived at the outbuildings. He crept up against the stone wall and slowly got to his feet. He moved on tiptoe through the gap between the wall and the barn, placing his feet carefully so that he made no sound.

When he reached the courtyard and its collection of cars he slowly scanned every inch, his eyes wide to pull in as much reflected light as possible. Only when he was sure that no guards had been posted did he turn right and slip along the rough wall towards the farmhouse. He drew level with a large window made up of four dirty panes of glass in a wooden frame and he peered inside. He could see metal barrels stacked on top of each other, thick wooden benches and a collection of farm tools. He eased himself past the window and reached a wooden door with ornate metal hinges. There was an ancient keyhole and two bolts, one high up and one near the ground. He gingerly pushed back the upper bolt and was relieved that it moved silently and smoothly. Though the door was old and battered, it was obviously regularly opened. The second bolt was similarly quiet. He held his breath, seized the metal door handle and turned it slowly. It grated a little but not enough for the sound to carry and then he pushed the door inwards. It hadn't been locked and it opened with a mild creak. Nguyen slid inside and closed the door behind him.

The room smelt of dust and decay and there was a bitter chemical taste to the air. Nguyen went over to the barrels. Most of them were full and according to the labels they contained weedkillers of various kinds. He was glad that they weren't fuel drums because at this stage he wasn't planning to burn down the house, he simply wanted to prove to Hennessy how serious he was.

He knelt down on the concrete floor and took off his rucksack. He took out one of the pipe bombs, an alarm clock and two of the shortest coils of wire. The glass had already been removed from the clock leaving the hands exposed. Nguyen fastened one end of one of the coils of the wire to the hour hand of the clock, twisting the wire around three times and then spreading the copper strands out into a fan shape. He did the same with the other piece of wire and the minute hand. He cut the length of wire in half with his knife and bared the cut ends. He took one of the batteries from his pocket and connected the wire from the minute hand to one of its terminals, and the loose piece of wire to the other, before setting the clock to twenty-five minutes to five and checking that it was fully wound. He now had about fifty minutes before the two wires came together. He put the pipe next to the wall under the windows and then connected the two wires protruding from it to the timing circuit by twisting the ends together. When the minute hand had crawled round to meet the hour hand and the two bare wire ends touched they would complete the circuit between the battery and the flash-bulb detonator which would in turn explode the bomb.

He repacked his rucksack and put it on before he gently rolled four of the full barrels of weedkiller over and ranged them around the bomb in a semicircle which would have the effect of concentrating the blast against the wall where it would do the most damage. The hands of the clock were forty minutes apart when he edged silently through the doorway and bolted the door.

Nguyen retraced his steps, but he didn't begin crawling when he left the courtyard, instead he ran around the barns in a low crouch, dropping down only when he came within earshot of the cottage. When past the cottage he rose up again and jogged by the stables. The horses were locked inside and he heard snorts and whinnies but no panic. He reached a point in the field where he could see the entire front of the farmhouse and he dropped down into the grass. He took his binoculars out of the rucksack, put them on the grass in front of him, and looked at his watch. Eight minutes to go.

He lay listening to the night sounds: the hoot of a hunting owl, the bark of a faraway fox, the whup-whup of army helicopters. In his mind, Nguyen pictured the clock ticking away the seconds, and his concentration was so intense that it was almost as if he could hear the metallic clicks emanating from the storeroom, getting louder and louder until the air resonated with the beat and he was sure it would wake everyone for miles around.

The blast, when it came, shocked him, even though he was expecting it. From where he was he couldn't see the explosion but the farmhouse was silhouetted by the flash and a fraction of a second later he felt a trembling vibration along his body and a thundering roar filled the night.

He clamped the binoculars to his eyes and scanned the farmhouse. Within seconds a light went on in one of the upstairs rooms and a figure appeared at the window. Nguyen recognised the man as being one of those who had searched him at Hennessy's office. No other lights came on upstairs so Nguyen got to his feet and, keeping low, scurried back along behind the stables. He moved carefully but he was sure that all eyes would be on the shattered outbuilding which was now burning fiercely. He heard the horses neighing in their stalls and the thuds as they kicked out with their hooves. He dropped down and crawled because he realised that someone would probably go in to calm them down. He made his way past the cottage and didn't stop until he was in the orchard. He crouched behind an apple tree and examined the upstairs rooms of the farmhouse. The door of the cottage burst open and a middle-aged man in a striped dressing-gown came running out, shouting, followed by three bare-chested young men. Nguyen checked them out through the binoculars. They were holding guns.

A light had gone on in the window on the right-hand side of the building, the end nearest the outbuildings, and there were lights in the two rooms on the left. As Nguyen watched, a woman came to the window and opened it. She was middle-aged and dark-haired. A light came on downstairs and then the door opened and two figures appeared. One of them was the man he'd seen at the far side of the building, the other was Hennessy They ran towards the flames. A young woman ran out of the cottage and the middle-aged man shouted something at her. She changed direction and headed for the stables.

From the farmhouse four more men emerged, none of whom Nguyen had seen before. One of them was carrying a fire extinguisher and the rest had shotguns at the ready. The flames were flickering out of a jagged hole in the wall where the door and window had been. Most of the roof tiles had been blown off and were scattered around the courtyard and on the cars. The fire extinguisher spluttered into life and the man played foam around the hole. The girl ran out of the stables carrying another fire extinguisher and she gave it to the man in the dressing-gown. He joined in the fire-fighting. The woman shouted down and Hennessy waved at her and yelled something back. Probably his wife, thought Nguyen. One of the men went back into the farmhouse and reappeared with another fire extinguisher and before long the three columns of foam had the blaze under control. Nguyen decided he had seen enough. He crawled on his belly, away from the farm and into the darkness. There was a wedge-shaped copse of trees about a mile away that he'd earlier identified as a suitable place to lie up during the day and which would allow him to keep the farm under observation.

* * *

Murphy and Hennessy stepped gingerly over the broken brickwork and peered into the smoking wreckage of the outhouse. Steel barrels had been torn apart in the explosion and they were careful not to tread on any of the twisted shards. The blast had shredded the tough, wooden benches and chunks of wood were scattered around misshapen tools, what was left of them.

A slate from the shattered roof crashed down on to the floor and Murphy pulled Hennessy back. "Careful, Liam," he said. "We'd better wait until daylight before we go messing in there."

Hennessy nodded and followed Murphy back out into the courtyard.

"Jesus, Mary and Joseph, what in heaven's name is going on?" said Joe Ryan, standing with an empty extinguisher in his hand, his dressing-gown flapping around his legs. Ryan had been the manager of Hennessy's farm for more than twenty years. He'd been a little surprised when Hennessy and Mary had arrived with McMahon, Murphy and seven men from Belfast who were now standing around the courtyard carrying various weapons that obviously weren't for shooting rabbits, but Hennessy hadn't offered an explanation and Ryan hadn't asked for one.

Hennessy went over to his manager and put a reassuring arm around his shoulder. "My fault, Joe, I should have told you earlier. But I had no idea he'd follow me here." As they walked to the kitchen door of the farmhouse he explained about The Chinaman.

Mary was waiting for them in the kitchen in a green silk dressing-gown and slippers. She'd made a huge pot of coffee and had placed a bottle of Irish whiskey and a dozen glasses on the table for the men. She poured a generous measure into one of the glasses and gave it to her husband. She told Murphy to fill the rest of the glasses for the men who were filing in behind him. "Are you all right?" she asked Hennessy, touching his shoulder as she spoke, her concern obvious and genuine.

"I'm fine, right enough," he said.

"Another warning?" she said, and he wasn't sure if she was being sarcastic or not.

"He wasn't trying to kill anyone, if that's what you mean, Mary," he said, and took a mouthful of the smooth whiskey.

He turned to Murphy. "Get Kavanagh down here straightaway," he said. "Tell him there's no point in looking for The Chinaman in Belfast. And tell him to bring a dozen or so of his men here. Including Willie O'Hara." Murphy grunted and went out to use the phone in the hall.

Ryan pulled a chair out and sat down, helping himself to a mug of coffee. "Has this Chinaman got hand grenades or what, Liam?" he asked.

"Nitroglycerine," said Hennessy. "He made his own nitroglycerine in Belfast." The kitchen was full now, men standing or sitting, some of them still coughing to clear the smoke from their lungs. Ryan's daughter, Sarah, stood behind her father, smoothing down his hair, more to calm her own shaking hands than anything.

Hennessy stood with his back to the sink and cleared his throat loudly to attract everybody's attention. "We're all going to have to be on our guard," he said. "I've underestimated The Chinaman up until now, and that's not a mistake I intend to repeat. For the rest of tonight I want six of you on guard outside." He nodded or pointed to the six men to indicate those he'd chosen. "Jimmy McMahon can sleep in the kitchen and I'll have Christy Murphy stay by the front door. Joe, you and Sarah should lock yourself in the cottage, and keep Tommy with you. Everyone else try to grab some sleep. By tomorrow I'll have worked out what we're going to do."

The men assigned to guard duty finished their whiskey, checked their guns and went outside. Ryan and his daughter went back to their cottage with Tommy O'Donoghue in tow.

Murphy came back into the kitchen. "Jim's on his way."

"Good," said Hennessy. "Mary and I are going to bed. Jimmy'll sleep here tonight. Can you stay in the hall? We'll get a proper rota fixed up tomorrow after Jim gets here."

"Fine by me," said Murphy.

Hennessy and Mary went up the stairs together. She carried a bright-yellow mug of coffee cupped in both hands. To Hennessy, though, it appeared that she was more annoyed than upset by the disturbance. In the bedroom, she put the mug down on her bedside table and brushed her hair with short, attacking strokes.

"I don't think you should stay here, not with all this going on," said Hennessy, taking off his dressing-gown and hanging it on the back of the door.

"I was thinking the same myself," she answered, watching him through the dressing-table mirror as she brushed her hair. He walked over to the open window and looked down at the courtyard. There were two of his men there, one with a shotgun. They waved and he waved back before shutting the window to keep out the smell of smoke. He drew the curtains with a flourish.

"The house in town isn't safe, even while The Chinaman's here," he said. "Abroad would be best, just until we've solved this problem."

"This problem!" she said, and laughed, her voice loaded with irony. "This problem, as you call it, Liam, is stalking around our farm with nitroglycerine bombs intent on God knows what and you call it a problem. You can be so pompous at times!" She shook her head, sadly, while Hennessy stood confused, not sure what to say. She made the decision for him. "I thought I'd go and stay with Marie." Marie, their daughter, was studying sociology at university in London and there were still some weeks to go before summer holidays. They'd rented her a one-bedroom flat in Earl's Court and Mary had been to stay on several occasions.

"I'd prefer it if you went well away, to America or the Caribbean, London is still a bit close to home," he pressed.

She turned to look at him, still brushing her hair. "Liam, I'll be perfectly safe in London," she said frostily. "In the first place, he's hardly likely to know about Marie's rented flat, and in the second, it's you he's after, not me."

Hennessy couldn't argue with that, so he reluctantly agreed.

"Besides, I'll fly over and I'll make sure I take a very close look at everyone else who gets on the plane. If I see anyone who looks vaguely Chinese, I'll call you," she said. She put down the brush and switched off the light. He heard the rustle of silk against her skin and then she slipped under the quilt. He got into his side of the bed.

"Good night," she said. He felt a light kiss on the cheek and then she turned her back on him, drawing her legs up against her stomach. Liam lay on his back, his eyes closed tight.

The french window was wide open allowing the fresh river air to stream in along with the early morning sunshine. Denis Fisher sat on the white plastic chair, a stack of Sunday newspapers on the circular white table. He was wearing a white T-shirt and faded blue Levis and a pair of black plastic sunglasses. His feet were up on another chair, he had a cup of strong coffee at his elbow, and he appeared to be at peace with the world. He ran his fingers through his blond hair and stretched his arms above his head.

"How's it going?" he called into the lounge.

MacDermott, the one they called The Bombmaker, was sitting at the dining-table in front of a collection of electrical equipment, wiring, batteries and timers, and peering into the innards of a laptop computer.

"Fine. There's acres of space here. More than enough. What I'm trying to do is to use the computer's internal clock as a timer and to connect the detonator to its internal battery. If I can it'll save a hell of a lot of weight. All I'll be adding will be the explosive, the detonator and a few inches of wire."

By the side of the computer was an oblong slab of what appeared to be bright-yellow marzipan, covered in a thick film of plastic. It was less than one inch thick but almost nine inches wide and twelve inches long. On top of the block, under the plastic, was a white paper label with a black border containing the words EXPLOSIVE PLASTIC SEMTEX-H.

The explosive had come a long way. It had been manufactured years earlier in the Semtex factory deep in the woods in western Czechoslovakia in the days when it had been behind the Iron Curtain. Production of the high-performance military explosive stopped in 1980, but between 1975 and 1981 the Czechs sold 960 tons to Libya for six million US dollars through the Omnipol trade agency and several tons of that had found its way to the IRA. The Libyan leader Colonel Gaddafi had filled six brick and sandstone warehouses a few miles outside Tripoli with boxes of the high explosive. The Libyan leader had been a staunch supporter of the IRA throughout the early seventies, but it was after the siege of his embassy in London in the summer of 1985 that he began to help them with a vengeance, as a way of getting back at the British Government.

In October 1986, six months after President Reagan ordered a US bomber strike on Tripoli, a converted oil industry safety ship sailed into Libyan waters and over two nights took on board eighty tons of weapons, including a ton of Semtex. The Semtex was unloaded at a small beach in southeast Ireland and over the next year or so much of it was secretly transferred to caches in Britain. The two packages on the table were from the 1986 consignment.

Fisher put down his *Independent on Sunday* and walked back into the flat. He watched over The Bombmaker's shoulder.

"It looks hellishly complicated," said Fisher.

"I've never done anything like this before," said Mac-Dermott. "I'm testing it with this torch bulb here until I'm sure it'll work. The timing is the crucial thing. The amount of explosive we'll be using is so small that it won't do much damage if it goes off in the wrong place. And there's no room for booby traps or secondary circuits."

"How much will you use?" asked Fisher.

"Two hundred grams is more than enough to blow a hole in the fuselage and cause decompression. It was three hundred grams that brought down the Pan Am jet at Lockerbie. Mind you, it's the Lockerbie fiasco that's making it so hard now."

"What do you mean?"

"You remember that doctor whose daughter died on the flight, the one that took a fake bomb on a BA jet to New York to show how lax security was? He filled a radio with marzipan and a battery but he proved his point and now the airlines routinely check all electrical equipment."

"Does that mean they'll take it apart?" said Fisher, frowning.

"They won't take it apart, but they will ask to see it working, and they'll peer through the grilles and any gaps. And they'll X-ray it. Before the summer of 1990 they'd let you take them on board without putting them through the X-ray machine, but the Secretary of State for Transport changed the rules."

"Won't the explosive show up?"

"It's supposed to on the new models, but I'm hollowing out the transformer and taking out the modem circuit and packing most of it in there. It'll look OK, no matter how good their equipment is, don't worry. Anyway, this is the sort of thing they expect people to take on planes, so if it works OK and the right person is carrying it they won't suspect anything. And it will work, I'll make sure of that."

Fisher put his hand on MacDermott's shoulder and squeezed. "If anyone can do it, you can. How's the Ascot bomb coming on?"

The Bombmaker nodded at a metal camera case on the floor. "That's child's play in comparison. I'll finish it tonight."

Fisher smiled, satisfied.

"Have you any idea which plane yet?" asked The Bombmaker.

Fisher shook his head. "We're going to have to be careful, bloody careful," he said. "We can't hit a flight where there could be Irish on board, or Americans, or kids. What I'm really after is a plane in the Queen's Flight, or one carrying the Prime Minister or any of the Government bastards. Or maybe an RAF plane. I just want to have the bomb ready so that we can use it immediately we get an opportunity. And a mule. We need a mule to carry it on board. Someone with access. A pilot, a journalist, a policeman, someone who can get close without raising suspicion."

"It's risky, mixing with people like that when we're trying to keep a low profile."

Fisher grinned. "I know it's risky, but think of the rewards. Just think about it. It'd be like another Brighton bombing, another Mountbatten."

The phone rang and O'Reilly put down the gun he was cleaning, a Smith & Wesson 9-millimetre automatic pistol, on the coffee-table. "Shall I get it?" he asked, but Fisher already had it in his hand.

"Yes, yes, understood. Yes," he said to the voice at the other end and hung up.

"Interesting," he said, rubbing his chin. O'Reilly and The Bombmaker looked at him expectantly. "The codeword has been changed," he explained. "As of tonight."

"Good of them to let us know," smiled O'Reilly as he picked up the automatic and began stripping it down. "They might not have taken us seriously."

Hennessy was alone in the large pine bed when he awoke. He bathed and dressed and went downstairs to find his wife in front of their stove frying eggs and bacon and grilling toast. Jim Kavanagh, Willie O'Hara, Christy Murphy and Jimmy McMahon were sitting around the table drinking coffee.

Despite the bomb shattering their sleep, Mary looked radiant and seemed to be relishing her role as a short-order cook.

"Right Christy, here's yours," she sang, and plopped down a plate of bacon and eggs in front of him. Willie O'Hara was already halfway through his breakfast, mopping up egg yolk with a piece of fried bread. Kavanagh had finished and was buttering a slice of toast. Liam had heard him arrive in the early hours and he didn't look as if he'd had any sleep, either. Mary broke another two eggs into the pan and put them on the burner, took four more slices of toast from under the grill and slotted them into the toast rack on the table.

"Good morning, Liam," she said cheerfully, and poured him a glass of orange juice. "What would you like?"

"Just toast," he said. He had never been a big eater, and considering the stress he was under just now he doubted if he'd be able to force down much toast. "Thanks for getting here so quickly, Jim," he said to Kavanagh.

"I'm just mad at myself for not getting him in Belfast, then none of this would've happened."

"Where are the men who came down with you?"

"They've relieved the guys who were on duty during the night, and they're over in the cottage having breakfast. We didn't think it fair to all impose on yez good lady wife."

"Nonsense," said Mary, walking over with another plate of food. "Jimmy, here's your breakfast."

Hennessy pulled out a chair and sat down. "How many men are here at the moment?" he asked Kavanagh.

"There's the six that came down with me, plus the seven who came down with ye and Christy. And there's three farm-workers who we can use if necessary. And Mr Ryan and his daughter have offered to help. I think they're a bit reluctant to be out working the farm with this Chinaman on the loose."

Hennessy nodded thoughtfully and sipped his juice. "We can't use the farmworkers, or the Ryans, not for this. If we need more men we'll bring them in from Belfast. So we're talking about thirteen men, plus you four." He saw a look of panic pass over O'Hara's egg-streaked face. "Don't worry, Willie, I won't be asking you to carry a gun." Willie O'Hara was notoriously afraid of firearms, despite being one of the organisation's foremost explosives experts. "And Christy, I want you to take Mary to London later today."

"Och Liam, he doesn't have to go all the way to London with me," chided Mary over her shoulder as she fried more eggs.

"To London," insisted Liam. Murphy nodded. "Jimmy, you'll be driving them to the airport." McMahon grunted through a mouthful of food.

Hennessy asked Kavanagh how many men it would take to make the farm secure.

"Nothing can ever be secure, ye know that," he answered. "Yez could put a hundred men on guard but a determined man could still get through." He could see that Hennessy was not pleased with his answer so quickly added: "Three guards could secure the courtyard, but there's a risk then that he could throw something in through one of the windows of the outside of the building, or get to the barns. Yez'll need a man guarding the barns, two by the stables, one in the courtyard, and three covering the front of the farm."

"So seven men in all?"

"That's at night. During the day four should do it because this place is surrounded by fields and yer'll see him coming for miles."

"That's still eleven men and that doesn't include sleeping time."

"That's right enough. Yer'll need at least twenty-two, and if it goes on for any length of time, Liam, yer'll need as many again because they're going to get tired and careless."

Hennessy slammed his hand down on the table, rattling the breakfast plates. "Damn this man, damn him," he cursed.

Mary put a filled plate in front of Kavanagh and he thanked her. "Are you sure you don't want anything else, Liam?" she asked, and when he said no she took off her apron and put it over the back of a chair. She was wearing tight ski pants and a blue sweater and Hennessy could see O'Hara and McMahon watch her backside twitch as she walked to the door. Did she know that men took such pleasure from watching her move? Hennessy was pretty sure that she did. While he took pride in having such an attractive wife, many were the times that he wished she'd age just a little faster, that she'd look a little less attractive so that men would stop looking at her with lust in their eyes. He wished she'd join him in middle-age and not keep acting like a teenager. Maybe she'd give him more of herself then.

"Christy, get on the plane with her and see her all the way to my daughter's flat. If at any time you even remotely suspect that The Chinaman is anywhere near, get to a safe place and call for help. Don't take any risks. This bastard is out to get me and he might just decide to hurt me through my family."

Murphy put his knife and fork together on his plate. "She'll be safe with me, Liam, I promise you."

McMahon drained his coffee cup and stood up. "I think

I'll take the car to the garage in the village and fill her up so that we don't have to stop on the way. Are they open on a Sunday?"

"The sign'll say closed, sure enough, but sound your horn and old man Hanratty will come out and serve you," said Hennessy.

McMahon wiped his hands on his trousers and went out into the courtyard. They heard the car start up and drive out of the courtyard.

"Willie, I want you to go through what's left of the outbuilding and find out what caused it, whether or not it was one of the home-made bombs you described. Then I think we ought to arrange a . . ."

His words were cut short by the echoing thud of an explosion in the distance, as if a huge pile of earth had been dropped from a great height. Kavanagh got to his feet first and he led the way as they rushed through the hall and out of the front door.

The Jaguar was lying on its side in the field next to the track about fifty yards before it joined the road. There were clouds of steam coming from under the bonnet which had burst open and the engine was racing. Three of the IRA guards were already running down the track to the car and two more came running from the stables, guns at the ready. One of them reached through the side window and switched off the engine.

"Oh God, Jimmy," said Hennessy under his breath as he began jogging towards the Jaguar. By the time he arrived there, with O'Hara in tow, they'd pulled McMahon out of the car and lain him on the grass. His face was cut in a dozen places, there was blood on his shirt and he was mumbling incoherently. Hennessy knelt down by McMahon and held his hand. It was covered in blood.

"Get a car here, we'll have to take him to hospital," he said to Michael O'Faolain, the gangly, red-haired youth who'd come down from Belfast. "We don't have time to wait for an ambulance." O'Faolain ran back down the track towards the farmhouse. "Willie, find out what the hell happened," he said to O'Hara. O'Hara went to look at the car, but Hennessy had already seen the crater in the track and knew what it meant. "The fucking Chinaman," he hissed.

McMahon groaned but didn't open his eyes. His trousers were burnt and ripped and through the slashed material Hennessy could see blood pouring from the injured legs.

O'Hara appeared at his shoulder. "Nitroglycerine bomb by the look of it, Liam, buried a couple of feet down in the track. Detonated by wire."

"That means he was close by."

"Still is, I reckon. Depends how long his wires were." He pointed across the field towards a distant copse. "The wires run in that direction. If you move fast . . ."

"Christ, what was I thinking of!" Hennessy blurted. "We should be after him now." He called Kavanagh over and told him to take all but three of the men and follow the wires and to go after The Chinaman. As an afterthought he told Murphy to stay behind because after what had happened he was even more keen to get Mary out of the way.

O'Faolain arrived in the Range Rover and Hennessy, Murphy and O'Hara helped lift McMahon on to the back seat. There was a large tartan blanket there and they used it to wrap him up in. Hennessy delegated another of the young men to sit in the back and make sure that McMahon wasn't tossed around too much on the drive to the hospital. The Range Rover roared off as Hennessy shielded his eyes and looked at the group of men running across the fields, fanning out the further away they got from the track. Of The Chinaman there was no sign, but he had to be out there somewhere.

Nguyen had begun to crawl through the grass as soon as he had detonated the pipe bomb. The wires had been about fifty yards long which put him about halfway across the field, but he could move quickly on his stomach and by the time the front door of the farm had opened he had reached the relative safety of a hedgerow that cut it off from the neighbouring field where a flock of sheep and lambs grazed and played.

He'd set the bomb in the early hours of the morning before the sky had streaked with red and the sun had made its first appearance. He'd planned to dig down into the track but as it turned out there had been no need. It cut across the field with a narrow ditch on either side to keep the rain running off it during the wet weather. In places, the earth by the side of the track had begun to crumble into the ditch and Nguyen found a spot where he could pull out handfuls of soil with a minimum of effort. He scooped out enough to hide one of the pipe bombs, and he carefully ran the wires down into the ditch and through the grass as far as they would go. The grass was barely tall enough to conceal him but the ground was uneven and towards the road it sloped steeply away from the farm so Nguyen knew that, so long as he kept low, he'd be able to reach the hedgerow without being spotted. He'd lain flat on the ground for about six hours, not moving. He'd seen the sun come up and heard the birds begin their dawn chorus and counted half a dozen helicopters flying overhead before the Jaguar had come down the track.

After he detonated the bomb he rolled under the hedge and found a gap big enough to squeeze through and then began crawling away from the road, back towards the farm. After he'd travelled two hundred yards he peeked through the hedge. He could see Hennessy kneeling on the ground cradling the driver. Nguyen doubted that he would be badly hurt, the bomb had been too far underground to do too much damage. He'd been careful to detonate it just under the front bumper, not so far ahead that the blast would send the windscreen glass spinning into the driver's face, but not so far back that the petrol tank would be ignited. Nguyen didn't want to kill unless it was absolutely necessary, he still hoped to get what he wanted by pressurising and intimidating Hennessy. If that didn't work then he'd rethink his strategy.

A small, thin-faced man was bending over the crater in the track. He knelt down and picked up something and looked at it and then went over to look at the blasted car. He examined the damage to the underside of the car and then walked back to the crater. He looked into the ditch and then jumped over it and began searching the grass. Nguyen knew that he was looking for the wires and that before long he'd find them. He cut away from the hedgerow and ran with his back to the farm-buildings, his rucksack banging on his shoulders. He tramped across a small stream and vaulted over a five-bar gate into a field containing a dozen or so brown and white cattle, breathing heavily because he wasn't used to running. He reached the edge of the copse where he'd hidden the previous evening and slipped into the cool undergrowth before looking behind him. The field was clear, and so was the one behind that, but it was only a matter of time before they came after him. Not that Nguyen was worried. He'd only seen ten men in the courtyard dealing with the fire last night and he doubted that Hennessy would allow them all to go tramping through the fields and woods, leaving the cottage unprotected. Five, or maybe six, that would be all, and Nguyen knew he was more than capable of handling that many because they'd have to spread out.

The copse covered several acres and was on land which was obviously too wet for grazing sheep or cattle. He'd spent several hours getting to know his way around and could move confidently through it, knowing where the best hiding places and vantage points were. The trees were a mixture of oak, horse chestnut and beech, all of them old and draped in moss and surrounded by bushes and brambles. The canopy of branches overhead blocked out much of the sunlight and the air was filled with the chatter of birds jostling for territory. Nguyen made his way towards the middle of the copse, being careful not to break branches or leave obvious signs of his passage. In the distance he heard shouts. They'd be able to follow the wires to the place where he'd lain in the grass and then they'd be able to see where he'd crawled to the hedge-row, but unless they were expert trackers they wouldn't be able to see where he'd gone from there. They'd see the trees but they wouldn't be sure if he'd gone to ground there, or if he'd run through or passed by, so they'd probably split up. Two, maybe three. It would be easy.

A rustling sound to his left made him drop into a crouch, senses alert. A grey squirrel sprinted out from underneath a bush, its tail streaming behind it like a banner, and it ran headlong up a tree with something held in its jaws. Nguyen relaxed and as he did he heard more shouts, heading in his direction. A meandering trail roughly bisected the wood, it was nothing more than a flattening of the soil where countless generations of feet had used it as a shortcut through the trees. By the side of the trail was a huge oak, a centuries-old tree which was gnarled and misshapen with age. It was a good twelve feet across at the base and its roots were as thick as a man's waist before they dived down into the earth. Behind the tree, on the side furthest away from the path, was a deep split where the wood had cracked, half covered with a rambling bramble bush with sharp thorns. Nguyen had marked it out as a good place to hide because anyone searching the copse would probably take the easy way and follow the path. Some fifteen feet or so either side of the tree he'd tossed small, dry twigs along the path which were sure to crackle and break when stepped on so he'd be able to hear them coming no matter how careful they were. He'd prepared traps along the trail in places where it narrowed. Nothing elaborate because he hadn't had the time, just holes dug in the earth, a foot or so deep, with sharpened sticks, smeared with his own excrement, pointing upward. The holes had been covered with a mesh of fine twigs and leaves and overlain with soil, and overnight they had blended in perfectly with the rest of the trail. Even Nguyen himself could see no traces of the traps.

He slipped by the brambles and edged into the hole in the tree, first removing his rucksack so that it wouldn't snag. He unclipped his knife and held it by his side, breathing slowly and evenly. There were more shouts to his left, outside the wood, and then a yelling voice to his right. There were more voices, closer, whispering. He heard someone forcing his way through the undergrowth, but moving away from him, and then a similar noise to his left, also moving away. Two men at least, then. They had entered the copse together and had split up either side of the trail and were moving through the trees. The shouting continued in the distance so he had been right, some of the men had gone by the copse and were probably even now running across the fields and checking the hedgerows.

Nguyen let his mind totally relax so that he could concentrate on listening for his pursuers. They moved like large animals through the trees, pushing branches out of the way, not caring where they trod, and he had no problem in pinpointing their positions. He closed his eyes and let his mind roam the woods. He heard the dry crack of a twig and homed in on the sound, twenty, perhaps twenty-five feet away, someone moving slowly and carefully, somebody who cared how and where he walked. There was a pause of perhaps ten seconds then a second sound, the rustle of a leaf being disturbed.

Nguyen blanked out his mind, wiping away all thoughts and concentrating only on the approaching man. He tried to make himself invisible. Nguyen had once tried explaining it to the instructors from the 5th Special Forces Group at Recondo School outside Saigon, how his sixth sense worked and how he would shield his own thoughts from pursuers so that he could blend into the jungle and not be seen or felt. They'd laughed, thinking he was talking about magic or voodoo, but Nguyen was serious. His talent had saved his life, and the lives of his men, many, many times. It wasn't a case of hearing, or smelling, it was sensing, but even Nguyen didn't know exactly what it was that he sensed. It was as if he could tune into the electrical field given off by a human being or an animal, as if he could detect their auras from a distance. And he believed that the reverse was true, that other animals and humans could detect his aura and home in on it unless he dampened it down.

He heard a small movement and knew that the man was now level with the tree, heading down the trail. Nguyen's mind was empty now, like a placid pool with not a single ripple disturbing its surface. He was no longer aware of the heavy knife in his hand or the pressure of the ground against his left knee as he knelt inside the tree trunk. He was invisible. He flowed out of the tree as gentle as a soft wind, brushing the brambles silently aside. His steps were small and only the balls of his feet made contact with the ground, his legs bent at the knees. The man on the trail was slightly taller than Nguyen. He stood with his back to him, wearing jeans and a dark-blue bomber jacket. In his right hand he carried a gun. Nguyen had planned to silence the man with his left hand and stun him by driving the handle of his knife against his temple but he couldn't risk it now because the man's finger would tighten involuntarily and the gun would go off. Still moving, he slipped the knife into one of the pockets of his jacket and moved behind the man, both hands out. Only at the last minute did the man sense his presence and begin to turn his head, but by then Nguyen was in position. His right hand moved down swiftly and clamped over the gun, fingers splayed so that he caught the hammer and prevented it from being released. His left hand simultaneously clamped over the man's mouth and nose. He pulled the nose between his thumb and the first joint of the opposing index finger while gripping the jaws between the heel of the hand and the remaining finger tips. The man tried to lash out with his left hand but Nguyen twisted away, out of reach. From experience Nguyen knew that it could take up to two minutes for the man to lose consciousness and he gripped tightly until the man sagged and the gun dropped from his nerveless hand. Nguyen put the gun into his jacket pocket and took out the knife. He let the man's dead-weight carry him to the ground. Killing him would have been easy; a quick slash across the subclavian artery would take just three seconds, cutting the carotid artery and jugular vein would kill within twelve. But Nguyen knew that killing the enemy wasn't always the best way, not when you were up against more than one. A dead comrade could be abandoned while the fight continued, but an injured one became a drain on the enemy's resources. He had to be cared for and transported out of danger, with the added psychological damage that a wounded man could do to the able-bodied. Time and time again Nguyen had seen it happen in the jungle. A group of Americans on a mission, the man on point would run into a booby trap, his leg blown off or a poisoned stick through his foot, and his screams and blood would terrify the rest. Not only that but the mission would be suspended while a helicopter was called in or the man was stretchered back to base. And next time a patrol moved down the trail they'd do so with twice the care at half the speed.

He heard a shout far to his right and an answer over to his left. He knelt down by the unconscious man and stabbed him twice in the upper thigh, not deep enough to cut an artery but enough to cause a considerable flow of blood.

The shouting was getting closer and Nguyen ducked behind the tree to pick up his rucksack and began to run down the track, keeping low. A gunshot behind him made him duck and he ran faster. Twice he jumped over places in the track where he'd earlier set spike traps. The man he'd ambushed must have come round because he heard frantic screaming. His screams and the gunshot would bring the rest of the men running to the copse, but Nguyen was still perfectly calm because he had many other hiding-places prepared. It would take a dozen men many days to search the copse thoroughly and they had no way of knowing whether he'd gone to ground or if he'd left the woods. They'd be sure to follow his tracks down the trail but there was a good chance that one of them would fall into one of the foot traps and that would slow them up even more. Everything was going to plan.

It seemed to Hennessy as if his life had been turned upside down. Mary had left with Christy Murphy in one of the Land-Rovers, driving over the fields for a mile or so before turning on to the road just in case The Chinaman had set other bombs. In a few hours she'd be in London where at least she'd be safe. Jimmy McMahon was in hospital where his condition, the doctors said, was as well as could be expected. They'd been told that a faulty generator had exploded because Hennessy didn't want the RUC sniffing around. The man who'd been stabbed in the wood had turned out to have superficial wounds despite all his screaming and they'd patched him up and he was being driven up to Belfast for treatment along with a teenager who'd put his foot through six wooden spikes smeared with what looked like shit. He could barely walk and he'd need antibiotics if the wound wasn't going to go septic.

In the space of an hour, three of his men had been injured and all they had to show for it was a description of a small Oriental man in camouflage gear carrying a rucksack. And if he wasn't armed before, now he had a gun.

Hennessy had posted four guards around the farm and everyone else was now indoors. Joe Ryan and Sarah were staying in their own cottage. With three men injured, one driving the car to Belfast, and Murphy on his way to London with Mary, it left Hennessy with just Jim Kavanagh and Willie O'Hara sitting at the kitchen table. He poured O'Hara and himself measures of whiskey and asked Kavanagh what he wanted.

"I'll make myself a brew, if that's OK with yez," Kavanagh said. He pushed back his chair and put the kettle on the stove.

"We're going to need more men," Hennessy said to his back. Kavanagh shrugged but didn't turn round as he busied himself washing the teapot and preparing a cup and saucer. "Can you arrange for half a dozen good men from Belfast?"

"I'm not sure if that's such a good idea, Liam," said Kavanagh quietly.

"What do you mean?" O'Hara emptied his glass and mumbled something about checking the bombed outhouse and let himself out of the back door. "What do you mean, Jim?" Hennessy repeated.

Kavanagh turned round, drying his cup with a big, white tea-towel. "I'm just not sure that we're going to be able to solve this just by bringing in more people, that's all. There were a dozen here last night and they didn't stop him."

"They weren't prepared," said Hennessy.

"They were prepared when they went into the wood," said Kavanagh. He put the cup and the cloth on the draining-board and sat down, looking earnestly at Hennessy. "Look, Liam, yer know that I'd do anything to protect ye, anything. But this isn't a question of numbers, it's quality not quantity. Yez could bring in a hundred men but they're used to the city, not the country. They're used to fighting in the streets not in the hills."

"So we bring in men from the farms. Come on Jim, that's not what's worrying you. Spit it out."

Kavanagh looked uneasy, as if knowing that what he would say would offend Hennessy. Hennessy found his reluctance to speak embarrassing, he'd always thought that they trusted each other implicitly.

"What's wrong, Jim?" he pressed.

Kavanagh leant back in his chair, as if trying to put as much distance as possible between the two of them. "This man, this Chinaman, has made it personal. It's ye he wants, right enough. Not the organisation. Ye. I just think that if ye use too many of the organisation's resources, it could backfire on yez."

Hennessy nodded. Kavanagh had a point. There were men in Belfast and Dublin who were looking for an excuse to discredit him. They were unhappy at the move away from violence and blamed Hennessy for the switch in policy.

"And the thing of it is, I don't reckon that bringing in more men is going to help. Look at it this way, he could travel ten miles or so in a few hours with no trouble at all. And a ten-mile radius from here will cover about three hundred square miles – that includes Newry, Castlewellan, and Warrenpoint, and most of the Mourne Mountains. There aren't enough men in the whole of Belfast to cover an area that large."

"So we don't search for him. OK. But I have to have guards here. I can't just sit here defenceless and wait for him to attack again."

"But how long do ye keep the guards here, Liam? A week? A month? A year? Round-the-clock protection from one man – think what a drain that would be on the organisation's resources. Think how it would look. I'm telling ye this as yer friend, yer understand? Playing devil's advocate, yer know?"

Hennessy nodded. "I know, Jim. I don't doubt your loyalty, you know that." He reached over and squeezed Kavanagh's arm. "I already owe you my life, you don't have to prove anything to me. And I know you have my best interests at heart. But what am I supposed to do? He obviously means business."

"If ye want my opinion, it was a mistake coming here. It's too open, there are too many places to hide."

"It sounds like you've had a change of heart, Jim. I seem to remember that it was your idea to get me out of Belfast in the first place." He said it softly, not meaning to criticise.

"That was then," admitted Kavanagh. "I thought it was a good idea because I didn't think he'd know about the farm. But now that he does know I think we should go back to Belfast. All yez need there is me and Christy, maybe a couple of others. Now that we know who he is he won't be able to get close to ye. He'll stick out like a sore thumb in Belfast." He held up his hands. "I know what yez going to say, that he managed to blow up yez office while we were there, but yer've got to remember that when he did that we didn't know what a threat he was then. It won't happen again."

Hennessy took a long, thoughtful swig from his glass.

"I don't know, Jim. He got to the car, didn't he? And he's obviously a patient bastard. He'll just wait until he gets another chance, sure enough."

"Yeah, but he'll be waiting in Belfast, not hiding in a wood. In the city we can search for him without worrying where we're stepping all the time."

The two men sat in silence for a while as Hennessy considered his options. He knew that Kavanagh was talking sense, but he knew too that there were advantages in keeping The Chinaman away from Belfast. God knows what it would do to his reputation if it became known that he was being stalked by a maniac with home-made bombs. The Press would have a field day. And so would his enemies within the organisation. Damn The Chinaman. Damn him for ever.

"There is something else yez should think about," said Kavanagh, interrupting Hennessy's thoughts. Hennessy raised his eyebrows quizzically. "The reason he's after yez," Kavanagh continued. "He wants the names of the team who're planting the bombs in London."

"We don't know who they are."

"No, but yer trying to find out. And yer'll find out eventually, they can't keep going for ever. Either we'll find out who they are or they'll make a mistake and the fucking Brits will get them. Either way that'll be the end of yez problem. All we have to do is to keep him off yez back until then. Liam, I know you're handling this yezself, but how close are ye to identifying them?"

Hennessy looked levelly at Kavanagh. He trusted the man sitting in front of him, but it was crucial that only Sean Morrison knew what he had planned. "At the moment we're no closer than we were a week ago," he said. "But if everything works out it shouldn't be much longer. Days rather than weeks. That's all I can say."

"That's good enough for me, Liam," said Kavanagh. The kettle began to shriek and he stood up and poured boiling water into the teapot. "Until then, we'll stick to yez like glue. When is Christy back?"

"I told him to take Mary all the way to London and to hang around for a while to make sure that she isn't followed. He should be back tomorrow night."

There was a scrabbling at the door and Jackie bounded in, her tongue lolling and her coat damp. She careered over to Hennessy and put her head in his lap; he stroked her absent-mindedly.

"I hear what you're saying," Hennessy said to Kavanagh. "Let's wait until Christy gets back until we decide what to do."

"It's yer call, Liam. But if I were ye I'd get a few more men around – not from Belfast but locals, workers from nearby farms maybe, fellahs yez can trust. They'll be used to dealing with poachers and the like and at least they'll be careful where they put their feet."

"That's a good idea, Jim. I'll make a few calls. It shouldn't be a problem."

Jackie growled softly, seeking attention.

*   *   *

Woody had the mother and father of all hangovers. His head felt twice its normal size, his mouth was dry and bitter and every time he moved his stomach lurched and only an intense effort of will kept him from throwing up. It was a normal Sunday morning. Saturday was always the paper's busiest day and once the presses started running and they'd checked that the opposition papers didn't have any earth-shattering exclusives then all the paper's journalists headed for the pub. The Saturday-night sessions in the King's Head were legendary, but Woody didn't just go for the alcohol and the company, he went because he had to keep in with the news desk and the paper's executives. The paper, along with most of Fleet Street, was cutting back all round, slashing a red pen through expense claims and reducing the number of casual shifts. It was like a game of musical chairs and Woody was fighting like hell to ensure that when the music stopped he'd be one of those left sitting at a desk. The hangover was a small price to pay.

He heard the phone ring on the floor below and one of the other tenants answered it and then he heard his name being called.

Woody groaned and pulled a pillow over his head. Footsteps clattered up the stairs and a hand hammered on his door and the student who lived in the bedsit directly below his yelled that the office was on the phone. If it had been anyone else Woody wouldn't have bothered answering, but a call from the paper probably meant there was a shift going so he coughed and forced himself to sit up, feeling waves of nausea ripple through his stomach. He breathed deeply and groped for a pair of jeans before padding slowly down the stairs, holding his head in his hands.

The phone was hanging down by the wall and he pulled it up and put it against his ear. His head swam and he closed his eyes.

"Ian Wood," he said, flinching as the words echoed around his skull.

"Woody?" said a voice. It was a man, but Woody couldn't place it.

"Yes?"

"Woody, it's Pat. Pat Quigley. I didn't get you out of bed, did I?"

Woody moaned and leant against the wall. "What the fuck do you want, Pat?"

"Jesus, Woody, you sound terrible. Are you sick or something?"

"Pat, you have exactly ten seconds before I go back to my pit. It's Sunday morning, you should be in church and I should be in bed."

"Got you, Woody. OK, listen. Do you remember those Sinn Fein guys you were asking me about a while back?" Woody grunted, but said nothing, so Quigley continued. "Well, there's something funny going on here. I've been told that someone has started some sort of vendetta against one of the men I told you about, Liam Hennessy. He's one of Sinn Fein's top advisers, and a leading lawyer here."

"A vendetta? What the fuck are you talking about?"

"Someone set off a bomb in his office. Just a small one, a chemical bomb I'm told, not high explosive. A warning, maybe. No one was hurt. It seems like a coincidence, you know, happening so soon after we spoke. That's all."

"I still don't see what you want from me, Pat." Actually Woody had a pretty good idea what was going on. As well as stringing for the *Sunday World*, Quigley filed copy for one of the daily heavies and they were probably pushing him for a Sunday for Monday story, what with it being a quiet news week and all.

"I was thinking that perhaps you passed Hennessy's name on to someone, someone who might want to, I don't know, put pressure on him, maybe. I mean, I'm told the attack wasn't sectarian, it was too amateurish for that. Come on Woody, what's going on?"

"Fucked if I know, Pat. Honest. Anyway, my notebooks are all in the office, I can't do anything now. But I'm sure you're barking up the wrong tree, mate. It was just a reader who wanted to contact someone in Sinn Fein, that was all."

"OK, Woody. I thought it was worth a try. Maybe I'll call you in the office during the week." He sounded disappointed, but Woody felt no urge to help him, not in his present weakened state. Besides, Woody could smell a possible story. What was The Chinaman's name? He couldn't remember so he stopped trying and instead concentrated on getting back to his room without throwing up over the threadbare carpet.

The taxi dropped Morrison close to the South African embassy in Trafalgar Square. A group of half a dozen demonstrators were outside, standing on the pavement close to the road. They were dressed like students, pale-faced girls with straggly hair and men with beards and John Lennon glasses. One of the women had a megaphone and she harangued two policemen who stood either side of the door to the building. "End Apartheid now!" she yelled, the electronically amplified shriek echoing off the stone walls of the embassy. Morrison wondered why they bothered. You didn't change things by standing on street corners with faded banners and shouting slogans. You changed things by taking action, by hurting those in power, and then by negotiating from strength. And by being committed to change. The anti-Apartheid movement in the UK had never really learnt that lesson, mainly because they had never experienced the discrimination they were protesting about. The vast bulk of them were from comfortable middle-class backgrounds or were working-class kids with chips on their shoulders. Most of them weren't even black. They'd be a hell of a lot more effective if they couldn't get work because they followed the wrong religion, if they didn't have a fair say in the running of their own lives, and if they and their friends and family could be beaten and tortured by the soldiers of an oppressive regime in a country that didn't even belong to them. The IRA was effective because its members cared and because they all stood to benefit if they were ultimately successful and the British pulled out of Ireland.

He crossed over the road and walked by one of the huge, majestic lions. It was surrounded by a group of Asian tourists laden with designer shoulder-bags and expensive camera equipment. A crocodile of Scandinavian sightseers were following a tour guide and Morrison stopped to let them go by. There were pigeons everywhere, fluttering through the air, sitting around the fountains and waddling along the floor. They had grown fat and lazy and had no fear of humans. On the contrary, they gathered in noisy flocks around the tourists who had paid for little tubs of bird seed and sat on arms and wrists while they fed.

Morrison looked around the square. He normally had a nose for plain-clothes policemen or off-duty soldiers, a sixth sense honed by years of surviving in Belfast. He tagged a man in his forties in a brown leather bomber jacket as one possibility, and he paid close attention to a balding man in a fawn overcoat, but both left the square eventually. Bromley got to within a dozen paces before Morrison realised he was the man he was there to see. Tallish with horn-rimmed spectacles and a well-trimmed black beard, Bromley looked more like a history professor than a Detective Chief Inspector with the Anti-Terrorist Branch. He was wearing a greenish jacket of some indeterminate material with baggy corduroy trousers and a brown wool tie. He was smoking a pipe. Morrison thought the pipe could be cover because it looked brand new, but the man appeared to have no problems inhaling and blew out a cloud of bluish smoke as he drew near.

"Detective Chief Inspector Bromley, I presume," said Morrison. He made no move to shake hands, and neither did the inspector. Each was highly suspicious of the other. Both knew that they could be under observation and whereas a clandestine meeting could possibly be explained, a handshake or any other sign of friendliness would be damning. And in Morrison's case, possibly fatal.

"How can I help you, Mr Morrison?" said Bromley with exaggerated politeness.

Morrison began walking slowly around the perimeter of the square. "It's about the bombs, the bombs on the mainland," he said. "We're not responsible."

"By we, who do you mean?"

"The organisation."

"Well, Mr Morrison, there appears to be some confusion here. The forensic evidence we have suggests that the devices are standard IRA type, and each time responsibility has been claimed they've given the correct codeword. Can you explain that?" Bromley shook his head and puffed on his pipe.

"We think there's a renegade unit behind it. We don't know who."

"Are you trying to tell me there's an active service unit on the loose and you don't even know who it is? Where are they getting their explosives from?"

"They've managed to gain access to several arms dumps in and around London. They have explosives, detonators and firearms. But they haven't been sanctioned by us. We're as keen as you are to see them stopped."

"And the codewords?"

Morrison nodded. "We think they're being helped by someone high up in Belfast or Dublin. But again, we don't know who."

Bromley thrust his hands deep into the pockets of his corduroy trousers and studied the ground as he walked. "You know they've taken explosives, but you don't know who they are?"

"We've checked out all our caches. Some ordnance was missing." Morrison chose his words carefully because he couldn't afford to give away any more information than was absolutely necessary. The IRA was still at war with the British Government, when all was said and done.

"Can't you just identify which IRA members are unaccounted for?"

"It's a big organisation. We're working on it."

"It's a big organisation but I doubt if you've that many bombmakers."

"You'd be surprised," said Morrison. "But with the organisation structured the way it is, it's harder than it used to be to get in touch with people. You of all people should know that."

Bromley grunted around the stem of his pipe. He knew what Morrison meant. Following several much publicised coups by the intelligence services in the late seventies and early eighties, the IRA had undergone a transformation, doing away with the old brigade command structure in favour of a more complex network of cells, each with different but often overlapping functions. Most of the units in Northern Ireland reported to the high command in Belfast, but in the country-side the chain of command was a great deal more flexible, harder to pin down. The cells were graded into four levels. The most important were active service units responsible for fund-raising robberies, assassinations, bombings and weaponry, numbering about one hundred of the organisation's most trusted members. At any one time at least half of them could be found in the H-blocks of Long Kesh.

The second level consisted of about three hundred and fifty men and women divided into small cells, all of them trained and ready to go into action but held in reserve until needed. They were generally less well-known to the security forces and it was members of the second level who were often sent into active service on the mainland or the Continent.

The third level comprised a small number of cells, mainly Dublin-based terrorists who were active during the sixties but who had effectively disappeared from the political scene and who did not appear on any current intelligence files.

The fourth level was made up of what Morrison thought of as the enthusiastic amateurs, usually Belfast teenagers who'd graduated from street fighting or youngsters from Catholic farming families helping with the organisation's smuggling operations. They were useful as couriers or lookouts, or for causing disturbances, but not sufficiently trained for anything more sophisticated. Most were expendable and would rise no higher in the organisation.

The structure had been set up so that if any one cell were exposed, its links with the rest of the organisation would be minimal. The system made the IRA much more secure, but it also made it difficult to run checks on who was doing what. Each cell had to be contacted individually, and that would take a great deal of time. And that wasn't allowing for the IRA members like Morrison who weren't even members of a cell but who worked alone.

"So what are you saying, Mr Morrison?"

"We have a plan," said Morrison quietly.

"We?"

That, realised Morrison, was the problem. "We" meant Hennessy and Morrison and nobody else, so he was going to have an uphill struggle to persuade Bromley to help. And it was made even more difficult by virtue of the fact that the policeman would also have to be sworn to secrecy. It was, whichever way you looked at it, an unholy alliance.

"The Provisional IRA is not responsible for the bombings, that I can promise you. They're using our ordnance and our codewords, but they are acting without official sanction. We plan to change the codeword, but different codes will be given to each member of the high command. When they claim responsibility for the next bombing, we should know who their link is."

Bromley bit down on the pipe, his brow furrowed. "You mean you want the police to tell you which codeword we get?"

Morrison nodded. "That's all you have to do. Give us the word, we'll do the rest."

"That's all I have to do!" exclaimed the policeman. "All I have to do is to co-operate with the IRA! Can you imagine what would happen if that ever got out?"

Morrison stopped walking and confronted Bromley, putting his face close up to the policeman's. "And can you imagine, Detective Chief Inspector Bromley, how long I'd have to live if anyone in the organisation knew what I was proposing? My life is on the line here, so don't give me any crap about your reputation being at risk."

"You're asking me to co-operate with you in a bombing campaign. You're asking me to give you confidential information on an investigation." A pigeon fluttered noisily over Bromley's head, saw he had no seed and flapped away.

"The bomb will go off anyway, whether or not you decide to help, Bromley. I don't know when, I don't know where, but there will be another bomb and people will probably die. There's nothing we can do to stop it, but maybe, just maybe, we'll be able to stop the one after that."

Bromley returned Morrison's gaze with steady, hard eyes. "Who else, Mr Morrison? Who else is involved?"

Morrison swallowed. He had hoped to persuade the policeman without bringing Hennessy's name into it, but he could see that it would not be possible. Bromley wouldn't believe this was a serious operation unless he knew who was running it. "Liam Hennessy," he said slowly. He was rewarded by the sight of Bromley's eyes widening with surprise.

Bromley turned away and Morrison walked with him. They passed a line of tourists queuing up to buy seed to feed the pigeons and neither of the men spoke. Two uniformed policewomen walked by, a blonde and a brunette, and Morrison wondered how they'd react if they knew that a member of the IRA and a Detective Chief Inspector from the Anti-Terrorist Branch were considering working together. Bromley waited until they were some distance from the policewomen before speaking again.

"When do you plan to change the codeword?" he asked.

"It's already done," replied Morrison. "Hennessy did it yesterday. Himself. Only he knows who was given which word. Even I don't know."

Bromley knew of Hennessy, and of his role as Sinn Fein adviser to the Belfast IRA council. He was one of the most powerful men in the organisation, just one step away from the seven-man Dublin-based army council. He was listened to by the council in Belfast but held equal sway over the headquarters staff in Ireland, the men who ran the active service units across Europe.

What Bromley really wanted was the list of men in the high command and the codewords they'd been given, but he knew Morrison would not hand out information like that. He would have to play by the rules Morrison was laying down or not play at all. Could he risk it? Could he afford not to? Morrison hadn't asked him how close the authorities were to catching the bombers. He hadn't needed to. They were no nearer identifying the active service unit behind the bombs now than they were when the campaign started. And it wasn't as if enough resources weren't being put into the investigation. Joining in the hunt for what was in all probability a small, self-contained unit, were the combined resources of Bromley's own Anti-Terrorist Branch, MI5, the Metropolitan Police, Special Branch, the Secret Intelligence Service, the SAS and the Defence Intelligence Service, not to mention the RUC in Northern Ireland. Actually, mused Bromley, combined resources wasn't the correct phrase because all the various anti-terrorist operations tended to work alone and to jealously guard whatever intelligence they collected.

"When I give you the codeword, what happens then?" asked Bromley.

Morrison noticed how the Detective Chief Inspector had said "when" and not "if". The decision had been made. "We'll track down the leak and interrogate him," he answered.

"Which will lead you to the bombers?"

"If Hennessy is right, yes."

"And then?"

"Then?" Morrison was confused.

"I don't think you've thought this through. How are you going to eliminate the unit that is setting these bombs? You can't send another IRA active service unit into London to knock out the first, can you? Or maybe you think you can." Bromley thought for a while. "How do I know that this is Hennessy's idea?" he said.

Morrison shrugged. "You're going to have to trust me on that," he said. "There's no way on God's earth that he can be seen with you. He'd never be trusted again. And that's assuming they didn't just kill him."

Bromley went quiet again and puffed on his pipe. "Very well. I agree. I'll tell you which codeword is given after the next explosion. But on two conditions. And they're not negotiable."

Morrison raised his eyebrows quizzically.

"When you find out where the bombers are, you tell me. You let the authorities handle it."

"The authorities?"

"Whoever it takes. Police. SAS. Whoever. It has to be that way. You can't handle it, not in London."

Morrison nodded. Hennessy had intended from the start that the Brits would clear up the mess, because if it was ever discovered that the IRA had betrayed its own, the organisation would be fragmented beyond belief. It had taken years of diplomacy and compromise to weld the various factions together and Hennessy did not want to undo it all because of a handful of lunatics. "And the second condition?" he asked.

"You give me a telephone number where I can call Hennessy. I'll only give the codeword to him. We'll share the risk."

They walked in silence again until Morrison reached his decision. "OK," he said. He gave him the number of Hennessy's farm and Bromley wrote it down in a small leather-bound notebook.

"I hope I never have to make the call," said Bromley.

"So do I," said Morrison. "But you will."

They parted without a handshake.

Woody didn't usually go into the office on Monday, most of the freelance shifts were towards the end of the week, the paper's busy period, but Quigley's phone call had intrigued him. The security guard on duty nodded good morning over the top of his copy of the *Sun*, he was used to journalists coming and going at all hours.

Woody helped himself to a plastic cup of machine coffee and then began rummaging through the drawer of the filing cabinet where he stored his old notebooks. He found the one he'd used the week The Chinaman had called and flicked through the pages. Among his spidery shorthand he saw "Chinaman" and a telephone number. He couldn't find an address, nor any note of the man's name. There was one name there among the hieroglyphics: S. J. Brown. Or Browning. Woody couldn't make it out.

He racked his memory while he dialled the telephone number. After ten or so rings a sleepy voice answered. "Double Happiness Take-Away," a man said. Woody scribbled down the name.

"My name is Ian Wood," he said. "Are you the gentleman who came to the *Sunday World* about the reward?"

"No," the voice said, and hung up.

"Terrific," said Woody to himself. He picked up a

telephone directory and went through it. There was only one Double Happiness Take-Away, it was in Clapham and the number matched. What he needed now was The Chinaman's name. He rang down to the cuttings library but there was no one there so he went himself and pulled the file on the Knightsbridge bombing. There were two foreign names among the dead: Nguyen Xuan Phoung and Nguyen Kieu Trinh. Woody wrote them down in his notebook and underlined Nguyen.

The knock on the door startled Morrison because he hadn't ordered anything from room service and he wasn't expecting any visitors. He was lying on his bed in a white towelling bathrobe, his hands clasped behind his neck. He sat up and looked at his watch. Ten o'clock. He'd been in no rush to get dressed because he was still waiting for instructions from Hennessy. Morrison had phoned him twice the previous day. The first time there had been no answer, and the second time he'd sounded strained and it was obvious that there were others in the room with him. Hennessy had told him to stay put and that he'd call on Monday. Something was wrong but Morrison realised he'd simply have to wait to find out what it was. The knock on the door was repeated, but harder and faster as if the caller was losing his patience. He felt a sudden rush of fear, thinking it might be the police or even a UDA hit-squad, but realised just as quickly that it was irrational, nobody knew where he was except for Liam Hennessy. Even so, he slid silently off the bed and padded to the door. He placed his hands flat against the wall either side of the door and eased his eye to the peep-hole. Even through the distorting lens he recognised her. She knocked again and he pulled the door open but kept his arm across the doorway as if blocking her way.

"Sean Morrison," she said, grinning.

"Mary Hennessy," he said. Morrison wasn't sure what emotions he felt as she stood in front of him. Pleased, for sure, but worried, too. Worried about what she was doing here. And guilt. Lots of guilt. And desire. Always desire. He'd never been able to look at Mary Hennessy without getting aroused, without wanting to possess her. There were other feelings too, regret, fear, sadness, all mixed up.

"Aren't you going to let me in?" she said.

He stepped to one side to let her pass and then closed the door behind her. She was carrying a white trench coat and she dropped it over the back of a chair before turning to look at him, hands on hips. She was wearing a white blouse with the collar turned up at the back and a soft skirt, patterned with large yellow flowers, and there was a small black bow in her brown hair. She was looking at him with a mischievous smile, her head on one side. Two years, he thought. They'd gone so quickly, so quickly that she hadn't changed one bit. He didn't know how old she was because he'd never cared enough to ask. He knew she was at least a decade older than he was but it hadn't shown two years ago and it didn't show now. Part of him had hoped that if he went away for a few years he wouldn't find her so attractive when he came back, that age would take away the desire, the lust. Her brown eyes sparkled as if she'd read his mind. She walked up to him, slowly, her hands still on her hips. Even with her high heels she had to tilt her head up to look in his eyes. She stood close to him, so close that he could smell her hair, clean and sweet.

"It's been a long time, Sean," she said softly. She reached up and rested her hands on his shoulders.

"I don't think you should be here," he said. The voice didn't sound like his own, it sounded thick and hesitant.

She raised her eyebrows. "Don't you?" she said. She stood up on her toes and put her lips up close to his. Their lips didn't touch but he could feel her warm breath. He swallowed. Even up close her skin was smooth and clear. The only signs of age were the laughter lines around her eyes and they just added to her attractiveness. "Don't you?" she repeated. She moved her head forward, just enough so that their lips touched. She opened hers slightly, but that was all. There was no pressure, no urging. She wanted him to prove how much he wanted her, to take the initiative. Part of him, the guilty voice in the back of his mind that had told him to go to New York, wanted to resist, but he already knew that he was lost. His lips parted too and his hands seemed to take on a will of their own, moving forward to link around her narrow waist. Still she stood on tip-toe waiting for him to make up his mind. He kissed her, once, a quick press of the lips, then he moved his head back and looked at her and then in a rush grabbed her and pulled her tightly to him, kissing her hard, forcing his tongue into her soft, moist mouth. For a few seconds she remained passive, allowing him to invade her, and then she began to kiss him back, returning his passion. He grunted as she kissed him and he closed his eyes as the urge to possess her washed over him again. She slowly put her heels on the ground so that he had to bend his neck to kiss her and she tried to pull away but he put his right hand behind her neck and pushed her head against his.

She used both her hands to push his shoulders away. A strand of hair had come loose, curling over her left eye, but she ignored it. She held him away, bending backwards slightly and pushing her groin against him. He felt as if he was on fire between his legs. Her eyes flashed. "Tell me you want me," she said.

"You know I do," he answered, and tried to kiss her, but she moved her head out of the way, pressing her thighs even harder against him.

"Tell me you want me," she said again. She moved her right hand slowly down from his shoulder and traced her fingernails across the hairs on his chest. He gasped as the sharp nails scratched against his flesh, parting his robe as they moved down between his ribs. She moved her hand lightly across his stomach and then down to his groin. "Tell me," she urged and at the same time took him in her hand. She squeezed him gently and he groaned and surrendered.

"I want you, Mary," he said. She pushed the robe off his shoulders so that he was standing naked in front of her and pulled his head down to hers, grabbing his hair so tightly that it hurt, forcing her body fully against his. He lifted her up and she raised her legs, gripping him around the waist and locking her ankles together. Now there was only one thought in his head. Her.

Nguyen lay motionless and listened to the birds singing in the treetops overhead. He'd made his way back to Tollymore Forest under cover of darkness and found the van exactly as he'd left it. There were a few things he wanted from the back of the van which he loaded into his rucksack, and he took a red can of petrol. He rejected the idea of sleeping by the van in case Hennessy should send a search party to the forest. It was an outside chance but not one worth taking because if they surprised him there would be no escape.

He found a safe place a hundred yards or so away and rested until mid-morning. He sat up and leant against a towering pine tree, the air thick with the smell of pine needles. He was surrounded by thousands of bluebells, shifting listlessly in the wind. He spent an hour or so cutting off the heads of three boxfuls of matches and crushing them into red powder which he carefully poured into one of the boxes. He cut a three-foot length of plastic-coated wire and then stripped off an inch of the plastic midway along it. With the point of his knife he made a hole at either end of the matchbox and threaded the wire through, knotting it so that the bared portion was in the middle, in contact with the powdered match heads. He stripped the ends of the wire clean of plastic and then coiled it up, wrapping it around the box. Nguyen removed the glass front from one of the plastic alarm clocks he'd brought with him and put it into the rucksack with the wired-up matchbox. Connecting the clock, the matchbox and a battery in a simple circuit would give him a basic timed fuse which would be more than sufficient to ignite the can of petrol.

The gun he'd taken from the man in the copse was a Browning HiPower automatic pistol which weighed about two pounds. Nguyen ejected the magazine and counted the bullets. Thirteen. An unlucky number for the Westerners, but not for a Vietnamese. He stripped the gun apart and cleaned it, checking that the mechanism worked. It was fine. The gun had two safeties, one worked by the thumb and one by the magazine, so that it couldn't be fired accidentally. It was a serious weapon. It was too heavy to carry around in his pocket for long so he put it in his rucksack. The smell of roast pork reminded him how long it had been since he had last eaten so he took out a carton of meat and one of rice and ate with his fingers. It had been a long time since he had eaten outside. What was it the Westerners called it? He'd seen the word in one of Kieu Trinh's English story books. Picnic, that was it.

As he ate he worked out what he was going to do next. One thing was for sure, he had to confront Hennessy one last time before he took things a stage further and that meant going back to the farm. Now that Hennessy had seen how much damage he could do, surely he would be more co-operative? Put anyone under enough pressure and they would bend. Not break, perhaps, but certainly bend.

Nguyen sighed and lay back in the pine needles. He took no pleasure in what he was doing. When he'd left Vietnam he'd thought that his days of fighting and killing were over, that he'd be allowed to raise his family in peace. When he saw the last helicopter leave the American embassy in Saigon he still had hopes of escaping from the North Vietnamese and eventually living in the United States. He'd fought alongside the Americans and had seen hundreds of American teenagers die in the fight for a free Vietnam so he didn't regard being left behind as an act of betrayal. He could see what a difficult logistical exercise it was for the Americans to pull out, and he knew that he wasn't the only one to have been left behind. It was only later, when Thi Manh and Mai Phoung died, that the resentment burst like a septic boil and he vowed never to seek sanctuary in the United States. They'd been surprised at the refugee camp in Hong Kong when he'd told them that he would go anywhere in the world but not to America. Officials from the United Nations High Commission for Refugees had interviewed him many times and had explained that because of his war record he would be welcomed with open arms in the United States but he had steadfastly refused and had been equally insistent that he would not explain his reasons. He had told them that two of his daughters had died on the voyage across the South China Sea but never detailed the circumstances. In Nguyen's mind, they had no right to know. They were so beautiful, Thi Manh and Mai Phoung, and even now, after more than ten years had passed, he could picture them clearly in his mind, jet-black hair, high cheek-bones, bright eyes and ready smiles, as pretty as their mother had been before the tough years had taken their toll. They had been such well-behaved children and it had been thoughts of them that had kept him going throughout his three years in the so-called "re-education" camps, working fifteen hours a day on a near-starvation diet, until the North Vietnamese were satisfied that he was a good Communist again.

There had been no doubt in his mind that he would be punished by the North Vietnamese but he had no idea of how severe that punishment would be. On the morning of April 30, 1975, he had slipped out of bed, leaving Xuan Phoung asleep clutching a pillow, and stood in the doorway leading to the alcove where his daughters slept together in a single bed, heads touching like Siamese twins. He stood there for more than an hour trying to imprint the scene on his mind, certain that it would be the last time he would see his daughters. The street noises had changed, there were no more helicopters whirring overhead, instead there was the far-off rumble of trucks carrying North Vietnamese troops and supplies into Saigon and the sound of cheering as the bo doi – the soldiers of the people – were welcomed by crowds of onlookers. In the early morning, while he was making love to his wife, Nguyen had heard tanks driving through the streets and the occasional rattle of machine-guns, but whether it was the North Vietnamese mopping up pockets of resistance or simply high spirits on the part of the victorious forces, he had no way of telling.

He dressed casually in washed-out cotton trousers, a faded checked shirt and an old pair of sandals. He'd dropped his army uniform in the street and he'd cleared all evidence of involvement with the US forces from their flat. They had made their plans long before the Americans pulled out, when it had first become obvious that there was no way the South could win the war. They had closed their bank account and transferred all their money into gold, knowing that when Saigon fell paper money would be virtually worthless. They had kept the gold in a safety-deposit box, along with several gold Rolex watches and pieces of jewellery that they had been able to buy on the black market with Nguyen's wages, and two weeks before the NVA arrived at the outskirts of Saigon they had taken everything out of the bank vault. They had already decided that Nguyen should go. It was the only chance the family had of surviving.

Xuan Phoung had friends who would help her to get a job as a kitchen worker and she would hide their savings under the floorboards until Nguyen was allowed to return, or until she got the opportunity to escape with the children. Before he left, Nguyen took a photograph from his wallet, a picture of Xuan Phoung and the two girls, and put it on the bed. He had carried it with him throughout the war but it would be dangerous for them to be caught with it now. He took all identification from the wallet, leaving only a small amount of paper money. It would not be long before a thirty-one-year-old man walking alone would be picked up for interrogation and anything in his pockets would be taken from him, so he left his wedding ring and his watch and his Special Forces cigarette lighter on the bed next to the photograph before kissing his wife once, on the cheek, and then dashing downstairs before he could have a change of heart.

The streets of Saigon were every bit as packed as they had been the previous night, but whereas the rush then had been to escape with the Americans, now the crowds were there to welcome the NVA. Children were waving NVA flags – red and blue with a gold star – and it seemed as if every shop in the city had managed to get a photograph of an unsmiling Ho Chi Minh in its window. Battered lorries covered with thick red mud rattled along loaded with troops, young men with baggy olive-green uniforms and rubber sandals, cheering and lapping up the attention.

He was picked up around lunchtime by a group of five teenage soldiers who prodded him with their guns and demanded his papers. He told them he'd been robbed two days earlier and they slapped him around the face and accused him of lying. They made him kneel on the ground, blindfolded him, handcuffed his hands behind his back and then dragged him roughly and threw him into the back of a truck. Throughout the day more men were thrown into the vehicle. All were blindfolded and manacled and told that if they spoke to each other they would be killed. When the truck was full they were driven for three days with just a handful of foul-smelling rice which they were forced to eat like animals, pushing their faces on to the floor to lick the grains up because their captors refused to unlock the handcuffs. Nguyen assumed they were being taken North and wondered why they bothered because the Communists now controlled the whole country. For a wild moment he thought that perhaps the NVA feared that the Americans would be back but in his heart he knew that could not be true. The evacuation of the embassy was not the action of an army planning to return.

He never discovered the name of the place he was taken to but there was no doubt that it was a prison, and had been for many years. He was thrown into a small cell, two paces by four paces, containing only a wooden bench and a bucket. They took off his blindfold and he saw that the bench was rubbed smooth from the bodies that had slept there over the years. It looked ages old and had obviously been used by the French to hold Vietnamese captives. The bench sloped so that any liquids would run off and there was a small drain hole at the bottom of one of the walls. There was no window in the cell, the only light came from the corridor through the open door and whenever it opened cockroaches ran for the dark corners. Nguyen was forced to lie on the bench and his feet were locked into a set of leg-irons which were fixed to the wall. They put the bucket within reach and took off his handcuffs and left without a word, locking the door behind them. They left him there for two weeks, opening the door only once a day to put down a handful of rice on a banana leaf along with a piece of stale bread. It was stifling hot in the cell and he was always thirsty but he was only given one earthenware jug of water to drink with his food. The cell stank of urine and sweat and decay. The cockroaches did not worry him, even when they ran over his body, but there were mosquitoes and he was covered in itching bites that made him want to scream. His legs were in pain too, rubbed raw by the metal leg-irons.

After two weeks of solitary confinement they dragged him out of his cell and into a room where he saw his first glimpse of the sun through a murky skylight. To the left of the skylight, set into the ceiling, was a large, rusty meat hook. Two NVA officers questioned him for an hour and then he was returned to the leg-irons and the darkness. A week later he was taken out and interrogated again. There was no violence, no threats, just a series of questions, almost identical to the ones he'd been asked on the first occasion, and he was sure that he gave the same answers. The same lies. He was a mechanic, he had never been in the army. He had no family. He had lost his papers. It was impossible to tell from the blank faces of his interrogators whether or not they believed him, and most of the time he could only look through squinting eyes because after the enforced darkness he found even the weak sunlight which managed to get through the dirt-encrusted glass blindingly bright.

They took him back to his cell and left him there for just three days before hauling him back to the interrogation room. By that stage he could barely walk and his gums were bleeding from malnutrition. He had diarrhoea and the backs of his legs and backside were a mass of sores. The older of his two interrogators, a kindly looking major with white hair, told him that they did not believe his story and that they would be grateful if he would tell them the truth this time. He insisted that he was not lying and they nodded, almost sadly. Four NVA soldiers came into the room, holding bamboo canes, and they beat him senseless. Then they threw a bucket of water over him to bring him round before beating him unconscious again and dragging him back to his cell.

For six days the process was repeated. They would ask him for the truth, he would stick to his story, the soldiers would beat him up.

On the seventh day, by which time he'd lost three of his

teeth and they had broken four of his ribs, they changed their tactics. They took a long piece of rope and bound his wrists behind him and then wound it excruciatingly tightly around his arms before hauling him up on the meat hook. It was strange, but he could not remember much about the days they tortured him. He could remember that he had never in his life felt so much pain and he knew that at one point it had been so bad that he'd pleaded with them to kill him, but now, as he lay on the pine needles and looked up through the branches to the clear blue sky above, it seemed as if it had all happened to someone else and that they were borrowed memories. Only one thing had got him through – the images of his wife as he left and his two daughters, asleep with their heads touching. Of all the images that stuck in his mind, they were the strongest, because throughout the torture he'd concentrated on them. They were the reason they could not break him.

He never knew whether or not they believed him, or whether they simply gave up trying to break him, but eventually the torture stopped and he was transferred to a re-education camp where he worked in the fields for fifteen hours a day but where at least there was food. He was forced to write endless self-criticisms which were duly filed away and he spent two hours each day sitting cross-legged on the floor with other prisoners being lectured to on the merits and ideals of Communism and being beaten with sticks if they nodded off. There were other punishments, meted out for the most trivial of offences. Men were shackled upside down and left hanging for days until their legs were weeping with gangrene, locked into cramped steel boxes in the sun or buried up to their necks in the ground. Nguyen was there for three years. Three years of living a lie. Three wasted years.

When he was finally judged to be a good Communist he was released on probation and was assigned to work on an irrigation project to the west of Hanoi. He had to report to a political officer three times a week for further indoctrination. He was lucky, he knew that, because tens of thousands of South Vietnamese were kept in the camps for much longer.

He fled one night and managed to get to Hanoi where he stole identification papers and money and journeyed south to Saigon. He lived rough in the city for several weeks before he dared approach Xuan Phoung and when he did it was at night. He knocked timidly on her door and when she opened it it was clear from her bewildered face that she did not recognise him. It was hardly surprising because he had lost so much weight and appeared to have aged ten years, but she took him in her arms and cried softly. She ushered him into the room and sat him down, knelt in front of him and held him around his waist, crying all the time and whispering his name. He realised then that however badly he had suffered it could have been nothing compared with what his wife had been through. At least he had been able to look forward to returning to her and the children. She had had no way of knowing if he was even alive.

She made him green tea and while he was drinking it she went into the bedroom and brought out a tiny child. A girl. The daughter he had never seen, conceived on the night that the Americans abandoned Saigon and now almost three years old.

"Kieu Trinh is her name," said Xuan Phoung. "But we can change it if you don't like it."

"It's perfect," said Nguyen. He held her in his arms and then his wife woke Thi Manh and Mai Phoung and brought them in to meet the father they barely remembered. He had been away for almost a quarter of their lives. Nguyen was so filled with happiness that he could barely speak, he just held all four of them. His family.

Before he could ask, Xuan Phoung said, "The gold is still here, and I know someone who can get us out."

"We must go soon," he said, his voice thick with emotion.

"I know," she said. "We were only waiting for you."

Nguyen and his wife and children travelled by night to a fishing port in Kien Giang province, all their valuables and papers in two canvas bags. They'd paid a deposit in gold to a middleman in Saigon and were told when and where they were to pay the rest.

They had to spend the night in a dirty hut that stank of

fish, sleeping on small cots with another two families who were also waiting for the boat. During the night little Kieu Trinh developed a hacking cough and when Xuan Phoung put her hand on the child's forehead it was hot and wet. She got worse through the night and kept them all awake. Nguyen stayed by her side, wiping her forehead with a cloth dipped in water and wafting her with a piece of cardboard. She got worse during the day. It was Xuan Phoung who said it first, even though Nguyen had already reached the same conclusion: the child was in no condition for a sea voyage, especially in an unhygienic boat crammed to the gills with refugees. Xuan Phoung suggested they wait in the village until the child was well enough to travel, but Nguyen pointed out that if they did they'd lose their deposit. And it represented a big chunk of their hard-earned savings.

"You must go ahead, with Thi Manh and Mai Phoung," she said. "We will join you in Hong Kong."

He'd refused at first, but eventually realised that what she said made sense. If he went with the two teenage girls, he was sure the captain could be persuaded to accept the deposits of all five of them towards the cost of the trip, leaving more than enough money for Xuan Phoung and Kieu Trinh to buy their passage when the child was well again. When the captain came for them later that evening, Nguyen explained what had happened and eventually he agreed that the five deposits could go towards the three fares, albeit with an extra ounce of gold thrown in. For another ounce he agreed to bring in a doctor to tend to the child.

When Nguyen saw the vessel that was supposed to take them across the South China Sea to Hong Kong, he almost had second thoughts. The boat was about fifteen metres long, its hull rotting and repaired in many places. There were already thirty or so refugees sitting or squatting on its deck and Nguyen and his two children and the two families that had shared the hut had to squeeze between them to find space. The boat was worryingly low in the water.

The captain was joined by a crew of three, men barely out of their teens in ragged T-shirts and cut-off trousers. It took half an hour of patient coaxing to get the engine started and it chugged uneasily out to sea as the huge orange sun sat low in the sky.

There was a hatchway in the deck leading to a hold containing a dozen camp beds where the refugees took it in turns to sleep. There was a small stove there and the women cooked what little food the crew had brought with them: some rice, strips of dried fish and a sack of green vegetables. Some of the men rigged up fishing lines and from time to time pulled in fresh fish to supplement the meagre rations, but mainly they fished to fight the boredom. Most of the days were spent cross-legged on the deck, watching the horizon and hoping that the boat would stay afloat.

Water was rationed and they were each given just a cupful every four hours, carefully meted out by a crewman using stained tin mugs. A blanket had been stretched out from a mast and tied down with ropes to provide some shade during the day and shelter from the occasional rain storm. Conditions were so grim that Nguyen was glad that Kieu Trinh had stayed behind.

They were three days out from Vietnam when they met the fishing boats. There were three of them painted in identical colours as if part of the same fleet. The decks were painted red and piled high with plastic barrels and coils of rope, and the wheel-houses were white. The hulls were pale green and there were lines of white Thai writing on the bows. The crews seemed friendly enough, smiling and waving as they drew close, and they shouted to the captain that they had water and ice to sell. The captain waved them away but a few of the refugees shouted to him that they would pay for it. Nguyen could see that the captain was uneasy and he whispered to the refugees to keep quiet, that the Thais could be trouble, but they ignored him and began calling over to the fishermen. The captain shouted at the man who was on the wheel and the old boat started to turn away but even Nguyen who had little sailing experience knew that there was no way they could outrun the fishing boats if they gave chase. He stood up and as he did he saw one of the Thais produce a rifle and put it to his shoulder. Nguyen yelled a warning but he was too late, there was a loud bang and the captain took the bullet in his chest. More rifles were produced and the wheel-house was riddled with bullets, killing the two crewmen inside. The refugees began to scream as the boat drifted aimlessly. Nguyen frantically looked around for a weapon, but there was nothing at hand. One of the Thai boats drew up alongside and the fishermen used poles with hooks on the end to secure the boats together.

The refugees moved away to the opposite side like cattle shying away from a snake and the boat tilted alarmingly. Women and children were crying, the men shouting, wanting to put up a fight but not knowing how to, not when all they had were their fists and the Thais had guns and hatchets and hammers. Nguyen found himself separated from his daughters, unable to move closer to them because of the crush.

A second boat cut across their bow and half a dozen menacing Thais jumped across, stocky men toughened by years at sea, their faces and bodies darkened by the sun and scarred from fights and accidents with the nets and ropes.

They moved through the refugees, separating the men from the women and the children, killing anyone who protested or tried to stop them. One of the Thais, a swarthy, thickset man with a huge tiger tattoo across his chest, looked down into the hatch. He shouted down in bad Vietnamese that all the women and children were to come up. There were screams and sobs from down below but no one appeared so a fisherman with a rifle jumped over from the boat alongside and fired twice into the hold. There were more screams and shouting and then three women and a young girl came up. One of the women was in her sixties and the fisherman cursed her in Vietnamese and stabbed her in the stomach, twisting the knife right and left before kicking her back down into the hold.

There was an uproar among the refugees and they began to surge forward but a volley of shots rang out and four of the men fell to the deck, screaming in pain. The Thais began searching the men, taking from them their watches, jewellery and any other valuables they had before throwing them down into the hold. Those that put up a fight were killed and thrown over the side. Some of the younger women were grabbed and carried screaming on to the Thai boats where more fishermen were waiting with their arms outstretched to take them. Nguyen watched in horror as the men began tearing the clothes off the women, slapping and hitting them if they struggled too much, before throwing them down on to the deck and raping them. He saw one girl who couldn't have been more than fifteen years old held down by two men while a third climbed on top of her. Her screams chilled him, and then he heard his own daughter, Mai Phoung, screaming for him. Two Thais had her and were taking her to the bow of the boat where more fishermen waited, lust in their eyes.

"She's only thirteen!" Nguyen cried.

"The youngest fruit is the sweetest," said one of the Thais in rough Vietnamese and slammed the butt of his rifle into Nguyen's sternum so that he collapsed to the deck, gasping for breath. Through a red haze he saw Thi Manh dash over to claw at the men in an attempt to save her sister. The men laughed and one of them grabbed her. He seized her shirt and pulled it savagely, the buttons popping off like small gunshots, revealing her small breasts and smooth skin. He was joined by two other men who used large fishing knives to cut away the rest of her clothes. She was screaming hysterically, begging Nguyen to rescue her. He staggered to his feet and pushed his way through the refugees who were still on the deck. Mai Phoung had been thrown across to the Thai boat and was being stripped and beaten by a group of three Thais who were snarling and growling like wild dogs. She too was calling for her father. Nguyen stepped forward towards the men holding Thi Manh but as he moved one of the Thai fishermen appeared in front of him holding a rifle. It was pointed at Nguyen's chest and the man was laughing, his finger tightening on the trigger. Nguyen leapt as the man fired, he felt the blast and a searing stripe of pain across the side of his head and then he was under water, choking and coughing, his head a mass of pain and the taste of blood in his mouth. He surfaced, spitting out salt water and when his eyes cleared he saw the Thais setting fire to the boat and rushing back to their own vessels.

Nguyen trod water, fighting to stay conscious. He would

never forget the horrified screams from the hold, and the howls from the women on the Thai boats. He never saw his daughters again. Part of him wished that he could die too, but his survival instincts took over. There were many bodies floating in the waves and Nguyen used his belt to tie two of them together. He clung to the macabre raft for more than fifteen hours before he was picked up by a British freighter on its way to Hong Kong.

He was told that he was lucky to have been spotted, but Nguyen didn't feel lucky. He felt ashamed, he felt that he'd betrayed his daughters, that he should have saved them or died trying. The guilt of that day had lived with him for-evermore. He'd reacted instinctively, without thinking, and not a day went by, not an hour, when the events of the last few minutes on board the refugee boat didn't flash through his mind.

He opened his eyes and looked up through the branches above his head. His arms were shaking and his breath was coming in ragged gasps. He wanted his time over again, he wanted to be back on the boat, because he knew this time he would make the right choice, that he would die trying to save his daughters rather than leaping over the side to save his own life.

He would not fail this time.

Mary Hennessy lay with her head on Morrison's shoulder and made small circles on his chest with her index finger. He kissed her on the top of her head and she smiled up at him.

"It's been a long time, Sean Morrison," she said.

"It has that, Mary Hennessy," he said lazily. He looked at his watch. Eleven o'clock.

"My time's not up, is it?" she said. She ran her hand slowly down through the hairs on his chest. "I bet I could change your mind . . ."

Morrison laughed and reached down and intercepted her wandering hand. "Mary, even you can't raise the dead."

She giggled. "Not dead, just resting," she said, but she put her hand back on his chest. "You're not going to throw me out, are you?"

"I'm waiting for somebody to call me," he said.

"A girl?"

"There's no girl, Mary Hennessy."

They lay together in silence for a while, enjoying each other's warmth.

"You shouldn't have left me, Sean," Mary said eventually, so quietly that at first Morrison thought that she was talking in her sleep. "There was no need for you to have gone."

He sighed. "There was every need."

"Because of Liam?"

"Because of us. Because it was wrong."

She laughed harshly. "The way the world is and you worry about the right and wrong of what goes on between a man and a woman. You amaze me sometimes."

"And you, Mary Hennessy, are a constant source of wonder to me."

"I didn't even know how to get hold of you in New York."

"That was the idea," he said. "Out of sight, out of mind."

She shook her head. "Absence makes the heart grow fonder."

"You were the one who wouldn't leave her husband," said Morrison "You were the one who said that an affair was fine but that it couldn't go any further."

"I've been married for a long time, Sean. A long time."

"I know. I know that."

She sighed and he felt her warm breath on his chest. "If I was free, you know that I'd be with you like a shot. If you wanted me."

"If!" he exclaimed.

"I'm so much older than you, Sean."

He squeezed her and stroked her hair. "It never mattered in the past, and it doesn't matter now."

"But it might in the future. It might."

Morrison closed his eyes. This discussion was a repeat of thousands they'd had before. Sometimes, before he'd left

New York, it seemed to him that they'd spent more time discussing the relationship than living it.

"I wish Liam was more like you," whispered Mary.

"What do you mean?"

"Stronger. Harder."

He laughed and she slapped his chest. "That's not what I meant, idiot. He's changed, he's gone soft. Soft on the Cause. I used to be so proud of him, he had power and he wasn't afraid to use it. Now he'd rather talk, negotiate. He acts like an old man, trying to make his peace with the world." Her voice was becoming increasingly bitter and she spat out the last few words like an angry cat. Morrison didn't know what to say so he lay in silence and concentrated on smoothing her hair, trying to calm her down physically rather than by talking to her.

"I've never forgiven him for Gerry, you know," she said. Her brother had been shot and killed by a Protestant death squad three years earlier. Four men in balaclava masks had forced their way into his house and shot him in front of his wife and three children on Christmas Eve. Mary had been there delivering Christmas presents and she'd been splattered with his blood. Morrison had seen her in the City Hospital several hours later, standing with Liam in the white-tiled corridor with flecks of blood over her dress, a red smear across one cheek, her eyes puffy from crying. That's when he'd fallen in love with her, he realised now.

"He found out who did it, you know?" she said.

"Yes. I know."

"They killed a farmer on the border a month later and got caught, stupid bastards. I begged Liam to have them killed before they got to court. He said no. They're in Long Kesh now, all four of them, and still he won't do anything. One of them is studying sociology with the Open University, Sean, can you believe that? Gerry's dead and buried and he's getting a fucking degree. And Liam says that justice has been done and that the time for revenge is past, or some such philosophical crap. He's lost his fire, and he lost it when I needed it most."

Morrison could feel her heart pounding against his chest and he kissed her softly on the top of her head.

"That's why I'm here, you know. In London. Because he's running away from a bloody Chinaman. One man and he's hiding like a frightened child. And he wants me to hide, too."

"What do you mean?" Morrison asked.

Mary sat up. "Of course, you don't know. He followed us to the farm. He blew up one of the outbuildings and the car. Jimmy's in hospital."

"Is he OK?"

"I don't know, I left right after he blew up the car. Liam thought it would be safer if I came to London. I didn't argue because I knew it would give me the chance to see you." She straddled him and kissed him and then rolled off the bed and skipped into the bathroom. He heard the shower kick into life.

The phone rang and Morrison jumped involuntarily. Guilt? Probably. He reached for the receiver. It was Hennessy.

He told him about the car bombing and the attempt to flush The Chinaman out of the woods and how it had ended in disaster. Morrison expressed surprise and asked who had been hurt even though he'd already been told by Mary.

As he talked, Mary came out of the bathroom wearing a towelling robe that was far too big for her. She was rubbing a towel through her hair. Morrison felt a sudden rush of guilt and he turned to one side so that he didn't have to look at her.

"We're obviously after a man who is used to fighting, some sort of terrorist maybe. Maybe he has jungle warfare experience, you know. Malaysia maybe," said Morrison. Mary had finished drying her hair and she began to brush it slowly, watching Morrison in the dressing-table mirror.

"The area around the farm is hardly a jungle," said Hennessy.

"It's not a jungle, I agree, but there's acres of woodland and a million and one places to hide. A man who knew what he was doing could stay put for weeks, living off the land, hiding during the day and making a nuisance of himself at night. And the more men you send in looking for him, the more damage he'll do."

"That's pretty much what Jim Kavanagh's been telling me. He says we should go back to Belfast. He says it'll be easier to protect me there."

"That's true, but at least you know where he is now. If you can deal with him in the countryside you should be able to keep a lid on it. In Belfast it could turn into a blood-bath." Mary stopped brushing her hair and sat looking at Morrison.

"You have a suggestion?"

"Set a thief to catch a thief. We send in one man, a man who's an expert at tracking, and we let him get on with it. No manhunt, just sit tight and let our man winkle him out."

"Come on, Sean. Where are we going to find such a man?"

"What about Micky Geraghty?"

"Retired," said Hennessy.

"Well un-retire him, Liam," said Morrison, exasperated. "He's the perfect choice. He was a gamekeeper as a kid, his father was one of the best in Ireland." Gamekeeping wasn't the only talent Geraghty had, but his skill as an IRA assassin wasn't the sort of thing to be discussed on an open telephone line. Morrison knew of at least three kills he'd been responsible for, two long distance with a rifle and one close up, a senior RUC officer who'd blinded a young Catholic during a particularly nasty interrogation. The boy had been a second cousin to Geraghty and he'd asked for the assignment. It had been personal, but professional. If he had truly retired, it was one hell of a loss to the Cause. "Doesn't he work as a deer tracker or something in Scotland now?"

"He's retired," Hennessy repeated. Mary stood up and walked over to where Morrison was sitting on the bed. He looked up at her and smiled and she shrugged off the robe so that she was standing naked in front of him. His mind whirled and he fought to keep his voice steady, certain that Hennessy would be able to sense that something was wrong.

"The sort of skills he's got you don't forget." Morrison wasn't just referring to gamekeeping, and Hennessy knew it.

"I don't mean retired from work, Sean, I mean he retired from the Cause."

"Nobody retires from the Cause," said Morrison. Mary pushed Morrison back on to the bed and pulled his robe apart. He closed his eyes and almost gasped when he felt her take him in her mouth. Her soft hair brushed his groin and as she caressed him with her mouth she ran her hands up and down his chest, gently scratching him. She was making small groaning noises and he was sure Hennessy would be able to hear her.

"He was a special case," said Hennessy. "His wife died five years ago. Cancer. It was very, very bad. He lost heart after that. He was no more use to us."

"So who decided he could retire?"

Hennessy didn't reply, which gave Morrison the answer. "It was you, wasn't it, Liam?" Still Hennessy said nothing. "If it was you, he owes you a favour. All you have to do is to make it personal. And let's face it, this is as personal as you can get." Mary began moving her head up and down, running her tongue along the whole length of him. He wanted her to stop but at the same time he didn't, and his confusion was compounded by the overwhelming guilt of it all, talking to Hennessy while his wife knelt naked in front of him.

"He might agree to help track this man down, but that's all. He wouldn't take it any further."

"OK, but that's a start. At least let me talk to him. He might jump at the chance of helping his old friend." A thought suddenly occurred to Morrison. A solution. "In fact, I'll ask him to take me with him. He can find him, I'll do the rest."

Hennessy thought about it for just a few seconds and then agreed. He told Morrison to wait while he rummaged through his desk and dug out an old address book. Morrison could feel himself about to come and reached down with his free hand to stroke Mary's hair and to gently push her away. She slid him out of her mouth and moved over him, licking her lips like a satisfied cat, her eyes flashing. He knew what she was going to do and he shook his head and tried to roll away but she pushed him down and continued to move over his body until her thighs were either side of his hips. She seemed to be revelling in his discomfort, knowing that he couldn't resist too much while he was on the phone, and knowing too that deep down he didn't want to resist, that he wanted her as much as she wanted him. She held him with one hand and positioned herself above him, rubbing him against herself, allowing him inside but only an inch or so and then easing herself away, teasing him and watching his face all the while. Hennessy came back on the line.

"He still does some deer tracking, mainly for Japanese tourists, but he also runs a survival school for executives, based near Thurso," he said.

"Thurso?" replied Morrison and as he spoke Mary pushed herself down so that he was completely inside her. He gasped involuntarily. She moved slowly up and down, grinding her pelvis against him, her eyes half closed, her mouth open and panting.

"It's in the far north of Scotland, about as far north as you can go before you hit the sea." He gave Morrison the address and a telephone number. Morrison told him he had to get a pen and paper. Mary stopped moving and, with him still inside her, leant over to the bedside table and gave him a black ballpoint pen and a sheet of hotel notepaper. He asked Hennessy to repeat the details and he wrote them down, thankful that Mary had at last stopped moving. He felt as if his groin was about to explode.

"And Sean, don't push him, OK? If he doesn't want to do it, forget it."

"OK, Liam," said Morrison. Mary squeezed him with her internal muscles and began to ride him again, throwing her head back and gripping him tightly with her thighs.

"How did the meeting with Bromley go?" asked Hennessy.

"Fine," answered Morrison, closing his eyes and concentrating on his breathing and trying with all his might not to come. "But when he gets the codeword he'll call you direct. He insisted."

"That's OK."

"Everything ready at your end?"

"Yes. I've given out the words. All we can do now is to wait for the next bomb. See you soon, Sean."

"Will do, Liam. Take care." He threw the phone to one side and reached up to caress Mary's breasts. She took one of his hands and placed two of his fingers in her mouth, sucking and licking them as she rode him.

"You, Mary Hennessy, are a bitch. A teasing, dangerous, gorgeous bitch." She laughed throatily and rode him all the harder.

Afterwards, she lay curled up with her back against him, her skin moist with a thin film of sweat. Morrison licked her back, enjoying the salty taste of her.

"That's nice," she whispered.

"I wish you'd come to New York with me," he said.

She sighed, and pushed herself back against him. "Don't start, Sean," she chided. "Just enjoy the time we have together. You already have more of me than anyone else in the world."

"Except your husband."

"You wouldn't want to swap places with him, believe me."

Morrison knew that they were going over old ground, replaying the same arguments they'd had before he left for the United States, but he couldn't help himself. It was like picking the scab of an old wound.

"How did Liam sound?" she asked, changing the subject.

"Worried. Very worried."

"About The Chinaman?"

"Yeah, and the London bombings. I'm not sure which worries him the most."

"Do you think he'll be able to find out who has been setting off the bombs?" She reached behind herself and began stroking his thighs with the back of her hand.

"It's the only chance we've got," he said.

"That's what Liam says, too. But do you really think his plan will work?"

"If there is another bomb, and if the bombers give the codeword when they claim responsibility, it'll lead us straight to whoever's behind it. With a bit of luck, it'll work."

"I hope so," she sighed.

Her hand became more insistent but he pulled himself away from her. "I'm going to have to go," he said.

"Where?"

"Scotland. To talk to a man who might be able to track down The Chinaman for us. What will you do?"

"I'm to stay in London until Liam says it's safe to go back. So if you're not here I'll just have to amuse myself."

Morrison went to the bathroom where he shaved and showered and when he came out Mary had dressed and was brushing her hair. She stood up on tiptoe and kissed him full on the mouth. "It's good to have you back," she said. "Don't stay away so long next time." She turned and picked up her trench coat and blew him a kiss before closing the door behind her.

Morrison shook his head, trying to clear her from his mind. Two years, and it seemed as if he had never been away. If anything he wanted her more now than before. He forced himself to concentrate on the job at hand. He wondered why the normally confident Hennessy was so touchy on the subject of Geraghty and if it really had been the painful death of his wife that had led to his exile in Scotland. He looked at his watch. Two o'clock. He hadn't a clue how to get to Thurso, or how long it would take, but he knew he had to speak to Geraghty in person, it would be too easy for him to decline on the phone. He rang down to reception and told them he'd be checking out and also asked if they'd find out the quickest way to get to Thurso.

"Is that in Cornwall?" the girl had asked. She said she'd phone back once she'd checked with a travel agent and Morrison began to pack his suitcase. He'd just about finished when the girl rang to say that he could go by train but that he wouldn't get there until the following day. The best way would be to fly up to Inverness and go the rest of the way by train or hire a car and drive. Morrison said he'd fly and asked her to arrange for a car to take him to the airport and have it put on the bill.

* * *

Woody was, as usual, short of cash, so he took the Tube to Clapham.

An unsmiling middle-aged Oriental woman was serving behind the counter of the Double Happiness Take-Away, and when it was Woody's turn he asked her for sweet and sour pork and chips. "Is the owner here?" asked Woody.

"Huh?" she said, her mouth dropping open.

"The owner. Can I see the owner?"

"In kitchen," she said.

"Yes . . . right . . . OK . . . could you ask him to come out? Tell him it's Ian Wood, from the newspaper."

"Ian Wood. Newspaper," she repeated. She stuck her head through the serving hatch and shouted. There was an equally raucous reply and she turned to Woody again.

"He busy," she said.

"I know, he's cooking my food," said Woody. "Look, he knows me."

"He say he not know you," she said emphatically and folded her arms across her chest.

Woody waited until his order arrived and she plonked the carrier bag on the counter in front of him. He paid for it and then asked to see the owner again. She glared at him before yelling through the hatch once more. This time a bald, Oriental giant came out carrying a huge carving knife. He stood next to the woman and barked: "I here. What you want?"

Woody looked at the couple, confused. "I'm sorry, you're not the man I wanted to see. I wanted Mr Nguyen." He had assumed that The Chinaman owned the restaurant because of all the cash he had, but perhaps he was an employee. "Does Mr Nguyen work here?" Woody asked.

"No," said the man.

"Do you know where he is?"

"No."

Woody was taken aback. He took his notebook from his pocket and looked at the telephone number that Nguyen had given him. He picked up one of the printed menus off the counter and compared the telephone number there. They were the same. He held the notebook out to the man. "Look, I spoke to Mr Nguyen at this number. Here."

The man didn't look at the notebook. "I own Double Happiness now," he said.

"So Mr Nguyen was the previous owner?"

"He own Double Happiness before. He sell to me."

At last Woody understood. "But you don't know where he went?"

The man shook his head.

"He was very upset about what happened to his family," said Woody. "Do you know if that was why he left?"

"No."

"No you don't know why, or no that's not why he left?"

"No," the man repeated. "I busy, you go now." He made to go back to the kitchen.

"Do you have a photograph of him?" Woody asked.

The man's eyes screwed up. "What do you mean?"

Woody drew a square in the air with his hands. "Photograph. A picture. Click, click!" He mimed using a camera.

The man nodded enthusiastically. "Ah! Picture!" he said.

"You have?" Woody asked eagerly.

"No," he answered, shaking his head.

Woody saw the doorway that led off from behind the counter. "He lived upstairs?" he asked, and pointed.

"My house now," said the man emphatically.

"Can I look?" Woody asked.

"No."

"I'll pay," said Woody, reaching across to lift up the counter.

The man raised the knife and it glinted under the shop's fluorescent lighting. "This my house now. My restaurant. My house. You go now."

Woody held up his hands, admitting defeat. He left the shop, thought about eating the sweet and sour pork but decided against it and dropped it into a rubbish bin before walking back to the Tube.

* * *

Hennessy sat at the kitchen table with Jackie sprawled at his feet and a pile of typewritten sheets in front of him. Except for the dog he was alone. Jim Kavanagh was in the next room, while Willie O'Hara had gone upstairs for a few hours' sleep after volunteering to be on guard duty overnight.

The papers Hennessy was studying were the lists of the munitions supplies that had been secreted in mainland Britain. There were sixteen lists in all. Most had arrived at his office before they'd left Belfast and he'd requested that the few remaining lists be delivered to the farm. Of the sixteen, five had been raided with about thirty-five pounds of Semtex in all unaccounted for. Detonators had been taken, and some ammunition, but no guns or rifles were missing. What worried Hennessy was that there appeared to be no common thread linking the arms dumps that had been tampered with, either geographically or in terms of people who knew about them. Hennessy was starting to think that perhaps more than one person was involved, or that security among the high-ranking IRA officials wasn't as secure as it should have been. And there was the added complication that whoever was behind the bombings could have lied when compiling the list of the contents of his own caches. He slammed the table in frustration and Jackie jerked awake, ears back. To have gone to all that trouble for nothing, cursed Hennessy. Jackie got to her feet and put her head in his lap, whining for attention, and he stroked her flanks.

Kavanagh popped his head around the door. "There's somebody coming," he said.

Hennessy gathered the papers together and put them into one of the drawers of the Welsh dresser. "It looks like Hugh McGrath. It's his car, anyway."

Hennessy went with Kavanagh through the hall to the front door. Two of the guards had already stopped the blue Volvo some fifty yards or so from the house. There were four men in it, including the driver. Hennessy used his hand to shield his eyes from the afternoon sun and recognised the grey, slicked-back hair and angular features of Hugh McGrath, wearing the tinted glasses that gave him what Mary always mockingly referred to as his Clint Eastwood look. McGrath .

owned a farm to the south-west, several hundred acres but little in the way of crops or livestock. Instead he earned a small fortune taking advantage of the price differentials between the North and South. That's how McGrath would have explained it. Hennessy called it by its true name – smuggling.

Price anomalies between the two parts of the divided Ireland meant that McGrath could always make a turn somewhere, be it on wheat, pigs, milk or petrol, or by smuggling things like contraceptives to the south or antibiotics to the north.

Hennessy had always been unhappy at McGrath's smuggling operations but he was a powerful man within the organisation and had many supporters. His role as liaison officer with the Libyans was also vital to the IRA, and he was one of the few men from the organisation who had actually met with Gaddafi. McGrath knew his value and capitalised on it.

The Volvo pulled up in front of the farmhouse and McGrath unwound his angular frame from the back seat. He was a good head taller than Hennessy, even with his slight stoop. He held out his hand and his grip was strong and confident.

"Liam," he said. "How are you this fine afternoon?"

"Fine," said Hennessy. "Come on in." McGrath's driver and his two bodyguards stayed in the car as Hennessy led him into the lounge. Hennessy waved him towards the floral-patterned sofa in front of the unlit fireplace.

"Drink?" he asked, and McGrath asked for a whiskey. Hennessy half filled two crystal tumblers before settling down into a leather wing-tipped chair opposite the sofa. Jackie butted the door open with her head and lay down at Hennessy's feet after first sniffing at McGrath's legs and accepting a pat on the back.

"How goes it?" asked McGrath.

"It's going OK."

"You checked out my arms dumps?" McGrath had been responsible for three arms caches, all close to London, and according to the reports Hennessy had received one of them was missing two packages of Semtex.

Hennessy nodded and told McGrath what his searchers had found. Or rather, what they hadn't found.

"I can't believe that one of mine has been touched. Do you have any idea yet who's behind this, Liam?"

"Not yet, no."

"It makes a mockery of our security, right enough. I know we don't see eye to eye on the question of mainland bombing campaigns, but this looting of our supplies is something else. We have to know who we can trust, Liam. Our organisation depends on it."

Trust and fear, thought Hennessy. In equal amounts usually, though in McGrath's case it was mainly fear. He came from a long line of Catholic landowners. His father was one of the driving forces behind the removal of many Protestant farmers from the border country. His method had been simple and brutal. He had targeted all the farms in the area where there was only one son and he had had them systematically murdered. When the parents became too old to work the farm and they were put up for sale, he made sure that there were no Protestant offers. Those farms where there were several children waiting to claim their inheritance were forced out of business by arson and poisoning campaigns and they, too, were sold to Catholic buyers. McGrath's own farm had once belonged to a Protestant family until their only son was shot through the back of the head as he sat on a tractor eating his lunch one day. The farm was put up for auction a year later and the sealed bid from McGrath's father was the highest, just as he knew it would be. Ironically, McGrath was an only son himself, with three sisters as siblings, but in his case it had been an advantage – not a death sentence.

"I gather you're having a wee spot of bother," said McGrath, stretching out his long legs.

"It's nothing I can't handle," said Hennessy.

"An explosion in your office, your farm and car bombed, Mary whisked off to London, and now Jim Kavanagh is trawling around the farms looking for men to guard you at night. I don't doubt that you can handle it, whatever it is, but I thought I might be able to help."

"I'm working on it," said Hennessy. He was worried about showing weakness in front of McGrath. He was one of the most political, and ruthless, men in the organisation, and always called in his debts. Accepting favours from Hugh McGrath was like doing a deal with the devil himself.

"Do you want to tell me about it?" McGrath asked.

Hennessy knew there was nothing to gain by not telling McGrath, because the man's intelligence network was second to none. He'd find out everything anyway. Hennessy explained about Nguyen and how his questions had turned into threats and how his threats had become reality. McGrath listened, occasionally grunting.

"Would it help if I seconded a few of my men?" McGrath asked once Hennessy had finished.

Hennessy shook his head. "No thanks, Hugh. Jim Kavanagh is getting a few of the local lads in. And I'm hoping to bring Micky Geraghty over. He should be able to track the bastard down, sure enough."

"Geraghty? Will he come back?"

"I hope so. I reckon he'll stand more chance than a group of townies trampling over the fields."

"I hope it works out. But let me know if you need help, OK?"

"I will, Hugh. I will."

McGrath drank his whiskey. It seemed to Hennessy that he had something on his mind.

"Is there something else, Hugh?"

"I don't know, Liam. It's this whole business of bombing on the mainland. Maybe we're going about this the wrong way. Maybe now is the time we should be applying pressure, not pulling back. Now is just the time to show our strength. To show that we're serious. And to give the British public a taste of their own medicine."

Hennessy raised his eyebrows. "What do you mean?"

"Let them have roadblocks on their roads, armed troops in their towns, body searches before they go into shops. Let them feel what life is like under an oppressive regime."

"I don't doubt that the bombs on the mainland will result in an over-reaction from the Government, and I know that'll probably result in a backlash of public opinion, but what about the damage the bombs are doing to our image? They're killing civilians, Hugh. With no warnings. They're not legitimate targets. You know as well as I do what we say in the *Green Book* that we give to volunteers. The only civilian targets that are legitimate are the Establishment, those who have a vested interest in maintaining the present status quo in Ireland: politicians, media, judiciary, business elements and the British war machine. That's virtually a direct quote."

McGrath shook his head. "There are no soft targets, no hard targets. Just targets. The Brits elected their Government, so they're responsible for it. They are all legitimate targets, every bit as legitimate as those in Ulster."

"And no warnings?"

"That's what makes them so effective. You should be embracing these bombers, Liam. You should be grateful to them, for the way they're raising the profile of the Cause around the world."

Liam looked incredulous. "By killing civilians?" he said. "What do you think that does for our reputation?"

McGrath held up his hand as if to calm an impatient child. "It doesn't matter. It never has. That's the big mistake everyone makes, Liam, they assume that when we kill what you call a soft target everyone turns against us. It doesn't happen. We kill a couple of tourists by mistake, we blow up a child, we shoot an old woman, it has no effect. It doesn't affect the votes we get at election time, it doesn't make a blind bit of difference to the amount of money we raise. In fact, you know as well as I do that a big bomb on the mainland, aimed at civilians or the army, often results in more money flooding in from the States, not less. It proves to them that we're serious, that we're prepared to fight for what we believe in."

McGrath shook his head, almost sadly. "Liam, I can't believe we're having this conversation, I really can't. It used to be you who had the drive, the energy. It was you who put the fire into the boys. Have you forgotten? Aldershot 1972? The M62 bombing in 1974? The Guildford pub bombings the same year? The Hilton bomb in 1975? You were with us then, Liam, you were the one who was calling for an escalation of the campaign, right enough."

"That was then, things have changed," said Hennessy. "There's a time for violence and there's a time for negotiation." He sounded tired.

"The Regent's Park bandstand bomb in 1982? The Brighton bombing in 1984? Have you forgotten that you were involved, that you pushed for them? What was it you said then, when Thatcher escaped? They were lucky. They'll always have to be lucky, but we only have to be lucky once. Christ, Liam, you knew what you were talking about then. And it holds true now."

Hennessy said nothing and McGrath continued. "Look what the ANC achieved in South Africa, through violence, look at Israel, founded on bloodshed."

Hennessy stood up and went over to the window. McGrath's bodyguards and driver were sitting patiently in the Volvo. One of them looked up when he saw the movement at the window.

"You've not forgotten what we're fighting for, have you, Liam?" said McGrath quietly.

Hennessy whirled round and jabbed his finger at McGrath. "That's not bloody fair!" he shouted. "I won't have you questioning my loyalty. Not now, not ever. There's no one who's done more for the Cause than me and my family. It's not three years ago that I buried my own brother-in-law, and before that my father and two cousins. My family has shed more than its fair share of blood." He stepped towards McGrath as if about to attack him. "And, I might add, my family hasn't been profiting from the border. We've given our lives in the struggle for a united Ireland, not set out to make fucking money from it. So don't you ever, ever, ask me if I've forgotten what we're fighting for!" He loomed over McGrath, his cheeks red and spittle spraying from his mouth. His fists were bunched and his shoulders quivered with tension.

McGrath looked stunned. He opened his mouth to speak but then seemed to think better of it.

"God damn you, McGrath!" shouted Hennessy. "Get out

of my fucking house. Now!" He stood glaring at the man sitting in front of him and then turned and stormed out of the room. He waited in the kitchen until he heard McGrath leave the house and the Volvo start up and drive down the track. Hennessy stood over the sink, gripping the edge of the draining board with his shaking hands. He felt the acidic taste of vomit in the back of his throat and he retched several times but nothing came up from his stomach. He poured himself a glass of water and was drinking it when Kavanagh came into the kitchen.

"Are ye all right?" he asked Hennessy.

"A wee exchange of words with Mr McGrath," said Hennessy. "I lost my temper with him." Hennessy tried to get his thinking straight. What had upset him so much? Part of it was McGrath's total unwillingness to even consider his point of view, and his almost inhuman eagerness to see innocent bystanders murdered. There was also the bitter memory of the friends and relatives who'd died, deaths that Hennessy had never really gotten over, like Mary's brother, Gerry. That was another reason for the burning anger coursing through his system, Hennessy realised. Mary.

"Jim, did anyone speak to McGrath on the way in?"

"Just one of the men on guard. He recognised him straight-away and let him through."

"No one else? Did you say anything to him?"

Kavanagh looked mystified. "I didn't, Liam. I'll ask the others. What's wrong? What d'ye think might've been said?"

Hennessy took another mouthful of water and swilled it round his gums before spitting it into the sink. The sour taste was still there, washing wouldn't get rid of it.

"He knew Mary was in London," he said quietly. "I want to know how he knew."

Even with the address Hennessy had given him, Morrison had a hell of a time finding Geraghty's house. The village it was supposed to be near was just a sprinkling of stone cottages in a valley sheltered from the biting winds of the North Sea and none of the roads seemed to have names. Geraghty was supposed to be living at Garryowen Farm but there was nothing even remotely like that on the map Morrison had bought in Inverness. It was dark and there were spots of rain flecking the windshield. Morrison decided to try the local pub, a weathered stone building with leaded windows that glowed yellow like the eyes of a wild animal. He parked his hired Rover next to a collection of mud-spattered farmer's vehicles and didn't bother locking his door. Above him the pub's sign – a fox with a dead chicken in its jaws – creaked in the wind. He pushed open the gnarled oak door and more of the yellow light oozed out, bringing with it the hubbub of pub conversation, predominantly gruff, masculine voices discussing sheep prices and football. It all stopped when he stepped over the threshold. It was, Morrison realised, like the scene in a vampire film when the stranger asks for directions to Dracula's castle. At a table near a shoulder-high hearth four old men in tweeds had been playing cards, but they had all stopped and were looking at him, wondering who he was. Under the table lay a black and white sheepdog, its ears up as it sniffed in his direction. A line of four younger men standing at the bar with pints of beer in front of them turned as one to look at him and even the barmaid, blonde haired and rosy cheeked, checked him over as she pulled a pint.

Morrison smiled at no one in particular and closed the door behind him. There was a thick mat just inside the door and Morrison carefully wiped his feet on it.

The card game began again and the dog settled its head down on to its paws with a sigh. Morrison walked over to the bar and put down the map.

"Good evening," said the barmaid. She finished pulling the pint and handed it to an old man wearing a grubby tartan cap. "Here you are, Archie," she said.

The pub was similar to those in farming communities all over Scotland and Ireland, the sort of pub where everyone knows everyone else and strangers are regarded with suspicion bordering on hostility. It was one large room, a handful of wooden tables worn smooth with age ranged against the outer wall and a bench seat either side of the fireplace which was unlit but contained a couple of roughly hewn logs on a blackened metal grate. The bar ran parallel to the wall, the full length of the room, and behind it was a door that obviously led to the landlord's private quarters. The walls of the room had once been painted white but had been stained a deep yellow by years of cigarette and pipe smoke and fumes from the fire. The floor was stone-flagged with a large, rectangular carpet of some long-faded red and blue pattern under the tables. On the gantry behind the bar was an impressive collection of malt whiskies, many bearing simple black labels with white lettering identifying the distillery that had produced them.

"What can I be getting you?" the barmaid asked, and Morrison indicated one of the Islay malts.

He savoured the bouquet of the deep-amber liquid before sipping it.

"Good?" asked the barmaid. She began drying glasses with a white cloth.

"Magic," he said. "Could you help me? I'm trying to find Micky Geraghty's house. Do you have any idea where it is?"

"To be sure," she said. She put down the cloth and reached for the map. She looked at it carefully, frowned, and then giggled. "I can't make head nor tail of this," she said. She held it out to one of the men standing at the bar. "Here Scott, can you show me Micky Geraghty's house?"

The man took the map, studied it and nodded. He put it down on the bar and pointed. Morrison looked over as the man ran his finger along a thin black line.

"Follow the road outside for about half a mile until you get to this crossroad here. Go left and then left again where the road forks, here. About two hundred yards later there's a single track to the right, you'll see a white post each side of the entrance. Micky's about half a mile down the track."

"It's no wonder I couldn't find it," said Morrison, taking another pull of the whisky. He offered to buy the man a drink and quickly extended it into a general offer for his three companions.

"You know Micky?" Morrison asked the man who'd given him directions.

"Sure, he's usually in here a couple of times a week. And every now and then his escapees will find their way here."

"Escapees?"

The man laughed. "He runs one of them Outward Bound places but for middle-aged executives. Teaches them survival stuff, rock-climbing, sailing, things like that. Sometimes he makes them spend a couple of nights on one of the islands, or dumps them miles away with just a compass and a pack of Kendal mint cake. The lucky ones manage to stagger in here to beg Tess for a drink."

The barmaid giggled. "They don't have any money, but we always give them credit. And they always come back and settle up. They're so grateful, bless 'em."

Morrison finished his whisky and said his goodbyes. He followed the man's instructions and ten minutes later he was outside a two-storey grey stone building with a steeply sloping slate roof. There were four cars parked outside the house and Morrison drove slowly past them. The track curved around the house, leading to a large, stone barn which had been converted into flats, and a short row of cottages. There were more cars parked there, all new models, so Morrison reckoned that Geraghty had a group of executives under his wing.

He found a parking space next to a white BMW and walked back to the front door of the house and pressed the bell.

The door was opened by a chestnut-haired girl in tight jeans and a green and white checked shirt. She looked at him with clear blue eyes and raised eyebrows.

"Is Mr Geraghty at home?" Morrison asked.

"Yep, come in," she said, and moved to let him into the hall. She closed the door and led him down a wood-panelled corridor. "My dad's in the study," she said over her shoulder. "Who shall I say is here?" Her accent was north Belfast, as far as Morrison could tell, but soft and with a gentle lilt.

"Morrison. Sean Morrison."

"From Belfast?" she asked.

"That's right." He wondered how come she was so willing

to let a stranger into her house, especially a stranger from over the water. Surely she must know of her father's past and that he'd always be at risk from Protestant extremists? They reached a door and she pushed it open. A grey-haired man with a weather-beaten face was sitting behind a desk talking into a phone. The girl showed Morrison in.

"I'll leave you here," she said. She left the door open and went back down the corridor. Somewhere in the distance he could hear a television set.

Geraghty waved at Morrison with his free hand, indicating a leather chair to the side of the desk, and Morrison sat in it.

"I'm booked pretty much solid now until the end of August," Geraghty said into the phone. He listened, frowned, and looked at a large book on the desk in front of him. "What, the twenty-eighth? Yes, we could do that. Until the eleventh? OK, I'll pencil your group in for that. Can you drop me a letter confirming it? Yes, yes, I'll look forward to it. Take care." He replaced the receiver.

"You'll be Sean Morrison?" he said, taking Morrison by surprise. Geraghty laughed at his discomfort. "Liam was on the phone to me earlier, said he didn't want me worrying overmuch when a stranger arrived on my doorstep. More likely didn't want me taking your head off with a twelve-bore. Good to see you, anyway, Sean. There's a bottle by the table next to you, pour yourself a drink, and one for me, too."

Morrison poured two measures of Irish whiskey. "I'm surprised we never met in Belfast," he said as he poured.

"I was what you might describe as low profile," laughed Geraghty. "I was always kept pretty much in the background."

"I know of the work you did, of course. You were one of my heroes."

"I'm sure you don't know half of it," said Geraghty, raising his glass. "But thanks anyway."

They drank. The study was very much a man's room. Floor-to-ceiling bookshelves lined one wall, every inch filled with a mixture of paperback novels, leather-bound classics and wildlife reference books. The other three walls were wood panelled, much the same as the hall outside, with several framed prints of hunting dogs. The furniture was sturdy, well-worn leather and wood that had long since lost its shine, comfortable chairs, a spacious desk with a brass reading lamp and three small circular tables. It was a room in which Morrison felt secure. To the right of the desk was a small window overlooking the line of cottages. A light winked out and Morrison could imagine an exhausted executive collapsing on to his bed.

If the study inspired a feeling of security, the man himself suggested a quiet confidence, that Micky Geraghty was a man who kept his word, a good guy to have at your back in a fight. He looked to be in his early fifties, broad shoulders and strong hands. His hair was grey but it was thick and healthy and his skin was wrinkled from exposure to the elements rather than age. His blue eyes were set aside a nose that had been broken several times. It was a strong, good-looking face, one that Morrison was sure would go down well with Japanese tourists wanting a set of antlers to take back home.

"Did Liam tell you why I was coming to see you?" Morrison asked, and Geraghty nodded.

Morrison continued: "The idea is for you to go in with me. You find him, I'll do the rest." From the look of it Hennessy's reservations were groundless, Geraghty appeared to be enthusiastic about the idea. Morrison relaxed, settling back in the chair and sipping his whiskey.

Geraghty laughed, his eyes sparkling. "I'd love to help, Sean, God knows I owe Liam a favour or two, but you're going to have to count me out."

Morrison frowned. "I don't understand, what's the problem?"

Geraghty leant back in his chair and swung his left leg up on to the desk. It was covered in greying plaster from his toes to just above his knee. He slapped the cast and pulled a face. "This is my problem," he said ruefully. "I broke it two weeks ago. The Doc says it'll be a couple of months yet before the cast can come off. Until then . . ." He shrugged.

Morrison's heart fell. For a wild moment he thought that perhaps Geraghty was making it up, that the cast was fake and he was just using it as an excuse to back out, but his disappointment seemed genuine, and so did the cast. It had been autographed in several places and the plaster was crumbling a little around his toes.

"How did it happen?" he asked.

"Teaching a group of sales reps to climb. I went up a rock-face to knock in a bit of protection and the guy who was paying out the rope lost concentration. I slipped and he let me fall about thirty feet further than he should have done. Problem was, I was only twenty-five feet above the ground. He was very upset about it."

"I bet," said Morrison. "Who's running things while you're out of action?"

"The admin and the lectures I can handle myself, and I've a couple of instructors working with me. And my daughter, Kerry, the girl who let you in, knows as much as I do."

Geraghty saw the look on Morrison's face and he smiled. "I hope that wasn't a chauvinistic comment I saw forming on your lips," he said. "Kerry knows as much about tracking as I do, and she's been teaching survival courses with me for five years or more. And if the truth be known, she's a darn sight fitter than I am, even without the cast."

"Why, Dad, you've never said that to my face," said a voice from behind Morrison, and he turned to see the girl, standing in the doorway with her hands on her hips and her eyebrows arched.

"How long have you been there, girl?" asked Geraghty. He didn't appear annoyed and Morrison knew that from where he was sitting he could see the length of the corridor leading away from the study so there was no way she could have crept up on them without him seeing her. In fact, the chances were that Geraghty had paid her the compliment knowing that she was within earshot. Morrison wondered how much she knew about Geraghty's past.

"I just came to see if you and Mr Morrison wanted a cup of tea, or something. God forbid I should eavesdrop." She shook her hair back from her face and swept it behind her ears. She had her father's eyes, and the same confident way of holding her head with the chin slightly raised. Her skin was healthy and bronzed and she was wearing hardly any make-up, just a touch of blue eye-shadow and mascara.

Morrison put her age at about twenty-five. Geraghty was right, she looked fit. She caught him looking at her and she grinned at him. He looked away.

Geraghty held up his whiskey glass. "We're doing just fine," he said.

"And I," said Morrison, getting to his feet and putting his glass on the table, "must be going."

"I'll show you out," said Kerry. Morrison shook hands with Geraghty, who wished him well, and then followed Kerry back down the hall. She wasn't wearing shoes and her bare feet brushed against the carpet. "Uncle Liam wanted my dad to do something for him, is that right?" she asked.

"Something like that," said Morrison.

She turned to look at him, stopping so suddenly that he almost bumped into her. Her clear blue eyes bored into his. "What did you want him to do?" she asked. "It must have been important for you to have come all this way. Important for the Cause."

Morrison looked at her, unsure how to react. She had called Hennessy "Uncle" and she was undoubtedly her father's daughter, but he didn't know her well enough to discuss IRA business with her. "We needed his help, but his leg puts paid to that," he said.

Her eyes sparkled and she reached forward, touching his arm. "Don't go yet," she whispered. "Come with me." She took him past the front door and into a comfortably furnished lounge. The television was on but the room was empty. She nodded towards an overstuffed sofa. "Wait there for a while," she said. "Let me talk to my dad. OK?"

"OK," Morrison replied, bemused. He sat down and crossed his legs and wondered what the hell she was up to.

Kerry walked back to the study where her father still had his leg on the desk. He had a knitting needle in one hand and was wiggling it down inside the cast trying to get at an itchy place. He grinned at her apologetically. She was forever warning him that scratching would only make it worse.

She leant against the door jamb and folded her arms across her chest.

"Uncle Liam needs our help, yes?" Liam Hennessy wasn't

a blood relative, but he was just as close. He was her godfather and when they'd lived in Ireland barely a month went by when she didn't see him. He'd taught her to ride on his farm, had given her the run of his rambling library and spent hours just talking with her when her mother was in hospital and dying bit by bit. Kerry loved Liam Hennessy fiercely and would do anything to protect him.

"He needs my help," said Geraghty.

"It's been five years since we were in Ireland, so I guess it's something they think only you can do, something that you can't do with a broken leg? Something to do with tracking, is that it?"

Geraghty sighed. "Why don't you just ask me what it is they want, Kerry? It would save us both a lot of time."

"You'll tell me?" she said, surprised.

"Try me," he answered.

"What is it Uncle Liam wants?"

To her surprise her father explained about The Chinaman and how Hennessy was stuck in his farm. "He wanted me to go with Morrison, to go into the countryside and flush him out."

"And then what?"

Geraghty fixed his daughter with his eyes, suddenly cold and harder than she'd seen them for a long time. "If he's lucky, Liam will hand him over to the police. If he's unlucky, well, you know that some of Liam's friends can play pretty rough, Kerry. It could get nasty."

"But the man's trying to kill Uncle Liam, that's what you said. So he's only got himself to blame."

"Whatever. But it's all immaterial anyway, Kerry. I can't do it, they'll just have to find someone else."

She leapt to her feet and leant over the desk, her hair swinging from side to side.

"No!" said Geraghty before she could speak.

"But I'm perfect for it," she said, exasperated. "You've taught me everything there is to know about tracking, and yet you never let me prove how good I am. You never let me take the hunting parties out on my own."

"You know why that is. The Germans and the Japs pay top

whack to be taken out by a traditional Highland gamekeeper, tweeds and flat cap and all. It's part of the enjoyment for them, it'd spoil it if their tracker was a pretty girl young enough to be their daughter."

Kerry ignored the compliment, realising she'd been side-tracked into an old argument.

"I know about tracking, and I know the area around Uncle Liam's farm, probably better than you do. I've ridden and walked over every inch, I know every hiding place."

"It's several hundred acres, my girl, I doubt if you know every inch."

"It's three hundred and twenty-four acres, Dad, and I know it like the back of my hand."

"It'll be dangerous," he warned, and she knew then that she'd won the argument about whether or not she had the ability.

"Dad, which of us is the best shot?"

"I can't fault your marksmanship Kerry, but I'm not having you trekking around the Irish countryside with a hunting rifle. It's practically a war zone."

"All right then, I won't take my gun. But it's Uncle Liam this man is after, not me," she pressed. "He'll be focused on him, not me." She waved her hand at the books lining the wall to her left. "I've read every book on trapping and tracking on those shelves, and I read most of them before I even went to school."

It was true, Geraghty acknowledged. Even as a child she'd had a fascination for the books, and she'd taught herself to make snares and simple traps and learnt to recognise spoors and tracks from the diagrams they contained. There were other books, too, manuals on warfare and booby traps and explosives, some that he'd bought out of curiosity and others that he'd acquired in connection with his work for the IRA, and she'd read them just as avidly. But unlike Geraghty, almost all her knowledge of booby traps was theoretical and not practical.

Kerry could see that her father was wavering so she decided to raise the stakes.

"It's not just a question of helping Uncle Liam," she said.

"I want to do something to help the Cause. I didn't stop you when you said you wanted to leave Ireland after Mum died, but you know that deep down I wanted to stay in Belfast and help in any way I could. I feel as strongly as you do about getting the British out of Ireland. You know that." Geraghty could feel the intensity of her conviction burning across the desk, and he remembered how, years before, he had felt the same desire to see a united Ireland. "Let me do this, for the Cause if not for Uncle Liam. This is something I can do, something that's a hell of a lot more constructive than throwing petrol bombs at troops or harassing the RUC."

Geraghty closed his eyes and rubbed them with the backs of his hands. He sighed deeply and Kerry knew that she'd almost won. One more push and he'd agree. It was time to play her trump card. She sat back down in the chair, pulled it closer to the desk, and leant her elbows on it so that her head was on a level with her father's. "And," she said thoughtfully, "it would get me away from here for a while." She paused, for emphasis. "From him," she added, just in case he didn't get the message.

"You're not still seeing him, are you?" Geraghty asked.

"I'm trying not to," she answered. For almost a year she'd been having an on-off affair with a British Telecom engineer who lived nearby. He was married but couldn't make his mind up whether to leave his wife or stop seeing Kerry. He'd sworn that he hadn't touched his wife in years, but midway through the affair he'd confessed that she was pregnant and that he couldn't abandon her. "I suppose it'll be a fucking virgin birth," she'd screamed, and thrown an ashtray at his head, but the following week she'd phoned him and their love-making had been better than ever.

Geraghty had made his disapproval plain, but had also refused to interfere, knowing that his daughter was old enough to make her own mistakes. He figured that she'd realise what a hopeless situation she'd gotten herself into and that she'd come to her senses. He was right. It had been almost two months since she had seen him, though she was still at the stage where she had to keep fighting the urge to call him and jumped whenever the phone rang. She knew that if she saw him again she'd end up in bed with him. Geraghty sensed the pressure she was under and thought that perhaps she was right, a spell in Ireland might be just what she needed to get the man out of her system once and for all.

"If you go, you're going to have to be careful," he said.

"I will be," she said earnestly.

"I mean very careful," he said. "It's not a game there, you know. It's not too far from the border. It's a war zone. You don't carry a gun, under any circumstances. You track him, and that's all. You don't take any risks, understand?"

She nodded furiously. "I promise. Can I go?"

Geraghty smiled, but it was an uncertain smile. "Yes," he said. "You can go."

She whooped, and grinned, and reached over the desk to hug him and kiss him on the cheek.

"Go and get Morrison for me," he told her. "I want a word with him."

Geraghty watched her rush down the corridor. He wasn't surprised at her keenness to return to Ireland, or to help the Provos. She'd put up a hell of a fight when he'd first decided to leave Ireland, and she'd come close to staying behind. Kerry had a stubborn streak, and he guessed that she'd got it from him. She had a hard side, too, a tendency to viciousness which went beyond simple devotion to the Cause. There had been times in Belfast when he'd felt she was actually enjoying taking on the army and the RUC, that she was getting some sort of kick out of the Troubles. Despite his apparent change of heart he was still reluctant to allow her to go back to Belfast and its violent influences, but he owed Liam Hennessy. He owed him a great deal. Besides, he knew that if she really set her mind on going back, he wouldn't be able to stop her. He knew his daughter, and he knew that she wasn't above telephoning Hennessy herself and offering her services. And if things were as bad as they sounded, he doubted if Hennessy would turn her down. And if Hennessy asked him if it was OK for Kerry to go back, could he refuse? Could he refuse any request of the man who held his life in his hands? No, he could not. And she knew that, his darling daughter. She knew that full well.

Kerry found Morrison still watching television. "Dad wants to talk to you," she said. "He says I can come with you."

"You?" said Morrison, surprised.

"To help you track down the man who's trying to hurt Uncle Liam."

A bemused Morrison followed her back down the corridor and into Geraghty's study.

"Leave us alone, Kerry, and shut the door this time," Geraghty told her. He waited until she'd gone before speaking. "She wants to help you, Sean," he said.

"Can she do it?" asked Morrison.

"Oh yes, she's a first-class tracker, I've taught her everything I know. She often comes with me out on to the moors after deer. She's a good shot, too. That's what I want to talk to you about. I don't want her carrying a gun out there. Under any circumstances. I don't want her put in any danger."

"I'll take care of her. I promise."

"There's something else." Geraghty scratched his chin and scrutinised Morrison. "I'm not sure how to put this, Sean. Kerry can be a bit, er, overenthusiastic sometimes. Do you know what I mean?"

Morrison shook his head, mystified.

"She's always idolised Liam, and me, and ever since she was a kid she was on the fringes of the Organisation, running errands, taking messages, the sort of stuff we all went through, you know? Throwing stones at the troops, giving the RUC a hard time. But I never wanted her to get drawn into the real rough stuff, the sort of things I was involved in. I mean, she has a pretty good idea of what I did, and I think she wishes she could be more like me."

Morrison laughed. "Jesus, Micky, it's hardly a secret, is it? There's barely a pub in Derry where they don't sing songs about you on a Saturday night when the beer's flowing."

"Aye, Sean, that's right enough. And I'm not ashamed of what I did, far from it. We're at war with the fucking British and I'd do it all over again, the killing and everything. But my family has given enough. I don't want Kerry to get any more involved. I didn't then and I don't now. I promised my wife,

God rest her soul, I promised her before she died that I'd take Kerry away from Belfast before she got in too deep. I don't want her to go back."

"You're going to stop her?" said Morrison, frowning.

"No. No, I can't stop her. But you must make sure she realises that this is a one-off. Don't romanticise it for her, don't pull her back. Just use her this one time, then send her back to me."

"I understand," said Morrison.

"Then good luck, and God bless. And take care of her. She's all the family I've got left." He swung his plaster cast off the desk and it thudded on to the floor. "It's late. You should stay here tonight and make an early start tomorrow. I'll get Kerry to cook us a meal. You might want to telephone Liam and let him know what's happening, if Kerry hasn't done so already." He reached for a set of metal crutches leaning against the wall and used them to clump out of the room.

Maggie linked her arm through Woody's as they stepped out of the cinema.

"Good film," she said. "Bit violent, but fun."

"Yeah, I've always liked a bit of mindless violence," laughed Woody. "You hungry?"

"Mmmm. Sure."

"Italian?"

"Italian would be great."

Woody suggested a place in Covent Garden and they walked together out of Leicester Square and down Long Acre. Maggie asked him how he was getting on at work and he told her about the stories he was working on. She was always interested in what he was doing at the paper and seemed to hang on every word. He told her about the phone call from Pat Quigley and the mysterious Chinaman. She raised her eyebrows when she heard about the money in the carrier bag.

"What do you think's going on?" she asked.

Woody shrugged. "I was thinking that maybe this China-man had paid someone to go after Liam Hennessy, some sort of hit-man."

"Wow!" she said.

"Yeah, wow is right. It'd be one hell of a story, if only I can nail it down."

They stood at the roadside and waited for a gap in the traffic before crossing.

"So what's the problem?" she asked.

"He's gone. Vanished. I went round to where he lives and he'd moved. No forwarding address. I don't even have his full name."

"You don't think that perhaps he's gone to Ireland himself?"

"Seems unlikely, doesn't it? I mean, a Chinaman in Belfast on the trail of an IRA leader. It's a bit unbelievable, even for our paper."

"I suppose so."

They walked in silence through the evening crowds, and then stopped to watch a man in a clown's suit juggling five flaming torches.

"Do you get to write much about the IRA?" she asked.

"Depends," said Woody. "I covered the Knightsbridge bombing, remember? The night I met you. Depends when it happens, you know."

"The *Sunday World* usually takes the Government line, doesn't it?" she said.

Woody nodded. "Slightly to the right of Attila the Hun, we are."

"What about you? What do you think?"

"Hell, Maggie, I don't know. I'm a reporter, not a poli-tician." The juggler put down three of his torches to scattered applause and then began fire-eating. "I guess I take the view that we should just pull the troops out and let the Irish sort it out themselves. You know the troops went to Northern Ireland in the first place to look after the Catholics. To protect them from the Protestants. And now it's the IRA who want them out. It doesn't make sense. It isn't something the British

Government can sort out, that much I'm sure. It's an Irish problem. What about you?"

"I suppose you're right. At the end of the day whatever the MPs in Westminster say isn't going to make the slightest difference. Maybe your paper should say that."

Woody laughed. "I don't think many MPs would take any notice of what appears in the *Sunday World*. *The Times* maybe, or the *Telegraph*." Something tingled at the back of Woody's mind. Something to do with an MP. He watched the clown blow flaming liquid up into the night sky, a glistening bluish stream which flared into orange and yellow. Of course, thought Woody. S. J. Brownlow, the name in the notebook. Sir John Brownlow. The Chinaman's MP. He'd said he'd written to his Member of Parliament and been to see him. With any luck he'd have The Chinaman's letter on file.

"What are you smiling at?" Maggie asked.

"Nothing," he said. "Come on, let's go eat. I'm starving."

As the darkness crept through the forest, Nguyen opened one of the containers of chicken and ate it slowly, along with a container of boiled rice. When he'd finished he scraped leaves away from the forest floor and buried the remains in the soil. He drank from one of his canteens and put it in the rucksack alongside the components of his firebomb detonator and the stolen gun. The can of petrol was too bulky to fit into the rucksack so he was forced to carry it. He waited until the sun had gone down before moving through the forest. The can slowed him, not because it was heavy but because it was awkward and forever catching in the undergrowth, but once he left the trees and was out in open fields he picked up speed.

He varied his route slightly this time, cutting through different fields and crossing the B8 further north than he'd crossed the previous night. Once he almost stumbled into an army patrol, half a dozen teenage soldiers walking along a narrow country lane, their faces blackened and their rubber-soled boots making almost no noise. They were strung out over fifty feet, walking in two lines. Nguyen was heading in the opposite direction, on the other side of a hedgerow looking for a gap so that he could cut across the track, when he heard one of the men sniff. Nguyen froze and as he did the petrol slapped against the side of the can. The field he was in had recently been ploughed and offered little in the way of cover but there was nowhere else for him to go so he dropped and rolled into a deep furrow and flattened himself down. He was invisible. He heard them go by, and heard the man sniff again. He stayed where he was for a full thirty minutes just in case they retraced their steps.

It was after midnight when he eventually reached the hill overlooking Hennessy's farm. He lay down close to the summit, careful that he didn't break the skyline, and studied the farm buildings through his binoculars for more than an hour until he was satisfied that he had spotted all the guards. The starlight wasn't strong enough to illuminate their faces but he could see that they were carrying shotguns. There was one in front of the cottage, another close by in the gap between the barns and the stables and three standing guard close to the farmhouse. One of them was smoking a cigarette, he could see the small red dot hovering in the air. He sniffed but could smell nothing. There had been times, Nguyen remembered, when he could smell a campfire two days' march away in the jungle, or smell the toothpaste or chewing gum or tobacco of an American who had passed by three hours before, but he was younger then and his senses were more acute.

During the hour he watched, the men walked up and down, occasionally talking to each other, but they did not bother patrolling the perimeter of the farm. Static sentries, thought Nguyen. The easiest to deal with.

He moved slowly down the hill and then crawled across the fields towards the barns, giving a wide berth to the stables and the cottage. He lay in the grass about a hundred yards from the barns and concentrated on them, checking that he hadn't missed a guard, and then began to crawl towards them. He moved only one limb at a time, left arm, right leg, right arm, left leg, keeping his body an inch off the ground to minimise noise while at the same time reducing his silhouette. It took him half an hour to cover the hundred yards to the nearest barn. He hugged the wall and slipped inside among the tractors and farm equipment. The barn was the furthest away from the farm but it would have been his first choice anyway because the other contained nothing but hay and the idea was to cause a diversion not to start a huge blaze that would have fire engines rushing over from the nearest town.

He put the can of petrol under a blue tractor and took off his rucksack. He knelt down and carefully removed the clock, the matchbox and its wire, and from his pocket he took out a fresh battery. He connected short lengths of wire to the hands of the clock and set them at quarter to and quarter past and then connected the battery and the matchbox and its match heads into a continuous circuit. He unscrewed the cap of the petrol can and poured half of it on the floor around the tractor then stood it under the cab. He lowered the matchbox into the can so that it was suspended above the liquid. It was important that the match heads were ignited in the vapour and not swamped with petrol or there would be no explosion. He wound the wire around the handle of the can so that the matchbox couldn't accidentally slip lower. He had thirty minutes to get into position. Plenty of time. He put his rucksack back on and eased himself out of the barn and slithered slowly along the ground, back the way he'd come, and then he crawled clockwise around the barns until he could see the side of the farmhouse and the gap that led to the courtyard.

He waited. The petrol bomb exploded with a whooshing noise followed by the crackle and hiss of the tractor burning. There were shouts and yells and the men at the front of the farmhouse ran towards the barn. Lights went on in the farmhouse and the door to the cottage flew open. When the guards had run through into the courtyard Nguyen made his way to the outbuildings and lay down in the shadows. Hennessy came out of the back door along with two other men, he in his dressing-gown, they in pullovers and jeans and holding handguns. Nguyen had planned to climb the drainpipe and get in through the bathroom window but he saw that Hennessy had left the back door open. The kitchen light hadn't been switched on so the doorway was in darkness. He waited until he was sure that no one else was coming out of the farmhouse and he moved along the wall, hugging the shadows like a cockroach, and then slipped through the door into the kitchen, listening carefully.

He moved on the balls of his feet, knees slightly bent, ready to move quickly if he had to, but it was all clear and he crept into the hall and up the stairs. The stairs turned to the left and he reorientated the map of the farmhouse that he held in his head and when the stairs opened into the first-floor hallway he knew immediately which way to move so that he would pass the bathroom and find Hennessy's bedroom. He unclipped the hunting knife from its scabbard on the strap of the rucksack and held it blade up as he put his hand on the bedroom door and pressed his ear to the warm wood. He hadn't seen the woman leave the house. She might have left during the day but there was a chance she was still in the room. He turned the doorknob slowly and smoothly and eased the door open. The light was on and the bed was empty. He pushed the door and stepped into the room. At the foot of the bed was a wicker dog basket and a brown dog growled at him and then began to bark. Nguyen closed the door as the dog got to its feet and moved towards him, barking and snapping, its tail down between its legs and the fur standing up along the back of its neck.

"Good dog," said Nguyen, holding the knife to his side.

Hennessy stood with his hands on his hips as he watched two of his men spray the burning tractor with fire extinguishers, the foam hissing and bubbling on the hot metal. Joe Ryan had run a hosepipe from the stables and he yelled over his shoulder for his daughter to turn the water on. The hosepipe squirmed and kicked and then water burst from the nozzle and he played it over the walls of the barn.

The rest of the men were busy moving equipment away from the fire, either to the far side of the barn or out into the courtyard. Kavanagh stood at Hennessy's shoulder. In the distance Hennessy heard Jackie bark. "Still think I've got enough guards, Jim?" he asked. Kavanagh remained silent, not sure if Hennessy was getting at him or not. "Any idea what caused it?" Hennessy asked.

"There's a can under the tractor and some melted plastic. It's The Chinaman, right enough. We were lucky that the can didn't explode, it could've been a lot worse. By the look of it the flames came shooting out of the top of the can like a jet engine, spraying fire across the wall and setting light to the tractor's tyres. It's a lot worse than it looks."

"He cocked it up?"

"Looks like it."

"Thank God he didn't set fire to the other barn. If the hay had gone up we'd have never got it under control."

The men with the fire extinguishers put out the burning tractor and moved to help Ryan douse the burning side of the barn. The tractor's tyres had melted and warped and the tractor was blackened and burnt and smeared with bubbly white foam. The smell of burnt rubber was choking and Hennessy and Kavanagh moved back into the courtyard. Hennessy looked up at his bedroom window. Jackie had stopped barking. "Still think we should go back to Belfast?" asked Hennessy.

"No question about it, Liam."

"And if he sets fire to my house? Could you stop him doing that?"

Kavanagh realised that whatever he said he'd be in the wrong, so he said nothing. They stood together and watched the men douse the final flames.

"Morrison should be back tomorrow," said Hennessy eventually. "He's bringing someone with him who might be able to help. Kerry Geraghty."

"Micky Geraghty's girl?"

"Yeah. She's going to try to track down The Chinaman. Micky was going to do it but he's got a broken leg, though from what Sean tells me she's every bit as good. We'll give her a go. While she's trying I'll have to stay here otherwise The Chinaman will just disappear, but if it doesn't work then we'll go back to Belfast and we'll handle it in the city. OK?"

"It's your call, Liam," said Kavanagh.

"You mean it's me he's after," said Hennessy. He smiled ruefully. "And you're right, of course. Look, there's nothing we can do here. I'm going back to bed and I suggest you do the same. I doubt if he's going to do anything else tonight and there's nothing we can do in the dark."

"I'll wait here until the men've finished," said Kavanagh. Hennessy began walking back to the farmhouse. Kavanagh called after him and Liam turned round. "I'm sorry about all this," said Kavanagh.

"Not your fault, Jim," said Hennessy. "And I didn't mean to imply that it was. I'm just a bit tense, that's all. This China-man is getting under my skin. I'll talk to you tomorrow."

He went into the kitchen and switched the light on. He poured himself a double whiskey and carried it upstairs to his bedroom. He hung his dressing-gown on the back of the bedroom door and placed the tumbler of whiskey on his bed-side table. Jackie lay on the floor at the side of the bed. Hennessy was disappointed that she hadn't welcomed him back with her normal tail-wagging and frantic licks. She was probably sulking because he'd kept her in the room. "Come on, Jackie," he said softly, and patted the bed. Mary didn't allow the dog into the bedroom, least of all on the bed, but when she was away Hennessy reckoned that he should be allowed to give Jackie a treat. He patted the bed again and clicked his tongue, but still she ignored him. He went over to her and knelt down. "Come on, Jackie, old girl," he said, and stroked her neck. There was no reaction and Hennessy began to panic. He stood up and switched on the bedroom light and immediately saw that there was blood pooling around the dog's neck. "Oh God, no," he groaned. He bent down to pick up the dog but as he did he realised that he was not alone in the room. In the gap between the large oak wardrobe and the wall he saw a pair of legs in baggy camouflage trousers and he looked up sharply.

"You!" he said.

Nguyen stepped forward out of the shadows. In his left hand he carried a gun which he pointed at the head of the kneeling man. In his right he held two wires between his fingers and around his neck was hanging what appeared to be a length of grey tubing. He'd used a length of insulation tape to suspend the tube so that it lay against his stomach. Various nails and screws had been stuck to the tube with more tape. To Hennessy it appeared that Nguyen had undergone a complete transformation. It wasn't just the outfit, though the camouflage and the gun gave him a military appearance that was a far cry from the down-trodden Oriental who had turned up at his office, it was more a question of bearing, the way he carried himself. There was a new air of confidence about the man and for the first time Hennessy felt afraid. He looked down at Jackie and ran his hand along her fur.

"You didn't have to kill my dog," he said, shaking his head sadly.

"He was barking."

"She. Not he. And you didn't have to kill her."

"I am sorry," said Nguyen. He walked behind Hennessy and bolted the bedroom door. "Please sit in the chair." He pointed with the gun at a pink armchair in a corner away from the window. The curtains were closed but Nguyen didn't want shadows to be seen by the men in the courtyard below. Hennessy stood up and slowly lowered himself into the chair. From where he was sitting he could see Jackie's head, her eyes nothing more than milky orbs, her tongue hanging grotesquely from the side of her mouth.

"Can I cover her?" he asked Nguyen. Nguyen took the dressing-gown from the hook on the back of the door and draped it over the dog's body.

"What is it you want?" asked Hennessy. He felt naked sitting in the chair wearing only his pyjamas.

"You must talk quietly," said Nguyen. He nodded down at the tube on his chest and held up the hand which was holding the wires. "This is a bomb, the same type I used to destroy the car. If anyone comes into this room all I do is put the wires together. Then we all die." He held up the gun. "And I have this. If we talk quietly nobody will hear us. Do you understand."

"Yes," sighed Hennessy. "I understand. But what do you want to talk about?"

"The names. I want the names."

"I cannot help you."

"You know that I am serious. You have seen what I can do."

"Yes." Hennessy looked down at the dead dog. "Yes, I know now what you can do."

"So you know that I can kill you? That I will kill you?"

"Killing me will make no difference, no difference at all. You see, I have absolutely no idea who is behind the London bombings."

Nguyen looked confused. "They are in the IRA?"

"Maybe."

"I do not understand."

Hennessy sighed because deep down he didn't understand either. "I'll try to explain," he said. "They're saying that they are in the IRA, but I don't know who they are. Nobody in the official IRA knows who they are. You must believe me, we don't want to kill innocent citizens. I'm doing everything I can to find out who's responsible."

Nguyen walked from the wardrobe to the end of the bed and sat down, facing Hennessy. Hennessy could see light glistening on the sweat that covered the man's hands. The wires that would set off the lethal package were less than two inches apart. Nguyen saw him looking at the wires and smiled. "Do not worry," he said. "It will only explode if I want it to explode."

"Killing me won't get your family back," said Hennessy quietly.

"I do not want to kill you, Mr Hennessy. But I cannot allow the men to be unpunished."

"This is getting us nowhere," sighed Hennessy.

"The explosives the men use. Do they make their own?"

Hennessy shook his head. "They've been using our explosives. We have it stored in several places in Britain. It looks as if they've been stealing it."

"Semtex?"

"Yes."

"Which sort? Semtex-H?"

"Yes."

"It would be," said Nguyen. "Everything moves in circles."

"You know about Semtex?"

Nguyen smiled tightly. "I know about Semtex-H," he said. "Hexagen is added, that is where the H comes from. Very stable explosive, but very powerful, more powerful than TNT."

Hennessy's mouth dropped open. "How come you know so much about Semtex-H?"

"I use many times in Vietnam."

"In Vietnam?"

"You do not know your history, Mr Hennessy. Semtex-H was made for the Vietnamese during the war. It is our explosive. They made it for us, the Chax."

"Czechs, you mean. It was made in Czechoslovakia."

"Yes. The Czechs. They made it. Before, when the French were in Vietnam, then we used a French plástic explosive. When the French left we asked the Czechs to make same style for us. They made Semtex-H. Very good for making bombs and for traps. Many Americans were killed by Semtex-H. Now the IRA uses it to kill my family. That is, how do you say, ionic."

"Ironic," said Hennessy. "The word is ironic."

"Yes, it is ironic. Vietnamese explosive kills Vietnamese family."

"I am sorry about what happened to your family. But it is not my fault."

Nguyen pointed the gun at Hennessy's throat. "You will tell me who killed my family. You will tell me or you will die. And when you are dead I will go and ask someone else. I will find out eventually." He said the words in a cold, flat voice and Hennessy knew that he meant it. The gun was cocked and ready to fire and he saw Nguyen's finger tighten on the trigger. Hennessy held up his hands as if trying to ward off the bullet.

"No!" he said.

"Then tell me," hissed Nguyen.

"I don't know," said Hennessy.

"Then die," said Nguyen.

Hennessy turned his head away, his eyes tightly shut. "I don't know but I'm trying to find out," he said, his voice shaking with fear.

"What do you mean?"

"I've set a trap for them. If it works I'll know who they are."

"When will you know?"

Hennessy stopped flinching from the gun, sensing that Nguyen was taking him seriously. Perhaps he had a chance after all. "When the next bomb goes off."

"What is your plan?"

"When they claim responsibility for the bomb they give a codeword that tells the police that they are with the IRA. I have changed the codeword and the one that they use will tell me who has been helping them."

"And then what?"

"We'll give their names to the police. And they will end it."

Nguyen thought about what Hennessy had told him, but the gun never wavered. Eventually he nodded to himself as if he had come to a decision.

"Very well," he said. "I will give you three days. In three days I will come back. But if you do not have the names by then, I will kill you."

"But what if they haven't set off a bomb by then?" protested Hennessy.

"That is your problem," said Nguyen.

"That's not fair!" protested Hennessy.

"Fair? Nothing that has happened so far has been fair, Mr Hennessy." Nguyen stood up and backed to the door. He reached for the light switch and plunged the room into darkness.

"Why are you doing this?" Hennessy asked quietly.

"You killed my family."

"There's something else. Something you're not telling me."

Nguyen moved silently to the window and pulled back one of the curtains. There were only two men in the courtyard below. One was carrying two fire extinguishers, the other was rolling up a hosepipe. He heard the back door of the farmhouse slam shut. The two men in the courtyard walked over to the cottage and Nguyen let the curtain swing back into place.

"I mean, I've lost relatives in the Troubles, my own brother-in-law was killed not so long ago. Almost everyone I know has had someone they know killed or maimed, but I've never met anyone who has taken it so . . . so personally . . . as you have."

"Perhaps if you did take it personally, the war in Ireland would not have dragged on for so long."

"What do you mean?"

"What are you fighting for?"

"To get the British out of Ireland. To be allowed to live our own lives without prejudice or persecution."

"So why do your people not take up arms against the British and drive them from the country?"

"Many do."

"But not enough. Not enough people care. Not enough take it personally. The Vietnamese fought the French until they left the country. And the Communists fought the Americans and the army of the South until the Americans left. They won because the desire to be one country was stronger than anything else. It seems to me that you will never force the British to leave Ireland. Not enough people care. You play at war."

"And you? Why are you doing this?"

Nguyen ignored him. He put his ear to the door and listened. He heard nothing. He turned to Hennessy. "I will go now. Do not shout, I still have the bomb and I will kill anyone who comes after me. I will be back in three days." He slipped the bolt back and opened the door, looked left and right down the corridor before easing himself out of the bedroom, keeping close to the wall. He went silently to the bathroom and put the gun in the rucksack and disconnected the wires before he stepped on to the toilet and climbed out of the window. He held the drainpipe and shinned down, taking care not to scrape his feet against the wall. When he reached the ground he pressed himself against the wall and checked out his surroundings. There was a lingering smell of burnt wood and scorched metal in the courtyard but there was no sound. He crept between the cars, keeping low, and made his way to the stables. Inside he heard the horses snorting and he wondered if they could sense that he was there. He heard footsteps by the cottage so he moved in the opposite direction and left the courtyard between the stables and the far end of the farmhouse.

Hennessy sat in the bedroom, slumped forward with his head in his hands. Part of him wanted to sound the alarm immediately but he knew that The Chinaman had meant what he'd said. He would use the gun and if that failed he would set off the bomb killing God knows how many. He gave him five minutes then switched on the light and went down to get Kavanagh who was stretched out on a sofa in the lounge. By the time Kavanagh had gone out to warn the men on guard duty Nguyen was long gone, slithering through the grass as silently as a snake.

O'Reilly caught the 10.33 a.m. train from Waterloo station and found himself a seat towards the front in a carriage full of men in morning suits and women in long dresses and expensive hats. Two of the couples in his compartment were obviously travelling together and one of the men had produced a bottle of champagne and four glasses and made a big show of opening it. Champagne sprayed out and as the man held it to one side it splashed over O'Reilly's aluminium camera case.

"Sorry old man," said the racegoer.

"No problem," said O'Reilly. He looked out of the window as the train pulled out of the station. Ascot was forty minutes away so he settled back in his seat and let his mind drift. In the inside pocket of his blazer was a badge to get him into the Members' Enclosure, which he'd bought from a ticket agency a week earlier. He'd wanted to get in on Ladies Day but hadn't been able to get a ticket for Thursday and had settled for Tuesday instead. Tuesday or Thursday, it didn't really matter, because a successful bombing at Royal Ascot would be news around the world.

The camera case at his feet was the sort professionals used to carry their equipment, about two-feet long, a foot wide and eighteen-inches deep, with a thick nylon carrying strap. The Bombmaker had stripped out the lining of the case and fitted slabs of Semtex, ten pounds in all, around the sides and the bottom. There were two detonators, each connected to a single timer made from a small electronic travel alarm. The alarm had been set for 2 p.m. and the bomb was armed. O'Reilly was tense but not over-anxious. He'd carried live bombs before and he had complete faith in The Bombmaker. The lining had been replaced over the explosive with alterations made where necessary, and it now contained two camera bodies, a selection of lenses, a light meter and boxes of film. Around his neck was a Nikon with a telephoto lens and a pair of binoculars in a leather case. Attached to the binoculars were a dozen or so badges from earlier race meetings and that, and the trilby hat, marked O'Reilly out as a regular racegoer and not just a social butterfly hoping for a glimpse of a famous face at Royal Ascot.

The train arrived at Ascot station at 11.15 a.m. and O'Reilly joined the crowds flocking to the racecourse. There were plenty of police around but most of them were wearing yellow reflective jackets and were directing traffic with bored faces and aching arms. O'Reilly stood with a group waiting to cross the road. A middle-aged man in a morning suit saw a gap in the traffic and started to cross but a young constable in the middle of the road shouted at him to get back. "Bollocks," muttered the man in the morning suit. He looked to be twice as old as the constable, a roughly hewn face and shoulders that strained at his jacket.

The policeman motioned at the traffic to keep moving and walked over to the man. "Have you got a problem?" he asked, jutting his head forward, his cheeks reddening. He had a thin moustache and the manner of an adolescent with something to prove.

"I think I'm old enough to cross the road on my own," said the man with barely restrained anger. He looked like a man more than capable of looking after himself in a fight and O'Reilly knew he'd be able to handle the copper with one hand.

"That's not what I asked you. I want to know what you said." He was glaring at the man, his teeth clenched together and a vein was pulsing on the side of his forehead. O'Reilly wondered what his problem was because his reaction was out of all proportion to what the man had said.

"Nothing," said the man through tight lips. "I didn't say anything."

The policeman stared hard at the man for several seconds and then nodded slowly as if satisfied. "Good," he said, then walked back into the road and continued directing traffic. The racegoer got a few sympathetic glances from pedestrians around him and he shook his head, exasperated. The Great British Bobby, thought O'Reilly. An angry young man with authority he couldn't handle. It was something he'd grown up with in Ireland, where the Protestant police and the teenage British soldiers would exercise the power of their uniform just for the hell of it, just to feel good. He was used to being stopped on the street and given a hard time from RUC officers who didn't say "sir" and didn't bother to keep their contempt out of their voices, and even as a schoolboy he'd been thrown against walls and roughly searched by gum-chewing soldiers in camouflage jackets. The abuse of authority was nothing new to O'Reilly, and it was with no small feeling of satisfaction that he now saw it spilling over to Britain.

Eventually the policeman held up his hand to stop the traffic and allowed them to cross. He seemed to be glaring at them all, as if blaming them for having to stand in the road.

Despite the strong police presence – there seemed to be hundreds organising the flow of coaches and cars into the carparks around the racecourse – O'Reilly saw no sniffer dogs at the entrance. There were two policemen there but they seemed to be more concerned about eyeing up two pretty blondes in white, figure-hugging dresses and floppy hats. The girls were twins, barely in their twenties, tanned and draped in gold. One of the policemen smiled and touched his helmet in salute. The girls smiled and giggled, and one of them looked back over her shoulder as they walked towards the grandstand.

A steward in a bowler hat squinted at O'Reilly's badge and waved him through the gate and then another steward who looked about seventy years old asked if he'd mind opening up his case. The police stood watching the twins, their long, lithe legs moving with the grace of thoroughbred racehorses.

"Security, you understand," said the old man apologetically.

A couple of middle-aged women in tweed suits were looking into handbags but the checks were nothing more than a cursory glance. O'Reilly wondered what the hell they expected to find – a black ball with "BOMB" written on it and a burning fuse maybe. The steward in front of O'Reilly rubbed his moustache and smiled and O'Reilly smiled back and put the case on the grass and clicked it open. The old man peered inside.

"Nice equipment," he said approvingly. He looked up at O'Reilly with watery eyes. "I do a bit of photography myself."

"It's a great hobby," said O'Reilly. He took out one of the camera bodies and showed it to the old man. "I always use Nikon," he said. "What about you?"

The man looked pleased about being asked his opinion. "Canon," he said. He handed the Nikon back to O'Reilly. "Enjoy yourself today," he said.

"Got any tips?" asked O'Reilly. He stashed the camera body away, and as an afterthought took the other Nikon from around his neck and put that away, too. He grunted as he picked up the case and slung its strap over his shoulder.

"You could do worse than back Eddery in the third," said the steward. Pity, thought O'Reilly, who wasn't planning to be around for the third race. In fact if everything went the way Fisher had planned it, there wouldn't be a third race.

He bought a race card and walked for a while among the crowds, listening to the plummy voices and girlish giggles. The idle rich at play, he thought. Who else could afford to walk around in thousands of pounds' worth of high fashion and jewellery in the middle of the week? Champagne corks were popping everywhere, and everyone he looked at had the glint of gold on their wrist or around their neck. Some of the women were simply stunning, like the coltish blonde twins he'd seen at the gate, but in the main they were overdressed, overweight and wore too much make-up. They stood in groups, eyeing up the competition; reading the price tags on their outfits every bit as easily as they identified the brand names. They looked fearful, thought O'Reilly. Fearful of what they might lose.

He took his place in the grandstand and scanned the crowds through his binoculars. He spotted a couple of minor starlets who were wearing considerably more than they did in their movies, and several captains of industry who presumably had nothing better to do at the office. There was minor royalty around, too, but he couldn't see any of the heavyweights. He wondered what the chances would be of catching one with the blast but knew that the likelihood was remote. Not that it mattered, the fact that a bomb went off at an occasion attended by the Royal family would be more than enough to guarantee worldwide coverage. He checked out the positions of the television cameras, which were there to cover the crowds as much as the horses. They'd have no problems recording the explosion and its aftermath.

He studied the race card for a while, though he didn't plan on placing any bets. The steward had been right, though, Eddery did look a sure thing in the third race. O'Reilly looked at his watch. Half past one. The aluminium case was under his legs, silently counting off the seconds. Part of him wanted to go now, to get as far away as possible from the bomb before the alarm clock completed the circuit, but he knew that if he left it unattended for any length of time there was a risk that it might be discovered. Fisher had been quite specific about the timing, and, besides, McCormick wouldn't be outside until exactly five minutes before two. He re-read the race card and surveyed the crowds again, anything to keep his mind off the bomb. Once or twice he found himself eaves-dropping on the chatter going on around him but he stopped himself and blocked out the conversations. His neighbours in the stand would be at the centre of the explosion and he didn't want to know anything about them. He didn't want it to be personal.

The minute hand on his watch gradually crept around to ten to the hour and he stood up, stretched, and lifted his case on to the seat. He took off his hat and placed it on top of the case and then moved himself along the row to the aisle, apologising all the way and looking for all the world as if he was on a pre-race visit to the toilet or the Tote. He walked up the aisle, passed the bar and took an escalator down to the ground floor. He slowed down and ambled across the grass to the pre-arranged exit, some way along from where he'd come in so that he wouldn't be recognised by the stewards. The pavements outside were still thronged with racegoers waiting to get in and he pushed through, smiling apologetically.

The green and white Yamaha 750 purred up to the kerb. McCormick was wearing black leathers and had on a white helmet with a tinted visor. A second helmet was attached to the side of the bike and McCormick unclipped it and handed it to O'Reilly. He put it on and fastened the strap under his chin as he slipped on to the seat and found the foot rests. McCormick clicked the bike into gear and drove off towards London. The roads away from Ascot were clear but he stuck to the speed-limit because there were so many police around. Even so, they were still four miles away from the racecourse when the bomb exploded.

Woody was in the office early so that he could hit the phones before Simpson and the rest of the news desk staff arrived. He wasn't surprised that he couldn't get through to Sir John Brownlow himself because the *Sunday World* didn't usually get to the top of the lists of calls to be returned by Members of Parliament. Woody's luck was in, though, because he did get to speak to Sir John's assistant, a pleasant-sounding girl called Ellen. She remembered The Chinaman coming to see her boss, but like Woody couldn't remember his name. He told her that the family name was probably Nguyen and she went off to check the MP's correspondence files. A few minutes later she was back on the line.

"His name's Nguyen Ngoc Minh," she said. "I've got his letter here." She read out the address on the letter and Woody checked it against the address of the Double Happiness Take-Away. They matched. He asked Ellen to spell out Nguyen's full name and he wrote it down in his notebook and then he asked her to read the letter out to him. It was pretty much the same story that he'd told when he visited the *Sunday World*'s office, and there didn't appear to be any information in the letter that would help Woody track him down.

"Can you remember anything else about this Chinaman?" Woody asked. "Anything at all?"

"Well for a start, he isn't Chinese," said Ellen. "He was Vietnamese, that's what he told Sir John. I can't remember if he said he was from the north or the south, but I certainly got the impression he was a refugee. You know, one of the boat people. He has full British citizenship."

"Anything else?"

"I'm sorry, that's all I can remember," she said. "Wait a minute, I've just had a thought. Why don't you try the Home Office?"

"The Home Office?"

"Sure. If he was a refugee then they'd have to have a file on him. It wouldn't matter if he was Chinese or Vietnamese or whatever. There's a hell of a lot of paperwork to go through to get citizenship."

Woody thanked her gratefully and flicked through his contacts book. He'd met a Government Information Officer who worked in the Home Office some years earlier when he'd been chasing up a story on immigration and he'd taken her for a couple of boozy lunches afterwards to thank her. He couldn't recall her name but he'd filed her under "Home Office" in his book. Annie Byrne. She wasn't there when he called but he left a message and he passed the time reading the morning papers and drinking coffee until she called back.

"Woody, long time no hear," she said. She seemed genuinely pleased to hear from him and Woody tried to remember why he hadn't kept in touch with her. He explained that he was trying to get information on a refugee but skipped over the IRA connection. Was there any way that he could get to see the man's file?

"Certainly not officially, no," she said. But she suggested that Woody came round to her office at lunchtime anyway, which Woody took as a good sign.

While Woody was on the phone the news desk drifted in one by one and when he hung up Simpson waved him over.

"You're in early, Woody," he said. "Got much on?"

"A couple of things. I'll let you know when they harden up."

"OK, I've got something here that needs knocking out, something worthy of your talents."

Woody sensed a trap.

"Don't look so nervous, Woody. You're gonna love it. I want you to give me fifty places where you can take the kids over the summer holidays. You know, a guide for the little horrors that the parents can cut out and keep."

"Thanks, mate."

"Come on, Woody, cheer up. A shift is a shift, it's all money in the end."

"Yeah, yeah, yeah," said Woody, and slouched back to his desk.

He left the office just before noon and took the Tube to St James's Park. He'd assumed that Annie was just after a lunchtime drink and a chance to catch up on Fleet Street gossip so he was pleasantly surprised to be shown into her office. She was a short, bouncy girl and she shook him firmly by the hand. She spoke like a head girl and laughed a lot and Woody wondered how long it would be before she was snapped up by one of the Civil Service high-flyers and installed in a country house where she'd breed children and horses. She was a very attractive girl but Woody remembered why he'd never tried to see more of her. She was, he realised ruefully, totally out of his league.

There was a blue cardboard file on her desk and she tapped it with her left hand. An engagement ring glinted under the lights. It was a big diamond. The girl had done well. "Nguyen Ngoc Minh," she said. "I tell you, Woody, this is one damned interesting file. It's just a pity that I can't let you see it. Home Office regulations, you understand. It'd be more than my job's worth. And you know how much my job means to me." She grinned and then looked at her watch. "Golly, is that the time. Look, Woody, I've got a meeting to go to. Can you amuse yourself for a while? I'll be gone for about half an hour. OK?"

"OK. Do you want me to wait outside?"

Annie walked around her desk and patted him on the shoulder as she headed for the door. "No, Woody, you stay where you are. I'll be back."

She closed the door behind her and Woody leant over and picked up the file. It wasn't the first time a civil servant or a police officer had shared information by leaving an open file on a desk, and Woody was sure it wouldn't be the last. At some point in the future he knew Annie would call in the favour. Besides, she'd already read through the file to check that it contained nothing secret or damaging to the Government. He opened it and began leafing through a sheaf of forms and written reports with a growing sense of wonder.

There were reports from the United Nations High Commissioner for Refugees in Hong Kong and from the Hong Kong Government's Security Branch, documents from the US Consulate, photocopies of service records and signed statements from senior American army officers detailing Nguyen's time with the US forces. One of the sheets was a photocopy of the inside of a British passport with Nguyen's photograph and there were photocopies of two awards made to his unit in Vietnam. There was a Meritorious Unit Commendation and a Republic of Vietnam Gallantry Cross Unit Citation, along with a memo from a US colonel recording the fact that Nguyen's unit had the highest body count in Vietnam during the first half of 1973. By the time he'd finished reading the file he was shaking his head in amazement. The man was a bloody war hero, a trained assassin and an expert in jungle warfare.

He went back through the papers, filling his notebook with dates and copying down quotes from the reports. God, it was good stuff. Amazing. The story in the file was award-winning copy in itself. If Nguyen really was after the IRA, it would be dynamite.

It was a very thick file, sheet after sheet. Even in the early eighties, when Nguyen was in a refugee camp in Hong Kong, all incoming Vietnamese boat people were given a thorough grilling to check that they weren't Communist spies or simply criminals on the run. Nguyen Ngoc Minh's story was so complicated, and, Woody had to admit, so frankly unbelievable, that he was interviewed many times. Officials from the UNHCR and the Hong Kong Government's Security Branch had gone over his story again and again, cross-checking and cross-referencing in an attempt to catch him out, until eventually they believed him.

Woody flicked through the file, taking down details of Nguyen's switch to the South Vietnamese and his time with the Long Range Reconnaissance Patrols. The fact that Nguyen had been left behind by the Americans and his time in prison and the re-education camp were detailed in the matter-of-fact reports. Woody could only imagine the horrors the man had endured before he'd finally managed to escape. There were few details of the actual journey to Hong Kong, though it was clear that two of his daughters had died. Nguyen had refused to expand on what had happened and the psychiatrist reckoned that Nguyen was trying to block out painful memories.

Woody wrote quickly. By the time Annie returned to the office the file was back on her desk and Woody was sitting reading through his notes.

"Sorry about that," she said.

"No problem," he smiled.

"I hope you weren't too bored. Right, come on, you can buy me lunch."

Morrison and Kerry arrived at Belfast airport late in the afternoon. Willie O'Hara was there to meet them with the Range

Rover. Morrison got in the front passenger seat while Kerry climbed in the back. She noticed a large black stain on the seat and O'Hara explained that they'd used the car to take Jimmy McMahon to the hospital.

"How is he?" Morrison asked.

"On the mend, thank God. If the bomb had gone off a second later it would've taken his legs off. But it looks as if he's going to be OK. This focking Chinaman is bad news, I can tell you. He was at it again last night."

"He was?"

"Yeah, he set fire to one of the barns. And killed Hennessy's dog."

Kerry leant over the seat. "Jackie? He killed Jackie?"

O'Hara nodded. "Slit its throat."

Kerry slumped back into the seat, her hand over her mouth. To Morrison it seemed that she was more upset about the dead dog than about the man in hospital. They drove in silence down the M2 towards the city. When they passed the ferry terminal Kerry leant forward again. "I'm going to need some things. Can we drive into the city?"

"Yeah, good thinking," said Morrison. O'Hara turned off the motorway and guided the car through central Belfast. They had to pull to one side when a fire engine came up behind, lights flashing and siren blaring. In its wake followed two armoured RUC Land-Rovers. They parked the car and walked to a shopping centre, a pedestrian road sealed off with a metal fence at either end. To get in they had to pass through a turnstile and two surly RUC officers checked through Kerry's handbag and body-searched Morrison and O'Hara. Kerry had said she wanted to go to a sports shop, the sort that sold skiing equipment, and O'Hara took her to one that he knew of.

"I've got to be honest, Kerry, but you're not likely to see much in the way of snow in County Down at this time of the year," said Morrison as she examined a selection of ski-poles. She took one from the rack and held it, feeling its weight. She wasn't satisfied and replaced it with another, slightly longer, version.

"We'll need tracking sticks," she explained. "Walking

234

sticks will do but ski-poles are the best. You can use them for moving vegetation, and they stop you getting tired. Choose one for yourself, pick one that feels sturdy but not too heavy. This one's fine for me."

Morrison followed her advice while she went over to a display of American baseball caps. When he caught up with her she was looking at herself in the mirror, a blue cap on her head.

"Cute," he said.

"You'll need a hat to shade your eyes from the sun. It makes it easier to follow tracks in bright sunlight. You should get one."

"Whatever you say, Tonto."

By the time he'd found a cap that fitted she was looking at a black squash racket. "Don't tell me," he said, "you use it for filtering soil looking for clues."

She laughed and shook her head. She put the racket back on its stand. "Come on. That's all we need from here. Unless you want to stock up on ski masks for the boys."

Morrison paid for the purchases and followed her out of the shop. "Anything else?" he asked.

She nodded. "Elastic bands, a tape measure, couple of notebooks and pens. And torches."

"I won't ask," he said.

When they'd bought everything that Kerry wanted they went back to the car and continued their journey south.

Fisher and McCormick sat on the leather Chesterfield watching the television. O'Reilly was on the balcony, sunbathing. They each had a can of Guinness and McCormick was smoking. The news came on and the Ascot bombing was the first item. Eight people died, the newsreader said, and fifteen were injured, six of them seriously. McCormick whooped and O'Reilly came inside to watch. There were shots of the dead and injured being carried to ambulances and a shot taken from a helicopter giving a bird's eye view of the damage to the grandstand. Fisher and McCormick clunked their cans together and then both did the same with O'Reilly.

"Great crack," said Fisher. "Those pictures will go around the world."

A senior policeman with a suitably dour expression was being interviewed. The IRA had not claimed responsibility, he said, but there were similarities between this bombing and the previous attacks.

"Yeah," said O'Reilly. "When do we make the call?"

"You can do it now," said Fisher. "But this time don't give a codeword. Just tell them that it was an active service unit of the Provisional IRA, and tell them where and when the bomb was planted. You can also say how much explosive it contained."

"Ten pounds," said The Bombmaker, who was sitting at the dining-table, probing into the laptop computer with a voltmeter.

"Tell them ten pounds of Semtex," said Fisher. "And tell them there will be more bombings until the British Government withdraws its armed forces from Ulster. They'll believe you."

O'Reilly frowned. "Why aren't we using the codeword?"

Fisher waved his can of Guinness in the air. "Change of strategy," he said. "I had a phone call from Ireland while you were out. No codewords from now on."

"Did they say why?"

"Does it matter?" asked Fisher.

O'Reilly grinned. "Not really." He picked up the London street atlas. "Where shall I make the call from this time? How about Barking? I've never been to Barking."

Fisher shook his head. "There are times, O'Reilly, when I wonder if you're quite right in the head."

Hennessy heard the Range Rover crunching down the track and went to the front door to meet it. He was too late, the car had gone round the back to park in the courtyard so he went back through the house and out of the kitchen door. By the time he reached the car Kerry had already got out. She rushed up to him and hugged him.

"Uncle Liam," she said, holding him tightly.

"Kerry, thanks for coming." Over her shoulder he greeted Morrison. "Was your flight OK?" he asked Kerry.

She released him from the hug and stood back, still holding his shoulders. "Uncle Liam, I'm so sorry about Jackie. She was a lovely dog."

"She was that," agreed Hennessy. He'd buried Jackie himself in a patch of rough ground just beyond the vegetable garden. He helped Kerry in with her bag while Morrison carried his own and O'Hara held the ski-poles. Morrison saw the curious look that Hennessy gave the poles and he shrugged. "Don't ask," he said.

Hennessy took Kerry up and showed her the bedroom he'd prepared for her. She'd stayed there many times, especially when she was a teenager. It was a small, pretty room, with pink curtains and pine furniture. She put her case at the foot of the bed and looked out of the tiny window. "Is Auntie Mary here?" she asked.

"No, she's gone to visit Marie in London."

"That's a pity," she said.

"We thought it best. Why don't you freshen up and join Sean and me downstairs," said Hennessy. "I've put some clean towels in the bathroom for you. And you know where everything is."

He went downstairs. Morrison had put his bag in the lounge. "There's a bedroom upstairs ready for you, Sean," Hennessy told him. "Second on the left at the head of the stairs, when you're ready."

"Great, thanks, Liam."

"You know there's been another bombing?"

"Yeah, Willie said on the way in. Blew up your barn, he said."

Hennessy sat down. "No, I mean another bombing on the mainland. At Ascot. Today. Eight killed."

"Has Bromley phoned?" Morrison asked, dropping into an easy chair opposite Hennessy.

Hennessy shook his head. "Not yet."

"I wonder what he's playing at."

"He definitely said he'd go for it?"

"No question about it."

"Then we just have to wait."

"Yeah. I gather The Chinaman was in the house last night. Willie said he was in your room with a bomb."

"Unbelievable, isn't it. Got in and out of the house without anyone seeing him."

"So the fire in the barn was a diversion?"

"I think so, right enough. He said he wanted to talk."

"And?"

"And he's given me three days to find out who's behind the bombings. Then he's going to kill me." The dispassionate way Hennessy described the threat belied his true feelings. "Do you want a drink?"

Morrison shook his head. "No, Kerry says she wants to have a look around while the light is still good. I'd better keep a clear head."

Kerry appeared at the door and the two men got to their feet. She'd changed into jeans and a dark-blue sweatshirt. "You're starting already?" asked Hennessy. "Are you sure you don't want a bite to eat?"

"It's the light, Uncle Liam. The best times to see tracks are early in the morning and late in the afternoon. It's to do with the angle of the sun and the shadows it casts. We've only got an hour or so. Is there someone who can show me where they saw him?"

"Jim Kavanagh knows where the car bomb was triggered. And he can show you where one of our men was attacked."

"Right," she said, rubbing her hands together, "let's get started. Sean, where are the poles and stuff?"

"Willie put them in the kitchen."

"Come on then." She led the way to the kitchen leaving Hennessy and Morrison smiling at each other.

"Looks like she's taken charge," said Hennessy. "I think you might have to watch yourself there."

They walked into the kitchen to find Kerry putting the two poles on the table. She slipped off the discs from the end of each of the poles, the bits that stopped the poles from sinking too deep into the snow. "I forgot to get some binoculars, do you have some?" she asked Hennessy, and he produced a pair in an old leather case from the hall. She opened the case and slotted in a notebook and pencil and the tape measure. She took one of the torches and handed the other, and a notebook and pencil, to Morrison. "Right," she said. "Let's go."

Morrison found Kavanagh at the front of the house and he asked him to show them where The Chinaman had been when the bomb had destroyed the Jaguar. Of the Jaguar there was now no sign, Ryan had towed the wreckage away with one of the tractors and put it in one of the barns, away from the prying eyes of army patrols and low-flying helicopters. The crater had been filled in with soil but was still obvious, like a gaping wound.

"Your hat," said Kerry, holding it out to Morrison as they walked down the track. He took it and put it on.

"Cute," she said.

"That's not a word we normally use to describe Sean Morrison," said Kavanagh, grinning. "But yez right, he does look cute."

"Thanks guys," said Morrison dryly. "Can we just get on with the business at hand."

Kavanagh took them up to the filled-in crater and then led them through the grass. It was trampled down in many places and even to Morrison's untutored eyes it was obvious that a number of men had been there, presumably chasing The Chinaman. Morrison couldn't stop thinking of Nguyen as The Chinaman, even though he knew he was from Vietnam.

"We found a battery here," said Kavanagh, indicating a flattened-down area. "And it's where the wires ended. He lay here until he saw that the car was over the bomb, detonated it, and then ran that way." He pointed towards the hedgerow.

"Ran?" asked Kerry. "You saw him?"

"Well, crawled, I suppose. We didn't see him, not then, but we were too busy trying to get Jimmy out of the wreckage. We saw the wires and guessed that he'd gone that way."

"Where did you first see him?"

"I didn't. We saw some tracks leading to that copse," he

pointed again, "but we didn't know if he'd gone into the trees or run by and gone through the fields. We split up, I went that way, three of the men went into the woods. He attacked one of them and stole his gun, the other two saw him running away, then they lost him again."

"OK, show me which way he went."

Kavanagh led the way, following the trampled grass to the hedge and showing her where the gap was. She examined the broken twigs and the mud by the hedge's roots. "It looks like an army went this way," she said. "They've obliterated any tracks there might have been."

"Hey, we were chasing the bastard, not tracking him!" said Kavanagh angrily. "We'd just seen Jimmy get blown apart, we weren't too concerned about where we were putting our feet."

Morrison put his hand on Kavanagh's shoulder. "OK, Jim, cool down. She wasn't getting at you, she's just trying to help."

"I only meant that it's easier when there's one set of tracks, Jim," she said.

Kavanagh shrugged off Morrison's hand. "Yeah, OK, I'm sorry I snapped at yez. We're all under a lot of pressure, and we didn't get a lot of sleep last night."

"Forget it," said Morrison. "Show us which way he went."

Kavanagh took them through another field, towards the copse he'd pointed at earlier. "I went that way, but three of the men went in to check out the woods." He pushed through some waist-high bushes until they were standing on a pathway that wound through the trees. "The way they tell it, the three of them split up, and one of them, the one that got stabbed, went down the path."

Kerry knelt down and looked at the ground. It was criss-crossed with a multitude of footprints, but she said nothing.

"Where was he stabbed?" asked Morrison.

"In the leg," answered Kavanagh.

Morrison laughed sharply. "I meant where in the woods was he attacked."

"Oh right, I see what yez mean. This way." He took them along the path and showed them. The soil had been flattened and there was a rusty discoloration. Dried blood, Morrison realised.

"Right," said Kerry. "Can you two gentlemen please get the hell off the path?"

Morrison and Kavanagh stepped to one side while she scrutinised the tracks. She walked back down the path a few paces and then squatted down and squinted, moving her head from side to side as she scrutinised the footprints and the place where the man had lain on the ground. She switched on her torch and shone it along the path, altering its angle as she played the light over the soil.

"Any good?" asked Morrison.

She shook her head and stood up. "What happened then?" she asked Kavanagh.

He nodded down the path. "He went that way. One of the others saw him and fired a couple of shots but didn't hear anything. They chased him down the path until one of them got caught in a trap."

"A trap?"

"A hole in the ground with small stakes in it. Smeared with shit, believe it or not."

"How far?"

"A hundred yards or so. But be careful, there could be others. Yez wouldn't want to put yez foot in one of them."

She motioned for them to stay where they were and went down the trail, prodding carefully in front of her with the stick. She came upon the trap and crouched down beside it. There were still too many footprints to be able to tell which belonged to The Chinaman. She continued along the path but found nothing to help her. She did find another trap, though, and she cleared the soil away from it so that nobody would step in it.

She went back to Kavanagh and Morrison and began examining the vegetation either side of the path, using the ski-pole to move brambles aside. "He must have hidden somewhere to have caught your man by surprise," she murmured. "Somewhere where he couldn't be seen but from where he could reach the path quickly – and quietly."

"What are you looking for?" asked Morrison.

"Bruised stems, broken twigs, pebbles that have been moved. It's hard to say, I'll know it when I see it. Problem is, he was here two days ago which means a lot of the traces will have gone. We're lucky that it hasn't rained, but the wind obliterates a lot of stuff and any soil he kicked up will have dried out long ago."

She bent down and looked at the brambles. "Come on, Chinaman, where were you hiding? Where would you feel safe?" She was talking to herself and Morrison could only half hear. She turned round and began searching the opposite side of the path. There was a large spreading oak tree and she scrutinised the brambles at its base.

"Sean, come and look at this."

He stood next to her and looked down at the tangle of thorny strands.

"What am I looking at?" he asked.

She pointed with the end of her pole. "See that bit there, see how it's stuck under that thorn?"

"Yes," he said hesitantly, not sure what she was getting at.

"See how it's under tension," she continued. "It's slightly distorted, it's been pushed into that position and the prickles on that bit are holding it down."

"Which means what?"

She sighed and gave him a withering look. "It means, Sean, that something, or somebody, pushed it into that position. Watch." She used the ski-pole to push the bent strand and it sprang free and wavered in the air like the antenna of a huge insect. Kerry began pushing more of the brambles to the side. "Help me, Sean," she said.

Together they cleared a section of the undergrowth away from the earth. "There! See?" she said. There were two smudges in the soil. "He was walking on the balls of his feet." She held the torch down and shone the light at an angle to the impressions, the shadows highlighting the marks.

"Yes, I see it now. God, you're right. He must have been hiding behind the tree, and attacked our man from behind."

"Come on, we'll go round the tree in the opposite direction, see if there are any better footprints there."

She and Morrison pushed the brambles apart and followed

the curve of the tree around. She found the crack in the trunk and moved aside to show Morrison. In the soft earth were clear signs that The Chinaman had waited there, a number of footprints and a circular indentation which Kerry explained was probably made by his knee. She showed him places on the trunk where he had leaned against it and scraped away parts of the lichen on the bark. She pointed at the best example of a print with her pole. "Now we use our notebooks," she said, opening the binoculars case. She took out her notebook and pencil and with painstaking concentration made a drawing of the print, using the tape measure to ensure that it was an exact copy. She watched as Morrison did the same, correcting him over the shape of the heel of the boot and the pattern of the sole. "We do this so that we'll always know from now on if it's his footprint that we're looking at," she explained. "And when we've finished this we'll draw a print of him walking on the ball of his foot."

When they'd finished the drawings to Kerry's satisfaction, she took the two men along the edge of the path, following the prints of running men past the two exposed traps. After a hundred yards or so the trees thinned out and they were standing in a large field, lush, green grass peppered with daisies and dandelions.

"Question now is which way did he go when he left the woods?" she mused. She pulled the peak of her cap down and scanned the horizon. "Come on, Chinaman, which way would you go? You'd be pretty exposed crossing the field wouldn't you, even if you waited until it was dark. So you'd look for cover, wouldn't you?" She turned to Kavanagh. "Did your men go after him, across the field?"

"No, we reckoned he went to ground somewhere in the copse, but we couldn't find him. We didn't have enough men."

"And were there any animals in the field?"

Kavanagh scratched his head. "I don't think so."

Kerry dropped down low and scanned the field, moving her head slowly but keeping her eyes fixed ahead.

"What are you doing?" Morrison asked curiously. She kept turning her head left and right as she answered. "Changes in colour," she said. "Easier to spot when your eyes are moving. If he went through the grass he'd alter the way the blades lie. The underside of a blade of grass is a bit lighter than the part that faces the sun. You won't notice one or two but you can spot a trail through long grass. That's one of the ways we track deer. Trouble is the grass reorientates itself fairly quickly, just a few hours if it isn't too badly damaged. It depends how tall it is. This is quite long so it could take a while before it reverts to the way it was. Damn, I can't see anything. Come on, walk over here."

She took him a few paces to the left and tried again. She slapped her thigh in frustration. "Damn," she said. She stood up and arched her back, her hands on her hips. "The light's starting to go," she said. "Let me just check the edge of the wood and then we'll call it a day."

She began walking slowly along the perimeter of the copse with Kavanagh and Morrison following behind. She scrutinised the ground and the vegetation overhanging the grass. Several times she stopped and bent down to examine a fallen leaf or a twig, causing the two men to pull up short, but she found nothing to give an indication that The Chinaman had passed that way. Then, just as she was about to give up, she saw a large leaf that had been pressed into the ground. She picked it up and held it out to Morrison. "Yes!" she exclaimed. "See how it's bruised, how it's been crushed across the middle?" she said. "That's a sure sign that it's been trodden on." She turned it over. There were several grains of soil pressed into it. "See that? You can tell by the state the leaf's in that it happened within the last day or two. See how it's still fairly fresh?"

Morrison nodded. "But couldn't it have been an animal?"

"It would have had to have been a fairly large animal, I mean the bruising couldn't have been done by a rabbit or a fox. I reckon this is where The Chinaman came out of the wood. Now, did he go across the field, or did he walk along the edge to that hedgerow?" She scanned the field again with her strange fixed stare. "No, not that way," she murmured. She continued along the side of the copse, pushing straggling vegetation to the side with her pole.

"Got him!" she cried, and waved the two men to come and stand beside her. She grinned and pointed down. At some point in the past a tree stump had been poisoned to kill its roots and the earth for some distance around it was devoid of grass. There, in the soil, were two prints, a left foot and a right foot, less than a metre apart. She took her notebook out and compared the prints to her drawing. They matched.

She slipped two elastic bands on the ski-pole, twisting them around so that they gripped tightly, then held it above the two footprints, parallel to the ground and an inch or so above the soil. She put the tip of the pole above the back of the heel of the front print and slid one of the bands to mark the position of the tip of the toe of the rear print. Morrison watched her, enthralled. Kerry moved the pole so that it ran through the centre of the rear print and she slid the second elastic band down to mark the position corresponding to the rear of the heel, so marking the length of the stride. She stood up and showed her pole to Morrison. "Did you follow that?" she asked, and he nodded. "OK, you have a go then." She watched over his shoulder as he positioned two elastic bands on his own pole.

When he'd finished he got to his feet. "Do you want to tell me what we're doing?" he asked.

"Now we've got a record of the length of his stride, and the length of his footprint. And you can use the stick to get an idea of where the next footprint is when you're following a trail. I'll show you tomorrow."

"You didn't learn that following deer around the Highlands," said Morrison.

"I got it from a book," she said. "A guy called Jack Kearney wrote it. My dad has it in his collection."

"And where did he learn a trick like that?"

"He was a border guard in southern California. He spent more than twenty years hunting down Mexicans who tried to get into America illegally, and he used to help track down missing kids and the like. Come on, I just want to see which way he went when he got to the hedgerow. My bet is that he turned right and headed east." She was right. When she reached the hedge she followed it along and eventually discovered a footprint. "Look, let me show you how to use the stick," she said. She put the two elastic bands on either end of the print. It was a perfect fit. "You can see from the way the heel is slightly deeper than the sole that he was walking, rather than running. So if we put the toe marker on the front of the print, and swing the pole around in an arc, we know that the next print should be within the area it covers. There you are. See?"

Morrison looked and saw the rounded mark of a heel in the ground, not as clear as the first print but definitely there, nevertheless.

Further on the ground sloped sharply down. Kerry held up her hand to stop the two men and she spent a lot of time examining the slope.

"That's interesting," she said, indicating a bluebell that had been crushed against the grass.

"He went that way?" asked Morrison.

"Look at the way it's been trodden on," she said. She sat down on the grass next to it and Morrison joined her.

"I don't follow you," he said.

"The head of the bluebell is higher up the slope than the stalk. That means that whatever squashed it was moving up the slope, not down. If it was The Chinaman, he was coming this way, not going."

"You mean it would be the other way if he'd been going down the slope?"

"Think about it, Sean, picture a foot coming uphill. It'll push the stalk up. And a foot going down would push the stalk down."

"Was it definitely him?"

"Can't say for definite. The grass is too thick and springy, there are no marks in the soil. But if it is him, he's going back the same way he came, he's not just running away. He's returning somewhere." Kerry looked up at the darkening sky. "We might as well go back," she said. "We'll make an early start tomorrow." Morrison stood up and helped Kerry to her feet.

"Shouldn't we go on?" Kavanagh asked.

"We need a good light," she explained. "Otherwise we'll

miss something. We know which way he's headed now, we can pick his trail up at first light."

The three of them walked back to the farmhouse together. Hennessy was waiting for them in the kitchen. Sarah Ryan was there and she rushed over to hug Kerry and kiss her on both cheeks.

"Liam didn't tell me you were coming," she cried. Sarah was a couple of years younger than Kerry and when they were teenagers they had spent a lot of time together during the school holidays, riding and picnicking in the countryside around the farm.

'God, it's been so long," Kerry said.

"I've a few more wrinkles," laughed Sarah.

"Twenty-two years old and you talk about wrinkles, wait until you hit twenty-four!" They hugged each other again.

"Do you want some sandwiches and coffee?" Sarah asked, and Kerry and Morrison both said yes.

O'Hara came in from the hallway as Sarah busied herself with the food. "Any luck?" he asked.

"More than I would have thought possible," said Morrison, leaning his pole against the Welsh dresser next to Kerry's. He held out his notebook.

"Very good," said O'Hara. "By Sean Morrison, aged four."

"It's a drawing of his footprint, you prat," laughed Morrison. He handed it to Hennessy. "Kerry found the spot where he was hiding in the woods. And we think we know which way he went." He took off his baseball cap and dropped it on the table.

"Uncle Liam, do you have a map of the area? A large-scale one," asked Kerry.

"I think so," he said, and went through to the lounge. He returned with several maps including a large one rolled up in a cardboard tube. He popped it open and pulled it out and she helped him spread it over the kitchen table. Morrison used a cruet set to anchor it down at one side and Sarah gave them two knives to weigh down the other side.

Kerry sat down in front of the map while Morrison and Hennessy looked over her shoulder. She traced out the route they'd taken with her finger, down the track, across the field to the copse, around the edge of the trees and to the hedgerow. "We got as far as here," she said, tapping the map. "But the light was starting to go and I didn't want to make any mistakes. We'll start again first thing in the morning. The interesting thing was, Uncle Liam, there were signs that he was going back the way he'd come. As if he had a base somewhere, you know what I mean?"

"That's a thought," said Hennessy. "He must be staying somewhere. I suppose I just assumed that he was living rough."

"What about the van?" said Kavanagh. "He'd need somewhere to store the stuff he used to make his explosives. And the landlady in Belfast said he drove away in his van."

Kerry took one of the small-scale maps and spread it out on top of the first map. She drew a line on it in pencil. "This is the way he was heading," she said. The line cut across the B8 and B180 and through Dundrum Bay. "That's his general direction, so if we assume that wherever he was heading was twenty degrees or so either side of that line, we're left with this," she said, and drew two more lines either side of the original one, creating two wedge shapes.

"That's still a hell of a lot of countryside," said Kavanagh, unconvinced.

"Agreed, but he's not likely to be travelling too far, not at night. Let's say two hours, six miles maximum. That would put him in this area." She made a curving line that cut across the first three lines.

"That includes a good piece of the Mourne Mountains. And a fair smattering of villages," said Kavanagh.

"He's not likely to leave his van where it would be seen," said Morrison. "He's not stupid. He'll know that the army is all over the place and that they don't take kindly to strange vehicles."

"The van is the key," agreed Kerry. "Assuming he has the van, he must have driven it to where he hid it, which means it can't be too far away from a road. I don't think he'd hide it in the mountains, even if he could drive there. I think we should look for a wooded area with a road nearby. I reckon this is the best bet." She pointed at the Tollymore Forest Park.

Sarah put mugs of coffee on the table and mouthed "See you tomorrow" to Kerry before slipping out of the kitchen door. Kavanagh looked at the map and scratched his head.

"Yez making a lot of assumptions," he said. "The Chinaman could've doubled back, he could've ended up by going west, not east. He might've ditched the van. He could be holed up less than half a mile away, Christ, he could be back in the copse, he could even be watching the house right now."

"You're so bloody defeatist!" snapped Kerry, surprising them all. She realised her show of temper had shocked them so she smiled in an attempt to defuse the situation. "You're right, of course," she said. "But I don't think west is likely. One, because he headed in the opposite direction, and two, because going west would mean crossing the River Bann, either by bridge, where he'd risk being seen, or through the water, which would be perfectly possible but uncomfortable."

"And he did say that he'd be back in three days," said Hennessy.

"Three days?" said Kerry.

"He said I had three days to tell him who's behind the bombings in England," explained Hennessy. "He said that if I didn't have the names by then that he'd kill me."

"Oh God, Uncle Liam. That's terrible."

Hennessy shrugged. "It'll be OK, Kerry. Don't think about it. But the fact that he's given me the deadline means there's no need for him to stay close by. And I don't think he'll dump the van. How else is he going to get away when all this is over? I think you're right, Tollymore looks the best bet. Castlewellan Forest Park is another possibility, but that's a mile or so further away."

"I'm not sure what you're suggesting," Morrison said to Kerry. "I thought the idea was to track down The Chinaman."

She nodded quickly. "Yeah, yeah, but a two-pronged attack doubles our chances. You and I go after him, following his trail as best we can. But at the same time I think you should send some men to check out the forest and come at him from behind."

"But the forest is several square miles," O'Hara protested. "It would take for ever."

Kerry shook her head. "You're forgetting the van," she said. "If we're right and he's hidden the van among the trees, then he must have driven it off the road. All you'll have to do is drive along slowly looking for places where he could have turned off. You've got to think like your quarry, put yourself in his place. It might come to nothing, but it's worth a try. And what's the alternative?"

"She's right," said Hennessy. "Jim, can you take three of the guys tomorrow morning? Use two of the cars and take a run through the forest. No guns, just in case you come across the army. Just the shotguns, we've got licences for them."

"Sure, Liam. Whatever ye says." Kavanagh still sounded decidedly unconvinced.

Kerry sipped her coffee. "Right, that's all I can do tonight," she said. "I'm going to get an early night."

Hennessy raised his eyebrows. "It's only nine o'clock, Kerry."

"When I said we'll make an early start, I meant it," said Kerry. "We'll be up at five."

"Five!" snorted Morrison.

Kerry stood up and grinned at him. "Say goodnight, Sean," she said and leant over to kiss Hennessy on the forehead. "Goodnight, Uncle Liam."

Hennessy reached over and held her hand. "Goodnight, Kerry. And thanks. For everything."

"I haven't done anything yet," she said. "But it's going to be all right, I promise."

The four men watched her go.

"She's one hell of a girl," said Morrison.

"She's her father's daughter, all right," agreed Hennessy. "It must be in the genes."

"Oh yes," said Kavanagh, watching Kerry's hips swing. "It's definitely in her jeans."

"You, Jim, are a sexist pig."

"We all have our faults, Sean."

"If you two children are going to squabble all night I'll leave you to it," said Hennessy, getting up from the table and gathering the maps together. He left the three of them sitting together, drinking coffee and reminiscing about the old days.

Morrison woke to the smell of freshly made coffee. He screwed up his eyes and squinted at Kerry, who was sitting on the edge of his bed holding a steaming mug.

"Rise and shine," she said, and waited until he hauled himself up into a sitting position before handing him the mug. She pulled the curtains open but the sky was just a smudgy grey.

"What time is it?" he asked.

"Four thirty," she said.

Morrison groaned. He gulped down his coffee and gave her back the empty mug. "How come you look so wide awake?" he asked.

"I'm used to it. When we run the executive courses, Dad always gets me to do the night-time marches and stuff like that. It's great fun, we send them to bed at midnight and then wake them up at three in the morning and take them for a six-mile hike. They look like death when they get back."

Kerry looked nothing like death, just then, Morrison thought. Her blue eyes were bright and clear and she seemed to be bursting with energy, her chestnut hair was still damp from the shower and she'd even put on make-up, a little mascara and a touch of lipstick. He doubted that it was for The Chinaman's benefit and he felt suddenly pleased that she'd made the effort for him.

"What are you thinking?" she asked. "You've a wistful look about you, Sean Morrison."

"I was just thinking how dog-tired I am," he lied. "Right, get out of my room and let me wash. I'll be downstairs in five minutes."

"Do you want breakfast?" she asked.

The mere thought of food at that time of the morning made Morrison's stomach lurch and he declined, but said he wouldn't mind another coffee.

When he walked into the kitchen, drying his hair with a blue towel, it was waiting for him. Kavanagh was there, along with three men he'd decided to take with him to the woods: Roy O'Donnell, Tommy O'Donoghue and Michael O'Faolain, all of whom looked totally wrecked. Hennessy was there, too, sitting at the table with a collection of guns and walkie-talkies in front of him. As Morrison sipped his coffee, Hennessy handed him one of the guns, a small automatic. "Be careful," warned Hennessy. "Any sign of the army and dump it fast."

Morrison nodded, more interested in the two other guns on the table. They had short, wide barrels and looked as if they fired just one cartridge. He realised what they were just as Hennessy began to speak. Flare guns. Hennessy was a keen sailor and they were obviously guns for firing distress flares.

"I want you to take one of these, Sean, and let it off if you get close to The Chinaman and need help. You can call in with the radio, but that won't identify your position, so call us up and then fire the flare. I'll give you half a dozen cartridges."

"Do we take the other one?" asked Kavanagh.

"No, I've only got the two and I'll need one here to signal to Sean and Kerry."

"But we'll have the walkie-talkie," said Morrison.

"Yes, but only to call me, you won't be able to leave it on receive in case you get close to The Chinaman and he hears it. If I want to contact you I'll let off a flare and you can call me up on the radio when you're sure it's safe. You'll only use the walkie-talkie if I signal you with the flare or if you've dealt with The Chinaman."

"Dealt with?" said Kerry.

"Captured," said Hennessy. "Or whatever." He held out two of the walkie-talkies to Kavanagh. "You can use these, Jim, keep one in each car. If you catch The Chinaman you call me and I'll contact Kerry and Sean. Does that make sense?"

"It sounds hellish complicated," said Morrison.

"Uncle Liam's right though," said Kerry. "Out there in the countryside sound travels a long way, especially electronic noise."

"And don't forget the army monitors all radio frequencies so we'll have to keep all transmissions to a minimum anyway," added Hennessy. He gave a small canvas haversack to Morrison. "You can use this for the flare gun and the radio," he said.

Kerry picked up the ski-poles from beside the Welsh dresser and stood by the kitchen door.

"What about food, and water?" Morrison asked.

She patted a small rucksack slung over her shoulder. "Here," she said. "And the maps. And torches. And anything else we might need. Come on, Sean, time to saddle up and move out."

"Yes, Tonto," he laughed. He packed the walkie-talkie and the flare gun and slipped the automatic into the inside pocket of his bomber jacket. It was heavy and the jacket bulged.

"This might be more comfortable," said Kavanagh, and slid a clip-on holster across the table. Morrison slotted the gun in and then clipped the holster to the back of his jeans.

"Better?" asked Kavanagh.

"Much," said Morrison. "Good hunting, OK?"

Kavanagh made a gun with his hand and sighted down it at Morrison as he and Kerry went out of the door.

"You lads had better be careful, too," warned Hennessy. "We've got licences for those shotguns but don't go waving them around the Brits, for God's sake. The last thing we need right now is trouble with the army."

"Don't yez worry, Liam, we'll be just fine," said Kavanagh. "We'd better be off." Kavanagh took the three men out into the courtyard and shortly afterwards Hennessy heard the two Land-Rovers start up and drive off. Willie O'Hara, his hair tousled and his eyes bleary, staggered into the kitchen and slumped into a chair.

"What's all the noise, Liam?"

"The lads on the way out after The Chinaman. Do you want coffee?"

"A whiskey'd go down a treat, right enough."

"Aye, you're right. I'll join you."

As Hennessy poured the whiskey into two tumblers, Kerry and Morrison walked across the fields towards the copse. The grass was covered with a sheen of morning dew that glistened in the early light. This time there was no need to walk through the trees so Kerry took him around the perimeter of the copse and along the hedgerow. When they arrived at the slope where they'd examined the squashed bluebell the previous evening, Kerry slowed the pace right down and began walking slowly, her eyes scanning the ground left and right like a fighter pilot scrutinising the sky. Morrison followed behind her and slightly to her left.

"What exactly do I look for?" he asked.

"If we're lucky we'll see a clear sign, like the footprints we saw yesterday, or vegetation that's been trampled. But signs like that'll be few and far between. Generally all we can expect to see are slight changes, small things. It's hard to explain. Sometimes it's just a feeling that something isn't right."

"What sort of changes?"

Kerry prodded the ground with her pole and knelt down to inspect the grass. "Differences in texture or colour of the vegetation, any regular marks in the ground that aren't natural, flattening of leaves or dirt, twigs or stones that have been moved. Anything that he might have dropped. None of those things in themselves prove that he's gone this way but taken together they all add up to a trail." She turned round as she crouched and pointed back the way they'd come. "You can't move across a field without leaving some sort of trace," she said.

Morrison turned and looked. Two lines of footprints were clearly marked in the damp grass stretching back across the fields as far as he could see.

"The obvious signs will disappear as the sun evaporates the dew over the morning, but you see what I mean." She began walking again. "A lot of it is common sense, too," she said. "You've got to think like your quarry. If you come to an obstruction, like a hedge or a river, then you've got to be able to guess what he'll do, whether he'll go to the right or the left, whether he'll go through a group of trees or round them, what he'll do if he comes across a cottage or a farm. In some ways it's easier to follow a man than a deer. A man usually has a reason for going somewhere, unless he's lost, and if he's lost then he's pretty keen to be found. A deer is trying to avoid humans and most of the time it's probably just grazing."

"You've hunted humans before?"

Kerry laughed. "Not with a gun, no. Even the Germans draw the line at deer, but it's a thought, isn't it? We could even arrange for the ears to be mounted."

"Yeah, OK, hunted was the wrong word. Tracked, then."

"From time to time a tourist will get lost in the mountains and the mountain rescue team will call up my dad and ask him for help. I've been with him a couple of times. But like I said, it's one thing to track someone who's hoping to be found, it's quite another to trail a man who wants to hide. And The Chinaman is certainly going to be hiding. At least the weather's going to be good. I suppose you know how the Blackfoot Indians forecast the weather?"

"What?"

"Weather forecasting, Indian-style. Here, I'll show you." She bent down and picked up a small stone and twisted a piece of grass around it so that it was hanging like a conker on a string.

"That's it?" asked Morrison, intrigued.

"That's it," she said. "You hold it in front of you like this, and you watch it. Here, you hold it."

She handed it to him and Morrison studied the stone. "Now what?" he asked.

"Well, first you touch it. If it feels dry, the weather is fine. If it feels warm, it's a hot day. If it turns white, it's snowing. And if it's wet, it's raining. Then you look at it. If it's swinging from side to side, it's windy."

Morrison laughed, realising he'd been taken for a ride.

"And, Sean . . ."

"Yes," he said warily.

"If you can't see it, it's probably foggy." They both dissolved into laughter.

* * *

The telephone rang in the hallway. "I'll get it," said O'Hara, who was sitting closer to the door than Hennessy. He picked up the receiver and then put his hand over the mouthpiece. "It's for you," he called. "Won't give his name."

Hennessy pushed himself up from the table and took the phone from O'Hara. "Liam Hennessy," he said.

"It's Bromley," said a gruff voice. Hennessy reached behind him and closed the door on O'Hara, not wanting him to hear.

"They called?" Hennessy asked.

"They called, but they didn't give a codeword. What's going on, Hennessy?"

Hennessy was confused and he put his hand to his head. "Look, Bromley, if they didn't give the codeword, maybe it wasn't them."

"It was them all right. The Press Association took the call last night. It was a man, Irish accent, and he said there would be no further co-operation with the British security forces and no more use of the codeword system."

"So how do you know the call was kosher?"

"He knew exactly where the bomb had been placed and how much explosive was in it. And with all the other bombs they claimed responsibility within twenty-four hours. We had the normal hoax calls but that was the only one that had enough details to convince us that it was genuine."

Hennessy closed his eyes. This wasn't what he had expected at all.

"Somebody talked," said Bromley.

"That's not possible," insisted Hennessy. "Only two people knew what was happening. Me and the man you met in London, Sean Morrison."

"Well, one of you isn't to be trusted. And only you know which one it is."

"I brought Morrison back from the United States especially for this. He'd been away for two years, so there's no way at all that he could be involved with the active service unit."

"Maybe you talk in your sleep," said Bromley.

"I'll treat that remark with the contempt it deserves,"

replied Hennessy, but something cold ran down his spine and settled in the pit of his stomach.

"So what do you think went wrong? Do you think it was just coincidence, that they decided on a whim not to use the codeword so soon after you changed it?"

"No, of course not. We've changed it twice before this year and each time they've picked it up immediately. No, you're right, they've been warned off. But for the life of me I can't think who it might be. Look, give me a number where I can reach you. I've got some thinking to do."

Bromley read out a number and Hennessy wrote it down. "I can get you there day or night?" he asked.

"If I'm not there, they'll be able to get hold of me."

"I'll call you as soon as I find out what's happening."

"For your sake I hope it's not too late," said Bromley.

"What do you mean?"

He heard Bromley click his tongue as if thinking, and when he spoke again his voice was hesitant. "The climate is changing here, Hennessy. These bombings have been so vicious that public opinion is turning against the IRA in a way that I've never seen before. We're not just talking about right-wing MPs calling for the death penalty or sending in the SAS, this is different. Part of it is the lack of warnings, but a lot has got to do with the choice of targets. When the IRA killed MPs like Airey Neave and Ian Gow you might have been able to justify them as political killings, and the Stock Exchange and the Carlton Club could just about be described as establishment targets, but these latest atrocities, I mean, Bank Tube station, for God's sake. And Ascot. I'll tell you, Hennessy, if much more of this goes on you could find the rules changing."

"What do you mean, rules changing?"

"I mean that, despite what you might think, in the past the IRA has had a relatively easy ride from the British Government."

Hennessy snorted. "Bullshit. The Catholics in Northern Ireland have been ridden rough-shod over in a . . ."

"We're not talking about Catholics, we're talking about the IRA. And all I'm saying is that you and your friends in Dublin, if you're serious about not being involved in these bombings, are going to have to pull your fingers out, or you'll feel a backlash the likes of which you've never known before."

"I hear what you're saying, Bromley. And I've got your number." The line went dead. Hennessy went back into the kitchen, where O'Hara was sitting at the table spooning cornflakes into his mouth.

"Trouble?" he asked, seeing the worried look on Hennessy's face.

"It's OK, Willie. Nothing I can't handle." Oh really? said a voice in his head that sounded disturbingly like Mary's.

Christy Murphy arrived at the farm just before ten o'clock. Hennessy was making coffee when one of the guards knocked on the kitchen door and announced that somebody was driving down the track towards the farm. A few seconds later a car crunched into the courtyard and Murphy let himself into the kitchen.

"Christy, just in time for coffee," said Hennessy, waving the large man to a chair. "Come on, sit down. How's my wife?"

Murphy stood where he was, clenching and unclenching his hands like a prize-fighter about to get into the ring. His big, square face was creased into a frown and for a moment Hennessy feared that something had happened to Mary.

"Mary's all right, isn't she, Christy?"

"She's fine, Liam, but . . ." His voice tailed off.

Hennessy pushed his plate away. "What's wrong, Christy? Cat got your tongue?"

Murphy seemed to be struggling for his words, and although he was normally a quiet man this was something different. He was acting like a small boy who wanted to confess to breaking a window but who was worried about being punished.

"Can I speak to you, Liam. In private?" he said.

"Of course, of course. Come through to the lounge." Hennessy got to his feet and took the big man through the hallway.

As the morning sun climbed higher and higher in the sky, Kerry found it progressively harder to follow The Chinaman's trail. Morrison didn't have to ask why, she'd already explained about the importance the angle of the sun played in defining footprints. Eventually, after it had taken her the best part of an hour to cover a hundred yards, she called a halt.

"I think we should rest for a while," she said. She indicated a leafy birch tree in the middle of a hedgerow. "Let's sit in the shade," she said. They dropped down into the cool grass and she opened her rucksack. She took out a pack of sandwiches and two cans of ginger beer. "I knew we'd be out here for some time," she said.

"How long do you think it'll take?" he asked, helping himself to a sandwich.

"The trail is cold," she admitted. "He's still heading for the forest, by the look of it, and if he is we've a better chance of finding him among the trees. It's harder to move through woods without leaving signs."

"Can't we just go straight there?"

Kerry shrugged. "We could, but we'd be taking a risk. There's still a chance he might turn north or south before we get there, and even if he doesn't we won't know for sure where he went into the trees. You can't take shortcuts, Sean. If we make a wrong call, we might have to spend hours backtracking." She popped open the can of ginger beer.

"You know best," he said. He held up his sandwich. "These are good," he said. "You make them?"

"Yeah, I had plenty of time while you were still in the land of Nod."

They ate together in silence, enjoying the feel of the fresh summer breeze on their faces.

"You live in New York now?" Kerry asked, brushing crumbs from her trousers.

Morrison nodded. "Yeah, raising funds, flying the flag, telling the Yanks where their money is going."

"Don't you miss it?"

"Miss what?"

"The crack. The kick from being in Belfast, where it's all happening." She frowned. "You know what I mean, surely. The fight is in Northern Ireland, not in the States, and certainly not in Scotland." The look of intensity was back in her eyes.

"There are different ways of helping the Cause," he said quietly, aware once again how quickly her temper could flare, how she'd snapped at Kavanagh in the farmhouse.

"Like my dad, you mean. Hiding in Scotland. And keeping me with him."

"Hey, come on now, Kerry. Your father has heard the rattle of soil on too many coffin lids to deserve that. No one has done more for the IRA than Micky Geraghty, you shouldn't forget that."

She shook her head. "I know, that's not what I meant. It's not so much that he's out of it now, it's more that he won't let me get involved. He's so fucking protective."

Morrison looked at her and immediately felt protective towards her himself. Her cheeks were flushing, her chin was up and her eyes flashed fire. She looked as if she was ready to fight the whole world. She was keen, there was no doubt about that, but he also knew that Long Kesh was full of men who had failed to temper enthusiasm with wisdom. "You should be glad you're out of it," he said quietly.

"I'll never be glad until the British are out of Ireland. It's our country, Sean, our country and our religion. You know what I mean, I know you do. You feel the same as I do when you see the black bastards swaggering through the streets in their bowler hats and sashes, their flutes and drums, ramming their religion down our throats. Did it never happen to you, Sean? Being grabbed by the bastard Billy boys and being forced to say 'Fuck The Pope' and 'All Catholics Are Shit'. Tell me that never happened to you. Tell me that your bile doesn't rise when you see an Orange parade."

Morrison said nothing, because he knew she was right.

"I want this Chinaman," she said. "I want to show Uncle Liam what I can do. If I can prove myself just this once, he'll let me do more for the Cause, and it won't matter what my dad thinks."

In the distance to the west a white star climbed into the sky leaving a greyish-blue trail zig-zagging behind it. The star popped with the sound of a bursting balloon.

"That's Uncle Liam!" she said.

Morrison took the walkie-talkie out of the haversack and switched it on. "Are you there?" he said. No names were to be used because the army constantly swept the airwaves.

"I want you back here," said Hennessy's voice. "Now."

"OK, we're on our way. Have you found him?"

"No, I just want you back."

"Understood." He switched off the receiver.

Kerry had heard and she sat forward. "I wonder what's happened?"

"No idea," said Morrison.

"Look, Sean, I think I should stay out here. Uncle Liam said they haven't found The Chinaman yet. And you can see how slowly it's going. I want to keep at it, you can come back here once you've sorted out what he wants."

"How will I know where you are?" he said. "You're the tracker, not me."

"I'm not going to be moving that fast." She picked up a long twig from the hedgerow. "I'll leave sticks like this sticking up every hundred yards or so, and I'll drag the pole through any patches of soil I pass. You'll have no problems finding me again. And I'm not likely to stumble across him, am I? This trail is dead cold. It'll save time."

"I'll have to check with him," said Sean, and switched the receiver back on. "Are you there?"

There was a delay before he heard Hennessy reply. "I'm here."

"I'll come back alone."

"Is that wise?"

"It'll save time later and we are quite sure there's no danger out here. Unless there's a problem."

Hennessy was quiet for a while as he considered Morrison's suggestion. "Be careful," he said eventually.

"Yeah!" said Kerry.

"Any doubt at all and you both come in," Hennessy said to Morrison.

"Understood," he replied, and switched off the receiver again.

"Like he says, be careful," Morrison said. He opened the haversack and took out the flare gun and the cartridges. He handed them, and the walkie-talkie, to her. "You'd better take these," he said.

"What about the gun?" she asked.

Morrison shook his head emphatically. "No, no gun," he said. "Liam was quite clear on that score. And if you think you're getting close and there's any chance of you finding him, then pull back and call me on that." He nodded at the walkie-talkie. "I'll be back once I've found out what it is that he wants."

"It must be important otherwise he'd have told you on the radio what it was," she said.

Morrison thought about that as he jogged back to the farm-house. Though they had been out for more than five hours they had covered just three miles and it only took him forty minutes to get back.

He was in good condition and he'd barely worked up a sweat by the time he walked into the courtyard to find O'Hara there with two men carrying shotguns. The guns were broken, the barrels pointing down to the ground, but Morrison could see the brass ends of cartridges in place.

"Liam's in the lounge," said O'Hara.

"Everything OK?" asked Morrison, hoping for some clue as to what was going on.

"Fucked if I know," said O'Hara. The two men with shot-guns said goodbye to O'Hara and walked across the courtyard towards the cottage. Morrison felt himself sigh with relief. For a wild moment he had thought that they had been waiting for him. An armed escort.

He wiped his feet carefully on the mat by the kitchen door and walked through to the lounge. The door was half open and he walked in to find Hennessy sitting in one of the arm-chairs by the unlit fire. He didn't get up as Morrison entered. "Sit down, Sean," he said. He seemed distant, almost shocked, and the one thought in Morrison's mind was that there had been another bombing. As he went over to the sofa he realised there was somebody else in the room, standing by the door. It was Christy Murphy.

"Christy!" he said, surprised. "When did you get back?"

Murphy looked away from Morrison and seemed ill at ease.

"Christy, you can wait outside," said Hennessy, and Murphy practically ran out of the door so keen was he to get out of Morrison's presence. Hennessy studied Morrison with unsmiling eyes as Murphy closed the door and Morrison began to worry, but the fear was a shapeless, nameless thing, made all the more terrifying by his inability to identify it. He wanted to speak, to ask what was wrong, but felt that to do so would be to imply guilt and that his interests would be best served by keeping quiet. He could feel sweat on the palms of his hands but he resisted the urge to wipe them on his trousers. Liam Hennessy might look like a kindly grandfather but he had the power of life and death and would have no compunction at all about killing somebody who he thought had crossed him. Thoughts of Mary Hennessy flashed into his mind and he felt his cheeks redden.

"The bombers have claimed responsibility for the Ascot bomb," Hennessy said flatly.

Morrison frowned, because that surely was good news, and yet Hennessy said it as if he was announcing the death of a close relative. "And?" he said.

"And they didn't use the codeword. In fact, they said they weren't going to co-operate with the authorities any more and that there would be no more use of the codeword system."

Hennessy looked at Morrison with cold, unblinking eyes and Morrison fought to keep his own steady on the older man's face, trying to stay cool. Eventually he weakened and looked out of the window. The two men with the shotguns were back. He looked at Hennessy again.

"Which means that somebody tipped them off," said Hennessy. He continued to stare straight at Morrison and again

Morrison was forced to avert his gaze. "The problem is, only two people knew about the reason for the change in the code-word. You. And me."

Morrison held up his hands. "I don't know what you're thinking, but I didn't tell anyone, Liam. I knew how important this was. I spoke to Bromley, and that was all. I swear, on my mother's eyes, I swear it."

Hennessy steepled his fingers underneath his chin and studied Morrison as if he was an undecided juror.

"You must have said something to somebody, Sean. Think very carefully."

The two men sat in a silence which was disturbed only by the ticking of a grandfather clock in the corner. Morrison was genuinely bewildered, because he knew that he hadn't broken Hennessy's confidence. He was sure of it. And yet Hennessy seemed so convinced.

Morrison shook his head, not knowing what Hennessy expected to hear.

"Would it help if I told you that I had Christy follow Mary in London?"

Morrison felt as if he'd been kicked in the stomach. He would have been able to face it better if Hennessy had shouted or banged his fist or thrown something at him, but he did none of those things, he simply sat in his easy chair and waited for a reply. It was his quiet acceptance of the facts, an acceptance that bordered on apparent indifference, that made the man seem all the more menacing. Morrison wondered if he was about to die, shot in the back of the head because he'd slept with another man's wife. He thought of lying, of claiming that she had just popped round to the hotel as a casual visitor, but he knew that it wouldn't work. Murphy wasn't stupid, he'd have found out that she'd gone to his room and would have known how long she was in there.

"Liam, I'm sorry . . ." he began to say, but Hennessy held up a hand to silence him.

"I don't want apologies, I don't even want to know what happened in your room. We'll leave that for some other time. All I want to do right now is to establish what went wrong, how they found out what we were up to. I know Mary was in 'your room on Monday morning, what I don't know is what you said to her. What you talked about."

"You don't suspect Mary, surely?" said Morrison.

"At the moment I don't know who to trust, you've quite clearly demonstrated that I'm no judge of character," said Hennessy savagely. "Now don't fuck with me, Sean. Did you or did you not discuss our plan with Mary?"

"No," said Morrison immediately. "I mean yes, sort of. She already knew what you were doing."

"She did not," said Hennessy emphatically. "I told no one. And I mean no one."

"But I'm sure..." He lapsed into silence, trying to remember exactly what she'd said as she lay in his arms in the afterglow of their love-making. "She seemed to know already."

"Think carefully about what she said. We spoke on the phone, remember? Could she hear what we were saying?"

It all came back to Morrison with a rush, him lying on his back talking to Hennessy on the phone as Mary made love to him. "Yes, she could hear us," he said. His voice sounded a million miles away. He wondered if Hennessy could see into his mind, if he knew exactly how he'd been betrayed. "And you're right, it was afterwards that she mentioned the codeword."

"She steered the conversation?"

Morrison nodded. "She made it sound as if you'd already told her what was going on. Most of the time I was just agreeing with what she said."

"She is good at manipulating people," said Hennessy, his voice loaded with sadness. Morrison suddenly felt sorry for the man. And guilty. And afraid.

"You think that Mary told the bombers?" asked Morrison. The possibility seemed so remote it was almost laughable.

"Not directly, no. But I think she found out from you what we were planning, and I think that she passed that information on to someone else."

"Who?"

Hennessy fell silent again. He leant forward in his chair, his elbows on his knees. He took a handkerchief from his top pocket and wiped his brow. "Do I trust you, Sean? After the way you've betrayed me, can I trust you?"

"My loyalty to the Cause has never been in question, Liam. The thing with Mary, that's different. I never meant to hurt you, I didn't plan for you to know. We were always very careful."

"You lied to me, you went behind my back. And now I'm supposed to trust you?"

"Liam, I'm sorry. If it makes a difference, it was one of the reasons I went to the States. To put distance between Mary and me. To stop it."

"You mean she wanted to continue the affair?" Hennessy sounded wounded, hurt.

Morrison realised he was making it worse by talking about it. Maybe Hennessy hadn't even considered that the affair had been going on before he went to New York. "We decided it was best," he lied. "Liam, whatever happened is in the past, what matters now is to get these bastards and to put an end to the bombings. To do what we set out to do. We can deal with our personal problems afterwards."

Hennessy nodded and settled back in the chair. "Maybe you're right, Sean. All right, we'll put that to one side. For the moment we'll concentrate on minimising the damage, maybe even turning it to our advantage."

"What do you mean?"

"I had a visitor before you and Kerry arrived. Hugh McGrath. He knew Mary was in London, but there was no way he could have known that."

"Unless she told him?"

"Unless she told him," agreed Hennessy. "She spoke to you, she tricked the information out of you, and then she called him." Hennessy let it sink in, and then twisted the knife. "She used you, Sean." There was bitterness in his voice, a nasty edge which cut through Morrison. He wondered then whether Hennessy really was prepared to put the affair behind them while they sorted out the bombing business. But he knew that Hennessy was right. Mary had bedded him and used him, barely waiting for him to leave before ringing McGrath. Another thought wormed its way into his mind. Maybe she was also McGrath's lover. Maybe she did to McGrath the same things she did to him, gave him her kisses, her passion, her energy, the things he thought she saved solely for him. He thought of her sitting astride McGrath, his hands on her breasts, her riding him until she came, and he felt the anger burn inside and realised for the first time exactly how bitter and betrayed Hennessy must have felt.

"I know she was angry, but I never thought she'd go that far," said Hennessy, almost as if he was talking to himself, or unburdening himself at confession. Morrison couldn't think of anything to say, knowing how easy it would be to provoke the man. "Mary never forgave me for not going after the men who killed her brother."

"They're all in Long Kesh, aren't they?"

"You know as well as I do that we could get to them, wherever they are, H-blocks or no H-blocks. She knew that, too. She never let me forget it. We've been arguing for months. Years."

"Arguing?"

"Mary's always been one hundred per cent behind the Organisation, much more than most people realise. We used to have the most fierce arguments, she couldn't understand why I was trying to take a more conciliatory line with the Protestants. She was always pushing me to gear up the campaigns, to turn the screw, to drive the British out. And that was before Gerry was killed. His death pushed her over the edge, I guess. I should have realised, I should have talked to her more. But by then I suppose we'd stopped talking. Really talking, you know what I mean?"

Morrison nodded, but he was fearful of being forced into the role of confessor. Hennessy was a man who guarded his secrets jealously.

"McGrath was always a possibility, anyway," continued Hennessy. "He makes more money out of the border than anyone else in the organisation, and he has strong links with Gaddafi. It'd also explain why we haven't been able to pin down the active service unit's bombmaker. It could be a complete outsider, someone that McGrath sent to Libya for training without telling us."

"Is that possible?" said Morrison, eager to turn the conversation away from Mary.

"Perfectly. We've always given him a lot of leeway when it came to dealing with the Libyans."

"But why would he have to take explosives and equipment from our stocks? Couldn't he just bring in his own supplies?"

"Some, maybe, but not on any large scale. He'd have to use our established routes to get it into the country and he couldn't do that without us knowing. And he'd know that if he was discovered organising secret deliveries that we'd know what he was up to. He wouldn't want to take the risk. Much safer to take what he needed from existing caches."

"OK, so assuming it is McGrath, what next?"

"He has to tell us where the bombers are," said Hennessy. "We get him here and we get the names from him."

"He's a powerful man, Liam. He carries almost as much influence with Dublin as you do, and he's virtually got his own private army on his farm. We can't just wade in and expect him to open up to us."

"I know, I know. I'm going to speak to Dublin now. And McGrath is going to come to us. I want you to call him and tell him that I've called an emergency meeting of our top officials here at the farm. Tell him it's about a change in our bombing strategy, that should bring him running. Tell him the boys are coming down from Belfast and the meeting is for noon."

"Sure," agreed Morrison. He felt somewhat easier now that Hennessy was concentrating on McGrath but he knew that underneath his neutral exterior the man must be in turmoil. Liam Hennessy was well used to concealing his emotions in the courtroom, and his big advantage had always been that his opponents never knew what he was thinking. He was a difficult man to read, but, no matter how calm he looked, the business over Mary would be gnawing at his insides and at some point it would emerge into the open. Morrison would have to be careful, very careful. One of the men with shotguns was looking into the window and he caught Morrison's eye. The man winked. Morrison didn't feel any better.

Fisher stood on the balcony with half a loaf of stale bread on the table next to him. He picked up a slice and tore it into small pieces and tossed them out into the air. A flock of unruly seagulls sitting on a barge across the river came squawking over and swooped and soared around him. He picked up another slice and ripped it into small bits and threw them one at a time high into the air so that the birds could catch them on the wing.

"You know what I'd like?" said McCormick behind him.

"What's that?" Two of the black-headed gulls collided in mid-air with the sound of a quilt being thumped.

"A twelve-bore shotgun," said McCormick. "Then we could have some real fun."

"You, McCormick, have no beauty in your soul." Fisher tossed out a handful of bread and birds swooped from all directions, beaks wide and wings flapping. When all the bread had been devoured, he went back into the flat.

"It's done," said The Bombmaker.

Fisher sat down and looked at the laptop computer. "It looks so inoffensive, doesn't it?" he said, running his hand along the smooth plastic. "And it works just as it did before?"

"Sure. There's no way of discovering that it's been modified unless it's taken apart. And they won't do that."

"Excellent," said Fisher.

"I've even fixed it so that the time is set by using the keyboard. It's a trick the Libyans taught me, a relatively simple program incorporated into the disk operating system. Once we know when we want it to explode, I call up the program and input the time. The computer does the rest."

Fisher grinned. "I'm impressed," he said. "And it'll get through the X-ray machines?"

"Even the new models. The only drawback is that there's

no room for a barometric device. We can't use altitude to detonate it, so we have to be sure of the timing."

Fisher nodded. "I don't see that being a problem, so long as we stick to a scheduled flight. What about the mule?"

"I've narrowed it down to two. A journalist and a cameraman who works for Thames TV. What about you?"

"There's a girl, an investment banker, who says she'll be going to Paris next week. She always flies British Airways, she says. I think we take the first one to confirm a flight, agreed?"

"Fine by me," said The Bombmaker.

Woody worked flat out to finish the school-holidays feature because he hadn't been told yet whether or not he was working the Saturday shift and the news desk weren't at all happy about his three-hour lunch with Annie. He was determined to keep in their good books, at least until they'd drawn up the weekend rota, but he was suffering. He was all too well aware that he hadn't become a journalist twenty years earlier to end up writing crap like that, but, as usual, he needed the money. He'd cashed two cheques at separate pubs and promised that he'd have enough money in his account to cover them by the end of the following week. He'd been fighting to keep his head above water financially for the last two years but he was getting nowhere. He needed a staff job, but Woody was a realist, his age and his track record were against him. What he needed was a big one, an exclusive story that he could sell for big money and which would restore his tarnished reputation. Yeah, he thought, dream on. Number forty-eight. Take them to the zoo. And feed them to the lions, he typed, and then just as quickly deleted it. It'd be just his luck for something like that to get into the paper.

He finished the feature and as he sent it into the news desk queue the phone on his desk rang. It was Pat Quigley, calling from Belfast.

"Hiya, Woody. I wasn't sure if I'd catch you in, this early

in the week, but I remember you didn't like being bothered at home."

Woody leant back in his swivel chair and put his feet on the desk. "No need for sarcasm, mate. You caught me at a bad time. Anyway, how's it going?"

"Not so bad, Woody. I'm calling about the Hennessy thing."

"Yeah?" said Woody, suddenly interested but trying to conceal it.

"His driver's in hospital. Somebody bombed his car. I'm told by a really good source that it happened on his farm. I started making a few enquiries and it seems that two more of his men are in hospital here in Belfast. One's been stabbed, the other has some sort of strange wounds in his foot. It's bloody curious, Woody, especially after the attack on Hennessy's office. Do you have any idea what's going on?"

"Sounds bloody mysterious to me, Pat. Are you sure it's not the Protestants?"

"Doubtful. There hasn't been much aggro between the guys at the top, not for a while. I suppose it could be starting up again, but it doesn't feel right. There haven't been any other attacks, either on the IRA or the UDA. It looks like a one-off."

"I don't know what to say, Pat. I don't see how I can help."

"You said you'd have a look for the name of the reader who was asking about Hennessy."

"He wasn't asking about Hennessy. He just wanted to write to a few Sinn Fein officials. I really don't think he's your man."

"OK, fine, but can you at least dig out his name for me?"

"I tried, but I can't find it in any of my notebooks. I did look, Pat, honest. It's just one of those things, you know?"

"OK, Woody. Fair enough. I thought I'd check." Woody could tell he wasn't convinced, but there was nothing he could do. Like Woody he was a freelance and dependent upon the paper's goodwill, he couldn't afford to offend anyone, even another freelance, especially a freelance who was doing regular shifts at head office. Quigley rang off.

When Woody went over to the news desk, Simpson was

leaning back in his chair, his immaculate shoes on the desk.

"Good piece, Woody, a classic!" he shouted, giving Woody the thumbs up.

Woody gave him a mock bow from the waist and pulled his forelock before approaching the desk. "About that story idea I had," Woody said.

"Pull up a pew," said Simpson and kicked over a chair.

Woody sat down. "Remember that guy who came to the office trying to offer a reward over the Knightsbridge bombing?"

Simpson screwed up his face like a baby about to cry. "The Chinaman?" he said.

"Yeah, The Chinaman. Only I've found out he's Vietnamese, not Chinese. His wife and daughter were killed in the bombing and he wanted to get the men responsible."

"Thousands of pounds in a carrier bag, right?"

"Right. He rang back a while later, said he wanted to talk to the IRA direct. He wanted names of people high up in the organisation."

"And you gave them to him?"

"Right. Not the IRA, because you know what they'd do to him, but I gave him a few names of the top Sinn Fein people. Now someone is running some sort of vendetta against one of the men, Liam Hennessy. His office has been bombed, his car has been hit and three of his men are in hospital. And the man that came to see me has disappeared."

"Disappeared?"

"He used to own a Chinese take-away in Clapham. He's sold up and vanished."

"And you think he's in Belfast?"

Woody nodded. "If he was crazy enough to offer a reward, he might just be crazy enough to take matters into his own hands."

"But you said Hennessy's office was bombed. You think this Chinaman has got hold of bombs?"

Woody leant forward, his eyes sparkling. "That's the kicker. He's a Vietcong assassin! The bastard can kill with his bare hands, he can make bombs, booby traps, the works."

"Woody, someone's been pulling your chain!"

Woody explained about the Home Office file and Nguyen's life story. When he'd finished, Simpson picked up a ballpoint pen and began chewing the end. "So what are you suggesting, Woody?"

"Let me go to Belfast and sniff around."

"Expensive," said Simpson.

"If the paper'll pay for my flight and cover my expenses, I'll take the fee as lineage. No story, no payment." Simpson agreed. "But if I get a splash, I want serious money. You'll have the best exclusive this year."

"If you're right."

"If I'm right. Is it a deal?" he asked.

"I've got a better idea, a better deal."

"What?" said Woody, warily.

Simpson reached for a letter on his desk and handed it to Woody.

"We've been invited to a conference in Rome. A security conference. All the top guys are going to be there, including David Tucker, the head of Scotland Yard's Anti-Terrorist Branch and a couple of MPs. Some of Europe's top terrorist experts are going to be speaking. It's supposed to be about computerised intelligence systems, but we've been tipped off that they're going to announce a new international database to help in the hunt for terrorists worldwide."

"Government tip?" asked Woody.

Simpson grinned. "Who else? We might show a fair bit of tits and bums but politically we're right behind the Government, and we've got several million readers. The Government wants a big show from this conference, so a few select newspapers have been invited along. They're offering to fly us out on a chartered flight with some of the speakers, all we have to do is cover expenses."

"And report the Government line."

"Don't bite the hand that feeds you, Woody," replied Simpson.

"Perish the thought," said Woody. He waved the letter. "You want me to go to this? You know the flight is to-night?"

"Yeah I know. We were sitting on it but in view of what

happened at Ascot, we'd be crazy to turn it down. I was thinking about sending Williams but he's gone down with the flu. You'll get a bloody good story out of the conference, and you're sure to pick up some juicy stuff behind the scenes. And while you're there you can pick their brains about what's going on in Belfast. I'd be amazed if they hadn't heard something."

Woody nodded his head thoughtfully. It made good sense. "And what about me going to Belfast?"

"Fly straight there from Rome when the conference is over. We'll fix up the ticket for you. Can you fly direct?"

"I dunno, I'll find out. So it's a deal?"

"It's a deal, Woody. Just one thing."

"What's that?"

"Keep off the sauce."

"You know me," said Woody, heading back to his desk.

"Yeah," muttered Simpson. "Too true I do."

Woody went back to his desk just in time to answer his phone. It was Maggie. "Hello, Woody. Do you fancy a drink some time tomorrow?" she asked.

"I can't, I'm afraid. I'm off to Rome tonight. You must be psychic, I've only just been told."

"What time are you going?"

He looked at the letter. "Eight thirty, so I'll have to get to the airport about seven, I suppose. And then I'm going to Belfast."

"Belfast?" she said. Woody explained briefly about the conversation he'd had with Pat Quigley.

"Wow, so you're going after The Chinaman? Hey, if you need any help while you're over there, you should call my cousin, he's a freelance journalist there. God, it's quite a coincidence, he was in London a couple of weeks ago."

"In Belfast? What's his name?"

"Eamonn McCormick, do you know him?"

"No, but it'd be useful to meet up with him. I'll need some help while I'm there. I should even be able to put some money his way, too." It would be best to keep out of Pat Quigley's way when he arrived in Belfast so another contact would be useful.

"Great. He left some stuff with me. You could give it to him when you see him. He's a really nice guy, you'll like him. Look, I tell you what, why don't I pop round and give it to you tonight, before you leave?"

"Lunch would be better." Woody looked at his watch. It was 11.30 a.m.

"I can't, I'm tied up. Why don't I come round to your house? Give me the address."

Woody gave her the address of his bedsit in Fulham.

"What time did you say the flight was again?"

"Eight thirty. It's a special Government charter, high security and all that. I mustn't be late. I'll have to leave the flat by five thirty, just to be on the safe side."

"That's OK, I'll come round about four thirty, maybe five."

"Aren't you working?" he asked.

"I'm supposed to be visiting clients so it's no problem. I might have to sell you an insurance policy, though."

"With my lifestyle, I don't think I could afford the premiums." He laughed and they said their goodbyes. Woody smiled as he replaced the receiver. Maggie was great fun and he was looking forward to seeing her again, even though it was likely to be a fleeting visit. He had yet to get beyond the kiss-on-the-cheek stage, but he lived in hope.

Morrison stood by a window in one of the front-facing bedrooms looking down the track that led to the road. It was just before noon. He saw McGrath's Volvo estate with four men in it and he ran to the door. "He's coming," he shouted downstairs and then rushed back to his vantage point.

Two of Hennessy's men walked towards the car and flagged it down, checking the occupants. Morrison saw the rear window being wound down and then the glint of sunlight off McGrath's glasses. He felt his heartbeat increase and his mouth went dry and he recognised the signs of his body preparing itself for violence. It had been four years since Morrison had killed a man, and then it had been in the heat

of a fire-fight at the border near Crossmaglen, but the deaths
he was responsible for caused him not one night's lost sleep
and he was quite prepared to kill again. He had made the
mental switch many years earlier, suppressed the values he'd
been taught by the priests and by his teachers at school in
favour of the creed of the political terrorist, that violence was
justified in the quest for self-determination. When Morrison
finally met his maker he would do so with a clear conscience
and an untarnished soul, he was sure of that. The death of
McGrath, if Hennessy ordered it, would be an added bonus
and would go some way to quenching the jealous fire that
burned through his mind. As he watched the Volvo bounce
down the track and slow to crawl around the filled-in hole
that marked the scene of the earlier bombing, images of
McGrath and Mary filled his mind again, the two of them
naked, enjoying each other, her arching her back and calling
out his name.

"Are you OK?" asked a voice behind him, and he turned
to see Murphy standing by the door, a large automatic in his
hand.

"I'm fine," he said. Morrison was no longer sure how to
react to Murphy. They had never been especially close. They
were about the same age yet Morrison had gone much further
in the organisation, taking a great deal of responsibility at an
early age, while Murphy had remained as little more than
a bodyguard. Morrison often felt that Murphy begrudged
Morrison the access he had to Hennessy and to the other top
IRA officials, but now he had something on which to pin
his envy. He would never forgive Morrison's betrayal of his
employer, and Morrison would forever have to watch his back
when the man was around.

Murphy looked at Morrison for a second or two with cold
eyes and then nodded, just once. "Liam says he wants us
downstairs, in the lounge," he said.

Morrison followed him down the stairs where Hennessy
was waiting for them. He took them into the lounge and
showed them where he wanted them to stand, just behind the
door. The lights were switched on because he'd drawn the
curtains so that no one could look in from the courtyard.

"I'll lead him in, you close the door behind him," Hennessy said. "He doesn't normally carry a gun, but I want you to frisk him, and don't be gentle with him. I want him off balance, disorientated, OK?"

The two men nodded.

"If I say hit him, hit him. If I say shoot him in the knee, you do it. No hesitation, no argument. He must know that I am totally serious and that if he doesn't co-operate he will be killed."

"And will he?" Morrison asked.

"Oh yes, Sean. Quite definitely. But we both know that anybody can be made to talk eventually, don't we? Every man has his breaking point. And McGrath is used to giving pain, not receiving it. I think that the mere threat of violence will be enough, but if it isn't he must have no doubt that I mean what I say."

They heard the Volvo drive into the courtyard. "Right, I'll bring him in," said Hennessy and left them. The two men avoided looking at each other and Morrison wondered if Murphy had already been told what Hennessy had planned for him, and if those plans included a bullet in the back of the neck. He shrugged off the morbid thoughts, knowing that there was no point in dwelling on them. Whatever his fate, there was nowhere he could run, Hennessy would have the full backing of the IRA High Command. Morrison was just one man. That thought brought The Chinaman to mind, one man who was taking on the organisation, and who had so far come out on top. He wondered how Kerry was getting on. There were voices in the corridor and then McGrath entered the room, closely followed by Hennessy.

"This is hellish short notice, Liam. When will the rest be getting here?" McGrath said as Hennessy closed the door.

Morrison stepped up behind McGrath and pressed his gun against the man's neck.

"Don't make a sound, Hugh. Don't say a word," said Hennessy.

Morrison moved round in front of McGrath, keeping his gun against his throat, pushing hard so that his head was forced back. Murphy went behind McGrath and kicked his legs apart and then roughly searched him, going through all his pockets and then slapping down his legs and his arms.

"He's clean," said Murphy.

"Now listen to me, Hugh, and listen good. We're going to walk through into the kitchen and we'll stand at the back door. You're going to tell your men that you'll be staying the night and that you'll be going up to Belfast with me tomorrow. Then you and I are going to come back here and have a wee chat. If you try to warn them, they'll be shot. If you try to run we'll shoot you in the legs and then we'll bring you back here and we'll still have a chat, except this time you'll be in a lot of pain. Whatever you do, it's going to end the same way. Do you get my drift?"

"Have you lost your mind?" hissed McGrath.

"No," said Hennessy levelly. "I've lost my wife."

"Is that what this is about? Mary? I don't fucking believe it. I don't know what you're playing at but there'll be all hell to pay when Dublin finds out about this."

Morrison pushed the gun hard into McGrath's throat and made him wince.

"Once your men have gone you can call Dublin and you can speak to whoever you want. But it should be obvious to you that I wouldn't be doing this without their approval. And I'd better warn you, Hugh, they've given me *carte blanche*. Now, are you ready to speak to your men?"

McGrath glared at Hennessy as if about to refuse but suddenly the fight seemed to go out of him and he agreed.

Morrison slid his gun into the pocket of his bomber jacket, making sure that McGrath saw what he was doing. Hennessy opened the door and led the way. Morrison pushed McGrath ahead of him and Murphy fell in behind, his gun held behind his back. They went through the kitchen in single file and Hennessy unlatched the door. McGrath's driver and two bodyguards were in the car, laughing at something. Beyond the car, McGrath saw two of Hennessy's men carrying broken shotguns.

He and Hennessy walked over to the car while Morrison and Murphy remained in the doorway. The window wound down and McGrath put his hand on the roof of the car and dipped his head.

"I'm going to stay over with Liam, and we'll be going up to Belfast tomorrow. You lads can go back to the farm, I'll call you when I get back." His voice sounded to Hennessy as if it was about to break up but his men didn't appear to notice that there was anything amiss. They asked him if he was sure, McGrath insisted, and they started up the car and drove out of the courtyard. Morrison stepped out of the kitchen and around McGrath, shepherding him back inside. Murphy took off McGrath's glasses and threw them on the ground. He stamped on them, grinding the pieces into the ground with his boots, then followed him down the hallway, pushing him roughly in the back.

McGrath tried to talk to Hennessy as the group moved back into the lounge but he was ignored. Morrison recognised the technique of sapping the man's confidence to make him more susceptible to questioning. He took a wooden chair from the kitchen and placed it in front of the fire, facing Hennessy's favourite easy chair. Morrison and Murphy shoved McGrath on to the chair and then stood behind him. He began to turn round but before he did Murphy clipped him a glancing blow with the barrel of his gun. McGrath yelped involuntarily and put his hand to the side of his head. It came away bloody.

"Liam, what the fuck do you want?" He squinted over at Hennessy, trying to focus. The tinted glasses weren't just for show, McGrath was also quite short-sighted.

Hennessy ignored him and went over to the window. He untied two thick cords which were used for holding back the curtains, and he threw them over to Morrison. "Tie his hands behind him, and tie his legs to the chair," he said. Morrison did as he was told while Murphy held his gun against the back of McGrath's head. Hennessy sat down in his armchair.

"Is this about Mary?" asked McGrath. "Is that what that line about losing your wife was about? You're not losing her, Liam. She'll never leave you, she made that clear right from the start."

Anger flared inside Morrison and he stepped forward and smashed his gun across McGrath's face. It cut deep into his cheek and blood spattered across the carpet as Morrison raised his gun again.

"No!" shouted Hennessy. "Leave him be."

Morrison let the gun hang by his side. He was breathing heavily, his heartbeat pounding in his ears.

"We know what you're fucking angry at, don't we, Morrison?" taunted McGrath. Morrison whirled around and slapped him across the face so hard that McGrath keeled over, taking the chair with him and slamming into the floor.

"Sean!" said Hennessy. "You do that again and there'll be hell to pay. Get him up."

Morrison pulled McGrath and the chair back upright. McGrath was dazed and he spat blood on to the floor, groaning and shaking his head.

Hennessy waited until McGrath seemed to regain his senses before speaking again. "This is not about Mary, Hugh. Or at least not in the way you mean. It's about the bombings. The London bombings."

"I don't know what you mean," said McGrath.

"Hit him," Hennessy said to Murphy, and Murphy smacked his gun across McGrath's head.

"This is me asking you nicely," said Hennessy. "In a while I'm going to stop asking you nicely and Sean here is going to blow one of your kneecaps off. He's good at that, is Sean. He's done quite a bit of kneecapping in the past, though sometimes I think he's forgotten where his roots lie. But kneecapping is a bit like riding a bike, once you've got the hang of it you never lose it. And I think we both know that Sean might have personal reasons for enjoying putting a bullet or two in you. In fact, I might have trouble persuading him to keep his aim low. You get my drift, Hugh?"

"Yes, Liam. I get your drift," mumbled McGrath. He seemed to have difficulty moving his lips, and there was blood trickling down his chin. Morrison realised then what a devious, cunning bastard Hennessy was. McGrath was frightened, not just because of the threat of torture, but because he was being put in the hands of the man he'd betrayed most in all the world, the one man who really wanted to kill him with his bare hands, to tear him apart and to eat his raw flesh. McGrath could see the bloodlust in Morrison's eyes and it was infinitely more terrifying than Hennessy's threats.

Morrison was being used by Hennessy almost as cynically as he'd been used by Mary. He knew that, but at the same time he didn't care. He just wanted to see McGrath in pain, and he hoped with all his heart that he'd refuse to answer Hennessy's questions.

"What is it you want to know?" McGrath asked quietly.

"You are behind the bombings?"

"Yes."

"Why?"

"Because I think it's the only way to defeat the British."

"There's more to it than that. There must be."

McGrath shook his head.

"Where did you get the people from?"

"A couple from Scotland, two from Southern Ireland. I got to them before they joined the organisation, told them there was more they could do for the Cause by working directly for me. I sent them to Libya for training, then sent them to London to establish cover stories, to blend into the community."

"Where did the money come from? You couldn't touch IRA funds without it being noticed."

"I used my own money."

"Very noble of you. Hit him, Christy." The gun smashed into the back of McGrath's head again and he moaned and sagged in the chair. Murphy seized him by the hair and pulled his head back. "Where did the money come from, Hugh?" said Hennessy. "I'm about to stop asking nicely."

"Some of it from Libya," said McGrath. "But most of it came from the Iraqis. They channelled the money through Libya."

"You took money from the fucking Iraqis?"

"It's not where the money comes from that counts, it's what we do with it. You know that."

"How much did they pay you?" asked Hennessy.

"I don't know, it was . . ."

"Shoot him, Sean," said Hennessy quietly.

"No!" screamed McGrath. "For the love of God, no. Two million. That's what they paid. Two million pounds." Morrison squatted down and pressed the barrel of his gun behind McGrath's left kneecap. "Get him away, for God's sake get him away." He was screaming and crying and straining against the cords.

"Where's the money?"

"A Swiss bank account. It's yours, Liam, I promise. You can have the fucking lot. Just get him away from me, get him the fuck away from me!"

Hennessy waved Morrison away and he reluctantly took his gun away from McGrath's leg. Hennessy picked up a notepad and a pen. "I want the number of the account, and I want the names and addresses of the bombers."

"What then?" asked McGrath. "I give you the names and then what?"

"I won't kill you," said Hennessy. "You give me the names and I'll take you down to Dublin and you can plead your case to the High Command. That's the only deal you're going to get from me. Now do I get the names?"

McGrath swallowed and coughed, and spat out more bloody saliva. "You get the names," he said.

Despite the sun being almost directly overhead, Kerry began to find the going easier, helped by the fact that The Chinaman appeared to be heading due east, albeit sticking to the hedgerows wherever possible. It would have been harder to follow him if he'd cut across the fields where the grass was thick and springy. As it was she found several good examples of his footprints in muddy places formed where rainwater ran off into the ditches.

It was just after 12.15 p.m. when she came across the B180 and Tollymore Forest Park beyond. She pulled a twig from the hedge and stuck it into the ground like a miniature bonsai as she'd done every hundred yards or so as a signpost for Sean. She took a plastic bottle of water from her rucksack and drank as she planned her next move. He'd obviously crossed the road but it would take some time to find out where. The better bet would be to cross the road straightaway and check the trees where she was more likely to spot evidence of his passing on the forest floor.

"Sean Morrison, where the hell are you?" she said to herself. She wanted to go into the trees immediately, knowing that he'd be certain to be hiding somewhere in there. She felt the same as she did when she got within shooting distance of a deer that she'd stalked for hours, the adrenalin flowed and the desire to get in close was so strong that she could almost taste it. Only one thing held her back, once in the woods she wouldn't be able to see the flare and she'd have to keep the radio off at all times because she'd have no way of knowing if The Chinaman was within listening distance. She could sit down and wait, but she didn't want to. She took out the walkie-talkie and switched it on and pressed the talk button.

"Can you hear me?" she asked, remembering Sean's instructions not to use any names over the air. There was no answer, just static. "Is there anybody there?" she asked. When no one replied to her third attempt she took that as a sign that she was on her own and that Sean Morrison had no one to blame but himself if he couldn't find her. She put the walkie-talkie and the bottle of water back into the rucksack, waited until the road was clear and then dashed across, into the cool, enveloping greenness of the woods.

Hennessy left Morrison and Murphy in the lounge as he went to use the phone. He took the notebook because the four names McGrath had given him were new to him. He dialled the number and it was answered by Bromley himself.

"It's Liam Hennessy," he said.

"Yes," said Bromley. Hennessy heard the sound of a pipe being tapped against an ashtray. The thought suddenly came to him that Bromley probably recorded all his calls, but he'd gone too far now to worry about that. He read out the list of names and gave Bromley the address of the flat in Wapping where McGrath said they could be found. Bromley repeated

the names and the address back to Hennessy and then asked
if there was anything else.

"Such as?" asked Hennessy.

"Such as the name of the man in your organisation who
planned all this?"

"You'll have to leave that side of it to us, Bromley. We'll
be washing our own dirty linen."

"You won't even give me the satisfaction of knowing who
it was?"

Hennessy laughed harshly. "No, I'm afraid I won't. Just be
assured that we'll take care of it."

"Permanently?"

"You have what you wanted, Bromley. Just do what you
have to do." He replaced the receiver.

He went back into the lounge.

"What are you playing at?" said McGrath, squinting up at
Hennessy.

"Gag him," Hennessy told Murphy.

"Oh for the love of God, Liam, you won't be needing a
gag," said McGrath, panic mounting in his voice.

"Gag him," Hennessy repeated. Murphy took a large green
handkerchief from his pocket and forced it between
McGrath's teeth before tying it behind his head. McGrath
grunted and strained, but nothing intelligible emerged. His
eyes were wide and frightened, but Hennessy ignored his
pleas. "Christy, take him out and shoot him."

Murphy didn't express surprise or argue, he'd killed on
Hennessy's orders before, always without question. He moved
to untie McGrath from the chair, but the man went wild,
thrashing about like a mad thing and trying to scream through
the gag. Murphy calmly clipped the butt of his gun against
McGrath's temple, knocking him senseless without so much
as a whimper.

"Here, let me help you," said Morrison as Murphy slung
the unconscious man over his broad shoulders.

"No, Sean, you stay with me," said Hennessy. "Do it in
the barn, Christy. You can bury him in one of the fields
tonight."

Hennessy waited until Murphy had carried McGrath outside before speaking again. "I want to explain why McGrath is being killed, so that you don't get the wrong idea," he said quietly.

"Wrong idea?"

"Dublin were quite explicit about what they wanted doing. They wanted the bombings stopped and they wanted the man responsible out of the way. I explained that I thought McGrath was the man, and they said that didn't make a difference."

"But you told him he'd get a chance to plead his case."

"That was to encourage him to talk, to give him hope. But they'd already said that if I was one hundred per cent certain then he was to be taken care of here. No appeal, no trial, no publicity. No corpse."

"Why did he do it?"

Hennessy shrugged. "I guess the money helped persuade him. Gaddafi and Hussein have their own axes to grind against the British Government, and someone like McGrath would be a godsend. McGrath earns a small fortune from his smuggling operations, he's been playing the border like a bloody one-string fiddle. But most of that disappeared with the European Community's single market, so recently he's had to depend even more on his other sources of income in Belfast, and they in turn depend to a great extent on the Troubles. He's behind a number of protection rackets in the city. Most of the cash goes into IRA funds, but I doubt if he passed it all on. I'd be very surprised if some of it didn't find its way into his Swiss bank account, along with the Libyan and Iraqi money."

"His men won't be happy."

"Dublin will take care of that. Anyway, that's not the point. The point I'm trying to make, Sean, is that McGrath is being killed because he was a traitor to the Cause, because he betrayed the IRA, not because of Mary."

They heard a muffled pistol shot in the distance, but neither of them showed any reaction to the noise.

"I love Mary," said Hennessy. "Despite everything. We've been together a long time, and sometimes I think I know her better than she knows herself. I'm the rock over which she breaks, if you understand what I mean. I give her stability, a base, security, but she's always needed more than that, more than I can give her." His voice began to falter. "I'm not explaining myself very well," he added.

Morrison felt embarrassed. It wasn't often that Liam Hennessy was lost for words, his oratory skills were legendary in the courts of Belfast. Morrison didn't know what to say and he looked out of the window, hoping that he would finish and he could get back to Kerry and the hunt for The Chinaman, where at least he'd be out doing something. "What I'm trying to say is that you don't have to worry. I'm angry, sure enough, but not to the extent that I'd tell Christy to take you out to the barn. I'm angry at Mary, too, but that's something I'm going to have to work out myself. You've hurt me, Sean, but I've been hurt before and I'll get over it. And your loyalty to the Cause has never been in question. Neither has hers, funnily enough. McGrath might have been doing it for the money, but Mary I'm sure was doing it because she felt it was in the best interests of the Cause. And for revenge, maybe. Because of that I'll try to protect her, though God knows it's going to be hard."

He looked at Morrison, his face unsmiling, but there was no hatred in his eyes, just sadness. In a way, thought Morrison, hatred would have been easier to deal with. Compassion and understanding just made him feel all the more guilty.

"One more thing," Hennessy added. "When all this is over, I'd be happier if you went back to New York, but I guess that's what you'd want, anyway."

Morrison nodded. "Liam, I'm . . ."

"Don't say it," interrupted Hennessy. "I don't want your pity, Sean. Just help me get The Chinaman out of my hair and then go back to the States."

Morrison realised there was nothing more to be said so he went through to the kitchen. Hennessy's walkie-talkie was lying on the kitchen table and he picked it up. He tried to call Kerry but got no reply and that worried him. Surely she wouldn't have left it switched off, not when she was out there on her own? He retrieved his ski-pole and the canvas haversack, checked his gun and stepped into the courtyard. Murphy walked over from the barn. He appeared to be totally impassive, no sign that he'd just taken a man's life.

"You're off then?" he said to Morrison, his voice cold.

Morrison wondered what Murphy was thinking, and how he would have reacted if he'd been told to take Morrison into the barn and put a bullet in the back of his neck. He wondered too how much he could actually trust Hennessy now and what would happen once The Chinaman had been dealt with. He would have to be very, very careful.

"Yeah, I've got to catch up with the girl."

"Be careful," said Murphy. Morrison smiled, but he realised as he did so that he had no way of knowing if Murphy's words were a genuine expression of concern, or a threat.

Roy O'Donnell was driving one of the Land-Rovers while Kavanagh sat in the passenger seat scanning the roadside. The Land-Rover containing Tommy O'Donoghue and Michael O'Faolain was about a quarter of a mile behind them. They drove slowly and on many occasions impatient drivers had sounded their horns and they'd had to wave them on. At one point a convoy of army vehicles had come up behind them and they'd had to speed up so as not to attract attention. A Lynx helicopter flew low above the army patrol, keeping watch. That had cost them half an hour because when they'd eventually found a place where they could turn off they had had to wait until the convoy was well out of sight before they could drive back along the road and restart the search.

Now they had an excuse to dawdle because ahead of them rumbled a large, mud-covered red tractor. Kavanagh was looking for gaps in the yellow-flowered gorse and the trees, anywhere where a van could be driven. They'd stopped at half a dozen possibilities on the right-hand side and gone into the woods as far as they could but found nothing. Kavanagh's plan was to go all the way through the forest and then to drive back, westwards, checking the other side of the road.

"Slow down," he said to O'Donnell. "Och, too late. Do a U-turn and go back." O'Donnell indicated and pulled hard on the steering wheel. The Land-Rover behind them copied the manoeuvre. "There," Kavanagh pointed.

"I don't see anything," said O'Donnell, screwing up his eyes. "What am I looking for?"

"There's a track there. Look." They drove by a gap between the trees.

"Could be, I suppose," said O'Donnell. "Shall we go down it?"

"Let's give it a go," said Kavanagh. They did another U-turn and this time when they reached the gap O'Donnell indicated a left turn and drove slowly between the trees. When both Land-Rovers were off the main road Kavanagh told O'Donnell to stop the vehicle and he got out. He waved at O'Donoghue and O'Faolain to come over. The four men stood on the track with their shotguns, like a group of country farmers out on a rabbit shoot. Kavanagh looked down at the muddy ground, but he wasn't sure what he was looking for. There were some tyre tracks but he had no way of knowing how long they had been there or what had made them.

"We'll leave the Land-Rovers here and walk," he said. "Spread out and keep your eyes open."

Nguyen heard them coming from almost a quarter of a mile away. He was sitting next to a thick gorse bush by a patch of bluebells eating rice and chicken with his fingers. The first thing he heard was a group of startled birds flapping out of the trees. He put the cartons of food on the ground and stood up. He listened carefully, moving his head from side to side to get a bearing on where they were coming from. Eventually he heard the crunch of a boot on a twig and a sniff from the direction of the track. He couldn't tell how many there were because he was too far away, but he was sure there were more than one. He put the lids back on the foil cartons and packed them in the rucksack next to the pipe bomb. There was no point in using the bomb, for it to be effective it had to be in a confined space. The gun would be better. He checked the magazine before slipping the rucksack on his back and moving in a crouch through the undergrowth towards the track. There was no point in running blindly away, first he had to see who it was. It might be nothing more sinister than a group of forestry workers.

He moved parallel to the track, placing each foot carefully so as to make no noise, stopping and listening every few steps. He took cover behind a leafy horse chestnut and waited for them to draw level with him. There were four of them, three well-built men and a thin youth, all of them carrying shotguns. He recognised one of the men from Hennessy's farm. They were moving slowly, watching the ground more than the forest, and Nguyen doubted that they would fail to find the van, despite the effort he'd made in covering his tracks. None of the men spoke and they were obviously trying to make an effort to move quietly, but to Nguyen they sounded like water-buffaloes. Feet were crunching on twigs, kicking leaves aside, squelching into damp soil. Nguyen could have followed them with his eyes closed.

He crept from tree to tree, flitting from cover to cover like a shadow. The men came to the point where he'd driven the van off the track, and for a moment he hoped that they'd missed it because they continued on, but then the man who appeared to be the leader of the group held up his hand for them to stop. The man knelt down and studied the ground and then went back along the track. He motioned for them to gather around him and then began to whisper earnestly, making small movements with his hand. Nguyen was too far away to hear what he was saying but it was clear that he was telling them that they were to spread out and move through the trees.

Nguyen knew that he had to make a decision now. He could abandon the van and vanish into the woods until the time came to confront Hennessy again, but that would mean that when it was all over he'd have nowhere to go, no way of getting out of the country. He'd be stuck with only what he was wearing and what he carried in his rucksack. And while that was ideal for living rough it would give him a lot of explaining to do when he tried to board a ferry or a plane. But if he killed the men it wouldn't be too long before Hennessy would send more to investigate. And he doubted that he'd be able to conceal four bodies plus whatever transport they had arrived in, not well enough to survive a full-scale search of the woods. He could kill them and then bring his plans forward, go back to Hennessy's farm for the final confrontation. But if he did that then there was a good chance that Hennessy would be none the wiser about the bombings and he'd have to kill him and start all over again with one of the other Sinn Fein names that the London journalist had given him. He'd have to move to a different hiding place, take his van somewhere else. It was possible, he decided. He heard an excited shout and realised that his van had been discovered. He took the safety off the Browning and crept towards them. The leader was standing by the front of the van, pulling away the ferns and branches Nguyen had used to conceal it. He was joined by the red-haired youth and then the two heavyweights came trampling through the undergrowth. They cleared away all the vegetation covering the Renault while Nguyen moved as close as he could without being seen. He hid behind a bush half a dozen steps from the rear doors of the van.

"Open the bonnet, Tommy," he heard a voice say. "And, Michael, check what's in the back."

The gangly youth walked round to the rear of the van. He transferred his shotgun to his left hand and with his right twisted the door handle. It wouldn't move, because Nguyen had locked it. Nguyen put the safety back on and stuck the gun into the waistband of his trousers before slipping the hunting knife out of its scabbard on the rucksack strap. He was reluctant to go in shooting because it was one against four and as soon as they heard a shot they'd all start firing.

He held his left hand up in front of him, his right ready to stab with the knife, because a stab always went deeper than a slash. He took three quick steps, centre of gravity low.

"It's locked," the youth called.

"Well force it," the leader shouted. "Are yez stupid or what?" There was a smash of glass as one of the other men broke the driver's window with the butt of his shotgun.

Nguyen sprang the remaining distance and forced his left wrist across the youth's trachea and simultaneously drove the knife horizontally into the kidney. He twisted the knife to do the maximum amount of damage. The wrist across the windpipe stopped all noise but Nguyen could feel him struggle and tense and then relax and slump as he died. He eased the body on to the ground and put the knife back into its scabbard.

The man who'd smashed the window had opened the door and was looking for the bonnet-release catch. Nguyen took one of his throwing knives and moved to the right-hand side of the van. He risked a quick look and saw that the man had his back to him. Nguyen ducked away, took out the gun and slipped the safety off once more, holding the gun in his left hand.

There was a loud click and the man shouted: "That should do it." Nguyen stepped from behind the van, the knife ready. He was holding the blade about two inches from its tip, the handle upwards. The man closed the van door and as he did, Nguyen had a clear view of the side of his head and his neck and he threw hard. The blade thudded into the man's throat and blood gushed down his chest. Nguyen began moving as the man's mouth opened and closed with no sound because the blade had speared his Adam's apple. He transferred the Browning to his right hand, side-stepped across the rear of the van and moved up the left side. The two men at the front had opened the bonnet and had their heads over the engine. "What do you reckon, pull out the spark-plug leads?" one said.

"Yeah. And let down the tyres. That should fix the bastard."

There was a thud as the man with the knife in his throat fell to the ground, his shotgun scraping against the side of the van.

"What's up, Tommy?" said one of the men.

Nguyen stepped swiftly up to the front of the van, knowing

that the two men would be distracted by the noise of the falling body.

"Tommy?" said the man again, and it was followed by a curse. As Nguyen got to the front the two men had their backs to him as they moved towards their dying friend. Nguyen put the barrel of his gun up against the head of the man nearest to him and fired. The shot was muffled as the bullet smashed through the skull and exploded out of the man's face in a red and pink shower of blood and brains. The other man whirled around but before the shotgun could point at Nguyen he fired the Browning a second time, hitting the man in the dead centre of his chest. He fell backwards, a look of surprise on his face and blood blossoming on his shirt, the shotgun dropping from nerveless fingers.

It had taken less than a minute but all four were dead. Nguyen took no pride in the achievement. When he'd first travelled over to Ireland he'd hoped to get what he wanted without killing anyone. He knew that people would have to be hurt before they'd take him seriously, but he'd taken enough lives during his time in the jungles of Vietnam and he hadn't wanted to add to his body count. They'd forced him into it, he said to himself. It was their fault.

He stood over the body of the last man he'd killed and listened. The forest had gone silent but gradually the birdsong and insect noise returned and when he was satisfied that all was well he turned towards the corpses.

Kerry heard two gunshots, the second louder and more distinct than the first. It sounded as if they came from two different guns. She had gone about eight hundred yards into the forest and was making progress, albeit slowly. She'd found where Nguyen had entered the trees but had lost his trail soon after and had wasted more than an hour doubling back and then searching backwards and forwards in an arc shape until she picked it up again. There was no obvious path for The Chinaman to follow and he had constantly had to change direction to get around large trees or bushes. And her task was made harder by the fact that Nguyen had travelled in both directions. Half the signs that she found were actually made when he had been going west, towards the farm, not into the depths of the forest.

The shots had come from the east, but she had no way of knowing how far away they had been, or even if they had been the result of Nguyen firing a gun or being shot at. If Nguyen was under fire then there was a chance that he'd now be running through the forest in the other direction, putting even more distance between them. If she carried on at her snail's pace she'd never catch up with him. But if she hurried towards the source of the shots and it turned out to be nothing more than poachers or Uncle Liam's men letting off their guns, accidentally or otherwise, then she risked losing the trail.

She tried to think what her father would do. Stick with the tracks or go after the shots? She thought of the tracking expeditions with her father, usually taking rich Germans and Japanese out into the Highlands to kill deer, looking for the spore and the tracks until they were close enough for the kill. Sometimes he'd take shortcuts, ignoring the signs because he felt that he knew instinctively where the deer were. That's how it felt now, she realised. She knew the shots came from Nguyen. She felt it inside. She began to run eastwards, towards where she thought the shots had come from.

Sean Morrison had heard the shots, too. He was almost a mile from the forest, faithfully following the trail Kerry had left for him. He immediately recognised the sounds as coming from a pistol rather than a shotgun or rifle, and guessed that it had been Nguyen. Kavanagh and the boys had taken shotguns and a poacher or farmer wouldn't use a handgun.

He ran for the trees. He saw a twig that Kerry had placed in the gap between two sycamore trees but he ignored it, taking the path of least resistance through the undergrowth. It was never easy to judge how far away a noise like a gunshot was, but Sean didn't reckon it could have been much more than three miles away, possibly closer. He ran for all he was worth because there had only been two shots and whereas Nguyen was armed he knew that Kerry didn't have a gun.

Nguyen dragged the bodies one by one into the undergrowth, putting his arms under their shoulders and letting their heels scrape along the ground. There was no point in going to the trouble of digging graves for them because any serious search would see the disturbed soil, so he made do by hiding them inside a large patch of brambles and covering them with ferns. When he'd finished there were eight wavy lines carved in the mud by their feet and he used a leafy branch to wipe them away.

He went back along the track to find out what transport Hennessy's men had used and came upon the two Land-Rovers. They were blocking the track so he'd have to move them when he wanted to drive the van out, but it made more sense to take them further into the forest right away.

Luckily both sets of keys had been left in the ignition. He climbed into the first and started the engine. His hands began to shake and he gripped the steering wheel tightly, the tension making the veins stand up on the backs of his hands. He struggled to control himself, not sure what was causing the nervous reaction. It could have been delayed shock, but it had never happened to him before after combat, and he had no remorse for what he'd done. He had no doubt at all that the four men would have taken his life without a second thought. So what was the problem? He closed his eyes and felt the vibrations of the diesel engine through his arms, making the bones shudder. He had to regain control of himself, he owed it to his family.

Kerry heard an engine start up and a few minutes later a vehicle growl through the trees. She headed towards the noise and in the distance she saw a Land-Rover. In the driving seat

was a small, Oriental man dressed in a camouflage uniform.
"The Chinaman," she said under her breath. She crept
forward and hid behind a sycamore tree. She watched as
Nguyen stopped the Land-Rover under a spreading horse
chestnut at the edge of a clearing and got out. He walked off
into the woods and a few minutes later returned with an armful
of ferns which he spread over the roof, bonnet and wheels. He
then placed branches against the sides of the vehicle before
standing back to inspect his handiwork. On his back was a small
rucksack, similar to the one she was using to carry her equipment. Stuck into the waistband of his trousers was a large gun
and the sight of it reminded her that she didn't have a weapon.
Damn Sean Morrison, she thought. Damn him for not leaving
the gun. One shot and it would all be over.

Nguyen walked off into the trees again and Kerry followed
him. She didn't want to get too close because she was aware
that her feet were making a noise as she moved through the
undergrowth, no matter how much care she took. She lost
him but then heard another engine start up and saw him drive
a second Land-Rover along the track. She'd seen it before,
parked in the courtyard of her uncle's farm, and with a rising
sense of fear she wondered what had happened to the men
who'd been driving in the vehicles. Surely The Chinaman
couldn't have killed them all? Besides, there had only been
two shots.

She crept from tree to tree though with less urgency this
time because she knew where he was going. She caught up
with him as he was stacking more ferns on the Land-Rover's
bonnet and knelt down behind a tree to watch. He walked off
into the undergrowth again, presumably for more branches,
and he was soon out of sight.

She looked at her watch and wondered where the hell Sean
Morrison had got to. The thought suddenly came to her that
she hadn't left a trail for him to follow. Would he be smart
enough to spot where she'd run through the forest? Had she
taught him enough in their few hours together? The only way
she had of showing her position was to fire the flare gun, and
she couldn't do that without alerting The Chinaman. Her
breath quickened at the thought of the flare gun. What if she

were to bring in The Chinaman herself? The flare gun would be just as threatening as a pistol. She slid the rucksack off her back and undid the cords at the top. As she put her hand in and groped around for the flare gun she heard a click behind her and found herself looking down the barrel of an automatic pistol.

"Stand up, slowly," said Nguyen. He kept the gun trained on her face as she got to her feet, still holding the rucksack. She clutched it to her chest like a baby. "Who are you?" he asked.

She thought frantically. "I'm a . . . I'm a . . . er . . ." she stammered. "I'm a birdwatcher. Watching birds. My binoculars are in here." She nodded at her rucksack. "Let me show you." Her shaking hand tightened around the handle of the flare gun, but she suddenly realised that it wasn't loaded, the cartridges were loose in the rucksack.

Nguyen held out his hand. "Give me," he said. She handed over the rucksack. "Drop the pole. And move into the clearing," he said, gesturing with the gun. They walked together out of the shade of the trees and he made her stand by one of the Land-Rovers.

"How old are you?" Nguyen asked, frowning.

"Twenty-four," she said.

"I had a daughter who would be twenty-four this year," said Nguyen. He stepped back and put the rucksack on the floor, kneeling down beside it. She wondered if she could rush him, but he never took his eyes off her, using his hands to search the rucksack. He pulled out the case containing the binoculars and opened it.

"Bird-watching," repeated Kerry, willing The Chinaman to believe her. She was finding it hard to breathe and her mouth had gone dry.

Nguyen nodded, placed the case on the ground, and continued to rummage inside the rucksack. He took out the walkie-talkie and examined it and put it next to the binoculars. Again his hand went in like a conjuror looking for the white rabbit, though this time he came out with Kerry's notebook.

Kerry began to say that it was for drawing birds she had seen but Nguyen ignored her and slowly turned the pages.

He saw the sketch she'd made of his footprint and he nodded to himself. "Birdwatching," he mused.

They both heard a crashing noise from the depths of the forest, the sound of a man running. Nguyen looked over his shoulder, then back to the girl, obviously unsure what to do. Kerry knew that The Chinaman was considering shooting her, or maybe using the big hunting knife fastened to the strap of his rucksack. Her stomach turned liquid.

The crashing noise got louder and Nguyen moved away from Kerry, deciding that she was the lesser threat. He ran in a crouch to the edge of the clearing, his gun at the ready. As he ran, Kerry grabbed her rucksack and groped for the flare gun and a cartridge. Her hands were trembling and it took several attempts before she managed to open the gun and force home the cartridge.

She moved to the side so that she could see over The Chinaman's shoulder. He was standing about fifty feet away from her, cocking his head and listening, and then raising the gun as Morrison came into view. Kerry saw him at the same time as Nguyen did, his dark hair waving in the wind and his haversack banging on his hip as he ran. Nguyen ducked behind a tree and Kerry stepped forward, aiming the flare gun with both hands.

Morrison saw her and shouted, and began waving frantically.

"Sean, watch out!" she yelled, as Nguyen moved from behind the tree and pointed his pistol at Morrison.

"Nguyen, it's all right! It's all over!" Morrison yelled, and The Chinaman lowered his gun. As he did, Kerry pulled the trigger.

"Kerry! No! No!" Morrison screamed.

The pistol kicked in her hands but she kept it steady and there was a loud whooshing noise as the flare erupted from the barrel and hurtled through the air leaving behind a trail of white smoke in the still air. It smacked into the rucksack on Nguyen's back. Nguyen whirled round and pointed his gun at Kerry. She flinched, throwing her hands up in front of her face, knowing that he wouldn't miss at that range. Nguyen's finger tightened on the trigger but he couldn't do it, he couldn't bring himself to shoot her. Not a girl. He could smell the burning flare and his ears were filled with the hiss of melting nylon and he knew that she had killed him, that there were only seconds before the heat ignited the bomb in the rucksack. He dropped the Browning and struggled with the straps of the rucksack, yelling at her to get away from him.

Morrison burst into the clearing and saw Kerry kneeling on the ground, her head in her hands. At first he thought that she'd been shot but there was no blood and he hadn't heard The Chinaman fire his gun.

"Go away, go away!" screamed Nguyen. "Bomb! Bomb!"

Suddenly Morrison realised what was happening, why The Chinaman had thrown his gun on the ground and why he was now frantically fumbling with the nylon rucksack. Morrison rushed forward and grabbed one of the straps, forcing it down off his shoulder. The Chinaman was gasping for breath, twisting and turning to get the deadly package off his back. The heat from the flare seared Morrison's hands and he saw the hairs on his wrists shrivel and blacken, then he was hit by a wave of pain that made him cry out. The white light was blinding and he closed his eyes as the rucksack pulled away from The Chinaman's shoulders and he slumped to the ground. Morrison swung the burning mass as hard as he could and let it fly up into the air, hissing and spluttering into the trees, and then he dived over to shield Kerry, falling against her and knocking her to the ground, then lying across her and shouting at her to keep her eyes closed and her face covered.

The explosion came within seconds, the blast deafening and vibrating the ground like a small earthquake, followed by a barrage of twigs and chunks of wood that fell like a tropical rain shower and then stopped just as suddenly. The forest was silent, as if the bomb had killed every living thing for miles. Morrison rolled off Kerry and helped her to her feet. In the distance a bird whistled and was answered by another. Short, nervous calls as if they were testing the silence. Satisfied that Kerry hadn't been hurt, Morrison went over to The Chinaman, who was rubbing his eyes with the knuckles of his hand, coughing and retching.

"Thank you," he said, surprising Morrison with his politeness.

Morrison heard a metallic click and he turned to see Kerry, her hands dwarfed by the big Browning.

"Move away, Sean," she said quietly. "I've got the bastard covered."

"Easy, Kerry," said Morrison. "Put the gun down. He's not going to hurt anyone." The Chinaman showed no fear. He looked at Kerry, his face expressionless.

"I'm going to kill him," she said, her voice oddly flat. Morrison wondered if maybe she was in shock. Her eyes were cold, almost blank, as if she was sleep-walking, but she seemed to have no trouble in keeping the gun pointed at the centre of The Chinaman's chest.

"It's over," said Morrison, holding his hand out for the gun. "We've found out who the bombers are. We know who was backing them. It's finished. We can all go home."

"It's not over!" she hissed. "It won't be over until he's dead."

Morrison looked at The Chinaman. He was standing with his hands loose at his side, his head slightly bowed but his eyes fixed on Kerry's face as if willing her to shoot, as if he wanted her to end it. There was, Morrison thought, a sadness in his eyes, a look that said that there was nothing else they could do to him. Morrison looked back at Kerry, his hand still outstretched.

"Kerry, he could have shot you. He didn't. You can't kill him. He's not armed, he's not a threat." He stepped forward and she took half a step back. "He had a deal with Liam, and we're going to stick to it. It's over. Give me the gun and we can go home."

Her finger began to squeeze the trigger and Morrison knew that she was about to fire. Still The Chinaman stayed rooted to the spot. "Kerry, if you do this you're doing it for the wrong reason. You're not doing it for Liam Hennessy, or for your father, or for the IRA," Morrison said. He took another step forward. "You're doing it for yourself." Another step. The gun was almost within reach. "It'd be on your conscience for ever. It's not worth it. Trust me, I know. It's not worth it."

He moved quickly, bringing down his right hand and forcing the gun to the side, away from The Chinaman, and then he grabbed it and twisted it out of her grasp. She tried to get the gun back but he held it out of her reach. She yelled in frustration, then drew back her hand and slapped him across the face, hard, and began to sob. He stepped forward and took her in his arms, holding her close but being careful to keep the gun where she couldn't grab it, just in case. She put her head against his shoulder and he could feel her body shudder as she cried. He turned with her slowly, as if they were dancing to a slow song, until he was facing The Chinaman.

"Go," said Morrison.

"You said you had the names?"

Morrison told him the names of the bombers, and the address of the flat in Wapping where they were based, and Nguyen repeated them to himself, imprinting the information on his memory.

"Thank you," Nguyen said.

"Don't thank me. Just go."

Nguyen turned and walked into the undergrowth, leaving Morrison and Kerry alone in the clearing. She had stopped crying and he could feel her chest rising and falling in time with her breathing. "I'm sorry, Sean," she whispered. "I'm so sorry."

He smoothed her hair and kissed her on the top of her head.

"It's OK," he said. "Sometimes it gets you like that. The violence. It gets a grip on you without you realising it. It's like a drug, it pulls you along . . ."

She turned her head up and pushed her lips against his, kissing him hard, reaching around his neck with her arms. Her baseball cap fell off and her hair swung free. Her tears wet his cheeks as they kissed and she pressed herself against him. He threw the gun away and then held her with both hands, touching and caressing as her tongue found its way into his mouth, probing, teasing, exciting him until all thoughts of The Chinaman evaporated and he concentrated on her, the feel of her, the smell of her, the taste of her. She pulled him down on to the ground, her hands groping for his belt, her breath coming in small gasps as she said his name over and over again. He made love to her quickly but gently, in the grass, under the trees, next to The Chinaman's gun.

Nguyen couldn't believe that the man would let him go. He was sure that he planned to shoot him as he left the clearing, but there was no gunshot, no thump in the back, he just kept on walking. Once he was sure they really were releasing him he began to run through the forest towards the van. It would only be a matter of time before the four bodies were discovered and when that happened he doubted that Liam Hennessy would be as generous. Nguyen wasn't surprised at how easy it had been to kill the men, he'd always been good at it, all that was required was the mental switch. He'd fought against it when he first started out, but now that he'd killed he knew that he would follow it through to the end. He would avenge his family, he knew that with a diamond-hard certainty. He would do whatever it took, and there would be no remorse, no guilt. Afterwards, when he'd finished, then he'd worry about his own future, but at the moment he could look no further than the flat in Wapping and the IRA bombers.

He opened the back door of the van and quickly threw out all the supplies inside. He stripped off his camouflage gear and changed back into jeans and a pullover, checked that his money was still under the front seat with his passport, and then he drove the van back down the track and on to the main road and headed for the airport.

They travelled in three Range Rovers with a police motorcycle escort, roaring down the outside lane of the M40 at more than ninety miles per hour. The flashing blue lights and the howling sirens forced a clear path through the early afternoon traffic on the motorway, though there were plenty of resentful looks from the company reps in their Sierras and Escorts as the men in the unmarked Range Rovers went by. Pulling over for fire engines and ambulances was second nature, but nobody liked to move out of the fast lane without knowing why, and there was nothing about the vehicles that identified the men inside as belonging to the SAS.

There were four men in each vehicle, tough-looking men with broad shoulders, but as they hurtled towards London they were laughing and smiling and looked no more threatening than a group of miners on a coach trip to the coast. Mike "Joker" Cramer was in the front passenger seat of the first Range Rover, laughing at a particularly foul joke that the driver, Pete Jackson, had spun out over the last two miles. The men were tense as they always were when going into action, but they used humour to keep themselves from worrying.

In the back seat were Sam "Bunny" Warren and Rob "Ginge" Macdonald. Bunny was tapping the back of his hand against the window and he wasn't as quick to laugh at Jacko's joke as the rest were.

Joker, the assault-team leader, was the leanest of the four men, well over six-foot tall, with a thin face that always appeared haggard no matter how much sleep he got. He looked over his shoulder at Bunny, a swarthy, stocky man with piercing green eyes. "Is that Morse code, or what, Bunny?" he said.

Bunny stopped tapping. "Sorry, Joker. Habit."

"You want some gum?" Joker asked, holding out the packet of Wrigley's which he always carried with him now that he'd given up smoking.

"Cheers," said Bunny, taking a piece. "We nearly at the RV?"

"Not far," said Joker. He leant forward and picked up the A to Z map of London. The Colonel had called from London and given them an address in Rotherhithe Street, alongside the Thames, where they were to meet. The convoy left the A40 and they motored along Marylebone Road, along Euston

Road past King's Cross and then they followed City Road to the Thames. The motorcycle riders worked in teams, rushing ahead to hold up the traffic whenever the lights weren't in their favour, then remounting and following up behind like pilot fish busily swimming around prowling sharks. When they reached the river the motorbikes peeled off by arrangement, leaving the three Range Rovers to make their own way across London Bridge to Bermondsey and then left along Jamaica Road to Rotherhithe.

They drove by new wharf-style blocks of riverside flats and then came to the building where the Colonel said they were to meet.

"This is it," said Joker. The three vehicles pulled up at the pavement. Joker climbed out and looked up and down the road. There were no signs that an operation was under way, no police cars, no ambulances, no nothing, just the sound of the Thames lapping against the banks.

The men got out of the cars and stood on the pavement. They were, Joker had to admit to himself, a motley crew. The one thing they had in common was that they were all in the peak of condition and trained to kill. I don't know what they'll do to the enemy, thought Joker, but they scare the shit out of me. He tried to remember who'd said that first, whether it had been Wellington or Napoleon, because he was sure he'd heard it somewhere. Whatever, that's exactly how he felt about the eleven men who began pulling their kit-bags out of the back of the cars.

"Where do we go?" asked Reg Lawrence, another assault-team leader.

"Fifteen B," said Joker. "This one here."

He pushed the button by Fifteen B and a light clicked on. There was a television camera behind a glass panel and a red light came on above it and then he heard the Colonel's voice tell him to come up. The door buzzed and Joker pushed it and the men filed through and followed him upstairs to the third-floor flat.

An intelligence officer in his distinctive green beret had the door open for them.

"The green slime gets here first for a change," jeered a

voice from the back, but when Joker looked to see who it was he was met with blank, innocent faces.

The flat was spacious, white-painted walls and ceilings and polished wood floors, a fully fitted kitchen but no furniture, and there was a "For Sale" sign in one of the bedroom windows overlooking the street.

The Colonel was in the lounge looking through a powerful pair of binoculars mounted on a tripod. A large blackboard was leaning against one wall and, as the men stood around, the intelligence officer began drawing a map of the flat under surveillance in white chalk. The Colonel looked up and nodded at Joker. "Fancy a look?" he asked.

The binoculars were trained on a modern wharf on the north side of the river and when Joker looked through them he saw a large french window and a lounge beyond it, a rectangular room with three men sitting around. The television was switched on but Joker couldn't see what was on the screen. In front of the window was a balcony, twelve-feet square, with a couple of white chairs and a circular table. Joker moved the binoculars sideways. The building was mainly featureless brick wall and double-glazed windows, but two-thirds of the way along the architect had obviously decided to introduce a little variety and he'd staggered the flats so that the one to the left of the flat under observation was about twelve feet further back and the one to the right was an equal distance closer to the river. While it made the building easier on the eye it made it impossible to enter the balcony from either side. There was no flat above the one under observation, but the architect had built a penthouse flat at the right-hand side of the building and its extra-large balcony overlooked it. It was immediately apparent to Joker that the penthouse was the way in. It would be a simple matter to jump down to the balcony below, they wouldn't even have to abseil.

The buzzer sounded from the hallway and the intelligence officer went to open the front door and let in two men from D11, the Metropolitan Police firearms team. They stood at the back of the group of the SAS men, their rifles slung over their shoulders. The Colonel nodded a welcome and went over to the blackboard, chalk in hand.

Woody panicked a little when he opened the door to his bedsit. Clothes were strewn all over the floor, a week's worth of newspapers were piled up under the room's one window, and there was a collection of empty lager cans and a three-quarters empty bottle of Bells by the side of the bed. It looked as if a burglar had wreaked vengeance on the place after finding there was nothing worth stealing, but Woody knew it had been in exactly the same state when he left that morning. He rushed around picking up the rubbish, putting the cans and the papers into an old carrier bag, and was just about to carry them downstairs to the dustbin when there was a knock on the door. He cursed and shoved the bag under his bed and smoothed down the quilt. The knock was repeated as he popped into the alcove where there was a mirror above a small wash-basin. He gave his hair a quick comb and then opened the door. It was Maggie in a dark-green suit, her red hair tied back in a ponytail. She was carrying a black leather briefcase and could indeed have been there to sell him insurance, except the smile she gave him wasn't the professional "have I got the policy for you" type, it was warm and genuine.

He stepped to the side and waved her in. "It's not much," he apologised.

She looked round and nodded. "You're right," she said.

"It's temporary."

"It would have to be," she laughed. "Does it have a bar?"

Woody laughed with her. "Yeah, there's some whisky. Let me wash a couple of glasses." He picked up a glass from off his dressing-table and went back into the alcove. There was another glass on the shelf under the mirror containing his toothbrush and a tube of toothpaste. He tipped them out and washed both glasses, carried them back, and poured them both a drink.

They clinked glasses. "Sit down," said Woody.

Maggie looked around the tiny bedsit. "Where?" she said. There was only one chair and that was covered with a pair of jeans and a couple of shirts that looked the worse for wear. She put her briefcase on the floor by the door.

"It'll have to be the bed, I'm afraid," said Woody.

She smiled and sat down and Woody joined her.

"So, Rome, then Belfast. You get around."

"Yeah, I'm sorry it's such short notice."

"A security conference, you said?"

"Yeah, lots of top guys. And with any luck there'll be a big story, too."

"I'm pleased, you deserve it. Why is it so hot in here?"

"I told you," he said. He tapped the wall behind them. "It's the immersion heater. It's really cosy in the winter."

"I bet, but this is the middle of summer, Woody."

"Let me take your jacket," he said, and helped her slip it off. She opened the top button of her blouse and waved the material back and forth to cool herself. She looked up and caught Woody watching her. She didn't say anything and Woody leaned over and kissed her on her left cheek, close to her mouth.

"Woody, no," she said softly, but she didn't move away so Woody kissed her again, closer to her lips. He reached up and cupped her breast and tried to kiss her on the mouth but she moved her head and his lips brushed her hair.

"Woody, don't," she said, but her hand fell into his lap and stayed there and he could hear her breathing heavily. He massaged her full breast through the soft material of the blouse and he felt her nipple stiffen and when he tried to kiss her again this time their lips met.

He unbuttoned her blouse as they kissed. Her bra fastened at the front and after a couple of attempts he undid that, too. Her breasts fell free and he leant forward and kissed them as she cradled his head in her hands.

"Woody, we don't have time," she said, running her fingers through his hair and kissing the back of his head.

He pressed his fingers against her lips. "Shhh," he said, and kissed her again as he slipped her blouse off her shoulders. She wriggled her arms out of her sleeves and then she helped him off with his shirt and they lay down next to each other, kissing and caressing. Woody broke free and took off his shoes, socks and trousers and then lay down on top of her.

"Woody, we can't," whispered Maggie as he began to push her skirt down her hips. She lifted her backside to make it easier for him and he used his foot to push it the rest of the way down her legs.

"It's all right," he said, kissing her again and running his hands down her legs. She was wearing stockings and they rasped against his fingers. He slipped his hand into the top of her briefs.

"No, it's not," she said. "We can't make love."

He removed his hand and raised himself up on one elbow. "You're not a virgin are you?" he asked.

She collapsed into giggles. "That's very flattering, Woody, but no I'm not." She reached up and linked her arms round his neck and pulled him down on top of her. "It's the wrong time of the month," she whispered into his ear. "I'm sorry."

Not half as sorry as I am, thought Woody. "That's OK," he said, but his voice was heavy with disappointment.

Maggie wrapped her legs around him and held him. She kissed him hard, her tongue probing deep into his mouth and then whispered into his ear again. "Lie on your back," she said. He did as he was told and she lay next to him, her hand moving gently between his legs. He groaned and she moved up the bed slightly so that her breasts were level with his mouth. "Kiss them," she said, while her hand became more insistent, moving faster and harder. "Kiss them while I make you come."

The British Airways stewardess stood to one side to allow the passengers to disembark, a flurry of briefcases and forced smiles. She smiled and said goodbye to an Oriental man in a duffel coat, but he looked right through her. He wasn't carrying any luggage and he was scruffily dressed, jeans and a pullover under the coat. There were streaks of dirt across his face as if he'd washed in a hurry and, not to put too fine a point on it, he stank to high heavens. One of the passengers who had been sitting on the same row had asked to be moved and the stewardess had had to agree. The smell turned her stomach, the bitter aroma of skin that hadn't seen soap and water in a long time. The man had been hungry and had wolfed down the tray of cake and sandwiches put in front of him, keeping his coat firmly buttoned up throughout the flight. She'd pointed the man out to the chief steward but he'd told her not to worry, security checks on the flights between Belfast and London were second to none and he looked more like a man taking his first flight than a potential hijacker. The smell? Well, that was a nuisance, but what could you expect, she was told. Nguyen left the plane at a brisk walk. He had to get to central London before the shops closed.

Woody stretched and looked at his watch. "Christ, is that the time?" he said.

"What time is that?" asked Maggie. She was lying with her back to Woody, her head in the crook of his right arm.

"It's six o'clock. I'm going to have to run." He slid his arm out from under her neck and kissed her shoulder. She turned and kissed him on the lips and his hand went to her breasts again and he moved on top of her. "I wish I could make love to you," he sighed.

"You will," she said. She hadn't allowed him to remove her briefs or stockings but she had made him scream with pleasure with her hands, extending his pleasure until he was exhausted. He'd asked if he could make her come but she refused, saying that she'd rather wait until they could make love properly and fully. "When you get back from Belfast," she'd promised.

Woody sat up and pulled on his underpants, then his socks, then his trousers. Maggie sat up while he went to his wardrobe and took out a clean shirt. She made no attempt to cover herself and Woody turned to admire her breasts while he buttoned his shirt up and put on a tie. She laughed and leant over to pick up her briefcase and swung it on to the bed. She clicked open the case and took out a piece of paper. "Here's the address and phone number of my cousin. I rang him this afternoon and said you'd be coming over and that you'd call him some time."

Woody walked over to take the sheet of paper but as he reached for it she moved it away, catching him off balance. "Ask nicely," she teased. He leant forward and kissed her and she put her arms around his neck, pulling him down on the bed. Woody pulled away and this time she gave him the paper. "And can you give him this?" she said, reaching into the case. She took out a laptop computer and put it on the bed beside her. "He asked me to get it repaired. He bought it in London last year and couldn't get it fixed in Belfast. It's OK now. Do you mind? I know it'll mean taking it all the way to Rome and then back to Belfast, but I don't trust the Post Office."

Woody shook his head. "Of course I don't mind." He picked it up and put it in his overnight bag along with a change of clothes and his washing kit. Maggie made no move to get out of bed so Woody asked her what she planned to do.

"Can I stay here for a while?" she asked. "I'll let myself out."

"Sure," said Woody, looking at his watch again. "Christ, I'm going to have to dash. I'll call you from Rome. What's your home number?"

She grimaced. "My phone's out of order. I'll call you from a call box. What hotel will you be staying at?"

"Hell, I don't know. Call the office, they'll tell you." He picked up his bag and kissed her. He blew her another kiss from the door and closed it behind him.

She lay back in the bed and put her hands over her eyes. She felt sticky and dirty being with the grubby man in his grubby room, relieving him with her hands and pretending to love it. She shuddered. "The things I do for you, Denis Fisher," she said to herself.

She slid out from under the quilt and padded over to the

sink, washing herself as best she could. She caught sight of herself in the mirror and pulled her tongue out. "Whore," she said to herself, and then laughed. She dried herself and put her clothes back on but she still didn't feel clean.

She took the towel and carefully rubbed it everywhere she'd touched, removing all trace of her fingerprints. Only when she was totally satisfied did she pick up her briefcase and let herself out of the room, not forgetting to wipe the door handle.

Woody made it to the airport with time to spare. He could barely keep his eyes open. He'd had a rough drinking session the night before, but it was Maggie who'd sapped his strength. He had no idea as he sat on the bed and tried to kiss her just how enthusiastic she'd turn out to be. He was quite surprised, and pleased. And knackered.

He was met by a Home Office press officer, a colleague of Annie's, a young guy who used to work for the *Daily Telegraph* and who Woody vaguely remembered meeting several years earlier.

"I'm sorry, Woody, there's been a change of plan. The jet we've chartered has had engine problems so we're putting everyone on scheduled flights. I've got you a seat on a plane leaving in forty-five minutes." He handed Woody a ticket. "It's Economy I'm afraid."

"No sweat," said Woody. "Are you going on the same flight?"

The man nodded. "Yeah, and I'll be around to look after you at Rome airport."

"We're not sitting together?"

At least the guy had the grace to look shamefaced as he admitted that he was flying Business Class. They joined the queue to have their overnight bags X-rayed. Woody filled his mind with images of Maggie as he waited.

His turn came and he handed his bag to a uniformed guard who put it on the conveyor and watched it disappear as he stepped through the metal detector. His bag was pulled out by a squat, middle-aged woman with a pointed face and a flat chest and put on one side with half a dozen others. It seemed that they were pulling out one in three bags for hand inspection, which Woody guessed was a result of the bombing campaign. It wasn't so long ago when it was a rarity to have one of the guards go through your luggage and then it was usually because they'd seen something they didn't recognise on the scanner.

A short youth with a pencil-thin moustache and sideburns gave him a crooked smile and asked him if the bag was his. When Woody said it was, the guard put it down on the counter and asked him to open it. Woody did and the boy thrust his hands into it as if he was about to deliver a baby. He pulled out Woody's wash bag, unzipped it and examined his can of shaving foam and toothpaste. He carefully pushed aside Woody's underwear and shirts and then his hands appeared with the computer. He looked at it front and back, peered inside the ventilation grille, and shook it.

"Can you switch this on for me, sir?" he asked.

Woody opened the machine, revealing the screen and the keyboard, and groped at the back where he knew the on-off switch would be. The screen flickered into life. Woody had used portables many times so he had no difficulty getting the computer to flash up a directory. The guard peered at it, and pressed a few keys at random.

"That's fine, sir," he said, allowing Woody to switch it off and put it back in his bag. Woody picked it up and slung it over his shoulder. "Have we got time for a drink before we board?" Woody asked the press officer.

"Probably several."

"You're talking my language," laughed Woody.

Joker stood by the french window and looked over the river towards where he knew the Colonel would be. He couldn't tell which of the many windows the Colonel was behind, but that was to be expected. He'd be well back from the window with the rest of his team. If Joker could see him, the IRA would be able to spot him, too.

As he waited for instructions he hummed to himself quietly. There was nothing else to do. He'd stripped and cleaned his Heckler & Koch MP5, the German-made 9-millimetre machine gun that the SAS favoured, reassembled it and replaced the magazine with its thirty rounds. He adjusted his assault waistcoat, more from habit than because of need, and flicked the safety catch off. Ginge stood by his side, while Bunny and Jacko waited behind. There was only enough space for two of them to jump down on the balcony at the same time so they'd agreed that Joker and Ginge would go first. Bunny and Jacko would follow as back-up.

During the briefing, the Colonel had made it clear that only one four-man team would actually be going into the flat and Joker had held his breath, fearing that he'd be going back to Hereford without seeing action. He needn't have worried, because the Colonel knew that Joker's team had been pulling the best scores in the killing house. The other two assault teams had groaned but knew better than to complain. One four-man team was sitting in a Range Rover in nearby Wapping Lane, parked up and listening on the radio to the Colonel's instructions, ready to give chase just in case something went wrong. The remaining four were in plain clothes, two in Wapping High Street and two down by the river in front of the target flat, but well out of sight.

"Stand by," said the Colonel's voice in Joker's earpiece. "We think we have a clear shot." The two D11 marksmen were the only police representatives Joker had seen, and at first he'd assumed it was because the Colonel wanted to keep the operation low-key and not risk having the terrorists tipped off by too much woodentop activity. During the briefing, however, it became clear that there was another reason for the minimum police presence. The Colonel had stressed that they were not planning to take any prisoners. The operation was to be a hit and run, leaving no martyrs alive in mainland prisons as a focus for future terrorist actions, though the

Colonel had stressed that one of the terrorists had to be interrogated to discover if there were any devices already planted that hadn't gone off yet. The Colonel suggested that The Bombmaker should be left alive, but that it was Joker's call. Obviously if she was armed she'd have to be taken out immediately.

"They've just switched the lights on. There are three men in the lounge area," said the Colonel in Joker's ear. "One sitting at the table, one on the couch, one standing in the hallway. There's still no sign of the girl.".

Another voice in Joker's ear, this time one of the men in the Range Rover, cut in. "She's coming. A taxi just pulled up in front of the building. It's her. She's going in."

There was silence for a minute and then the Colonel's voice spoke again. "One of the men is opening the door. Yes, it's her. The two of them are going into one of the bedrooms. OK, stand down. We can't move while two of them are out of sight."

Joker and Ginge went back into the flat to wait.

Fisher took MacDermott in his arms and held her. "Did it go OK?" he whispered.

"It was horrible, horrible. I don't ever want to have to do anything like that again. He was all over me, Denis, like some sort of slobbering animal."

He kissed her ear. "Come on, kid. It had to be done, you know that. And think of the prize. If what he told you is right, that plane is going to be the biggest coup we've ever had. And we get to take out some of our worst enemies. Anyway, it's not as if he was grotesque or anything. He was a good-looking guy."

She pulled away and glared at him. "That's not the fucking point, Denis. I had to spend weeks around him, fending him off, toying with him, waiting for the opportunity to use him. I feel dirty, really dirty."

Fisher held up his hands to calm her down. "OK, OK, I'm

sorry. Don't take me the wrong way. We're all proud of you, really proud. And we know what you went through."

"Do you Denis? Do you really?" She shook her head and there were tears in her eyes. "I'm going to shower," she said, pushing past him.

"Stand by," said the Colonel. "We see the girl, coming out of the bedroom. She's going into the bathroom. The man is out of the bedroom, too, he's walking towards the lounge. OK, we have all three men in view. We'll wait for the girl to come out. Get ready, Joker."

Another voice broke in, this time one of the SAS men on foot. "There's somebody walking along Wapping High Street," he said. "A man. Anyone else see him?"

"We see him," said the watcher in the Range Rover. "He's heading towards the block. No, it's OK, it's a delivery. He's carrying a box. He's a Chink, by the look of it. Yeah, I can see Chinese writing on the box. Somebody's ordered a Chinese take-away by the look of it. Nothing to worry about."

"It can't be for our targets, we saw them eating earlier on," said the Colonel. "Keep an eye on him, just in case."

"He's outside the block," said the man in the Range Rover. "He's going in."

Nguyen hefted the box in his left hand and reached for the doorbells with his right. There were more than twenty individual buttons and he was about to press a few at random to see if anyone would let him in through the security door when he saw movement in the hallway and a second later the door pushed open and a middle-aged man carrying a small terrier went by him. Nguyen caught the door before it swung shut and slipped inside. At the end of the hallway was a lift with its doors open and to the left was a stairway. He headed up

the stairs, carrying the box in both hands. He was after Flat
19 but had no way of knowing which floor it was on, so as he
reached each landing he quietly eased open the door and
checked the numbers of the flats. On the fourth floor he saw
a door with 19 on it and he jerked back out of sight. He was
almost there. It was almost over.

"Get ready, Joker. The girl is coming out of the bathroom.
She's wearing a bathrobe, a white bathrobe, and she's heading
for the lounge. This could be it. Where's the guy with the
dog?"

"He's well away," said the watcher in the Range Rover.

"No sign of the delivery man?"

"Still inside."

"OK. She's sitting down on the left in the armchair by the
television. Hang on, the man at the table appears to have
a gun, an automatic, but he's not holding it. It's on the
table."

The four soldiers looked to their right at a large drawing
of the flat below. The Colonel had copied it from the diagram
on the blackboard, including details of where the furniture
was. It was pretty much a copy of the flat they were in, though
smaller. Joker used the barrel of his gun to indicate where
the four terrorists would be. Ginge nodded.

"I'll take the man at the table, and the guy on the couch,"
said Joker. "The one in the hallway is yours. Don't forget, we
try to take the girl alive. We've got some questions for her."

"We think we have a clear shot at the man in the hallway.
Stand by," said the Colonel.

"Mine is the couch, yours is the table," corrected Joker.

"Right ho," said Ginge.

"Move out on to the balcony," said the Colonel.

Joker felt the adrenalin surge as he prepared for action. He
and Ginge stood side by side waiting for the word. They both
cocked the actions of their MP5s, slotting home live rounds
into the chamber. They both had their safeties off and their

fingers on the trigger guards so that there was no way the guns could go off accidentally when they jumped. There were live rounds in the chambers of their holstered Brownings but they'd kept the safeties on. They were wearing assault waistcoats loaded with stun grenades over black overalls. They had both chosen to wear light body armour and had discarded the high velocity body armour with its tough ceramic plates that they'd brought with them, partly because there was no sign of anything bigger than a handgun in the flat below and because they didn't want to be burdened down with too much weight when they jumped.

"Prepare to jump," said the Colonel. The two SAS men eased themselves over the blue-painted metal railings, facing forward and holding on with one hand. The drop was about twelve feet which was easy enough, but they had to twist through ninety degrees to the right as they jumped so balance would be a problem. Joker would be able to land by the side of the white plastic table and chairs but Ginge would drop behind them so he wouldn't be able to move inside as quickly, he'd have to go round. Bunny and Jacko moved up behind them to stand on the balcony.

Nguyen placed the box on the floor and squatted next to it. He took out the cartons of food, long since gone cold, and stacked them against the wall. At the bottom of the box, in pieces, was a replica of a Kalashnikov AK-47. He'd arrived at the shop minutes before it was due to close, out of breath because he'd run down the Strand, and paid in cash. It was realistic down to the last detail, a perfect copy of the Russian-designed 7.62-millimetre automatic rifle that he'd used in the jungles of Vietnam. He assembled it with an efficiency born of familiarity, screwing home the wooden stock and slotting in the magazine. The weight felt slightly wrong but it looked real enough, and the men he was up against were professionals, they would assume that anyone who moved against them would be using the real thing. He'd have preferred to have used the Browning but he'd left that behind in the forest, and besides, there was no way he could have got any weapons at all through the airport security. Anyway, there was a certain irony in using the AK-47, which is why he'd chosen it over the rest of the range of replica guns the shop had in stock. That and the fact that it was the gun he felt most comfortable with. So long as he kept moving, so long as he didn't give them time to think, they wouldn't realise that it was a replica, they wouldn't notice that the barrel was solid metal and that the gun could never in a million years be used to fire bullets. They'd be off-guard, defensive, and scared, and he'd be able to use their confusion to take their own weapons from them. They'd be sure to have guns, and once he'd taken them from them he'd have no further need of a replica. And if he was wrong, if there were no guns in the flat, then he'd use the knives he'd also bought at the shop.

Nguyen no longer gave any thought to his own future, to what would happen if he should succeed. He didn't care any more. He'd given up any hope of justice being done, all he wanted now was revenge. He wanted nothing less than the death of the four bombers and he had no interest in what lay beyond that. His life was over.

When the weapon was ready he put the cartons back in the box and stood up. He slid the rifle inside his coat, barrel down, and held it in place with his right arm and then picked up the box with his left. It felt awkward, but it wouldn't be for long.

MacDermott ran a towel through her red hair. The shower had helped, she was more relaxed now and the hot water had made her feel a little cleaner, on the outside anyway. She jumped as the doorbell buzzed. Fisher frowned. It wasn't the bell at the entrance to the main security door, it was the doorbell, which meant that whoever was ringing was already inside the building, outside the flat. He motioned to McCormick to pick up the gun as he moved towards the door.

McCormick took the automatic in his hand, clicked off the safety and held it under the table.

Fisher walked down the hallway on tiptoe. He put his eye to the security viewer and a distorted Oriental face looked back, grinning. Fisher saw the man press the doorbell again and it buzzed. The man was holding a box with what looked to be cartons of Chinese food.

"What do you want?" Fisher shouted through the door.

"You order Chinese food?" said the man.

"No, you must have the wrong flat," Fisher shouted back.

"I not hear you," the man said.

"Wrong flat," Fisher repeated, his eye still pressed to the peep-hole.

He could see the Oriental shake his head and step back, looking confused. "I not hear you," he said.

Fisher reached for the lock and turned it. "It's OK," he called to the others. "Some guy trying to deliver a Chinese take-away. He's got the wrong flat, that's all." He unlocked the door and turned the handle, stepping to the side as he did. In the lounge, McCormick relaxed and took his finger off the trigger of his gun. O'Reilly grinned and patted his chest with the flat of his hand.

MacDermott began drying her hair again and then suddenly stopped, her heart pounding as realisation hit her like a kick in the chest. She gasped for breath, her mind whirling as if she was falling from a great height, full of images of Woody's Chinaman, the man on the trail of the IRA, knowing that he was the man outside the door but unable to form the words that she could shout as a warning. All she could think to yell was "No! No! No!" and her screams echoed around the flat, startling them all. McCormick flinched and began to get out of his chair as Nguyen kicked the door open, sending Fisher sprawling across the hallway.

Nguyen threw down his box and grabbed for the Kalashnikov, swinging the barrel up at waist level. He stepped into the hallway and kicked Fisher, knocking him away from the door, keeping him off balance so he wouldn't be able to get a good look at the gun. Over Fisher's shoulder he saw a man at a table, pushing himself to his feet and pointing a handgun towards him. "Drop the gun!" shouted Nguyen, aiming his useless replica at the man's chest and stepping forward. The man looked confused and began to lower the weapon.

"We have another target in the flat," said the Colonel's voice in Joker's ear, calmly and controlled. "I repeat, there are now five in the flat. Three in the lounge, two in the hall." There was a pause, and then he spoke again. "One of the targets in the hallway has an assault rifle. OK, Joker, we have a clear shot at the men in the hall. We'll take them both out from here. Jump on my command." Another pause, enough for three heartbeats. "Go!" said the Colonel. "Go, go, go!"

Joker and Ginge dropped together, and a fraction of a second after they let go of the rail they heard the double crack of two high velocity rounds splitting the air.

To Joker it seemed that time slowed right down as they pushed themselves out and twisted in the air, knees slightly bent to absorb the shock. They hit the ground together and slipped their fingers over the triggers of their MP5s. It took a fraction of a second for Joker's brain to register the scene in the room. There were three of them, two men and a girl, and they all had their backs to the window. The man on the couch was halfway up, the woman was holding a towel over her mouth. The man at the table had a gun in his hand. All were looking at the hallway where a blond-haired man was slumped against the wall, his hand clutched to his blood-smeared chest, obviously just seconds from death. Another man, an Oriental, stood in the hallway with what looked like a Kalashnikov in his hands and blood pouring from a wound in his shoulder. The man's mouth was opening and closing and he had a look of amazement on his face. He saw Joker, saw the MP5 and then looked down at his own gun as if seeing it for the first time. Joker fired instinctively and put three bullets into the man, two in the chest and one in the head, sending him slamming backwards.

The man at the table began to turn but before he could

bring his gun up Ginge hit him with four rounds. Joker took out the man on the couch before he even turned round and he died without knowing what had hit him.

Joker stepped into the room first, followed by Ginge, and Jacko and Bunny dropped down behind them. The girl began to stand up but Ginge pushed her back down. "You fucking Brit bastard!" she screamed, and Ginge slapped her so hard that she was almost knocked out of the chair. A thin dribble of blood ran down her chin. Her eyes blazed and she stood up, her hands hooked like claws, and she lashed out at Ginge's eyes. He swayed backwards, easily avoiding her attack, and prodded her in the stomach with the barrel of his gun. She doubled up, gasping for breath and retching, and Ginge threw her back into the chair.

"Stay where you are you fucking bitch or you're dead!" he warned. He kept the gun trained on her while Joker moved along the hall, stepping over the bodies of the two men, checking the kitchen, bathroom and three bedrooms. Jacko and Bunny moved behind him. They were a well co-ordinated team, they'd spent hundreds of hours training together in the killing house at Hereford, breathing in lead fumes and smoke as they pumped round after round into cardboard cut-outs of Russian storm-troopers. Compared with the killing house, this was a breeze.

"Clear," said Joker when he was satisfied.

"You have the girl?" the Colonel's voice asked.

"Secured," said Ginge.

The Oriental groaned, murmured something in a language none of the men could understand, and then went still, blood seeping from between his lips, his chest a mess of mangled flesh and pieces of ribcage.

The three SAS men joined Ginge in the lounge. Jacko and Bunny checked the bodies while Joker began to search the room, quickly and efficiently. He found the Semtex in a cupboard below a bookcase in the lounge, along with some detonators and several electric clocks. In a walk-in cupboard in the hall, by the front door, he found an empty box that once contained a laptop computer. Inside the box was an instruction manual, still sealed in its polythene wrapping, and pieces of plastic-coated wire. He took it into the lounge and threw it at the girl's feet.

"What's this?" he shouted. "Is this the next bomb, you Irish whore?" His words came out in short, staccato bursts like bullets from his MP5.

The Bombmaker wiped the back of her hand across her mouth, smearing the blood across her lips like a manic clown's make-up. "Fuck off," she said. "And I'm Scottish you ignorant bastard." Joker stamped on her instep and she screamed in pain. As she bent down to rub her foot Joker slammed his fist into her face and she hurtled back into the chair. Tears streamed down her cheeks and she covered her face with her hands. Ginge grabbed her hair and yanked her head back.

Joker put his face up close so that she could smell his breath. "Listen you bitch. We've killed your friends and unless you talk to me you can join them."

He nodded at Ginge and he dragged her by the hair over to where Fisher lay face down in a pool of his own blood. Ginge threw her on top of the body and rubbed her face in the blood. Joker walked over and kicked her in the back, over her kidney where he knew the pain would be excruciating.

"Get her on her knees," Joker said, and Ginge hoisted her up by her hair. Joker stood in front of her and levelled the gun at her mouth.

She shook her head from side to side. "You're too late," she whispered.

"Stand to the side," Joker said to Ginge. "I'm going to blow her fucking head off." Ginge moved from behind her and Bunny and Jacko went to stand by the window.

"There's nobody who'll know that you didn't die when we stormed the flat," he told her menacingly. "There are no witnesses. This isn't going to be another Gibraltar."

"You're too late," she said. "It's set to go off in less than five minutes. They won't be able to land in time."

"A plane?"

"No shit, Sherlock." She cleared her throat and spat down on the floor, not to insult him but because her mouth was filling up with blood and saliva.

"Which plane?"

She was talking now, because she figured that whatever she told him it wouldn't make a difference. She wanted him to know, and to know that there was nothing he could do to stop it. She told him it was a special flight to Rome, that a journalist called Ian Wood was carrying the bomb, and that everybody on board the flight was as good as dead. She began to laugh sourly until Joker hit her on the side of her head with his gun as Ginge began relaying the information to the Colonel.

Woody was on his fourth whisky when the "fasten seatbelt" light went on and the front of the plane dipped down.

"Ladies and gentlemen, this is the captain speaking. There is some turbulence ahead and we are descending to avoid it. Please make sure your seat is upright and your seat-belt is fastened."

Woody frowned. He'd flown often enough to know that the normal procedure was to fly over bad weather, not under it. He fastened his seat-belt and sipped his whisky. Better to drink it rather than to take the risk of spilling it, he decided.

"Would passenger Ian Wood please make himself known to the cabin crew," said the captain. Woody didn't realise at first that it was his name that had been called, but he heard it when the message was repeated. The plane had gone into a steep descent and the stewardesses were briskly moving down the aisles checking that seats were upright and passengers strapped in. Woody could also see that they were scanning the passengers to see if anyone was reacting to the final announcement. He waved to a pretty blonde stewardess. She came over, eyebrows raised.

"I'm Ian Wood," he said. The woman in the seat next to him was openly listening, curious to know what he'd done.

"Mr Wood, do you have any baggage in the hold?" the stewardess asked briskly. Woody could tell from her tone that something was very badly wrong, so he answered immediately, suppressing his first instinct to make a joke.

"No," he said. There was a cold feeling of dread in his stomach.

"Could you give me all the cabin baggage you have, please," she said. She was smiling but he could tell that it was an act to put him at his ease and get his co-operation, the girl was frightened shitless. So was Woody.

"Oh God," he moaned, and reached between his legs to pick up his bag.

The bomb exploded.

Joker and Ginge kept Maggie covered as they waited for instructions from the Colonel. They had made her lie face down on the bloodstained carpet next to Fisher, with her hands clasped behind her neck. She had a good body, thought Joker. Good legs, firm arse, just the way he liked a woman to be. He looked at his watch.

The Colonel's voice spoke in his left ear. "The plane has gone down. We assume with all lives lost. Operation is discontinued. No loose ends. I repeat, no loose ends."

Joker looked across at Ginge to see if he had heard. Ginge nodded and made a small motion with his MP5, his way of saying that Joker could do the honours. Joker fired once into her back, just over where her heart was.

She didn't die straightaway, they never did. In books they often said that people who were shot died before they hit the ground. It never happened that way, Joker knew. Joker had killed people in Belfast, in the Falklands, in the Middle East, and once in Spain, and he'd yet to see anyone die straightaway, no matter where they were shot. If the bullet went through the heart or the lungs then the brain kept sending out messages for up to a minute or so before their eyes glazed over and they finally died. If they were shot in the head and the brains were splattered over the floor, then the heart continued to pump and the limbs twitch for a while until they realised that it was all over. That's what it was like in real life. Not many people knew the difference between death in books and movies and death in real life. But Joker knew.

When the bullet tore through her back and punched a ragged hole in her chest, her arms flailed out and she grunted. Some time after that she died in a pool of blood, her arms and legs drumming against the floor, saliva dripping from her mouth and panic in her eyes. Joker didn't stand over her and watch while she died, he stood with his back to her, looking out over the river as he waited for the banging and wheezing to stop. Slow deaths always embarrassed him.

Jon Simpson stayed late in his office so that he could see the second editions before going home. His own paper wasn't printed for another seventy-two hours but he wanted to see how the dailies treated the bombing of the jet and the SAS operation against the IRA bombers. News of the bombings had broken too late for the papers to do much in their first editions, though most had managed to get in a few pars.

A copy boy came through the double doors with a stack of papers under his arm and dropped them on to the desk. Simpson separated the tabloids from the broadsheets and went through them first: the *Sun*, the *Daily Mirror*, the *Daily Mail*, the *Daily Express*, the *Daily Star* and *Today*. They all had pictures of the wreckage in the sea, and the head-shots of the active service unit. They had all used the girl Bombmaker's photograph big on their front pages because that was the obvious one to go for, and both the *Express* and the *Mail* had used Woody's picture on the front along with the story of how he'd been duped into carrying the bomb.

Yeah, Simpson thought, that's how he'd do it. The bombing, the betrayal, the SAS operation on the front, along with the girl's picture. Inside, backgrounders on the bombing campaign and the SAS, biogs of the bombers and lots of political reaction. A great story, just a pity that it hadn't happened on a Saturday night. The two pictures of Woody looked up at Simpson. Simpson shook his head sadly. "Well, Woody, you finally made the front page," he said to himself. He gathered the papers up and took them home to read in detail.

The call to attend the meeting in Whitehall came as Bromley was reading the morning papers at his breakfast table. The bombing of the jet was on the front of every paper, along with a graphic account of the SAS operation against the bombers in Wapping. From the amount of detail in the reports it was obvious that Ministry of Defence press officers had been hard at work pushing the Government line. There was no mention of The Chinaman in any of the stories. His life, and death, would remain a secret for ever. Another basic fact missing from all of the stories was how the authorities had managed to locate the active service unit. Intelligence, was the nearest thing to an explanation. The press officers knew exactly how to handle the Press, to spoonfeed them with more information than they could handle so that they'd forget to ask the basic questions.

He put his jacket on, kissed his wife on the cheek and went out to the garage to check the underside of his car. He peered through the driver's window to check that the onboard detection device showed that his car hadn't been tampered with and when he was satisfied he took several steps backwards and clicked a small remote-control device that started the car automatically. Only when he was satisfied that his car was safe did he unlock the door and get in. The safety precautions were second nature to him, and had been long before the car-bomb deaths of Airey Neave and Ian Gow.

The early morning phone call meant that he'd have to completely reschedule his day, but a call from the Co-ordinator of Intelligence and Security took precedence over everything else. The Co-ordinator answered to only two higher authorities – the Prime Minister and the Permanent Secretaries Committee on the Intelligence Services. His main role in life was to ensure that all the different intelligence agencies worked together, an uphill struggle at the best of times.

Bromley was one of the last to arrive at the conference room and he eased himself into an empty chair. The room was almost filled by a long, oval table of highly polished mahogany around which sat many familiar faces, several of whom nodded to Bromley. The room itself was typical Whitehall, an ornate fireplace, a smattering of respectable oil paintings in gilded frames and fussy patterned carpets. The man who stood at the head of the table was also typical Whitehall, pin-stripe suit, crisp white shirt, dark-blue tie, neatly combed hair that was greying at the temples, ramrod-straight back behind which were clasped hands with immaculately mani-cured nails. The Co-ordinator was a career civil servant for whom the fight against terrorism was merely a stepping stone to the knighthood that he regarded as his birthright, but he was every bit as committed to the task as the men who sat waiting for him to speak. They represented, Bromley knew, the cream of the country's anti-terrorism agencies, though he was somewhat surprised to see that there were no heads pre-sent, they were all number twos or personal assistants to the chiefs. They were all grim-faced, most had lost colleagues or friends on the doomed flight. He recognised representatives from MI5 and MI6, the Defence Intelligence Staff, several members of his own Anti-Terrorist Branch, and there were men he didn't know. Some were high-ranking police officers, others were men with military haircuts and bearing who he guessed were SAS or SBS.

There were no name-cards identifying those present, nor was there any writing equipment on the table – just a few crystal jugs of water and upturned glasses. There were, he noticed ruefully, no ashtrays.

One or two latecomers filed through the double doors lead-ing to the room, smiling apologies at the Co-ordinator. As they took their places two men in dark suits went out, closing the doors behind them.

"Gentlemen," said the Co-ordinator, "thank you for coming. Let me say first that no notes are to be taken of this meeting, and it must not be the subject of any memos or written reports. You should also not record this meeting in your diaries. This meeting never took place. Is that understood?"

He waited for all the men to nod acceptance.

"Thank you. This is by way of a briefing for the various security and intelligence services, and for those police authorities which will be affected by what I am about to tell you. You are free to verbally brief your superiors on the nature of this meeting, but there is to be no down-the-line transfer of the information. This, as you will appreciate when I have finished, is on a need-to-know basis. And those with a need to know are a very, very select group."

He had the undivided attention of every man in the room now. There was no fidgeting, no coughing, no one looked anywhere except at the face of the Co-ordinator.

"You will all have heard about the horrifying events of yesterday evening. Tragic, absolutely tragic. It did, however, bring about the demise of the active service unit which has been behind the recent atrocities, and for that we are all grateful to Special Branch and to the SAS." He nodded to representatives of both organisations, including Bromley.

"As you know, one hundred and thirty-six people died in yesterday's plane crash. That includes twelve children and three nuns, as well as the Members of Parliament and civil servants who were on the flight. The public backlash against the IRA has already started. Not just in the Press, though obviously all the newspapers are clamouring for something to be done, including the normal misguided calls for the return of the death penalty. It goes beyond that. This time there is a groundswell of public opinion against the IRA, a feeling that something should be done, that something must be done."

He paused again, looking round the table at the men who were hanging on his every word. "Gentlemen, we have here a window of opportunity. Our experts tell us that the reaction against the terrorists will be at fever pitch for the next ten days, possibly two weeks. When the IRA hits a soft target, or kills innocent bystanders, they normally follow quickly with a highly visible attack on a legitimate target. It restores their credibility, as it were. Public opinion is notoriously fickle, but this time they have gone too far. Now, we around this table know that it was a rogue IRA active service unit responsible for the bombing campaign, that in fact it had not been sanctioned by Belfast or Dublin. That information has been kept from the Press. So far as the public is concerned it was an official IRA operation.

"The decision was taken late last night, at the highest level, to take positive action against senior members of the IRA and Sinn Fein. Over the next seven days the top echelons of the organisation will be eliminated, at a time when public opinion will be totally, one hundred per cent, against them. That is the window of opportunity I spoke about. Anything we do now, right now, will have the unqualified backing of the public. This is not, I repeat not, a shoot-to-kill policy. It is a shoot-to-kill operation. A one-off. We have drawn up a list of the twenty-five men, and women, who we see as being the key members of the IRA, without whom we feel the organisation would no longer be a viable terrorist force. A combined, and highly secret, task-force of SAS and SBS operatives will move against them. Wherever possible it will be made to seem like an accident, a car crash, a drugs overdose, a fall downstairs, but if it cannot be done tidily it will be a straightforward assassination made to look as if it is the work of Protestant extremists. Once the operation is over, the IRA will no longer be an effective threat. Then we can take them on using more legitimate methods, including the formation of a new Anti-Terrorist Task-Force, a single national task-force to counter terrorism. That, however, will be the subject of further meetings later this month. Now, are there any questions?"

Most of the men sitting around the table seemed stunned, though Bromley knew that they would all wholeheartedly support the plan put forward by the Co-ordinator. Most of them had privately been pushing for such a policy for many years, determined that the only way to defeat the IRA was to match their ferocity.

"I would appreciate it if you would confine your comments to questions," the Co-ordinator continued. "This is not a discussion forum, there is nothing to be voted on, no consensus is needed. The decision has already been taken at a much higher level. The highest level."

One of the uniformed police officers coughed and raised his hand. "When does the operation start?" he asked.

The Co-ordinator looked at a slim gold watch on his wrist. "It started ten minutes ago," he said quietly.

Another hand went up. One of the MI6 representatives. "Can we be told who is on the list?" he asked.

"Officially there is no list," the Co-ordinator said. "Nothing has ever been put down on paper, there will be no written record. However, I am able to tell you the names of the twenty-five IRA members that we feel the organisation can least afford to lose."

The names were all known to those around the table, so there were no raised eyebrows of surprise, just nods of approval. Bromley put his hand in his pocket and took out his pipe. He tapped the stem against his teeth as the names rolled on. Liam Hennessy came somewhere in the middle. Sean Morrison was the last name to be spoken.

THE TUNNEL RATS

For Maureen

I am indebted to Alistair Cumming for keeping me on the right track regarding the work of the British Transport Police, and to Mr Hoang, who took me deeper into the Vietnamese tunnels than I really wanted to go. I read and reread the definitive work on the Cu Chi tunnel complex – *The Tunnels of Cu Chi* by Tom Mangold and John Penycate, first published by Hodder & Stoughton in 1985 – and unreservedly recommend it to anyone who wants to know more about one of the most remarkable battlefields of the Vietnam War.

The scorpion's jet-black endoskeleton glistened as it scuttled away from the anvil-shaped rock. It moved quickly, its stinger arched over its back, leaving a trail in the sandy dirt the only record of its passing. The jungle at dusk was usually a noisy place, with birds and insects marking their territory before the final rays of the reddish sun disappeared below the horizon, but for several minutes there had been a heavy silence as if the whole world was holding its breath.

A small indentation appeared in the dirt in front of the rock, as if a ghostly finger had scratched the surface. The indentation formed a straight line and grains of dirt dribbled down into the crease. A second line appeared, eighteen inches away from the first and running parallel to it, then a third line appeared, and a fourth, and the lines slowly grew together until they formed a rectangle in the dirt. There was a gentle scraping sound from somewhere under the ground, then the rectangle of dirt lifted up. Grains of soil spilled around the sides as the rectangle tilted, revealing a bamboo hatchway into which dry leaves had been intertwined. The hatch was thrown to the side, uncovering a square hole.

A soft peaked cap made of camouflage material appeared, and then a face. The face was striped with light and dark green paint and there was no way of knowing where the flesh ended and the cap began. Narrowed eyes scrutinised the surrounding area for several minutes. Only when the man was satisfied that it was safe did he leave the hole, crawling on his belly like a snake, a silenced automatic in his right hand, an unlit flashlight in his left. As he crawled away from the hatch, a second figure appeared, another man wearing identical gear, but with a scarf of camouflage material tied around his head instead of a cap.

The first man knelt in the shade of a thick-trunked tree around which vines wound like the veins in an old woman's arm. He made an 'okay' gesture with the thumb and first finger of his left hand and beckoned for the second man to come out in the open, all the time his eyes scanning the jungle, alert for any sign of danger. The second man joined him, a sawn-off shotgun cradled in his hands like a valuable antique. The second man nodded at the first, then moved off to the right.

A third head emerged from the hole. The third man wasn't wearing a cap, and his short, dark, curly hair was the only sign that he was of a different race to the first two, because every inch of his exposed skin was covered in camouflage paint. He crawled out, an M2 carbine with a paratrooper stock in his right hand, closely followed by a fourth man.

They fanned out until the four men were equally spaced around the hatch, far enough apart so that they couldn't all be taken out with a single hand grenade or a spray of automatic fire. The men were used to working together as a team and communicated only with small hand movements and nods. They remained immobile for a full minute until they were satisfied that they were alone in the jungle, then the man with the flashlight crept back to the hatchway.

A fifth man appeared at the entrance, his face contorted with pain, and the man with the flashlight helped him out. The fifth man could barely walk, and even with the other man's help he stumbled and fell face down into the sandy dirt. The back of his shirt was ripped and torn in more than a dozen places and streaked with still-wet blood. The man with the flashlight knelt down by the side of the injured man and checked his wounds with a professional eye. He patted the man's neck and whispered something in his ear, then went back to the hatchway where a sixth man was already crawling out into the open.

The eyes of the sixth man were wide and staring, the whites exaggerated by the camouflage paint smeared over his flesh. He stumbled to his feet and looked around anxiously as if wondering which way to run.

The man with the flashlight holstered his gun and gripped the shoulder of the sixth man, pulling him close so that their faces were only inches apart. 'It's okay,' he hissed. 'We're out.' The sixth man opened his mouth but no words came. The man with the flashlight glared at him with a fierce intensity. 'It's okay,' he said. 'Tell me it's okay, Rabbit.' He tightened his grip on the man's shoulder.

The sixth man visibly relaxed. 'It's okay,' he whispered. 'Again.'

'It's okay,' said the sixth man, slightly more confident this time. 'I'm sorry, Doc. I lost it.'

The two men stared at each other for several seconds, then the man with the flashlight nodded. 'We all lost it,' he said. He took his hand away from Rabbit's shoulder and stared at his palm. It was red with blood. 'Are you hurt?' Doc asked.

Rabbit shook his head. 'No. It's . . .' He shook his head as if trying to rid himself of a bad memory.

A seventh man climbed through the hatchway, a green headband holding his dirt-encrusted hair flat against his scalp. He had a rope tied around his waist and it tightened as he crawled away from the hole. 'Help me,' he said, through tightly gritted teeth.

Doc and Rabbit grabbed the rope and pulled, grunting with exertion. 'Are you sure he's . . . ?' began Rabbit, but Doc silenced him with a threatening look.

Together they hauled in the rope. Attached to the other end was the body of another soldier. The rope had been looped under his arms and they heaved the body out of the hole. The neck was a mass of torn flesh as if it had been hacked with a dull blade and the shirt was caked with dried blood.

The seventh man took an eighteen-inch-long knife from a scabbard on his leg and used it to cut the rope from around his own waist. As he replaced the knife in its scabbard he saw that the back of his hand was covered with blood. He knelt down and wiped his hand in the dirt. His skin was a dark olive colour and even under the camouflage make-up his high razor-sharp cheekbones hinted at his Latino ancestry. 'Now what?' he said, looking up at Doc. His voice was flat and cold and his eyes were equally emotionless.

'Put the hatch back,' said Doc.

The man in the headband nodded and did as he was told.

Doc went over to the injured man and knelt down beside him again. 'On your feet,' he whispered. 'We can't stay here.'

The injured man murmured something incomprehensible and struggled to stand. Rabbit came over to help and together with Doc he pulled the man upright. In the distance there was a low rumbling growl as if a thunderstorm was approaching. 'I'm all right,' said the injured man.

'Can you walk?' asked Doc.

'Don't worry about me,' he said.

The Latino slotted the hatch into its original position and smoothed dirt over it.

Doc looked over his shoulder. 'Sergio, put the rock over it. Rabbit, give him a hand.'

The two men pushed the rock over the hatchway. Doc looked towards the horizon, smeared blood red by the dying rays of the sun.

'That was bad, Doc,' said the injured man.

'I know.'

'Real bad.'

'Forget it,' said Doc, cocking his head and listening to the approaching thunder.

Rabbit and Sergio joined Doc and the injured man. Doc motioned for the three other men to join the group and they stood in a circle, avoiding each other's gaze as if fearful of what they might see in their eyes. The sun began to slip below the horizon and the shadows of the seven men faded on the sandy ground.

'That goes for all of us,' said Doc. 'We forget it. We forget it ever happened.'

'There'll be questions,' said Sergio.

'And I'll answer them. No one gets blamed. No recriminations.' He looked across at the mutilated corpse. 'What happened down there stays dead and buried.' He looked back at the men. 'Any arguments? If there are, I want to hear them now.' All six men shook their heads. Doc reached towards Rabbit and seized his hand. He wiped his forefinger across Rabbit's bloody palm, then smeared the blood across Sergio's right hand. He did the same to all the men, then held out his own hand, palm down. Sergio put his hand on top of Doc's, and one by one the men followed suit until there were seven hands piled one on top of the other. Below their feet the earth began to vibrate.

'Not worth a rat's ass,' said Doc. 'Let me hear you say it.'

One by one the men repeated the phrase.

Doc took his hand away from the bottom of the stack. 'Let's go,' he said. 'We've got a long walk home.'

The men unlinked their hands.

'Shit,' said the injured man, his hand reaching up to his neck.

'What?' asked Doc.

'My dogtags. They've gone.' His head swivelled around and he stared at the rock and the covered hatch. He took a step towards the rock.

Doc gripped the man's arm. 'Leave it.'

A sudden explosion far off to their right knocked them to the ground. It was followed swiftly by a second and a third.

'B-52s!' shouted Sergio. 'They're dumping their shit!'

Doc got to his feet and helped the injured man up. 'Let's get out of here,' he shouted.

There were more explosions off to their left. The last of the sun disappeared below the horizon as the seven men regrouped. Rabbit helped Doc with the injured man and together they headed south, away from the falling bombs.

The scorpion emerged from underneath a twig torn from a tree by the force of the explosions. Doc raised a booted foot and stamped on it, squashing it flat without breaking stride.

The old lady muttered to herself as she walked along the street pushing a supermarket trolley, and passers-by gave her a wide berth. She had a red woollen scarf tied around her head and a thick tweed coat that reached down almost to her ankles. She was wearing scuffed leather boots with bright yellow shoelaces and from around her ankles protruded pieces of newspaper. One of the wheels on her trolley kept sticking and she had to concentrate hard to keep it moving in a straight line. The trolley contained everything she owned, packed into plastic carrier bags which were stacked on several sheets of cardboard.

She stopped next to a rubbish bin and began searching through it. Her first major find was a copy of the *Daily Telegraph*, rolled up tightly. She unrolled it carefully and flicked through it. She beamed with pleasure as she saw that the crossword hadn't been done, and refolded it, slipping it into one of the carrier bags. Deeper inside the bin she came across a Burger King carton containing a barely touched cheeseburger and a pack of French fries, along with an unopened sachet of tomato ketchup. She giggled and did a little jig around the bin, then packed her treasure into another carrier bag and resumed her journey. There were more than a dozen rubbish bins along the one-mile stretch of road and she checked them twice each day.

Small drops of rain began to patter around her and she glared up at the leaden sky. A raindrop splattered on her spectacles and she took them off and wiped the lenses with a pale blue handkerchief. After she'd put her glasses back on she untied a large golfing umbrella from the side of her trolley, unfurled it, and jammed the handle down among the carrier bags so that she had some shelter as she walked.

T he train lurched to a halt, throwing a Japanese tourist off balance. Her husband steadied her by the elbow as the doors opened and half a dozen passengers spilled out on to the platform. The doors closed and the Tube train swiftly accelerated towards the next station. Tommy Reid rested the back of his head against the window and exhaled through clenched teeth. He'd been riding the Circle Line train for more than two hours and he was dog tired. He had a bottle in a brown paper bag, which he raised to his lips, taking a couple of swallows. He narrowed his eyes and stared at the map on the wall of the carriage opposite him. Bayswater was the next station. He sighed mournfully. The muscles in his backside ached and his ears hurt from the near-constant noise. He scratched the two-day growth of beard with the palm of his hand and grinned across at the blind man sitting opposite him, a thirty-something man in blue wrinkled linen jacket and black jeans, holding a white cane between his legs.

The train began to slow as it approached Bayswater. Reid's earpiece crackled. 'We have a possible contact,' said a voice. 'Three white males. Black motorcycle jacket, red baseball jacket with white sleeves, green anorak.' The three muggers had struck four times in the last week.

Reid sniffed and took another swig at the bottle as the train slowed then stopped.

'Fourth carriage,' said the voice in his ear. Reid was in the fifth carriage from the front. He swivelled his head. Through the window in the connecting door he saw the three teenagers board the carriage and huddle together, laughing at something Anorak had said.

The doors closed and the train lurched forward again. Motorcycle Jacket took a stopwatch from the back pocket of his jeans and nodded at Anorak and Baseball Jacket. All three of the teenagers pulled out black objects from inside their jackets, the size of flashlights with small metal prongs on the end, and spread out along the length of the carriage. Baseball Jacket clicked the trigger on his and blue sparks arced across the prongs.

Reid got to his feet and went over to the connecting door. Two schoolgirls moved away uneasily. He slowly buttoned up his thick overcoat, figuring it would offer at least some protection against the stun guns. Reinforcements would be waiting at Paddington, and all Reid had to do was to make sure that no one got hurt.

A businessman handed over his wallet. Anorak took it and put it into a green Harrods carrier bag. A housewife fumbled in her shopping bag while Baseball Jacket stood over her menacingly. An elderly black man was waving his hands and shaking his head, clearly unwilling to give up his money. Anorak walked quickly over to him, thrust the prongs of his stun gun against the man's thigh and pressed the trigger. The man screamed and then stiffened, his whole body shuddering involuntarily.

'Oh shit,' said Reid. The muggers had never actually used their stun guns before – the threat alone had always been enough to frighten their victims into submission. He gripped the metal handle and pulled open the door. The noise of the rolling gear rattling down the rails was deafening. He opened the door leading to the adjoining carriage and stepped across the gap.

The three teenagers looked up. Reid held out the bottle and grinned blankly. 'Wanna drink?' he asked, pretending to lose his balance. Reid figured they were about thirty seconds away from Paddington – all he had to do was to keep them distracted.

Suddenly the door at the far end of the carriage opened and two men in leather jackets and jeans burst in. Reid cursed. They might as well have been wearing uniforms.

'Cops!' yelled Motorcycle Jacket. 'Run for it!'

All three teenagers hurtled down the carriage, towards Reid. Anorak reached him first. Reid stepped to the side and slammed his bottle against the teenager's head. Anorak slumped to the side, falling against two young men in suits who grabbed him and wrestled him to the ground.

Reid tried to bring up the bottle for a second time but Baseball Jacket ran into him, slamming him against the carriage door, then stabbed the stun gun against Reid's shoulder and pressed the trigger. Reid felt as if he'd been kicked by a horse. He tried to breathe but his lungs wouldn't work and the life seemed to drain out of his legs. Baseball Jacket yanked open the door and he and Motorcycle Jacket spilled into the next carriage. Reid heard the brakes begin to bite as the train approached Paddington.

They rushed along the carriage, pushing the two school-girls out of the way, the two plainclothes policemen about ten paces behind. Ahead of them the blind man was getting to his feet, one hand gripping his white cane, the other outstretched. The train burst out of the tunnel and the platform flashed by.

'Out of the way!' Baseball Jacket shouted, pushing the blind man to the side as the train came to a halt and the doors opened. Baseball Jacket stepped out, but as he did so, a hand grabbed his hair and yanked him back.

'You're under arrest,' said the blind man, slamming Baseball Jacket against the side of the carriage. The white cane dropped to the floor.

Motorcycle Jacket skidded to a halt and held out his stun gun. 'You're not blind!' he shouted.

'It's a miracle,' grinned the blind man, jerking Baseball Jacket's arm up behind his back until the teenager yelped in pain.

Motorcycle Jacket glared at the blind man, then spat at his face and jumped out of the carriage. The blind man pushed Baseball Jacket towards the two plainclothes policemen, who grabbed his arms, then he tossed his sunglasses away and chased after Motorcycle Jacket.

The uniformed inspector shook his head in frustration as he stared at the closed-circuit television monitor. The teenager in the motorcycle jacket was cannoning down the platform, pushing people out of his way and waving his stun gun in the air. Nick Wright was in pursuit, his arms pumping furiously as he ran. On another monitor Tommy Reid stumbled out on to the platform, still holding his bottle, and was almost bowled over by the fleeing mugger.

'Keystone bloody Cops,' muttered the inspector.

'Sorry, sir?' said the shirtsleeved officer sitting in front of him.

'Where are the reinforcements?' said the inspector, putting his hands on the back of the officer's chair and leaning closer to the rank of monitors.

'Main ticketing area, sir,' said the officer. He pressed a button on the panel in front of him and the image on the central monitor changed to show half a dozen uniformed British Transport Police officers sprinting towards the top of the escalators.

The inspector straightened up and ran a hand through his thinning hair. He watched the mugger run into one of the exits, closely followed by Wright. At least Wright appeared to be gaining on him.

Nick Wright exhaled through clenched teeth as he ran, his lungs burning with each breath. He swung around a corner just in time to see Motorcycle Jacket collide with a guitar-playing busker, scattering a tin can of coins across the tiled floor.

'Stop him!' Wright shouted, but no one moved to help. His quarry sprinted to the escalators and ran up, pushing people out of the way.

'Police!' yelled Wright. 'Move, people, please!' Again his pleas were ignored and he had physically to force his way up the escalator after the teenager.

Motorcycle Jacket was halfway up the escalator when a

group of six uniformed officers appeared at the top and fanned out. The boy snarled at the waiting officers, then leaped off the escalator and on to the concrete stairs. He sped down the steps, taking them five at a time, as the policemen rushed to the down escalator.

Wright vaulted off the escalator and on to the stairs, twisting his leg as he landed. Passengers on both escalators watched in amazement as the teenager cannoned down the steps with Wright in pursuit.

As they neared the bottom of the stairs, Reid appeared around the corner. His jaw dropped as he saw Motorcycle Jacket running towards him, and before he could react, Motorcycle Jacket ran into him, knocking him to the side.

The teenager was a good fifteen years younger than Wright, and Wright cursed the age difference as he ran. He took a quick look over his shoulder, flashing Reid a sympathetic smile. In his earpiece, Wright could hear the inspector giving instructions to his men, but there was no sign of the uniformed officers. Motorcycle Jacket reached a crossroads and dashed off to the left, forcing his way between two students with rucksacks. The tunnel led to a platform which Motorcycle Jacket sprinted along. Closed-circuit television cameras stared down at them as they ran along the platform.

Motorcycle Jacket slowed as he realised that there were no more exits off the platform, and all that lay ahead was the train tunnel.

Wright slowed, too. In his earpiece, the inspector told his men which platform Wright was on. He heard footsteps behind him and he turned to see Tommy Reid jog on to the platform, some distance behind him.

'I've got him, Tommy,' Wright shouted. Reid waved his bottle in acknowledgement.

Motorcycle Jacket turned to face the two men, holding his stun gun in front of him, then jumped down on to the track and began to sprint towards the tunnel mouth.

Wright took a quick look up at the digital display above the platform – the next train wouldn't be along for six minutes. He ran after Motorcycle Jacket, into the blackness of the tunnel, then gradually slowed and stopped.

The teenager was bent double, his hands on his knees, fighting for breath. 'What are you waiting for?' shouted Motorcycle Jacket.

Wright jumped as if he'd been pinched. He swallowed. His mouth was dry yet his whole body felt as if it was drenched in sweat. He tried to step forward, but his legs wouldn't move. Reid had jumped down on to the track and was walking uncertainly towards him.

Motorcycle Jacket grinned. 'What, afraid of the dark, are we? Jesus, are you in the wrong fucking job or what?' Laughing, he turned his back on Wright and began to jog down the track, into the blackness.

Wright closed his eyes, willing himself to follow the teenager, but he simply couldn't move. His legs remained locked. A hand fell on his shoulder.

'What's up, Nick?' asked Reid, and he moved to stand in front of Wright. 'You're soaking wet,' he said.

Wright opened his eyes. 'He got away,' he said.

'Don't worry about it. We'll get the bastard.' Reid held up his bottle. 'How about a drink?'

Wright shook his head. He took one last look into the black depths of the tunnel, then turned and walked towards the platform. Back into the light.

T he old lady splashed through a puddle and grimaced. The newspapers lining her leather boots kept her warm but they didn't keep out the water. The rain was pouring down, and even with the golfing umbrella over her head, she was still getting soaked. Ahead of her lay the mouth of the tunnel she knew would provide her with warmth and sanctuary.

She rattled the trolley along the side of the railway line, the rails crusted with dirt and rust from years of disuse. The wheels of her trolley skidded across a patch of gravel and then locked as they bit into damp grass. The old lady whispered soft words of encouragement and coaxed the trolley into the tunnel. It was suddenly quiet. One by one she removed the carrier bags, then she carefully placed her sheets of cardboard and three blankets on the ground and sat down on them with a grunt.

She leaned over to the carrier bag where she'd put the Burger King carton. She opened the carton with an expectant smile on her face, then took out the burger and sniffed it. It couldn't have been more than a couple of hours old; it was still warm. She took a bite and chewed slowly. Something moved at the tunnel entrance, something small and black that kept close to the rail furthest from her. It was a rat, almost two feet long from nose to tail. The old woman watched it go. She had no fear of rats, and no revulsion either. Like her, it was only seeking food and shelter. She tore off a small piece of hamburger and tossed it over to the rat, but it ignored the tidbit and hurried by.

The man woke as the first rays of the morning sun hit the tops of the New York skyscrapers. Down below, the city's garbage trucks growled through the streets and far off in the distance a siren howled like a lovesick dog. As soon as his eyes opened he sat up and swung his legs off the single bed. There was no clock in the small room and no watch on the man's wrist but he knew exactly what the time was. He walked naked to the bathroom, his feet padding across the bare wooden floorboards. He stood under a cold shower and washed methodically from his head down. He rinsed and dried himself before going back into his tiny room and opening the door to the wardrobe. A single grey suit hung there, with three identical long-sleeved white shirts that had been laundered and were still in their polythene wrappings. A tie rack on the back of the wardrobe door held a solitary tie. At the bottom of the wardrobe were two drawers. The man pulled the top one open. It contained a dozen pairs of khaki shorts. He slipped on a pair, then took the sheets, blanket and pillowcase from the bed and put them in the wardrobe.

Behind the bathroom door was a black plastic bucket and a wooden-handled mop. The man filled the bucket with water and swabbed the wooden floor. When he'd finished with the floor, he used a cloth meticulously to clean the toilet, basin and shower.

16

The cleaning over, he went back into the room and sat down on a wooden chair, his hands on his knees. In an hour's time he would exercise for thirty minutes, then he would go to a local diner and eat breakfast. He would only leave the room twice, both times to eat; the rest of the time he would spend exercising and waiting. Waiting for the call. The man knew the call would come eventually. It always had in the past.

The rat scurried purposefully down the disused rail track, its nose twitching as it scented the air ahead. It could smell something sweet, something nourishing, something that it hadn't smelled in a long time. It was joined by a second rat, a female several inches shorter. A third rat emerged from the darkness to their left, its eyes glinting and its ears forward.

The three rats began to run, their paws crunching on the gravel around the sleepers. Soon they were among more rats. A dozen. Twenty. All heading the same way. Before long the tunnel entrance was nothing more than a small squashed circle behind them. The three rats stopped running: there were too many furry bodies ahead of them to keep up the pace. They slowed to a walk, then they had to push their way through the mass of rodents to make any progress. The sweet smell was stronger, driving them into a frenzy. Food. The food was close by.

Superintendent Richard Newton stirred his tea thought-fully as he watched the video recording. He looked up as his secretary entered his office and placed a plate of assorted biscuits on his desk. 'Thanks, Nancy,' he said, using the remote control to switch off the recorder. He sighed and leaned back in his executive chair. 'I suppose you'd better send in the clowns,' he said.

Nancy opened the door and ushered in Nick Wright and Tommy Reid. They stood in front of his desk, unsure whether or not to sit. Newton continued to stir his tea, a look of contempt on his face. Reid had changed out of his tramp's disguise, but his brown suit and stained tie weren't much of an improvement. Wright was as usual the better dressed of the two, but there were dark patches under his eyes as if he hadn't slept for a week. Both men studiously avoided Newton's stare, their eyes fixed on a point in the wall behind him.

'Tell me, Tommy, what does the word "assistance" mean to you?' Newton asked.

'Help?' said Reid, hopefully.

Newton nodded. 'Help would do. Support. Aid. All perfectly reasonable alternatives. So when the Moles asked for assistance, what do you think they expected to get?'

'Help, sir?' said Reid, frowning.

'Exactly,' said Newton. 'Help. Not hindrance, not a foul-up, not two of my men making fools of themselves. What happened down there? How did he get away?'

'The guy was fast, sir. That guy could run for England.'

Newton sniffed and wrinkled his nose. 'Maybe if you two spent more time in the gym and less time in the pub you'd have been able to keep up with him.' He picked up his spoon and started to stir his tea again. 'What was in the bottle, Tommy?'

After several seconds of silence, Reid shrugged. 'I was supposed to be an alkie, sir. I could hardly have carted around a bottle of Perrier, could I?'

'Inspector Murray said you'd been drinking on the job. So I'm asking you on the record, what was in the bottle? On the record, Tommy.'

Reid looked across at his partner, then back at the superintendent. 'Ribena, sir.'

Newton put the spoon down and sipped his tea. 'Ribena?' he said, as if it was the first time he'd ever heard the word. 'That would account for the smell on your breath, I suppose,' he said dryly, then opened the top drawer of his desk and took out a pack of Polo mints which he rolled across his desk towards Reid. 'We're going to need an artist's impression of the one that got away. There's nothing usable on the video.' He dismissed them with a tired half-wave, then had a change of mind. 'Nick, stay behind, will you?'

Newton waited until Reid had closed the door before asking Wright to sit down on one of the two steel and leather chairs facing the desk. 'Are you still living with Tommy?' he asked.

Wright nodded. 'Yes, sir.'

'How long's it been now? Three months?'

'Five.'

Newton traced his finger along the edge of his saucer. 'What about getting a place of your own?'

Wright pulled a face as if he was in pain. 'It's a question of money, sir. Things are a bit tight just now.'

'Your divorce came through, right?'

Wright nodded again. 'Yeah, but she's still after more money. There's the house payments, child support, she wanted double-glazing put in.' Wright held his hands out as if warding off an attack. 'I'm sorry, I shouldn't bring my problems into the office.'

'You've nothing to apologise for, Nick. Divorce is becoming the norm these days. Unfortunately.' He stared at the cup with its pattern of roses. 'Five months is a long time to be living with Tommy. He's one of our best detectives, but his personal life leaves a lot to be desired. You've got a lot of potential, Nick. I wouldn't want any of his – how shall I put it? – habits, rubbing off on you.'

'Understood, sir.'

Newton's telephone rang and he waved for Wright to go as he reached for the receiver.

The old woman muttered to herself as she threaded a plastic-covered chain around the shopping trolley and padlocked it to the lamp-post. She checked that it was securely fastened before walking into the police station.

A uniformed sergeant looked up as she approached the counter. He smiled politely. 'Hello, Annie, how are you today?' he asked.

'I've seen Jesus,' said the old woman. 'On the cross.'

'That's nice,' said the sergeant. He was in his early fifties, with greying hair and a tired face from years of dealing with irate members of the public, but the smile he gave the old lady seemed genuine enough. 'How about a nice cup of tea? Two sugars, right?' The sergeant called over a WPC, a slim brunette, and asked her to fetch the old woman a cup of tea from the machine in the reception area. The sergeant reached into his pocket and gave the WPC a few coins. 'Milk, two sugars,' he said. The WPC gave the old woman a quizzical look. 'Annie Lees, she's a regular,' the sergeant explained. He lowered his voice to a conspiratorial whisper. 'She's harmless.'

The old woman stood up straight and glared at him through the thick lenses of her spectacles. 'Young man, I am not harmless,' she said, her voice trembling with indignation.

T he doctor unscrewed the cap off the tube of KY Jelly and smeared it over the rubber glove, making sure there was plenty over the first and second fingers.

His patient hitched his gown up around his waist and bent over the examination couch. 'I had hoped that by the time I became Vice President I'd be past the stage where I'd have to let people shove their hands up my backside,' he joked.

The doctor smiled thinly and put down the tube. He knew how concerned his patient was, but he also knew that there was nothing he could say to put him at ease. The examination was purely routine, and neither man was expecting a change in the prognosis. 'Okay, Glenn, you know the drill. Try to relax.'

The patient chuckled dryly and opened his legs wider. 'Relax, says the man. You know when I last relaxed?' He grunted as the doctor inserted two fingers into his rectum.

'Try to push down, Glenn. I know it hurts.'

'Pete, you have no idea.' The patient forced his backside down on to the probing fingers, biting down on his lower lip and closing his eyes. The doctor's fingers moved further in and a long, low groan escaped the patient's mouth. 'I can't believe that some men do this to themselves for pleasure,' he said.

'No accounting for folk,' agreed the doctor. He moved his fingers gently, feeling for the hard mass that the Vice President's prostate had become. The patient tensed and gripped the sides of the couch. The doctor continued to probe the mass for several seconds and then slipped out his fingers. He stripped off his gloves and dropped them into a bin before handing his patient a paper towel to wipe himself with.

'How've you been feeling, Glenn?'

The patient shrugged. 'As well as can be expected, considering I've got terminal cancer.' He forced a smile. 'Sorry, shouldn't let the bitterness creep in, right?' He finished cleaning himself and changed back into his clothes. 'It's the unfairness of it, you know?'

'Yeah, I know. There's nothing fair about prostate cancer, I'm afraid.'

'I can't believe the speed of it all. Six months ago, I was fine. Now . . .' He smiled ruefully. 'Now I'm not so fine, right?'

The doctor made some notes on a clipboard. 'It's bigger.'

'A lot bigger, right?'

The doctor nodded. 'It's just about doubled over the past month.'

'That's what's so unfair,' said the patient. 'Mitterand's cancer took years to kill him. Hell, he even stood for re-election knowing that he had it. But mine . . .'

'There's no predictable pattern, Glenn. I told you that.'

'I know, I know.' The patient adjusted his tie and checked his appearance in the mirror above the washbasin. 'So what do you think?' he said, his voice matter-of-fact but his eyes fixed on the doctor's reflection. 'How long?'

There was no hesitation on the doctor's part. The two men had known each other for many years and had developed a mutual respect that the doctor knew merited complete honesty. 'Months rather than weeks,' he said. 'Nine, possibly.'

'Nine productive months?'

'That would be optimistic. Four would be more realistic.'

The patient nodded. He turned around. 'Enough time to get my affairs in order,' he said. 'Ensure a smooth transition and all that.'

'How's Elaine taking it?'

A sudden sadness flashed across the Vice President's face. 'She's only just gotten over her father,' he said. 'I intend to spend as much time with her as possible before . . .' He left the sentence hanging and gave a small shrug. 'I'll see you next week, then, Pete.' He headed for the door. 'Give my love to Margaret.'

Two Secret Service agents in dark suits were waiting for the Vice President in the reception area. They escorted him to the elevator, one of them whispering into a concealed microphone as they walked.

Tommy Reid carried two plastic cups of coffee over to his desk and sat down heavily. His desk was pushed up against Wright's and they shared three telephones between them. Reid looked over his shoulder and reached into the bottom drawer of his desk. He took out a quarter bottle of vodka and winked at Wright as he poured a slug into his cup. He held up the bottle, offering Wright a shot, but Wright shook his head. Wright was trying to arrange a photofit artist but no one was available. A bored secretary had put him on hold and for the past six minutes he'd been listening to a computerised rendition of something that a child could play with two fingers. He watched Reid sip his laced coffee.

Reid put down his coffee. 'What?' he said.

'What do you mean?' asked Wright.

'You were staring at me like I had something in my teeth.'

'Nah, I was just thinking.'

Reid passed over Wright's cup of coffee. 'Yeah, well, you don't want to be doing too much of that.'

Wright slammed down the receiver. 'It's a plot by British Telecom, that's what it is.'

'What is?'

'The music they play to keep you hanging on. In the old days they'd say that they'd call you back. Now they put you on hold for hours. Who profits, huh? British sodding Telecom, that's who.'

Reid grinned. 'The old days,' he said. 'How old are you, Nick?'

'Old enough.' The middle of their three telephones rang. Wright raised an eyebrow. 'I suppose you want me to get that?' he said.

'Wrong, Wright,' said Reid. He picked up the receiver as he took another sip at his coffee.

Wright began pecking away at his computer keyboard. He was working on a report of the morning's undercover operation and had come to the section where he had to explain what had happened in the tunnel.

Reid replaced the receiver. 'That can wait, Nick. We've got a body on the line.'

Wright stopped typing. 'Jesus. Another? That's three so far this month and we haven't even had a full moon yet.' He picked up his notebook. 'All the pool cars are taken. Can we take your car?'

'Sure. I could do with the mileage.' The detectives were supposed to use pool cars when available, but if they had to use their own vehicles they were paid a substantial mileage allowance.

They went down together to the car park. Reid's car was a four-year-old Honda Civic with forty-three thousand miles on the clock and a back-seat littered with empty fast-food containers.

They drove out on to Tavistock Place, headed south to the River Thames and turned right along the Embankment. It began to rain and Reid switched on the wipers. They smeared greasily across the glass.

Wright flicked open an *A to Z*. 'Where are we going exactly?'

'Nine Elms, not far from New Covent Garden Market.

Nearest road is Haines Street, off Nine Elms Lane. I thought I'd swing across Vauxhall Bridge and double back, the traffic'll be lighter.'

Wright tossed the street map on to the back seat. 'I don't know why you bother having an *A to Z*,' he said. 'You know every bloody road there is.'

'Just one of my many talents, Nick. You hungry?' Wright shook his head. 'Thought we might stop off at a pub or something.'

'Maybe afterwards,' said Wright.

Reid snorted contemptuously. 'What, want to see it on an empty stomach, do you?'

Wright said nothing. It wasn't his stomach he was thinking about: he was more concerned about his partner turning up on a job smelling of drink.

It took them a little under twenty minutes to reach Nine Elms. They saw two police vans and a white saloon parked at the roadside, and Reid pulled in behind them. Wright climbed out of the Honda and peered down an embankment overgrown with nettles. A beaten-down pathway through the vegetation showed where the occupants of the vans had gone down to the tracks. The sky was a dull grey and a fine drizzle gave the scene the feel of a washed-out watercolour painting.

'I thought you said this was a body on the line?' said Wright.

'That's right,' said Reid, opening the boot and taking out a pair of mud-covered Wellington boots. 'What's wrong?'

'See for yourself,' said Wright.

Reid took off his shoes, pulled on the Wellingtons and joined Wright at the edge of the embankment. The two lines down below were crusted with rust and dirt. 'Ghost train?'

said Reid. He popped a mint in his mouth and started down the slope. Wright followed him, his shoes slipping on the muddy path.

At the bottom they looked up and down the tracks, unsure which way to go. To the south, they could see several hundred yards before the lines were swallowed up in the drizzle; to the north, they curved to the left. Wright looked down at his feet. A trail of muddy footprints led north. He nodded in their direction.

Reid grinned amiably. 'You ought to be a detective,' he said.

They followed the trail. Moisture flecked Wright's suit and he put his hands in his pockets and shivered. Reid was wearing a brown raincoat which fluttered around his boots, and from somewhere he'd produced a battered tweed hat. He looked like a farmer setting out to market.

As they walked around the bend they saw a young uniformed policeman in a fluorescent yellow waterproof jacket standing at the entrance to a tunnel. The tunnel entrance was of weathered stone crisscrossed with veins of moss and overgrown with ivy and brambles. The policeman tensed as the two men approached.

'British Transport Police,' said Reid, taking out his warrant card and showing it to the constable. 'Tommy Reid. This is Nick Wright.'

'Reid and Wright?' The constable rubbed his hands together. 'Sounds like a comedy act.'

'Yeah, yeah, yeah, we've heard all the jokes,' said Reid wearily.

'Our guys are already inside,' said the constable.

'Then they're wasting their time, it's a BTP case,' said Wright.

'There hasn't been a train along here for ten years,' said the constable.

Wright shrugged. 'Makes no odds. It's Railtrack property, so it's ours.' He put his head on one side and listened to a rumbling noise from inside the tunnel. 'What's that?' he asked.

'Generator,' said the constable. 'The SOCO boys brought it with them to run the lights.'

Reid stepped into the tunnel. Wright stayed where he was. 'Nick?' said Reid.

Wright swallowed. 'Yeah, coming.' He followed Reid into the tunnel mouth. He shivered involuntarily. Ahead of them they could see white, ghostly figures moving around, and beyond them, a bright wall of light. Wright stopped. He could feel his heart pounding.

'Nick, are you okay?'

Wright took a deep breath. 'Yeah.' He shook his head and started walking briskly down the line, towards the lights. As they got closer, they saw that the ghostly figures were Scene of Crime Officers in white overalls and boots, gathering evidence. Two dark silhouettes carrying flashlights walked towards Reid and Wright, tall men with their hands in the pockets of their raincoats. Wright recognised them immediately and his heart sank. The slightly shorter of the two, Inspector Gerry Hunter of the Metropolitan Police CID, was a good-looking man in his mid-thirties with black curly hair and tanned skin. His sidekick was Detective Sergeant Clive Edmunds, slightly older with receding hair and a thickening waistline.

'What brings you on to our turf, lads?' asked Reid goodnaturedly.

'A uniform found the body and called it in,' said

Hunter. He nodded at Wright. 'Thought we'd have a look-see.'

'What was the uniform doing down here?' asked Wright. 'Having a kip?'

Hunter smiled coldly and ignored Wright's sarcasm. 'A down-and-out name of Annie Lees was sheltering from the rain a couple of days back.'

Edmunds lit a cigarette. 'She's a bit crazy. She kept talking about finding Jesus.' He offered the pack of cigarettes to Reid and Wright but both men shook their heads.

'Jesus?' repeated Reid.

'You'll understand when you've seen the body,' said Hunter. 'No one took her seriously at first.'

'Where is she now?' asked Reid.

'We've got her back at the factory. We'll keep her for you.'

Reid nodded. 'Cause of death?'

Edmunds chuckled. 'Well, it wasn't suicide.'

'The doctor's there now,' said Hunter, 'but I think it's safe to say we've got a murder enquiry.'

'We?' said Wright quickly. 'This is our case.'

'Yeah, handled many murders, have you?' asked Edmunds.

Wright felt Reid's hand on his shoulder. He realised he was glaring at Hunter and he forced himself to relax.

Hunter started to walk away and he motioned with his chin for Edmunds to follow him.

'Don't forget your gloves, lads,' said Edmunds.

Wright was about to reply when Reid squeezed his shoulder. 'Don't let them get to you, Nick. They're just taking the piss.'

They continued along the tracks towards the lights. There

29

was a flash, then, a second later, another. 'What's that?' asked Wright.

'Photographer,' said Reid. They walked by a small generator. A white cable snaked away towards two large fluorescent lights mounted on tripods.

A woman came down the tracks towards them. She was in her forties with greying blonde hair tied back in a ponytail. She was wearing disposable rubber gloves and carrying a large moulded plastic briefcase.

'Excuse me, are you the doctor?' asked Reid.

'Pathologist, actually,' she said brusquely. 'Anna Littman.'

'Tommy Reid and Nick Wright,' said Reid. 'British Transport Police.'

'I've already spoken to your colleagues,' she said briskly, and stepped to the side to walk past them.

'They're not our colleagues,' snapped Wright.

She raised her eyebrows and stared at Wright with the greenest eyes he'd ever seen. 'I've known Gerry Hunter for three years,' she said. 'I can assure you he's a detective.'

'He's with the Met, Dr Littman,' said Reid. 'We're British Transport Police.'

'Sounds like too many cooks to me,' she said.

'Can you tell us what we've got here?' asked Wright.

'What we've got is a dead white male, late forties, I think, and he's been dead for several days.'

'It's murder?' asked Reid.

'Oh, there's no doubt about that.'

'Murder weapon?' asked Reid.

'A knife, I think.'

'You think?'

'The body's in a bit of a state. The rats have been at it.

I'll know better after the post mortem. Now if you'll excuse me . . .' She brushed past Wright.

The two men turned to watch her go. 'Nice legs,' said Reid.

'I'm off women just now,' said Wright.

Reid sighed and turned up the collar of his raincoat. 'Why would anyone dump a body down here?'

'What do you mean?'

'Bound to be found eventually. If you really wanted to hide a body, you'd bury it, right?'

They walked down the track, their feet crunching on gravel. 'No footprints,' said Reid. 'And none outside if it was two or three days ago.'

'No drag marks either. So how did they get the body in here?'

'Carried it, maybe.'

'Which brings me back to my first point. Why carry it in here? Why not bury it?'

A Scene of Crime Officer stood up and stretched. He was in his fifties with steel-grey hair and thick horn-rimmed glasses. 'Nice day for it,' he said.

'Found anything?' asked Wright.

'Lots of stuff. Problem is knowing what's relevant. Down-and-outs have been sleeping here, kids playing around, dogs, cats, rats. There's litter, used condoms, sweet wrappers, empty bottles, cigarettes. We'll bag it and tag it, but as to what's relevant and what isn't, well, your guess is as good as mine.'

'No sign of a murder weapon?' asked Wright.

The man snorted softly. 'No, and I haven't come across a signed confession. But if I do . . .'

Reid and Wright walked past one of the tripod lights. A

woman in white overalls was kneeling down, examining a wooden sleeper. Wright flinched at a bright flash of light. The photographer was a small, squat man in a dark suit, standing with his back to them. He took a step back, adjusted his focus and took another picture of something against the tunnel wall.

Wright moved to the side to get a better look. 'Jesus Christ,' he whispered.

'Yeah, practically crucified,' said the photographer laconically. 'I don't think they cut Jesus's dick off, though, did they?' He turned his camera side on and took another photograph. 'Who are you guys with?' he asked.

'British Transport Police,' said Reid.

'Don't think he was hit by a train,' said the photographer.

A young man in blue overalls joined them carrying a large metal suitcase. He placed it on a sleeper and opened it to reveal a large video camera and a halogen light. 'Are you going to want the video, then?' he asked, pulling the camera out of its foam rubber packing.

'Yeah,' said Wright, handing him a BTP business card.

The body was naked, spreadeagled against the wall, the hands impaled on thick nails. The man's groin was a mass of blood, and strips of flesh had been ripped from his chest, arms and legs. A knife had been thrust into the chest.

'That's not what I think it is in his mouth, is it?' asked Reid.

Wright lean forward. Between the man's teeth was a piece of bloody flesh. Wright's stomach lurched. He screwed up his face in disgust. 'What sort of sick bastard would do that?' he whispered.

'Black magic?' said Reid. 'Some sort of Satanic ritual?'

Wright shook his head. 'There'd be symbols. Candles. Stuff like that. This guy's been tortured to death.' He took a step closer to the body. There was something impaled on the knife. A playing card. Blood from the man's face had trickled down over the card. Wright reached out his hand.

'Don't even think about touching that!' boomed a voice.

Wright looked around. The grey-haired man in overalls was standing behind Wright holding a polythene evidence bag. 'I wasn't going to touch anything,' said Wright defensively.

'Who are you anyway?' asked the man. 'Gerry Hunter's already been over the crime scene.'

'I'm Nick Wright. This is Tommy Reid. British Transport Police.'

'Been at many crime scenes, have you, Mr Wright?'

'What?'

The man sealed the evidence bag. Inside was a cigarette packet. 'Standard procedure is for detectives to wear gloves and shoe covers before they go trampling over a crime scene.'

'Yeah, well, we'll watch where we put our feet,' said Wright. 'And it's Sergeant Wright. What about the victim's clothes?'

'No sign of them. Assuming he didn't walk in naked, the murderer must have taken them with him.'

Wright put his hands in his pockets and turned to look at the body again. He peered at the playing card. 'Ace of spades,' he said. 'Now what the hell's the significance of that?'

'Bridge game got a bit nasty, do you think?' said Reid.

'It must mean something, Tommy. Someone went to a lot of trouble to stick that on his chest.'

Kristine Ross opened the UPS package, taking care not to damage her blood-red fingernails. Inside was a manila envelope, with the senator's name and 'PRIVATE AND CONFIDENTIAL' typed across it. She picked up the UPS wrapper and looked at the name of the sender. Max Eckhardt. It wasn't a name she recognised. The address was an apartment in London, England. The space for the sender's telephone number had been left blank. She clicked her mouse on the logo for the senator's contacts book and entered the name Eckhardt. Nothing. She scrolled through the Es, just to be on the safe side, but there was no name that was even remotely similar. It wasn't unusual for members of the public to mark their mail private and confidential in the hope of reaching the senator's desk unopened, but it was Kristine's job to make sure that he made the maximum use of his time. Whoever Max Eckhardt was, he wasn't known to the senator and so his envelope was fair game. She slit open the envelope and peered inside. All it contained was a Polaroid photograph. Kristine closed the envelope and tapped it on her desk, a tight feeling in her stomach. She doubted that it was a wedding picture. There was no letter, no card, just the photograph, and the fact that it was a Polaroid meant that it probably wasn't the work of a professional photographer.

People sent strange things to the senator. His mail was

scanned before it reached Kristine's desk, but X-rays couldn't weed out all the nasty surprises. In the twenty-two months she'd been working for Senator Dean Burrow she'd seen pornographic pictures of housewives offering themselves to him, hatemail written in crayon, obscene drawings, and on one occasion a small bottle of urine from a woman who said that the FBI were trying to poison her. Anything threatening was passed on to the Secret Service; anything obscene went into the shredder. Kristine sighed through pursed lips and tilted the envelope so that the Polaroid slid out, face down. She turned it over. For a second or two she stared at the image, unable to believe what she was looking at, then she felt her stomach heave.

'Oh, sweet Jesus,' she whispered.

Tommy Reid dropped Nick Wright at the door to Battersea police station and went looking for a parking space. Wright waited until the grey-haired duty sergeant had finished taking details of a stolen bicycle from a young girl before showing his ID and asking to see Annie Lees.

The sergeant's face creased into a grin. 'What, has she been fare-dodging now, then?' he asked.

Wright smiled coldly. 'She's a witness in a murder investigation,' he said.

The sergeant's grin vanished. 'I know that, son. I was just pulling your leg.'

The door opened behind Wright and Reid joined him at the counter. From somewhere he'd managed to buy a portion of fish and chips. 'Hello, Reg,' said Reid, shoving a chip into his mouth.

'Bloody hell, Tommy Reid,' said the sergeant. 'What've you been doing with yourself?'

Reid offered his fish and chips and the sergeant helped himself to a handful of chips. Reid gestured at the fish and the sergeant broke off a piece. 'Same old rubbish,' said Reid. 'I thought you'd retired.'

'Next year. You on this murder enquiry?'

Reid pushed a chunk of fried cod into his mouth and nodded.

'I'll let you in,' said the sergeant. He disappeared from behind the counter and unlocked a side door. Reid and Wright went inside. 'Second interview room on the right,' said the sergeant.

Annie Lees was sitting at a table, her hands cupped around a mug of weak tea. She looked up as the two detectives walked into the room. 'Where are my things?' she snapped.

Wright stopped in his tracks. 'I'm sorry?'

'My things. They said I could have my things.' She scrutinised Reid with wary eyes. 'What's that you're eating?'

'Fish and chips. Want some?' Reid put what was left of his meal on the table and wiped his hands on his coat.

The old woman picked up a chip between her first finger and thumb and inspected it closely before taking a bite.

'Annie, did you see anyone near the tunnel?' asked Wright.

The old woman's eyes narrowed. 'What tunnel?'

Wright sat down opposite her. 'The tunnel where you found the body.'

She averted her eyes and concentrated on selecting the best chips. She ate several more before speaking. 'I've already told that other detective everything.'

'Other detective? What other detective?'

'Gerry. He's such a nice young man, isn't he?'

'Gerry Hunter?'

'Inspector Gerry Hunter,' she said, stressing the title. 'He's very young to be an inspector, isn't he? Are you an inspector?'

Wright's jaw tensed. 'No,' he said. 'I'm not an inspector.'

D ean Burrow was bored out of his skull, but the three women sitting opposite him would never have known. Burrow had smiled his way through more than a decade of television interviews, rubber chicken dinners and factory openings. He'd perfected the technique with the aid of a style coach, the same woman who'd shown him how to walk with authority, how to shake hands sincerely, how to show concern and sympathy when the occasion warranted. He smiled and from time to time he nodded to show that he agreed with them, giving them all equal eye contact so that none of them would feel slighted. They'd wanted to talk to him about abortion, a subject close to Burrow's heart, and they represented a group of more than five hundred churchgoing middle-aged women from Burrow's home state. Five hundred votes was worth twenty minutes of anybody's time.

Burrow had been consistent on his views on abortion.

In public he was against it; in private he thought it was a necessary evil: his own wife had had an abortion soon after they'd married, and his former secretary had been persuaded to have one three years ago. Both women had agreed to the abortions for financial reasons – his wife because they were struggling to meet the payments on their first house; his secretary because he'd paid her fifty thousand dollars. She wasn't his secretary any more; she'd opened her own beauty salon in Cleveland and Burrow remained convinced that she'd deliberately become pregnant in the first place. Burrow wondered what his three visitors would do if they discovered that their pro-life senator was responsible for two aborted fetuses.

The woman who'd been doing most of the talking, a stick-thin black woman with swept-back hair and tortoiseshell spectacles, stopped speaking and looked at him expectantly.

Burrow nodded urbanely. 'I couldn't agree with you more, Mrs Vine,' he said, even though he hadn't been listening. 'You can rest assured that we are of one mind on this issue.' He stood up and adjusted the sleeves of his jacket. 'It's been a pleasure, ladies. I want to thank you all for the time and trouble you've taken to come and see me.'

The three women stood up and he shook them by the hand. His handshake was as practised as his smile, strong enough to show strength of character and determination, but not too overpowering. He escorted them to the door and opened it, giving each of the women a warm smile as they left.

Kristine Ross was standing in the outer office, holding a manila envelope. Burrow gave her a genuine smile and looked her up and down. With her long tanned legs, full figure and shoulder-length blonde hair, Kristine could have worked as a catwalk model. Not that Burrow would ever do anything more than look – he'd learned his lesson the hard way and he didn't want to throw away another fifty thousand dollars. She looked worried.

'Something wrong, Kristine?' he asked.

She gestured with the UPS package. 'Can I have a word with you, Senator?'

'Of course,' he said, ushering her into his office. He watched her walk over to his desk. She had a sexy, sensual walk, slow and easy as if she knew that men liked to watch her move. Burrow made sure that his gaze was levelled at her face when she turned to face him.

'This came in the morning mail,' she said as Burrow went back behind his side of the large oak desk. 'It was addressed private and confidential, but office policy is to—'

'I know, I know,' he said brusquely, adjusting his cuffs. 'What's the problem?'

'It's a photograph.'

'So?' Burrow was starting to find the secretary's reticence annoying. She gave him the envelope, a look of disgust on her face, then looked away as he opened the envelope and took out a Polaroid photograph. Burrow grimaced. It was a human figure, spreadeagled, dripping with glistening blood, the flesh made ghostly pale by the camera flash. 'Why would anyone . . . ?' he began, then he noticed something impaled in the chest. He held the photograph closer to his face and squinted.

'I wasn't sure whether I should give it to the Secret Service or—'

'How was it delivered?' interrupted Burrow.

'UPS. From London, England.'

Burrow clicked his fingers impatiently. 'Get me the pack it came in. You've still got it, don't you?'

'Yes. Yes, I do.' She backed away from him and then walked quickly out of the office. For the first time ever, Burrow didn't watch her go. He continued to stare at the photograph. His heart was racing and his palms were damp with sweat.

Kristine returned with the UPS pack, and Burrow practically ripped it from her hands. He scanned the label. 'Max Eckhardt,' he whispered.

'I couldn't find his name on the computer,' said Kristine. 'That's why I opened it. I didn't do anything wrong, did I?'

Burrow put the UPS pack down on the desk and leaned back in his chair. He smiled as if he didn't have a care in the world. 'Probably a crank,' said Burrow. 'Nothing to worry about, Kristine.'

'Shall I give it to—?'

'No, it's nothing. There wasn't anything else in the envelope, was there? No note or anything?'

'Just the photograph,' said Kristine.

Burrow shrugged dismissively. 'So it's nothing.'

Kristine brushed a stray lock of hair away from her face. 'You're sure?' she asked.

Burrow crinkled his eyes slightly. It was his serious, sincere look. 'Absolutely,' he said.

Kristine looked as if she wanted to say something else, but she could tell from Burrow's demeanour that the conversation was over. She left the office. This time Burrow watched her leave, but his eyes were cold and hard as if his mind was elsewhere. As soon as the door closed, he picked up the photograph again and stared at it.

R eid and Wright got nothing of value from the twenty minutes they spent with Annie Lees. The old lady was showing all the symptoms of Alzheimer's disease and seemed unable to concentrate for more than a few minutes at a time. Several times during the interview she wasn't even able to recall finding the body, and once she'd burst into tears. They left her with a uniformed policewoman and the remains of the fish and chips.

'She needs to be in a home,' said Wright as they closed the door to the interview room.

'Care in the community,' said Reid. 'Part of the cutbacks.'

Wright shook his head sadly. 'She needs looking after. Her family should be taking care of her.'

Reid snorted. 'Come off it, Nick. Who'd take care of you if you went crazy? Do you think your ex-wife would put you in the spare room? What about your son? He's what, seven? And even if he was older, kids don't take care of their parents any more. Those days went out with the village bobby and free school milk. It's every man for himself nowadays. Little old ladies like Annie Lees fall through the cracks and the cracks just get bigger and bigger.'

'Yeah, well, isn't that a cheery thought?' said Wright.

Reid clapped Wright on the back. 'Come on, old son, you're never going to reach retirement age anyway.'

Wright shrugged him off. He didn't feel like laughing.

They headed down the corridor towards the reception

area. Gerry Hunter came out of an office, a large envelope in one hand, a cup of coffee in the other. 'Any joy?' he asked.

Reid shook his head. 'Nah. She thinks the world of you, though. Said she wanted to adopt you.'

'What can I say? Must be my boyish charm.' He gave the envelope to Reid. 'Pathologist's report. She didn't know where to contact you.'

'Tavistock Place,' said Wright.

Hunter looked pained. 'I know that, but she didn't. She hasn't dealt with BTP before, so she called us to attend the post mortem. It was straightforward, nothing out of the ordinary.' He nodded his head towards the interview room. 'Do you need Annie for anything else?'

'No, we're through with her,' said Reid. He tapped Wright on the shoulder with the envelope. 'Come on, Nick, let's go.'

Hunter disappeared back into his office. Wright and Reid walked towards the door, but before they reached it, someone called out Wright's name. It was Clive Edmunds, his tie loosened and the tail of his shirt flapping over his trousers. He waved a sheet of paper at Wright as he walked towards them.

'Thought this might help with your investigation,' he said, handing the paper to Wright. He walked quickly away and disappeared into a side office.

Wright scanned the sheet. Across the top, in typed capital letters, were the words 'QUESTIONS TO ANSWER'. Underneath, in a single column, was a list of words. 'Who? When? How? Why?' Wright felt a surge of anger.

Reid read the list over Wright's shoulder and snorted. 'Ha bloody ha,' he said.

Wright screwed the sheet of paper into a tight ball and threw it down the corridor. 'I bet Hunter put him up to it,' he said.

'Nah, Edmunds is enough of a twat to have thought of it himself. Come on, forget about it. Do you want a drink?'

Wright shook his head and reached for the envelope. 'You drink too much,' he said.

'Yeah, well, you snore but you don't hear me complaining.'

The duty sergeant unlocked the door for them. 'Where's the nearest pub, Reg?' asked Reid.

'Bull's Head,' said the sergeant. 'Left, then first right.'

The two detectives walked there. It was an old-fashioned public house with a smoke-stained plaster ceiling and a long wooden bar that had been varnished countless times and was now almost black. A shirtsleeved barman was pulling a rack of steaming glasses from a washing machine under the counter and nodded a greeting. 'Be with you in a minute, gents,' he said.

'What do you want?' asked Reid, leaning nonchalantly against the bar.

'I want to go back to the office,' said Wright, looking at his watch.

'Don't be a party-pooper, Nick. We're allowed a lunch hour.'

Wright could see that it was pointless to argue and sighed in resignation. 'Lager shandy,' he said, then went over to an empty table and sat down. He read through the pathologist's report until Reid came over with their drinks. Wright looked at Reid's double vodka and tonic and shook his head admonishingly.

Reid pretended not to notice. 'Wasn't sure if you wanted

ice or lemon. Or a cherry.' He sat down, took a deep pull at his drink and smacked his lips as if deliberately trying to antagonise Wright. Wright looked down at the report again. 'So what does the delightful Dr Littman say?' Reid asked.

'Sixty-three cuts, a dozen of which could have been the fatal one. Three different blades used.'

'Three?' repeated Reid incredulously.

'He was dead when his dick was cut off.'

'That's a relief, then.'

'And his vocal cords had been cut. Presumably so he couldn't scream.' Wright dropped the report down on top of the envelope. 'Who the hell would torture a man in that way, Tommy?'

Reid shrugged and drained his glass. 'Whoever it was, they went to a lot of trouble. Three knives. The nails. Something to bang them in with. Something to put the clothes in. And the playing card. Another?'

Wright looked up sharply. 'What?'

'Another drink?' said Reid, tapping his empty glass. He stood up, grunting from the effort.

Wright refused the offer. He rested his head against the back of his seat while Reid ambled across the carpet to the bar.

Superintendent Richard Newton pushed the photographs with his index finger and grimaced. He'd seen more than his share of mutilated bodies during his twenty-year career, usually suicides who'd decided to end it all by throwing themselves in front of a train, but the injuries of the man in the tunnel were all the more horrific because of the way they'd been inflicted. This was no sudden death: the wounds had been inflicted one at a time, methodically, over a period of time. He shuddered.

The door to his office opened and his secretary showed in Tommy Reid and Nick Wright. Reid's cheeks were red and the superintendent could smell his minty breath from across his desk as the two men sat down. 'Well?' said Newton. 'What's the state of play?'

'White male, mid to late forties, multiple stab wounds and mutilations,' said Reid. 'That's all we know.'

'No identification on the body?' asked Newton.

'No, nothing,' said Reid. 'No clothes, no wallet, no jewellery.'

Newton slid one of the ten-by-twelves across the desk to Reid. 'Is that what I think it is in his mouth?' he asked disdainfully.

Reid nodded.

'A warning?'

'Maybe.'

'And the playing card?'

Reid shrugged.

Newton nodded thoughtfully. 'It's a messy one,' he said.

'I think it's a serial killer,' said Wright. It was the first time he'd spoken since entering the office.

Newton settled back in his chair and tapped his fingertips together as he studied Wright. Wright shifted uncomfortably under the superintendent's gaze. 'Why do you say that, Nick?'

Wright pointed at the glossy photographs. 'It's too . . .' he struggled to find the right word '. . . formal.' He frowned and ran a hand through his fringe.

'Formal?' said Newton. He raised his eyebrows archly.

'Organised,' said Wright hurriedly. 'It's too organised to be a gangland or a drugs killing. The way the body was nailed to the wall, it was as if someone was creating an image.' Wright's voice tailed off as he struggled to express himself.

'But I've not heard of any similar killings,' said the superintendent. 'And that would be a prerequisite for a serial killer, wouldn't it?'

The sarcasm didn't appear to register with Wright. 'It could be the start,' he said.

'It could,' said Newton, unconvinced. 'But at present we have a single killing. I think the time to start speculating about a mass murderer would be if and when there's a second victim. Until then I suggest you treat it as a straightforward murder investigation.' Newton tapped his fingertips on the desktop like a concert pianist warming up. 'I've been considering letting the Met continue with the case,' he mused.

Wright looked across at his partner for support. 'We've already started the preliminary work.'

'Nevertheless, the Met is geared up for murder investigations, and with the best will in the world—'

'We cracked the Everton case last spring.'

'The guy was caught with the knife in his hand,' said Newton patiently.

'It was still murder.'

'Manslaughter,' corrected the superintendent.

'Murder, manslaughter, what's the difference? This is a BTP case, sir,' said Wright. We can handle it.'

'Whatever happens, it's going to be a joint investigation,' said Newton.

'I understand that, sir, but it should be a BTP case first and foremost, with you as governor.'

'Nice of you to be so keen to increase my workload, Nick.' Newton kept his eyes on Wright as he gathered up the photographs. He stacked them neatly, then handed the pile to Wright. 'Okay. Have it your way. Tell Ronnie I want to see him,' Newton said eventually. 'He'll be liaison officer. Use the conference room in the basement as the incident room. I'll draw up a rota of officers to be assigned to the case. I'll arrange for temporary transfers and authorise the necessary overtime.' He took a deep breath as if reconsidering his decision. 'Ronnie can talk to the Met and have their officers sent over here, and I'll have half a dozen uniforms assigned. Oh, and the press have been on asking for details. I've arranged a press conference for four o'clock. The two of you can handle it. Ronnie's going to be too busy getting the incident room sorted out. Just give them the basics, and put out an appeal for witnesses. Don't mention the playing card. Keep that in reserve.'

'Our ace in the hole?' said Reid, deadpan.

Newton looked at him icily. 'And no mention of a serial killer.'

Reid and Wright stood up. 'Thank you, sir,' said Wright.

Newton acknowledged Wright's gratitude with a slight nod. 'It's not open ended, Nick. If it looks like you're not making any progress, the case goes to the Met.'

'Hey, Gerry, take a look at this!' Clive Edmunds gestured with a lit cigarette at the wall-mounted television above the office coffee machine. 'Those railway wankers are on Sky news.'

Gerry Hunter stopped pecking at his computer keyboard and looked up. 'Turn the sound up, will you?' he asked.

Edmunds looked around for the remote control and increased the volume. Tommy Reid was reading a prepared statement while Nick Wright sat next to him, toying with a ballpoint pen. Behind them was a blown-up map of the area where the body had been found. Hunter couldn't help smiling at Reid's appearance: the man's hair was damp as if he'd splashed water on it in an attempt to make it lie flat. Stray strands of hair were already coming adrift at the sides. He'd fastened the top button of his shirt but his collar was a size too small and clearly pinching his neck. Reid finished reading the statement and asked the assembled reporters if they had any questions.

'Do you have any motive for the killing?' asked a redhead holding a small tape recorder.

'Not as yet,' said Reid.

'And no suspect?'

Reid's jaw tightened. 'We're appealing for anyone who was in the vicinity of the tunnel to come forward,' he said. 'Even if they don't think they saw anything of significance, we'd still like to talk to them.'

'In fact, you don't even know who the victim is, do you?' pressed the redhead. Reid pretended not to hear her.

A middle-aged man in a crumpled blue suit raised an arm. Hunter recognised him as a crime reporter on one of the tabloids. 'When are you going to call in the Met?' he said.

Edmunds nudged Hunter in the ribs. 'The guys are running a sweepstake on that very question,' he chuckled.

'This is a British Transport Police investigation,' said Wright.

'We will be liaising with the Metropolitan Police,' said Reid. 'Officers from the Met will be assigned to the case.'

'Any other questions?' asked Wright, looking around the room.

'Do you think the killer could strike again?' asked a local radio reporter.

'It's a possibility,' said Wright.

Reid stiffened and put a hand on Wright's arm. Wright shrugged him off.

'A serial killer?'

Before Wright could answer, Reid stood up. 'I'm afraid that's all we have time for, gentlemen.' He added as an afterthought, 'And ladies.'

Wright looked up at his partner as if preparing to argue, but Reid gave a small shake of his head. The news broadcast cut away to a studio presenter.

Edmunds muted the sound and flicked ash into a waste-paper bin. 'They haven't a clue,' he said.

'It's a tough case, Clive.'

Edmunds snorted dismissively. 'Those two couldn't crack a fucking egg.'

'Maybe.' Hunter put his hand in his pocket and pulled out a crumpled ball of paper which he tossed to Edmunds. 'That wasn't funny,' he said.

Edmunds held his cigarette between his lips and flattened the sheet of paper. It was the list he'd given Wright earlier. 'Made me laugh,' he said.

'Yeah, well, go easy on him, will you? He's pissed off enough at me as it is.'

Edmunds folded the sheet into an aeroplane and threw it towards a wastepaper bin. 'Well, you are sleeping with his wife, Gerry.' The plane missed the bin by several feet and ploughed into a grey carpet tile. He took the cigarette between his forefinger and thumb and blew a smoke ring. 'When all's said and done.'

'Ex-wife,' said Hunter. 'Just leave him alone, huh?'

Edmunds held Hunter's look for several seconds, then realised that his partner was serious. 'Okay,' he said. 'They can have all the rope they need.'

'We were set up,' hissed Wright as he stormed down the corridor. 'It was that bastard Hunter. I'm sure of it.'

'Calm down, Nick.' Reid caught up with his partner and walked beside him. 'It wasn't too bad.'

Wright waved his hand in the air dismissively. 'You heard that shit from the *Mirror*.' He contorted his face and mimicked the crime reporter. '"When are you going to call in the Met?"'

Reid held up his hands in mock surrender. 'Hey, I'm on your side.' He went over to the coffee maker and filled two polystyrene cups. He took them back to the desk and poured in large measures of vodka, then passed one over to Wright.

Wright glared at his partner for several seconds, then

relaxed. It wasn't Reid he was mad at. He raised his cup and banged it against Reid's. 'Cheers,' he said, and drank gratefully. 'Are you working tomorrow?'

'What else is there to do on a Saturday? What about you?'

'Oh yeah, I'll be in. I need the overtime.' Wright flicked through his desk diary then groaned. 'Hell, I forgot, tomorrow's my day with Sean.'

'No sweat. Where are you going to take him?'

Wright closed his diary. 'I don't know. Trocadero, maybe. He likes video games. Where did you used to take Craig and Julie?'

'The old favourites. British Museum. Science Museum. The zoo. Football.'

'Been there, done that.' He reached over and took the prepared statement from Reid. He'd spent an hour working on it before the press conference but he still hadn't been happy with it. Wright was as aware as the journalists that the investigation had stalled before it had even started.

'All right, lads?' said a deep, Glaswegian voice.

Reid and Wright looked up. It was Detective Chief Inspector Ronnie Dundas, the fifty-year-old Glaswegian Newton had appointed as liaison officer on the investigation.

Wright put down his cup guiltily. 'How's the incident room going, sir?' he asked.

'Computers are in, HOLMES is up and running and there's a PNC terminal on line. We'll have two NCIS terminals connected by this afternoon.'

The Home Office Large Major Enquiry System would be used to collate all the evidence and interviews produced during the investigation, and the Police National Computer and National Criminal Intelligence Service would provide online databases and criminal intelligence.

'Who's office manager?' asked Reid.

'Are you putting yourself forward, Tommy?' Dundas perched on the edge of Reid's desk. His hair and moustache were unnaturally black, and he was rumoured to be dyeing both.

Reid flashed the chief inspector a sarcastic smile. 'You know me, Ronnie. I'm much more a foot-in-the-door man.'

'Arse on a bar stool, more like,' said Dundas. The banter was good natured: the two men had worked together for more than a decade. 'Anyway, Phil Evans has already been assigned.'

'He's well suited,' agreed Reid.

'What about the Met?' asked Wright. 'Have they said who they're sending over yet?'

Dundas shook his head. 'Only numbers. A DCI, two DIs, three DSs and six DCs. Same as us.'

'So when do we move downstairs?' asked Wright.

'Give it a couple of hours. They're still moving desks and getting the phones connected.'

'Time for a pint, then,' said Reid.

Dundas grinned. 'You read my mind,' he said.

The two senior officers looked expectantly at Wright, who sighed mournfully. 'Okay, I suppose so.'

There was a timid knock on the door and Dean Burrow looked up from the papers he was reading. Kristine Ross popped her head around as if she was trying to keep her body concealed from him. 'I'm the last one here, Senator,' she said. 'Is there anything you need?'

Burrow took off his reading glasses. 'Any sign of Jody Meacher?' he asked.

'He said he'd be here by seven, Senator.'

Burrow looked at his watch. It was half past seven. 'Okay, Kristine. You can call it a night.'

She flashed him a nervous smile and closed the door. Burrow toyed with his spectacles. Kristine was obviously still upset at the photograph. He wondered how she'd feel if she knew the real significance of the mutilated corpse. Then she'd really have something to worry about.

He was still daydreaming when there was a second knock on his door, louder and more confident than the first. The door opened wide and Jody Meacher strode in. He was a big man, at least twenty stone, with a waistline that was still expanding. He was balding with a greying beard and cheeks pockmarked with old acne scars. Meacher was one of the smartest men Burrow had ever met, and was a shrewd political operator. In his younger years he'd had his own ambitions of office, but his looks had been an insurmountable barrier and he'd settled for being one of the best spin doctors in the business instead. He'd helped two men get into the Oval Office already, and if everything went to plan, Burrow would be the third.

Meacher glided across the plush blue carpet. He moved majestically, with surprising grace for a man of his size. Burrow went around his desk to meet him and they shook hands firmly.

'Thanks for coming so quickly, Jody,' said Burrow. He

went over to his drinks cabinet and poured two measures of Jack Daniels, each with a single cube of ice. He handed a glass to Meacher and they toasted each other silently. Burrow waved Meacher over to two green leather couches placed at right angles to each other at the far end of the room. While Meacher eased his vast bulk down on to one of the couches, Burrow walked over to his desk and picked up the UPS package and the manila envelope.

'Something's cropped up,' said Burrow, going over to sit on the second couch. He put the package and the envelope on a low oak coffee table.

Meacher watched him with unblinking eyes and the same coldness with which an entomologist might study a beetle. Meacher rarely smiled, and on the few occasions that he did, the expression never looked sincere. To strangers he appeared aloof, hostile even, but Burrow knew that the man's facial expressions often belied his true feelings. It wasn't that he wore a mask, it was as if he simply didn't care how he looked, that his intellect was his only concern.

'I received something in the mail today,' Burrow continued. He opened the flap of the envelope and slid out the Polaroid photograph. He handed it to Meacher.

Meacher's expression didn't change. He studied the photograph for a full five seconds, then looked at Burrow expectantly. 'Everything,' he said softly. 'Tell me everything.'

Burrow spoke for ten minutes while Meacher listened, his hands in his lap as if meditating. When he had finished, Burrow drained his glass and went over to the drinks cabinet to refill it. Meacher's glass remained untouched on the coffee table.

'Remember what I said to you when I first agreed to join your team?' Meacher asked.

'Yes. I remember.'

'So why did you withhold this from me?'

Burrow sat down and adjusted the creases of his trousers. 'Jody, this all happened a long time ago. A lifetime ago.'

Meacher held out the Polaroid photograph so that it was just inches from the senator's face. 'And this? When did this happen?'

Burrow felt his face redden. 'I don't know.' He took another mouthful of Jack Daniels.

Meacher tossed the photograph on to the coffee table. 'You know what this means?'

'You don't have to spell it out for me, Jody.'

'Everything we've worked for, everything we've done, it'll all be for nothing if this gets out.'

'I know, Jody. I know.'

Meacher sat in silence, staring into the middle distance. Burrow crouched forward, his elbows on his knees. Burrow could practically hear Meacher's mind working.

'Who else has seen the photograph?' Meacher asked eventually.

'My secretary. Kristine Ross.'

'Would you miss her?'

Burrow flinched at the question. 'Is there no other way?'

Meacher's pale blue eyes bored into Burrow's. 'Senator, you know as well as I do the state of the Vice President's health. He's going to have to step down within the next few months, and you are the frontrunner to take his place.' He nodded at the Polaroid. 'What do you think will happen if what you've told me becomes public knowledge?'

Burrow drew a finger across his throat. The end of his career. The end of everything.

'So don't ask me if there's any other way out of this. There's only one way. My way.'

Burrow held Meacher's gaze for several seconds, then he nodded slowly. 'Whatever it takes, Jody,' he said, and drained his glass.

Tommy Reid grunted and fumbled in his pockets for his keys. Nick Wright beat him to it and slotted his Yale into the lock. He pushed open the door and allowed Reid in first. The two men walked down the narrow hall to the sitting room. Reid stopped dead. The room was a mess, with empty fast-food cartons on the floor, stacks of newspapers and magazines on a coffee table and a pile of dirty laundry in the corner by the television.

'Shit! We've been burgled,' said Reid. 'Call the cops.'

Wright pushed him in the small of the back. 'You always say that,' he said. 'If it annoys you so much, get a cleaning lady.'

'Who said it annoys me?' He staggered over to the window and pulled the curtains shut with a flourish. Dust drifted down around him. 'Is it snowing?' he asked.

'You're pissed,' said Wright, dropping down on to a sofa that had once been beige but had long ago turned into a dirty brown.

Reid exhaled and looked around the room. There were two overstuffed leather armchairs next to the sofa, both scuffed and worn from years of abuse, facing a portable television on a black plastic stand. 'What's on the box?' he asked.

Wright ran his hands through his hair. 'Who cares?' he said. The two men had spent several hours in a local Indian restaurant, challenging each other to increasingly hot curries and cooling themselves down with half pints of lager. All Wright wanted to do was sleep.

'Do you want a nightcap?' Reid asked. Wright shook his head. 'Okay, I'll get myself a beer and head off to bed. See you tomorrow.'

Wright gave Reid a small wave. He heaved himself up off the sofa and went over to the pine shelving unit which had been amateurishly screwed into the wall opposite the window. On the middle shelf, surrounded by well-creased paperbacks, was a mini stereo system. Below it were several dozen CDs, mostly jazz. Wright ran his finger along the cases and pulled out a Billie Holiday recording. From the kitchen he heard a dull thud as a can of beer hit the floor followed by a muffled curse. Wright slotted in the CD and pressed the 'play' button.

'Goodnight, John Boy,' shouted Reid as he ambled down the hall to the bedroom.

'Goodnight, Grandpa,' Wright replied unenthusiastically. He was starting to think that Superintendent Newton was right, that he had indeed been living with Reid for too long. Even the jokes were becoming stale. He pulled the cushions off the sofa and unfolded the bed where he'd slept for the past five months. It was small and uncomfortable, but cheaper than paying for a place of his own.

He went to the bathroom, cleaned and flossed his teeth, then took his quilt and pillow from the airing cupboard. As he returned to the sitting room, Billie Holiday was singing 'Lover Come Back To Me'. Wright threw the bedding on to the sofa and sat down to remove his shoes. He looked around the cramped room and a wave of hopelessness washed over him. His wife, his son, his house, his car; he'd lost everything. He'd been working for more than ten years and all he had to show for it were the two suitcases of clothes he'd taken from the house and the ageing Ford Fiesta he'd driven away in.

Wright went back over to the shelving unit and picked up a harmonica. He sat down on the edge of the sofabed and played along with the recording, the mournful notes echoing down the hallway.

The elevator wasn't working, and by the look of the rusting gate, it hadn't been used for several years. Jody Meacher took the stairs one at a time, resting for breath every couple of dozen steps. When he reached the third floor he took off his overcoat and draped it over one shoulder. By the time he was on the fifth floor, he had to mop his forehead with a large white linen handkerchief. The man he was looking for lived on the ninth floor, but Meacher doubted that he was ever fazed by the long climb. Len Kruse was a fitness fanatic and probably raced up all nine floors at the double.

Meacher transferred his black leather briefcase to his left hand, pulled out his gold pocket watch and flipped it open. It was five o'clock in the morning. Meacher had driven from Washington to New York. He hated driving but he didn't want to use an official car and there was a good chance he'd be recognised if he travelled by train or plane. The fewer people who knew he was in New York, the better. He leaned against the whitewashed wall and exhaled deeply. At his feet was a discarded used condom, glistening wetly like a trout that had just been pulled from a stream. Meacher grimaced and carried on climbing. He smelled stale urine and put his handkerchief over his mouth as he walked by a yellow stain on the wall.

There were no numbers to indicate the floors, but Meacher had been keeping count during his ascent. He pushed open a door and stepped into a corridor. The smell wasn't much better than in the stairwell. The corridor had a low ceiling with dim lights every fifty feet that did little to illuminate the drab walls and black-painted doors, every one of which appeared to have a minimum of three locks, and strips of metal along the jambs to prevent them being forced. Meacher walked slowly down the corridor, his heart still racing from the exertion of the climb.

He found Kruse's apartment at the end of the corridor, on the left. He stuffed his handkerchief into his trouser pocket and knocked gently on the door. Meacher waited. The paint was peeling off the ageing wood and a small glass lens stared blankly back at him. There were three locks in the door: a Yale and two high security locks. Meacher knocked again.

'It's open,' said a voice.

Meacher pushed the door. It squeaked open.

Kruse was sitting on a wooden chair in the corner of the room, his back ramrod straight and his hands resting on his knees. He was naked except for a pair of khaki boxer shorts, and his eyes were closed. It had been a little under three years since Meacher had seen Kruse but he didn't appear to have changed. His upper body was trim but muscular, his thighs thick and powerful. His hair was close cropped, light brown and flecked with grey at the temples, and there were lines around his eyes and mouth that made him look older than his twenty-eight years.

'Hello, Len,' said Meacher.

The room was little more than a cell, three paces wide and four paces long with a single bed that had been stripped of its bedding, a cheap wooden wardrobe and a door which Meacher presumed led to a bathroom. A bare lightbulb hung down from the middle of the ceiling. There was no curtain at the window, though a thin wire had been strung across the top of the frame as if one had once been there.

'Hello, Jody.' Kruse slowly opened his eyes. 'Long time, no see.' His face crinkled into a smile but there was little warmth in it, and the expression vanished just as suddenly as it had appeared.

Meacher walked into the room and closed the door behind him. There was no carpet, just bare floorboards, but they had been polished to a shine. Kruse was a fanatic when it came to cleanliness, and Meacher knew that if he ran his fingers along any surface they'd come away spotless. Kruse remained seated and watched Meacher with dispassionate eyes as he waited for him to speak.

Meacher smoothed his beard with his right hand. 'How've you been, Len?'

The corners of Kruse's lips turned down a fraction. 'Same old, same old.'

Meacher lifted the briefcase. 'Are you available for a short-term contract?'

The smile appeared again. 'Who do you want me to kill this time, Jody?' Kruse asked. His chest shuddered as he laughed, a dry, rasping chuckle that sounded more like a death rattle.

'D ad!' Sean's voice jolted Wright out of his reverie. He turned and grinned at his seven-year-old son. The boy ran forward for a hug and Wright scooped him up off the floor. 'Hiya, Dad,' said Sean, throwing his arms around Wright's neck.

'Whoa, you're choking me,' said Wright, but he didn't try to break free. Over his son's shoulder he saw Janie, her face a polite mask. She looked pointedly at her wristwatch.

Wright set his son down. He stepped forward, prepared to kiss Janie on the cheek, but her eyes hardened, leaving him in no doubt that the gesture wouldn't be appreciated. Wright's stomach lurched at the thought that she couldn't even bear to touch him any more. 'Do you want a coffee or something?' he asked.

Janie shook her head and looked at her watch again. 'I'll pick him up here at six.'

'That's okay, I can drop him off at home.'

'No,' she snapped. Her lips tightened as if she was holding something back, then she forced a smile. 'Here's fine.' She knelt down beside Sean. 'Give Mummy a kiss,' she said. Sean kissed her dutifully on the cheek. 'Be good,' she said.

Wright watched her go, her heels clicking on the tiled floor of the burger bar. He ruffled his son's hair. 'What do you want to eat?'

'Mummy gave me breakfast already,' said his son.

'Yeah? What did you have?'

'Muesli.'

'Rabbit food,' said Wright scathingly. 'Wouldn't you like a cheeseburger?'

'Mummy says red meat is bad for you.'

'Burgers aren't red. They're brown.' Sean giggled and Wright's spirits lifted. He might have lost his wife, but his son was still very much his son. Even if he was having muesli for breakfast. Flecks of rain peppered the window. 'So, where do you want to go?' Wright asked.

'Anywhere.'

'What about the Trocadero? We could hit the video games.'

'Mummy says I shouldn't play video games,' said Sean.

'She said what?'

Sean wiped his nose with the back of his hand. 'She says they encourage violence.'

Wright snorted softly. He knew that he shouldn't contradict his ex-wife, but sometimes she talked absolute nonsense. What did she hope to achieve by feeding the boy muesli and keeping him away from video games? She'd be putting him in a dress next. 'Okay,' he said. 'What do you want to do?'

Sean drummed his fingers on the table, his brow furrowed. 'We could go to the zoo,' he said eventually.

'You want to go to the zoo?' said Wright, surprised.

'Fine. I guess.'

'Okay, it's the zoo, then.'

They went out to the car park. Wright opened the door to the Fiesta for Sean and waited until he'd fastened his seatbelt before getting in himself. It took several turns of the key before the engine burst into life. Wright drove to Regent's Park, doing his best to keep the conversation going. His son seemed happy enough, but it was clear from the number of questions that Wright had to ask how little they knew about each other.

'Here we are,' said Wright, stopping in the zoo car park. As they walked towards the entrance, spots of rain began to fall. Sean pulled up the hood of his blue anorak. 'You're not cold?' asked Wright.

'I'm okay,' said Sean.

Wright looked up at the clouds gathering overhead. They were grey rather than black and the rain didn't seem to be getting worse, but Wright wondered if he should suggest going somewhere else. The problem was, he couldn't think of a single place to take a seven-year-old boy on a wet Saturday morning.

He paid for them to get in and they walked together towards the large cats enclosures, which was always Sean's favourite part of the zoo. They passed several other father-and-son couples. The zoo was a popular place for divorced fathers to go with their children.

'Can you see them?' Wright asked.

Sean shook his head. 'Lions don't like the rain,' he said.

Drops of rain began to pitter-patter on the hood of Sean's anorak and water trickled down the back of Wright's neck. 'I'm sorry,' said Wright. He put his hand on his son's shoulder.

Sean looked up at him. 'What for?'

'The rain.'

Sean smiled up at him. 'It's not your fault.'

In the distance there was a flash of light followed a few seconds later by a roll of thunder. Wright and Sean hurried back to the car as the skies opened.

Sean looked out of the window as Wright drove towards Tavistock Place. 'Where are we going?' he asked.

'It's a secret,' said Wright.

It was only when Wright pulled up in front of the Gothic-style brick building in Tavistock Place that Sean realised what their destination was.

'It's your office,' he said, his eyes wide.

'Smart lad,' said Wright. 'You should be a detective.' The black metal gate rattled up and Wright drove through to the courtyard. There were fewer than a dozen cars parked there and Wright pulled up next to Tommy Reid's Honda Civic.

They found the man himself in the CID office, slouched in his chair with a naked foot propped up on his desk, clipping his toenails. He seemed totally unfazed by the appearance of Wright and his son and continued to drop pieces of clipped nail into a wastepaper bin. 'I thought you were playing video games,' he said.

'Nah, they encourage violent tendencies,' said Wright.

Reid raised his eyebrows in surprise. 'Do they now?' he said. 'I must remember that.'

'Then Sean here said he wanted to see animals. So I thought . . .' He gestured around the office.

'What better place?' Reid finished for him with a wry smile. He put down his clippers and pulled on his sock. 'How are you doing, Sean? My name's Tommy.'

Sean said hello but he was more interested in a large whiteboard which Reid had placed in front of the window on an easel. On it Reid had stuck a photograph of the body in the tunnel. 'What's that?' asked Sean, pointing at the photograph. 'It's a body, isn't it?' he said, stepping forward for a closer look.

Too late, Wright realised what Sean was looking at, and dragged him away. 'What the hell's that doing up here?' he yelled at Tommy. 'It's meant to be in the incident room. That photo's enough to give the boy nightmares.'

'They've only just finished connecting the phones and computers downstairs.' Reid went over to the coffee machine. 'I'm still checking lists of missing persons on the Police National Computer.'

'Any joy?' asked Wright.

'Do you have any idea of how many middle-aged men go missing every year?'

'A lot?'

'Yeah. A lot. Mind you, I thought of doing a runner when my wife set her solicitor on me. You were probably the same, right?' He froze as he realised that Sean was listening. He looked across at Wright, who shook his head admonishingly. 'Do you want a coffee?' asked Reid.

'Sure,' said Wright coldly.

Reid made a gun of his hand and pointed it at Sean. 'Coke?'

'Yes, please,' said the boy. Sean looked up at his father, his face suddenly serious. 'You're going to find the man who did it, aren't you?'

Wright nodded. 'Sure I am.'

Jody Meacher pulled the door closed and walked down the dimly lit corridor. He took his pocket watch out and opened it. With luck he'd be back in Washington for lunch.

A door opened to his right and Meacher flinched, but a single eye glared at him for a second and then the door slammed shut again. Meacher put his watch away and pushed open the door that led to the stairs. This time the smell didn't seem as bad.

He switched the briefcase to his right hand. The briefcase had been mainly for show, a badge of office. The briefing he'd given Kruse had been entirely verbal: no papers, no photographs, not even a copy of the Polaroid that had been sent to the senator. Kruse had listened in silence as Meacher explained what had to be done. There had been no questions, a credit to the thoroughness of Meacher's briefing and the sharp intelligence of the man who had been nicknamed 'Missile' during his brief time in Special Forces. Kruse hadn't even asked how much he'd be paid this time.

Meacher wasn't concerned by the man's apparent lack of enthusiasm. Or by his curious living arrangements. Meacher knew that between missions Kruse simply shut himself down, like a piece of machinery that was surplus to requirements.

Meacher knew that in his resting phase, Kruse was almost robotic; but primed and briefed, given an objective, he became a human juggernaut. His personality underwent a transformation, too, like an actor assuming a role. Kruse would produce whatever characteristics were necessary to get the job done, almost on demand.

Meacher walked slowly down the stairs, taking care not to touch the walls. He had come across Kruse five years earlier, shortly after he'd left the army. Kruse had served with distinction in Desert Storm and had stayed behind in Saudi Arabia as part of a special anti-terrorist unit protecting the Saudi royal family, but one of his best friends had been killed by a suicide bomber. Kruse's retaliatory attack had killed three Iranian terrorists, but bad timing had led to two innocent bystanders being injured, one of them a Saudi prince. The Americans pulled Kruse out before the Saudis discovered that he was involved.

On his arrival back in the States Kruse was given a battery of psychological tests, the result of which was a recommendation that he be removed from Special Forces. He'd quit the military a week later, and according to an FBI report that had passed across Meacher's desk, he'd tried to begin work as a contract killer. He approached a New York Mafia family but they were suspicious of the non-Italian and sent three of their own men to kill him. They were found two days later in a dumpster, shot with their own guns. That was when Meacher approached Kruse, offering him a chance for occasional work on condition that he worked solely for him. The arrangement had worked perfectly so far.

Kruse didn't know the reason for the missions he was given, and as far as Meacher knew, Kruse was unaware that Meacher worked for a US senator. The man simply didn't care. All he cared about was being given the chance to use the skills he had. Killing skills.

W right dropped Sean back at McDonald's to meet Janie, then after spending a lonely and depressing evening in an Indian restaurant he drove back to Tavistock Place, parked his car in the BTP courtyard and walked up to the CID office, showing his warrant card to the security guard at the entrance. The guard was reading a first edition of the *News of the World*, his feet on the desk. He nodded a greeting at Wright and then went back to his paper.

Wright went up to the first floor, but the CID office was deserted and the whiteboard had gone, so he took the stairs down to the incident room in the basement. He took off his coat and dropped it on the back of a chair, then went over to the whiteboard and stared at the photograph of the mutilated corpse for several minutes, rocking backwards and forwards on his heels. Wright picked up a black marker pen and drew an ace of spades next to the photograph on the whiteboard, carefully shading it in. He stood back and admired his handiwork. The playing card was the key to solving the murder, he was sure of that.

He tapped the pen on the palm of his hand as he nodded slowly. He smiled tightly, then stepped forward and began writing on the board in large capital letters. WHO? he wrote. WHEN? HOW? WHY? He circled the last word. Then he circled it again. And again.

Superintendent Newton pushed open the door to the incident room. It was seven o'clock in the morning and he didn't expect to see anyone in before him, but to his surprise Nick Wright was sprawled in a chair, his head slumped down on his chest. He was wearing a pale green cotton shirt rolled up to the elbows and khaki Chinos, and scuffed, dirty Nike training shoes. Newton frowned and his pale lips tightened into a straight line. It was most definitely not the standard of clothing he expected to see his plainclothes operatives wearing. Newton walked over to Wright and stood looking down at him. Wright continued to snore quietly. A thin dribble of saliva had run down his chin and plopped on to his shirt. Newton clasped his briefcase to his chest and coughed. Wright shifted his legs. On Wright's desk was an opened can of Coke and a plastic-wrapped sandwich. The superintendent realised that Wright must have spent the night in the office. He coughed again, louder this time. When Wright still didn't react, Newton gently kicked his leg.

Wright opened his eyes sleepily. 'Huh?' he said, trying to focus. 'What?'

'What are you playing at, Nick?' asked Newton.

Wright sprang to his feet. He ran a hand through his unkempt hair and grinned shamefacedly. 'Sir? Sorry. I was, er . . .' He swallowed and realised there was saliva on his chin. His hand flew up to cover his embarrassment and he wiped away the mess.

'Have you been here all night?' Newton asked.

Wright wiped his hand on his trousers. 'I must have fallen asleep,' he said. He picked up his can of Coke and drank, swilling the cola around his mouth before swallowing. 'Sorry,' he said. 'My mouth felt like something died in it.'

'When I said that you should move out of Tommy's place, I didn't mean to suggest that you should take up residence here,' said Newton dryly.

'Oh no, I wasn't—' began Wright, but he stopped short as he realised that the superintendent was joking. 'I'll go home and change,' he said.

Newton looked at Wright through narrowed eyes. 'Are you okay, Nick?' he asked.

'Yeah, really. I fell asleep, that's all.'

Newton nodded at the whiteboard covered with Wright's doodles. 'The tunnel case?'

Wright put down his can of Coke. 'I was going through the PNC, checking missing persons.'

Newton waved for Wright to sit down. Wright dropped down into his chair and Newton perched on the edge of his desk, his briefcase still in his arms. 'How far have you got?' he asked.

'Based on what little we've got, the PNC computer's generated some two hundred-odd possibilities,' said Wright.

'That seems a lot,' said Newton.

'That's the number of men aged between forty-two and fifty-eight who've been reported missing and who haven't been accounted for yet,' said Wright.

'Nationwide?' asked Newton.

'Except Northern Ireland,' said Wright, picking up a print-out of names and addresses. 'Trouble is, it's not an exhaustive list. A lot of men that age go walkabout and nobody misses them. Single men, contractors, tramps.'

'And you can't be more precise about the age?'

'Pathologist reckons fifty, give or take five years. We widened the age range a bit, just to be on the safe side.'

'And you're telling me that two hundred men in their forties and fifties have gone missing?'

Wright handed the print-out to the superintendent, who ran his eyes over it as Wright talked. 'They've been reported missing within the last three months, but a lot will have turned up, it's just that the police weren't told. People are quick to call up if someone goes missing, but not so quick to phone to say that the guy's turned up again. I've been going through the list, checking to see who's still not been accounted for and requesting photographs where possible. The problem is, sir, the face is in a real mess and I don't think we can rely on getting a match from a photograph. I want to narrow it down before we start bringing in people to identify the body.'

'Agreed,' said Newton. 'The last thing we want is a stream of people filing past the corpse wondering if it's their nearest and dearest. What about identifying marks on the body?' He smiled thinly. 'And I don't mean the fact that his dick was cut off.'

'The post mortem mentions some scars on his back but doesn't go into detail. We weren't in on the post mortem because the pathologist called in the Met instead. I'm going to talk to her to see if there's anything else that might give a clue as to who he is.'

'What about a search of the crime area?'

'We had a fingertip search of the tunnel and a general sweep outside, but there wasn't anything. It was well planned, his clothes had been taken away, there were several knives used. Anyone who went to that amount of trouble isn't likely to have left anything lying about outside.'

Newton exhaled deeply. 'And no witnesses?'

Wright shook his head. 'There are no houses or gardens overlooking the area, and anyone using the road can't see down into the culvert. There was some dog shit around so we've got a man there interviewing any dog walkers. We're going to start a house-to-house once we've got the rotas worked out.'

Newton stood up and went over to the whiteboard. He looked at the words Wright had written, and at the ace of spades he'd drawn. 'Who, when, how, why?' Newton read. 'Well, answer those questions, Nick, and the mystery is solved.' He turned around. 'I saw you on TV.'

'Ah.' Wright looked embarrassed.

'At least you didn't allow yourself to be drawn on that serial killer question.' Newton sighed despondently. 'I suppose I should be grateful for small mercies. Go home and change, Nick. You've got a busy day ahead of you.'

Kristine Ross rolled over and hugged her pillow, luxuriating in the warmth of her bed. She opened one eye and looked at the clock radio on her bedside table. It was just after two a.m. She closed her eye and tried to get back to sleep. Her alarm was set for six a.m. so that she could be in the office by seven thirty. She listened to her own breathing, then jerked involuntarily as she heard a soft scraping sound from the far side of her bedroom, as if the door had opened and brushed against the carpet. She opened both eyes. The door was closed. She sighed and tried to slip back into sleep.

Sleep wouldn't come. She tossed and turned and rolled on to her side. Working for Senator Burrow was demanding, both physically and mentally, and normally she was so tired that she dropped off as soon as her head touched the pillow. The skin on her back tingled as if she was sleeping in a draught. She pulled up the quilt and drew her knees up against her stomach, curling up into a fetal ball. It was no use. She was wide awake. She opened her eyes. Immediately she stiffened. There was a dark shadow in the corner of the room in a place where she'd never seen a shadow before. She frowned, wondering what it was, cursing herself for being so stupid, but then the shadow moved and she gasped.

'I've got a gun,' she said. 'If you don't leave now I'll shoot.'

There was a soft chuckle from the shadow. 'You didn't have a gun when I checked this morning, Kristine. I hardly think you bought one on the way back from the office.'

He knew her name, but Kristine was sure that she didn't know who the man was. She sat up, holding the quilt up to cover herself. Suddenly she realised what the man had said. He'd been in her apartment before. She began to panic and her hands shook uncontrollably. 'Take what you want,' she said.

'I intend to,' said the man. He walked over to the light switch and flicked it on.

Kristine blinked and tried to focus on the man. He was wearing a grey suit and a white shirt and a conservative tie in muted reds and greens. He looked more like a stockbroker than a burglar or a rapist, but then she'd seen enough police documentaries to know that burglars, rapists and even serial killers didn't always conform to type. His light brown hair was greying prematurely and it was cut short in military style. He was trim and fit but not over muscular, and he was, Kristine realised, the type of man she often went out with.

'Just don't hurt me. Please.' She felt weak and vulnerable and hated herself for it.

'I'll try not to,' he said.

Kristine was seized by fear. 'Oh God. Please, take what you want and go!'

The man pursed his lips and pressed his index finger to them. He was wearing gloves, Kristine realised. Tight-fitting black leather gloves. 'Try to keep your voice down, Kristine. I know how stressful this is for you, but if you raise your voice I'm going to have to use more force than I want to. Do you understand?' He raised his eyebrows and nodded and Kristine found herself nodding along with him. 'I want you to get dressed,' he said. 'There's a blue cotton dress in your wardrobe, the one with the white flowers. Put that on. Are you wearing underwear?'

'What?'

'Are you wearing underwear?'

'No,' she said, her voice trembling.

'Put a bra and panties on. White.'

She slid out from underneath the quilt and scampered across the thick-pile carpet to the chest of drawers where she kept her underwear. He watched her, but there was nothing salacious about the way he looked at her. She turned her back on him while she pulled up her panties and put on her bra.

'Do you work out?' the man asked.

'What?'

'Do you work out? Exercise? You've got a great body.'

'Thank you.' The words came out instinctively and she mentally cursed herself for thanking the intruder. She went over to the mirror-fronted wardrobes and pulled open the doors. The blue dress was on a hanger. She took it out and put it on.

'Let's go to the kitchen,' said the man.

Kristine was confused. 'What?'

'The kitchen. Now come on, Kristine, you're not being a very good host, are you?'

He was so close that she could feel his breath on her face. Kristine stared down at the man's jacket. She had seen enough Secret Service agents around Senator Burrow to know that no matter how well a weapon was concealed, there was always a telltale bulge.

The man smiled. It was an easy smile, showing perfect teeth. 'I don't need one,' he said, as if reading her mind.

'What?'

'You keep saying that, Kristine, and frankly I don't think it's especially polite. Didn't your mother teach you to say, "I beg your pardon" or "Excuse me"?'

Kristine shook her head, now totally confused and unable to speak.

'Let's try, shall we?' said the man. 'You can say, "I beg your pardon?" can't you?'

Kristine felt suddenly light headed and for a moment she feared she was going to pass out. She fought to steady herself. 'What do you want?' she asked. This wasn't a robbery. Did he want to kidnap her? That didn't make any sense: she wasn't married and her parents didn't have money.

'I think you need a drink,' he said. 'There's wine in the kitchen.' He held the door open for her. 'After you.'

He followed her along the hall to the kitchen. 'You know where most accidents happen?' he asked as she switched on the overhead fluorescent lights.

Kristine shrugged. 'The roads?' she guessed.

The man pointed a gloved finger at her. 'That's what everyone thinks. But it's the home. Home sweet home. More people are hurt at home than anywhere else. Homes are dangerous places.'

'Red or white?' she asked. She was feeling braver. He'd

made no move to hurt her and seemed to be going out of his way to put her at ease.

'You choose,' he said. Kristine pulled a bottle of Chianti from the rack by the door and picked up a silver-plated corkscrew, a housewarming present from her mother. She removed the cork and reached for two glasses. 'Just the one glass,' he said.

'You don't want any?' she said. It was important to keep him talking, she knew. She'd seen an Oprah Winfrey show once about how to deal with attackers, and a policeman had said that it was important to establish a rapport with the criminal.

'I don't drink,' he said.

Kristine half filled the glass, and raised it. 'Cheers,' she said. 'Do you have a name?' She stared at his face, trying to imprint it on her memory. It was important to remember details that couldn't be changed, the detective had said. Not clothing, or jewellery, which is what most witnesses fixated on. Things like the dimple in the centre of his chin. The light brown hair that was starting to grey. The pale hazel eyes.

'Len,' he said. 'Short for Leonard. Let's go into the lounge. Bring the bottle with you.'

He held the door open for her and she smiled at him as she walked by. 'Thanks, Len,' she said. Use his name if you knew it, the policeman had said. Make the process as personal as possible.

He followed her into the lounge and closed the door, then switched on a table lamp. 'Have some more wine, Kristine.'

She turned to face him. 'I don't want any more. I've had enough.'

'Do it for me anyway,' he said pleasantly.

Kristine shook her head. 'Please, really, I've had enough.'

The man's smile widened but all the warmth vanished. It was a cold, harsh smile, the smile of an attacking shark. Kristine shivered. 'I'm asking you nicely, Kristine, and I expect you to do as I ask. If you don't, I'm going to rape you, then I'm going to fuck you up the arse and then I'm going to shove a carving knife so far up your cunt that you'll get a nosebleed.' The warmth seeped back into his smile. 'So drink up. Please.'

Kristine drained her glass and refilled it with shaking hands. She forced herself to drink but she almost gagged and wine spurted from her mouth. 'I'm sorry,' she said.

The man ignored her apology. 'Keep drinking,' he said. He perched on the back of her sofa with his arms folded and watched as she forced down the wine.

Kristine began to giggle. Her stomach felt as if it were glowing and she could feel the alcohol coursing through her system. The most she usually drank was a couple of glasses of wine and that was while she was eating. She poured the last of the wine into the glass and put the empty bottle on to the coffee table.

'Very good, Kristine,' said the man. 'What about some music?' He nodded at the stereo. 'Something mellow.'

Kristine walked unsteadily over to the Panasonic stereo system and looked through the rack of CDs. Her mind was in a whirl as she frantically searched for a way out of her predicament. The wine was making her dizzy and she knew that she wouldn't be able to run. Besides, even if she was sober she doubted that the man would have any problem catching and restraining her. There was a telephone in the bathroom – if she could convince him that she had to go to the toilet then perhaps she could call the police. She chose a Lloyd Cole CD and slotted it into the player.

'I need to use the bathroom, Len,' she said. She brushed a stray lock of blonde hair from her face and tried to make herself look as appealing as possible. Make them think you were co-operating, the policeman had said. Then choose your moment.

'Later,' he said. 'There's still some wine in your glass.'

He turned on a table lamp and walked over to the sliding window that led to the balcony. He flipped the lock and slid the window open. Kristine frowned, wondering what he was doing. She picked up her wine glass. Despite the threat he'd made in the kitchen, he clearly wasn't going to rape her; he'd had every opportunity to do that in the bedroom. And if he was planning to rob her, why make her drink the wine? Maybe he thought the wine would knock her out so that he could make a clean getaway. But that didn't make sense either because all he had to do was tie her up.

'Beautiful view, isn't it, Kristine?' said the man. He had his back to her as he stared out at the lights of the nation's capital. 'Come and look.'

Kristine was totally confused. He was treating her more like a girlfriend than a hostage. She walked slowly across the room, both hands cupped carefully around the wine glass as if it was a sacred chalice.

The man moved to the side and gestured with his left arm for her to go out on to the balcony. It was a big balcony with room enough for a white-painted cast-iron table and three chairs, and was one of the main reasons she'd chosen the apartment. 'It's a beautiful home you have,' he said. 'Are you buying or renting?'

'Buying,' she said.

'You're a very lucky girl, Kristine,' said the man.

Kristine opened her mouth to reply, but before she could speak she felt a thump in the small of the back and she stumbled forward. Her arms flailed as she tried to regain her balance, but she was pushed again, this time harder, and she pitched across the waist-high rail, falling towards the car parking area eight floors below. She tried to scream but her throat was full of wine and vomit and all she could manage was a terrified gurgle before she slammed into the tarmac.

Nick Wright handed a cup of coffee to Tommy Reid, who looked at his wristwatch theatrically. 'Wet leaves on the line?' Reid said.

Wright sipped his coffee and sat down. 'I didn't leave until seven o'clock this morning,' he said. 'I got back to the flat just after you'd left.'

Reid snorted. 'I assumed you'd pulled a bird,' he said. He pointed at the polythene-wrapped sandwich on Wright's desk. 'I suppose that's still fresh, then?'

Wright shook his head in disgust. He tossed the sandwich to his partner.

Reid caught it one handed. 'Hey, I could have just eaten it before you got here.'

'That would've been theft,' said Wright. He took another sip of coffee. 'And I would've pressed charges.'

Reid unwrapped the sandwich and took a large bite out of it. 'You came back here last night?'

'Yeah.'

Reid gestured at the whiteboard. 'That's your artwork, then?'

Wright nodded. 'I was brainstorming.'

He picked up the list of missing middle-aged men. 'I've managed to eliminate a dozen names so far,' he said. 'I want to eliminate a few more before we start bringing people in to look at the body,' said Wright. 'We know our man's fingerprints aren't on file with New Scotland Yard's Fingerprint Bureau, so I want to check if any of those missing have had their prints taken. Any that have, we can eliminate.'

Reid nodded. 'Makes sense.'

'I've arranged for a DNA sample to be sent to the DNA database at Priory House in Birmingham but they're struggling with a backlog and it'll be at least five days before they get back to me. And I'm going to see the pathologist. See if there's anything else she can tell me about the body. Stuff that might help us identify him. Or at least rule out some of the names on that list.'

'Busy, busy, busy,' said Reid. He handed the list of names back to Wright and picked up the second sandwich.

'What about you?' asked Wright. 'Any thoughts?'

'Ronnie's asked me to canvas the area again for witnesses and check with the uniforms, the ones checking dog-walkers. But according to Ronnie, the Met boys'll be in later today and they'll probably take over that end of it. He says we'll stick with the crime scene and the forensic, the Met will handle the trace and any witnesses.'

'That's bollocks,' said Wright. 'We've already started trawling missing persons. Hell, between us we've already discounted twenty per cent of the names.'

'Don't argue with me, mate, speak to Ronnie.'

'Speak to Ronnie about what?' boomed the chief inspector from the doorway.

Wright twisted around in his seat. Dundas was carrying a pale blue file and a carton of milk. He had recently acquired an ulcer, and a pint of milk a day was his one concession to his doctor's plea for a change in lifestyle.

'I think we should handle the identification of the body,' Wright said.

'What, you've started so you want to finish?'

'Exactly.'

Dundas pretended to consider what Wright had said. He drank from the carton, leaving a smear of milk across his upper lip. 'Remind me again how you got on with your inspector's exam, Nick?' he said eventually.

Wright scowled but didn't reply. There was no need to. Dundas knew exactly how badly Wright had done.

'Oh, I remember,' said Dundas, waving around his carton of milk. 'Not an inspiring performance, was it?'

'And your point is?' sighed Wright.

'That when you're a chief inspector, you can call the shots. Until then . . .'

'Okay, okay, I get the drift,' said Wright. 'Do you have any objections to my going to see the pathologist? See if I can get any more physical characteristics?'

'Now you're sulking,' said Dundas. He gestured at Reid. 'What do you think, Inspector Reid?' he said, stressing Reid's title. 'Should we allow Sergeant Wright to go to speak to the nice pathologist?'

Wright shook his head in disgust.

Dundas and Reid exchanged grins. 'Might keep him out of trouble,' said Reid.

'Thanks, partner,' said Wright.

'What about you, Tommy? Any thoughts?'

'Thought I'd have a go at following up the playing card. The forensic boys haven't got any prints off it, but it must have come from somewhere.'

Dundas nodded approvingly. He looked around the incident room. There were half a dozen detectives sitting at desks and three female uniformed officers working on the computers. 'Lads and lassies, could I have your attention for a few moments, please,' he boomed. All heads turned to look at Dundas as he took another drink from the carton. 'Just to let you know that the Met team will be arriving later this afternoon. Twelve officers in all, the brightest and the best, no doubt.' He grinned and there were several guffaws from around the room. 'Most will be coming from the Battersea station and you'll probably recognise a few familiar faces. I see you've spread yourselves out but it might make more sense to stake a claim to one side of the incident room and let them have their desks together. They're a sensitive bunch and they feel happier in a pack. Phil, make sure they have enough phones and terminals, will you? I don't want them complaining that they're getting the short end of the stick.'

Phil Evans flashed Dundas a thumbs-up.

'Now, you know as well as I do how this is going to work. It's a joint investigation, with the BTP and the Met working hand in hand, brothers-in-arms in the fight against the forces of darkness. That's the PR shit. In reality we'll tell them fuck all and they'll treat us like mushrooms. I know I'm pissing in the wind, but please try to remember that we're supposed to be co-operating. Try to share something with them, otherwise we'll have two investigations going and that's not going to help anyone. Any questions?'

'Who's on the Met team?' asked Wright.

Dundas opened his file and held out a sheet of paper on which was a typed list of names. Wright scanned the list. His heart fell. The third name on the list was Detective Inspector Gerry Hunter. The sixth name was Detective Sergeant Clive Edmunds. He handed the list back to Dundas who gave it to Phil Evans. Dundas smiled at Wright. 'Any problems?' he asked.

'No, sir,' said Wright.

'Glad to hear it,' said Dundas. He left the incident room, humming to himself.

'Hunter's on the case?' asked Reid.

'Yeah.'

'That should produce a little creative tension, wouldn't you say?'

Wright drank the rest of his coffee and stood up. 'Maybe.'

On the way out, Wright checked his mailbox by the door. There was a single envelope, blindingly white, with his name and the address of the office typed on the front. He ripped it open on the way to the elevator. It was from the Child Support Agency, asking for details of any savings accounts he had. It was the third letter from the agency that he'd received that month. He treated it exactly the same way as he'd treated the previous two. He screwed it into a tight ball and tossed it into a wastepaper basket.

A middle-aged man wearing a bloodstained dark green glossy apron over light green scrubs squinted at

Wright's warrant card and told him that Dr Anna Littman was in the middle of a post mortem but that he could go in if he wanted. He nodded at a pair of green-painted swing doors with metal protective strips at waist height. Wright shook his head and said that he didn't mind waiting. The man pulled off bloody rubber gloves and dropped them into a bin, then stripped off his gown and put it in a black bag before going over to a stainless-steel sink and carefully washing his hands. 'Don't see many of you chaps here,' he said. 'What happened? Somebody fell under a train?'

'Murder,' said Wright. 'I'm Nick Wright.'

The man nodded. 'Robbie Ballantine.' He wiped his hands on a towel. 'Oh, of course, the body in the tunnel. Gruesome business that.'

'You saw it?'

'I helped Anna with the post mortem, actually. Is there a problem?'

'No, not really. I just wanted more information, that's all.'

'The report seemed comprehensive to me.'

'It's not that. I'm more interested in seeing if there was anything about the body that might help me identify the man.'

'You still don't know who he is?'

Wright shook his head. 'Can you think of anything? The scars on his back, for instance.'

Ballantine raised his eyebrows. 'Ah yes. The scars. They're in the report, aren't they?'

'The report refers to them as old scars, but doesn't say how they got there.'

'No real need to,' said Ballantine. 'They were very old

wounds. At least twenty years, I'd say. No connection at all with the crime.'

'Knife wounds?'

'Oh no,' said Ballantine. 'They were too jagged for that. Fragmentation scars, I'd say.'

'From a grenade? A war wound?'

'Could be.' He looked up at the ceiling and waggled his head from side to side as he thought about it. 'An explosion of some sort, certainly. It could have been a gas cylinder exploding, something like that.' He looked at Wright again. 'I actually hadn't given it much thought. Why are you so interested?'

'Because if it was a grenade I'd be looking for someone with a military background. If it was a bomb, then he could have been caught up in a terrorist incident.'

The swing doors behind Wright banged open and Anna Littman burst into the room, her gloved hands held out in front of her. Her hair was covered with a green plastic cap and she was wearing scrubs and a bloodstained green apron. 'Nick Wright,' she said. 'Rank unknown. To what do I owe the pleasure?'

Wright was surprised that she'd remembered his name. Surprised and flattered. She turned her back on him as she stripped off her protective clothing.

'It's sergeant,' said Wright. 'And I need your help.'

'Take two aspirins and call me tomorrow.' She took off her cap and her greying blonde hair spilled out. She looked over her shoulder at him and winked mischievously. 'That's a doctor joke,' she said.

'I just came to tell you that your car's been towed away,' he said.

'I only . . .' she began, but she stopped when Wright's face broke into a grin.

'That's a policeman joke,' he said.

Her green eyes flashed, then she smiled. It was an open, honest smile, thought Wright. He decided that he liked Dr Anna Littman. She seemed a lot less prickly than when they'd met in the tunnel. She went over to the sink and washed her hands.

'He was asking about the tunnel corpse,' said Ballantine, putting on a fresh apron.

'Was he now?' said Dr Littman. She pulled her hair back into a ponytail and fastened it with a small black band. 'You got my report?'

'Eventually,' he said.

'Oh yes, I'm sorry about that. I didn't know where to send it, so I figured that Gerry could hand it on to you.'

'The report was fine,' he said, putting his hands in his pockets. 'I just wanted to pick your brains.'

Ballantine pulled on rubber gloves. 'Duty calls,' he said to Wright, and used his shoulder to push his way through the swing doors.

'So, Sergeant Nick, pick away.' Dr Littman leaned back against the sink and watched him with amused eyes.

'I'm having trouble identifying the body,' said Wright. 'The face was messed up so badly it's impossible to get a match from photographs. Hundreds of men go missing every year, and other than the scars on his back there don't seem to be any identifying features. Robbie there was saying he thought they might be shrapnel scars. An old war wound. Or an accident. Something like that could help me identify him.'

'I see. Do you want a coffee?'

86

The change of subject took Wright by surprise and for a moment he was flustered. 'Coffee? Sure. Yeah, that'd be great.'

'Come through to my office.'

Wright followed her down a corridor. Even in the shapeless scrubs it was clear she had a good figure. Wright wondered how old she was. Late thirties, certainly. Maybe early forties. At least six or seven years older than he was. She opened a door and he followed her into a small office with a single window overlooking a car park. There were several feminine touches: a fern in a pot, a watercolour of a young girl playing with a puppy, and several framed photographs on the desk. One of the pictures was of a good-looking man wearing gold-rimmed spectacles with two young boys in his lap. Dr Littman poured two cups from a coffee-maker on top of a filing cabinet. 'No milk, but I've got Coffeemate,' she said.

'Coffeemate's fine,' said Wright.

'Sit,' she said. 'Sugar?'

'No, thanks,' said Wright, sitting in a leather armchair. On the wall to his right was a poster of a rock group, half a dozen beefy men with long hair and leather waistcoats holding their musical instruments in phallic poses. Wright wondered if Anna Littman had a thing about rock musicians. The poster certainly seemed out of place in the office.

She stirred white powder into the coffees, gave him his cup and then sat in the high-backed swivel chair behind the desk. 'I'm not sure how much of a help the scars on his back will be,' she said. 'They were very old, hardly noticeable. A wife would probably know about them, but they wouldn't be common knowledge.'

'Pity,' said Wright. 'Was there anything else that you

saw, maybe something that wasn't in the report but which I could use to narrow down the possibilities?'

Dr Littman looked at Wright over the top of her cup. Small frown lines appeared across her forehead. She put down her cup. 'He was circumcised,' she said. 'That should help. I think you'd probably be able to eliminate two thirds of the possibilities on the basis of circumcision alone.'

She warmed her hands on the steaming cup of coffee and chewed on the side of her lip, deep in thought, staring into the middle distance as she tried to recall the body.

'Contact lenses,' she said. 'He had contact lenses. The disposable type, the ones you wear for a day and throw away.' Suddenly her eyes widened. 'Oh God, I clean forgot. I think he played bass guitar.'

Wright burst out laughing. 'Come on, Anna. What on earth makes you say that?'

She looked at him seriously. 'I was checking his hands for defence wounds. They were soft, as if he wasn't used to manual work, but the skin on the fingertips of both hands was hard.'

Wright shook his head, still chuckling.

Her eyes flashed and she flicked her hair to the side like a horse swishing its mane. 'Do you want my help or not, Sergeant Nick?'

Wright did his best to stop laughing. 'I'm sorry,' he said, 'but that's a feat of deduction that Sherlock Holmes would be proud of.'

Dr Littman pointed at the poster. 'See the guy third from the left. With the bass guitar?'

Wright looked at the musician. A tall, good-looking man in black leather with shoulder-length jet-black hair and a white guitar thrusting up from his groin. 'Yes . . .' he said, not sure what she was getting at. Dr Littman turned the framed photograph of the man with two children around so that he could see it more clearly. He did a double-take. 'My God,' he said. 'You married a rock and roll star.'

'He used to dye his hair,' she said. She smiled at the photograph. 'And he has to wear glasses these days.' She looked up at Wright. 'He still plays. And I'd know a bass guitarist's hands anywhere.'

'Okay, I'm convinced, but why are you so sure he played bass and not lead guitar?'

Dr Littman sat back in her chair, smiling broadly. 'Lead guitarists use plectrums, so the skin isn't so hard on the fingertips of their right hands. And Spanish guitarists have long nails on their right hands so that they can pluck the strings.' She gave an exaggerated shrug. 'What can I say? I've been married a long time. My husband could probably tell you half a dozen causes of hypertension.' Wright was suddenly very envious of Dr Littman's husband. Her love and affection for him was written all over her face. Wright doubted that Janie had ever felt the same way about him. 'So, have I been of any help?' the pathologist asked.

Wright grinned. 'Of course you have,' he replied. 'I'm looking for a short-sighted, circumcised bass player. How hard can that be?'

W hen Wright got back to the office, Tommy Reid was devouring a carton of Kentucky Fried Chicken. 'Wanna piece?' asked Reid, offering a leg.

Wright shook his head. He sat down and studied a note that had been left on his desk. His ex-wife had called. Three times. Wright held up the note.

'Yeah, she's not a happy bunny,' said Reid. He wiped his greasy lips with a paper napkin.

'Did she say what it was this time?'

Reid picked up a handful of French fries. 'Nope.' He slotted the fries into his mouth and chewed contentedly. 'How did it go with the lady doctor?'

'I think I can narrow the list down quite a bit. Our man played bass guitar.'

'Yeah? What colour?'

'I'm serious. Playing the guitar affects the fingers, apparently.'

Reid pulled a face. 'You learn something every day,' he said.

'What about the card?' asked Wright.

Reid reached for his notebook and flicked through it. 'I had no problem identifying it. I took it to a magic shop in Kensington and the guy there knew what it was straight away. It's a Bicycle brand, one of the most common brands, unfortunately. Manufactured in Ohio by the United States Playing Card Company. They make millions of the things.'

'Any chance of telling where our card was bought?'

'If we had the box they came in, maybe. But not from the card itself. Game shops, department stores, magic shops, newsagents, they all sell playing cards. And a hell of a lot of them sell the Bicycle brand.'

Wright heaved himself out of his chair and went over to the whiteboard. He massaged his temples with his knuckles as he stared at the photograph of the mutilated corpse. 'I wonder what it's like to die like that?' he mused. 'To have your skin peeled off, bit by bit.'

'Hey, I'm eating here,' complained Reid. Wright turned and was about to apologise, but his partner was already biting into his chicken leg.

T here were two detectives, big men in cheap suits with the careworn faces of cops who had been on the job long enough to have seen it all. They were polite enough, and the senior of the two, an inspector called O'Brien, had shaken the senator by the hand after they'd shown him their identification. The questions were routine, O'Brien had said, and he didn't expect to take up too much of Burrow's time. They'd rejected his offer of coffee and O'Brien's partner had taken out a pen and notebook after they'd seated themselves in front of the senator's desk.

'How long had Kristine Ross been working for you, Senator?' asked O'Brien.

'Just under two years.'

'As your secretary?'

'As one of three secretaries. Four, if you include my office manager, Sally Forster.'

'Did she seem depressed?'

Burrow leaned forward. 'I thought it was an accident? She tripped, I was told.'

O'Brien made a patting motion with his hand and shook his head emphatically. 'These are standard questions, Senator. Whenever we get an accidental death, we have to rule out any other possibilities. I wouldn't be doing my job if I did otherwise.'

Burrow sat back again. 'I understand, Officer, but Kristine was a delightful, high-spirited, wonderful girl, and I wouldn't want it to get around that she might have killed herself. No, she was most definitely not depressed.'

'To the best of your knowledge, did she have a drinking problem?'

'A drinking problem? Absolutely not. Why, was drink involved?'

'She'd drunk a bottle of wine before she fell.'

Burrows shrugged. 'That surprises me,' he said.

'Was she under a lot of stress here?'

'No more so than the rest of my staff. We all work long and hard here, Inspector O'Brien, but it goes with the turf. Kristine knew what was involved before she joined. She didn't appear to me to have any trouble coping, but Sally would know better than me. You should speak to her.'

'We have, Senator, and she agrees with you.'

Burrow held his hands out, palms upward. 'There you are, then.' He stole a glance at O'Brien's partner. The detective was scribbling in his notebook. He finished writing and looked up. Burrow flashed him a confident smile.

O'Brien stood up and held out his hand. Burrow shook it again and looked the detective in the eye. The senator knew how important eye contact was: it demonstrated sincerity and openness, qualities that Burrow was a master at projecting.

'Terrible business,' said Burrow.

'Accidents happen,' said the detective. His partner put away his notebook and nodded a farewell to the senator. 'Did you know that more accidents happen in the home than on the roads?' O'Brien asked.

'Is that so?' said the senator. 'I had no idea.'

He walked the two detectives to the door and showed them out. Sally Forster was waiting to escort them out of the main office. Burrow closed the door and sighed deeply. His heart had been pounding throughout the interview, even though he knew that Jody Meacher would have left nothing to chance. There wouldn't be anything to connect Burrow to the murder, and it was a murder, he was sure of that. Meacher hadn't said what he was going to do, or when it would happen, but Burrow knew that Meacher was behind Kristine Ross's death. More than that, Burrow didn't want to know. All that mattered was that Meacher was taking care of things, just as he'd promised.

Nick Wright spent the afternoon methodically working through his list of missing persons. The list had been generated by the Police National Computer after details of the corpse had been fed in: height, weight, eye colour, age, and distinguishing features. The wide age bracket was the main reason that the list was so long, but he hadn't wanted to narrow it any further. Each missing man had his own page giving physical details, the name and telephone number of the investigating officer and a PNC code that identified the police station involved in the enquiry. What the PNC didn't supply was a photograph, or details of next of kin; for that Wright had to contact the officer handling the enquiry. It was slow, methodical work. Often the officer involved wasn't available, so Wright had either to leave a message or find someone else who could pull the file for him. If there was a photograph available, Wright arranged to have it sent to Tavistock Place, either through the Photophone system that the Force Intelligence Bureau had on the third floor, or by faxing it to one of the two fax machines in the incident room. Sometimes he was able to eliminate a possibility solely on the basis of a photograph, but the mutilation of the face and the poor quality of the photographs meant that more often than not Wright would have to telephone the next of kin for further details.

At first he'd felt a little embarrassed asking relatives if the man who'd gone missing was circumcised, and several times he'd been accused of being a pervert and had had the phone banged down on him. Despite his embarrassment, he'd already ruled out more than twenty names. Wright was about to dial another number when the phone rang. He picked up the receiver and his heart fell as soon as he heard his ex-wife's voice.

'What the hell are you playing at, Nick?' she hissed. Janie rarely shouted. If anything, the angrier she got, the quieter she became.

Wright was stunned. He had no idea what he'd done to upset her. 'What's wrong?' he said.

'What did I say to you about telling Sean war stories?' she said. 'He had nightmares all last night and I had to take him to school with bags under his eyes. What the hell did you think you were doing?'

'He wanted to—'

'Just how long do you think the judge is going to allow you to see our son if he finds out the sort of photographs you've been showing him? Crime scene pictures, for God's sake. You showed him a photograph of a dismembered corpse.'

'Okay, I'm sorry.'

'Sorry doesn't cut it. I'm supposed to be able to trust you with Sean. I specifically told you not to talk about that case.'

'Janie, it was raining, the zoo was a washout, I couldn't think what else to do with him. It was a mistake. I'm sorry. What do you want me to do, open a vein?'

'An artery would be nice,' she said. 'Don't do it again, Nick.'

The line went dead. Wright banged the receiver back on its cradle. He put his head in his hands and closed his eyes. 'Shit,' he whispered. He stood up and went over to the coffee machine and poured himself a cup. He sipped it but the hot, bitter liquid couldn't shift the bad taste in his mouth. Wright went over to Reid's desk and pulled open the bottom drawer. The bottle of vodka was wrapped in a Kentucky Fried Chicken bag. Wright took it out and poured a slug into his coffee, then drank half of it in one gulp. He added more vodka, then put the bottle away and closed the drawer. Reid was out trying to interview dog-walkers and wasn't planning to put in an appearance that afternoon. More than likely he'd be in a pub somewhere. Wright raised his polystyrene cup in a silent salute to his absent partner.

Wright sat down at his own desk and ran his finger down the list of missing persons. He'd already discounted most of the names on the first sheet. As he flicked over to the second sheet, his mobile telephone rang. The noise startled him and coffee slopped over his hand. He cursed, put the cup down and licked his hand as he picked up the phone and held it to his ear. He had a sinking feeling that it was his ex-wife, but the voice on the other end of the line was cultured and soft-spoken, the sort of voice that might belong to the wife of a Conservative Member of Parliament. 'Sergeant Wright?' she said.

'Speaking,' said Wright.

'You left a message for me to call you,' she said. 'My name's May Eckhardt.'

Wright ran his eyes down the sheet. No Eckhardt. 'Do you by any chance have a relative missing, Mrs Eckhardt? A man?'

'My husband,' she said hesitantly. 'Have you found him?'

Wright found the name on the fourth sheet. Max Eckhardt. A forty-eight-year-old American living in Maida Vale. May Eckhardt didn't sound at all American, her accent was pure Home Counties. 'I just wanted to ask you a few questions about your husband, Mrs Eckhardt.'

'Have you found him?' she repeated, a harder edge to her voice this time.

'Mrs Eckhardt, at this stage all I'm trying to do is to eliminate names from a list of missing persons. A body was found in a railway tunnel and I'm trying to identify it. Could you tell me, was your husband circumcised?'

'Excuse me?'

'Your husband. Was he circumcised?'

She hesitated for several seconds. 'Oh, I see. Yes. Yes, he was.' She had obviously realised why he had asked the question, for which Wright was immediately grateful.

'Did he wear contact lenses?'

'Yes. Yes, he did.'

'And were there scars on his back? Old scars, small ones.'

'Oh my God,' she whispered.

'Mrs Eckhardt, did he have scars on his back?'

'Yes, he did. It's him, isn't it?'

'I really couldn't say, Mrs Eckhardt, but I would like you to come in and take a look at the body we have.'

'You think it's him, don't you?'

'It's a possibility,' Wright admitted.

'What about his wallet? He had a driving licence, his press card, his credit cards.'

'There were no personal effects on the body, Mrs Eckhardt.'

'But you said he was found in a tunnel. He was hit by a train, wasn't he?'

'No, he wasn't hit by a train. Look, Mrs Eckhardt, I really don't want to say any more until you've had the chance to identify the body.'

'When?'

'As soon as you can,' said Wright. He gave her the address of the mortuary and arranged to meet her there within the hour. Wright put his mobile phone into his jacket pocket. He drank the rest of his coffee, but the bad taste was still in his mouth. He hoped that the body wouldn't be that of May Eckhardt's husband, but he had a feeling that his search was over.

Wright arrived at the mortuary in St Thomas's Hospital fifteen minutes before he was due to meet Mrs Eckhardt. He wanted to check with Dr Littman that the corpse was in a fit state to be viewed. The last time Wright had seen it the face was cut to ribbons and smeared with blood. Dr Littman wasn't there but Robbie Ballantine was, washing up after yet another post mortem.

'What state's the tunnel body in after the post mortem?' Wright asked him. 'I've got a possible relative coming to identify him.'

'The face was pretty cut up,' said Ballantine. 'We've put it back together as best we can, but it's still a mess.'

'Recognisable?'

'I should think so. How close a relative?'

'Wife.'

'Poor cow,' said Ballantine sympathetically.

'If it's her,' said Wright. He looked across at the large clock on the wall over the sink. 'I'd better go along to reception. Can you get it ready?'

'Sure,' said Ballantine. 'Does she know about the injuries?'

'Not yet.'

'Because the body isn't . . . complete. If you see what I mean. His dick's in a specimen jar, to put it bluntly,' Ballantine said. 'So if she's any thoughts about checking up on other parts of his anatomy to confirm that it's him, I'd think twice before you let her pull the sheet back.'

Wright walked through to reception. There were two uncomfortable-looking orange plastic chairs to the left of the main entrance with a metal coffee table on which lay a few well-thumbed magazines. A bored receptionist was pecking away at a computer keyboard and she looked up as Wright walked up to the counter.

'I'm waiting for a Mrs Eckhardt,' he said. 'She's here to view a body. Can you point her in my direction when she gets here?'

The receptionist nodded but didn't say anything.

Wright went over to a window which overlooked the car park. Dark clouds rolled slowly overhead, threatening rain. A black VW Golf cabriolet nosed into the car park, driven by an Oriental girl. The top was down and as she parked she cast a nervous look at the sky. 'Yeah, it looks like rain,' Wright said out loud. 'Better safe than sorry.' He smiled to himself as she put the top up.

Wright picked up the magazines, wondering what sort of reading matter was thought suitable for a mortuary. Most of them were old copies of *Hello!*

He looked up as the Oriental girl walked in. She was a little under five feet six, with shoulder-length glossy black hair. As she approached Wright he realised that she was older than he'd first thought, certainly in her late twenties, maybe older. The fringe and her small frame gave her the appearance of a schoolgirl from a distance, but she walked with authority and he saw the swell of firm breasts under her open fawn Burberry raincoat. She had an expectant look on her face and Wright figured that she worked in the mortuary. He was about to point to the receptionist when she spoke.

'Sergeant Wright?'

Wright's mouth fell open in surprise. The cultured upper-middle-class voice was totally at odds with the petite Oriental. 'Yes?' he said, momentarily confused.

'May Eckhardt.' She held out her hand. 'We spoke on the phone.'

She seemed to be deliberately trying to put him at ease and he realised she must have sensed his confusion. 'I'm sorry,' he said, trying to regain his composure. 'Of course, Mrs Eckhardt, I'm sorry, my mind was elsewhere.' He immediately regretted the words. It was possibly the worst day of May Eckhardt's life and he'd told her he was thinking about something else. 'I'm sorry,' he repeated. He shook her hand. It felt tiny within his own, but it was strong and firm and he felt her nails press against his flesh. The sensation was decidedly sexual and he felt a slight tingle down his back. She withdrew her hand quickly and seemed flustered herself as if she'd sensed what he was thinking. 'Thank you for coming,' he added, and felt another surge of embarrassment. It wasn't as if he'd invited her to a party.

Wright took her down the corridor to the viewing room in silence. He didn't trust himself to speak without making a fool of himself again. The viewing room was little more than a cubicle, about six feet wide and ten feet long, painted a putrid yellow. The only furniture was a narrow table on which stood a white oval vase containing a bunch of faded silk flowers. Set into one of the walls was a white-framed window, and on the other side was one of the post mortem rooms. Robbie Ballantine was waiting on the other side of the glass. Wright nodded that they were ready and Ballantine pushed a trolley over.

The body was covered with a sheet the same colour as Ballantine's scrubs. He slowly pulled back the sheet until the face was revealed. It was considerably less bloody than when Wright had last seen it, but the cuts were clearly visible in the pale dead flesh.

Wright looked across at May Eckhardt. She was staring at the body, her face devoid of expression. 'Is it your husband?' he asked.

She didn't reply and Wright wondered whether or not she'd heard him. He was going to ask her again when she gave a small shake of her head. 'I'm not sure,' she said, her voice a hoarse whisper.

Ballantine looked at Wright expectantly. Wright shrugged. 'Take your time,' he told her.

She wrapped her arms around herself as if she was feeling the cold. 'It's just . . .'

She didn't finish, but Wright knew what she was trying to say. People never looked the same after death. 'There's no rush, Mrs Eckhardt.'

She turned to face him. 'Can I get closer?'

Wright wanted to dissuade her, but he knew that her request made sense. 'Okay,' he said. 'Come this way.' He took her along the corridor to the post mortem room. Ballantine had realised what was happening and was holding the door open for them. He flashed Wright a warning look as he went by, a silent reminder not to allow her to pull back the sheet. Wright nodded.

May seemed not to notice the non-verbal communication between the two men, and walked hesitatingly over to the trolley. She stared down at the body for a few seconds, then looked up at Wright. Her lower lip was quivering. She tried to speak, but words wouldn't come and she just nodded. Wright reached for her arm, wanting to guide her away from the trolley, but she took a step back, leaving him grabbing at empty air. She turned, bent down and kissed her husband on the forehead. Her hair swung across the corpse's face, then she straightened up and walked quickly out of the room.

Wright gave a small sigh of relief. He had feared that she might break down and he wasn't sure how he would have dealt with that. Her high heels click-clacked along the tiled floor and Wright had to jog after her as she hurried along the corridor. She rushed through the door to reception and it slammed in Wright's face. He pushed it open and called after her. She stopped in the centre of the reception area, facing away from him. The receptionist was engrossed in her computer.

Wright walked up behind her. 'I'm sorry, Mrs Eckhardt,' he said, 'but I have to ask you, for the record. Is that your husband in there?'

She spun around, her eyes filled with tears and contempt. 'What do you think?' she spat.

Wright held up his hands as if trying to ward off her rage. 'Please, Mrs Eckhardt, I have to ask. I can see you're upset . . .'

'Upset!' she hissed. 'Upset? That's my husband in there and you can see that I'm upset?'

Wright ran a hand through his hair, wondering what he could possibly say that would calm her down. 'I'll be asked at the inquest, Mrs Eckhardt. I'll be asked if you positively identified the body as being that of your husband, and it won't be enough for me to say that you reacted as if it were. I have to hear you say the words. I'm sorry.' He kept his head close to hers and his voice down to a hushed whisper.

She took a deep breath, and gradually regained her composure. 'No,' she said. 'I'm the one that's sorry. You're right, of course. Yes, that is my husband. Max Eckhardt.'

The strength seemed to fade from her legs and Wright reached for her as her eyes closed and she fell forwards. He grabbed her around the waist. She was as light as a child and he swept her up and carried her over to the chairs, where he sat her down and loosened her coat.

Wright looked over his shoulder; the receptionist was continuing to type obliviously. 'Excuse me, do you think you could get me a glass of water?' Wright asked her.

The receptionist gasped when she saw May slumped in the chair. 'Oh my goodness,' she said. 'That's the third one this week.'

'A glass of water,' said Wright. 'If it's not too much trouble.'

He fanned May's face with a copy of *Hello!* until the receptionist returned with a plastic cup of tepid water. By then May had opened her eyes again and she sipped gratefully at the water. 'What happened?' she asked.

'You fainted,' said the receptionist. 'You're the third one this week.'

Wright glared at her and she shrugged carelessly and went back to her desk behind the counter. He took the cup off May. The rim was smeared with pink lipstick.

'What happened to Max?' she asked.

Wright shook his head. 'I'm afraid he was murdered, Mrs Eckhardt.'

'Murdered?' What little colour remained in her face visibly drained away and Wright put a hand on her shoulder, afraid that she was about to faint again.

She shook him away. 'I'm all right,' she insisted, but she took the cup off him and drank again.

'Is there someone I can call for you? A friend? A relative?'

She shook her head. 'I don't have any friends in London,' she said. 'We've only been here a few weeks. And I don't have any relatives.'

'What about on your husband's side of the family?'

'He left home when he was a teenager.' She snorted softly. 'Not that he ever called it home. He hasn't spoken to his parents for thirty years, doesn't even know if they're alive.' She bit down on her lower lip. 'Didn't,' she corrected herself. 'He didn't even know if they're alive.' She looked at Wright with large, tear-filled eyes. 'When do you start thinking about them in the past tense?' she asked.

Wright took one of her small hands in his own. This time she didn't seem to resent the physical contact. 'It takes a long time,' he said. 'Sometimes you never get to think of them in the past.'

She shuddered and slowly withdrew her hand, a faraway look in her eyes. Wright gave her back the cup of water and she sipped it. 'What am I going to do?' she asked.

Wright didn't know what to say.

'I have to go home,' she whispered. 'I have to take the car in for its service. I have a lot of things to do.' The words came out singly, each separated by a distinct pause.

'Are you going to be all right?' he asked, the words sounding woefully inadequate.

She looked up at him as if she'd forgotten that he was there. 'I'm sorry?' she said, frowning. 'What did you say?'

'Will you be all right?'

She stood up and adjusted the belt of her raincoat. 'I'll be fine,' she said, her voice robotic.

'I'll need to talk to you again,' he said. 'There are questions I have to ask you.'

She turned away. 'Of course,' she said.

'I'll telephone you tomorrow,' he said.

She pushed open the door. 'Do that,' she said. The door swung closed behind her.

Wright went over to the window and watched as she went over to her car. He half expected her to break down in tears, but she opened the door, climbed in, and a few seconds later she drove away. She didn't look in his direction.

Ballantine walked into the reception area. 'Did she identify him?'

'Yeah. It's her husband. Max Eckhardt.'

'Okay, I'll do the paperwork. Do you want to stay and watch a post mortem? I've got a victim of parakeet poisoning.'

Wright frowned. 'Don't you mean paraquat?'

'Nah, someone shoved a parrot down his throat.' Ballantine chuckled and slapped Wright on the back. 'Just trying to lighten the moment, Nick.' He walked away, still chuckling.

Wright drove back to the office. Reid was squinting at his VDU and cross-checking a list of names against a computer printout.

'The victim is Max Eckhardt,' said Wright. 'Definitely.'

'Thank God for that,' said Reid. He sat back and massaged his right shoulder. 'I think I'm getting RSI,' he complained. 'You want to contact the press office?' He shook his hands, then clicked his knuckles.

'I think I'll wait until I've interviewed his wife.'

'Widow,' corrected Reid. 'Speaking of ex-wives, your solicitor rang.' He handed Wright a piece of a Burger King wrapper on which he'd scrawled a telephone number.

'Did he say what he wanted?'

Reid shook his head.

'Great,' sighed Wright. He was sure of one thing: it wouldn't be good news. 'Where's Ronnie?'

Reid gestured upwards with his thumb. 'With the governor.'

'I'd better tell him I've identified the body.' The door to the incident room was pushed open. 'Speak of the devil,' said Wright as Ronnie Dundas stepped into the incident room, closely followed by Superintendent Newton.

Wright got to his feet. 'Sir, we know who the victim is. Max Eckhardt. Number sixty-three on the PNC list.'

'Great,' said Dundas. The chief inspector turned to the superintendent. 'At least we can show the Met boys something, Governor,' he said.

Newton nodded, his mouth a tight line. 'Where are they going to sit?' he asked.

Dundas pointed at a group of desks that had been pushed together to the right of the door. 'We've given them their own HOLMES computer and I've asked Phil to assign two uniformed WPCs to input their statements and reports. I don't think they'll have any reason to moan.'

Newton pursed his lips as he looked around the incident room. He looked at his wristwatch. 'They're due in at three,' he said. 'Bring their chief inspector up to see me when they get here.' He turned and left the incident room.

Dundas went over to his desk and picked up a carton of milk. 'Okay, tell me about Eckhardt,' he said.

Wright logged on to the PNC terminal and called up Eckhardt's details. 'Forty-eight years old, American, married and lives in Maida Vale.'

Dundas cursed as his fingers slipped and the carton fell to the ground. Milk splattered over his shoes as he retrieved it. 'Why the hell do they make these damn things so difficult to open?' he asked. He took a long drink and wiped his moustache with the back of his hand. 'Missing since when?'

'A week ago. His wife reported it on Tuesday.'

'Did she say why he was in Battersea?'

'I haven't interviewed her yet,' said Wright. 'She was

pretty shaken up. I thought it best if she went home. I'll go along and see her later.'

'Okay,' said Dundas. 'Get a picture circulated. The Met boys'll be handling the house-to-house in Battersea. They'll be glad of the overtime.'

'Couldn't we handle that?' asked Wright. If there was going to be an early break on the case, it would probably come from a witness who'd seen the killer in the vicinity.

'It's a joint investigation, Nick.'

'Yeah, yeah, yeah.'

'I'm serious.' Dundas held his arm up in the air. 'That goes for everyone!' he shouted. 'I know we're not the best of buddies with the council cops, but the key word here is co-operation. Everything goes into HOLMES. Everything. No holding back tidbits for yourself. And at morning prayers we share ideas, not hurl insults. Is everyone clear on that?'

There were assorted mumblings from the detectives in the room.

'Good!' Dundas shouted. 'Just make sure we solve the case before the bastards!'

R oy Casper's office was little more than a broom cupboard, with half a window that looked down on a street of shops, most of which had 'For Sale' or 'To Let' signs in their windows. The office had once been twice the size but a plasterboard wall had been fitted, splitting it down the middle. There were no pictures or framed certificates hanging on the wall and Nick Wright wondered if the solicitor had been warned that it wouldn't take the weight. The few qualifications that Casper had hung on the wall by the door. Wright had never looked at them; for all he knew they could have been primary-school swimming certificates.

The office furniture wasn't dissimilar to that in Wright's own office: a cheap teak-effect desk, three shoulder-height metal filing cabinets, and swivel chairs covered in grey fabric. The solicitor had a computer on his desk but it was probably a decade older than the one Wright used. Casper hadn't even switched it on.

Casper was smoking a cigarette that he'd rolled himself and scattering ash over the file he was reading. Wright waited impatiently, knowing that he could only have been summoned to the poky little office to hear bad news.

'Here it is, sorry,' said Casper, pulling out a letter. Casper was only a few years away from retirement and Wright had the feeling he was coasting. Everything about the man suggested he'd given up taking care of his appearance. In a perfect world Wright would have had a more high-powered solicitor, but Casper was all he could afford.

Casper squinted at the letter, clicking his teeth as he read, and Wright had to fight the urge to grab the letter from him. Casper looked up at him. 'She wants to cut back on your visitation rights . . .'

Wright jumped to his feet so quickly that his chair flew backwards and banged into the wall. 'She what?' He grabbed for the letter, almost tearing it out of Casper's hand. His whole body shook as he read it.

'Calm down, Nick,' said the solicitor.

'Once a month!' Wright spat. 'She wants me to see him

once a month! For God's sake, he's going to forget who I am. She can't do this.'

Casper began rolling another cigarette. 'She can try,' he said. 'Read on.'

Wright read through to the end. Janie was claiming that Sean was having nightmares after the unauthorised visit to his office. 'This is bullshit,' said Wright.

Casper used a red plastic lighter to light his cigarette and he blew smoke over the file. 'Did you take Sean to your office?'

'Yes. I'd taken him to the zoo, it started raining, I figured he might like to see where I worked, that's all.'

'But your ex-wife specifically told you not to?'

Wright shook his head vigorously. 'No, that's not what happened at all. Look, whose side are you on?'

'You're paying my bill,' said Casper. 'Though I should mention that I'm still waiting for your last account to be settled.' He took a long pull on his roll-up. 'Your ex-wife alleges that your last visit has had a detrimental effect on your son's mental wellbeing. Accordingly, she wants to decrease your exposure to him.'

'Can she do that?'

'It'll have to go before a judge. But if she gets a medical report on her side, I wouldn't be surprised if the judge decided in her favour.'

Wright tossed the letter back on to the solicitor's untidy desk. 'Terrific,' he said bitterly.

Casper put the letter back in the file. 'How do you want me to proceed?' he asked.

Wright put his hands either side of his head and massaged his temples. 'What are my options?'

'I can say that we'd like our own psychologist to examine

your son. They'll have to agree to that, and by the time he's been examined, he'll probably be over the nightmares.' Casper put up his hands as Wright scowled at him. 'That's my recommendation, anyway.'

'I've a better idea,' said Wright. Casper raised his eyebrows expectantly. 'I could kill her.' Wright bared his teeth in a semblance of a smile. 'I'm only joking, Roy,' he said. 'Honest.'

M ay Eckhardt's address was an apartment in a four-storey mansion block in Maida Vale. Her black VW was parked in the road and Nick Wright pulled in behind it. The exterior of the mansion block was orange brick and white-painted pebbledash with a slate roof that looked brand new. There was a narrow well-tended strip of garden in front of the block and a black and white cat with pale green eyes watched him from the safety of a small chestnut tree as Wright walked towards the front door. There were eight bells and a brass speakerphone to the right of the door. Most of the bells had brass nameplates, but the one under the Eckhardt bell was written on cardboard. Wright pushed the bell. There was no answer and he pressed it a second time. There was still no reply, but the door lock buzzed and when he pushed the front door it swung open. He looked around and saw a closed-circuit television camera tucked away at the top of the entrance alcove. She'd obviously seen him on that. He smiled up at the lens, and immediately regretted it. He wasn't there on a social call.

There were two apartments on each floor. Wright walked up to the second floor where May Eckhardt already had the door open for him. She was wearing a baggy white sweatshirt with Exeter University on the front, the sleeves pulled up to her elbows, and blue Levi jeans. Her hair was tied back in a ponytail and she had dark patches under her eyes.

'Sergeant Wright,' she said flatly. 'I thought you said you'd telephone.'

'I'm sorry, but I was passing and . . .'

She turned away and walked down the hall, her bare feet slapping on the polished pine floorboards. Wright closed the door. When he turned around the hall was empty. There was a stripped pine door to the left and Wright peered around it into a big room with a bay window overlooking the street. May was sitting on a beige sofa, her knees drawn up against her chest. Apart from the sofa there were two armchairs in matching fabric and a Chinese-patterned rug on the floor. A big screen TV sat in one corner and a JVC stereo with waist-high speakers in another. An alcove opposite the door had been lined with shelves on which were stacked hundreds of records. Frank Sinatra was playing on the stereo.

'I thought I'd try, on the off chance . . .'

'It's all right,' she said. There was a bottle of white wine on the floor by the sofa and a half-filled glass.

'How are you?' he asked, sitting down in one of the armchairs.

Her eyes narrowed. 'How do you think I am?' she asked.

'I'm sorry, stupid question.' He looked around the room. A black bass guitar hung on the wall behind the sofa where May was sitting.

'Is that your husband's?' asked Wright.

May twisted around and stared at the guitar for several seconds as if it was the first time she'd seen it. 'Yes,' she said.

'He was a musician?'

She turned around again. 'No, it was a hobby. He was a photographer.'

Wright took out his notebook and a pen. 'Who did he work for?'

'Agence France Press. It's a news agency. He was moved to the London bureau three months ago.' She leaned forward and picked up the wine glass. 'We've only just moved into the flat. Half our things are still in storage.'

'When did he go missing?'

'Last Monday. He'd been sent to Brighton for the Conservative Party conference. The office wanted him to stay in Brighton rather than coming back to London each night.' She sipped her wine. 'He was supposed to be back on Monday but didn't show. That's not unusual so I didn't worry. But on Tuesday the office called me asking where Max was. He'd left Brighton on Monday. I thought perhaps he'd had an accident, and started calling around the hospitals. Then I called the police.' She finished her wine with several gulps and refilled her glass before holding out the bottle. 'Would you . . .?' she said.

Wright shook his head. 'I wouldn't mind a drink of water, though,' he said.

She began to get up but Wright beat her to it. 'Tap water will do just fine,' he said.

May settled back and looked at him over the top of her glass. 'The kitchen's first on the right,' she said.

Wright went along the hallway. The kitchen was all stainless steel and shiny white worktops and it reminded

Wright of the post mortem room, stark and functional. He picked up a glass off the draining board and ran the cold tap. There was a pine knife block to the left of the sink in which were embedded five knives, all with black handles. There was a space for a sixth knife. Wright put down the glass and pulled out one of the knives. It seemed to be a pretty good match to the one that had been impaled in Eckhardt's body. He took out a second knife. It was a bread knife with a serrated edge. Wright wondered which knife was missing from the kitchen block. He pushed the two knives back into the block and filled his glass from the tap. As he did, he looked down into a plastic washing-up bowl. Lying next to a toast-crumb-coated plate was the missing knife. Wright took it out of the bowl and slotted it into the block. It was a perfect match. Wright felt an inexplicable sensation of relief wash over him.

He went back into the sitting room with his glass of water. May didn't appear to have moved at all. Wright sat down and sipped his water. 'Was he driving back from Brighton?' he asked.

'No. He was taking the train.'

'So why did you think he might have been involved in an accident?'

She frowned as if she didn't understand the question. 'I don't know. I suppose I thought he might have had a heart attack or something. You know what flashes through your mind when someone goes missing. You always assume the worst.' She began to shiver and she gripped the glass so hard that Wright feared it would shatter. 'Who would do that to him?' she whispered. 'Why would anyone want to kill my husband like that?'

'Did he have any enemies?' asked Wright.

'Good God, no. Oh no. You don't think that someone who knew Max would . . . ?' Her voice tailed off.

'Is it possible that he was working on a story that brought him into contact with dangerous people?'

'Like the Conservative Party?' She smiled thinly. 'What is it they call it? Gallows humour? Isn't that what police are famous for?'

'Sometimes it makes it easier to deal with the sort of things we come across,' said Wright.

'Well, Max is . . . I mean, Max was . . . a senior photographer with the agency. They wouldn't have him doorstepping gangsters or drug dealers. Most of the time he covered wars. Crazy, huh? I never worried about him when he was here. It was always when he was abroad that I was scared. And we haven't been here long enough to have made enemies. You could talk to the office, though. His boss is Steve Reynolds.'

'Where were you before you moved to London?'

'The States. New York.'

'He was an American?'

She nodded.

'And you? If you don't mind me asking, where are you from?'

'Sale. Just outside Manchester.' She smiled tightly. 'Sorry to disappoint you if you thought I was from somewhere more exotic.'

'Oh, it's not that,' he said quickly. 'I know lots of Asians are born here these days—'

'Oriental,' she interrupted.

'I'm sorry?'

'I'm Oriental,' she said. 'Asians are Indians or Pakistanis.' She shook her head. 'It doesn't matter.' Her eyes glazed over

114

and it was obvious her mind was elsewhere. They sat without speaking for several minutes. Frank Sinatra began to sing 'New York, New York'. One of life's little coincidences, thought Wright.

'He must have died in such pain,' May said eventually. 'I wonder if . . . ?' Tears welled up in her eyes.

Wright uncrossed and crossed his legs, embarrassed by the strength of her emotion. He looked down at his notebook and to his surprise saw that he'd been doodling, boxes within boxes.

'Why would anyone torture him like that? Why would anyone cut him so many times?'

'I don't know,' said Wright lamely. He knew that she wasn't fully aware of the extent of her husband's injuries and he didn't want to make her any more upset than she already was. 'It could have been a random killing. Someone who just wanted to kill, and your husband was in the wrong place at the wrong time.'

'Poor Max,' she said. 'Poor, poor Max.'

Wright and Reid had to wait in the reception area of Agence France Press for almost twenty minutes before a balding man in his late thirties ambled out. His jacket collar was up at the back as if he'd pulled it on in a hurry and one of his shoelaces was undone. 'Hiya. Steve Reynolds,' he said, holding out his hand. He had an American accent.

'Tommy Reid,' said Reid, shaking his hand. 'This is Nick Wright. Thanks for seeing us.'

Reynolds opened a glass door for them and they walked together down a white-walled corridor and through another set of glass doors into a large open-plan office full of shirtsleeved young men and women sitting at desks in front of VDUs.

Reynolds's office was to the left with a glass wall over-looking the main working area. 'Can I get you coffee or something?' he asked. Both detectives nodded and Reynolds asked a young blonde secretary for three coffees. Reid and Wright sat down opposite Reynolds's desk. Wright took out his notebook as Reynolds closed the door and sat down on the other side of his desk. 'So how can I help you guys?' Reynolds asked.

'We're looking for a reason why anyone would want to kill Max Eckhardt,' said Reid.

Reynolds grimaced as if he had a bad taste in his mouth. 'It's a mystery to all of us here,' he said. 'Max was the nicest guy you could imagine.'

'How long have you known him?'

'Personally, three months. That's when he moved here from our New York bureau.'

'He was a photographer?' asked Reid. The two detectives had agreed beforehand that Reid would lead the questioning and Wright would take notes. It was their usual way of operating, mainly because Reid's handwriting was so bad that he often had trouble reading back his notes.

'That's right. He's been with the company for more than fifteen years.' He reached across his desk and picked up a green file which he handed to Reid. 'This is Max's personnel file. I thought it might speed things up a little.'

Reid gave the file to Wright. 'The job he was on just before he died. The Conservative Party conference. Was that typical of the sort of work he did?'

'Good Lord, no,' said Reynolds. 'In fact, he fought like hell not to go.'

'Labour supporter, was he?'

Reynolds grinned and shook his head. 'War photographer. Max always wanted to be where the bullets were. Panama. Grenada. Kuwait. Northern Ireland. Bosnia. Never happy unless he was wearing a flak jacket.'

'That's why he requested a transfer from New York? To be closer to the hot spots?'

'Partly,' said Reynolds. 'He reckoned that Europe and the new Russia were going to be the major areas of conflict over the next decade. He tried to get a transfer to our Paris office, but there are no openings there.'

Wright looked up from the file. 'So it wasn't because of his wife?'

'His wife?'

'May Eckhardt. She's British. I thought maybe she wanted to come home.'

The blonde secretary reappeared with three plastic cups of coffee. Reynolds gestured at the file. 'There's a memo in there from Max requesting the London posting. He doesn't mention May. I don't think she had a problem travelling with him. She's a computer programmer, she can work pretty much anywhere. I don't think she especially wanted to come back to the UK.'

'You said he covered Northern Ireland. Is it possible he crossed one of the terrorist organisations?' Reid asked.

Reynolds leaned forward, his shoulders hunched over

the desk. 'Not really,' he said. 'Max was a photographer, not a reporter.'

'He could have photographed something he shouldn't have.'

Reynolds shook his head. 'Unlikely,' he said. 'He's been on soft jobs for the last month. Besides, terrorists would have just shot him or put a bomb in his car. They don't go in for torture.'

Reid nodded. 'You said he didn't want the Brighton job. Why did you send him?'

'We had a couple of guys off sick. And you can't cover wars all the time. It's not good for the soul.'

'And how was Max's soul?' asked Reid.

'That's a searching question,' said Reynolds, picking up a pen and twirling it around his thumb. 'Very philosophical.'

'For a policeman, you mean?'

'For anyone,' said Reynolds. 'Max was a driven man, you know? As if he was aiming for something, something that was always beyond his reach.'

'Or running away from somebody?'

The pen flew off Reynolds's thumb and landed on the floor. He bent down and retrieved it. 'Max was one of the most centred people I know. He wasn't a man on the run, he wasn't living in fear, he was just a bloody good photographer. He worked hard, harder than almost anyone I know, and I don't know anyone who didn't like or respect him. Most journalists, reporters and photographers are driven by something. They have to be. Long hours, low pay, no respect from the public, they have to have their own reasons for doing the job.'

'Tell me about it,' said Wright bitterly.

Reynolds grinned. 'I suppose there are a lot of similarities between our jobs,' he said. 'The search for the truth. The accumulation of facts.'

'The fiddling of expense sheets,' added Reid.

The three men laughed. 'Seriously,' said Reynolds, 'you'd be wasting your time looking for someone who wanted to kill Max.' He pointed at the file in Wright's hands. 'Look at his yearly evaluations. Every boss he's ever had has given him glowing references professionally and personally.'

'Could we look through his desk?' asked Reid.

'Sure,' said Reynolds. He stood up and took the two detectives out into the open-plan office. Several heads turned to look at them. They walked to the far end of the office where two white-shirted men bent over a light box studying a strip of negatives. Reynolds introduced the two men to Reid and Wright. The taller of the two was Martin Staines, the bureau's picture editor, the other man was his assistant, Sam Greene.

'They're investigating Max's murder,' Reynolds explained.

Staines nodded at the desk nearest the window. 'We weren't sure what to do with his stuff.'

'No one's touched it?' asked Reid, sitting down at the desk and pulling open the drawers.

'Nobody wanted to,' said Staines.

'Was it bad?' asked Reynolds. 'The papers didn't give too many details.'

'Yeah,' said Wright. 'It was bad.'

'You might want to look at his locker,' said Greene. He nodded at a line of light blue metal lockers. 'Max's is third from the left.'

Wright went over to the lockers. There was a combination padlock on Max's locker. 'Six two five,' said Greene. Wright raised an eyebrow. 'He left his address book in it one night and phoned me to get a number he wanted,' explained Greene.

Wright took the lock off and opened the locker door. Inside was a yellow waterproof jacket hanging from a hook and a pair of green Wellington boots. There was an extendable metal pole at the back of the locker. Wright took it out and examined it.

'It's for supporting a long lens,' said Staines. 'Max had some pretty heavy equipment.'

Wright replaced the pole. He checked through the pockets of the waterproof jacket but there was nothing there. 'What about the rest of his equipment?' asked Wright. 'His cameras and stuff?'

Staines and Greene exchanged looks. Staines shrugged. 'Photographers are responsible for their own gear,' he said. 'He took everything he needed with him to Brighton.'

Reid walked over to join Wright. 'Is that his wife?' he asked Wright, tapping a photograph that had been taped to the inside of the locker door.

Wright hadn't noticed the black and white photograph. It was May Eckhardt, smiling nervously at the camera as if she'd been caught unawares, one hand up to her face, the fingertips close to her lips. It was a good photograph; it had captured the softness of her skin, and the fact that it was in black and white emphasised the blackness of her hair against her pale skin. 'Yes. That's her.'

'I didn't realise she was Asian.'

'She's not,' said Wright quickly. 'She's Oriental.'

'What?'

'It doesn't matter.' Wright closed the locker door and

turned to look at Reynolds. 'Did you speak to Eckhardt after he'd finished in Brighton?'

'I spoke to him,' said Staines. 'He called to say he was leaving Brighton on the afternoon train.'

'Didn't he drive?' asked Reid.

'He did as a rule but he went down with one of our reporters, Pete Thewlis. They used Pete's car and were planning to come back together, but Pete was sent on to another job. Max was a bit pissed off, but it's not as if he was in the Outer Hebrides. We told him we'd pay for him to come back first class on the train.'

'And that was the last you heard of him?' asked Reid.

'That's right,' said Staines. 'That was on the Monday, and he was due in the office that afternoon. When he didn't show we assumed he'd missed the train, either by accident or design.'

'I don't follow you,' said Reid.

'Like I said, he was a bit annoyed at having to take the train. We thought maybe he'd gone AWOL as a sort of silent protest. When he didn't turn up for work on Tuesday, we called his home. That's when we realised he'd gone missing.

'To be honest, we weren't that worried,' said Greene. 'It wasn't unusual for Max to go chasing after his own stories. He always checked in eventually.'

'What about this Pete Thewlis, can I talk to him?'

'He's in Islington on that explosives seizure,' said Reynolds. 'He wont be back until late. I can give you his mobile number, though.'

'Would Thewlis have taken Eckhardt's camera equipment with him?' asked Reid.

'Definitely not,' said Staines. 'Photographers are very

possessive about their gear. They don't even like sharing lenses and stuff. Besides, Thewlis didn't know how long he'd be away.'

'So he'd have taken it with him on the train?' asked Wright.

'Sure,' agreed Staines.

'How much gear would he have had?' asked Wright.

Greene bent down and picked up a large canvas holdall. It was heavy and he used both hands to lift it on to the desk next to the light box. 'This is about par for the course,' he said. 'Three or four camera bodies, half a dozen lenses, a tripod, film. Max had a bag like this, and two leather cases containing his really long lenses.'

Wright put his notebook away and looked at Reid. His partner nodded. 'Okay, well, thanks for your time,' said Reid. He handed BTP business cards to the three men. 'If you should think of anything else, give me or Nick a call.'

Outside the AFP offices, Reid said, 'Can you call that guy Pete Thewlis? Check when he last saw Eckhardt?'

'Sure,' said Wright. 'What about checking the station to see if Eckhardt caught the train from Brighton? We've got to find out how he ended up at Battersea.'

'Yeah, okay. We'll go down this afternoon. We should do a sweep of the train, too. We'll need a few more bodies. Half a dozen, maybe. Can you clear it with Ronnie? We'll do the train that he was supposed to catch, and the ones either side. Oh yeah, and make sure someone goes to Edbury Bridge and views the Victoria surveillance tapes. They're supposed to hold them for twenty-eight days before wiping them, but put in a call today just to make sure.'

'I'll arrange it.'

Reid looked up and down the street.

'I hope you're not looking for a pub, Tommy,' said Wright.

'Last thing on my mind,' said Reid.

'They're not open yet.'

'I know a place. Just around the corner. Come on, hair of the dog.'

Wright shook his head emphatically. 'I'll see you back at the office.'

'Ah, come on, Nick,' Reid whined. 'You've got the car, how am I going to get back?'

'Well, duh, Tommy. What's wrong with the Tube?'

'You know I hate public transport,' scowled Reid, but Wright was already walking away.

Wright collected his Fiesta from the underground car park and headed back to Tavistock Place.

Wright got caught in heavy traffic and it took him the best part of an hour to get back to the office. Superintendent Newton was in the incident room, studying a whiteboard on which the various assignments had been written up. Ronnie Dundas was hovering at the superintendent's shoulder and he winked at Wright.

'Morning, Nick,' said Newton.

'Morning, sir.'

'Tommy not with you?'

'We were at Eckhardt's office. Tommy's checking his personal effects.'

Newton looked at Wright with slightly narrowed eyes, his

lips pressed so tight together that they had practically disappeared. Wright instinctively knew that the superintendent didn't believe him. Dundas grinned and made a cut-throat motion with his hand.

Wright ignored the chief inspector's antics and took out his notebook. 'We know what train he was supposed to be on. We'll do a sweep of the stations, and we'll put men on the trains interviewing passengers. I'll get the video surveillance tapes from Victoria and have them checked. If he got on the train at Brighton it could be he was forced off at Battersea.'

'The train doesn't stop there, does it?'

'No, but it goes close by and sometimes the trains are held up if Victoria's busy.'

Newton nodded his agreement. 'Any sign of a motive?' he asked.

'I'm afraid not, sir.'

Newton turned to Dundas. 'Any progress on the knife?'

'It's a common kitchen knife,' said Dundas. 'We've identified fifteen different suppliers in London alone, including three chain stores. The Met boys'll continue looking, but I don't see it providing us with a lead.'

'When Eckhardt went missing he had a bagful of camera equipment with him,' said Wright. 'I'm going to arrange a sweep of secondhand shops to see if I can turn it up.' For the first time Wright realised that the superintendent was holding a sheet of paper. It was a fax.

'Well, maybe the cavalry will help,' said Newton dryly.

'Cavalry?'

Newton held out the fax. 'An FBI agent, on secondment from FBI headquarters in Washington.'

Wright took the fax and scanned it quickly. It was a brief

memo from an assistant director of the Federal Bureau of Investigation, notifying the BTP that a Special Agent James Bamber was being sent to assist in the investigation and to act as liaison with the FBI.

'Is this normal?' asked Wright. 'Do the FBI usually send people over on murder enquiries?'

'Eckhardt was an American citizen,' said Newton.

'Yes, but even so. Do we send cops over to investigate deaths overseas?'

Newton took back the fax. 'It's not unknown,' he said. 'To be honest, we should just be grateful for the additional manpower.' He gestured with his thumb at the list of assignments. 'We can't keep this many detectives assigned to the case indefinitely.' The superintendent went back to his office.

'You missed my briefing this morning,' said Dundas.

'Yeah, sorry. We went straight to AFP to talk to Eckhardt's boss.'

'Just so you know, the Met team is handling the house-to-house, the knife, and they'll look into Eckhardt's background. We'll concentrate on the forensics, the playing card, and anything else that turns up in the tunnel. We'll be sharing information on a daily basis at morning prayers, and we'll all have access to the HOLMES database. I've recommended that the two teams eat together in the canteen to talk informally but I won't be holding my breath. If you think there's anything that they should know about urgently, tell me and I'll brief my opposite number, Chief Inspector Colin Duggan, aka the Welsh Wizard. He's a twenty-year-man with a lot of murder enquiry experience and if your paths cross I'd recommend treating him with kid gloves. Okay?'

'Okay,' said Wright unenthusiastically.

'I gather there's a bit of friction between you and Gerry Hunter,' said Dundas.

'A bit.'

'Well, I know you're man enough not to let it interfere with the job,' said Dundas. 'There really shouldn't be any reason for the two of you to talk, you'll be following separate lines of enquiry.'

'It won't be a problem,' said Wright.

'Glad to hear it,' said Dundas. He took another swig from his milk carton and went over to one of the HOLMES terminals.

Two BTP DCs were sitting at neighbouring tables, their faces close up against VDUs. They were both in their late twenties, but other than their jobs, that was all they had in common. Dave Hubbard was tall and bulky and played rugby in his spare time. Julian Lloyd was anorexically thin and was one of the best amateur squash players in the South of England. They'd been assigned to checking on sexual offenders with a record of attacking men. It had been Reid's idea, but hadn't provided any tangible leads so far.

'Hey, guys, can one of you call Victoria, see if you can get the surveillance tapes for last Monday,' Wright shouted. 'Eckhardt was supposed to catch an afternoon train from Brighton. We might get lucky.'

Lloyd waved, his eyes still on his screen. 'I'll do it.'

There were more than a dozen surveillance cameras around Victoria, and with a four-hour window, that would mean around fifty hours of tape to view. Tapes were rarely easy viewing, either, especially when you were trying to identify one face among thousands. With his holdall and two leather cases, hopefully Eckhardt would be relatively easy to spot, but even with half a dozen officers it would still take the best part of a day to go through the tapes. And all that would prove was whether or not Eckhardt had arrived at Victoria.

'Get back here by noon,' said Wright. 'We're going down to Brighton to do a sweep through the station and then we'll be coming back on the train. Dave, we'll need you. Tommy's coming, and we'll need another four bodies. See who you can round up.'

'Will do,' said Hubbard.

Wright sat down and flicked through his notebook. He found the number of Pete Thewlis's mobile and dialled it. Thewlis answered, his voice a Liverpudlian drawl. Wright told the journalist who he was and asked him when he'd last seen Max Eckhardt. Thewlis said they'd had breakfast together in their Brighton hotel and that Thewlis had left first, driving to York. Wright made a note of the hotel and thanked the journalist for his help.

He was about to call the hotel to find out exactly when Eckhardt had checked out when Reid walked into the office and flopped down into his chair. He pulled open his top drawer, took out a pack of mints and popped two into his mouth. 'So, what's new?' he asked.

'The Yanks are coming,' said Wright, putting down his phone.

'What?'

'The FBI are sending an agent over. To help. I guess they think we Brits aren't up to solving the case.'

Reid put his mints back into the drawer. 'Yeah, well, they can join the queue, can't they?'

'Line,' said Wright. 'Americans call it a line.'

'Yeah? Well, we're really going to have problems if I tell

127

him I want to smoke a fag, right?' He opened his bottom drawer and looked into it. 'Fancy a coffee?' he asked.

The occupant of seat 17A was practically the perfect passenger. If Gwen could have her way, only men like him would be allowed to fly. He'd smiled politely when he'd boarded, had no carry-on luggage with him, and hadn't asked for a thing to eat or drink. There had been no salacious looks, no clumsy attempts to chat her up, just a small shake of the head when she'd offered him his dinner tray. Gwen wondered what he did for a living. His clothes gave nothing away: a nondescript grey suit, white shirt and a neatly knotted tie. He looked like the typical business-class passenger. What wasn't typical was his lack of a briefcase or laptop computer. Most businessmen had come to regard the cabin as an extension of their office, and those who didn't work caught up on their sleep. Passenger 17A didn't work or sleep, nor did he bother to use his inseat entertainment. He kept his seat up and simply stared ahead of him, his hands together in his lap, almost as if he was meditating. He wasn't in a trance, though, because whenever Gwen spoke to him he answered immediately.

'What do you think about the quiet one, Tony?'

Tony Kelner was working business class with her, and was a good judge of passengers. He was gay and had the inbuilt radar which allowed him to spot other gays without a word being spoken. He pouted as he looked over her shoulder. 'Definitely my type, darling,' he said. 'But he's definitely hetero. Cruel lips.' He mimed a shiver. 'Oooh, I think I'd better go and lie down.'

'Not until you've helped get the breakfasts ready,' laughed Gwen. 'What's his story?' It was a game she and Tony often played, making up fictitious backgrounds for their passengers.

Tony folded his arms and put his head on one side. He pressed a finger against his lips as he studied the passenger. 'He works out,' he said. 'Look at those thighs. What is he, twenty-seven, twenty-eight?'

'His hair is starting to go grey,' said Gwen.

'Prematurely, darling,' said Tony. 'Nothing a little Grecian Two Thousand wouldn't hide.'

'Is that what you use?'

'Bitch!' hissed Tony playfully. He ran a hand through his own unnaturally blond and coiffured hair. 'A little peroxide, that's all I allow near my locks.' He put his forefinger to the side of his face as he glanced at the profile of the passenger. 'He's a professional footballer,' he said eventually. 'Played for a first division club, but was plagued by injury—'

'Didn't have a limp,' interrupted Gwen.

'Is this my story or yours?' asked Tony. 'Knee problems, or Achilles tendon. Nothing serious, but enough to keep him from giving his best, so he decided to quit playing before he was over the hill. He's just joined a second division club, as assistant manager.'

'Oh, did I mention that he was American?' said Gwen.

'They play soccer in the States,' said Tony. 'All right, Miss Know-it-all, what do you think?'

'Mafia hitman,' she said. 'Look at his eyes. Cold, cold eyes. That man could pull the trigger and not care. The Mafia send him all over the world to get rid of people who are causing them problems. He gets well paid for what he does, but he doesn't do it for the money.'

Tony raised his eyebrows. 'Interesting,' he said. 'I wonder if I could persuade him to indulge in a little S and M.'

Gwen giggled and Tony gave her a playful push. The man in 17A turned his head slowly and looked at them across the cabin. His eyelids were half closed and his face was devoid of any emotion, but Gwen and Tony both stopped laughing immediately. Tony shivered, and this time Gwen knew he wasn't faking it. He turned away and began to busy himself with one of the trollies. The passenger held Gwen's look for several seconds, but to the stewardess it felt like an eternity. She was transfixed by his pale hazel eyes, unable to tear herself away. The man smiled, but his lips didn't part. It was a humourless smile and it sent a chill down Gwen's spine. Eventually he looked away. Only then did she realise that she'd been holding her breath all the time he'd been staring at her, and she exhaled like a deflating balloon.

Tommy Reid put down a cup of coffee in front of Nick Wright. 'Morning prayers in five minutes,' he said.

Wright sipped his coffee. 'Yeah, I know,' he said. The two detectives went downstairs to the incident room. Most of the BTP detectives were already there, sitting on tables or standing around, drinking coffee or chewing on bacon sandwiches brought from the canteen. Only half of the Met contingent had turned up, but Hunter and Edmunds were there, huddled over a HOLMES terminal. Several of the detectives fidgeted with pens or pencils – Newton was a vehement anti-smoker and had banned smoking in the room. The detectives would have to wait until after the briefing before lighting up.

The superintendent walked in, a clipboard under one arm, followed by Ronnie Dundas and the Met's senior officer on the investigation team, Chief Inspector Colin Duggan, a balding Welshman in a dark blue suit. The assembled detectives stopped talking and waited while Newton studied his notes. 'Day eight, gentlemen. One week and a day. I have so far approved four hundred and eighty hours of overtime and I appear to have precious little to show for it. I know you're all keen to have that central heating installed or upgrade your car or pay for that foreign holiday next year, but the powers that be are going to want to see some sort of return on their investment. And frankly, so am I.' His upper lip barely moved throughout his speech, though his eyes fixed on each of the detectives in turn. Most of them averted their eyes under his stony gaze; they were all well aware of how slowly the investigation was proceeding.

'So, let's recap. We know that Max Eckhardt left his hotel intending to walk to the station, but none of the station staff remembers seeing him. Nick, have we spoken to every member of staff?'

'Everyone who was working on the Monday. And if he did buy a ticket, he didn't use a credit card.'

'We've interviewed passengers on the train that he should have caught,' said Reid. 'And the trains either side. We'll do another sweep next Monday, just in case there are passengers who only travel then. It's a long shot, but it's worth a try.'

'Agreed,' said Newton. 'Julian, any joy on the surveillance tapes?'

'Afraid not,' said Lloyd. 'We've been through all of them, but there's no man with a holdall and two leather cases. We're trying to decide whether we go through them again to see if he's lost the gear, but that's going to take days. We'd have to look at the face of every white male, and the quality's not that good.'

'I think we should,' said Wright. 'It's the only way we have of finding out if he arrived back in London.'

The detectives looked at Newton, waiting for him to reach his decision. His lips tightened to the point where they almost disappeared, then he relaxed. 'Okay. But organise it so it's done between other enquiries. No overtime. What about forensics?'

'Nothing,' said Reid. 'At least nothing that we can definitely say belonged to the killer. If we had a suspect, it's possible we might be able to link him to the crime scene.' He grinned. 'But then if we had a suspect, we could just beat a confession out of him anyway.' He held up his hands. 'Joke.'

The superintendent glared icily at Reid. 'As always, we're grateful for you trying to lighten the moment, Tommy. But I'd rather you left the song and dance act until we'd at least got some of the way towards solving this case.' Newton looked around the room as if daring any of the others to crack a joke. 'Gerry, anything new on the knife?'

'Nothing,' said Hunter. 'When we eventually get a suspect, maybe we'll be able to link them to the knife, but it's not going to point the way. I'm more concerned at the moment about finding Eckhardt's camera equipment. I've distributed serial numbers and descriptions. That equipment's worth over two thousand pounds, it must be somewhere.'

Newton nodded. 'Good,' he said. 'I want that equipment found, and found soon.' He looked around the assembled detectives before tapping his clipboard. 'Right, two more things. First, we're going to hold another press conference tomorrow. We'll announce that we've identified the victim, then release his picture and appeal for witnesses again. I'm also going to release details of the missing camera equipment. This time I'll conduct the press conference, along with a press officer. That's tomorrow at three. Second, Max Eckhardt's funeral is this afternoon. Tommy and Nick, I want you two to attend.'

'It's a bit sudden, isn't it, sir?' asked Wright.

'Not really. It's been more than a week, and the cause of death isn't going to be disputed,' said the superintendent. 'The pathologist says they don't need anything else, so they contacted the widow. She called in a firm of undertakers and they had a slot today. I gather there weren't any other relatives to inform, and it suits us to have the funeral before the press conference so that we don't have a pack of photographers pestering the mourners.' He looked around the room. 'Any other thoughts?'

None of the detectives spoke. The first few morning briefings had produced a stream of ideas and theories, but the initial flush of enthusiasm had faded and most of the detectives were now resigned to the fact that the case, if it was ever going to be solved, would be solved by routine investigation rather than a flash of deductive reasoning. That, or a lucky break.

The superintendent didn't appear to be surprised or disappointed by the lack of response. 'Okay, let's get on with it,' he said, heading for the door. 'Oh, by the way. For those that don't know already, an FBI agent has been seconded to the investigation. James Bamber's his name. He has no jurisdictional powers in this country. That means he has no powers of arrest, no right to acquire a warrant or to question suspects. That said, he's to be offered every assistance.'

The superintendent left the room, and half a dozen of the detectives immediately went upstairs to light up. Hunter and Edmunds took their coats off the rack by the door and headed out.

'Shit,' said Reid.

'What?' said Wright.

'I'm not wearing my black suit.' He grinned, expecting to get a smile out of Wright, but Wright wasn't amused.

'Newton's right, you know. Sometimes you're not funny.'

There was a single red rose on the polished pine coffin, and it vibrated as the wooden casket slid along the metal rollers and through two green velvet curtains. Recorded organ music oozed out of black plastic speakers mounted on shelves close to the ceiling. The vicar closed his leather-bound Bible as if impatient to get on with his next function, be it a wedding, a christening or a funeral. Wright wondered if the young vicar, who was still in his twenties, showed a similar lack of enthusiasm for weddings as he'd shown for the funeral service. It had taken a little more than ten minutes and he'd hardly looked up from the Bible, as if embarrassed by the handful of mourners who'd gathered to say farewell to Max Eckhardt. There were eight in all, including Reid and Wright, who stood together in the pew furthest from the vicar and his lectern, their hands clasped across their groins like footballers in a defensive wall.

May Eckhardt stood alone in the front pew, wearing black leather gloves and a lightweight black coat that reached almost to her ankles. Her hair was loose and she kept her head down throughout the service so that it fell across her face, shielding her features like a curtain. The rest of the mourners were Eckhardt's co-workers: Steve Reynolds, Martin Staines and Sam Greene were there, along with two young women who looked like secretaries.

'Not much of a turnout,' whispered Reid.

'She said he didn't have many relatives,' said Wright.

'None by the look of it. No friends of the family, either. Just colleagues.' The curtain slid over the rear of the coffin and the organ music stopped abruptly. The vicar looked at his watch.

Wright wondered how many mourners there would be at his funeral if he were to die tomorrow. His mother was in a nursing home in the West Country and he only visited her two or three times a year. He had a brother in Australia, but they hadn't spoken for more than five years. He looked across at Reid. His partner would be there, Wright was certain of that, probably wearing the same brown raincoat and carrying the same tweed hat. And Reid would probably twist a few arms to get some of his colleagues to attend. Superintendent Newton would be there, but out of duty rather than friendship. Would Janie attend? Probably, with Sean at her side. Wright could picture her in black, a comforting hand on their son's shoulder, telling him not to worry because Sean had another daddy who loved him just as much as his real daddy did. Wright shivered.

May Eckhardt was walking down the centre aisle, the vicar at her side. The top of her head barely reached the vicar's shoulder and he had to stoop to talk to her as they walked. She saw Wright and gave him the smallest of smiles. For a brief moment their eyes locked and Wright felt something tug at his stomach. Wright smiled back at her but she looked down as if the contact had frightened her.

The mourners filed out of their pews and followed May and the vicar out of the church. The vicar stood at the doorway with May and together they thanked each person for attending. Wright and Reid were the last to leave. Wright nodded at the vicar, but had no interest in talking to him. The service had been perfunctory and the man appeared to have been operating on auto-pilot throughout. Wright felt that May had deserved better.

'Thanks for coming, Sergeant Wright,' said May, and she held out a slim gloved hand.

He shook it. Her hand felt like a child's in his. 'How are you?' he asked.

She withdrew her hand. 'I don't know,' she said. 'How are people usually? After . . .' She faltered and put her hand to her head.

'I'm sorry,' said Wright quickly. 'Stupid question, really.' The news agency staff stood together on the pavement as if unsure what to do next. 'Is there a reception?' Wright asked.

May shook her head. 'No, I just wanted a service. In fact, I didn't really want that. Max wasn't one for religion. He always said that the Apaches had the best idea: lay the body on a rock and let the birds eat it.' She forced a tight smile. 'I didn't think Westminster Council would look too kindly on that. Besides, Steve Reynolds called me and said some of the people in the office wanted to say goodbye . . .' Her voice faltered again. She brushed away a tear.

Wright wanted to step forward and comfort her. She tensed as if she'd read his thoughts. 'What are your plans now?' he asked.

'I'm going to go back home. Then I . . . I don't know. I've been taking it one day at a time. His clothes are still on the chair in the bedroom . . .' She mumbled incoherently, then shook her head as if clearing her thoughts. 'I'll be fine, Sergeant Wright.'

'Nick. Call me Nick.'

She looked at him for several seconds until he began to feel that he was lost in her soft brown eyes, as if she was pulling his soul towards hers. He blinked and the spell was broken.

'Nick,' she said. 'Thank you for coming.' She thanked the vicar and then walked away.

The church was only half a mile from her flat so Wright assumed that she was going to walk, but then he noticed her VW Golf parked at the roadside. He watched as she unlocked the door and climbed in. She put on her seatbelt and started the engine. At the last moment she turned and looked at him. She flashed him a quick smile and gave him a half wave, then drove away.

Reid finished talking to the vicar and came up behind Wright. 'Okay?' he asked.

'Yeah. I guess.'

Wright turned and looked up at the outside of the church.

It was a modern building, all brick, the windows shielded from vandals by wire mesh screens. It looked more like a fortress than a place of worship, bordered by roads on three sides. A poster on a noticeboard by the door advertised the services of the Samaritans and next to it was a handwritten notice asking for donations of clothing to send to a church project in Africa. The young vicar disappeared inside and closed the door.

'He didn't even know her,' said Wright. 'There was nothing personal in the service.'

'That's the way it goes these days. People don't go to church, but they want weddings and funerals. I asked the vicar and he said he'd never seen the Eckhardts, didn't even know where they lived other than that they were local.'

'What happens to the coffin?' asked Wright. There was no graveyard attached to the church.

'It gets taken to the crematorium,' said Reid. 'Then she takes delivery of the ashes.'

'I wonder what she'll do with them?'

'Bury them maybe. There's a place at the crematorium. Or maybe he wanted them scattered somewhere.'

'Yeah? What would you want doing with your ashes?'

Reid rubbed his hands together. 'I'm going to have them thrown into my ex-wife's face,' he said. 'By a nineteen-year-old blonde with big tits.'

'You old romantic, you,' laughed Wright. They watched the AFP staff hail two taxis and climb into them. 'Not much to show for a life, is it?' asked Wright. 'Half a dozen mourners, a handful of ashes, then nothing.' He shivered, though it wasn't a cold day.

They walked together to Reid's Honda Civic. 'Can you do me a favour?' asked Wright.

'Depends on what you want,' said Reid, cautiously.

'I want to go and look at the tunnel,' said Wright.

Reid looked puzzled. 'What's the story?'

'No story. I just want to get a feel for what happened.' It was clear from Reid's face that he didn't understand. 'I thought it might help me get inside the killer's head.'

Reid looked even more confused but didn't say anything.

Wright felt that he had to justify his request, but words failed him. 'I can't explain it,' he said. 'I just feel that I have to go and have a look.'

Reid raised his eyebrows. 'Okay, if that's what you want, we'll go.'

'Alone,' said Wright. 'I want to go alone. Can I borrow the car?'

Reid rubbed the back of his neck. For a moment it looked as if he was about to argue, but then he handed the car keys to Wright. 'I'll get a cab,' he said.

'Thanks, Tommy. I'll see you in the office in a couple of hours.'

'Just be careful,' said Reid. 'With the car.' He walked away, but after a few steps he hesitated, then turned and shouted to Wright that there was a flashlight in the boot.

Wright got into the car and drove south to Battersea. He pulled up at the side of the road that ran parallel to the disused rail line. He retrieved the flashlight from the boot, and stood for a while staring down the overgrown embankment. A cold wind blew from his left, tugging at his hair and whispering through the grass and nettles that hadn't been trampled down by the investigation team. The sky above was pale blue and clear, but there was a chill in the air. Wright shivered inside his raincoat. He went down the embankment, his hands out at his sides for balance, skidding the last few steps and coming to a halt next to the rusting rails.

The cutting sheltered Wright from the wind, and there was a stillness around him as if time had stopped. Wright headed towards the mouth of the tunnel. As it came into view, he saw that a wooden framework had been constructed across the opening. Yellow tape with the words 'Crime Scene – Do Not Enter' had been threaded through the wire and the message was repeated on a large metal sign. Wright cursed himself for not realising that the tunnel would have been sealed off. He walked up to the wire and peered through it into the blackness of the tunnel. He heard a noise, a scuffling sound, and turned his head to the side, trying to focus on whatever it was, but the noise wasn't repeated. He remembered the rats and what they'd done to the body of Max Eckhardt.

Wright stood back and examined the barrier. It had been well put together and bolted into the stone of the bridge. He walked across the mouth of the tunnel, stepping over the tracks and running his left hand over the mesh so that it rattled and shook. He realised a doorway had been constructed in the barrier, a wooden frame with a double thickness of mesh, three hinges on one side, a bolt with a padlock through it on the other. Wright stared at the padlock. It was hanging open. He reached for it and unhooked it from the bolt. It didn't appear to have been forced. He put it in his coat pocket, then slid open the bolt. The door creaked on its hinges and Wright opened it just enough so that he could slide through the gap. His coat snagged on a piece of wire and he felt it rip. He reached behind his back and pulled himself free, then slipped inside.

The darkness was almost an impenetrable wall, a finite boundary that he hesitated to cross. He switched on the flashlight and a yellow oval of light appeared on the ground, illuminating one of the rails. He held the flashlight out in front of him but the darkness seemed to swallow up the beam. Wright felt his heart pound and he realised he was breathing faster than normal. He took slow deep breaths and tried to quell the feeling of unease that was growing stronger by the second. He closed his eyes. His fingers tensed around the body of the flashlight until it was the only thing he could feel.

He flashed back in his mind to another time when he'd faced darkness, to a time when he'd been eleven years old. It wasn't the mouth of a tunnel he faced then, it was an open door, a door that led down to the basement. The eleven-year-old Nick Wright took a step forward, then another, until he was standing on the threshold. The darkness was absolute as if the basement had been filled with tar, a darkness so thick and black that the eleven-year-old Nick was sure he would drown in it. More than twenty years later, the adult Nick struggled to remember where the light switch was, or even if there was one, but he could vividly recall the terror he felt as he dipped his right foot into the darkness and felt for the first step. He was alone in the house, of that he was certain. Alone except for what lurked in the basement, waiting for him. He put his weight on his right foot and probed with his left, both hands gripping the wooden rails as if they were a lifeline to the light behind him. He took a second step, and a third, and then the blackness swallowed him up.

Wright opened his eyes. His face was drenched in sweat and he rubbed his forehead with his sleeve. He pointed the flashlight at the floor and stepped in-between the rails. There was a damp, slightly bitter, smell to the air, a mix of stale urine and rotting vegetation, and Wright tried to block out the stench by breathing through his mouth. He stood with his feet together on an ancient wooden sleeper, like a high-diver preparing to jump. He took a step forward, concentrating on the rust-covered rails highlighted by the yellow beam of the flashlight. The light flickered. The batteries were old, Wright realised. He shook the flashlight and the beam grew stronger for a few seconds but then faded back to its original yellow glow.

Wright began walking, stepping from sleeper to sleeper. He wondered how long the batteries would last, and how he would react if the torch died while he was in the bowels of the tunnel. And he wondered why he was deliberately testing himself, pushing himself into a situation that was almost more than he could bear. It wasn't just that he hated tunnels. He hated all dark places. Dark places and confined spaces. He was thirty-two years old and he was scared of the dark, but today was the day that he was going to prove to himself that his fears were groundless.

Wright swung the beam from side to side. The walls of the tunnel were stained black, streaked with green moss and dotted with silvery cobwebs that glistened with moisture. Wright shivered. Last time he'd been in the tunnel he hadn't noticed how cold it was.

Suddenly he stopped. He'd heard something ahead of him. It wasn't the same sort of sound he'd heard outside the tunnel; this was a gravelly crunch, the sort of noise a foot might make if it slipped off a sleeper. A human foot. He crouched down and listened. All he could hear was the sound of his own breathing. He held his breath. There was nothing. He stared ahead but couldn't see anything outside the beam of his flashlight. He put his hand over the end of the flashlight so that the light glowed redly through the flesh. The darkness seemed to wrap itself tighter around Wright and he took his hand away. He crouched lower, instinctively trying to make himself a smaller target even though he didn't know what he was protecting himself from.

He listened, but the sound wasn't repeated. Something brushed against his cheek and he spun around, sweeping the flashlight beam around his head like a claymore, but he was alone. A large moth fluttered up to the roof of the tunnel where it dislodged flecks of soot that fell around him like black snow. Wright's panic gradually subsided and he stood up again. He looked over his shoulder. He'd only walked fifty feet or so into the tunnel. Through the opening he could see the lush green embankment and a strip of sky. Fifty feet. He could run that far in seconds, yet it felt a lifetime away. Part of him wanted to run back into the open, to get the hell out of the tunnel, but he knew that he had to fight his phobia; he had to break its hold on him before it gripped him even tighter.

Wright turned back. Someone was standing in front of him. Wright yelped in fright and dropped the flashlight. It crashed on to the rail and the light went out. Wright put his hands up to protect himself.

'Whoa, take it easy,' said the man. He had an American accent.

Wright tried to regain his composure. 'Who are you?' he asked, attempting to sound authoritative but all too well aware just how much his voice was shaking. The man was an inch or so shorter than Wright but his shoulders were wider and he stood confidently between the rails, his hands swinging freely at his sides. 'Who are you?' repeated Wright, with slightly more confidence this time.

'I was here first,' said the man. 'Maybe I should be asking you who you are.'

Wright wanted to pick up his flashlight but he was too close to the man to risk bending down. 'You're trespassing on Railtrack property,' he said. He could only make out the man's silhouette. He looked down at his hands, trying to see if he was carrying a weapon. There was something in his right hand, but Wright couldn't make out what it was.

'I might say the same about you,' said the man.

'I'm a policeman,' said Wright.

Bright white light suddenly blinded Wright and he turned his head. The light went off. Wright blinked, trying to recover his night vision. He took a step back as he realised how defenceless he was.

'You don't look like a policeman,' said the man. He sounded amused, and although Wright couldn't make out his features, he knew he was grinning.

'Look, I'm a policeman and you're trespassing. I want you out of here. Now.' He shouted the last word and it echoed down the tunnel.

The man stood where he was. When he spoke, his voice was a hushed whisper. 'Suppose I said no. What would you do then? Do you think you could make me?' He chuckled. 'I don't think so.'

Wright took another step backwards, then swiftly bent down and retrieved the flashlight. He flicked the on-off switch but it had no effect. The bulb must have broken. He tapped the flashlight against the palm of his left hand. It wasn't much of a weapon but it was all he had.

'Bet you wish they let you carry guns, huh?' said the

man. 'Never understood that. Ninety-nine per cent of people will do as they're told if you ask them the right way, but what do you do when someone just says no? You have to use necessary force, right? But how do you decide what's necessary? And what if the guy you're up against isn't intimidated by force?'

Realisation dawned and Wright sighed with relief. 'You're the FBI agent?'

'Jim Bamber at your service,' said the man.

'Why the hell didn't you say so?' asked Wright angrily.

'Hey, you weren't exactly quick to identify yourself,' said Bamber. 'Anyone can say they're a cop.'

'Yeah? Well, anyone can say they're an FBI agent.'

Bamber took his wallet out of his jacket pocket and switched on his flashlight. Wright squinted at the credentials, FBI in large blue letters and a small photograph of an unsmiling man in his late twenties with a strong jaw and a prominent dimple. 'Of course, you probably wouldn't be able to tell if it's real or not,' said Bamber. 'Same as if you showed me yours. How would I know, right?' The flashlight went off.

'Do you think you could leave that on?' asked Wright.

'Sure,' said Bamber. He did as Wright asked, keeping the beam low, illuminating the rails.

'I'm Nick Wright,' said Wright, realising that he still hadn't identified himself. 'Our superintendent warned us you'd be coming.'

'Warned?'

'Maybe warned's the wrong word. He said the FBI was sending someone over to work on the case.'

'And here I am,' said Bamber. He held out his hand, shining the beam of his flashlight on to it, and

Wright shook it. 'How come you're here, Nick?' asked Bamber.

'I just wanted another look at the crime scene,' said Wright. 'I had some crazy idea about getting a feel for the killer.'

'Not such a crazy idea,' said Bamber. 'That's what I was doing. The superintendent let me view the video and the stills, but that can't tell you everything. The smell, the sounds, the atmosphere, it's all part of it. You can feel what the victim felt, right up to the moment he was killed.' He looked around the tunnel. 'Not a good place to die, huh?'

'Is there a good place?' asked Wright.

'A five-star hotel room, in a king-size bed with busty blonde twins and a bottle of champagne,' suggested Bamber. He started walking deeper into the tunnel and Wright hurried after him. Bamber ran the flashlight beam along the bottom of the tunnel wall. A large brown rat scuttled along the floor, trying to escape from the light. 'They must have made a mess of the body,' said Bamber.

'Yeah. It was down here for a couple of days before it was found. Most of the lower parts of the legs had been eaten away.'

'According to the autopsy report, the body was already well mutilated.'

'Post mortem,' said Wright. 'We call them post mortems here.'

Bamber played the beam along the wall, back and forth. He picked out the rusty brown smears where the body had been and headed towards them. 'Must have taken some time,' Bamber continued. 'Do you reckon it was because they wanted information from him?'

'We're not sure,' said Wright. 'You said "they", do you reckon there was more than one?'

'How else would they get him in here?' said Bamber. He nodded at the entrance to the tunnel, a squashed oval of light in the distance.

'He could have been carried in, unconscious.'

'Maybe,' said Bamber. He stepped closer to the wall and played the beam down the bloodstains. There were scrape marks where the forensic people had taken away samples. 'It was all the same blood group?' asked Bamber.

Wright nodded. 'Have you ever come across anything like it in the States?'

'Not personally,' said the FBI agent, 'but I've only worked on a dozen or so homicides. I'm running a check through our Behavioral Science Services Unit. They'll spot any patterns that match similar deaths. Have you considered a Satanic connection? Ritual sacrifice?'

'We spoke to a few experts, and they said that Satanic symbols would have been used, candles and the like. Eckhardt was also the wrong sort of victim. Sacrifice would normally involve children or young women.'

'Drugs?'

'He certainly wasn't a user, and he didn't appear to be the sort who'd have drug connections.'

'He was a news agency photographer, right? Could he have been photographing the wrong people?'

'Nothing controversial,' said Wright. 'At least, not in the UK.'

'We're looking at his New York background, but I've already got a negative from the DEA and he doesn't have a criminal record, other than a few speeding tickets. He's just a regular citizen.'

'That's what we figured,' said Wright. 'An innocent bystander. Wrong place, wrong time.'

Bamber straightened up. 'I want to switch the flashlight off. Are you okay with that?'

Wright felt his chest tighten and his breath caught in his throat. He forced himself to relax. 'Sure,' he said.

The light winked off. Wright immediately felt as if he was falling. He gasped and put out his hands, but there was nothing to hold on to. He twisted around and fixed his eyes on the entrance to the tunnel, focusing all his attention on the patch of light, but that only made his disorientation worse. Time seemed to crawl by, and with each passing second the darkness seemed to become more and more stifling, a creeping cloud that threatened to suffocate the life out of him. The flashlight came back on and Bamber walked over to stand next to Wright again.

'Gives you a feel for what it must have been like,' said the FBI agent. He looked across at Wright. 'Are you scared of the dark, Nick?'

'Why do you ask?' asked Wright, defensively.

'Because it's as cold as a witch's tit in here, and you're sweating.'

Wright wiped his hand across his forehead. It came away wet. 'I'm a bit claustrophobic, that's all.'

Bamber chuckled. 'Yeah? That's funny, isn't it? You being a transit cop and all.'

'It's transport, not transit,' said Wright. 'And I joined for the trains, not the tunnels.'

'I didn't think of that,' said the FBI agent. He stopped laughing. 'Hey, you really are uncomfortable, aren't you?' He handed Wright the flashlight. 'Come on, let's get out of here.'

The two men walked back along the track and out into

the sunshine. Wright took the padlock from his pocket and relocked the gate.

'How did you get here?' Wright asked. 'I didn't see a car.'

'It's about half a mile away. I picked up a rental at the airport.'

They walked away from the tunnel. 'How long are you going to be in town, Jim?' asked Wright.

'As long as it takes. We don't take kindly to our citizens being murdered overseas.'

They climbed up the embankment. Bamber went first. He moved quickly and gracefully, with swift, sure steps that took him up the slope at twice Wright's speed, and whereas Wright was panting when he reached the top, Bamber wasn't affected at all. Bamber looked as if he worked out regularly; he wasn't over muscled, but he was lean and hard without a spare ounce of fat on his frame.

'Do you want to follow me back?' said Wright, figuring that Bamber would have difficulty finding his way across South London to the office.

'I thought I'd go and talk to Eckhardt's widow,' said Bamber.

Wright stiffened. 'Now's not a good time,' he said. 'The funeral was today.'

Bamber stood looking down at the tracks below. He wasn't wearing a coat and the wind was tugging at the lightweight material of his suit but he didn't appear to feel the cold. 'That's the best time,' he said. 'She'll be off balance.'

'She's not a suspect,' said Wright quickly. Too quickly, he realised.

Bamber turned to look at him. He didn't say anything

for several seconds, then he slowly smiled. 'Pretty, is she?'

'Don't be stupid,' Wright said brusquely. He could feel himself start to blush and he looked away.

'Stupid? I just meant that maybe she had a lover, maybe she wanted her husband out of the way.' He craned his neck forward, his head twisted to the side like a hawk eyeing up potential prey. 'What did you think I meant, Nick?'

'She's not a suspect,' Wright repeated. Bamber continued to look at him, smiling. 'It's not what you think,' said Wright.

'Yeah? What do I think?'

'You think I fancy her.'

'And do you?'

Bamber was still smiling. It was a good-natured, open smile, and Wright felt that the FBI agent wasn't being malicious. Wright grinned despite his embarrassment. 'Maybe,' he said. He shook his head. 'I don't know, it's weird. I keep thinking about her, you know? At night, when I'm driving, when I'm shaving. Pretty sick, huh? Her husband's only just been cremated and I want to get inside her pants.'

'Actually, it's understandable. She's vulnerable, she's hurting, it brings out the protective instinct in you. You want to take care of her. It's happened to me before, Nick.'

Wright rubbed his nose. 'Yeah. Maybe.'

'Okay, I'll follow you back to the office. I'll go get my car.' He walked away as Wright climbed into Reid's Honda. As he waited for Bamber to return, Wright thought over what he'd said about May Eckhardt. He wondered whether it had been a good idea to open up to the FBI agent, to a man he'd only just met. Bamber had been sympathetic, though, in a way that Reid would never have been. If Wright had told

Reid how he felt about May Eckhardt, his partner would have reacted with guffaws and sarcasm. Wright massaged the back of his neck, kneading his fingers into the base of his skull in a vain attempt to ease the tension that was building there.

Louise Malone had been a chambermaid for almost eight years but she had never come across a guest as strange as the man in room 527. According to the register he was an American, James Bamber, but he'd never spoken to her so she hadn't heard his accent. On the few occasions she'd seen him, he'd merely smiled and nodded. Hadn't said a word. That in itself was unusual because he was a good-looking guy in his late twenties, exactly the sort of man who'd normally make a pass at her. With her shoulder-length blonde hair, green eyes and curvy figure obvious even under her housecoat, Louise received more than her fair share of passes and she wasn't used to polite indifference. It was a shame that he wasn't interested, because she was between boyfriends and he had a firm, hard body and hazel eyes that made her go a little weak at the knees.

It was the state of his room that Louise found so unusual. She had come across all sorts during her years cleaning rooms, from an Arab who insisted on defecating in the wardrobe, to a family of wealthy Hong Kong Chinese who took the lightbulbs with them when they checked out, but she'd never encountered a guest who cleaned his own room. Louise prided herself on her standards, but she had to admit that his bathroom positively sparkled. He'd even cleaned the shower curtain and managed to dislodge the limescale that had discoloured the toilet overflow. There was never any rubbish in the litter bins, not even a scrap of paper, and his bed was always made, no matter what time of day she checked the room. If she hadn't seen him entering and leaving the room, she'd have been convinced that no one was staying there. She'd been so intrigued by the mysterious Mr Bamber that she'd gone through the drawers and the wardrobe looking for any clues as to what he did for a living, but there were no personal effects to be found, just a few items of laundered clothing, still in protective wrappers. Still, there was nothing wrong with being neat and tidy. Maybe he was gay. That at least would explain why he hadn't made a pass at her.

Two desks had been lined up in front of three large floor-mounted boards. On the centre board were the words 'British Transport Police' and underneath it was the force's logo. On the left-hand board was a photograph of Max Eckhardt, one of several that Nick Wright had borrowed from the widow, blown up to poster size. Underneath were photographs of camera equipment similar to that owned by Eckhardt. On the board on the right was a large photograph of the tunnel entrance and below it a map of the area. More than two dozen reporters and photographers were already in the room when Duggan and Dundas followed Superintendent Newton to their places.

A pretty brunette from the press office was handing out press releases and photographs of the victim. She flashed the superintendent a nervous smile and thrust the remaining press releases at a television reporter before chasing after the officers. She caught up with Newton as he sat down. 'Sorry, sir, could you just hang on a few minutes? Sky TV want to go live and they're having problems in the studio.'

Newton sighed heavily. 'Do we have to?'

'It's good coverage, sir. And they'll reuse it in their hourly bulletins.'

Newton looked at his wristwatch and sighed again. 'Okay, but we haven't got all day.'

The press officer held up her hands for silence and explained to the assembled journalists that the press conference wouldn't be starting for several minutes. There were grumbles from the newspaper reporters. 'Bloody Sky,' shouted one. The press officer suggested that the photographers use the opportunity to take pictures. Newton blinked under a barrage of photographic flashes.

Nick Wright stood at the side of the room next to Tommy Reid, looking at the reporters. They were a mixed bag: earnest young men in sharp suits, middle-aged women with tired skin, grey-haired men in sheepskin jackets. Most had notebooks and pens though several were also holding small tape recorders. A tall blonde wearing a black mini skirt was reading the press release and underlining parts of it. She crossed her long legs. Wright looked across at Reid. His partner was openly staring at the girl's thighs.

'Try to keep your mind on the job, Tommy,' whispered Wright.

A bearded man with a plastic clipboard made a thumbs-up gesture at the press officer. She took her place next to the superintendent and nodded at him. Newton stood up, took his glasses out of his top pocket, and read through the press release. It consisted of barely a dozen paragraphs, identifying the victim as Max Eckhardt, a brief biography, and an appeal for anyone who had been in the vicinity of the tunnels at the approximate time of the murder to call the incident room. They were also appealing for any motorists who had driven along the road that ran parallel to the disused line to come forward, in the hope that they had seen any parked vehicles. Eckhardt's missing camera equipment was listed on a separate sheet. The superintendent asked if there were any questions and there was a flurry of raised hands. They all started to shout at once, so the press officer stood up and pointed at one of the older journalists. Wright recognised him as a crime reporter from one of the heavier Sunday papers.

'Is it possible for us to speak to the man's widow?' he asked. 'It might add weight to the appeal if we could have a quote from her?'

'I'm afraid not,' said Newton. 'She's made it clear that she doesn't want to speak to the press. It's a very difficult time for her.'

'Can we at least have an address for her?'

'No, I'm afraid we can't release that information,' said the superintendent.

Two of the tabloid reporters exchanged hushed whispers. Wright knew that the Eckhardts were ex-directory, but most newspapers had contacts within British Telecom who'd be prepared to disclose the information for the price of a couple of bottles of Scotch. He made a mental note to warn her.

The blonde in the black mini skirt raised a languid hand. 'Are you any closer to discovering a motive?' she asked.

She had a strong Geordie accent which was at odds with her elegant appearance.

'We are pursuing several lines of enquiry,' said Newton.

The blonde uncrossed her legs and tapped her lips with a gold ballpoint pen. 'Have there been any similar murders in the past?' she asked.

'Similar in what way?'

She recrossed her legs. Wright looked across at Newton but the superintendent was staring fixedly at her face. Wright admired the man's self-control.

'The way the body was mutilated. I understand the man's penis was cut off.' Several of the male reporters laughed but the blonde wasn't distracted. She appeared to have the same degree of self-control as the superintendent. 'And then stuffed in his mouth.'

The guffaws intensified and the superintendent waited for the noise to die down before speaking. 'We haven't released details of the man's injuries,' he said.

'Yes, I know that. But we do have our own sources. Perhaps I should rephrase the question. In your experience, have there been any murders in the past where the victim's genitalia have been removed and placed in the victim's mouth?'

Wright and Reid exchanged looks. The blonde had good contacts, either within the police or the pathologist's department. Reid grinned wolfishly and Wright immediately knew what had passed through his mind. Her long legs and short skirts probably opened a lot of doors.

'No, we don't know of any murders which have involved injuries such as you described,' said Newton.

'But you can confirm that Max Eckhardt was mutilated in the way I've described?'

'I'll repeat what I said earlier. We haven't released details of the man's injuries.'

'Because?'

'Because we might need the information to identify the person responsible.'

One of the television reporters, a thirty-something man in a dark blue double-breasted suit, raised his arm and the press officer pointed at him. 'Have you had many hoax confessions?' he asked.

'Fifteen,' answered Newton. Duggan leaned across and whispered into his ear. 'Correction,' said Newton. 'As of today there have been seventeen.'

'Do you have an opinion on people like that who waste your time and resources?'

'Not one that you can print,' said Newton.

A man in a sheepskin jacket stood up. Wright recognised him as the reporter from the *Daily Mirror* who'd been at the last press conference and who had goaded him about the Met being called in. The press officer pointed at him. 'Ted Vincent,' she said to the superintendent out of the corner of her mouth. *'Daily Mirror.'*

'Other than the seventeen hoaxes, how many suspects do you have at present?' said Vincent.

It was a rhetorical question, Wright knew, serving no purpose other than to embarrass the superintendent. 'We are pursuing several lines of enquiry,' Newton said eventually.

'Yes, you said that,' said Vincent. 'But do you have any actual suspects?'

'No,' said Newton coldly. 'That's why we are making this appeal for witnesses. We want anyone who was in the area to come forward—'

'You're asking the public to solve the case for you,' cut in the reporter, punctuating his words with short jabs of his pen. 'This is the second appeal for witnesses in as many weeks. Isn't it time that this case was turned over to more experienced investigators? Such as the Met?'

'Mr Vincent, the Met are already assisting the BTP with this investigation. Officers from both forces are working together. We have more than two dozen officers on the case and are prepared to increase our manpower resources if necessary.'

Vincent shrugged and muttered something as he sat down. The questions continued for more than half an hour and Newton fielded them deftly. None of the reporters was as hostile as Ted Vincent had been, and the *Mirror* reporter made no move to ask any further questions.

When the press conference was over the press officer ushered the superintendent to the back of the room where the television crews wanted to record individual interviews.

Wright and Reid slipped into the corridor. Reid made a drinking motion with his hand and wiggled his eyebrows. 'Yeah, okay,' said Wright wearily.

They walked past the pub nearest their office, figuring that the press pack would be sure to pile in to compare notes before heading back to their papers. The one they chose was already filling up with office workers, and two waitresses in black and white uniforms rushed around with trays of food, everything with chips.

'Solids?' asked Reid disdainfully as they stood at the bar.

Wright shook his head. 'Just a Coke.'

'Bloody hell, Nick. You're over eighteen, you know. Have something stronger.' He waved a ten-pound note and a red-haired waitress in a white blouse gestured with her chin to let him know that he'd attracted her attention. 'Vodka and tonic, love. Make it a double.' He looked meaningfully at Wright.

'Okay, okay. Lager shandy.'

'Pint of lager shandy,' Reid relayed to the waitress, who was already putting his vodka and tonic on the bar in front of him. Reid sipped his drink and smacked his lips. 'How do you think it went?' he asked.

Wright grimaced. 'Better than the one we did, that's for sure.'

'Smooth, isn't he?'

'He's a politician. And he's been on courses for television, press conferences, the works.'

The waitress brought Wright's shandy over and Reid paid her. The two men turned their backs to the bar and leaned on it. The door opened and in walked Ted Vincent, his hands thrust into the pockets of his sheepskin jacket. The journalist grinned when he saw the two detectives.

'Men after my own heart,' said Vincent.

'Ideally with a stake through it,' said Wright.

Vincent laughed good naturedly. 'Can I buy you two gentlemen a drink?' he asked, edging between them and pulling out his wallet.

'That'd be fraternising with the enemy,' said Reid. He pretended to consider the offer for several seconds. 'Mine's a vodka and tonic. A double.'

'Funny guy,' said Vincent. 'Good to see you can keep your sense of humour in the face of adversity.'

'And what adversity would that be?' asked Wright.

'Come on, you know as well as I do that you're getting nowhere on this case.'

'It's early days,' said Wright.

Vincent ordered Reid's vodka and a beer for himself. He raised an eyebrow at Wright but Wright shook his head. 'It's been almost two weeks. What leads have you got?'

'You were at the press conference,' said Wright.

'You've got fuck all,' said Vincent. 'You've got fuck all and you know it.' Reid and Wright looked at each other, then together they turned their backs on the reporter. He wasn't fazed in the least by their show of indifference. He patted them both on the shoulders. 'Look, we're on the same side here, lads. We shouldn't be arguing.'

'How do you figure that?' asked Reid. His vodka and tonic arrived and he downed it in one swift gulp.

Vincent waved at the waitress, pointing at the empty glass and at his own. She brought fresh drinks. 'You want to solve the case. And I want to write about it. It's no bloody story if it stays unsolved. You can see that, right? You guys should learn how to handle the press.' He tapped a cigarette out of a pack of Rothmans and slipped it between his lips.

'A ten-foot barge pole springs to mind,' said Wright. His glass was only half-empty but he pushed it away. 'I've got to go.'

Wright's Fiesta was parked ten minutes' walk from the pub. He sat in the car for several minutes, wondering what he should do. Other than Reid's flat, he had nowhere to go, and he was in no mood to sit down in front of Reid's portable television with a takeaway meal in his lap and a can of supermarket lager on the arm of his chair. He decided to go to see May Eckhardt.

The early afternoon traffic was heavy but flowing smoothly and he reached Maida Vale in twenty minutes. A Suzuki Jeep was pulling out of a pay and display parking place close to the Eckhardts' mansion block and Wright eased his Fiesta into the gap.

As he walked towards the block he realised that he was too late. Half a dozen photographers were clustered on the pavement, five men and a girl, all with cameras and lenses hanging around their necks. They all wore thick jackets and one of the men was pouring steaming coffee from a Thermos flask into plastic cups. Wright put his hands into the pockets of his coat and slouched past. They didn't even look at him.

He walked up to the block and pushed the button for the Eckhardt flat. There was no reply so he pressed it again. And again. When she still didn't reply, Wright kept his thumb on the buzzer for a full minute. When it became clear that she was either out or ignoring the bell, Wright took his mobile phone and tapped out her number. She answered on the fifth ring. 'Yes?' she said.

'Mrs Eckhardt? This is Nick Wright.'

'Nick Wright?'

Wright felt an involuntary twinge of regret that she didn't recognise his name. 'Sergeant Wright,' he said. 'British Transport Police. I'm at the entrance to your block, can you buzz me in?'

'Are you the one who's been ringing my bell?'

'I'm afraid so.'

'There've been so many journalists trying to get in, I didn't . . .' Her words dried up. 'Okay, I'll let you in,' she said. The line went dead and a couple of seconds later the lock buzzed and Wright pushed the door open. He went upstairs. This time she didn't have the door open for him and he had to knock. She had a security chain on the door and it only opened a few inches. Wright caught a quick glimpse of May's face before the door closed again. He heard the rattle of the chain being taken off and then the door opened wide.

May Eckhardt was wearing a white towelling robe that was much too big for her. For a brief moment Wright thought that she'd just got out of the shower but her hair was dry, and then he noticed that she had jeans on under the robe. Her eyes were red and puffy and she turned her face away from Wright as she closed the door.

'Are you okay?' he asked, and immediately wished he'd bitten off his tongue instead. Of course she wasn't okay. Her husband had been brutally murdered and a pack of press photographers were camped on her doorstep.

She walked by him into the sitting room and curled up on the sofa again. There was a box of tissues on the coffee table. 'What do you want?' she asked.

Wright shrugged apologetically. 'I actually came to warn you that the press would be after you. It seems I was too late.'

'Yes, you were,' she said coldly. May leaned forward and picked up half a dozen sheets of paper. She held them out to Wright and he went over to her and took them. Their fingers touched and Wright felt a small shock, like static electricity. May didn't react and Wright wondered if he'd imagined it. He looked at the pieces of paper. They'd been torn from different notebooks and were offers of money in exchange for an exclusive interview. A woman reporter from the *News of the World* had written three times, each time raising her offer. The amount she finally offered was more than Wright earned in a year. 'They were ringing my bell and stuffing these into my letterbox for hours,' she said.

Wright nodded at the telephone. 'Have they phoned yet?'

May shook her head. 'No, we're ex-directory.'

'That won't stop them,' said Wright. 'Can I sit down?' he asked. She nodded and Wright dropped into one of the armchairs.

May brought up her knees against her chest and wrapped her arms around her legs. 'What am I going to do?'

'Is there somewhere you can go?'

'I told you before, I don't have any relatives here.'

'You said you were from Manchester. Can you go back there?'

She threw back her head and gave a short laugh that sounded almost like a cry of pain.

'Friends?'

She shook her head. 'We haven't really been here long enough to make any,' she said. She rubbed her cheek against the towelling robe. Wright realised it was her husband's robe and that she was inhaling his scent.

'I'm sorry,' said Wright lamely. He always seemed to be lost for words in her presence. She looked so small and helpless that he felt an overwhelming urge to protect her, yet he knew there was nothing he could do. The press had a right to pursue her, and they weren't breaking any law by posting messages through her letterbox or waiting on the pavement outside. 'They'll get bored eventually,' he said. 'It's a story today, but that's because there was a press conference.'

'A press conference? Why?'

'We were releasing your husband's name. And appealing for witnesses.'

She held her legs tighter and rested her head on her knees. 'So you're no closer to discovering who killed Max?'

Wright looked away. 'No, I'm afraid not.' There was a

photograph of the Eckhardts on one of the shelves in the alcove, both of them smiling at the camera. Wright didn't remember seeing it last time he was in the flat. 'By the way, an American might get in touch with you. An FBI agent.'

May's eyebrows knotted together and her forehead creased into a frown that made her look suddenly much older. 'FBI?' she said.

'Yeah, his name's James Bamber. The FBI have sent him over to help with the investigation.'

Her frown became even more severe. 'Why? Don't they think you can find Max's killer?'

'It's not that, he's just here to help co-ordinate with the Americans, Max being an American and all. He said he might want to talk to you.' Wright looked around the room, not wanting eye contact with her. Something strange happened to his stomach each time he looked into her soft brown eyes. 'Do you have food?' he asked. She looked puzzled. 'So that you don't have to go out to the shops,' he added. 'The photographers outside are waiting for a picture. If you stay inside, they'll go away eventually.'

'I've enough food,' she said. 'I don't have much of an appetite, anyway. How long? How long do you think they'll stay there?'

'A couple of days, then they'll be chasing after another story.'

'That's all Max's death is? A story?'

Wright sat forward. 'No, of course not,' he said earnestly. 'I meant that's how the media regards it. It's much more than that to me. And to my colleagues.' A tear rolled down her cheek. 'I will find his killer, May. I promise you.'

She rubbed her cheek against the robe. 'Thank you,' she whispered.

There were half a dozen empty glasses lined up on the bar and Tommy Reid tapped them one at a time, trying in vain to play a recognisable tune.

Vincent patted him on the back. 'My round,' he said. In fact, they'd all been Vincent's rounds. Alcohol loosened tongues, and loose tongues produced page leads. He winked at the waitress and she produced fresh drinks without being asked. 'Your partner's a bit touchy, isn't he?'

'Nick? He's okay.'

'Oh, sure,' said Vincent hurriedly, not wanting to offend the detective. 'But it's like he's got something to prove.'

'He's young.'

Vincent finished off his cigarette and stubbed it out in a plastic ashtray. 'Dog in a manger,' he said.

'Bollocks,' said Reid. 'He's co-operating with the Met team, and with the guy the FBI sent over.'

Vincent's heart began to race, but he kept his face expressionless. It was the first time anyone had mentioned an FBI involvement and he sensed a good story. He decided to use a softly-softly approach. Reid was drunk but he was clearly used to consuming large amounts of alcohol and Vincent didn't want to scare him off. 'He hasn't been on a murder case like this before, has he?'

'I don't think any of us has ever seen anything like it before,' said Reid. 'It's a one-off.' He gulped down his vodka and tonic and looked at his wristwatch.

'Not in the States, even? There's all sorts of weird stuff goes on there.'

'The FBI guy says no.'

'So why's he come over, then?' Vincent pulled a ten-pound note from his pocket and waved it at the barmaid.

'Because Eckhardt's an American.'

'They do that? They send over an FBI agent when an American dies?'

Reid shrugged. 'I guess so. I'd better be going.'

Their drinks arrived. 'You might as well have one for the road,' said Vincent, picking up his pint. 'So what's his name, this guy?'

'Bamber,' said a voice behind him. 'Jim Bamber.'

Vincent turned around. The speaker was a man in his late twenties, slightly shorter than Vincent with light brown close-cropped hair that was greying at the temples. Bamber's hand was outstretched. Vincent transferred his glass to his left hand and they shook. The American had a firm grip but Vincent had the feeling that he wasn't using all his strength. 'Ted Vincent.'

'Careful what you say, Jim,' said Reid. 'He's a journalist.'

'Yeah? Which paper, Ted?'

'The *Mirror*. Can I buy you a drink?'

'Sure. Scotch. On the rocks. How's it going, Tommy?'

Reid shrugged as Vincent ordered Bamber's drink. 'Did you see the press conference on TV?' asked Reid.

'Sure did.'

'So you know how it's going.'

Vincent handed Bamber his whisky and they clinked glasses. 'Cheers,' said Vincent. 'I was asking Tommy if it was normal practice to send an FBI agent over to investigate the death of an American national.'

'Depends on the circumstances,' said Bamber.

Vincent could already see the headline: 'Train Cops Call In FBI.' He sipped his beer, taking his time. 'And are you taking an active part in the investigation?'

'I'm asking a few questions, sure. This isn't an interview, is it, Ted? I wouldn't want to say anything on the record.'

'Sure, sure,' said Vincent dismissively. He pulled his pack of Rothmans from the pocket of his sheepskin jacket and offered a cigarette to Bamber. The FBI agent declined and Vincent lit one for himself. 'What's your perspective on this, Jim?' Vincent asked. 'How do you think the investigation's being handled?'

'It's a tough case,' said Bamber.

'Would they do it different in the States?'

'Like I said, it's a tough case. We just have to wait for a break.'

'Yeah? Well, without a witness and without some sort of forensic evidence, it all comes down to motive, that's what I reckon.'

Bamber sniffed his whisky but didn't drink it. 'You might be right, Ted.'

'So which office do you work out of?'

'Washington.'

'FBI headquarters?'

Bamber nodded but didn't reply.

'I've got to tell you, Jim, what I'd really like to do is have an interview for my paper. An exclusive.'

'I don't think so,' said Bamber quietly.

'It might help bring people forward. Any publicity is good publicity and all that.'

'I don't think so,' Bamber repeated. His voice was barely audible, little more than a soft whisper, but there was a hard edge to it.

Vincent sensed the man's reluctance and tried to put him at his ease by smiling broadly and squeezing him on the shoulder. Bamber didn't react to the physical contact. He stared unsmilingly at Vincent and the journalist took his hand away. 'How about another Scotch?'

The FBI agent smiled, but without warmth. 'I'm okay,' he said.

Vincent ordered another pint for himself and a vodka and tonic for Reid. 'So, how long will you be over on this side of the pond?' asked Vincent.

'Depends,' said Bamber.

'The Bureau's happy to leave it open ended? Some murder investigations take months.'

'And some are never solved,' said Reid. He ran his fingers along the top of his empty glasses. The waitress returned with fresh drinks and reached out to take the empty ones, but Reid waved her away. 'I need an A flat,' he explained.

'I mean, can you imagine the BTP sending one of their men to investigate a death in another country?' said Vincent. 'Wouldn't happen.'

'Nah, you're dead wrong there,' said Reid, banging the flat of his hand down on the bar. 'British cops have been sent to the Falklands, to Kenya, lots of places.'

'Yeah? But you're talking about real police, not the BTP.'

Reid looked sideways at the journalist. 'Hey, you don't hear me saying that the *Mirror*'s not a real newspaper, do you? You don't hear me saying that it's a comic with a reading age in single figures.'

'And I'm grateful for that, Tommy. You're all heart.'

Bamber put his drink on the bar. 'Do you two always fight like this?'

'This?' said Reid. 'This is just the warm-up.' He chuckled and rested his arms on the bar.

'It's a symbiotic relationship,' Vincent said to Bamber. 'We publicise their successes, we help with appeals for information, and in return they give us stories to help us sell papers. Which brings me back to you, Jim. I'd really like to do a story on you and your involvement in the tunnel murder.'

'I don't think so,' said Bamber.

'Come on, Jim. I don't actually need your co-operation, you know. Freedom of Information Act and all that. I can call Washington and get the scoop from them. They'll have a press office, right?'

'I'd rather you didn't, Ted,' said Bamber.

'So talk to me. Give me an interview. That way you'll be able to put your own slant on it.'

'No,' said Bamber. He took a step forward so that his face was only inches away from the journalist's. His pale hazel eyes stared at Vincent so intensely that the journalist flinched.

Vincent was a good two inches taller than the FBI agent and several pounds heavier, but he still felt intimidated by the man. 'I'm just trying to do my job, Jim,' said Vincent. He heard his voice wavering and laughed to cover his embarrassment. It was a hollow laugh and Bamber continued to stare at him. Vincent took a drag at his cigarette. His hand was shaking and he dropped it to his side, not wanting Bamber to see the effect his stare was having on him. Reid watched them in the mirrored gantry.

'Okay, I guess I'd better be going,' said Vincent, taking a step back.

'Yeah, see you,' said Reid unenthusiastically.

Vincent waved to Reid's reflection, still backing away.

'Nice meeting you, Ted,' said Bamber. He smiled and the hardness faded from his eyes. He seemed suddenly friendlier, and when he stuck out his hand Vincent shook it. Bamber put his left hand on top of Vincent's as they shook. 'It's been a rough day,' said the FBI agent. 'I didn't mean to offend you.'

Vincent felt suddenly relieved, as if a snarling dog had begun wagging its tail. He smiled gratefully at the FBI agent. 'No offence taken, Jim.'

L en Kruse pressed the doorbell. It buzzed and a few seconds later the hall light went on. The door opened and Ted Vincent peered out. 'Jim?' he said.

Kruse grinned good naturedly. 'Hiya, Ted. I wanted to apologise for giving you a hard time earlier.'

The journalist ran a hand through his unruly hair. He was still wearing his suit but he'd removed his tie. 'No problem.' He frowned. 'How did you know where I lived?'

'Tommy Reid told me.'

'Tommy knows my address?'

'I guess so. Look, I had a long talk with Tommy, and he convinced me that we've more to gain by co-operating.'

'Co-operating?'

'On your article. I thought maybe we could do the interview tonight.'

Vincent looked at his watch. From upstairs a woman called. 'Who is it, Ted?'

'It's okay, it's for me,' he shouted. He shrugged apologetically at Kruse. 'My wife,' he explained. 'Can we do this tomorrow?'

Kruse gave him a pained look. 'No can do. I'm heading up to Manchester tomorrow morning.'

'What's in Manchester?'

'A lead on the tunnel killing.' Kruse shivered. 'Can I come in?'

The journalist opened the door. Kruse walked into the hall. He looked up the stairs. There was no sign of Vincent's wife. On the wall alongside the stairs hung dozens of framed newspaper articles and photographs of Vincent in several trouble spots. In one Vincent was standing in front of three blazing oil wells. 'Kuwait?' Kruse said, nodding at the photograph.

'Yeah, I was there during Desert Storm.'

'Must have been hell,' said Kruse.

'It was rough,' agreed Vincent.

Kruse nodded. He could have told Vincent a few stories about how rough it had really got in Kuwait. As a journalist covering the war, Vincent would have been fed the Allied line: smart missiles, clean kills, the antichrist as the enemy. It wasn't as clear cut as that, Kruse knew, but he wasn't there to enlighten Vincent. 'It must have been,' he said.

Vincent closed the door. Upstairs, the landing light clicked off. Kruse wondered if the wife had been listening. 'Through there,' said Vincent, pointing towards a door. Kruse pushed it open. It was a sitting room, large and airy with white walls, pine furniture and lots of potted plants, with wooden blinds on the windows. More framed articles and photographs hung on the walls. Modesty clearly wasn't one of Vincent's qualities. There was a wedding photograph on top of a big-screen television, Vincent in his twenties about to kiss a frightened blonde. He looked more like a vampire about to go for the throat than a just-married groom preparing to kiss his bride.

'Pretty girl,' said Kruse. There were no photographs of any children and no toys in the room. 'No kids?'

'Not yet,' said Vincent. 'Still trying. Fancy a drink?'

'No, thanks,' said Kruse. 'But don't let me stop you.'

Vincent nodded at a mug of coffee on a pine table next to a crystal ashtray in which a half-smoked cigarette smouldered among a dozen or so butts. 'I was having coffee. Do you want one?'

Kruse waved his hand dismissively. 'Never touch it,' he said.

'Can I tape our conversation?' asked Vincent. 'My shorthand's a bit rusty.'

'Sure.'

Vincent went over to a rack of shelves filled with paperback books. There was a small tape recorder on one of the shelves. Kruse pulled a pair of black leather gloves from his suit pocket. He slipped them on and walked quickly behind the journalist. He clamped his right hand over Vincent's mouth and gripped the man's throat with his left, applying pressure to the carotid arteries with his fingers and thumb. Vincent tried to turn but Kruse pushed him forward, taking care not to bang his head against the shelves. Vincent clawed at Kruse's gloves but his strength was already draining away as the brain began to feel the effects of the curtailed blood supply. Kruse was more than capable of crushing the man's windpipe with his left hand but he didn't want to do major damage. A post mortem wouldn't show up tissue damage, but broken cartilage or bones wouldn't be missed. It was a delicate balance, but it wasn't the first time that Kruse had choked a man to death, and he knew exactly how much pressure to apply. Too much and there'd be small haemorrhages under the skin and pinpricks of blood in the whites of the eyes.

Vincent's chest began to heave. He let go of Kruse's gloves and started to flail around with his arms. Kruse pulled him away from the bookshelves until they were standing in the centre of the room. Kruse shuffled to his right so that Vincent wouldn't hit the coffee table when he fell. He felt the journalist's legs begin to buckle, and watched in the mirror over the mantelpiece as Vincent's eyes fluttered and eventually closed. Kruse let him slide slowly to the ground, maintaining the pressure on the man's arteries all the way down.

Kruse lay down next to Vincent, his hands still around the man's neck. If he kept the grip on long enough Vincent would die from suffocation, but that wasn't what Kruse wanted. There had to be smoke in the lungs, and corpses didn't inhale. He stayed curled against Vincent like an attentive lover until he was satisfied that the journalist was unconscious, then he took his gloved hands away and stood up.

He listened intently, but the only sounds he could hear were the clicking of the water heater in the kitchen and the rustle of leaves outside. He walked on tiptoe to the foot of the stairs, then crept up them, keeping close to the wall so that the stairs wouldn't creak. Four doors led off the landing, but only one was ajar. Kruse peeked in. Vincent's wife was lying in bed, reading a paperback by the light of a table lamp. He pushed open the door and walked quickly across the plush pile carpet.

'Who was it?' she asked, still reading.

Kruse said nothing. He moved around the side of the bed. The curtains were drawn. The woman lowered the book. Her eyes widened in terror and she opened her mouth to scream, but before she could make a sound Kruse sat down on the bed and put his left hand across her mouth and nostrils. She dropped the book and clawed at his face but he grabbed both of her wrists with his right hand and forced her arms down. She struggled but she was no match for him. He straddled her on the bed, taking care not to bruise her flesh. The fire would probably obliterate all traces of tissue damage, but Kruse took a professional pride in his ability to kill without leaving marks. He pinned the woman's hands to her stomach, gripping with his thighs so that he could use his right hand on her neck. He found the carotids with his thumb and fingers, pushing in between the muscle to block off the blood supply. The woman kicked and bucked but Kruse was too heavy and strong. The brain held only enough oxygen for between ten and fifteen seconds, and she was soon unconscious. Kruse waited a further minute, to be absolutely sure, before climbing off the bed.

He put the woman's book on the bedside table, then went downstairs. He picked up Vincent and slung him effortlessly over his shoulder. Vincent was breathing heavily. Kruse knew from previous experience that the man would be unconscious for at least fifteen minutes. He carried him upstairs and lay him down on the bed before stripping off all the journalist's clothes. There was a raffia laundry basket under the window and Kruse dropped Vincent's shirt, underwear and socks into it. He took a wooden hanger from the wardrobe and hung up Vincent's suit. Kruse put the shoes Vincent had been wearing at the bottom of the wardrobe next to three other pairs. He closed the wardrobe door and looked around the room. The tie was downstairs, on the back of the sofa, but Kruse decided to leave it where it was. He quickly checked through the drawers of the dressing table and a cupboard, but there were no pyjamas. Vincent obviously slept in the nude, as did his wife.

Satisfied that everything was as it should be, Kruse rolled Vincent under the quilt, lying him on his back. He went downstairs and stood in the centre of the sitting room, checking that nothing was out of place. He went through to the kitchen and locked the back door. In the sink there was a pile of dirty dishes but Kruse figured that Vincent was the type who'd have left them until the morning.

He switched off the kitchen light and went back into the sitting room. The cigarette was still burning in the ashtray. Kruse picked up the ashtray and a box of matches that were lying on the coffee table and took them upstairs.

He knelt down by Vincent's side of the bed, then pulled the man's arm from underneath the quilt and slid the lit cigarette between the first and second fingers. After a final look around the bedroom to check that everything was as it should be, he took one of the matches out of the box and lit it. He held it against the quilt cover. It went out almost immediately. He lit a second match. This time the cotton quilt cover began to burn.

The fire spread quickly across the quilt. Kruse knew that the room with its wooden furniture, woollen carpet and cotton curtains would be an inferno within minutes. He switched off the light and went downstairs. He pulled the front door shut behind him and walked quickly down the street, his footsteps echoing in the night air.

C live Edmunds stopped off at a video rental store in Camden High Street on his way home. He left his car on a double yellow line with his hazard warning lights flashing while he went inside. The girl behind the counter smiled, recognising him as a regular customer. 'Anything new come in?' he asked, heading for the new releases section.

'Not since you were last here,' she said. 'Well, there's another of them talking dog whatsits, but they're not really your thing, are they?'

'Bloody right,' said Edmunds, running his eyes along the video cases. He was an avid movie watcher and there was nothing on the shelves that he hadn't already seen or dismissed as not worth viewing. He pulled a face and went over to the action section. He fancied a good action movie, something with blood and guts. An early Schwarzenegger maybe, or a late Jean-Claude Van Damme. His eyes stopped at *Apocalypse Now*. It was the widescreen version, released after the film had won two Oscars in 1979, for Best Cinematography and Best Sound. It deserved more, Edmunds reckoned, but it was ahead of its time, before America was prepared to come to terms with Vietnam.

Edmunds turned the case over. On the back were two stills taken from the film, one of Marlon Brando, one of Martin Sheen. Edmunds scratched his bald spot. There was something at the back of his mind, something niggling him, that kept the video in his hands even though he'd seen it three times already, once on the big screen and twice on video. He tapped the video case against his forehead as he struggled to work out what it was about the movie that was troubling him, but the more he tried to concentrate, the more elusive the feeling became. It was like a mild case of *déjà vu*, but it wouldn't go away. He took the case over to the counter and handed it to the girl. 'I'll have this,' he said.

L en Kruse was in the middle of his third set of sit-ups when the telephone rang. He unlinked his fingers from behind his neck and reached over for the phone. 'Yes?' he said.

'Jim? It's Clive.'

Kruse got to his feet. 'Yes, Clive, what's up?' Kruse was bathed in sweat but there was no sign of strain in his voice. He stared at his reflection in the mirror on the front of the wardrobe. His face was a blank mask.

'What do you know about the Vietnam War?' asked Edmunds.

Kruse's face remained impassive. 'I know it's one we lost, Clive. What exactly do you have in mind?'

'Can you come around to my place now? There's something I want you to see.'

Kruse picked up a pen from the bedside table. 'Give me your address, Clive. I'll be right over.'

Nick Wright parked his car opposite May Eckhardt's flat and switched off the engine. He sat back in his seat, his hands gripping the steering wheel. He wasn't quite sure what he was doing. It was almost midnight. He should have been at home. Wright snorted. He didn't have a home any more, he thought ruefully. All he had was a sofabed in Tommy Reid's tiny flat. He looked across at the mansion block where May's apartment was. The lights were off and the curtains were open. The moon was reflected in the sitting-room window, glaring down at him like a single baleful eye. Wright wiped his hands on his face and then up through his hair. He'd actually been on his way home. Maida Vale was well out of his way, but he'd been struck by a sudden urge to see May Eckhardt.

May Eckhardt had been very much on his mind over the previous few days. He'd telephoned several times but there'd been no answer. There was something vulnerable about her, something that made Wright want to take care of her, to protect her from the world that had killed her husband. She was so different from his ex-wife.

Wright had never felt that Janie needing looking after, even when she was ill. Wright had once read in a magazine that couples were always referred to in order of dominance. He wasn't sure if it was true or not so he'd asked several of his friends and they'd all agreed that it was Janie and Nick. It had come as something of a shock because Wright had always felt that their marriage was a partnership of equals.

But the more he'd thought about it, the more he'd realised that when it came to making decisions, usually Janie got her way. She'd chosen the house, she'd had the final word on what car they bought, and it had been her decision to come off the pill when she did. They always talked through their problems, but it was always Wright who gave way. Because he loved her and she knew it.

He'd read in another magazine that the most successful marriages were where the husband loved the wife more than the wife loved the husband. Wright was living proof that the theory was flawed.

He wondered what May Eckhardt's marriage had been like. Had it been Max and May, or May and Max? He closed his eyes and rested his head on the back of the seat, trying to recall her face. Wright shivered. The car interior had cooled quickly with the engine off and he rubbed his arms, trying to keep warm. An old man wearing a raincoat and a flat cap walked by with a Yorkshire terrier on a bright red lead. He turned to look at Wright as he walked by. Wright smiled and gave him a small wave.

Wright looked up at the window again. The room was still in darkness. He checked the parked cars but there was no sign of her VW. Wright rubbed his chin. She didn't strike him as the sort who'd stay out late. He climbed out of his Fiesta and stretched, then locked the door and walked down the path towards the entrance to the mansion block. A light came on, presumably motion-activated because no one opened the front door. He ran his finger down the bell buttons, then frowned. The piece of cardboard with Eckhardt written on it had gone. He stared at the blank space under the bell, his forehead creased into a puzzled frown.

'Can I help you?' said a voice behind him.

Wright jumped as if he'd been poked in the ribs. He whirled around to see the man in the flat cap standing behind him, his dog cradled in his arms. The man was in his seventies and there was an aggressive tilt to his chin as if he suspected Wright of being up to no good. The dog yapped twice and the man put a hand on its muzzle to silence it.

'I'm a policeman,' said Wright, recovering his composure.

'Really,' said the man. 'Well, I'm with the Neighbourhood Watch and I've never seen you around here before.' The terrier struggled to escape the man's grip on its muzzle. 'Hush, Katie,' the man whispered.

'I suppose that's your guard dog,' said Wright good naturedly, but the joke fell flat.

The man tilted his chin higher. He was a small man, barely reaching Wright's shoulder, but he wasn't intimidated by Wright's relative youth or height. Wright had the feeling that he was a former boxer, and that if push came to shove he'd be prepared to take a swing at Wright, despite his age. Assuming he put the dog down first.

'I'd like to see your identification,' said the man.

'Sure,' said Wright. He reached into his inside pocket, took out his wallet, and opened it to show his warrant card and badge.

The man released his grip on his dog's muzzle and took the wallet. He stared at the warrant card as if committing it to memory. 'This says you're with the British Transport Police,' he said.

'That's right.'

The man compared the photograph on the card with

Wright's face, then handed it back. The dog growled softly. 'So you're not a real policeman, then?' he said.

Wright smiled tightly but said nothing.

'And who is it you're here to see, Sergeant Wright?'

'May Eckhardt,' said Wright. 'Flat four.'

The man smiled smugly. 'She's gone,' he said. 'Good thing too, the photographers were a bloody nuisance. Night and day, standing on the pavement, talking and laughing. Called the police but they said there was nothing they could do, they weren't trespassing.'

'Gone?'

'Moved out.'

'Do you know when?'

'Why? Is she a suspect now?'

'No, she's not a suspect, Mr . . .?'

'Jenkins,' said the man. 'I live in the flat below the Eckhardts.' He fished a key out of his raincoat pocket and Wright stepped aside so that he could unlock the door. 'Two days ago, that was when she left.'

'There's no "for sale" sign up,' said Wright.

'They rented,' said Jenkins.

'From who?'

'The landlord's a Mr Sadiq, I believe. Never met the man, though. He owns several flats in the area.' He pushed open the door and put down his terrier. It ran along the hallway and up a flight of stairs, its stub of a tail wagging furiously.

'I don't suppose you've got a telephone number for him, have you?' asked Wright.

The man shook his head, then pointed to a noticeboard on the wall. Several letters were pinned to it. 'The managing agents should be able to tell you. That's their address.'

Jenkins turned to follow the dog, but Wright asked him

if he could spare a few minutes. Jenkins looked at his wristwatch, then nodded.

'What sort of couple were they?' Wright asked.

Jenkins narrowed his eyes suspiciously. 'What do you mean?'

'I meant when they lived above you. Were they quiet? Did they argue?'

'Never heard a peep,' said Jenkins, taking off his hat and unbuttoning his raincoat. 'Hardly saw them. I was a bit worried when they first moved in, her being Chinese and all. I was a bit worried about the smell, you know?'

'The smell?'

'Cooking. Chinese food. The smell lingers, doesn't it? It was never a problem, though. Delightful girl. Spoke perfect English.'

'What about her husband?'

'Oh, he's American. Terrible English.'

'I meant what was he like?'

'A photographer. That's all I know. He liked jazz. I had to complain about the noise one Sunday, but generally they were perfect neighbours.' He looked at his watch again. 'Anyway, if there's nothing else, Sergeant Wright, I have to give my wife her medicine.'

Wright thanked him. Jenkins waited while he copied down the name and telephone number of the managing agent, then closed the door behind him.

D ean Burrow smiled at the office receptionist and wished her a good morning. He pushed through the glass door that led to his outer office and almost bumped into a black UPS deliveryman on his way out. Burrow held the door open for him and the deliveryman nodded his thanks.

'Good morning, Sally,' he said to his office manager. Sally Forster had been on his staff for more than fifteen years and was one of his most devoted staffers.

She looked up from the stack of mail on her desk and put a hand up to push her spectacles higher up her nose. 'Good morning, Senator,' she said brightly. A cigarette smouldered in a small brass ashtray. Sally smoked sixty cigarettes a day and the non-smoking members of staff had twice tried to declare the senator's office a no-smoking zone. They'd failed both times: Sally was as adept at office politics as she was at running the senator's diary.

'You work too hard, Sally,' said the senator. It was a common refrain. She generally put in a sixteen-hour day, and appeared to have no life outside the office.

She made a dismissive waving motion with her ringless left hand. 'Bullshit,' she said. 'If you want something doing . . .'

'And there's no one does it better than you,' said the senator. 'But you make me look bad by always getting in before me.'

She grinned slyly. 'I could give you an early morning alarm call, Senator.' She picked up her cigarette and inhaled.

Burrow chuckled. Sally was the only member of his staff who could get away with such teasing.

Burrow spotted a UPS document package on her desk and he twisted his neck to get a better look. It was from Bangkok. He reached for it but Sally beat him to it. 'It's not been scanned, Senator.'

'Who's it from?'

Sally read the waybill affixed to the package. 'Eric Horvitz. Bangkok, Thailand.'

Burrow felt a chill run down his spine. 'That's okay, I know Mr Horvitz,' he said.

She held the package out. 'You're sure that's his signature?'

Burrow didn't even look at the scrawl. 'Yes, don't worry, I've been expecting this.'

Sally let go of the package and Burrow took it. 'Coffee?' she asked.

Burrow shook his head. 'No, thanks. Maybe later.'

'There's a list of calls on your desk. And the *Washington Post* wants an interview. You've got a twenty-minute slot at three.'

'Three's fine. Who are they sending?'

'Jane Owen. With a photographer.'

Burrow nodded. 'Okay, go ahead and confirm. Better have Kimberly in to do my hair at two thirty.'

'Already booked,' said Sally.

Burrow acknowledged her mindreading ability with a slight nod and went through to his own office. He ripped open the package as he walked around his desk. There was only one thing inside – a Polaroid photograph.

Burrow stopped dead. For a second or two he felt faint and he reached out with his free hand to grip the desk. He stared at the image, his pulse pounding in his ears. It was almost identical to the previous Polaroid he'd received. A man, his flesh turned ghostly white, spreadeagled against a wall, shiny red blood smeared over his mouth and chest. Burrow narrowed his eyes as he looked at the face of the corpse. It had been more than a quarter of a century since he had last seen Eric Horvitz, but Burrow was reasonably sure that it was Horvitz in the photograph.

The senator dialled Jody Meacher's number and put the picture on to his blotter as the telephone rang. Meacher's answering machine cut in and Burrow left a brief message.

There was a discreet tap on his door as he replaced the receiver, and Sally popped her head in. 'Ready to go over your diary?' she asked.

Burrow opened the top right-hand drawer of his desk and tossed the photograph into it. 'Sure,' he said, closing the drawer and flashing his 'everything's all right with the world' smile. 'And I'll have that coffee now, too.'

There was an ambulance in the road outside Edmunds's house but the blue light wasn't flashing and the driver stood by the rear doors smoking a cigarette. Two police cars were parked on the opposite side of the road, both empty. Gerry Hunter climbed out of his car and locked the door. A group of housewives huddled together on the pavement, staring over the hedge at the front door. An old woman in a faded housecoat and slippers saw him coming and Hunter heard her say 'CID'. They all turned to watch him walk towards the gate.

'Isn't there something on television you could be watching?' shouted Hunter bitterly. One of the women had the decency to blush, but the rest were unfazed by his outburst. 'Go on, piss off!' he said.

One old woman tut-tutted and Hunter had a sudden urge to push her over the hedge, or better still to drag her into the house so that she could see for herself what was inside. Maybe if she came face to face with a few corpses she wouldn't be so keen to gawp. Hunter glared at her so aggressively that she took a step backwards.

He pushed his way through the onlookers and walked briskly down the path to the front door. It was ajar and he pushed it open with his foot. A uniformed constable was there, picking his nose. 'Get those people out of here!' Hunter barked. 'This is a crime scene, not a circus.' The constable opened his mouth but before he could speak Hunter cut him short with a warning finger. 'Just do it,' he said. 'Where's the body?'

'Upstairs, sir,' said the constable.

'Doctor?'

'She's there already, sir.' The constable edged past Hunter and out of the front door. Hunter closed it.

A second uniform came out of the sitting room, this one a sergeant. Hunter recognised him. 'Hiya, Mick,' said Hunter.

'Gerry. Have you been upstairs?'

'Not yet. What's the story?'

'Choked on his own vomit by the look of it.'

'Jesus.' Hunter walked through to the sitting room and looked around. He'd spent many an hour in that room, drinking and watching Sky Sport with his partner, their feet propped up on the coffee table. It was a comfortable room, a man's room, with cigarette burns on most of the furniture, and irregular-shaped stains on the brown carpet. Edmunds had never been married and his house was a female-free sanctuary for his friends and colleagues.

'Nothing suspicious?'

Mick shook his head. 'Made himself a snack and drank the best part of a bottle of whisky.'

Hunter rubbed his jaw. Edmunds was a heavy drinker, though he tended to drink in company rather than on his own. 'No visitors?'

'Doesn't look like it. Just the one glass.'

Hunter sighed. He wasn't sure if he'd have been happier if there had been suspicious circumstances. Dead was dead, when all was said and done. 'Okay, cheers, Mick. I'll go up and see the doc.'

Hunter went slowly upstairs, holding on to the banister as if afraid that he'd lose his balance. A third uniformed officer was in the bedroom, standing at the window and staring down at the street. He turned as Hunter walked into the bedroom. It was Sandy Peters, an old friend of Hunter's. They'd joined the force at the same time, and despite the fact that Peters had remained a constable while Hunter had risen relatively quickly through the ranks, they were still firm friends.

'Hiya, Gerry,' said Peters.

'Sandy. Thanks for the call.'

Dr Anna Littman was bending over the bed, examining the body. She nodded a greeting to Hunter.

Peters walked over to Hunter. 'Yeah, they said it was your day off, but I thought . . .' He shrugged, not sure what to say.

'I'm glad you did,' said Hunter.

'I'm sorry,' said Peters. 'He was a good guy.'

'Yeah. I know. Who found the body?'

'Me. His car was giving him trouble and I was going to pick him up from the garage. He didn't turn up so I came here. The curtains were drawn and I thought maybe he'd overslept. Tried his mobile, no answer.'

'How did you get in?'

'Broke a back window. I'll have it fixed.' He fiddled with his tunic. 'I'd better go downstairs, check that everything's sorted.'

Hunter nodded. He patted Peters on the arm as he went by.

Dr Littman stood up and draped the quilt over Edmunds's body. 'I'm sorry, Gerry.'

'Yeah,' said Hunter.

'You'd worked together for quite a while?'

'Three years. Give or take.' Hunter walked over to the window. Outside, the young constable was shepherding the neighbours away. 'What do they expect to see?' asked Hunter. The doctor didn't answer. 'What happened, Anna?'

'Choked on his own vomit. You'd be surprised how often it happens, Gerry. A lot of drunks . . .' She walked up behind him and put a hand on his shoulder. 'I'm sorry. I didn't mean that Clive was . . . you know what I mean.' She squeezed his shoulder gently. 'Are you okay?'

'It's such a stupid way to die,' said Hunter quietly. 'If he'd been on duty, if he'd been shot . . .'

'Then you'd have a murder to investigate. You'd be able to do something.'

Hunter sighed. 'Yeah, I guess that's it.'

'It's your day off, isn't it? Go home.'

'Yeah, and drink something sweet. A nice hot cup of tea. I know the routine.' He closed his eyes and massaged the bridge of his nose. 'I'm sorry, Anna. I didn't mean to snap.'

'I could give you something . . .'

Hunter shook his head. 'I'll be okay. I'll have to go and see his mother. She'll have to be told. Jesus, what do I tell her? He choked on cheese on toast?'

'Just say he died suddenly in his sleep. There's no need to go into details.'

'They always want details,' said Hunter.

The doctor took her hand away from Hunter's shoulder. 'Do you want a copy of the post mortem report?'

'Not unless there's anything unusual.'

'There won't be, Gerry. I'm sorry.' She went back to the bed and picked up her medical bag. 'Come on,' she said. 'Come downstairs with me.'

Hunter continued to stare out of the window. 'Just give me a few minutes,' he said.

He waited until she'd left the room before going over to the bed. He stared down at the bump in the quilt and reached out his hand, but then changed his mind. He didn't want to see his partner's corpse, he wanted to remember him as he had been. 'You stupid, stupid, bastard,' he whispered. Tears filled his eyes and he wiped them away with his sleeve.

Tommy Reid unscrewed the cap off his bottle of vodka and poured slugs into two polystyrene cups of coffee. He handed one to Nick Wright. 'Congratulations, partner,' he said.

They bashed their cups together and toasted each other.

'Never thought we'd get the bastard,' said Wright.

'All things come to him who waits,' said Reid, drinking his coffee and smacking his lips.

The mugger who had escaped from Wright during the undercover operation had finally been caught and was safely under lock and key in a custody suite at Edbury Bridge, the BTP's area headquarters. He'd almost killed an old man on the Victoria Line with his stun gun but had been overpowered by a group of rugby players on their way home from a training game. They'd almost broken one of the mugger's legs and blacked both eyes before handing him over to the British Transport Police. Reid and Wright had been over to identify him as the mugger they'd pursued through Paddington. It was definitely him – he was wearing the same motorcycle jacket. They'd left him screaming obscenities and threatening to sue the rugby players for assault.

Wright would have preferred to have caught the man himself, but he was happy to settle for second best. He sipped his spiked coffee and swung his feet up on to the desk.

'Hey, Nick, did you get the box?' called Dave Hubbard.

'Box? What box?'

Hubbard pointed over at the far corner of the CID office. 'Came first thing this morning.'

Wright pushed himself up out of his chair and went over to the large cardboard box and knelt down beside it.

'Not ticking, is it?' shouted Reid.

It had been delivered by a courier firm and Wright studied the documentation stuck to the top of the box. 'It's from my ex-wife,' he said.

'Bloody hell, it probably is a bomb!' shouted Reid. He

and Hubbard giggled like a couple of schoolboys and Wright scowled across at them.

He pulled open the box. Inside were pieces of model railway track and more than a dozen small parcels swathed in bubble-wrap. He picked one of them up and carefully unwrapped it. It was a green and black model steam engine.

'You bitch, Janie,' said Wright under his breath. Stuck into the side of the box was an envelope. Wright opened it, read it, and ripped it in half.

Reid walked over and looked down into the box. 'A train set?'

'Brilliant deduction,' said Wright sourly.

Reid knelt down and picked up the model locomotive. 'Beautiful,' he said.

'My dad's,' said Wright. 'It was in the loft. Janie's had a clear-out.'

'Must be worth a bit?'

'Probably.' He stood up and went over to his desk. He picked up the phone and banged out Janie's number. She answered after half a dozen rings. 'Janie, what the hell are you playing at?'

'I don't know what you mean.'

'The train set.'

'Good. It arrived, did it?'

'That's for Sean. You know I gave it to him.'

'Sean doesn't want it. He's too old to play with trains.'

'He's seven.'

'Exactly. Anyway, he doesn't want it. It was just cluttering up the attic.'

'That's what attics are for, to be cluttered up.'

'I'm having it converted,' she said. 'Into a sewing room.'

'Hell's bells, Janie. I wanted Sean to have it.'

'He doesn't want it.'

'Can I speak to him?'

'He's at school.'

'I'll call later.'

'If you like.' She hung up.

'Bitch!' shouted Wright. He slammed the phone down.

'Ex-wives, huh,' sympathised Reid. 'What can you do with them?' He leaned forward conspiratorially. 'I've got an idea.'

'What?'

'Why don't you kill mine, and I'll kill yours. Like in *Strangers On A Train*. The Hitchcock movie.'

Wright shook his head in disgust. As far as he was concerned, his ex-wife's vindictiveness was no laughing matter.

Phil Evans walked over, grim faced. 'Hey, did you guys hear about Clive Edmunds?'

'Yeah? What did he do?' asked Reid. 'Break the habit of a lifetime and buy a round?'

'He's dead, Tommy.'

Reid's face fell. 'Shit. What happened?'

'Choked on his vomit. Died in his sleep.'

'Bloody hell.' Reid looked across at Wright. 'Better make sure I kip on my stomach from now on.'

Evans glared at Reid. 'Gerry Hunter's been on the phone. The funeral's next Friday. The Super thinks we should be represented.'

'Is Newton going?' asked Wright.

'Nah. Budget meeting with Railtrack. Can either of you two make it?'

Reid and Wright shook their heads.

'Great, that makes a grand total of zero so far. At this rate I'm going to have to go myself.'

'Well, it's his own fault for being such an unlikeable bastard,' said Reid.

'Come on, Tommy, he's dead,' said Evans.

'I'll go,' said Wright.

'You sure?' asked Evans.

'Yeah. He was a cop, he deserves to have someone there from the office.'

'Cheers, Nick. I'll get the details for you.' He went over to ask Hubbard and Lloyd.

'I can't make you out,' said Reid. 'You hated him. He was forever taking the piss out of you.'

Wright shrugged. 'Professional courtesy.'

'You're a soft bastard.'

'Yeah, maybe you're right.'

Reid sipped his coffee. He groaned. 'Okay, you can stop looking at me like that.'

Wright raised an eyebrow. 'Like what?'

'Like a puppy that wants to go for a walk. Okay, I'll come with you. Just don't expect me to throw myself on the coffin.'

'You're a soft bastard, too,' said Wright, grinning.

Reid leaned forward. 'Maybe. But if you tell anyone, I'll kill you.'

Gerald Manville rolled over on to his back and stared up at the ceiling fan which was doing its best to keep the air circulating in the windowless room. He raised his arm and looked at his wristwatch. He'd booked the room for two hours and he still had fifteen minutes left. He dropped his arm and groaned. It was his fifth day in Pattaya and he was exhausted. Sun, sea, sand and sex – Thailand was the perfect holiday destination, especially for a man with needs like Manville's. Three times a year he flew over to the Land of Smiles, to enjoy the sort of sex he could only dream of back in Plymouth. He had hit the bars within hours of getting off the plane from Heathrow, and since then the days and nights had blurred into one long session of sex and drink, with the occasional visit to a restaurant for food.

He turned on to his side and ran his finger down the silky smooth back of the figure next to him. Thai skin was so unbelievably soft, like silk. Manville kissed the boy between the shoulderblades, revelling in the salty taste of the thirteen-year-old skin. He felt himself grow hard again but he hadn't the inclination to start something he didn't have time to finish. They'd soon be knocking on his door to let him know that his time was up.

He patted the boy on the hip and went over to the shower. He rinsed himself clean and wrapped a threadbare white towel around his waist. When he went back into the bedroom, the boy was already dressed in a T-shirt and shorts and was sitting on the edge of the bed. Manville picked up his jeans and pulled out his wallet. He gave the boy a five-hundred-baht note. The boy smiled and put his hands together in a 'wai' of thanks, bowing as if he was saying his prayers, then he scampered over to the door and rushed out.

Manville smiled to himself as he dressed. He loved

Thailand. He loved the food, he loved the climate, and he loved the boys. He had another six years before he could retire from his job on a halfway decent pension, then he'd be on the first plane out with a one-way ticket. He'd have more than enough money to rent a small house with a garden, close to the beach, to run a car and to buy himself all the companionship he needed. Six more years. It seemed like a lifetime.

He checked himself in the bathroom mirror, then left the room. The door opened out on to a small concrete area across which a thick purple curtain had been drawn. Many of the customers at the short-time hotel arrived in cars, and the curtain hid their vehicles from prying eyes. Manville had walked from the nearby bar so he put his hands in his pockets and strolled out into the sunshine. Two chambermaids in blue uniforms giggled as they hurried by with a cart piled high with sheets and towels.

Manville decided he'd have a drink on the beach before heading back to his own hotel. He walked along the narrow street that led to the beach road, shading his eyes from the bright afternoon sun with the flat of his hand. Two Thai boys sitting on a low wall smiled up at him hopefully. Manville had already been with one of the boys, but he didn't recognise the other. Neither was much older than fourteen. Manville arranged to meet them both later that night and gave them each a one-hundred-baht note to seal the deal. Both boys gave him a formal 'wai' and he was almost tempted to go back to the short-time hotel with them there and then.

He crossed the road and walked down on to the beach, where Manville bought a copy of the *Bangkok Post* from a newspaper vendor. Spread out across the vendor's table were a number of Thai newspapers, and several had photographs of a corpse splashed across them. The Thai newspapers were even worse than their British counterparts when it came to running blood and gore. Manville bent over the table to get a better look.

The largest of the photographs was of a light-skinned bearded man, his mouth a bloody mass and his eyes staring lifelessly at the camera lens. It looked as if the man was lying on his back, but as he looked more closely Manville realised that he was actually spreadeagled against a wall and that the picture had been twisted around for reasons of space. There was something familiar about the corpse. Not the face, but the injuries and the position of the body.

Manville frowned and gathered up copies of all the papers that carried the photograph, paid the vendor and went across the sand to a row of deckchairs. He sat down under a faded red and yellow striped umbrella and spread the Thai newspapers over the sand. An old Thai woman with skin like an old leather briefcase came over and asked him what he wanted to drink. Manville asked for a Singha beer, his eyes fixed on the newspapers. He flicked through one. There were more photographs on the inside pages. In one of them, a playing card was impaled on the victim's chest. Manville lifted the paper up and stared at the card. He couldn't make out what it was.

'Hello, Jack,' said a voice.

Manville looked up. It was Poonsak, an eighteen-year-old Thai boy whom Manville had known for several years. Poonsak knew him as Jack, as did most of the underage boys whom Manville took back to the short-time hotel. Poonsak had grown too old for most of the sex-tourists who visited Pattaya, and now made a living procuring younger boys.

'Hello, Poonsak. Come here, will you?' Poonsak squatted down next to Manville's deckchair. 'Translate this for me, please.' Manville tapped the headline and story around the picture of the brutalised corpse.

Poonsak put his head on one side as he read through the story. 'It say farang was killed. Someone cut him, very bad.' He looked up but saw from Manville's face that he expected more. He looked down at the paper again and tugged at his lower lip as he read. 'His name is Eric Horvitz. He's an American. He had a place for children with no parents.'

'An orphanage?'

'Yes. An orphanage. He was found in the *haung tai din*. The basement. The basement of the orphanage. He was tortured, with knives. Somebody cut off his dick and put it in his mouth.' Poonsak pulled a face. He peered at the photograph as if to confirm that that was indeed what had been done to the man, and grimaced.

'What does it say about the playing card?'

Poonsak read through the article. 'An ace of spades. It was stuck on a knife that had been stuck into his chest. Police say they think it was maybe a drugs killing.'

'Why do they say that?'

Poonsak read more, then shook his head. 'It not say, Jack.'

'When did it happen?'

'The body was found yesterday. They not know when he was killed.'

Manville flicked through the *Bangkok Post*. The English-language newspaper was generally less salacious than its Thai rivals. It seldom printed gory photographs and tended to hold back on the details of murders and rapes. He found the murder story on page three, with no photograph. There were only a dozen paragraphs giving details of the victim and his orphanage. The playing card was mentioned right at the end of the story, but no significance was attributed to it.

'Did you know him?' asked Poonsak.

The old lady brought Manville's beer to him on a battered tray. He took it and smiled his thanks. The woman gave him an ice-cold wet towel and he wiped his face and neck before handing it back to her with another smile.

'No,' said Manville. 'No, I didn't know him.'

Poonsak stood up, brushing sand from the knees of his jeans. 'Do you want me to get you a friend tonight? I know a new boy, only just arrived in Pattaya. Almost a virgin.'

Manville chuckled. According to Poonsak, virtually every boy he supplied was as pure as the driven snow. 'No, thank you, Poonsak. I'm fixed up tonight.'

Poonsak smiled. Manville patted him on the back of the leg. He really was a delightful boy. Pity he'd grown so quickly. Poonsak's smile widened and Manville realised he'd misunderstood the gesture. Manville shook his head and took away his hand. The teenager shrugged and wandered away towards a group of Scandinavian tourists who were paddling in the surf.

Manville gathered up the newspapers. He knew now why the photographs had seemed familiar. There'd been a similar murder back in England a month or so previously. A circular had passed across Manville's desk from a British Transport Police detective describing a torture-killing in South London and requesting details of any similar murders. Manville had drawn a blank and had replied on behalf of the Devon and Cornwall Constabulary. There had been several vicious drugs-related killings in Plymouth but the injuries didn't match those of the London murder, and no playing cards were involved.

Manville began tearing out the articles. He'd put them in the post when he got back to the UK. That'd be the best and safest way of passing on the information. He didn't want to have to explain why an unmarried chief inspector was holidaying alone in Thailand.

D ean Burrow walked across the grass, his hands thrust deep into the pockets of his cashmere overcoat. Over to his right two Secret Service agents stood by a nondescript saloon parked behind his limousine. A third agent walked some distance behind him. Washington at night wasn't the safest of cities, but Burrow had wanted some fresh air and the Memorial was as good a place as any to meet Jody Meacher. Sirens wailed in the distance, three police cars by the sound of it. Burrow shivered. It was a full moon but he only saw glimpses of it as thick grey clouds scudded across the night sky. He stepped on to the cobbled path that led down to the Memorial and walked by the metal lecterns containing the books listing all those who had died during the Vietnam War. Not long after the slabs of black marble had been erected, Burrow had spent hours poring over the books, checking that the names of the friends he'd lost during the war were included, then he'd gone to the Memorial and satisfied himself that their names were carved there and that they'd been spelled correctly. There had been no omissions, no mistakes.

The black marble glistened in what little moonlight managed to filter through the clouds. It was the simplicity of the Memorial that made it so effective. Just a list of names. Burrow wondered what the tourists made of it, the Europeans and the Asians and the Arabs who came to photograph it because it was on the list of things to see in Washington, a ten-minute stop on a tour of the nation's capital. To them it could be nothing more than a list of names, but to Burrow and to the rest of the nation's veterans, it was something far more poignant, far more meaningful. It represented legs blown off by landmines, heads splattered by snipers' bullets, chests crushed by exploding mortars. Countless images of dismemberment and death flashed through Burrow's mind as he walked past the marble slabs and their silent roll call.

A lone figure stood midway down the Memorial. There was no mistaking Jody Meacher's massive profile, swathed in a dark overcoat the size of a small tent. Meacher continued to stare at the Memorial as Burrow approached. 'What a waste,' he said.

'The war, or the Memorial?' asked Burrow.

'The deaths,' said Meacher.

'What would you have done, Jody? Negotiated?'

Meacher shook his head. 'Who knows, Senator? Twenty-twenty hindsight is a wondrous thing. What's past is past. It's the future we have to be concerned about.'

He held out his hand, his eyes still on the Memorial. Burrow reached inside his coat and took out the Polaroid photograph with a gloved hand and gave it to Meacher. Meacher studied it for several seconds, then pocketed it. Burrow opened his mouth to protest but Meacher shook his head.

'Leave it with me, Senator.' His hand reappeared from his pocket and he stroked his greying beard thoughtfully. 'Eric Horvitz, you said?'

'That was the name on the UPS package. And it's him in the photograph. Whoever it is, they're not going to stop, Jody. They're going to keep—'

'It's going to stop, Senator,' interrupted Meacher. 'Don't worry.'

The Secret Service agent who was following the senator had stopped some fifty feet away, though his head still swivelled from side to side and periodically he mumbled into his hidden microphone.

Burrow arched his back and rubbed his knuckles into the base of his spine. 'I should get more exercise,' he complained.

'We all should,' agreed Meacher. 'But we don't always do what's good for us.'

Burrow began to walk along the path, and Meacher fell into step beside him.

'The Vice President will be stepping down within weeks, Senator.'

Burrow's eyebrows shot up and he stopped walking. 'You know that for sure?'

'From the horse's mouth. Well, the horse's doctor's mouth. The cancer is growing faster than they'd thought and the Vice President wants to spend more time with his family.'

'Jesus,' said Burrow, shaking his head sadly.

'Don't feel too sorry for the man, Senator. At least he knows it's coming; at least he's got time to put his affairs in order and say goodbye properly. Most of us don't get the chance.'

Burrow began walking again. 'I was at Kristine Ross's funeral today,' he said.

'It had to be done, Senator. There's too much at stake.'

'I know, I know.' They walked in silence for a while, their breath feathering in the night air. 'How many so far?' Burrow asked eventually.

'Four. Including your secretary.'

'Who were the other three?'

Meacher hesitated as if reluctant to answer the question, then shrugged almost imperceptibly. 'A journalist and his wife. And a policeman.'

Burrow put a hand up to his forehead. 'A policeman? Oh God.'

'Policeman, secretary, dental hygienist, their career path doesn't make any difference, Senator. All that matters is that this doesn't get out. The policeman was getting close.'

'How were they killed?'

'Need to know, Senator. And you don't need to know.'

'That may be, Jody. But I want to know.'

'It's not in your best interest.'

'Damn you,' hissed Burrow. 'I deserve to know. He's doing it for me.'

The two men stopped walking again. Meacher stared at Burrow for several seconds, then nodded. 'It was an accident,' he said. 'I mean it was made to look like an accident. No one will ever know different.'

'And it was the same guy who killed Kristine?' Meacher nodded. 'Who is he, this man?'

Meacher turned away from the senator and began walking towards the Secret Service agent. The agent mumbled into his hidden microphone and headed back along the path. 'That really *is* need to know,' said Meacher.

'At least tell me something about him.'

'He was in Special Forces. His specialty was to make his assassinations look like accidents. Falls, car crashes, food poisoning. Now he works for me and a few other individuals who have need of his particular skills.'

The senator looked incredulous. 'The army has people like that?'

'Hopefully you'll never know half of what goes on in the military,' said Meacher. 'There are black departments in the Pentagon that answer to no one. Not even the President.'

'So how does this guy end up working for you?'

'A friend of his was killed in Saudi Arabia. Iranian suicide bomber, remember? Killed a dozen Marines.'

'I remember.'

'This guy found one of the men who'd planned the operation and tortured him until he gave up the names of the other two men in his cell. Then he doctored their car, fixed it so it'd crash when it hit sixty miles an hour. Worked perfectly, but when the car spun out of control it crashed into a Mercedes being driven by a member of the Saudi royal family. A prince. The prince ended up in hospital with a broken back. The military pulled their man out and sent him back to the States.

'How much have you told him?'

'The bare minimum to ensure that he gets the job done, Senator.'

They left the memorial behind and walked by the lecterns. The Secret Service agent was now off to their left. 'And what is his job, Jody?'

'His instructions are to take care of anyone who discovers your secret. It's open ended.'

'So he'll go to Bangkok?'

'Once we're sure that the London situation is under control, yes.'

They walked by the bronze sculpture of three war-weary American soldiers. 'What if whoever it is comes after me, Jody?'

'You're a US senator. You're well protected.'

'So why am I being sent these pictures?'

'To scare you.'

'It's working.' They walked together back to the road. 'Can I give you a lift, Jody?' asked Burrow, nodding at his limousine.

'No, thank you, Senator. I'm going to walk for a while.'

'Are you sure? Washington's a dangerous place at night.'

Meacher smiled thinly. 'Not just at night time, Senator.' The two men shook hands, then Meacher walked away as gracefully as a galleon under full sail.

Nick Wright lay on the folded-out sofabed, staring up at the ceiling. It had been one hell of a day. In between handling his regular caseload, his efforts to track down May Eckhardt had come to nothing. Neither the managing agents nor the owner of the Maida Vale flat had had a forwarding address for her. He'd contacted British Telecom but an extensive search hadn't produced a new telephone number for a May Eckhardt anywhere within the United Kingdom. He'd spent the best part of two hours trying to obtain a

National Insurance number or tax reference for her, but without success. He wasn't sure what else he could do.

He sat up and ran his hands through his unkempt hair. The cardboard box containing his late father's train set was by the side of the sofa. Wright had tried to speak to Sean on the phone more than a dozen times but Janie had insisted that he wasn't at home. First he was at school, then at piano practice, then at a friend's house. After nine o'clock in the evening all he got was the engaged tone. Janie had left the phone off the hook.

Clive Edmunds's funeral had taken place late in the afternoon, and it had been a depressing affair, hardly better attended than the funeral of Max Eckhardt. Wright and Reid had represented the British Transport Police, and there had been a dozen Met officers, including Gerry Hunter. There had been no relatives, and no grieving widow.

Wright swung his legs off the sofabed and went over to the stereo. He put a Muddy Waters CD on and turned the volume down so as not to disturb Reid in the adjoining bedroom. His harmonica was on the shelf above the CDs and he stood by the fireplace, playing softly. He figured that if he was feeling depressed, he might as well play the blues.

Len Kruse was midway through his second set of press-ups when the telephone rang. He locked his elbows. Naked except for his khaki boxer shorts, his body was bathed in sweat, though his breathing was steady, his chest barely moving. He supported his weight with his right arm and reached over with his left to pick up the telephone from the bedside table. 'Yes?' he said.

'Are you alone?' It was Jody Meacher.

'Yes.' Kruse lowered himself so that his chest was only inches from the carpet. His arm muscles bulged but there was no sign of strain on his face.

'There's been another event,' said Meacher. 'In Bangkok.'

Kruse pushed himself up until his arm was rigid. 'Can you send me details?'

'You'll have them tomorrow. Have things stabilised in London?'

'Everything's under control. I'll book my ticket.'

'It might be a good idea to get a visa for Vietnam while you're in London. Just in case.'

'Agreed.' Kruse replaced the receiver and continued his press-ups, increasing the pace until the muscles in his arm began to burn. The pain didn't bother Kruse. In fact, he welcomed it.

G erry Hunter parked his car as close as he could get to Clive Edmunds's house. None of the houses in the street had garages, and it was early evening so he had to walk almost a hundred yards to the front door. Hunter had been surprised on two fronts when the solicitor had telephoned: surprised that Clive had actually made a will, and even more surprised that he'd made Hunter joint executor of it.

For a man whose life appeared to be in a constant state of disorganisation, Clive had organised his death down to the last detail. He'd even paid for a burial plot in a graveyard in North London and listed the hymns that he wanted to be played at his funeral. He had a hefty mortgage on his house, but even so, his assets, including two life insurance policies, came to more than a hundred and fifty thousand pounds, the bulk of which he'd left to his three nieces in Australia. The will stipulated that Hunter take anything from the house that he wanted and arrange to have the rest sold or given to Oxfam.

Hunter had put off going there for as long as he could, but the solicitor had called to say that a buyer had been found for the house so Clive's belongings had to be cleared out. He slotted the key into the lock and pushed open the door. The air was stale and Hunter grimaced. He closed the door behind him and stood in silence for several minutes. The red light on the answering machine was blinking and Hunter realised that he'd forgotten to have the telephone disconnected. He pushed the 'play' button. It was a girl from a local video rental store, asking Clive to return a video. *Apocalypse Now*.

Hunter went through into the sitting room and knelt down in front of Clive's video recorder. He rifled through the cassettes stacked on top of the recorder but most of them were tapes that Clive had recorded himself. There was no sign of *Apocalypse Now*. He pressed the 'eject' button on the video recorder but no tape emerged from the slot. Hunter drummed his fingers on the top of the machine and looked around the room. He stood up. His fingertips were smeared with dust and he wiped them on the back of the sofa. He checked the sideboard, the bookcase, and the cupboard on which

Edmunds kept framed photographs of his parents and his brother's family. There was no videotape.

He went back into the hall and replayed the message. The girl didn't say which shop she worked for, but a quick flick through the *Yellow Pages* turned up four within half a mile. The third one that Hunter called had Clive down as a member and the man who answered the phone confirmed that he hadn't returned the video.

'There's a big fine,' said the man gruffly. 'And it's growing by two quid a day.'

'When did he take it out?' Hunter asked.

'Ten days ago.'

Hunter counted backwards in his head. 'Thursday?'

'Yeah. Thursday.'

Thursday was the day Clive died. 'Are you sure?'

'Of course I'm sure, it's all on computer. Now when am I going to get it back?'

'I'll see if I can find it for you,' said Hunter.

'Why can't Mr Edmunds tell you where it is?'

'Because Mr Edmunds is dead,' said Hunter, and slammed down the receiver.

He took Clive's keyring out of his pocket. His car keys were on it. Hunter tossed them in the air and caught them. Maybe Clive had left the cassette in his car. He went outside and found the car but there was no sign of the video cassette. Hunter went back to the house and sat down on the sofa with his feet on the coffee table, deep in thought. Assuming Clive had come straight home with the video, and assuming he'd watched it before going to bed, then the cassette should still be in the house. And if it wasn't, then somebody else must have taken it. But there were no signs of a break-in, and any self-respecting burglar would have taken the television and video recorder. Hunter couldn't imagine why anyone would want to steal a rental copy of *Apocalypse Now* and nothing else.

Wright put two cups of coffee down in front of his partner and blew on his fingers. 'That coffee's getting hotter and hotter,' he said. He picked up his own cup again and carried it over to his desk. A large white envelope was propped up on his computer terminal.

'I got your mail for you,' said Reid.

'You're all heart,' said Wright. He sat down, sipped his coffee, and picked up the envelope.

Reid looked across at the envelope in Wright's hands. 'What is it, a birthday card? It's not your birthday, is it?'

'No,' said Wright, ripping it open.

Wright pulled out the contents of the envelope. It was a collection of newspaper cuttings. He spread them out. Most of them were in a strange language, the letters totally different to the English alphabet with hardly any spaces between words. 'What the hell's this?' he muttered.

Reid stood up and peered over at the pieces of newspaper. 'What is it, Indian? Arabic?'

'No idea,' said Wright. Several of the cuttings had grainy photographs on them. Photographs of a corpse. Wright looked carefully at the pictures. 'My God,' he said. 'Look at this, Tommy.'

Reid hauled himself out of his chair and stood behind Wright. He looked down over his shoulder.

Wright pointed at one of the photographs. 'It's a playing card,' said Wright.

'Is it an ace of spades?' asked Reid.

Wright held the cutting closer to his face. 'I can't tell.' He handed it to his partner. 'What do you think?'

As Reid scrutinised the picture, Wright picked up the only cutting that was in English. It had been cut out to include the name of the newspaper and the date. The *Bangkok Post*. Twelve days ago.

'Thailand,' said Wright. 'They're Thai newspapers.' He picked up the envelope. The postmark was Plymouth.

'I can't see what card it is,' said Reid. He picked up another of the cuttings.

Wright scanned the *Bangkok Post* article. 'It's the same,' he said.

'What's the same?'

'A man in his forties, tortured and killed. His dick cut off and shoved in his mouth.' He reached the last paragraph. 'And impaled in his chest . . . an ace of spades.'

Reid stepped back theatrically. 'Coincidence? I think not!' he boomed.

Wright glared at his partner. 'Come on, Tommy. This is important.'

Reid went back to his desk. 'It's Thailand, Nick. It's the other side of the world. What do you think's going on? A serial killer who's collecting frequent-flyer miles?'

Wright waved the cutting in the air. 'It's the same man. He's killed twice. And he's going to kill again.'

'You don't know that.'

Wright stood up. 'There are times when you really piss me off,' he said coldly. Reid shrugged and sipped his coffee. Wright wanted to say more but he could see that he'd be wasting his time. He stormed off, the cutting clutched in his right hand.

Newton's secretary looked up from her typing as Wright walked up to the door to the superintendent's office. 'Yes, Nick, is there something I can do for you?' she asked.

Wright stopped dead. 'I have to see him, Nancy.'

'He's in a meeting,' she said.

'When will he be free?'

She looked at him over the top of her gold-framed glasses. 'I don't know,' she said. 'Would you like me to call you when he is?'

Wright looked at the cutting, then at the closed door. 'I'll wait,' he said.

'Nick, I don't know how long he's going to be.'

'I'll wait,' he repeated.

There were three hard-backed chairs against the wall facing Nancy's desk. Wright sat on the middle one. Nancy continued to watch him for several seconds, then she pushed her glasses higher up her nose with her forefinger and resumed her typing. Wright reread the cutting as he waited. The victim was an American, Eric Horvitz. He ran an orphanage in Bangkok and he'd been discovered in the basement. There weren't many details of what had been done to the body, but what there were tallied with the corpse that had been found in the tunnel near Battersea.

The door to Newton's office opened and two men wearing suits and carrying briefcases walked out. Wright stood up but the door closed firmly. He looked across at Nancy expectantly, who gave an impatient wave of her hand.

'Go on, go on,' she said.

'Thanks, Nancy,' said Wright. He knocked on the door and opened it without waiting for a reply.

The superintendent was dipping a biscuit into his cup of tea and he looked up guiltily. As he did so, half of the biscuit broke off. Newton stared distastefully at the cup. 'Yes, Nick?'

'Sir, I've had a lead on the tunnel murder.' He gave the cutting to Newton.

The superintendent took a pair of reading glasses from his shirt pocket and put them on. He read the cutting, grimaced, and gave it back to Wright. 'So?'

'So I was right. It's a serial killer.'

'No, Nick. It's two similar murders, five thousand miles apart.'

'Both with an ace of spades left on the corpse? Come on, sir. It's the same killer. It has to be. Sir, this is a break. I want to follow it up.'

'Nick, the simple fact is, we just don't have the resources to pursue this lead. We answer to different masters here, masters who are ultimately responsible to shareholders. It's all about money, Nick. I'm sorry, but that's the way it is.'

'So profits come before justice?'

'That's not what I'm saying,' said Newton. 'I'm saying that I have to operate within a strict budget. I can't afford to send you halfway around the world to follow up a lead that might prove to be nothing.'

Wright reached over and took the cutting back. 'Let me go over there, sir. I just know the murders are related, and I know I can crack the case. Just one week, and I promise I'll get a result. It'll reflect well on the BTP, you know.'

Newton hesitated for a few seconds, then leaned forward. 'Okay, you can go, but the Met boys will have to know about it, and I want you reporting back anything you find out immediately. You've got exactly one week.'

Wright punched his fist in the air. 'Thanks, sir.'

'Just be careful, Nick. And for God's sake, don't get into trouble out there. Thailand can be a dangerous place.'

There was something about the Oval Office that inspired respect, even when its occupant was less than presidential. Some of the most important decisions facing mankind had been taken in the office: wars had been started and ended, economies had been ruined or revived, men had seized the opportunity for greatness or lied their way into infamy. Dean Burrow could sense the history in the room, so strongly that he could virtually smell it, even above the oversweet aftershave of the man who stepped towards him, arm outstretched.

'Dean, good to see you,' said the President, smiling easily. The word on the cocktail circuit was that the presidential smile had cost somewhere in the region of thirty thousand dollars and that there was now so much metal in his mouth that the Secret Service had had to reduce the sensitivity of the metal detectors at the entrances to the White House. They shook hands. The President's grip was firm, his hand dry. 'How's Patricia?'

'She's fine, Mr President. Thank you.'

'And Bill? I gather he's top of his class at Yale.'

'We're both very proud of him.'

'You should bring him in for lunch some time. I'd like to meet him.'

'He'd be honoured, Mr President.'

The President patted Burrow on the shoulder and guided him to a chair. 'You're looking good, Dean. Real good.' The President gestured to his own ample waistline. 'That's the big drawback in this job: there's never enough time for exercise.' He sat down in a chair facing Burrow and crossed his legs. 'Your health is the most important thing, Dean. Nothing else matters. Money, power, none of it means anything if you haven't got your health.'

Burrow nodded. The meeting had been called at short notice, and there could be only one reason for it.

'Glenn's condition is deteriorating, Dean. He wants to throw in the towel now and spend more time with Elaine. She lost her father, you know.'

'Yes, Mr President.'

'Hell of a business, prostate cancer. Not an easy way to die.' The President shivered. 'I've asked him to hang on in there for two more weeks, until the China trade talks are out of the way. Glenn's always gone down well in Beijing, being fluent in Mandarin and all. He's agreed. God bless him for that.'

The President brought his sky-blue eyes to bear on Burrow. The effect was almost hypnotic and while the contact lasted it felt as if Burrow was the centre of the President's universe, that nothing else mattered to him other than the man sitting opposite him. It was something all the best leaders seemed to be able to do at will, a skill that Burrow himself was working to acquire.

'Forty-eight's a good age to be Vice President, Dean. Can you handle it?'

'Absolutely,' said Burrow. He felt a surge of elation which he fought to keep under control. He'd known he was front-runner, but he'd been counting chickens right up until the moment the President said the words. He wanted to leap up out of his chair and punch the air, but he confined himself to a tight, almost regretful, smile. When all was said and done, it was still a case of dead man's shoes.

'The timing's perfect from your point of view,' the President continued. 'Economy's on the up and up, the Middle East is as quiet as it's ever going to get, no dark clouds on the horizons, none that I'm aware of anyway. Two years' time, you could have this job.'

Burrow said nothing. He wanted the job more than he'd ever wanted anything in his life, but burning ambition was something best kept hidden, especially when the only obstacle to your desire was sitting just a few feet away.

'Two weeks today I'm going to be in Washington – I plan to announce it then. Clear your schedule for the day, and the day after. You're going to have the world's media on your tail. I'd appreciate it if you'd hold off from telling Patricia. You know how the girls love to talk.' He stood up and extended his hand again. The second handshake was as firm and dry as the first. Burrow could feel that his own palms were damp with sweat.

'Congratulations, Dean.' He put a reassuring hand on Burrow's shoulder. 'It's going to be good to have you on the team.'

'I won't let you down, Mr President.'

The President chuckled. 'I'm relieved to hear that.' He let go of Burrow's shoulder, but continued to shake his hand for a few seconds more. 'It goes without saying that I've had you checked out, Dean. And it also goes without saying that you passed with flying colours. First-class war record, which is more than I can say for myself, huh? Never been caught taking drugs, and other than a handful of parking tickets you're clean as a whistle.' He fixed his eyes on Burrow again. 'There was that business with your secretary, of course, but you handled that well.'

Burrow felt his chest go suddenly cold and he caught his breath. He forced himself to keep smiling. 'Secretary?' he said. Did he know? Did the President know about Kristine Ross? And if he did, why in God's name wasn't he being taken away in chains instead of being given the second most powerful job in America? The President was known as a vindictive man, but why on earth would he dangle the prize and then snatch it away?

'Mary-Louise Wilson,' said the President. 'She's been as good as gold since the . . . operation. She seems to have settled nicely in Cleveland.'

Burrow suppressed a sigh. The abortion. 'Yes, Jody Meacher paid her off.'

'And you haven't seen her since? She hasn't approached you?'

'She got what she wanted. There are no records, no written proof. In a worst-case scenario it would be her word against mine, and I doubt that the media would use it without some sort of corroboration. I can assure you there is no evidence that would back up her story – Meacher took care of that. Besides, it was a long time ago.'

The President nodded. 'And you can give me your cast-iron guarantee that no other skeletons are going to emerge from some long-forgotten closet?'

'Absolutely, Mr President.' Burrow returned the President's gaze and flashed him a confident smile, despite the images that flitted through his mind, whirling and twisting like bats at dusk. Bodies crucified, with bloody mouths and playing cards impaled on their chests.

'Because if there are, we should clear them out now.'

Burrow shook his head. 'I am as pure as the driven snow, Mr President.'

G erry Hunter tossed his jacket on to the back of his sofa and knelt down in front of his video recorder. He slotted in the tape. He'd had to visit three video rental stores before finding one that had a copy of *Apocalypse Now*. The store manager was a bearded man in his late twenties who had refused to allow Hunter to take away the tape until Hunter had filled out an application form and provided him with two pieces of identification. Hunter had shown him his warrant card and told him that he needed to borrow the tape as part of a murder investigation, but the manager had been adamant: no membership, no tape.

Hunter pressed the 'play' button and sat down on the sofa. The telephone rang and he cursed. He leaned over and picked up the phone.

It was Janie Wright. 'Hiya, honey,' she said. 'What are you doing?'

'I'm watching a video,' said Hunter, his eyes on the screen.

'Come and watch it with me,' she said.

'It's work related,' he said.

'That doesn't matter,' she said. 'Come on, Gerry. I haven't seen you for two days.' Hunter looked at his watch. 'I'll cook,' she said. 'Pasta.'

'It's late, Janie.'

'Please,' she whined. 'Please, please, please.' He could picture her pouting and swinging her shoulders from side to side, playing the little girl lost like she always did when she wanted to get her own way. It might have been attractive when she was in her teens, but Hunter was starting to find it irritating in a woman in her early thirties.

Hunter knew that it was pointless to argue with Janie when she was in one of her demanding moods. Besides, she was right, he hadn't seen her for two days, he'd been so tied up with work. 'Okay, I'll be there in twenty minutes,' he said.

'I'll open a bottle of wine,' she said.

Hunter retrieved the video cassette, grabbed his jacket, and drove to Janie's house.

He parked behind her car and walked up the driveway. She opened the door before he reached it. She was wearing a pink silk dressing gown and full make-up and she'd obviously just brushed her hair. Wright thought she looked gorgeous, and he knew immediately that she'd lied about the pasta. She was dressed for the bedroom, not the kitchen. Hunter kissed her on the cheek and caught her favourite scent. Her arms slid around his neck and she kissed him on the mouth, pressing her body hard against his. Hunter could taste wine as her tongue slid against his teeth.

'Thank you for coming,' she said when she eventually broke away.

He held up the video cassette. 'I have to watch this,' he said.

'Right now?'

'Right now. It won't take long.'

She took it off him and examined it. '*Apocalypse Now*?

That's at least two hours long, isn't it?' She held it behind her back. 'Bed first.'

'Video first,' Hunter insisted.

Janie could see that she wasn't going to get her way, so she gave him the video and flounced off to the sitting room. Hunter followed her and loaded the video into the recorder. He dropped down next to Janie on the overstuffed sofa opposite the television. A half empty bottle of wine and two glasses were on the coffee table next to Janie. The screen flickered into life and Hunter picked up the remote control and fast-forwarded through the piracy warning and trailers for other movies.

Janie picked up her glass and sipped her wine. She put her glass down and slid across Hunter, straddling him. Her dressing gown rode up her thighs as she put her hands on either side of his face and pressed her lips against his. Hunter tried to protest but as he opened his mouth wine spilled between his lips and he had to swallow. Janie thrust her tongue deeper into his mouth and ground her backside against his groin. Wine dribbled from between their lips and ran down Hunter's chin. Janie took her hands away from his face and wriggled out of her robe. She was naked underneath.

Hunter put his hands on her shoulders and pushed her away. She was panting and there was an almost manic gleam in her eyes. 'Janie,' he protested.

'Do as you're told,' she said. She seized his wrists and placed his hands on her full breasts. The nipples were hard and he couldn't stop himself caressing them. She smiled, sensing that she'd won, and slipped her hands down to his groin, rubbing and probing and making him hard.

'Where's Sean?' he asked.

'Sean's in bed, asleep.' She raised herself up and undid his belt. Her right hand found him and Hunter gasped. Janie pressed her mouth against his again and as she kissed him she slid him inside her.

The British Airways flight to Bangkok was full and Nick Wright was lucky to get a window seat. He was seated next to two Australian backpackers who seemed to be intent on drinking as much free beer and wine as they could. They were pleasant enough but there was no chance of Wright getting any sleep. Two hours into the flight he decided that he might as well join them in their binge, and together they downed the best part of a case of lager by the time they landed in Thailand.

It took more than an hour for Wright to clear immigration. The queues were long and the brown-uniformed immigration officials seemed in no hurry to process the arrivals. His suitcase was waiting for him on the carousel, so he collected it, handed in his Customs form and headed through the 'Nothing To Declare' exit.

Several Thai men in blue blazers and black slacks tried to shepherd him towards counters offering hotel and limousine services but the Australians had already warned him that they were overpriced. They'd told him to walk on to the public taxi counter and given him the names and addresses of several reasonably priced hotels to go along with those he'd already picked from the *Lonely Planet* guide to Thailand.

At the public taxi counter a young girl in a white blouse

tried to persuade him to accept a non-metered taxi, but the backpackers had told Wright to refuse and to insist on a taxi with a meter. Reluctantly, the girl handed him a chit stamped with 'Taxi Meter'. On it she'd written his destination, one of the hotels that the backpackers had recommended. It was off Sukhumvit Road, a mile or so from the orphanage where Eric Horvitz had worked.

A driver materialised at Wright's shoulder, a bulky Thai in his forties wearing a blue T-shirt and beige slacks. He took the chit, picked up Wright's suitcase and led Wright across the crowded terminal building. Wright stopped to change the sterling he'd brought with him into Thai baht then they walked outside.

He was hit by a wall of humidity that took his breath away. Beads of sweat gathered on his face and he wiped his forehead with his sleeve. He slipped off the blazer he was wearing.

The driver grinned at his discomfort as he held open the door of the white Toyota. 'First time in Bangkok?' he asked.

'First time in Asia,' said Wright. In fact, it was his first time outside Europe. Janie loved France and Italy, and apart from a couple of weeks in Spain, they'd spent most of their holidays there.

The driver put the suitcase in the boot, climbed into the front seat and drove off. Wright leaned forward and pointed at the meter. 'Meter,' he said.

The driver shook his head. 'Not working.'

The backpackers had told Wright that it was common practice to claim that the meter was out of order so that the drivers could negotiate a higher fare. Wright jabbed his finger at the meter. 'Use the meter,' he said.

The driver shrugged and pressed a button on the front of the meter. Red numbers glowed. 'You want massage?' said the driver.

'No,' said Wright.

'You want girl?'

'No.'

'Boy?'

Wright laughed and the driver laughed along with him.

The traffic was heavy and they soon slowed to a crawl. Cars and trucks seemed to stretch towards the horizon. In the distance tower blocks glinted in the early morning sun. The light was dazzlingly bright, a stark contrast to the grey drizzle he'd left behind in England. Wright settled back and dozed, his head resting against the window.

It took them almost two hours to get to the hotel, which as far as he could judge was only ten miles from the airport. Wright had become so used to the taxi stopping and starting that he didn't realise they'd arrived until the driver twisted around in his seat and pointed, saying, 'We here.'

Wright stretched and rubbed his eyes. They were in a narrow street in front of a five-storey building that had once been white but that was now a grubby grey. Streaks of rust ran down from leaking pipes and the windows were covered with a film of dust. Wright pulled out his wallet, paid the driver and carried his suitcase into reception.

A security guard in a blue uniform was fast asleep on a grey sofa, his peaked cap over his face, and the young girl at the reception desk had her head on her arms and was snoring softly. Overhead a wooden-bladed fan turned slowly and in the corner of the reception area a small television showed a Thai news programme, the sound muted. The girl opened her eyes and looked up at him sleepily. She smiled, reached under the desk for a check-in form and slid it across to him. She smiled again and put her head back on her arms.

Wright filled in the form, and just as he finished the girl opened her eyes and handed him a key. She was snoring once more as he picked up his suitcase and headed for the stairs.

His room was on the third floor, clean but basic with a double bed, two cane chairs and a small circular table, a mirrored built-in wardrobe, a television and a small refrigerator. Wright heaved his suitcase on top of the wardrobe and sat down on the bed.

Bangkok was six hours ahead of London, but despite not sleeping on the plane he didn't feel tired. There was a telephone by the bed and a *Yellow Pages*. He flicked through it but it was all in Thai. He took his notebook out of his blazer pocket and read through the notes he'd made on the Eric Horvitz murder. He'd managed to find a translation agency in the West End that had translated the Thai cuttings, and one of them had contained a quote from a policeman who was involved in the investigation. Wright reckoned he would be as good a place to start as any, but first he needed a contact number.

He showered and changed into a pair of brown slacks and a white shirt, then took his notebook down to reception, woke up the receptionist and showed her the policeman's name in his notebook. She frowned, not understanding. Wright pointed at the inspector's name and mimed using a telephone. The girl squinted at his writing, then smiled and shook her head. 'Not speak English,' she said.

'Directory enquiries?' asked Wright, pointing at her telephone, but it was clear from the look on her face that she didn't understand. The girl's smile widened, as if the smile would solve his problem. He banged his notebook against his leg as he considered his options. The orphanage where Horvitz had worked seemed the best bet.

He went outside and looked up and down the narrow street but there was no sign of a taxi. He headed for the main road and within seconds he was bathed in sweat. The Bangkok air assailed his nostrils, a stifling brew of exhaust fumes, sewage and fried food. He stepped across an open drain and as he looked down something moved in the grey sludge, something with a tail and hard, beady eyes.

A large Mercedes went by, the wing mirror narrowly missing Wright's arm. He walked by an open-fronted shop selling tinned food and canned drinks. He bought a can of iced coffee and sipped it as he walked.

The traffic on the main road was locked solid. Wright looked at his wristwatch. Nine thirty. Obviously still rush hour. In the distance a traffic light turned from red to green and the traffic began to crawl forward. A green taxi with white Thai writing on the side had its red 'For Hire' light on in its windscreen, so Wright flagged it down and opened the rear door.

'Sukhumvit Soi Two,' he read, hoping that he was pronouncing it correctly.

The young driver smiled and shook his head. Wright tried again. This time the driver made a waving motion with his hand. Wright showed him the notebook but the driver refused to look at it. Horns blared out behind them, illogical because the traffic was barely moving.

'Look, I want to go here. This is Sukhumvit Road, right? I want to go to Sukhumvit Soi Two. It can't be far away.'

The driver turned away and sat motionless with his hands on the wheel. Wright sat back and silently cursed. What chance did he have of solving the case if he couldn't even tell a taxi driver where he wanted to go? He got out of the taxi and walked back along the side street.

When he got back to his hotel the sleeping girl had been replaced by a young man in a black suit and a starched white shirt whose collar was about three sizes too big for him. He smiled at Wright and held out a key for him. 'Good morning, Mr Wright,' he said, flashing a grin of perfect white teeth.

'How did you know my name?' asked Wright.

'My colleague told me that you had checked in, and she described you as a good-looking man wearing brown trousers.'

Wright shook his head in amazement. Faultless English and flattery combined, it was almost too good to be true. 'What's your name?' he asked.

'Somchai,' said the teenager. 'At your service.' He bowed slightly, still holding out the key.

'Somchai, you're just what I need,' said Wright, showing him the notebook. 'I want to go to this address. Can you help?'

Somchai put the key back in its cubbyhole and studied the page. 'An orphanage?' he said.

'That's right.'

'Sukhumvit Soi Two. The main road is called Sukhumvit. The soi is the street off the main road. We are in soi twenty-six.'

'So how do I tell the taxi driver?'

'You say Sukhumvit Soi Song. And to get back here you say Sukhumvit Soi Yee Sip Hok.' He picked up a pen and a sheet of hotel notepaper and wrote on it in Thai. 'This will be better,' he said. 'Show the driver this, and when you want to come back, show him the printed address.'

'You're a lifesaver, Somchai,' said Wright, pocketing the piece of paper. He went through the notebook and found the name of the police inspector. He showed it to Somchai. 'I want to speak to this man. He's a police inspector. Can you get a telephone number for him?'

'Do you know which police station he is based at?'

'I'm afraid not.'

Somchai copied down the name. 'I will see what I can do,' he said. He smiled expectantly at Wright. Wright smiled back. Somchai's smile widened so that it seemed to encompass the whole of his jaw. Realisation dawned and Wright took out his wallet and gave the teenager a hundred-baht note.

This time Wright had no problem persuading a taxi driver to take him to the orphanage. It was only a mile or so away from the hotel but the journey took almost an hour. If it hadn't been for the searing heat and humidity, Wright could have walked it in less than half the time. Even the Thais seemed affected by the heat. A line of schoolchildren stood in the shadow cast by a telegraph pole; female office workers in pastel-coloured suits shielded their faces with their handbags as they walked along Sukhumvit Road; a crew of workers resurfacing a section of the road wore wide-brimmed straw hats and had swathed their faces with cloth to protect themselves from the sun.

The road was a mix of old and new: gleaming shopping malls with boutiques and ATMs, and small open-fronted shops where bare-chested old men worked on ancient Singer sewing machines. There were roadside stalls selling T-shirts and cheap watches, and others offering noodle soup and fried fish balls on sticks from the shade of spreading umbrellas.

The orphanage was in a quiet side street, barely wide enough for two vehicles to pass at the same time. Wright heard the sound of laughing children as he climbed out of the taxi and paid the driver.

The orphanage was surrounded by a high wall into which was set a pair of huge wrought-iron gates encrusted with dirt. A security guard in a pale blue uniform with a gleaming gold badge on the breast pocket opened the gate for Wright.

'Who's in charge?' asked Wright.

The guard smiled and worked a toothpick between his front teeth. Wright repeated his question but it was clear that the man didn't understand.

Wright looked around helplessly. The orphanage was a large concrete two-storey building, painted a pale pink colour with a red tiled roof. The laughter he'd heard came from one of the rooms on the ground floor. The windows were wide open and inside he could see children sitting at desks while a Thai nun in a white habit stood in front of a blackboard. The gardens around the building were well tended with neatly trimmed bushes and a large expanse of grass where the children could play. In the far corner of the garden, close to the wall, were a slide and a set of swings. It wasn't at all how Wright had pictured a Thai orphanage: he'd expected a drab, dreary place where hollow-cheeked malnourished children held up empty bowls and begged for more.

Wright nodded at the guard and headed along a flagstoned path that led to the main entrance. Two stone lions stood guard at the front door, each coming up almost to Wright's shoulder. He walked past them and into the building.

There was no airconditioning but large fans whirled overhead in the wood-panelled hallway and it was much cooler than outside. A highly polished rosewood table stood to the left, with a large visitors' book next to a vase of pink and white orchids.

'Can I help you?' asked a voice behind him.

Wright jumped. 'Jesus!' he exclaimed. He whirled around to find himself face to face with an amused European nun, a woman in her forties with striking green eyes and a sprinkling of freckles around her nose.

'Hardly,' she said. 'Though we do like to feel that we have his blessing in our work.' Her accent was Irish, a soft, feminine brogue that suggested she enjoyed teasing men.

Wright felt his cheeks flush with embarrassment. 'I'm sorry, Sister,' he said. 'You caught me by surprise.'

The nun clasped her hands together. She was wearing a white habit and stray locks of red hair peeped out from the cowl as if reluctant to stay hidden. 'And what brings you to our establishment, Mr . . .?'

'Wright. Nick Wright. Are you in charge?'

'For my sins,' she said. 'Sister Marie is my name. Taking care of children, my game. And you, Mr Wright?'

'I'm a policeman,' said Wright. He took out his warrant card and showed it to her.

She studied both sides, then handed it back to him, suddenly serious. 'It's about Eric, I suppose?'

Wright nodded. 'Is there somewhere we can talk?'

'My office,' she said. 'This way.' She swept down the hall, past an ornate crucifix and a small font, and down a second tiled hallway to a wooden door. She was a tall woman, the spreading cowl emphasising her height, and she had to duck slightly as she walked through the doorway. The habit concealed her figure and Wright couldn't help but wonder what Sister Marie's body looked like. He shook his head, disgusted with himself. She was a nun, for God's sake. A bride of Christ.

Sister Marie stood to the side and ushered him to a straight-backed wooden chair next to the window. She closed the door and glided over to her desk. 'Can I offer you a drink?' she said.

'It's a bit early for me,' said Wright.

'I meant water,' she said archly. 'Or iced tea.'

Yet again Wright was flustered. He was so used to Tommy Reid offering him a hair of the dog that refusals had become second nature. 'I'm sorry,' he said. 'Iced tea would be fine. Thank you.'

Sister Marie pressed a small button on the side of her desk and a moment later the door opened and a Thai nun opened the door. Sister Marie spoke to her in Thai and the nun nodded and closed the door. 'So tell me, Inspector Wright. Why is a transport policeman from England investigating Eric Horvitz's murder?'

A good question, thought Wright. And one that he wasn't sure how to answer. 'There was a similar murder some weeks ago. In London. I thought there might be a connection. The victim was also an American. His name was Max Eckhardt. I don't suppose you know if Mr Horvitz knew him, do you?'

'I don't think so,' said Sister Marie. 'It's certainly not a name I'm familiar with.' She opened one of the desk drawers and took out a Filofax. She flicked through it, then shook her head. 'No, there's no Eckhardt here. This is Eric's. Was Eric's, I mean.'

There was a timid knock on the door and the Thai nun carried in a tray containing a jug of iced tea and two glasses which she placed on the desk. Sister Marie murmured her thanks, and waited until the nun had left before picking up the jug. 'I suppose I'd better be mother,' she said.

Wright grinned. He couldn't help wondering why a sexy, self-assured woman like Sister Marie had turned her back on the outside world and offered her body and soul to Christ. He went over to the desk and took the filled glass from her. 'Cheers,' he said.

She raised her own glass. '*Slainte*,' she said, toasting him.

When he'd sat down again, Wright asked her what Eric Horvitz had been doing in Thailand.

'His job, you mean? He didn't actually have one. He ran the orphanage, took care of any repairs that needed doing.'

'And who paid his salary? Who did he work for?'

'Oh, didn't you know? This is his orphanage. He bought the building, he paid the running costs, sponsored the older children to go to university.'

'That must cost a fortune.'

'He never talked about money. But whenever we needed it, it was there. The Lord will provide, he used to say, but I know it was his own money.'

She went suddenly quiet and Wright could sense that she was uneasy talking about Horvitz, as if she was betraying his secrets.

'Do you know of anyone who might have wanted to kill him?' he asked. 'Anyone who would have profited from his death?'

'He left everything to the orphanage,' said Sister Marie. 'We haven't got the money yet, of course, things take time in Thailand. But his lawyer said we were the only beneficiary in his will.'

'And enemies?'

She smiled and shook her head. 'Eric had no enemies,' she said. 'He wasn't the sort to make enemies. He was quiet, even tempered, he was at peace with himself.'

'He was a religious man?'

'Oh no. He didn't believe in God, and I was never able to convince him otherwise.' She looked across at another chair, a leather armchair almost within reach of her desk, and Wright knew that that was where Horvitz used to sit whenever he visited Sister Marie in her office. He knew also that it would remain Horvitz's chair for a long time to come and that was why she'd shown him to the one by the window.

'How did you meet him?' asked Wright.

'I like to think that it was God who sent him to us, despite his lack of belief,' she said, fingering her glass of iced tea. Wright sipped his. It was sweet and sickly, but he was grateful for the ice. Like the rest of the building, Sister Marie's office had no airconditioning. 'Our order had an orphanage in Vietnam, in Saigon,' she continued. 'Or Ho Chi Minh City as they insist on calling it these days. Eric came with a group of Americans to look around. They were part of a goodwill tour arranged by some war veterans association. The idea was for the vets to come to terms with the war by meeting the people they'd once fought against. We were part of their itinerary. The orphanage had looked after hundreds of Amerasians who had been abandoned by their mothers.'

'When was this?'

'Seven years ago.' She frowned. 'No. Eight.'

'Sister Marie, Max Eckhardt wasn't on the tour, was he?'

She frowned and put a hand up to her cowl. 'No, I'm pretty sure he wasn't,' she said eventually. 'Actually, I can't be sure, because I wasn't told all their names. There was a guy called Lehman, Dan Lehman, and a man with an artificial hand called Larry.' She smiled as if recalling a fond memory. 'The reason I remember their names is because although they came as part of the goodwill tour they returned a few months later and gave the orphanage a lot of money.' She paused and sipped her tea.

'How much, if you don't mind my asking?'

She held his look for several seconds. 'A lot,' she said. 'Enough to solve all our financial problems. Dan and Larry stayed in Vietnam for a few months then returned to the United States. Eric stayed.'

'Do you know how I can contact them?' asked Wright.

She shook her head. 'I'm afraid not. We occasionally get Christmas cards from Dan, but he seems to move around a lot. Believe me, none of them would want to hurt Eric. You never saw such close friends.'

A bell began to ring and seconds later came the sound of children laughing and running down a corridor. It was a happy place and Wright felt that the atmosphere had a lot to do with the fact that Sister Marie was in charge.

'What happened to the orphanage in Vietnam?' he asked.

'Oh, it's still there, and our Order still runs it, but the Vietnamese made it harder and harder for foreigners like myself and Eric to stay there. It became increasingly difficult for us to get visas and the authorities made it clear they'd rather have the orphanage in Vietnamese hands. It's still a Communist country, you know, and the petty bureaucracy has to be seen to be believed. At first we paid off the right people, but after a while even that wasn't enough and we had to leave.'

Wright smiled at Sister Marie's admission of bribery, but he guessed that in her mind the end justified the means. Even so, he couldn't help but wonder what other transgressions there had been in the nun's life. He wanted to ask her if she'd always been a nun, or if prior to taking holy orders she'd had a normal life, of pubs and dances and boyfriends. Wright could imagine a lot of broken hearts when Sister Marie turned her back on the outside world and chose a life of chastity and prayer.

'Eric offered to set up a new orphanage here in Bangkok.' She waved her hand, indicating the room they were in. 'He paid for everything. The building. The staff. Medical care.'

'And no ulterior motive?' Wright regretted the words as soon as they'd left his mouth.

She stiffened and her eyes narrowed. 'What do you mean?' she said.

Wright smiled awkwardly. 'I'm sorry,' he said, 'but I think like a policeman. I'm not used to dealing with philanthropists. Everybody I meet has a dirty secret, an axe to grind . . .' He tailed off as he realised he was rambling.

'Not Eric Horvitz. He was truly a good man.'

'I'm sorry. I didn't mean to imply otherwise.'

She smiled and inclined her head, accepting his apology.

'You said his two friends went back to the States. What about here in Bangkok, does he have many friends here?'

'Some,' she said. 'He chose his friends carefully. He played jazz with a group at a bar in Lang Suan.'

'Lang Suan?'

'It's an area near the embassies. Upmarket nightclubs, expensive restaurants. Eric played at a club called Cowboy Nights. He sang and played percussion.'

'Drums?'

'No, not drums. The tambourine, and those things you shake.'

'Maracas?'

'That's right, maracas. He had a good singing voice.' She smiled at the memory.

'You went to a jazz club to hear him?' asked Wright, surprised.

Sister Marie raised an eyebrow. 'I'm not a prisoner here, Sergeant Wright. They do allow me out from time to time.'

'Could you give me the address?' he asked.

She reached for a sheet of paper and wrote on it. When she handed it to him he realised it was in Thai. 'You read and write Thai?' he said.

'And Vietnamese. I was always good at languages. I studied French and German at university.'

'Don't you miss it?' asked Wright. 'The real world?'

There was more laughter outside and running footsteps. Sister Marie smiled as if she had a secret only she knew. 'This is the real world,' she said softly. 'I'm not hiding under these robes. I chose them.'

Wright emptied his glass. She didn't offer to refill it. A sudden thought struck him. 'Oh, I've been trying to get hold of the policeman in charge of the investigation. I don't suppose you know who he is, do you?'

'Of course,' she said. There was a Rolodex on her desk and she flicked through it and pulled out a business card. 'He hasn't been in touch for a while,' she said. 'I think they

233

haven't made any progress and he's too embarrassed to tell me. It's a question of face, you see.'

She handed him the card and Wright studied it. There was an ornate crest and writing in Thai. He turned the card over. The man's name, title, address and telephone number were reprinted in English. Police Colonel Vasan Srihanam, the officer quoted in the newspaper. He slipped it into his wallet, put his empty glass on the tray and thanked her.

'I'll show you out,' she said.

'He was found in the basement, wasn't he?' asked Wright.

Sister Marie shivered but quickly regained her composure. Wright wondered if she had been the one who'd found the body. 'Yes,' she said quietly.

'Can I take a look?' he asked.

The nun shook her head. 'It's been locked and sealed by the police,' she said. 'Colonel Vasan said the seals mustn't be broken.'

Wright felt a sudden surge of relief. He hadn't relished the prospect of going down into the basement.

'Maybe you could ask him for permission,' said Sister Marie.

She walked him out of the orphanage and to the gate. A dozen children, boys and girls, were playing on the swings and the slide, laughing and giggling. She was absolutely right, Wright realised, this was the real world, children were all that mattered. He wondered how long it had been since he had heard Sean laugh. Far too long.

Sister Marie interrupted his thoughts. 'You were asking about Eric's motives for helping us,' she said. Her face was turned towards the children and he couldn't see her expression. Wright said nothing, sensing that there was

234

something she wanted to tell him. 'He had his own demons to deal with, that much I can tell you. He was at peace here, with the children, but I think that perhaps you're right, he was atoning for something, something in his past. He never spoke about the war, but I think that was where his demons lay. Whatever he did back then, he's more than made up for it since.' She turned to face him and the sun glinted off her white cowl so brightly that Wright had to avert his eyes. 'He was a saintly man,' said the nun. 'Maybe not a saint, but a saintly man.'

She left him at the gate and Wright watched her walk back to the building. Two children, a boy and a girl, both wearing white shirts and red ties, ran over to Sister Marie. They stood either side and she took a hand each and they walked together, a huge white mother hen and her clucking chicks. Wright felt an urge to see his son again, a longing so strong that it made him gasp.

G erry Hunter lay back on the sofa, the remote control in his right hand. Janie had gone upstairs to bed soon after they'd finished making love, taking with her the bottle of wine. It wasn't the first time that she'd taken the initiative so aggressively, but it had still caught him by surprise. He wondered if it had had anything to do with the fact that he'd been so keen to work on the Eckhardt case. Janie demanded constant attention and Hunter felt that she was as jealous of his police work as she would be if he looked at another woman. It was almost as if she wanted to prove to herself that he loved her more than his job, and once she'd proved it she was happy to go to bed alone.

Hunter watched the television and tried to push Janie out of his mind. He wouldn't need much encouragement to follow her upstairs and slip under the quilt with her. Janie had one of the sexiest bodies he'd ever seen, taut and soft, the skin flawless, her breasts soft but firm and showing no signs of her having had a child. And Hunter knew from experience that she was at her sexiest when she'd had a couple of drinks. Alcohol seemed to wipe away what few sexual inhibitions she had and it was all he could do to keep up with her. He sat up and forced himself to concentrate on the movie. He had all night to join her in bed.

He leaned forward with his elbows on his knees and his hands supporting his chin. Hunter wasn't a fan of war movies, in fact he didn't enjoy watching any films containing violence. He'd spent too much time clearing up the aftermath of violence to take any pleasure in watching it on the big screen, and he preferred comedies or historical dramas as entertainment.

His attention was caught by a scene early in the movie, at the start of Lieutenant Willard's journey down the river in search of Colonel Kurtz. He watched Robert Duvall striding through a Vietnamese village in the aftermath of an American attack. He was wearing a black cavalry officer's hat and a silk scarf wrapped around his neck as he strutted arrogantly past a line of corpses. A soldier ran up and handed Duvall a pack of playing cards. Duvall ripped the pack open and began throwing a playing card on to each body. Martin Sheen, as Willard, had picked up one of the cards and was staring at it. 'Death card,' said Sheen. 'Lets Charlie know who did this.'

Hunter sat bolt upright, his eyes wide. He scrambled closer to the television so that his face was inches from the screen. There wasn't an ace of spades and he couldn't make out what brand the cards were, but Hunter knew that if Edmunds had watched the movie he'd have seen the connection with the Eckhardt case. Hunter retrieved the remote control from the sofa and replayed the scene. Had Edmunds seen the movie on the night he died? Hunter wondered. And if he had, what had happened to the video cassette?

Hunter stood up and paced around the sitting room, all thoughts of Janie forgotten.

When Nick Wright arrived back at his hotel, Somchai had gone and his replacement, an elderly man in a stained T-shirt, was asleep with his head in his arms. Wright collected his key from behind the counter, then went upstairs and showered. He lay down on his bed, swathed in two thin towels.

When he opened his eyes again it was dark outside. He stared at his wristwatch. It said four o'clock. He frowned. Four o'clock in the morning? Impossible. Then he remembered that he hadn't reset his watch to local time. Bangkok was six hours ahead of London, so it must be ten o'clock at night. He'd slept for the best part of eight hours.

He sat up and swung his legs off the bed. It was sweltering in the room and his mouth was dry. He went into the bathroom and drank from the tap, then splashed water over his face.

He dried his face and looked at himself in the bathroom mirror. There was a small yellow sticker in the corner of the mirror warning guests not to drink the water from the tap. There was still a bad taste in his mouth and he took his washbag out of his suitcase and cleaned his teeth. His hair had dried in a mess, unkempt and spiky, and he dampened it and recombed it.

Wright's original plan had been to call on the police colonel, but that would have to wait until tomorrow. He changed into a fresh shirt and a pair of black Levis and left the hotel.

The first taxi driver that Wright stopped had no trouble reading the note that Sister Marie had given him. Wright flopped down in the back seat. The traffic was much lighter than it had been during the day, though the roads were still far from quiet. There were motorcycles everywhere, buzzing around the cars and trucks. Some were clearly being used as taxis, the riders wearing brightly coloured vests with numbers on; others were workhorses, piled high with cartons or bags.

The pavements were as busy as the roads. Small restaurants had been set up, with plastic chairs and folding metal tables, and old women ladied out noodles and roast duck and steaming vegetables. Lines of stalls sold T-shirts and cheap dresses and wristwatches, and vendors called out to the tourists who walked by. Small children ran around the stalls, laughing and playing, and skinny dogs with curly tails lay at the roadside, panting in the evening heat. At one of the makeshift restaurants two Thai businessmen in suits were eating noodle soup, their portable phones standing to attention on the table in front of them, while next to them two labourers in threadbare T-shirts and shorts argued over something they were reading in a Thai newspaper. It was like no other city Wright had ever seen, a jarring mixture of old and new, East and West.

They drove past a park where the trees had been bedecked with hundreds of tiny white lights. In the distance, Wright could hear a band playing, a tune he vaguely recognised but accompanied by Thai words.

'You want massage?' said the driver, his guttural voice lancing through Wright's thoughts.

'What?' replied Wright irritably.

'Massage,' repeated the driver, twisting around in his seat even though they were speeding down a main road. He handed a creased glossy brochure to Wright. 'Many pretty girls. We go now?'

Wright studied the brochure. It featured a massage parlour and the main photograph consisted of more than a hundred smiling Thai girls dressed in white togas, each with a numbered blue badge pinned to her left breast, presumably to aid in identification.

'Okay?' asked the driver, nodding vigorously. The taxi narrowly missed smashing into the back of a bus packed with strap-hanging passengers, but at the last second the driver looked back at the road and swerved across into the next lane. 'Okay?' he repeated.

'Not okay,' said Wright, giving him back the brochure. It seemed that every time he got into a taxi he was offered sex. He'd never complain about London cabbies and their banal chatter again.

'You not like Thai girls?' asked the driver as he powered through a red light.

A huge elephant stood on the pavement, a bare-chested man sitting astride its neck. A second man was selling small bunches of bananas to passers-by who took it in turns to feed the animal.

'I don't like paying for sex,' said Wright.

'Huh?'

'Sex. I don't want to pay for sex. Not give money for sex.' Wright realised that he was behaving like the typical Englishman abroad: if the natives don't speak English, talk loudly and slowly in the hope that they'll get it in the end. Surprisingly, it actually worked, and the driver began to laugh.

'Everybody pay,' he said. 'Nobody get free sex.' He slapped his leathery hands on the steering wheel and rocked backwards and forwards.

The driver was still chuckling when the taxi came to a halt outside a three-storey building which had been lined with wooden planks to make it look like a building from the Wild West. A group of young Thai men in leather jackets lounged around on motorcycles smoking cigarettes and drinking Thai whisky from a bottle. A lazy saxophone solo leaked out from the double doors which opened inwards saloon-style. To complete the Western motif there was a hitching post on either side of the doors, and a gold-embossed wooden sign across the middle of the building read 'Cowboy Nights'.

Wright paid the driver and climbed out of the car. The Thai motorcyclists stared at him but without hostility. The guy with the bottle raised it in salute and when Wright smiled they all smiled back.

He pushed open the doors half expecting to see men in cowboy hats and boots, but the people inside were conservatively dressed: Thai thirty-somethings in fashionable outfits, Westerners in suits, a group of teenage girls in short skirts and pullovers sipping Cokes through straws. The club was on two floors, with a wooden spiral staircase leading up to a second level from where balconies looked down on a dancefloor and a small raised stage where the band was performing.

Around the edge of the dancefloor a dozen large leather sofas were grouped around wooden coffee tables, and winged leather armchairs that would have been more at home in a London gentlemen's club filled the corners of the room. Framed oil paintings were hung around the walls, between brass light fittings with green shades. There were two bars, one on the far side of the dancefloor, where a group of Westerners sat on barstools holding bottles of beer and tapping their feet to the music, and a longer bar to the right where two waistcoated waiters juggled cocktail shakers. The nightclub was full, all the sofas and chairs occupied, and a sea of faces, mainly Thai, looked down from the balcony.

A young Thai waitress with her hair pinned up smiled at Wright and held up one finger. He nodded and she led him to an empty bar stool. Wright sat down and ordered a lager from one of the bartenders. A Heineken arrived and Wright followed the example of the Westerners and drank from the bottle.

He swivelled around so that he could watch the band perform. They were all Thais and Wright doubted that any of them was older than twenty-five. They were professional and played tightly, but they lacked emotion. It was as if they'd learned to play by listening to records, and though they could hit the right notes and keep the rhythm going, there was next to no improvisation. They didn't look at each other; each was concentrating intently on his own instrument, like session musicians who'd been brought together for a single gig.

Another waitress appeared in front of Wright, holding a

menu. She waited with her hands clasped behind her back while Wright read through it. It was in English and contained a selection of Western and Thai food. Wright realised the last thing he'd eaten was the tray of food he'd been given on the plane, and he'd left most of that untouched. He didn't want to dive into the unknown and order Thai food so he plumped for a club sandwich. The waitress frowned when he told her what he wanted, so he pointed at the menu. She nodded enthusiastically. Wright smiled. He felt that he was starting to get the hang of Bangkok.

The group finished the song to scattered applause, as if the audience realised that they'd been short-changed artistically. Wright wondered why there were so many people in the club, because what he'd heard so far couldn't in any way be described as a crowd-puller. The lead guitarist said something in Thai and the musicians began packing away their instruments. Wright looked at his watch. It was only eleven o'clock so presumably there'd be more acts to follow. He drained his bottle and ordered another. The man on the bar stool to his left accidentally knocked Wright's arm and he apologised, his accent vaguely French.

'No sweat,' said Wright. He introduced himself and the two men shook hands.

'Alain Civel,' said the man. 'From Montreal. Are you on holiday?'

'Sort of,' said Wright.

'You like jazz?'

'Love it.'

Civel was drinking a bottle of the local beer, Singha, and he waved it at the stage. 'That was *merde*. Crap.'

'It wasn't great,' admitted Wright.

'Now the next group, they really are something. Not

kids like that lot. You can't play jazz unless you've lived.'

'Unless you've suffered?'

'Life. Suffering. One and the same, Nick.' He pronounced it Neek.

'Can't argue with that,' said Wright, and the two men clinked bottles.

Wright's sandwich arrived. It was a massive triple-decker, filled with chicken, cheese and a fried egg, cut into four triangles, each of which was impaled on a miniature plastic sword, and served with a pile of French fries. Wright's stomach growled. He saw Civel looking covetously at the sandwich and Wright offered him a piece.

The two men chewed as a middle-aged Westerner and two Thais carried instrument cases on to the stage and opened them. The Westerner was in his late forties, the two Thais maybe a decade older. The bigger of the two Thais, a beefy man with a weightlifter's shoulders, was carrying a double bass, which he unpacked and began to tune. Two waiters put a dust cover over the drums that the previous band had used and pulled a cover off a second kit in the middle of the stage. It was considerably bigger than the first, a professional set-up that must have cost several thousand dollars. On the bass drum was the name of the band: The Jazz Club.

The Westerner had combed-back greying hair, a drinker's eyes, watery blue and flecked with red veins, and pale white skin as if he avoided going out in the sun. He opened his case and took out a saxophone.

'That's Doc Marshall,' said Civel. 'You've never heard anyone play a horn like Doc.'

A young waiter handed Doc a bottle of Singha beer, and

Doc drank it as he surveyed the crowd, nodding at familiar faces. The younger of the two Thai musicians, square jawed with an Elvis quiff and sideburns, opened a guitar case and took out a red and black guitar which he leaned against a stand at the side of the stage, then he went over to a pair of chest-high congas and stood behind them.

A Westerner in a wheelchair rolled across the dancefloor towards the stage. A big man with a round face, he had grown what hair he had left and tied it back in a ponytail. Behind him stood a hefty black man with a wide chest and powerful legs, and a stick-thin Latino who had also tied his glossy black locks into a ponytail. The two men lifted the crippled man and his wheelchair on to the stage and the Latino handed him the guitar.

'Dennis O'Leary,' said Civel, nodding at the man in the wheelchair. 'They say he played with Clapton once.'

'He's a regular here?'

'The whole band is. Been playing together longer than I can remember, and I've been coming to Bangkok for ten years, on and off.'

Wright leaned towards Civel, and lowered his voice. 'I don't suppose you ever saw a guy called Eric Horvitz play with them, did you?'

'The guy that was murdered? Damn right.' He drained his bottle and Wright bought him another. 'Great singer, voice that could rip your heart out.' He jabbed Wright's shoulder with a forefinger. 'Now Horvitz was a guy who'd suffered. You could hear it in his voice when he sang. Like a knife through your soul, man.'

On the stage, O'Leary began strumming on his guitar, his head tilted to the side as he listened to the chords. The big black man went to stand behind a keyboard and began to do what looked like martial art moves, presumably his own style of warm-up exercises. His hands moved through the air in a slow-motion dance, curving and flexing, first relaxed then tense, and even from across the bar the strength in his upper body was obvious.

'Bernie Hammack,' said Civel.

'And the drummer?' said Wright. The Latino had sat behind the drum kit and was adjusting a wing nut on top of one of the high hats.

'Sergio Ramirez.' Two fresh bottles of beer arrived and the two men clinked them together. 'The girls love him.' He nodded over at the group of Coke-sipping teenagers. 'His fan club.'

Ramirez was a good-looking guy with skin the colour of burnished oak, eyes of a brown so dark that they appeared black, and high cheekbones that a catwalk model would kill for. A silver crucifix glittered at his throat and he wore a tight polo shirt that showed off his chest.

The customers in the bar gradually fell silent and all faces turned towards the stage. The lights dimmed and the six members of the band were picked out in individual beams of soft yellow light. Ramirez started first, tapping a simple four-four beat on the high hat, his eyes half closed, nodding as he played. He brought in the bass drum with an off beat, and at the same time he was joined by the Thai on the double bass, laying down a solid rhythm with a simple bass riff.

O'Leary began to play along with them, picking out the notes with the ease that came from thousands of hours of practice, then Hammack joined in on his keyboard. Doc stood with his back to the audience, watching the band play. He nodded at the Thai percussionist, who started to drum the palms of his hands on the congas, a lilting

245

counterpoint to Ramirez's hypnotic beat. Doc listened to them play for several minutes, then he put the mouthpiece of his saxophone to his lips and turned and began to play.

Wright sat transfixed as he listened. The jazz the men played was on a whole different level to the Thai group. A whole different planet. It was like listening to a single entity, a single creature that could sing with different voices, each individual but connected, voices that took it in turns to lead and follow, to increase the pace and to slow it down. At first it seemed to Wright that the band members were deciding among themselves who should improvise, but he gradually realised that it was Doc who was running the show, communicating with the rest of the band with looks and signals so subtle that it was no wonder Wright had missed them. A sideways look at Hammack, and the black man would go off on his own, his huge hands moving confidently across the keyboard, his finger span so big that he barely had to stretch. Wright watched Hammack's face as he played: the man's eyes were open but he seemed to be staring off into space. He was chewing gum, and the faster he played, the harder he chewed.

Doc took the lead back from Hammack with no more than a nod of the head and a deep breath, then he took the tune into a short solo accompanied only by the Thai percussionist and the bass player before slowing the pace and moving into a Roland Kirke number that Wright hadn't heard for years. The transition was so smooth that Wright sat back in amazement.

'*C'est superbe, huh?*' said Civel, and Wright instantly resented the man's intrusion into his enjoyment of the music. Wright didn't take his eyes off the stage, just nodded to show that he'd heard.

Doc cued O'Leary with a quick glance. The guitarist had been watching for the gesture out of the corner of his eye and again the transition was seamless. The lights slowly dimmed until O'Leary was the only one picked out on the stage. He played for a full ten minutes, the rest of the band accompanying him so unobtrusively it was as if he was playing alone. It was the best live guitar playing that Wright had ever heard, and he'd seen all the greats.

When he finished playing the silence lasted several seconds as if the audience didn't want to believe it was over, then there was a sporadic clapping followed almost immediately by tumultuous applause. Wright clapped enthusiastically.

Civel nudged his arm. 'What did I tell you?' he said.

'Brilliant,' said Wright. 'Bloody brilliant.'

The spotlights came back on. Doc leaned forward to his microphone and thanked the audience, then introduced the band members one by one. They acknowledged the applause with a nod or a half wave, then at a nod from Doc they moved effortlessly into a Van Morrison number, 'Days Like This', with the saxophone taking the part of Morrison's voice. They played for almost an hour, everything from traditional jazz and blues to Lennon–McCartney, but with their own distinctive feel, nothing was predictable. Occasionally Hammack would sing, but usually they stuck to instrumentals, and Wright wondered how the band had sounded when Horvitz had sung along with them. He sang like a man who'd suffered, the Canadian had said. One thing was for sure, he'd suffered before he died.

Wright was jerked out of his reverie by ecstatic applause and he realised that the band had finished their set. He joined in, and when several of the Westerners in the audience began cheering, Wright cheered along with them.

'Thanks,' said Doc, unscrewing the reed from his saxophone and leaning towards his mike. 'And don't forget, tomorrow night's jam night, so come prepared to show us what you can do.'

The lights went down and conversation started up. The group of Coke-sipping girls clustered around the drummer, laughing and vying among themselves for his attention.

'They never do an encore,' said Civel. 'They play what they play, then they stop.'

'Best way,' said Wright. 'Leave the audience wanting.' He drained his lager and Civel ordered two more bottles.

Hammack and Ramirez helped lift O'Leary and his chair off the stage and went over to two green leather sofas placed at right angles to each other close to the bottom of the spiral staircase that led up to the balcony. Hammack and Ramirez sat down and O'Leary parked his wheelchair in the gap. A few seconds later they were joined by Doc. The two Thai members of the band headed for the doors, the big musician carrying his double bass as if it were no heavier than a briefcase.

When Wright's lager arrived he said goodbye to the Canadian, and went over to the table where the band were sitting and drinking beers. The four men looked up at him as he approached. 'Mind if I join you?' he asked.

Ramirez, Hammack and O'Leary looked across at Doc. Doc in turn squinted up at Wright. 'We know you?' he asked.

'My name's Nick Wright. I'm a policeman. From England.'

'Jolly old England, what?' said Doc in a passable imitation of an upper-class English accent. 'Hello, hello, hello, what's all this, then?' He laughed and his three companions laughed along with him. 'Do you have any identification, Mr Wright?'

Doc asked, his face suddenly serious and the English accent forgotten.

Wright showed him his warrant card.

'British Transport Police?' said Doc. 'Someone stolen a train, Sergeant?'

'It's more serious than that,' said Wright. He indicated an empty space on the sofa next to Doc. 'Okay if I sit down?'

Doc stood up. He was an inch or so taller than Wright, but thinner. 'If it's serious, maybe we should have a little privacy,' he said. He spoke in Thai to a waitress and she nodded at a door close to the bottom of the spiral staircase. Doc thanked her. 'There's a private room we can use over there,' he said, handing the warrant card back to Wright. Wright followed Doc as he weaved through the armchairs and sofas.

The far wall of the nightclub was filled with framed photographs of the bands that played there, and Wright saw several featuring The Jazz Club as he walked by. Doc was always centre stage, the focus of the group.

The thickly carpeted room that Doc led Wright into was gloomy and lined with books that appeared to have been bought by the yard. There were several leather armchairs and, incongruously, a pinball machine up against one wall.

Doc sat down in the armchair furthest from the door and lit a Marlboro with a Zippo lighter as Ramirez, Hammack and O'Leary made their way into the room. Hammack waited until O'Leary's wheelchair had crossed the threshold, then he closed the door and stood with his back to it. Again, the three musicians waited for Doc to speak.

Doc blew smoke through tightly pursed lips and studied the detective for several seconds. 'So what brings you to

Bangkok, Sergeant Wright?' He put his Zippo on the table next to him.

'I'm investigating a murder,' said Wright.

'Eric's?' said Doc.

'Maybe.' He squinted at the lighter. It was an old steel model, worn and scratched from years of use. Engraved on it was a cartoon rat, not a friendly rodent like Mickey Mouse but a shifty-looking creature with narrow eyes and a malicious grin. In one hand it held a flashlight, in the other a gun.

Doc said nothing, his watery eyes boring into Wright's.

'What do you mean, maybe?' asked O'Leary, but he was deterred from saying anything else by a quick sidelong glance from Doc, a look that could have frozen antifreeze.

'I'm investigating a similar murder that took place in London several weeks ago.'

'Similar in what way?' asked Doc.

'An American. Tortured and killed.' He paused. 'With an ace of spades impaled in his chest on a knife.'

Wright heard a slight gasp from behind him, but he had no way of knowing if it was O'Leary or Hammack. Wright kept his eyes on Doc. The man showed no reaction at all: his hands were rock steady, he didn't even swallow.

'According to the newspaper reports I've read, that's how Eric Horvitz died. I'm working on the theory that the murders are connected.'

Doc nodded slowly. 'And this American, the one who was murdered in London. What was his name?'

'Max Eckhardt.'

Doc's face was as unyielding as a granite cliff. He stared at Wright and took another long draw on his cigarette.

'Doesn't ring a bell,' he said. He flicked ash into a large crystal ashtray.

'Max Eckhardt,' repeated Wright. He spelled out the surname.

Doc shrugged. 'It's an unusual name, I'm sure I'd remember it.'

Wright turned around to look at O'Leary, who was staring at Doc with wide eyes. 'What about you, Mr O'Leary? Does the name Eckhardt ring any bells with you?'

O'Leary shook his head, but he kept looking at Doc, like a loyal Labrador waiting for instructions from its master.

'Are you sure?' pressed Wright.

O'Leary looked up at him. 'I'm sure,' he said, but Wright could sense the tension in his voice.

'And you, Mr Hammack?'

Hammack stood impassively, his massive arms folded across his chest. 'Not a name I'm familiar with,' he said. He grinned, but there was no humour in the expression. A gold tooth glinted in the left-hand side of his mouth.

Wright looked sharply across at Ramirez. 'Want to make it unanimous, Mr Ramirez?' he said.

Ramirez flashed Wright a movie-star smile but said nothing.

'Three wise monkeys,' said Wright. 'Hear no evil, see no evil, speak no evil.'

'There are four of us,' said Doc. 'Actually.'

'And you never met Max Eckhardt?'

'You won't get a different answer by asking the same question over and over again,' said Doc, stabbing out the butt of his cigarette.

'What makes you think it's the same killer?' asked O'Leary, a nervous tremor in his voice.

Wright turned to face him. O'Leary was clearly the weak link in the group. 'There are too many similarities for it to be a coincidence,' he said. 'The way the body was tortured, the playing card, the fact that the victim's penis was placed in his mouth, the fact that the body was found underground . . .'

'Underground?' repeated O'Leary. 'What do you mean, underground?'

'Horvitz was found in the basement of his orphanage. Eckhardt was tortured and murdered in a disused railway tunnel in South London.'

'A tunnel?' repeated O'Leary. His head swivelled around to look at Doc, who silenced him with a small wave of his hand.

'But you've no motive, no explanation of why someone would want to kill two men that way?'

'No,' admitted Wright. 'We've no motive.'

'And no suspect?'

'I was hoping that by finding a link between the two victims, I'd be able to come up with a motive and a suspect. It seems I was wrong.'

'It was worth a try, though,' said Doc, lighting up another Marlboro. 'I'm sorry we couldn't be of more help, but Eric's murder is a mystery to us, and we've never heard of Eckhardt.' He blew a thin plume of smoke up at the ceiling. 'Is there anything else we can help you with?'

'Yeah, just one thing,' said Wright. 'How come this place is called Cowboy Nights?'

Doc grinned. 'Used to be a country and western place, line dancing, banjos, the works. The Thai guy who owned it lost a bundle and sold out to the present owners. They liked the name, thought it had class, so they did up the interior and left the outside as it is. Typical Thailand.' He took another long pull on his cigarette, his watery blue eyes fixed on Wright's face. 'Okay?' he said.

Wright nodded and headed for the door. Of all the questions he'd asked of the four men, it was probably the only one that he felt had been answered truthfully. 'Thanks for your time,' he said, wiping his sweating hands on his slacks. 'And for the music.'

Hammack stepped to the side and opened the door for him, then closed it behind him.

Wright stood for a while, looking at the framed photographs that lined the wall at the bottom of the spiral staircase. He wondered what the men would say when they were alone. And he wondered why they'd lied to him. The proof that the four Americans knew Max Eckhardt was hanging on the wall among the scores of other photographs. One of the pictures was an old one of The Jazz Club, by the look of it taken more than a decade earlier. Eric Horvitz wasn't in the photograph, but Max Eckhardt was, standing next to Doc and cradling a bass guitar.

'Max is dead,' said Ramirez quietly. 'How could it have happened and we not know about it?'

'We're not his next of kin, Sergio,' said Doc. 'Why would anyone tell us?'

'We're family,' said Ramirez bitterly. 'We should have been at the funeral. We pay our respects to the dead, when it's family.'

'Doc, did you know what had happened to Max?' asked Hammack, who had remained standing with his back to the door.

Doc flicked ash into the ashtray. 'No, Bernie, I did not. Do you think if I had known, I'd have kept it from you?'

'First Max. Then Eric. Who's next, Doc?' O'Leary's voice rose in pitch and there was a look of panic in his eyes.

'We don't know that anyone's going to be next,' said Doc.

O'Leary gestured with his chin at the door. 'The Brit knows,' he said.

'He knows nothing,' said Doc calmly. 'Hell, Dennis, what do any of us know?'

'He's not dead,' said O'Leary. 'He didn't die down there and now he's coming back for us.'

'That's crazy talk,' said Doc.

'What, that's a professional opinion, is it, Doc?'

Doc looked at O'Leary through a cloud of cigarette smoke. 'Maybe it is, Dennis.'

Ramirez laughed sourly. 'Maybe I could prescribe him a little something, hey, Doc?'

Doc went to stand with his back to the pinball machine. 'Time for a sitrep,' he said. 'Eric was murdered in his basement, by a person or persons unknown. In a manner with which we are all familiar. We've just been told that Max has also been murdered under similar circumstances. Whoever killed them knows what we know, but there are no such things as ghosts, gentlemen. He died down there, he's dead and buried, so we have to look elsewhere for our killer.'

'The card, Doc?' said Ramirez. 'What about the card?'

'The card is being used for exactly the same reason that

we used to use it. The fear factor. Somebody's trying to scare us.'

'They're fucking well succeeding,' said O'Leary.

'Someone knows what we did,' said Hammack quietly. 'Someone knows what we did and is paying us back.'

'Maybe,' said Doc. 'So we've got to find out who it is, not worry about ghosts from the past. The dead don't walk, the dead don't talk. The dead don't send photographs in the mail. That's what dead means.'

'Maybe he's not dead,' said Hammack.

Doc's upper lip curled back in a sneer. 'Your memory playing tricks on you, Bernie?' he said.

Hammack shrugged. 'They were tough motherfuckers, Doc. We've seen them walk when they should be crawling, crawl when they should be dead.'

'After what we did?' asked Doc. 'Time for a reality check, gentlemen. Is there anyone here who seriously thinks that he's not dead?' He looked from man to man, and could see indecision in all their faces. He shook his head in disgust. 'I don't believe this,' he said.

'Who else could it be?' asked O'Leary. 'Who else knows what we did? Max? Eric? They're dead. The four of us? Well, I sure as hell know I didn't do it, and I'd trust you guys with my life.'

'There's Rabbit,' said Ramirez.

'Rabbit's in the States, hasn't been out here in more than twenty years. And he's too high profile these days. Are you suggesting that Rabbit flew to London to murder Max, then got on a plane to Bangkok and did Eric?'

Ramirez shrugged. 'I'm just listing the possibilities, Doc,' he said.

'Well, if you're doing that, what about Jumbo?'

'Jumbo?' repeated O'Leary.

'Yeah, maybe Jumbo wasn't dead. Okay, maybe we had his blood all over us, okay so his neck was hacked to bits, and I know I helped put the corpse on the helicopter myself, but maybe an angel came down and blessed him and gave him another chance, maybe the dead can walk again . . .'

'Jumbo's dead,' said Hammack flatly.

Doc clenched his left hand in frustration and banged it against the side of the pinball machine. 'I know he's fucking dead!' he hissed. 'That's what I'm trying to tell you. They're both dead, we all know they're both dead.' He turned his back to them and stared at the book-lined walls as if hoping to draw inspiration from the volumes.

'Doc, who else could it be?' asked O'Leary, hesitantly.

Doc turned around. 'I'm going to ask you one at a time. Do you think he's alive or not? Dennis?'

'I think he might be, yes,' said O'Leary, averting his eyes.

'Jesus H. Christ. Sergio?'

'I don't know,' said the Latino. 'I really don't know. Like Dennis said, who else could it be? There were only seven of us came out alive, and two have been murdered. That leaves five, and four of us are here. Rabbit's got no motive, and if he had, why would he wait so long? He's always known where we were.'

Doc blew cigarette smoke in Ramirez's direction and shook his head sorrowfully. He looked across at Hammack. 'Bernie?'

'Maybe,' said Hammack. 'Maybe he is, maybe he isn't. I wouldn't like to place a bet one way or the other.'

Doc dropped his cigarette on to the floor and ground it into the carpet with his heel. The emotion seemed to drain from his face and he visibly relaxed. 'Fine,' he said. 'We have a might be, a don't know, and a maybe. And as my vote is a definite no, that means we have nothing approaching a consensus.' He sat down and folded his arms. 'So what do we do now?' he asked them. 'I'm open to suggestions.'

'We could talk to the cops,' said O'Leary.

'And tell them what we did?' said Doc.

O'Leary shrugged. 'It was a long time ago, in a war situation.'

'And if someone is trying to kill us all, you think the Thais will protect us?'

O'Leary pulled a face. 'I guess not.'

'We could go back,' said Hammack.

'And do what?' said Doc.

'See if the body's there.'

'And if it's not? Then what?'

'Then at least we'd know,' said Hammack.

Doc leaned forward and scratched his neck. 'And if there's no body, Bernie? If it's not there?'

'Then at least we'd know,' said Hammack. 'Either way, we'd know.'

Doc said nothing. He stared at Hammack and the two men locked eyes as if both were unwilling to be the first to look away.

'Okay,' said Doc eventually. 'We'll vote on it. You first, Bernie.'

'I'm not exactly losing sleep over it, but the card business makes me think it's connected with what happened back then. Yeah, Doc, I wanna go back for a look-see.'

Doc nodded. 'Sergio?'

The Latino shrugged. 'Waste of time,' he said. 'It doesn't matter who did it, what matters is if they try again.

And there ain't nobody gonna get close to me to cut me up.'

'So you vote no?'

Ramirez nodded. Doc looked at O'Leary. 'Dennis?'

O'Leary slapped the wheels of his chair. 'What's the point of me voting? I'm not going back, am I?'

'Dennis,' said Doc quietly. O'Leary looked up. 'We're a team, Dennis,' said Doc quietly. 'You get to vote.'

O'Leary smiled tightly. 'Then I vote yes. I want to know if he's dead or not.'

Doc sat back in his chair. 'Two votes for yes, one for no,' he said. 'You're out of your minds.' He looked at Hammack and at O'Leary. 'Out of your fucking minds.' He turned to Sergio, and the Latino wrinkled his nose and shrugged. 'Okay, I vote yes,' said Doc. 'Is that okay with you, Sergio? No one's going to force you.'

Sergio laughed harshly. 'Think I'd let you two go back down there alone?' he said. 'You wouldn't last five minutes. Besides, have you taken a look in the mirror lately? You're both about twenty pounds heavier than you were back then.'

Doc stood up and went over to O'Leary. 'Okay, we go. We'll need visas, but I've got a guy who can get them for us pronto.' He held out his right hand, palm down. O'Leary reached out hesitantly and put his hand on top of Doc's. Hammack walked over and put his massive black hand down on top, and Ramirez did the same.

Doc nodded. 'Not worth a rat's ass,' he said. One by one the men repeated the phrase. 'You are a bunch of crazy bastards,' said Doc.

'Yeah,' agreed Hammack. 'But you love us really.'

W hen Nick Wright arrived back at the hotel, the elderly
man in the stained T-shirt was still fast asleep, slumped
across the reception desk. He'd been joined in his slumber by
the security guard who had reoccupied his spot on the sofa
and was snoring softly, his peaked cap pushed down over
his face. Half a dozen keys were lined up on the counter
and Wright took his.

Wright went up to his room and sat down on the bed,
wondering how he was going to deal with Doc and his band.
Why were they lying about not knowing Max Eckhardt? Did
they know who the killer was? If they did, why hadn't they
told the police? And if they didn't, what were they hiding?
None of it made any sense. He stood up and paced around
the room, then stood for a while staring out through the
window.

His room was at the back of the hotel and overlooked a
sprawl of tin shacks with corrugated iron roofs scattered
around a construction site where foundations were being
laid. Concrete columns intertwined with steel mesh sprouted
from the ground like stunted trees and a group of mangy dogs
sat staring at a cement mixer as if they expected it to provide
food at any moment. Wright ran his finger down the window,
then slowly traced out the word 'Why?' on the glass.

He went over to the wardrobe and took his harmonica
out of his suitcase, then stood at the window again. He
began to play, a slow mournful tune that he'd heard once
but never discovered the name of, his brow furrowed as he

concentrated. Down below, one of the dogs pricked up its ears and stared up at his window.

G erry Hunter lifted down the cardboard box and went through the contents. Several notebooks, a small tape recorder, a pencil sharpener with 'World's Best Uncle' on it, stationery and pens, and a couple of science fiction paperbacks. No video. Hunter hefted the box back on to the metal shelf. He'd cleared out Edmunds's desk the day after he'd died, but he hadn't known what to do with his stuff and had left it in the evidence room for safekeeping. Hunter stood with his hands on his hips, wondering if there was anywhere else Edmunds could have left the *Apocalypse Now* video. He'd searched his flat and his car and he'd asked all his colleagues and friends but none of them had been given a video by Edmunds.

Hunter went back to the incident room and sat down at his desk. The ace of spades playing card was in a clear plastic evidence bag, propped up against Hunter's computer keyboard. Hunter stared at it. It was crusted with dried blood and there was a jagged hole in the centre of the card where the knife had been. Hunter picked up the evidence bag and looked more closely at the card within. In the middle of the black ace was the ghostly figure of a woman, and the hole went through her chest. Was there any significance about the ace of spades? Hunter wondered. He knew that there was a death card in the Tarot pack, but he didn't know if the ace of spades was connected to death or murder. There hadn't been an ace of spades in the *Apocalypse Now* video; Duvall had been throwing down cards at random. He turned the card over. There was more blood on the back than the front, but there seemed to be nothing unusual about the card itself. It obviously meant something to someone, however. Had Edmunds solved the mystery? Hunter wondered. Had he uncovered the significance of the card before he died?

Hunter dropped the evidence bag on to his desktop and sat back in his chair, staring up at the polystyrene tiles above his head. A card had been left on mutilated bodies in South London and Bangkok. Playing cards had been left on bodies in the Vietnam War. What was the connection? He wondered if Wright's investigation in Bangkok had turned anything up yet.

He leaned forward and tapped out the commands on the HOLMES computer keyboard that called up the background notes on Max Eckhardt. He had been forty-eight years old. Old enough to have served in the Vietnam War. There was no mention of military service in the notes, but as it would have been a quarter of a century earlier, Hunter wasn't surprised. He called up the post mortem file and scanned it. There had been old scars in the man's back. Shrapnel wounds, perhaps. A war wound? Hunter took his notebook out of his jacket. He was a compulsive note-taker, had been ever since he'd been a twenty-year-old constable on foot patrol. There were two lines of enquiry that he wanted to follow: he had to find out if Max Eckhardt had served in the Vietnam War, and he had to nail down the significance of the ace of spades.

S omchai was back on duty when Nick Wright went down to reception. 'Good morning, Mr Nick,' the Thai said, smiling broadly. 'I have good news for you.'

'Good news?' said Wright. He was wearing a blue linen jacket, white shirt, light brown slacks and his BTP tie.

Somchai produced a sheet of hotel notepaper with a flourish. 'I have found the policeman you wanted. Colonel Vasan.' He handed the paper to Wright. In capital letters he'd written Vasan's name, a telephone number and an address, and he'd noted down the address in Thai. Wright didn't have the heart to tell him that he already had the man's business card in his wallet. He smiled and thanked the Thai teenager and gave him a five-hundred-baht note.

'Can you do me another favour? Can you call and fix up an appointment for me?' He looked at his wristwatch. It was ten a.m. 'Say in about an hour?'

'It will take you more than an hour, Mr Nick,' said Somchai. 'Traffic very bad today. Maybe an hour and a half.'

'Okay. Can you arrange it?'

'I can try,' said Somchai. He picked up the telephone and dialled Colonel Vasan's number. He spoke for a minute or two then was put on hold. After a few minutes he spoke to someone else and was then put on hold again. Somchai smiled apologetically.

Wright went over and sat on one of the sofas by the side of the entrance. He picked up a copy of the *Bangkok*

Post and tried to read an incomprehensible article on Thai politics. There had just been an election but with no outright winner all the participants were manoeuvring to put together a workable coalition. Wright found the story difficult to read: the English was unwieldy and the names of the people involved were so impossibly long and unpronounceable that he couldn't remember them from one paragraph to the next. From time to time he glanced over at Somchai who was waiting patiently with the phone held against his ear.

Wright read through the news section and then the sport section, which contained a surprisingly large number of stories on British football. He read the business section, then flicked through the classified advertisements. He looked at his wristwatch. Half an hour had passed and Somchai was still on the phone. Wright sighed and put his feet up on a small table. He closed his eyes.

He was woken up by someone shaking his shoulder. It was Somchai. Wright rubbed his eyes and took his feet off the table. 'What?' he said, momentarily confused. He looked at his watch again. He'd been asleep for half an hour.

'Colonel Vasan is very busy,' said the receptionist, 'but his secretary said if you come and wait, maybe he can see you.'

'So is that an appointment or not?'

Somchai's eyebrows knotted together. 'I don't understand.'

'If I go, will he definitely see me? I don't want to waste my time.'

'Maybe,' said Somchai, smiling ingratiatingly.

Wright hauled himself up off the sofa. His mind felt woolly and he was having difficulty concentrating. It was probably jetlag, he figured, coupled with the humidity and the alcohol he'd drunk the previous night. He thanked Somchai and went out in search of a taxi.

It was a swelteringly hot day and his shirt was soon drenched with sweat. He walked down the soi to Sukhumvit and stood at the roadside, trying to breathe through his nose because the air was thick with traffic fumes. A coach crawled by, the windows wide open and most of its passengers dozing in the heat. Black smoke belched from its exhaust and Wright stepped back. Emission controls were clearly not a priority in the city.

A motorcyclist in a wraparound helmet and wearing a bright green vest over a T-shirt stopped in front of Wright. 'Where you go?' he asked.

Wright shook his head. He peered down the traffic-packed road. The only taxis he could see were already occupied.

'Where you go?' the motorcyclist repeated. He was barely in his twenties with skin burned almost black from the sun. He wore ragged jeans and had rubber flipflop sandals on his feet.

Wright showed him the police colonel's business card.

'Forty baht,' said the motorcyclist. About one pound sterling.

Wright took another long look around. There wasn't an empty taxi in sight and the traffic was barely moving. 'Okay,' he sighed and climbed on the small motorcycle. The driver twisted around and handed Wright an old pudding-basin-type black helmet with a frayed strap. Wright inspected the interior for lice, found none, and put it on. It wasn't a bad fit. Before he could fasten the strap the motorcyclist pulled away from the kerb and began weaving through the traffic. Wright held on to the metal bar at the rear of the seat.

They made surprisingly quick progress. The cars and trucks all left plenty of space between their vehicles, giving the motorcyclists room to get by. On the few occasions they reached a blockage, the car drivers would do their best to create a gap so that the bikes could get through, acts of generosity that were acknowledged with nods of helmeted heads.

They reached a set of traffic lights where more than fifty motorcycles had already gathered, engines revving. Wright tried holding his tie over his mouth but it provided little in the way of protection from the fumes. The air was deadly, and he could understand why most of the traffic policemen he'd seen wore white cotton masks over their mouths and noses.

The lights turned green and Wright almost fell off the pillion as his rider sped away. All the girl passengers he saw were riding side-saddle, one leg on the foot rest, the other suspended in mid air, their handbags on their laps. Many appeared to be office workers or housewives in pastel-coloured suits. There were many child passengers, too, some so small that they sat astride the petrol tanks, their tiny hands gripping the handlebars as their fathers drove. On one 250cc Yamaha he saw a husband and wife and three children between them, packed like sardines on to the seat.

There seemed to be construction sites everywhere Wright looked, and the skyline was peppered with cranes atop half-built office blocks and apartments.

A Mercedes pulled out of a side street and the bike swerved to avoid a collision, but it all happened so quickly that Wright didn't even have time to be scared. They turned off Sukhumvit and roared down a four-lane road, but within half a mile hit another traffic jam and began weaving in and out of unmoving cars. At one point the driver took the bike up on to the pavement and drove slowly, nodding apologies to those pedestrians he inconvenienced.

Several times they were forced to stop at traffic lights and had to wait an inordinate length of time. The lights appeared to be operated almost on a random basis by brown-uniformed policemen who sat in glass-sided cubicles. At one intersection they were held up for a full ten minutes and when Wright looked over his shoulder he could see a queue of cars almost half a mile long.

They left the main road and sped through a network of narrow side streets. Behind walls topped with broken glass stood houses with red-tiled roofs, wide balconies, shielded by spreading palm trees. The air was fresher, though occasionally Wright was hit by the stench of an open sewer or the odour of overripe fruit or animal faeces. The small streets had no pavements and the driver kept having to swerve to avoid pedestrians. There were clusters of shops with apartments above them, high-class shops selling Italian furniture and Thai antiques, and others offering haircuts or same-day laundry.

Many of the side streets were one-way, being too narrow for cars to pass, and they had to zigzag left and right with little or no indication of who had the right of way. They cut through the car park of a large hotel where a security guard in a grey uniform and white gloves pushed a mobile barrier out of the way so they could get by, then joined another main road. Wright had lost all sense of where he was; the city seemed to be one huge sprawl with no obvious centre.

They eventually came to a halt close to a white three-storey building with a huge car park in front. Above the main entrance porch was a huge gold and red insignia and large Thai letters which ran almost the full length of the building. Brown-uniformed policemen manned the barrier restricting entrance to the car park. Wright dismounted and paid the motorcycle rider, then strode up to the barrier. The policemen smiled at him but didn't ask what he wanted so Wright walked by and headed for the main entrance. He pushed open a glass door and went inside.

A dozen or so Thais sat on several rows of wooden benches, and two men in denims lay on one of the benches, snoring softly. An elderly woman was peeling an orange and handing pieces of the fruit to a little girl in pigtails. The benches faced a wooden counter behind which stood half a dozen uniformed men and women. Two of them, young men with red braid on the left shoulders of their tunics and strips of bright-coloured medals on their breast pockets, were talking to visitors and taking notes but the rest didn't seem to be doing anything. Wright couldn't see a queuing system in operation so he walked up to the counter. A girl who was barely out of her teens smiled at him.

'Do you speak English?' he asked.

She smiled and shook her head.

'Does anyone here speak English?' asked Wright, pointing at the uniforms behind the counter.

Her smile widened. She shook her head again.

Wright and the girl stood smiling at each other. He wondered if it was a test of wills, if she was seeing how long he could wait with an inane grin on his face. If it was a test, Wright failed. He took out Colonel Vasan's business card and handed it to the girl.

'I want to speak to him,' he said.

She read the card and then looked at Wright with renewed respect, speaking to him in rapid Thai.

Wright shook his head. 'I don't understand,' he said. He was starting to feel helpless. The language was so unfamiliar, the sounds so strange, that he couldn't even begin to guess what she was talking about.

A female officer and a middle-aged man came over and took it in turns to read the card. The man spoke to Wright in Thai.

'I'm sorry,' said Wright. 'I don't speak Thai.'

'Name you?' said the man.

'Ah, yes,' said Wright. He took out his wallet and gave the officer one of his British Transport Police business cards. It was studied with equal solemnity.

'Sit, please,' said the man, indicating the benches.

Wright went and sat down. The officers talked among themselves, then the young girl picked up a phone. Wright sighed. That hadn't been too difficult.

Half an hour later he was still waiting. He went back up to the desk and in pidgin English tried to ask how long it would be before Colonel Vasan could see him. He was faced with more smiles and nods towards the benches. He went and sat down again.

Forty-five minutes later a matronly woman in a pale blue dress came up behind him. 'Mr Nick?' she said.

Wright stood up. 'Yes,' he said. 'Nick Wright. I'm here to see Colonel Vasan.'

'He is very busy today,' she said, handing him his business card. 'Can you come back tomorrow?'

'I don't mind waiting,' he said.

The woman hesitated, then smiled. She turned and went through one of four doors in the wall opposite the counter. Wright sat down. Behind him the two men continued to snore quietly. Wright wondered if like him they were also waiting to see someone, of if they had just come in to take advantage of the airconditioning.

It was a full hour before the woman returned. 'Colonel Vasan will see you now,' she said.

Wright followed her through the door, along a corridor, up a flight of stairs and along another corridor, lined on both sides with dark wooden doors bearing the names of police officers. The woman took Wright into an office which contained a desk and a dozen filing cabinets. On the desk was a photograph of two smiling children and next to it a gold Buddha statue around which had been draped a garland of purple and white flowers. She knocked on a door and disappeared.

When the woman reappeared a few minutes later she nodded at a chair by the door. 'Please wait here,' she said, smiling. 'He is busy again.'

Wright began to feel that he was getting the runaround, but he smiled and sat down as asked. He could only imagine what sort of reception a Thai detective would get if he turned up at BTP headquarters unable to speak a word of English, so he was prepared to be patient. He sat with his hands on his knees and resisted the temptation to keep looking at his watch.

The woman busied herself with paperwork, occasionally pecking at a large electric typewriter that shuddered so much that her desk vibrated every time she pressed a key. After fifteen minutes she stood up, opened the door to the colonel's office and told Wright that the colonel was ready to see him. There had been no phone call, no signal from the colonel, and Wright knew for sure that he'd been deliberately kept waiting in the outer office.

Colonel Vasan was a short, stocky man with jet black

hair that glistened as if it had been oiled and steel-framed spectacles that sat high up on a prominent nose. He wore a chocolate-brown uniform with gold insignia on the shoulders and a thick chunk of ribbon medals on his breast pocket. His left cheek was pitted and scarred as if it had been scraped against a rough surface a long time ago. He had a square face with a wide jaw that he thrust forward as he studied Wright. He had Wright's business card on his desk and he looked down at it and then back at Wright's face.

'Thank you for seeing me, Colonel Vasan,' said Wright, holding out his hand.

The colonel looked at the hand, then at Wright's card, then back to Wright's face. He spoke in Thai. Wright was about to say that he couldn't speak Thai when the secretary spoke behind him.

'Colonel Vasan prefers to conduct interviews in his own language,' she explained. 'I will translate for him. He asks that you sit down.'

Wright sat on one of two wooden chairs facing Vasan's desk. The secretary sat next to him, her hands clasped in her lap.

'I am Sergeant Nick Wright. I am a detective with the British Transport Police in London investigating a murder that took place several weeks ago.'

Wright waited for the secretary to translate. The colonel stood up as the secretary spoke and strode over to a window that overlooked the car park. Wright noticed a large holstered handgun on Vasan's right hip, and a radio transceiver hooked to his belt. His trousers were tucked into black boots that had been polished to a lustrous shine. He looked more like a soldier than a policeman.

'I understand from press reports that there has been a

similar murder in Bangkok. A man called Eric Horvitz. I was hoping that you might tell me what progress had been made on the case.'

When the secretary finished translating, the colonel turned. He spoke in Thai and the secretary turned to Wright.

'Colonel Vasan asks that you tell him about the case you are investigating,' she said.

Wright took an envelope out of his jacket pocket and handed it to Vasan. Inside was a printout of the pathologist's report, a description of the crime scene, photographs of the crime scene and the body, Max Eckhardt's biography and several newspaper cuttings. Vasan studied them. Wright wondered if he was able to read English or if he was only pretending to.

'The victim was a forty-eight-year-old American photographer, married but with no children. He'd only recently arrived in London. He had no enemies as far as we can see. Some camera equipment and his wallet were taken, but we don't think robbery was the motive. The wounds were inflicted over a long period and amount to torture.'

The colonel nodded, even though the secretary hadn't started translating. When she did begin talking, Vasan seemed more interested in the newspaper cuttings than in what she was saying. Wright reckoned the Thai policeman's English was more than adequate for a conversation, but that he preferred to use the woman as a buffer. Vasan waited until she'd finished before speaking to her in Thai.

'Colonel Vasan asks why there is no mention of the playing card in the newspaper articles you have given him,' she said.

Wright explained that investigating officers often withheld

information in the hope that it would help identify the culprit at a later date. The secretary translated and the colonel nodded. He sat down again behind his desk and spread the photographs out, studying them in silence for several minutes.

'What I'd like is to have a look at the evidence you collected from your crime scene, and perhaps to speak to your officers,' said Wright. 'It has to be the same killer.'

The secretary didn't start translating until the colonel looked up from the pictures. He replied in Thai.

'Colonel Vasan asks what is it that you want to know,' she said.

Vasan gathered up the photographs and handed them to Wright, but kept hold of the printouts and newspaper cuttings.

'The playing card,' said Wright. 'I'd like a look at it.'

Again, Vasan reacted before his secretary translated. He said something to her and nodded at a bank of filing cabinets. She went over to them and pulled out a drawer. She had a pair of spectacles hanging on a chain around her neck and she put them on, then riffled through the grey cardboard files. She took one out and gave it to Wright.

It consisted mainly of written reports, all in Thai, none of which made any sense at all to Wright. Most appeared to be handwritten. There was a hand-drawn diagram which he realised must be the basement where the body was discovered. 'Are there any photographs of the crime scene?' he asked.

Colonel Vasan shook his head before the secretary had time to translate.

'No, there are not,' she said.

At the back of the file was a plastic bag containing a

blood-stained ace of spades. The black ace filled most of the card and in the centre of it, where it had been punctured by a knife, was the ghostly figure of a woman. It was the same brand that had been found in the Battersea tunnel.

'It's the same,' he said. 'The card we found in London was the same as this.' He held it up.

The secretary translated.

'Would it be possible for me to have translations of these reports?' asked Wright, indicating the file.

The secretary spoke to Vasan, who shrugged and replied.

'It is possible, but it will take time,' said the secretary. 'If you tell us where you are staying, we will have them delivered to you.'

Wright nodded. 'Thank you.'

'There will be a charge for the service, however,' she said.

Wright was surprised but tried not to show it. 'Fine,' he said.

She spoke to Vasan and the colonel smiled.

'And I'd appreciate a look at the rest of the files on the case,' said Wright.

The secretary frowned. 'There is only the one file,' she said.

Wright was stunned. 'That's all there is?' he said. 'For a murder investigation? Are there no computer files? Witness reports?'

She translated and listened as the Colonel replied. 'That is the only file,' she said, 'but Colonel Vasan will answer any questions you might have.'

'Does he have a suspect? Any motive, a reason why anyone would want to kill Eric Horvitz?'

Through his translator, the Thai policeman said that enquiries were continuing, but so far they had no theories, that Eric Horvitz had been well liked, had no financial problems, and so far as the Thai police were concerned, no enemies.

'And what about the card? Do you have any idea of the significance of the ace of spades?'

The secretary translated and the colonel shook his head. Assuming that Vasan wasn't keeping anything back, the Thai police had made as little progress as Wright and his colleagues had on their case.

The colonel spoke to his secretary. 'Colonel Vasan asks if you know of any other connection between the two dead men,' she said.

A good question, thought Wright. He'd gone to the police station with the intention of sharing the information he had, and of telling Vasan that Eckhardt and Horvitz had both played with The Jazz Club in Bangkok, but now he was having second thoughts. Vasan seemed more concerned with playing power games than with solving the case. Wright shook his head. 'Not yet,' he said.

When he left the office, Wright didn't offer to shake hands.

Gerry Hunter got AFP's number from directory enquiries and called up Steve Reynolds. 'I'm calling about Max Eckhardt,' explained Hunter. 'Do you by any chance know if he served in Vietnam?'

'I've already been through this with another officer,' said Reynolds tetchily.

Hunter tensed. 'Who?'

'Edwards. A sergeant, I think.'

'Clive Edmunds?'

'That's it.'

'When was this?' asked Hunter.

'A while back, I think. He called late one evening just as I was on my way out of the office. Insisted I pulled Max's personnel file.'

Hunter gripped the ballpoint pen in his right hand so tightly that his fingers started to turn white. 'Can you remember what you told my colleague?' he asked.

'I know I was able to tell him that Max had been in Vietnam. Look, give me a second, I'll get the file.'

Reynolds was only away from the phone for a few seconds, but it felt like an eternity to Hunter. 'Yeah, here we are. He did a tour of duty in 'sixty-seven and 'sixty-eight.'

'Does it give any details of what he did?'

'No, it's an old CV, from the 'seventies, and back then people tended to gloss over what they did during the war. There was a lot of anti-war feeling in the States, right up until the Reagan years, I guess.'

'What about you, did you go?'

'Hell, no,' said Reynolds. 'I missed it by five years. Why are you so interested in what Max did during the war?'

'It's just a line we're following up,' said Hunter. 'Do you have any idea how I could find out more about his war record?'

'I can tell you the same as I told Edmunds,' said Reynolds. 'You should try the Pentagon. The Defense Department. I'm sure they'd have him on file. Edmunds said he would speak to your FBI agent about it. And there's May, of course.'

'May?'

'Max's wife. She'd probably know.'

'Oh, right, sure.' Hunter thanked Reynolds and hung up.

He sat staring at the wall, his mind in turmoil. Clive had been on to something, but what? He'd tied Eckhardt to the Vietnam War, a war where playing cards were used as death cards. Had Clive taken it any further before he died? Hunter picked up the evidence bag containing the ace of spades. There was nothing in the HOLMES file about Eckhardt's war service, and while Clive was notoriously lax at filling out his reports, Hunter figured that he must have been working on the Vietnam link just before he died. What else had he found out?

Wright pushed open the swing doors and walked into Cowboy Nights. He'd changed into a white cotton shirt and black Levi jeans. The crowd was pretty much the same as the previous night, and he recognised several faces.

The Canadian, Alain Civel, was standing at the bar and he waved at Wright. 'Ah, Neek,' he called, 'back for more?'

Wright joined him and ordered a lager. A waitress put a bowl of roasted peanuts down in front of him and he took a handful. 'What time are The Jazz Club on?' he asked.

'Ten minutes or so. You know it's jam night?'

'Yeah. Are you going to play?'

Civel grimaced. 'Not me, man. They're way out of my league.'

The Thai band finished their set to lukewarm applause. Wright carried his bottle over to the spiral staircase and examined the framed photographs hanging on the wall. The one featuring Max Eckhardt had gone. Wright methodically looked at all the photographs on the wall in case they'd been rearranged, but there was no mistake.

Wright turned around. Doc was standing on the stage, holding his saxophone. He was staring at Wright. Wright raised his bottle in salute and grinned. Doc flashed Wright a tight smile, then turned away.

Wright went back to Civel. 'You've been coming here for ten years, you said?'

'Oui,' said Civel. 'I work in Saudi, but every chance I get I fly over. Beer and women on tap, what more could a man want?'

The question was rhetorical, Wright assumed. 'Ever come across a guy called Eckhardt? Max Eckhardt. Played bass guitar.'

Civel shook his head. 'Don't think so. Why?'

'I saw his picture on the wall, playing with the band.' He nodded at the stage, where Hammack and Ramirez were lifting O'Leary's wheelchair. They spent a few minutes tuning their instruments while the audience waited expectantly.

The band went straight into 'Dimples', a John Lee Hooker song, with O'Leary stabbing at his guitar, rocking his head violently in time with the beat, and Doc's saxophone taking the place of the vocals. Then they eased into two more John Lee Hooker blues tunes, 'Walkin' The Boogie' and 'I See When You're Weak', both giving Doc ample scope to show

277

his flair and originality. Civel jabbed Wright in the ribs and Wright nodded appreciatively.

Hardly had the applause broken out than the band launched into a Muddy Waters classic, 'Got My Mojo Working'. Hammack sang as he played on the keyboard, chewing his gum between verses.

For half an hour the band jammed, and once again it was Doc who was firmly in control, allocating solos with nods and glances. They ended to tumultuous applause, and Doc introduced the members of the band. Then he announced that it was jam night, and that members of the audience were welcome to take part.

The first volunteer was a middle-aged Westerner in a Coca-Cola T-shirt and cut-off jeans. He played drums and Ramirez went over to stand with his fan club while the band ran through two Phil Collins numbers, 'In The Air Tonight' and 'Another Day In Paradise'. The drummer tried to be too clever and several times lost the beat after attempting complicated fills. He left the stage to supportive applause, but there was a self-satisfied look on Ramirez's face as he took his place behind the drum kit.

Next up was a stocky Japanese man in a shiny black suit, who sang 'My Way' in a near-perfect imitation of Sinatra, down to the phrasing and gestures of the great man. It owed more to karaoke than jamming, but The Jazz Club gave him musical and moral support, and joined in the applause when he finished the number. He beamed as he went back to a group of Japanese businessmen clustered around the bar and several of them slapped him on the back.

'Any more volunteers?' asked Doc.

'Here we go,' Wright said to the Canadian. 'Wish me luck.' He walked towards the stage, taking his harmonica from the back pocket of his jeans. Doc raised a querulous eyebrow. 'Okay?' said Wright, holding up the harmonica.

Doc gave him an exaggerated bow and made a sweeping gesture with his arm. 'Feel free,' he said.

Wright stepped up on to the stage. A spotlight moved across and settled around him. O'Leary was staring open mouthed. Wright was obviously the last person he'd expected to see on stage. Ramirez grinned and said something to Hammack and the keyboard player chuckled. '"Before You Accuse Me",' Wright said to Doc. 'You know it?'

'One of my favourites.'

'Guess we don't need to rehearse, then,' said Wright, raising his harmonica to his lips.

Doc looked at him with an expression that came close to amazement, then he shrugged and nodded curtly at Ramirez. The drummer came in quickly as if trying to catch Wright off guard, four taps of his sticks to get the beat and then straight into it. He was joined almost immediately by O'Leary.

Wright took the chorus, his harmonica taking the place of the vocals, and Doc stood at the side of the stage, listening and tapping his right foot. Wright closed his eyes and concentrated on hitting the notes right.

As he finished the chorus, Hammack joined in, but it was Doc who took the solo, turning his back on Wright and putting everything into it.

Doc turned sideways on and flashed a look at Wright, letting him know that the chorus was his again, but Wright didn't lift his harmonica. Instead he sang, with his eyes closed because he didn't want to see Doc's reaction or be distracted by it.

There was a whooping cheer from the far side of the bar

and Wright opened his eyes. It was the Canadian, pumping his fist into the air.

The bass player joined in as Doc took the next verse. Doc threw in a few improvisations as if trying to show Wright what he was capable of. Wright remained stony faced, his eyes fixed on the saxophone as he tried to get a feel for Doc's rhythm. Doc finished the verse and nodded at Wright. Wright raised the harmonica to his lips and played, this time keeping his eyes on Doc's face. Doc smiled and folded his arms around his saxophone. When Wright finished the chorus, Doc nodded again.

Wright stepped closer to his microphone, arching his neck up as he sang. Doc turned to O'Leary as the verse ended and nodded, then gave Hammack a sideways glance. They all hit the chorus together, and Wright joined in with his harmonica. They finished with a flourish and the audience erupted. Wright felt the appreciation wash over him. Ramirez was grinning and Hammack gave Wright an enthusiastic thumbs-up.

Doc walked over to Wright. 'A singing policeman,' he said. 'Where the hell did you learn to sing?'

'I was in a band at university,' said Wright. 'Pubs and stuff.'

'You're good,' said Doc.

'Nah,' said Wright.

'You wanna do another?'

'Sure.'

'You know "It's Rainin' In My Life"?' Doc asked.

'Yeah. Mine too.' Wright grinned. 'Yeah, I know it.'

Doc turned around and primed the rest of the band, then went immediately into it. Wright played harmonica, singing only when he came to the chorus, but when they moved seamlessly into 'Honky Tonk' Wright started to sing again.

Without a break they went into a medley of Howlin' Wolf songs. Wright felt as if Doc was testing him, seeing if he was able to spot the cues. Several times Doc threw solos at him, allowing Wright to jam on the harmonica, then quickly coming in on his sax, taking the lead back and switching tunes, then throwing it back to Wright. Wright enjoyed the challenge, and after half an hour was confident enough to be able to relax and enjoy himself. When Doc eventually brought the set to a halt, the nightclub burst into applause.

Wright went back to the bar where Civel hugged him and clapped him on the back. 'Bloody brilliant, man. *Fantastique.*'

Wright picked up his bottle and drank the last of his lager. Civel ordered him another.

'You can sing, man,' said Civel. 'You can really sing.'

'Thanks.'

The members of The Jazz Club were making their way over to their regular seats. Wright clinked bottles with Civel, then went over to join them.

Doc was whispering something to O'Leary, but he moved back as Wright approached. 'Pull up a chair, Nick,' said Doc.

'Nice harp-playing,' said Ramirez.

'It's just a hobby,' said Wright, sitting down on the sofa next to Hammack.

'You could do it professionally,' said O'Leary, pouring the contents of his bottle of Singha into a glass.

'You could, too,' said Wright. 'Why don't you?'

O'Leary shrugged. 'Not much call for wheelchair-bound

musicians,' he said bitterly. 'These days it's all pretty boys and dance routines.'

'Bullshit,' said Wright. 'You're a musician, a good one. You could play with any band in the UK or the States. Doc said you played with Clapton.'

'He was out here on tour and he dropped by one night, that's all.'

'You held your own, Dennis,' said Doc. He stabbed his cigarette at Wright. 'Clapton offered Dennis a gig in the States, but he turned him down.'

'It wasn't a definite offer, Doc,' said O'Leary.

'Damn was, Dennis, and you know it. You just didn't want to leave your wife alone.'

Ramirez's fan club clustered around him, four young Thai girls in short skirts and tank tops. They were flirting outrageously, vying for his attention, flicking their long hair and batting their eyelashes like crazy. Ramirez talked to them in Thai and they giggled.

'I went to see the cop who's investigating Eric Horvitz's death,' Wright said to Doc. 'He didn't seem to be making much progress.'

'And you're surprised at that?' asked Doc. 'Eric was a farang.'

'A farang?'

'It's what they call foreigners. Investigating the murder of a farang isn't exactly a money-making opportunity, so we're pretty low on their list of priorities.'

'What's money got to do with it?' asked Wright, confused.

Doc sighed as if he'd been asked by a child to explain why the sky was blue. 'People here don't join the cops out of a sense of public service,' he said.

'What, like they do in the States?' interrupted Hammack, his voice loaded with sarcasm. He spat the gum he'd been chewing into an ashtray.

Doc ignored him. 'They join for one reason – to make money. The traffic cops take bribes from motorists, the guys back in the station take a percentage, everyone gets a cut. The higher up the ladder they can climb, the more they get. You want to open a bar in Bangkok, you have to pay the cops. You want to start a business, you talk to the cops. You get arrested, you pay off the cops.'

'Are you saying they don't investigate murders here?'

'No, that's not what I'm saying. Most murders are domestics: a wife stabs her unfaithful husband, husband has one drink too many and hits his wife too hard, kids arguing with parents over money, and they get put away, though they usually serve less than ten years. No, what I'm saying is that if the crime doesn't solve itself, they're not going to put in any effort, not unless there's going to be a pay-off.'

'And where would the pay-off be in solving a murder?'

Doc looked across at Hammack and winked. 'The innocent abroad, isn't he?' He waved his bottle of Singha at Wright. 'Did you tie your white horse up outside, Nick? Checked your suit of armour at the door? You're not in bloody old England now. You can get someone killed in Bangkok for less than a hundred US dollars. Hitman on a motorbike, bullet in the back of the head.' He mimed pulling a trigger. 'Pop!' He took a swig from his bottle. 'Happens every day. Now, do the cops investigate? Yes, if the victim's rich or well connected, because if the victim's a somebody, then the guy who paid for the hit is probably a somebody, too. And being a somebody in this country means only one thing: money. So sure, they'll try to solve the murder then, because if they can come up with a suspect who's got money, they can take a bribe to let him off.'

'That happens?'

'Sure it happens. The hitman will probably go to prison for a few years, but the guy who paid him will take care of his family and give him a bonus. It's typical Thailand, everyone comes out of it making a profit.'

'Except the victim?'

'Yeah. Except the victim.'

'So you reckon this Vasan isn't going to solve Eric's murder?'

'Eric didn't have any rich enemies; hell, he didn't have any enemies at all. He wasn't the boss of a big company, the orphanage was a non-profit-making body.'

'He had money, though.'

'Who told you that?' asked Doc, leaning forward. He pulled a cigarette out of its pack, lit it with his Zippo, and put the red and white pack and the lighter on the low table in front of him.

'One of the nuns. She said Eric paid for everything.'

'He did, but through a trust fund he'd set up. No one could have made a profit from Eric's death.'

Wright put down his bottle of lager. 'Where did Eric get his money from?'

Doc shrugged. 'He never said. He turned up in Bangkok five years ago. Before that he was in Saigon. Before that he was in the States, living rough on the Canadian border.'

'Living rough?'

'I guess he went a little crazy after he got back home. Went off to live by himself in the woods.'

'Back home?'

Doc went suddenly still as if he'd just realised that he'd said too much. Hammack, Ramirez and O'Leary sat looking at him. Ramirez waved the girls away. They pouted and went over to stand by the bar. Wright waited, knowing it was a turning point in the conversation: Doc could either shut up, change the subject, or continue. It was a moment Wright recognised from countless interviews with suspects and witnesses and he knew there was no way he could influence the way Doc would jump. All he could do was wait.

Doc blew smoke out through his nostrils as he stared at Wright. 'Back to the world,' he said eventually. 'From Vietnam. He was a Vietnam vet, and he had a rough war. Post traumatic stress syndrome they call it now. Crazy, they called it back then. Eric went crazy, but no more than thousands of others. Did you know that fifty-eight thousand Americans died in the war? But many more than that went on to commit suicide after they got back. You don't see their names on the wall.'

'The wall?'

'The Vietnam War Memorial in Washington. All the names of the dead are on that wall, they say, but that's shit because they forget about the ones that took their own lives. Tens of thousands of suicides, probably more than a hundred thousand if you count all the car wrecks and drug overdoses. Where are their names, Sergeant Wright? Who remembers them?'

'What about your war, Doc?' asked Wright quietly. 'What was your war like?'

Doc looked at him, his eyes bloodshot and watery. He looked suddenly tired. 'You don't want to know about my war,' he said.

'I can't imagine what it must have been like, to have been sent thousands of miles away from your home to fight a war in a country you knew nothing about. I can barely walk through Bangkok without getting covered in sweat, it must have been hell to have been sent into the jungle carrying a gun. Being shot at.'

'Ever been in a war zone?' asked Doc.

Wright shook his head.

'So you'd never understand, even if I spent a hundred years trying to describe it.'

'And Eckhardt? What was his war like?'

Doc's eyes hardened. Wright could feel the barriers building up. 'How would I know?' asked Doc.

'I just thought that maybe he was a Vietnam War vet, too. That seems to be the common thread, right? You, Eric. And Bernie, Sergio and Dennis, you're all about the same age, all American, I just assumed . . .'

'You assume a lot,' said Doc coldly.

'What about you, Dennis?' Wright asked O'Leary.

O'Leary flinched as if he'd been struck. 'What?'

'Your tour of duty in Vietnam. Is that where you were injured?'

O'Leary looked at Doc. Doc gave a small shake of his head, the sort of gesture he used to such good effect when they were playing. O'Leary looked away and said nothing.

'Maybe it's time you left,' said Doc.

'Why did you take the photograph down?' Wright asked.

'What photograph?' asked Doc.

'You know what photograph. Did you think I hadn't seen it? Did you think that if you took it down I'd convince myself that I'd imagined it?'

Doc said nothing.

'What's going on?' Wright pressed. 'Why the secrecy? They were friends of yours and they were murdered. Don't you want to know who the killer is?'

'We know,' said O'Leary bitterly.

Doc flashed him a withering look and O'Leary put up his hands as if warding off an attack.

'Why don't we tell him?' asked O'Leary.

'This isn't the time or the place,' said Doc.

'You name it,' said Wright.

Doc glared at the detective. 'You're an outsider here, Sergeant Wright, and you've overstayed your welcome.'

'There are still some questions . . .'

'You're not in England now,' said Doc. 'We don't have to tell you anything.'

'I just thought . . .'

'You just thought that if you came along and jammed with us then we'd open up to you like shucked oysters.' Doc stood up. He looked across at Hammack. Hammack stood up, too, his massive arms swinging at his side. 'You can leave under your own steam, or I can provide an alternative. It's up to you,' said Doc.

Wright could see that it was pointless arguing. 'Okay, I can take a hint,' he said. 'Do you mind if I have a cigarette?' Before Doc could say anything, he leaned over and picked up the pack of Marlboro and the lighter.

'Didn't realise you smoked,' said Doc.

Wright took out a cigarette and lit it. He looked at the Zippo. The rat engraved on the side grinned up at him. Wright flipped the lighter over. A Latin phrase was inscribed on the back: *Non Gratum Anus Rodentum*.

Doc took the lighter and the pack from Wright. He nodded at the door.

Wright smiled thinly and held up his hands in mock surrender. 'I can tell when I'm not wanted,' he said. On his way to the swing doors he stubbed out the unsmoked cigarette.

The three flaming torches soared high in the air and the juggler looked up optimistically, his top hat perched precariously on the back of his head. He caught them one by one to scattered applause while a young girl with braided blonde hair walked around with a Harrods bag collecting change from the spectators. As he continued to whirl the torches around his head, the juggler flicked off his top hat and caught it deftly with his right foot.

Gerry Hunter walked behind the crowd and headed for a row of small speciality stores at the far end of Covent Garden. The shop he was looking for was in the middle. Game For A Laugh, it was called, and the window display consisted of board games and books, including more than a dozen different chess sets. Hunter pushed open the door and a bell ding-donged at the back of the store. A balding, overweight man in rolled-up shirtsleeves was sitting behind the counter reading a chess book. He looked up and nodded at Hunter, then went back to his book.

Hunter was the only customer. There were glass-display cases containing more chess sets and stacks of board games, some like Monopoly and Cluedo that Hunter remembered from his childhood, but many that he'd never seen before. Hunter went over to the glass counter. On a shelf below it he saw what he was looking for: dozens of packs of playing cards.

'Help you?' said the man, putting down his book.

Hunter showed him his warrant card. 'I'm interested in a playing card,' he said, taking the plastic bag containing the ace of spades from his coat pocket.

The man took it. 'Is that blood?' he asked.

Hunter nodded. 'Do you know who made the card?'

'Sure do,' said the man. 'The United States Playing Card Company. Biggest card company in the world.' He turned the card over. 'What made the hole?' he asked. 'A bullet?'

Hunter ignored the question. 'Is there anything special about the card?'

The man's lower lip jutted forward and he frowned, as if thinking was an effort. 'Not that I can think of,' he said. He scratched his bald head, and flakes of skin drifted down on to the counter. 'They've got several brands. This one they call Bicycle.'

'Any idea why?'

The man shrugged. 'Just a name, I think.' He showed the front of the card to Hunter. 'See the woman here? The white figure? That's only on the Bicycle brand.'

Hunter took the card off him. 'Do you know much about the cards?'

'I'm more of a chess buff,' said the man, indicating the display case full of chess pieces and boards. 'If I had my way that's all I'd sell, but there's not the call for them that there was. It's computers or fantasy games. Even playing cards don't sell like they used to. What is it you want to know?'

'That's the thing,' said Hunter. 'I'm not really sure.'

The man nodded at the card in Hunter's hand. 'It's a clue, right?'

Hunter smiled thinly. 'Yeah, it's a clue. A big clue. But I haven't the faintest idea what it means. Do you know of anyone who is a real card expert? Somebody who might be able to tell me something about the history of playing cards, stuff like that.'

'Try the card company,' said the man. 'Their head office is in Cincinnati, Ohio.' He scratched his peeling scalp again.

Hunter thanked him and headed back to his office. He wasn't sure what the time difference was between Cincinnati and London, but he figured it must be about six hours. He had time for a quick bite in the canteen before he called the company.

Wright managed to find a taxi driver who spoke reasonable English and he explained that he wanted to sit and watch the bar for a while. 'Five hundred baht for one hour,' said the driver.

'Whatever,' said Wright. He settled back in his seat. The driver tuned his radio to a Thai pop station and adjusted the airconditioning. After an hour, there was still no sign of the members of The Jazz Club leaving Cowboy Nights.

The driver turned around and held out his hand. 'One more hour, five hundred baht,' he said. Wright handed over another purple banknote.

Three elephants walked slowly down the road, trunks and

tails swinging in unison. Each had a man sitting astride its neck, and ahead of them walked a man carrying a string bag full of coconuts.

Thirty minutes later a grey minivan pulled up in front of the bar, driven by a middle-aged Thai man in a pale blue safari suit. The man went into the bar and a few minutes later the swing doors opened and he reappeared, followed by Doc, who was pushing O'Leary's wheelchair. They all headed over to the minivan. The driver climbed back into the cab and opened a side door. A lifting mechanism swung out and down and Doc pushed O'Leary's wheelchair on to it. The wheelchair slowly lifted into the air and back into the van. Doc climbed in with O'Leary and the two men were deep in conversation as the van pulled away from the kerb.

Wright pointed after the van. The driver nodded and followed.

O'Leary lived half an hour's drive from Cowboy Nights, in a row of modern townhouses in a quiet side street. Wright told the driver to keep his distance and they stopped at the end of the street, behind a black pick-up truck. The van parked and the safari-suited driver helped Doc unload O'Leary and his wheelchair. Doc pushed O'Leary up a ramp to the front door and into the house.

Wright's driver turned around and looked expectantly at Wright. The detective handed over another purple banknote.

Doc left the house fifteen minutes later. He climbed into the front of the minivan and it drove off down the road.

Wright waited a few minutes, then went over to the front door and knocked on it. A Thai woman answered it, barefoot in T-shirt and jeans. Wright told her who he was and said that he wanted to speak to Dennis. She stepped to the side to let him in.

Dennis O'Leary was sitting in his wheelchair at the far end of the room, a bottle of whisky on the table next to him. An Eric Clapton CD was playing on an expensive stereo system under one of the windows. Wright recognised the album. *Journeyman*.

'What do you want?' O'Leary asked.

'Just a chat,' said Wright. The girl who'd opened the door padded up an open wooden staircase and disappeared into a bedroom. 'Your wife?' asked Wright.

O'Leary shook his head. 'No. Not my wife.' He drank from a tumbler. 'Doc says we shouldn't talk to you.'

'Do you do everything Doc says?' asked Wright.

O'Leary put his head on one side as he considered the question. 'Pretty much,' he said.

The room was large, with dark wooden floorboards and rosewood furniture and several large Buddha statues, most of which looked very old. Thai embroideries hung on the walls. At one end of the room there were two guitars on stands, like sentries on duty. There was no airconditioning but two metal fans whirred overhead and the windows had been left open so that a gentle night breeze blew across Wright's back. Two doors led off the main room and both had been widened to accommodate O'Leary's chair. Across one of the doorways was a metal pole which Wright guessed O'Leary used for arm exercises, and in the far corner of the room was a set of dumb-bells and weights.

'Nice place,' said Wright.

O'Leary shrugged but said nothing. His face was flushed. He'd untied his ponytail and his long hair hung around his shoulders like some sort of Viking warrior. A crippled warrior, thought Wright. Maybe that was why he was drinking so heavily.

Wright gestured at the bottle of whisky. 'May I?' he said.

'I thought you were a lager drinker,' said O'Leary.

'I'll take what I can get,' said Wright.

O'Leary waved at the bottle. 'Help yourself,' he said.

Wright took a glass from a cabinet. There were several photographs in brass frames on a shelf below the glasses. Pictures of O'Leary with a pretty Thai woman and two children, a boy and a girl. In none of the photographs was O'Leary in a wheelchair.

'Yeah,' said O'Leary from behind him. 'That's my wife.'

'She's lovely,' said Wright. 'Great kids, too. How old are they there? Four and six?'

'The girl was five then, the boy seven. They're sixteen and eighteen now.'

'They don't live with you?'

O'Leary sneered and took another long pull at his whisky. 'No profit in it any more,' he said, and slapped the wheelchair. 'Half a man.'

Wright sat down on a wooden chair that had elephants stencilled into the back of it. 'I'm sorry about before, when I was asking if it happened during the war.'

'That's okay,' said O'Leary. 'In a way it would have been better if it had happened then. At least then I'd have got disability payments. Two tours of duty without a scratch and I have to fall off a fucking motorcycle.'

'It's not going to get better?' asked Wright.

O'Leary shook his head. 'I'm in this chair for life,' he said. 'My wife came to see me in hospital, spoke to the doctors, and I haven't seen her or the kids since. She sold my business, the house, the car, took the money and went upcountry. That was seven years ago.'

'That's rough,' said Wright.

'It's Thai style,' said O'Leary. 'No matter how much you think they love you, no matter how much you give them, they always want more. She knew I'd never walk again so she figured she'd better look for another man before she got any older.'

'And the kids?'

'She probably told them I'd died.' He drank and swirled his whisky around the glass as he stared into it. 'Might have been better if I had. Bastards.'

Wright wasn't sure who O'Leary was cursing. He went over and refilled the man's glass, then poured more whisky into his own.

'Thais,' said O'Leary, as if sensing Wright's confusion. 'Give them your finger and they'll take your hand. Give them your hand and they'll want your arm. Give them your arm . . .' He scowled. 'Been to the bars yet?'

Wright shook his head. He sat down again.

'Pat Pong, Nana Plaza, Soi Cowboy. The red light areas. You'll meet beautiful girls there, stunners, and they'll be all over you. They'll smile and they'll bat their gorgeous brown eyes at you and they'll fondle your dick and they'll take you for everything they can.'

'Yeah, but you're talking about hookers,' said Wright.

'Ha! They're all fucking hookers,' said O'Leary. 'Every last one of them. Any girl you see driving an expensive car in Bangkok has either fucked someone rich or is the daughter of someone who's been fucked by someone rich. It's all about money, and when my wife thought her gravy train had come off the rails, she ran like the fucking wind.'

'What about this?' said Wright, indicating the room. 'This is a nice place.'

'It's Doc's,' said O'Leary. 'He lets me live here. If it wasn't for Doc, I'd be on the fucking street.'

'It's a better place than where I'm living,' said Wright. He told O'Leary about his own domestic situation, about his divorce and the arguments over access to his son.

O'Leary nodded sympathetically. 'Yeah, it's the kids I miss most,' he said. 'Not knowing what they look like, what they're doing. Not knowing if they even know that I'm alive. Don't let her keep your son away from you, Nick. Do what you have to do. Fight and don't stop fighting, okay?'

Wright raised his glass in salute. 'Here's to that,' he said, and the two men toasted each other. Wright could feel the warmth of the spirit spreading comfortingly across his stomach and he stretched out his feet.

'Tell me about Doc,' said Wright.

'Like what?'

'You met him in Vietnam, right?'

'Yup.'

'And you've all stayed together for twenty-five years? I don't think I've any friends from twenty-five years ago. There must be something special between you all to keep you together.'

O'Leary flicked his hair away from his shoulders with a quick movement of his head. 'Do you know much about Vietnam, Nick?'

Wright shook his head. 'Not much.'

O'Leary helped himself to more whisky. The bottle was almost empty when he put it back on the table. 'Doc wasn't being facetious about it taking a hundred years to describe what it was like,' he continued. 'If you weren't there, you'd never understand. There's a bond formed with the people you fought with, a bond that's stronger than marriage, than family, than loyalty to your country.'

Wright cradled his glass with both hands. O'Leary stared at the floor, almost as if he was talking to himself.

'The VC had a network of tunnels right across the country, built when the French occupied Vietnam, and then expanded when we went in to help the South. By the time the war was almost over, they had hundreds of miles of tunnels, stretching from Saigon to the Cambodian border. They started off as a way of getting from village to village without being seen, but by the time we were there they had huge underground installations: training rooms, armament factories, bomb shelters, hospitals, dormitories. Thousands of VCs and civilians lived underground, coming out to fight at night, then disappearing as soon as they came under fire.'

A cockroach scuttled across the floor in front of O'Leary's wheelchair, a big insect several inches long, but O'Leary didn't appear to notice it.

'We all went down the tunnels, Doc, Bernie, Sergio and I. Max and Eric, too. Bernie, Sergio and Max were with the Twenty-eighth Infantry, First Engineer Battalion. Eric was with Special Forces, but he was attached to the Tunnel Rats for six months. I was supposed to be mapping the tunnel network. Doc was a medic. You asked what sort of war we had? It was a shitty, dirty, nasty war, Nick. A war fought underground, in the dark, with guns and knives because there wasn't room to use anything bigger, in a battleground totally of the enemy's making, booby-trapped, full of poisonous snakes and spiders and God knows what else.' He shivered and rubbed the bridge of his nose as if trying to stave off a sneeze.

'Five of us stayed in South-East Asia after our tour of duty: Doc, Bernie, Sergio, Max and I. Max went over to the States in the 'eighties, then we met up with Eric five years ago.'

'Why were you so reluctant to tell me that yesterday?' asked Wright.

O'Leary looked across at him, his jaw set tight. 'Why should we tell you anything? What happened back then is nothing to do with you.'

Wright didn't say anything for several seconds. O'Leary looked away and took a mouthful of whisky. He gulped it down.

'What did happen?' Wright asked eventually.

O'Leary didn't answer, nor did he look at Wright. The only indication that he'd heard the question was a slight shrug of his shoulders.

'Is it connected to the way Horvitz and Eckhardt died?' asked Wright.

O'Leary continued to avoid Wright's gaze.

Wright decided to try a different approach. 'Tell me about Doc's lighter,' he said. 'The Zippo.'

'What about it?'

'There's a rat on one side, a rat with a torch and a gun. And a Latin motto on the other.' He screwed up his face as he tried to recall the words he'd read. '*Non Gratum Anus Rodentum*. Rodentum is rat, I guess.'

O'Leary smiled. 'Not worth a rat's ass,' he said. 'More of a credo than a motto.'

'That's how you felt?' asked Wright.

'We lost a lot of friends down the tunnels,' said O'Leary.

'Were you volunteers?'

'The Tunnel Rats? Sure. There's no way they could force you down there.'

'So why do it?'

O'Leary pressed his glass against his cheek. 'That's the question,' he said quietly. 'If you could answer that, you'd know a hell of a lot about human nature.'

'Self-destructive, was that it? Some urge to punish yourself?'

O'Leary shook his head. 'We didn't go down there to get killed, or to punish ourselves. We fought to stay alive, we took every precaution we could.'

'But you didn't have to go down in the first place.'

O'Leary flashed Wright a lopsided grin. 'Doesn't make sense, does it?'

'What about Doc's motivation? Why did he join the Tunnel Rats?'

'He was already a veteran of the tunnels when I met him. I think he wanted to make sure we didn't get hurt. He likes to take care of people, does Doc. He likes to lead, he likes responsibility.'

'And Ramirez?'

'Ramirez? I think he just wanted to prove that nothing scares him.'

'Prove to who? To you? Or to himself?'

'Another good question.'

'Hammack?'

O'Leary swatted a mosquito that had settled on his left leg. 'Bernie wanted to be special. There weren't many blacks down in the tunnels.'

'What about Horvitz?'

'Eric was Special Forces. I think of any of us he was the one most reluctant to go. I don't think he had anything to prove. But he was a good soldier and he obeyed orders.'

'And Max?'

'I didn't really know Max, we only went on the one mission together.'

There it was, out in the open. Wright said nothing, allowing the pause to get longer and longer. O'Leary drained his whisky. He poured the rest of the bottle into his glass. A motorcycle roared by outside and Wright caught a whiff of exhaust fumes through the open windows.

'I can't tell you any more,' said O'Leary softly.

'You have to,' said Wright. 'You owe it to Eric and Max.'

O'Leary shook his head. 'We can't ever tell. Any of us.'

'But it was twenty-five years ago, Dennis. A quarter of a century.'

'I know,' said O'Leary bitterly. 'You think I don't know exactly how long it's been?'

'Two men have died, and it's connected with whatever happened in Vietnam. You said you knew who it was. Who, Dennis? Who's killing the Tunnel Rats?'

O'Leary drained his glass and looked mournfully at the empty bottle. 'A ghost,' he whispered.

'A ghost?'

O'Leary looked up, and there was no disguising the fear in his eyes. 'He isn't dead,' he said, his voice a dry rattle. 'He isn't dead and he's coming back for revenge.'

O'Leary slumped back in his chair and his eyes closed. Wright sat and watched him. After a minute or so O'Leary began to snore, and his head fell forward on to his chest.

He'd drunk almost three quarters of the bottle of whisky, plus several beers at Cowboy Nights.

Wright stood up. One of the two doors led through to a kitchen, beyond which was a patio with a barbecue pit. A brown and white dog looked up at Wright and then settled back to sleep. The other door led to a large bedroom containing a king-sized bed swathed in mosquito nets. The furniture appeared to have been designed with O'Leary's disability in mind: there was a dressing table built so that there was room for the wheelchair, and the wardrobes were all low so that O'Leary could remove his clothes while sitting. Wright went back into the main room and pushed O'Leary into the bedroom. He was a big man and it took all Wright's strength to lift him out of the chair and roll him on to the bed. He loosened O'Leary's shirt, then switched off the light and left.

International directory enquiries had no problem coming up with a number for the United States Playing Card Company. Hunter got through to a fast-talking girl in the public relations department whose enthusiasm came bursting out of the telephone with all the force of a tornado. She was even more excited when Hunter told her that he was a policeman investigating a murder, though considerably less pleased to discover that one of her company's products was involved. Hunter explained that he wanted to speak to someone about the playing cards in general, and in particular any role they played in the Vietnam War.

'I can't think of anyone in the company, not off hand,' she said, 'but we do have a museum devoted to playing cards. They've got more than a hundred thousand different decks. Why don't you call them?'

Hunter took down the number of the museum and thanked her. This time a man answered, and he spoke in slow, measured sentences as if he was considering each word before he allowed it to pass his lips. His name was Walter Matthau. 'Not the actor,' he said. 'But we do share the same birthday. My friends call me Wally.'

Hunter explained why he was calling and asked Wally if the Bicycle brand had played any special role in the Vietnam War.

'Sure did,' said Wally.

When Wally didn't elaborate, Hunter had to prompt him. 'Could you tell me exactly what that role was?' he asked.

'The ace of spades,' said Wally. 'It was the death card.'

Hunter felt a surge of excitement. 'Death card?' he repeated.

'They were left as calling cards by the Twenty-fifth Infantry Division. And by Special Forces in Operation Phoenix.'

Hunter was so shocked that for several seconds he couldn't speak. He hadn't expected to strike gold so quickly. 'What do you mean, calling cards?'

Wally sniffed before continuing, and Hunter suspected that the man had just wiped his nose. 'It was back in 'sixty-six, I think. The company got a letter from two lieutenants in the Twenty-fifth Infantry Division. Seems they'd been leaving the cards behind whenever they attacked the Viet Cong. They reckoned the VC were scared of the cards, you see? Part of their folklore, the ace of spades, it represents death. And the soldiers preferred the Bicycle brand because of the woman. The woman in white. The VC thought it was a ghost. You know what I'm talking about, Inspector Hunter?'

'Yes, I've seen the card. It was always the ace of spades? I was watching *Apocalypse Now* and in the movie they used all sorts of cards.'

'Yeah, I remember that scene. Robert Duvall, right? I don't know what that was about. I heard of one long-range reconnaissance patrol that used one-eyed jacks, but generally it was our ace of spades. It was started by the infantry but Special Forces started using it as well once they realised how effective it was. They were so popular that they wanted us to send them a thousand aces of spades.'

'A thousand?'

'That's right.'

'And the company was happy to help? Despite what they were being used for?'

'Our company has a long and proud history of supporting the military,' said Wally. 'We ended up sending several million aces of spades, in special packs. Didn't charge them a cent. We designed a special pack. "Secret Weapon, Bicycle Ace of Spades", it said. Don't know if they were all used. Is this of any use to you, Inspector Hunter?'

'A great help, Wally. Believe me. You said something about an Operation Phoenix. What was that about?'

'It was a plan to destroy the VC by getting rid of as many members as possible. They used bribery, military attacks, and there were rumours of assassinations. The South targeted some ten thousand VCs who were reckoned to be crucial to the organisation, from local politicians up to full generals. Thousands of them died.'

'Thousands of assassinations?'

'Depends who you believe,' said Wally. 'The official

line was that most were killed in military engagements. Jane Fonda and her lily-livered liberals would probably accuse our boys of personally torturing and butchering every last man.'

Hunter made copious notes in his notebook, grateful for the man's slow delivery. 'And who was involved in this operation?'

'Now, I'm no expert on the Vietnam War, Inspector Hunter. Playing cards are my specialty. You'd better talk to someone who knows what they're talking about. I wouldn't want to steer you wrong.'

Hunter clicked his ballpoint pen shut. 'Wally, I can't thank you enough,' he said.

Dennis O'Leary awoke, struggling to breathe. He tried to twist his head to the side but something was clamped across his chin, pressing him down on to the bed.

'Don't struggle, and don't make a noise, Dennis,' hissed a man's voice.

O'Leary tried to turn to face the man but he couldn't move his head.

'I mean it, Dennis,' said the man. 'I don't want to have to kill your maid or anyone else who's in the house, but I will if they wake up. Do you understand?'

O'Leary nodded.

'Now, I'm going to take my hand away, and I don't want you to make a sound until I've finished speaking, do you understand, Dennis?'

O'Leary nodded again. He didn't recognise the voice, but the accent was American.

'I've got a knife, Dennis, a very sharp knife, and I know how to use it. If I even think you're going to shout for help I'll slit your throat. Understand?'

O'Leary closed his eyes and nodded. The hand went from his mouth and he felt the man move around the bed and sit down on the edge of it. O'Leary opened his eyes. The man was in his late twenties with a military haircut and a prominent dimple in his chin.

'What do you want?' O'Leary whispered.

The man held a finger to his lips and held up a knife. It had a long, thin blade and was curved slightly at the point. 'I want you to tell me everything you told Nick Wright,' said the man. 'And then I want you to tell me everything that you didn't tell him.'

G erry Hunter dialled the number of Jim Bamber's hotel. The female receptionist who answered had an East European accent and spoke English that was slightly too correct, as if she'd learned from a textbook published in the 'fifties. Hunter asked to speak to Bamber.

'I am terribly sorry, but the gentleman is no longer resident at our establishment,' she said.

'Are you sure?' asked Hunter. The FBI agent hadn't said that he was planning to change hotels. It was unprofessional of him not to have informed the Met.

'I am certain. The gentleman checked out on Tuesday last.'

'Did he leave a forwarding number? Somewhere I can reach him?'

'I am afraid that he did not.'

Hunter thanked the girl and replaced the receiver. He called over to a WPC who was inputting data into her HOLMES computer and asked her if she had an up-to-date number for Bamber. She shook her head. Hunter had hoped that Bamber would be able to suggest the name of someone who could brief him on the Vietnam War and in particular Operation Phoenix. He also wanted to ask him if Clive had voiced any suspicions about there being a Vietnam connection to Eckhardt's murder. Reynolds had said that Clive was going to ask Bamber to help him get information on Eckhardt's war service record from the Defense Department. Now he'd have to wait until the FBI agent got in touch.

He decided to call his local library. There was a lady there, Miss Blackstone, who often helped him with enquiries. He'd never actually met her, but he pictured Miss Blackstone as a fifty-something matronly figure, several stones overweight with ornate spectacles and purple-tinted hair. She worked in the reference section, and always seemed pleased to hear from him; he felt that she probably enjoyed telling her friends how she helped Scotland Yard crack their most difficult cases.

'Why, Gerald, it's so nice to hear from you,' she said when he got through to her. She insisted on calling him Gerald, even though no one else, not even his parents, used the full version of his name. Hunter explained what he wanted. 'Operation Phoenix,' she whispered as if she was frightened of being overheard. 'What's the case, Gerald?'

'It's confidential at the moment, Miss Blackstone. I'll be

able to tell you more once I've got a suspect, but at the moment I'm just looking for background information.'

'We do have an extensive military history section,' she said. 'Let me see what I've got on the Vietnam War.'

'Could you do me a favour, Miss Blackstone? Could you fax me over anything you find?' He knew from past experience that the librarian would do such a thorough job that it could take her several hours. Miss Blackstone said she'd be delighted to and Hunter gave her the fax number before hanging up.

Hunter sat back in his chair. He was worried about Bamber checking out of his hotel without telling him. Everything else about the man had been extremely professional; it was out of character for him not to have been in touch. He obtained the American Embassy's telephone number from directory enquiries and asked to be put through to the FBI's office. He got through to one of the Bureau's representatives who introduced himself as Ed Harris, a legal attaché. Hunter explained who he was and that he was trying to track down Jim Bamber.

'Never heard of him,' said Harris.

'Are you sure?'

'Sure I'm sure. There are only five of us here in London. What office does he work out of?'

'Washington,' said Hunter.

'And he's here in what capacity?' asked Harris.

'Shouldn't you know? He's one of your agents.'

'Not necessarily,' said Harris. 'The London office is part of the FBI's legal attaché programme. We're here to liaise with the local police forces and security services. We exchange information, we don't investigate crimes.'

'But this guy Bamber, he said he'd been seconded here from Washington. He said—'

'Don't get me wrong, Inspector Hunter, I'm not saying it's not possible, I'm just saying that he's not working out of the London office. He could be reporting direct to Washington or to the Bureau's intelligence division. What exactly is he doing here?'

'He's helping us with a murder enquiry. An American by the name of Max Eckhardt. But he's checked out of his hotel and I don't know where he is.'

'Well, I can assure you he hasn't made contact with us,' said Harris. 'But I'll speak to headquarters, he shouldn't be too hard to track down. Give me your number and I'll get back to you.'

Hunter did as Harris asked and thanked him. He replaced the receiver. His stomach growled and he decided to pop over to the canteen for a quick meal. He had a hunch that it was going to be a long night.

Nick Wright was in a cold, dark place. His hands were shaking and his legs were trembling. He was afraid. 'Dad?' His voice echoed around the darkness, but there was no reply. 'Dad?' he called again. There was a ringing sound off in the distance, muffled as if it was coming through water. He opened his eyes. It was a telephone.

He groaned, rolled on to his stomach, and reached for the phone by his bed. He put it to his ear and heard a dialling tone. The ringing continued. He dropped the receiver back on its cradle.

The ringing was coming from Wright's suitcase. He pulled it down from the top of the wardrobe and opened it. It was his mobile ringing. 'Yeah?' he said, putting it to his ear.

'Nick?' It was Tommy Reid.

'Hey, Tommy.'

'Wasn't sure if your mobile would work,' said Reid.

'It's a GSM, same as yours,' said Wright. 'Should work anywhere in the world.'

'Satellites,' said Reid. 'Bloody marvellous, aren't they? How's it going, mate?' He was slurring his words. Wright looked at his wristwatch. It was just after midnight back in London. 'You alone, or have you got some lovely Asian babe with you?'

'I'm alone, Tommy. Alone and asleep. What do you want?'

'Just wanted to see how you were getting on.'

'Great. Eckhardt and Horvitz served together in Vietnam,' said Wright. 'In a unit called the Tunnel Rats. Something happened twenty-five years ago, something they want to keep secret.'

'Yeah? What was that?'

Wright closed his eyes. 'Tommy, if they want to keep it a secret, why the fuck would they tell me?'

'Because of your smooth tongue? Because they like you? Because you're a sodding policeman?'

'Yeah, well, I was talking to one of them tonight, a guy called O'Leary, but he'd only open up so much.'

'What about the Thai police? Are they any help?'

'Don't seem interested. But I did have a look at their file on Horvitz's murder, and guess what: the card on the chest is exactly the same.' Wright heard the chink of glass against glass. Reid was obviously pouring himself another drink.

There was a knock at the door. Wright went over to answer it, but realised he was naked and hurried to the bathroom for a towel.

'Hold on a minute, Tommy,' said Wright. He pulled open the door.

Jim Bamber was standing there, an easy grin on his face. The grin disappeared when he saw that Wright was on the phone.

'Fuck me,' said Wright.

'But you're so far away, darling,' said Reid, giggling.

'Not you, you soft bastard. Jim. Jim Bamber. He's here.' Wright opened the door for the FBI agent. Bamber was wearing his usual grey suit and white shirt and he looked fresh and relaxed as if he'd just showered. Wright gestured at the phone. 'Tommy,' he mouthed.

Bamber nodded and went to stand by the window.

'What's he doing there?' asked Reid.

'Tommy wants to know what you're doing in Bangkok,' said Wright, closing the door.

'The second murder,' said Bamber.

'Same as me,' said Wright into the phone. 'The second killing.' Bamber was standing looking out of the window, his arms folded. 'Look, tell Hunter what I've told you, will you? I'll talk to you tomorrow, okay?'

'Ah,' moaned Reid. 'Can't you read me a night-night story?'

'Goodnight, Tommy,' said Wright.

'Goodnight, John Boy.'

Wright cut the connection and put the telephone on the dressing table. 'Sorry about that, Jim. Tommy likes to talk when he's pissed.'

'Pissed?' Bamber turned around, frowning. 'What's he pissed at?'

'Pissed. Drunk.'

Bamber smiled. 'Oh, right. I get it. Two nations divided by a single language.'

'Something like that. When did you get to Bangkok?'

'Three days ago. I didn't realise you'd come to Thailand. Who told you about the murder in Bangkok?'

'Anonymous tip-off,' said Wright. 'Someone sent in some newspaper cuttings.'

'So Superintendent Newton sent you to Bangkok?'

'He's as keen as I am that the BTP solve this case.'

'Seems a little unusual, that's all. An American murdered in Bangkok. Not really your jurisdiction.'

'The two cases are obviously connected,' said Wright. 'It's got to be the same killer.'

'No doubt about it', said Bamber. 'That's what I told my bosses. So what progress have you made?'

'O'Leary's one of four Americans who play together at a club called Cowboy Nights.'

'Near Lang Suan. I know.'

'Yeah, there's Dennis O'Leary, a guy called Doc Marshall who's sort of the group leader, Bernie Hammack and Sergio Ramirez. And the victims both played with the band. Not together, Eckhardt left before Horvitz arrived, but they all knew each other in Vietnam, twenty-five years ago. They were all Tunnel Rats, fighting the Viet Cong underground.'

Bamber raised an eyebrow, clearly impressed. 'You've found out a lot in a short time,' he said.

'I was lucky,' said Wright. 'I saw a photograph of Eckhardt with the band in Cowboy Nights, and I managed to get O'Leary to talk to me a little. We've both had woman troubles. And he'd been drinking. What about you? What have you found out?'

Bamber adjusted the cuffs of his jacket. 'I'd pinned down the Tunnel Rats connection. Our Washington office checked up on the service records of both men and discovered they'd served together for a time towards the end of the war. I haven't approached the four surviving members in case one of them is the killer.'

'What?' said Wright, stunned.

Bamber frowned. 'Hadn't you considered that? It seemed obvious to me. Either Marshall, Hammack or Ramirez could be behind the murders. O'Leary we can rule out because of the chair, but the others are definite suspects. Immigration is doing a check for me to see if any of them were out of the country at the time Eckhardt was killed.'

Wright sat down on the edge of the bed. 'But whatever it was that happened twenty-five years ago, they've all kept the secret. Why start killing now?'

'I don't know, Nick. But I did find out something else. They're all going back to Vietnam. Back down the tunnels. All except O'Leary, of course.'

'Why?'

'I'm not sure. All I know is that they've already applied for their visas and have booked tickets on Wednesday's Thai flight to Saigon.'

'How the hell did you find that out?'

'We've had them under surveillance,' said Bamber.

Wright rubbed his eyes. 'This is crazy, Jim. If one of them is the killer, why would he want to go back down the tunnels?'

'Maybe he wants to finish the job.'

'So why would the other two go? Why put themselves in harm's way?'

Bamber opened the minibar. 'Okay if I have a soda?' he asked. Wright nodded. Bamber took out a can of Sprite and popped the tab. He sipped it. 'Nick, you're asking questions that I don't have the answers to. But I know for sure that the solution lies down in the tunnels. We have to go, Nick. It's the only way we're going to solve this case.'

Wright's jaw dropped. 'You have got to be joking!' he exclaimed.

Bamber drank from his can. 'It's the only way,' he said.

Wright shook his head emphatically. 'O'Leary said there were hundreds of miles of tunnels, all the way from Saigon to Cambodia. How are you going to find out where they're going?'

Bamber grinned, crushed his empty can and tossed it into a wastepaper bin. 'I'm getting a map sent over. The Defense Department mapped a big chunk of the tunnel network, and the mission that Horvitz, Eckhardt and the rest went on was recorded. I'm getting the file pulled from the Pentagon, and it and the map are being sent over to our office here.'

'And you're going down the tunnels?'

'Not just me. We. It's going to take two, Nick. I need you down there with me.'

Wright swallowed. His mouth had gone completely dry. 'I'm not sure if I'm up to it,' he said.

Bamber looked at him levelly. 'You want to solve this, don't you? That's presumably why you came.'

'Yes, but . . .'

'There are no buts. The answer lies down in the tunnels. That's where they're going and that's where we have to go. Okay?'

'Okay,' said Wright, reluctantly.

Bamber walked over to stand in front of Wright. The detective looked up at him. For a wild moment he thought that the FBI agent was going to strike him. The feeling was so strong that he had to force himself not to flinch. 'I mean it, Nick. I need you on this. I need you to be one hundred per cent committed.'

'I am,' said Wright, more sure this time.

'Good man. I'll arrange the tickets. I've already got my visa for Vietnam, I can pull a few strings to get yours done quickly. I'll need your passport.'

Wright got his passport from his dressing table and handed it to Bamber.

'One more thing,' said the FBI agent. 'Keep a low profile for the rest of the time you're in Bangkok. Don't go back to Cowboy Nights, don't speak with The Jazz Club, or the police. And don't mention me to anybody. I don't want anyone to know that the FBI's involved.'

Wright nodded. 'I understand.'

'Be ready to leave on Wednesday.'

Wright nodded again. His stomach began to churn.

Bamber went over to the door. He made a gun with the fingers of his hand and pointed it at Wright. He made a clicking noise, then let himself out.

Gerry Hunter sat down at his desk and drank from a can of 7-Up.

'Anything good in the canteen?' asked Steve Denning, a middle-aged DS with a thickening waistline and a tendency to snack on Mars bars during periods of stress.

'If there was, I missed it,' said Hunter, massaging his stomach.

'What did you have?'

'Sausage and chips, but I'm regretting it. Anyone call for me?'

Denning shook his head but pointed at a wire basket on the desk next to Hunter's. 'Fax came for you, though.'

Hunter reached over and retrieved the stack of pages. There were almost two dozen in all. Miss Blackstone had done him proud. There were photocopies of articles from several encyclopedias and selected pages from military history books and biographies.

He read through the pages and from time to time he made notes in the margins and underlined words and phrases that he thought might be significant. Hunter himself hadn't even been ten years old when South Vietnam fell, and for him the conflict was as distant an event as the First and Second World Wars. Many of the references to people and events meant nothing to him.

Gradually Hunter began to build up a picture of Operation Phoenix and its significance. It came towards the end of the war, when it was clear to most commentators that the

United States wasn't capable of winning by conventional means. The army thought that a change of tactics might produce results, and in 1968 Operation Phoenix was born. The aim was to identify and target specific members of the Viet Cong infrastructure: its fighters, its political cadres and its rank and file members. It was initially set up as a means of pooling intelligence information, which up until then had rarely been shared. The Americans didn't trust the South Vietnamese, and vice versa, and both sides guarded their intelligence jealously. Operation Phoenix set up official guidelines on how information was to be shared, and once targets had been identified they were arrested and interrogated. Some eighty Operation Phoenix offices were set up around South Vietnam, collating information with the aid of computers.

If proven to be Viet Cong sympathisers, targets would be either imprisoned or persuaded to change sides. It was, Hunter realised, the same technique that the British had used against the Provisional IRA in the 'seventies. In Northern Ireland the technique had paid dividends, with a number of notable successes, but in Vietnam, Operation Phoenix was regarded as a failure. There were allegations of torture and assassination, and time and time again Operation Phoenix was described as a front for government-sponsored assassination. Included among the photocopies were articles from American newspapers alleging that Operation Phoenix was primarily an assassination plot and that the CIA was targeting individual members of the Viet Cong and murdering them. All such allegations were denied by Defense Department spokesmen. The official view was that any deaths were the result of military action, not assassination.

According to some of the articles Miss Blackstone had photocopied from encyclopedias, Operation Phoenix wasn't regarded as a success because of all the negative publicity it generated, but it did come close to achieving its objectives. In 1968, almost 16,000 Viet Cong cadres and fighters were either captured, killed or switched sides. In 1970 the number was 21,000, and US intelligence experts estimated that over the four years that Operation Phoenix was underway, the Viet Cong infrastructure was reduced by a total of almost 75,000 men.

Nowhere in the information Miss Blackstone had sent was there any mention of the ace of spades death card. Wally Matthau had said that Special Forces had used the card, but there was no mention of Special Forces involvement in Operation Phoenix.

By the end of June 1972 all American advisers had been pulled out of South Vietnam, and a few months later the Saigon government ended Operation Phoenix.

Hunter sat back in his chair and stared up at the ceiling. What did he have so far? He had a dead middle-aged American, tortured and killed in London with a card impaled in his chest which had been used as a death card in the Vietnam War, and another in Bangkok which Wright was following up. Eckhardt had served in the Vietnam War. Had he come into contact with the soldiers using the death cards? Had Max Eckhardt himself been involved in Special Forces operations in Vietnam? Jim Bamber would probably be able to find out, but until Hunter could get in touch with the FBI agent he'd have to pursue his own line of enquiry, and the dead man's widow seemed the best bet. He picked up his coat.

'I'm going to see Eckhardt's widow,' he told Denning.

316

'You want company?' asked the detective sergeant.

'Nah. If Jim Bamber calls for me, tell him he can get me on my mobile.'

Denning gave him a thumbs-up without taking his eyes off his computer screen.

Hunter drove to the Eckhardts' flat in Maida Vale and parked in front of it. He walked down the path and peered at the doorbells. None bore the name Eckhardt. He took his notebook out of his raincoat pocket and checked the address. It was the right building. One of the bells didn't have a name attached to it and he pressed it hopefully. There was no response and he didn't bother pressing it again. Hunter heard a noise behind him and he turned to see a postman walking down the path pushing a mail cart. He showed the postman his warrant card and asked about May Eckhardt.

'Haven't had anything for them in a few days,' said the postman. 'I think they've moved.'

'Did they leave a forwarding address?'

The postman shook his head and began slotting letters through the communal letterbox. 'You could try asking old man Jenkins, Flat Two. He's the local busybody.'

The postman pushed his trolley back down the path and Hunter pressed the bell for Flat 2.

'Who is it?' asked a disembodied voice.

'Police,' said Hunter.

'Your name, please,' said the voice.

'Gerry Hunter. Inspector Gerry Hunter.'

'Hold your warrant card up to the camera behind you, please,' said the voice.

Hunter did as asked, suppressing a smile.

'Thank you,' said the voice. The door lock buzzed. 'You can come up.'

Hunter pushed open the door and went upstairs. He knocked on the door to Flat 2 and it was opened by a man in his seventies.

'Are you Mr Jenkins?'

'Yes,' said the old man, scrutinising Hunter through narrowed eyes. A security chain prevented the door from being opened more than a few inches. A dog yapped from somewhere behind him. 'Hush, Katie,' said Jenkins. 'It's only the police.' The dog continued to bark.

'Can I have a word with you about one of your neighbours?' said Hunter.

Jenkins undid the security chain and opened the door for Hunter. The flat stank of vomit and disinfectant and the detective wrinkled his nose at the smell.

'First on your right,' said Jenkins. 'It's about the Eckhardts, I assume,' he said as he followed Hunter into the sitting room. It was akin to stepping into a time warp. The wallpaper, carpets and furniture all seemed to be relics of the 1950s, clean but shabby. A gas fire surrounded by a green-tiled fireplace hissed like a deflating balloon and in the corner a six-foot-tall grandfather clock ticked off the passing seconds. 'Sit down, please,' said Jenkins, indicating a green velvet sofa that had worn bare in places.

Hunter sat down. Jenkins was wearing a blue dressing gown and tartan slippers, one of which had a hole in the toe through which poked a gnarled, yellowed toenail.

'I spoke to a Sergeant Wright some time ago,' said Jenkins. 'Of course, he wasn't a real policeman. Transport Police, he was.'

'That's right,' said Hunter.

'He was a rum sort,' said Jenkins. 'I couldn't understand why a transport policeman was involved in a murder investigation.' He drew out the word 'murder' as if reluctant to finish saying it.

'The body was found in a railway tunnel,' explained Hunter.

'Oh, I know that,' said Jenkins. 'But murder requires real police work, doesn't it?' Again he drew out the word 'murder' as if relishing the sound.

A bell tinkled and Jenkins flinched as if he'd been slapped. 'My wife,' he explained. 'She needs her medicine.'

Hunter felt suddenly sorry for the old man, living out his final years with a yappy dog and an invalid wife. It had been more than six months since Hunter had seen his own father, the detective realised. Six months was way too long. He sat and listened to the hissing gas fire and the ticking clock until Jenkins returned carrying a Yorkshire terrier. He perched on the edge of an armchair at the side of the fire, his back ramrod straight.

'So do you happen to know where Mrs Eckhardt is?' asked Hunter.

'Haven't seen her for a few weeks. Her car's not outside so I presume she's moved. Is she a suspect?'

'We just want to ask her a few questions,' said Hunter. 'Did she leave a forwarding address?'

'Not with me. As I told Sergeant Wright, the landlord or the managing agent might know. The agent's name and address is on the noticeboard by the front door.'

'What about her furniture? Did a removal van call?'

'Didn't see one, but I think they rented the flat furnished.'

'And you've no idea where she might have gone?'

Jenkins stroked the Yorkshire terrier behind the ears. 'Maybe she went home to China,' he said absentmindedly.

'China?' said Hunter. 'What makes you say that?'

'She was Chinese. Didn't you know? Spoke perfect English, but she was Chinese.'

'Are you sure she was from China?' asked Hunter.

'Well, she was Oriental, no mistaking that, but she wasn't Japanese, I'm damn sure.' The old man shuddered. 'I spent two years in a Japanese POW camp so I know what bloody Japs are like.' The old man shrugged. He looked suddenly older and there was a faraway look in his eyes as if his mind was elsewhere.

Hunter stood up. He thanked Jenkins for his help and shook his hand. His grip was surprisingly strong for a man of his years, and the memory of it and the smell of sickness stayed with Hunter for the rest of the day.

K ruse settled back in the taxi and closed his eyes. His meeting with Nick Wright had taken a completely unexpected turn and he had a lot of thinking to do. He'd gone to Wright's hotel room intent on killing the British detective, but the phone call had put paid to that. Kruse couldn't risk being associated with Wright's death, whether or not it looked like an accident. Tommy Reid might have an alcohol problem, but he wasn't stupid. The idea of taking Wright with him to Vietnam had come out of the blue, but Kruse was used to thinking on his feet and he knew it made perfect sense. Down in the tunnels anything could happen, and there'd be no witnesses. Getting a visa for Wright at short notice wouldn't be difficult: anything could be obtained in Bangkok for a price, and Jody Meacher had made it clear that money was no object.

Kruse went over the conversation he'd had with Wright, looking for any slips he might have made. He hadn't liked having to lie about getting information from the Pentagon, because that could be checked, but it was the only way he could think of explaining how he knew about the service records of the members of The Jazz Club. And he needed an explanation for the map that he'd taken from O'Leary's house. Suggesting that one of the surviving members of The Jazz Club might be the killer had been a flash of brilliance. It would keep Wright off balance, trusting no one.

The question of who the killer was still troubled Kruse. His thirty-minute conversation with O'Leary had provided no clues. Kruse knew exactly what had happened down the tunnels a quarter of a century ago, and he understood why the men needed to go back, but he didn't believe in ghosts and he didn't believe that dead men waited twenty-five years before coming back for revenge. The killer was real, flesh and blood, and Kruse knew that when the men went down the tunnels, the killer would be going too. Kruse smiled to himself. The witnesses would be there, the killer would be there, and the detective investigating the case would be there. And once Kruse had finished his work, all would be dead and buried deep below the earth. It was perfect, so perfect that the anticipation was almost painful.

The loud knocking on Wright's door woke him from a dreamless sleep, the taste of vomit still at the back of his mouth. 'Yeah, who is it?' he called. There was no reply and the banging continued. Wright wrapped a towel around his waist and opened the door.

Two policemen in dark brown uniforms stood there. The taller of the two was wearing Ray-Ban sunglasses. He spoke to Wright in Thai.

Wright frowned. 'You'll have to speak English,' he said.

A third figure moved into view behind the two policemen. Somchai. He looked worried. 'They want you to go with them, Mr Nick,' he said.

'Why?' queried Wright.

'They won't say.'

'Tell them to wait while I get dressed,' he said. He moved to close the door but the smaller policeman stuck out his arm and held it open.

As he dressed, Wright looked at his watch. It was ten o'clock in the morning. He'd only slept for two hours after Bamber had left and he was exhausted. He ran a hand over his jaw and wondered if he should shave, but the policeman in sunglasses made an impatient clicking sound and motioned with his hand for Wright to hurry up, so Wright threw on his jacket and followed them down the corridor.

A white police car and a uniformed driver were waiting outside the hotel. Wright got into the back with the smaller of the men; the one with sunglasses climbed into the front. A garland of purple and white flowers and a small gold Buddha in a transparent plastic case hung from the driver's mirror. Wright knew it was pointless to ask any questions so he stared silently out of the window as they drove through the crowded streets.

It wasn't until the car turned into the small side street that Wright realised they were heading for O'Leary's house. Three other police cars and a Jeep were parked haphazardly outside the building, red lights flashing on their roofs, and two brown-uniformed police motorcyclists in knee-high boots and white helmets were talking to a small group of onlookers, obviously telling them to keep back.

The car stopped behind the Jeep and the cop next to Wright pointed at the front door. Wright got out of the car, a sick feeling in the pit of his stomach. He'd liked Dennis O'Leary, and this amount of police activity could only be bad news.

Colonel Vasan was in the main room, standing by O'Leary's desk and watching two uniformed officers rummage through the drawers. They weren't wearing gloves, Wright noticed. Vasan looked across at Wright, then turned his head away, deliberately ignoring him. Wright waited by the door, not wanting to walk across the room without being asked.

After several minutes Vasan walked over, his gleaming black boots squeaking on the wooden floor. He stared at Wright through the lenses of his steel-framed spectacles, but said nothing. He was, Wright realised, trying to intimidate him with silence.

Wright smiled. 'Is there a problem, Colonel Vasan?' he said.

The colonel said nothing. He nodded at a uniformed officer who was standing by the kitchen door. The officer opened the door and ushered out the maid who'd admitted Wright the previous night. She'd been crying.

The colonel spoke to her in Thai. She looked at Wright and nodded tearfully. He said something else to her and she hurried back into the kitchen and closed the door.

The colonel scratched his pitted cheek and studied Wright with hard eyes. 'Why were you here last night?' he said.

'I wanted to talk to Mr O'Leary.'

'About what?' Any pretence that Vasan wasn't able to speak English had disappeared.

'About the murder of Eric Horvitz. They played together in a band. Horvitz was a singer, O'Leary—'

'Played guitar. Yes. I know the connection between the two men.'

'Was there an ace of spades?' asked Wright.

Deep furrows appeared on Vasan's forehead.

'On the body. Was there an ace of spades?'

'How did you know he had been killed?' asked Vasan. 'I didn't say he had been killed.'

Wright sighed patiently. 'The maid's in tears, your men are all over the place and there's no sign of a robbery.'

Vasan glowered at Wright. 'You are quite wrong,' he said. 'There has been no murder.'

A sudden thought struck Wright and he caught his breath. 'He didn't kill himself, did he?'

Vasan shook his head. He turned his back on Wright and walked towards the door to O'Leary's bedroom. Wright followed him. Vasan pushed upon the door. A uniformed officer was going through O'Leary's wardrobes, patting down the pockets of his clothes. Another policeman stood guard at the open door to the bathroom. Vasan motioned for Wright to take a look.

O'Leary was sprawled on the floor next to the toilet, his head up against the wall, his neck at an awkward angle. The belt to his trousers was undone and his flies open. The wheelchair was on its side, next to the bath. The man had soiled himself in death and Wright put his hand over his mouth, trying to block out the smell of urine and faeces.

'Mr O'Leary had been drinking?' said Vasan.

'Yes. Almost a full bottle of whisky.'

'He was trying to use the toilet. He must have overbalanced.'

'It certainly looks that way,' said Wright.

'Bathrooms can be dangerous places, even for those who aren't in wheelchairs.'

Wright tried to remember where he'd left O'Leary's wheelchair when he put the man to bed. Had it been within reach? Had O'Leary woken up, levered himself into the chair and rolled himself into the bathroom? It was possible, he decided. An ugly, unnecessary accident. Guilt washed over Wright. He'd allowed O'Leary to get drunk in the hope that he'd talk. Encouraged him, even. He was partly to blame for the man's drunken state, and that meant he was partly responsible for his death.

'Is there something on your mind?' asked Vasan, looking at Wright over the top of his spectacles.

'It seems such a waste,' said Wright, backing out of the bathroom.

The colonel stroked his chin. 'Did you obtain anything useful from him? During your talk?'

'No,' said Wright. He went through the bedroom. The policeman who had been going through the wardrobes was slipping something into his own pocket. Wright flashed a look at the colonel, but Vasan appeared not to have noticed what the man was doing.

'According to the maid, you were with him for almost an hour.'

'Thirty minutes, at most.'

They went through to the main room. More uniformed policemen arrived, all with holstered guns and radios on their belts. They were walking around and examining O'Leary's possessions as if they were at a jumble sale.

'And you learned nothing of interest?'

Wright was determined not to tell Vasan anything. Nothing he'd seen so far had suggested that the colonel was anything other than incompetent. Even if O'Leary's death was an accident, there was no excuse for allowing so many men to be trampling around the house. 'He confirmed that Horvitz had no enemies, and he couldn't think of any reason why anyone would want to torture and kill him. The rest of the time we talked about music.'

'Music?'

Wright nodded at the two guitars. 'He played guitar. He was good, he played with Eric Clapton once.'

'Eric Clapton? Who is Eric Clapton?'

'A famous guitarist. It doesn't matter.'

Vasan nodded. His hand rested on the butt of his gun as if reassuring himself that it was still in its holster. 'So you talked about music, then you went back to your hotel?'

Wright shrugged. 'That's about it.'

Vasan stared at Wright, who held the colonel's gaze. 'I would prefer that you inform me in advance of any future interviews you wish to conduct,' Vasan said eventually. 'I would like one of my investigating officers to be present.'

'I have no problem with that.'

A uniformed policeman picked up one of O'Leary's guitars and strummed it. Vasan looked across at the man, but there was no trace of annoyance on his face.

'In my opinion you would do best to visit our temples,' said the colonel. 'Maybe go and see the pretty girls we have in Pat Pong, then go home.'

Wright ignored the suggestion. 'Is it okay if I leave now?' he asked.

'My men will drive you back to your hotel,' said Vasan. He turned his back on Wright and went through to O'Leary's bedroom, his shiny black boots squeaking like hungry rats.

Tim Marshall was updating the medical records of the patient he'd just seen when the intercom on his desk buzzed. 'Yes, Ma-lee?' he said, storing the file.

'There are two men to see you, Dr Marshall. They don't have an appointment but they say they are friends. Mr Hammack and Mr Ramirez. I have asked them to wait in reception.' Ma-lee had only been with the surgery for three weeks and was already proving herself an asset. She was university educated and spoke good English, and wasn't in the least intimidated by farangs.

'Thank you, Ma-lee, you can show them in.'

A few seconds later the door to his consulting room opened and Bernie Hammack and Sergio Ramirez came in, both men visibly shaken. 'It's Dennis,' said Hammack as he closed the door. 'He's dead.'

'What!' said Doc. 'What happened?'

'An accident, according to the cops,' said Ramirez. 'We went around to pick up the map and the police were all over the house.'

'Seems he was drunk and he fell out of his chair trying to use the toilet. Broke his neck.'

Doc sat back in his chair and ran his hands through his thinning hair. 'Shit. Poor Dennis.' He narrowed his eyes. 'There's no doubt about this? About it being an accident?'

'They seem sure,' said Hammack.

'Just a lousy coincidence?'

Ramirez sat down on a low sofa by the window. 'I don't think it is a coincidence, Doc. Max, Eric, now Dennis. What are the odds, huh?'

'Pretty extreme, I'd say,' said Doc. 'But if it's the same killer, why make it look like an accident? He tortured Max and Eric, ripped their bodies apart and left a calling card. Why go to all the trouble of making Dennis's death look like an accident?'

'None of this makes any sense,' said Hammack. 'Question is, what do we do now?'

'Did you get the map?'

'They wouldn't let us into the house. Besides, I wouldn't know where to look.'

There was a small red birthmark on the back of Doc's neck and he scratched it, deep in thought. Ramirez and Hammack sat in silence, waiting.

'We don't need the map,' Doc said eventually. 'We can find our way back.'

'We're still going?' asked Ramirez.

'We took a vote,' said Doc.

'I think we should make a stand here, in Bangkok,' said Ramirez. 'On our turf. If it is him, if he has come back, I'd rather face him out in the open.'

'We took a vote,' Doc repeated, a harder edge to his voice. 'We go back.'

Ramirez's jaw tightened and for a moment it looked as if he was going to argue, but then he relaxed and nodded. Doc looked at Hammack. The black man nodded, too.

'I'm pretty sure I can remember the layout. What about you, Bernie?'

'Ain't never gonna forget,' said Hammack. He grinned and his gold tooth glinted at the side of his mouth.

'Sergio?'

The Latino sighed. He nodded slowly. 'I might have trouble finding the entrance, but once I'm down there, I'll know my way around.' He smiled ruefully. 'A map would have been nice, though.'

'Like Bernie said, we don't even know where Dennis kept it.' Doc stood up. 'I'm getting the visas tonight. We fly out tomorrow at eleven. We'll pick up the equipment we'll need in Saigon.'

'What about weapons?' asked Ramirez.

'We won't need them,' said Doc. He stood up. 'The only thing we're going to find down there is a skeleton.'

'I meant for the snakes and stuff. The VC might have moved out, but the wildlife's going to be well entrenched by now. Scorpions, rats. The works.'

Doc nodded. He took off his white coat and hung it on the back of the door. 'There's no way we can get guns through the airport, and I wouldn't know where to go about buying them in Vietnam. We can get knives in Saigon, that's about it.'

'I'd feel happier with a gun, Doc.'

'I hear you, Sergio, but I don't see how it's going to be possible.'

'And if he's not down there, Doc,' said Hammack. 'What then?'

'Let's cross one bridge at a time, gentlemen. One bridge at a time.'

Nick Wright spread the typewritten sheets over the bed. There were more than twenty in all. They had been delivered by a young uniformed policeman who had demanded five thousand baht before handing them over. Wright hadn't had enough cash in his wallet and he'd had to go to an ATM to withdraw Thai money. The officer turned out to be a motorcycle policeman and he'd offered Wright a lift. It had been almost surreal, driving through the traffic along Sukhumvit Road, riding pillion behind a traffic cop. The policeman had even turned on his flashing red light, forcing traffic to pull to the side to allow them to pass. After he'd withdrawn the money, the cop had driven him back to the hotel, and laboriously written out a receipt before taking the money and handing Wright the manila envelope containing the translated reports. He'd even saluted Wright.

Wright was surprised at the thoroughness of the reports. There was a summary of the post mortem, and the injuries were identical to those of Max Eckhardt's. The body had been discovered by a nun just after breakfast, and there was a statement from her and from the rest of the nuns in the orphanage including Sister Marie. Neighbours had also been interviewed, but to no avail. No one had seen or heard anything unusual. There was a breakdown of Horvitz's financial situation and photocopies of bank statements from Thai Farmers Bank and Bangkok Bank. Horvitz had had almost a quarter of a million dollars on deposit. There had been no major withdrawals before or after Horvitz's death. Extortion or robbery had been ruled out as a motive. Doc had been interviewed, but not the other members of The Jazz Club. Doc had told Vasan as little as he'd told Wright on their first meeting. Wright could find nothing in the report about the playing card, other than in the description of the crime scene. Vasan had obviously decided that it wasn't a clue worth following up.

He went over to the minibar and took out a can of lager and a can of Sprite and mixed himself a shandy. Wright stood looking out of his window as he drank. A group of bare-chested children were running around a corrugated-iron shack, laughing and giggling. Wright wondered what Sean was doing. He looked at his watch. It was just after two o'clock in the afternoon. Back in London, Sean was probably getting ready for school.

He sat down on the bed and began to read through the translated reports again, hoping to find something that he'd missed on his first reading. If he could come up with a clue as to who the killer was, maybe he wouldn't have to go down the tunnels.

He toyed with the idea of phoning Hunter, but remembered

that he'd already asked Tommy to update him on what he'd found out so far.

There was a knock on the door and Wright went over and opened it. Jim Bamber stood there, a black holdall in one hand.

'How's it going, Nick?'

'Fine,' said Wright. He closed the door and handed the typewritten sheets to the FBI agent. 'Colonel Vasan sent over a translation of his file on the Horvitz killing, but there's nothing of any use.'

'Did you really expect there to be?' asked Bamber. He unzipped the holdall and handed Wright his passport and a folder containing an airline ticket.

Wright opened his passport and flicked through it. The Vietnam visa filled an entire page, blue writing with a large red seal.

'The guys are flying out tomorrow morning on Thai Airways. We're booked on the flight after them. It's Vietnam Airlines, I'm afraid, but there's no way we can travel on the same flight.'

Wright picked up his glass of shandy. 'Jim, I'm having second thoughts about going down the tunnels.'

'We've no choice,' said Bamber. 'The answer to the murders is down there. We have to go.'

Wright began to pace up and down in front of the window. 'Look, you know I'm claustrophobic. You know the state I was in when you switched off your torch in the tunnel. Think how bad I'm going to be underground.'

Bamber grinned. 'I think I've solved that,' he said. He reached into the holdall and pulled out what looked like a bulky pair of binoculars. He handed them to Wright. There were two lenses and an adjusting knob, and a black rubber facepiece with webbing straps to hold it in place. 'It's a nightsight.'

'Yeah, I know.' Wright had used something similar on night-time anti-vandal surveillance operations. 'But they won't work underground.'

'What do you mean?'

'They work by gathering what light's available and amplifying it. Starlight, whatever. But underground there's a total absence of light. Nothing to amplify.'

Bamber shook his head. 'That would be true for the passive systems, but these operate on infra-red. They'll work. Took me ages to find. I've got two sets, plus a stack of batteries. Has the bathroom got a window? Try them in there.'

Wright went into the bathroom, switched on the light and closed the door. He put the goggles on and adjusted the straps, then switched the unit on. It took ten seconds or so to warm up, whining in a high-pitched tone that was almost out of his hearing range, then the eyepieces flickered and he had a white-flecked green view of the bathroom. He switched off the light and moved his head from side to side. They were heavy and the view was initially a little disorientating, but they worked.

'Yeah, they work,' he shouted.

'Should hope so,' said Bamber.

Wright opened the bathroom door. 'How long do the batteries last?'

'The guy said six hours. That probably means four.'

Wright took off the headset. 'How long are we going to have to be underground?' he asked.

'Twelve hours or so, max.'

Wright's mouth opened in surprise. He wondered if he'd misheard. 'Twelve hours?'

'Twelve hours, maximum. But probably less.'

'Twelve fucking hours!'

Bamber held out his hand. 'I'll look after them until we get there,' he said.

Wright gave the headset to the FBI agent. 'Jim, I can't stay underground for twelve hours.'

'That's what it's going to take,' said Bamber. 'The main tunnel complex is about two miles from the entrance they used. It's a communications tunnel, but it's the only way to the complex. The only way that's been mapped, anyway. Down in the tunnels you can make about half a mile an hour. And that's assuming we don't make a wrong turn along the way. So it's going to take about three hours just to get there.' He put the headset into the holdall.

Wright pressed his glass against his cheek. 'Twelve hours,' he said.

'Twelve minutes, twelve hours, twelve days. It takes as long as it takes, Nick. Do you want to crack this case or not?'

'You know I do.'

'So we go down the tunnels. We find out what's so important that Marshall, Hammack and Ramirez feel they have to go back after twenty-five years.'

Wright nodded. 'Yeah. You're right.'

'I know I'm right. You'll be just fine. And I'll be with you every step of the way. It'll be a walk in the park, Nick.'

Wright drained his glass. Despite Bamber's confidence, he was gripped by an overpowering feeling of dread. He smiled weakly. 'If you say so, Jim.'

G erry Hunter was putting on his coat ready to go home when Steve Denning shouted across to him that he had a call.

'Who is it?' called Hunter.

'FBI,' said Denning. 'Guy called Harris.'

Denning transferred the call to Hunter's extension. 'Hiya, Ed. Thanks for calling back,' he said.

'Yeah, sorry I didn't get back sooner,' said Harris. 'It took longer than I thought. Can I just confirm the spelling of this guy's name. B-A-M-B-E-R, right? First name James?'

'That's it,' said Hunter.

'In that case, we have a problem,' said Harris. 'There's only one agent of that name in the FBI, and he's a twenty-year veteran working out of our San Francisco office. I spoke to him an hour ago.'

'So the James Bamber who's been part of our murder enquiry team is an impostor?'

'Looks that way, Gerry. You saw his ID, right?'

'Not personally, but I'm sure it must have been looked at somewhere along the line. This doesn't make any sense. Why the hell would anyone want to sit in on a murder enquiry that's going nowhere?'

'Maybe he wants it to stay that way,' said the FBI agent. 'Look, we'd like to speak to this guy, whatever his motives. If nothing else, it's a federal offence to pass yourself off as an FBI agent. Have you got an address?'

'He checked out of his hotel last week. I haven't a clue where he is now.'

'What about fingerprints? Have you got anything he touched? A cup, a typewriter?'

Hunter looked around the incident room. Bamber had only visited the room twice and he couldn't recall him touching anything, and the hotel room would already have been cleaned. 'I don't think so,' said Hunter. 'If I think of anything, I'll let you know.'

Hunter replaced the receiver and slipped off his coat. He slumped down into his chair and ran his hands through his hair. There were so many strands to the investigation that his mind couldn't cope with them all. He picked up a pen and a sheet of paper. He wrote the name JAMES BAMBER at the top. Underneath he wrote MAX ECKHARDT. Then MAY ECKHARDT. Then ERIC HORVITZ. Underneath that he wrote the name of his dead partner. He stared at the five names and chewed the inside of his lip. James Bamber, an American claiming to be with the FBI. Max Eckhardt, an American brutally murdered. An American who had served in the Vietnam War. A playing card impaled on his chest that had been used as a death card by American Special Forces. May Eckhardt, an Oriental girl married to the victim, vanished. Clive Edmunds, dead after renting a Vietnam War movie. No sign of the video cassette. The cassette disappears, so does Jim Bamber. Hunter drew an arrow connecting Bamber to Edmunds. Was the timing coincidental? He remembered Eckhardt's boss Reynolds saying that Edmunds was going to check with Bamber for details of Eckhardt's Vietnam record, and he shuddered involuntarily. He drew another arrow between Bamber and May Eckhardt. Were their disappearances connected in some way? He drew a third arrow linking Bamber to Max Eckhardt, and a fourth between Bamber and Horvitz. Was Bamber the killer? Was his desire to be part of the murder enquiry some perverse voyeurism? He underlined Bamber's name several times. Hunter had a growing sense of dread, a fear that perhaps his partner's death wasn't a tragic accident.

He drew a circle around May Eckhardt's name. Where had she gone? Had she too been killed? He wondered if it would be worth getting a search warrant and giving the flat a going over, but decided against it. If she had moved out, the landlord would have checked the premises. Besides, Jenkins had said that her car was missing, so presumably she'd driven away.

'You okay, Gerry?' asked a Welsh voice.

Hunter looked up to see Colin Duggan scratching his fleshy neck.

'That guy Bamber, apparently he wasn't with the FBI. I've just been on to their London bureau and they've never heard of him.'

'Fuck me,' said Duggan. 'Who the hell is he?'

'No idea. But he had to have some reason for hanging around.'

'Jesus, they say that murderers always return to the scene of the crime, but this is the first time I've heard of one joining the investigating team. Put a couple of guys on it, will you? Unless you fancy taking it on?'

'I want to chase up May Eckhardt. She's gone AWOL, too.'

Duggan ran his hand over his bald patch. 'What a fucking mess,' he said. 'This Bamber, it was the BTP that brought him in initially, right? Nothing to do with us?'

Hunter nodded. 'Newton introduced him,' he said. 'I've

got a memo somewhere saying that we should offer him every assistance.'

Duggan winked at Hunter. 'Not our fault, then, huh? If the shit hits the fan we're in the clear. Dig out the memo and send it to me, will you?'

As Duggan left the room, Hunter went over to a HOLMES terminal and logged on. He pulled up the interviews that Nick Wright had done with May Eckhardt and read through them. There was nothing untoward and the BTP detective had done a professional enough job. There were no details of her family, but according to the background, she'd studied at Exeter University. Hunter looked at his watch. It was too late to call the registrar's office, he'd have to do it first thing in the morning.

D oc handed the three passports and tickets to the girl behind the check-in desk. 'Three seats together,' he said.

She smiled and began tapping away at her computer console.

Doc turned around to look at Ramirez and Hammack. 'Okay, guys?'

The two men nodded. 'I could do with a beer,' said Hammack.

'We've plenty of time before we board. We can get a drink airside.'

'Any bags to check in, sir?' asked the Thai Airways girl.

'Just hand baggage,' said Doc. 'We won't be staying for long.'

From their vantage point up on the second floor, Wright and Kruse looked down on the three Americans as they walked away from the check-in desk towards immigration. 'They're travelling light,' said Wright.

'They're not planning to stay long,' said Kruse. 'Straight up to the tunnel complex, then down.'

The men walked through the barrier to the immigration area and passed out of sight. 'Are you sure we won't lose them in Vietnam?' asked Wright.

'We know where they're going. The map I've got is incredibly detailed. We can find the entrance, and once we're in the tunnels we know where they're going.'

'They're going to have a hell of a start on us.'

'Not really,' said Kruse. 'We'll get to Saigon about three hours after them, and they don't seem to be taking much in the way of equipment with them. They're going to be picking up their supplies in Saigon, say an hour. Maybe two.' He kicked the metal suitcase at his feet. 'We've got all the stuff we need right here. I reckon we'll reach the tunnel entrance an hour or two after they get there. They'll only be half a mile or so ahead of us, and that's not too big a margin. Sound will travel down there, so we won't want to get too close.'

Wright rubbed his chin thoughtfully. 'What are we going to find down there, Jim?'

339

'The answer,' said Kruse. He leaned on the rail that ran around the balcony. He already knew what the Americans hoped to find when they reached their destination, deep underground. A body. O'Leary had told him everything before he died: where the map was; where the body was buried; what had happened twenty-five years earlier and why the Tunnel Rats were so convinced that their past had come back to haunt them.

Kruse didn't believe in ghosts. He didn't care who was responsible for the murders, but he needed to know the identity of the killer and he needed to make sure that everyone who knew the secret of the tunnels was silenced for ever. He looked across at Wright and smiled. Kruse's speciality was making deaths look accidental, but down in the tunnels that wouldn't be necessary. 'What say we get breakfast, Nick? We can't check in for a couple of hours yet.'

The Thai Airways 737 turned off the main runway and headed for the terminal. 'Never thought I'd be back,' said Hammack. 'Once I was on the Freedom Bird, I swore that was it.'

'I don't think any of us ever expected to return, Bernie,' said Doc, peering out of the window. The plane taxied past curved concrete shelters that had protected US warplanes from VC mortar attacks during the last years of the wars. Most stood empty and were overgrown with weeds but a few contained small cargo planes. At the peak of the war, Saigon airport was the busiest in the world, with huge transporters ferrying in the hundreds of thousands of troops and all the armaments and equipment needed to keep them in combat, and bombers queuing up to drop their loads on whatever targets the top brass had earmarked for devastation that day. The airport was still busy, but now it was civilian airliners that were rolling up and down the taxiways.

The plane stopped and three buses pulled up next to it. The passengers poured off the plane and were ferried to the terminal, where they handed in yellow health forms that said they had no contagious diseases, and then joined the queues for immigration. Most of the passengers were Japanese and Chinese businessmen, though there were a few Westerners, mainly backpackers.

'Just like Bangkok, huh?' said Ramirez, nodding at the queues.

'I guess we make it just as hard for foreigners arriving at JFK,' said Doc.

They waited for more than an hour before handing their passports and visa forms to a stony-faced immigration officer in a green military-looking uniform, then passed through Customs where another green-uniformed official gave their holdalls a cursory inspection after passing them through an X-ray machine.

The three men walked out of the terminal into blinding sunshine, and stood in silence, looking out over the acres of tarmac, filled with gleaming taxis and chauffeur-driven luxury cars. Drivers in blue trousers and white shirts waited expectantly. Beyond them were large billboards advertising Japanese computers and American cigarettes. All were struck by the same thought: they'd left a war zone, and returned to an economic boom town.

Two Vietnamese girls walked by wearing the traditional *ao dai* costume – long blouses slit up the side over flowing, baggy pants. They were carrying cans of Coke and sipping their sodas through straws. From the open window of one of the taxis came the thumping beat of an Aerosmith song.

'Remind me again who won, Doc,' said Hammack. 'It was the Communists, right?' He ripped open a pack of chewing gum and slotted a piece into his mouth.

A young Vietnamese man came over. 'Taxi?' he asked.

'We want to go to the Rex Hotel,' said Doc. 'How much?'

'All taxis have meters, sir,' said the man. He motioned with his arm to the queue of taxis where a driver had already opened his boot for them.

'Beats Bangkok,' said Ramirez. 'You always end up bargaining with the cabs at the airport.'

They loaded their holdalls into the boot and climbed into the back of the Toyota taxi. The airconditioning was on and the interior was spotless.

It was a half-hour drive to the hotel. The bulk of the traffic on the roads was of the two-wheeled variety, bicycles and motorcycles. Unlike Bangkok, the traffic flowed freely and the air didn't shimmer with exhaust fumes. Construction seemed to be going on all around them and the skyline was littered with cranes and the skeletons of half-completed tower blocks. The three Americans stared out of the windows. The last time they had seen Saigon it had been a military town, packed with Jeeps and trucks and US military personnel. Now the only uniforms were worn by the policemen standing in the middle of the crossroads directing traffic. They drove by a sidewalk café where waiters in white shirts and black trousers served coffee to a group of businessmen, then by a line of shops filled with lacquerware and rosewood furniture. The car slowed as they eased through a group of young women pedalling old bicycles, all wearing pastel-coloured *ao dais* and what appeared to be long evening gloves, presumably to protect their hands and arms against the fierce Vietnamese sun.

It was a city in transition. One block would consist of a gleaming office tower with smartly dressed secretaries carrying briefcases, the next a boarded-up tenement block with peeling paint and rusting balconies, obviously awaiting demolition. Alongside modern stores with expensive display cases stood open-fronted shops selling secondhand motors covered in grime and oil, and advertising hoardings promoted everything from vitamins and baby powder to cigarettes and cognac.

'It's not what I expected,' said Hammack.

'What did you expect?' asked Doc.

'I dunno. Everyone in Mao tunics, maybe. The NVA on the streets. Tanks. Communist slogans. Martial music broadcast through loudspeakers. This is just like Bangkok.'

'It's capitalism, but under Communist control,' said Doc. 'They're trying to bring in Western products but without Western politics. Same as China.'

'And foreigners can go anywhere? No restrictions?'

'Pretty much,' said Doc. 'They're trying to encourage tourists. And that's what we are, tourists.'

The taxi turned down a tree-lined avenue. Ahead of them a sandy-coloured building sported a huge crown. 'The Rex Hotel,' said Doc. 'It was where the military used to brief the press corps. I thought it was appropriate. We can have a final briefing here before we head upcountry.'

It was a long time since May Eckhardt had worn an *ao dai*. The silk was soft against her skin and it rippled in the warm wind that blew down Nguyen Hue Boulevard from the Saigon River behind her. In front of her stood the red-roofed white and yellow building that was the Hôtel de Ville, home of the Ho Chi Minh City People's Committee. The Vietnamese flag, a yellow star on a red background, fluttered above it. To her left was the Rex Hotel. She stood astride her Yamaha scooter, her sandalled feet flat on the ground. No one gave her a second look in her pale blue *ao dai* and conical hat, she was just one of many. A small beggar boy, nine years old at most, held up a handful of packs of chewing gum. She shook her head. *'Toi khong muon . . .'* she said, but he pouted and pushed the gum at her.

She relented. She didn't want the chewing gum but she could remember when she was nine years old and alone on the streets of Saigon. She gave him one US dollar and took a pack. He grinned, showing a mouthful of yellowing teeth, then skipped away to bother an overweight German couple who were loudly bargaining to buy an opium pipe from a roadside trader.

May stared up at the Rex Hotel. She'd followed the three Americans from the airport, keeping close behind them on her scooter, until she was sure of their destination. She was disappointed that the one called Rabbit wasn't with them. She'd hoped that by sending him photographs of what she'd done, he would have contacted the others and travelled to

Vietnam with them. She'd been wrong. Still, there was a certain irony in leaving him until last, because he was the one she hated most. She kicked the scooter into life and drove away from the kerb. She weaved between the packs of cyclists making their way towards the Hôtel de Ville, and turned left on to Le Loi Boulevard, then into the narrow side street where she'd rented a small house. In front of the house was an Isuzu pick-up truck, the red paintwork starting to rust. She parked the scooter behind the Isuzu and went inside to change. The Americans wouldn't stay in the hotel for long, she knew. And where they were going, her *ao dai* would be useless as camouflage.

T he woman in the registrar's office wouldn't take Gerry Hunter's word that he was a detective inspector and insisted on taking down his warrant card number and calling him back. When he picked up the receiver again she apologised profusely but explained that a year ago a jilted boyfriend had obtained confidential information from the university by falsely claiming to be a police officer. Hunter told her that he was trying to track down a former student who had studied computing at the university. 'Her name's May Eckhardt but she's married and I'm afraid I don't know her maiden name,' he said.

'Do you know when she was here?' asked the woman.

'About fifteen years ago, but could you check five years either side?' said Hunter. Wright had shown her date of birth as September 1965, but there was nothing in his report to say when she'd gone to university. 'I think her parents were from Sale in Cheshire. She's Oriental. Chinese, maybe.' He gave the woman May Eckhardt's date of birth, and she promised to check with the Department of Computer Science and get back to him as soon as possible.

Nick Wright scratched his ear with his pen. 'So many bloody forms to fill in,' he complained. 'Customs, immigration, health.'

'You've got to remember it's still a Communist country, Nick,' said Jim Bamber. 'The bureaucracy controls everything.'

Wright finished copying down his passport details on to the immigration form and put away his pen.

A stewardess with bright pink lipstick smiled and asked Wright if he wanted another drink. He shook his head. They were about halfway through the eighty-minute flight from Bangkok.

'Tell me about the tunnels,' Wright asked.

'What do you want to know?'

'O'Leary said they had all sorts of stuff underground. Factories, hospitals, training areas. How come the Americans didn't just blow them up?'

'They tried,' said the FBI agent. 'Cu Chi, to the north-west of Saigon, is riddled with tunnels. They reckon the network there is more than a hundred and fifty miles long, spread over something like three hundred square miles of an area they called the Iron Triangle. The Americans knew the tunnels were there, and they sent in tens of thousands of troops, but they uncovered only a tiny fraction of the network. They bulldozed the jungle, they sprayed the area with defoliants, practically killed every tree and blade of grass, but still they couldn't find the tunnels. Bomber pilots returning to Saigon were told to dump their unused bombs and fuel on the area, and then they started carpet-bombing with B-52s. Couldn't move the VC, though. They just dug in, deeper and deeper. The only way to get them out was to send in American soldiers.'

'The Tunnel Rats?'

'That's right. Hand-to-hand combat, deep underground.'

'Maybe I'm being obtuse, but why didn't they just pump the tunnels full of gas?'

'They tried, but the tunnels were built with water traps so that the gas could only go so far. Like a sink trap. Then they tried using dogs, but so many were killed by booby traps that they had to stop. They tried filling the tunnels with explosives and setting them off, but there are so many kinks and bends that the damage was always limited.'

'What I can't work out is why they're going back. What can be down there that's so important?'

'If we knew that, Nick, we wouldn't have to go down ourselves.'

Wright shivered. 'What about the reports you were getting from the Defense Department?'

'My people are having trouble tracking them down. They hope to have them by the time we get back to Bangkok.'

'But you've got the map, right?'

'Sure.'

'Can I see it?'

Bamber looked around. The plane was full. 'I'd rather wait until we've got a bit more privacy,' said Bamber.

'I guess so,' said Wright. 'But we're going to Cu Chi, right?'

'About thirty miles further north,' said Bamber. 'Cu Chi has been turned into a tourist area, believe it or not. They've widened some of the tunnels, even installed electric lighting. The tunnels that our guys are heading for haven't been opened up, and have probably been deserted for the last twenty-five years.'

A thin sheen of sweat had formed on Wright's face. A male steward offered him a cold towel with a smile and Wright accepted it gratefully. 'What sort of state are they going to be in?' he asked. 'Won't they have collapsed?'

'Shouldn't have,' said Bamber. 'The earth is mainly soil and clay, but it doesn't soak up water so most of the time it's as hard and dry as brick. It's softer during the rainy season, which is when the VC did most of the digging, but at this time of the year it's rock hard. It's perfect for tunnelling: it doesn't turn to mud, yet it doesn't crumble. The water table is about fifty feet below the surface, so they don't flood. The network we're going to is more than ten miles from the Iron Triangle, so it should have escaped the bulk of the B-52 bombing. Even so, the tunnels were so well built that even a bomb from a B-52 would only affect the upper levels.'

'I don't understand this business about levels,' said Wright.

'I'll be able to show you better on the map,' said the FBI agent. 'But basically the upper levels were communication tunnels, linking villages, firing posts and all the trapdoor entrances. They were usually about ten to fifteen feet down.

There are trapdoors leading down from the communication levels to the second level, about thirty feet below the surface. That's where they had sleeping chambers, air-raid shelters, training rooms and hospitals. Even further down, forty or fifty feet, were the command headquarters and storage areas.'

'Sounds like a whole city underground.'

'It was, Nick. At one point there were supposed to be something like twelve thousand VCs based in the various tunnel networks.'

A stewardess interrupted their conversation, asking them to put up their tray tables and to make sure that their seatbelts were fastened as they were preparing to land. Wright wiped his face with the cold towel. He was still sweating. He stared out of the window at the rice fields below and wondered what it would be like to be deep below the surface, crawling through the earth like a tunnelling animal. He shivered.

Sergio Ramirez and Bernie Hammack were already sitting around a wrought-iron table with cups of coffee in front of them when Doc walked on to the terrace. They had ordered a cup for him and it sat with its aluminium coffee dripper on top of it. He lifted the dripper off and poured milk into the inky-black brew.

'Rooms okay?' asked Doc. He sipped his coffee. It was bitter and strong.

'Hard to believe it's Saigon,' said Hammack. 'It's as good as anything in Bangkok.'

'And they speak better English,' said Ramirez.

A group of Japanese businessmen were sitting at a neighbouring table, peering at a blueprint. Two Chinese entrepreneurs in polo shirts and Chinos slurped noodles and argued over a balance sheet. Doc could almost smell the money being made. The terrace bar was tacky in the extreme, with garishly painted statues of animals, including two grey elephants and a white horse, standing amid tubs of ornately clipped bushes, and around the perimeter of the roof faded flags fluttered gently in the wind. At the far end of the terrace was a statue of a crouching Oriental archer, drawing back his bow. A Japanese girl posed next to it while her boyfriend snapped away with a small camera.

'I've booked the rooms for three days,' said Doc. 'I expect to be back here tomorrow, so if everything goes smoothly we can have a couple of days R and R.'

'If,' said Hammack. 'That's a big if, Doc.'

'We go down, we check it's still there, and we come back.'

'And if he's not there?' said Hammack. 'If he's not dead?'

'Then I'll eat my fucking hat, Bernie.'

'That's not what we should be worrying about,' said Ramirez. 'If he's not dead, if he is the killer, then it's going to be easy enough to protect ourselves. But if it's not him, then we have a big, big problem. Who killed Eric, Max and Dennis?'

'Dennis was an accident,' said Doc.

'Maybe,' said Hammack. 'But the point is, someone knows what we did. And someone wants to make us pay.'

'Whatever, we take this one step at a time. And step one is to get ourselves equipped. There's a market not far away where we can get everything we need.' He took a sheet of paper from the pocket of his denim shirt and dropped it on the table in front of Ramirez and Hammack. 'I've drawn up a list of what I think we'll need. Can you see anything I've missed?'

Ramirez ran his finger down the list. 'A double-action Smith & Wesson .44 magnum would be nice,' he said.

Doc smiled thinly. 'Much as I'd like to oblige, short of stealing one, we're not going to get a gun.'

'String,' said Hammack. 'You forgot the string. And rope.'

Doc took a pen out of his pocket and added string and rope to the list.

'How are we getting up to the tunnels?' asked Ramirez.

'Bikes,' said Doc. He smiled when he saw the look of disbelief on Ramirez's face. 'Motorbikes,' he clarified. 'Foreigners can't hire cars without a local driver, but we can rent motorbikes. I asked reception and there's a place around the corner that can help us.'

The three Americans went down together in the lift and walked through the marble-floored foyer where a group of Taiwanese tourists were checking in. There was a line of white Toyota taxis outside the hotel and they climbed into the first one. Doc told the driver where they wanted to go and he smiled and flicked on the meter. It was, thought Doc, a pleasant change from Bangkok where more often than not getting into a taxi meant several minutes of bargaining, depending on how heavy the traffic was and whether the driver wanted to go in a particular direction.

'You tourists?' asked the driver. He was in his fifties with greying, spiky hair and skin that was as leathery and weatherbeaten as an old saddle.

'Sort of,' said Doc.

The driver looked at them in his rearview mirror as he negotiated a way through several dozen bicycling schoolchildren.

'You here during war?' he asked.

The Americans looked at each other. Doc shrugged. 'Yeah,' he said.

'American GIs, Number One!' he cackled.

They passed two cyclos, hybrids of bicycles and rickshaws, with two thin Vietnamese teenagers pedalling hard up an incline, ferrying two obese tourists in T-shirts and shorts who were filming each other with video cameras. A beautiful young girl in a pale green *ao dai* and black evening gloves drove by on a Honda moped. She smiled at Ramirez and he beamed back.

'You were a soldier?' asked Hammack.

'Damn right,' said the driver, cackling again.

'What, with ARVN?' The Army of the Republic of South Vietnam. The soldiers who were supposed to be fighting alongside the Americans, but who more often than not proved to be a liability rather than an asset.

The driver laughed louder. 'No, me VC!' he said, thumping his chest.

'You've got to be joking,' said Ramirez.

'VC. Damn right!' He twisted around in his seat. 'We won, huh?'

'Yes, you did,' said Doc. He looked across at his two companions. Hammack and Ramirez sat stony faced, their arms folded across their chests.

The driver dropped them in front of a bustling market with stalls bedecked with clothes and shoes, vendors selling food, and tables strewn with cheap plastic toys. The three

Americans threaded their way through to the rear of the indoor market where most of the clothing was in camouflage fabric and the plastic toys and electrical equipment gave way to war surplus equipment. There were lines of old gas masks, combat boots, webbing belts, canteens, flashlights; enough equipment to outfit an army. Hammack and Ramirez stood with surprised looks on their faces.

'How did you find out about this place?' asked Hammack.

'It's in the guide book, believe it or not,' said Doc. 'Dan Sinh Market. Most of it is reproduction, tourists love it.'

Ramirez was looking at a rack of field stretchers and a medical kit with a red cross on it. 'This looks genuine,' he said.

'Some of it is, but a lot of it is made here.'

Ramirez tossed him the medical kit and Doc opened it. Inside were bandages, dressings, sutures and hypodermics. The quality looked as good as anything he had back in his surgery in Bangkok. He wondered whether buying it would be taken as a bad omen by his two companions, but he decided that it would be essential, to deal with the cuts and bruises they'd get just negotiating the tunnels. He bought it, along with several tubes of antiseptic ointment and mosquito repellent from a neighbouring stall.

The three Americans chose the clothing they'd wear, all opting for T-shirts and jeans, knowing how hot it would get underground. They selected small nylon rucksacks, checking them for fit, and plastic canteens because they'd sweat like crazy and dehydration would be one of their biggest problems.

Ramirez found a stall selling knives and they argued for a while over which would be the best type to buy.

Ramirez wanted a killing weapon, but Doc's view was that they'd be most useful for probing for booby traps and hidden trapdoors. Eventually they agreed to differ: Ramirez selected a large hunting knife, Doc chose a bayonet-type knife and Hammack a smaller weapon in a plastic scabbard. A neighbouring stall sold compasses, including several aviation models that appeared to have been stripped from planes. They chose the most rugged and easy-to-read models they could find.

Doc took out a pen and crossed off the items they'd purchased. 'Flashlights,' he said.

They bought flashlights and spare batteries, three green canvas kitbags with 'USMC' stamped on them, and the rest of the equipment that was on the list. The last thing that Doc bought was a small folding shovel. Hammack and Ramirez looked away as Doc put it in one of the kitbags with the rest of his purchases.

It took Nick Wright and Jim Bamber more than an hour to pass through immigration, and it was another hour before their bags rolled out on to the carousel. They carried their bags over to Customs where two green-uniformed young women with waist-length hair helped load them through an X-ray machine.

'This doesn't make sense,' said Wright. 'Shouldn't they be X-raying luggage before it goes on the plane?'

'It's not about safety, it's about contraband,' said Bamber.

'There's a lot of duty imposed on stuff brought into the country, computers and the like.'

One of the girls pointed at Bamber's case as it rolled out of the X-ray machine. 'I bet I know what this is about,' he sighed. He popped the locks and opened the case. She went through his clothes and pulled out the two sets of infra-red goggles. Bamber smiled easily. 'Binoculars,' he said, miming putting a pair to his eyes and looking through them. 'For night-time. For watching birds at night-time.'

She held out her hand for the Customs form he was holding. Wright's suitcase emerged from the X-ray machine and a middle-aged man with a squint motioned for Wright to open it. He riffled through the contents and took out Wright's portable telephone and charging unit.

'You have receipt?' the girl asked Bamber. The FBI agent shook his head. She pointed at the form. 'You have to put down how much they cost.'

Her colleague held Wright's form a few inches away from his face. 'Fill in form properly,' he said.

Wright borrowed Bamber's pen, detailed the phone and charging unit on the back of the form. They handed over their forms and were told they could go. They walked out into the arrivals area.

'Are we going to hire a car?' asked Wright.

'No can do,' said Bamber. 'Guide book says you can't drive here. Cops'll stop any foreigner they see at the wheel. We have to take a taxi.'

They went outside and Wright was hit by a wave of heat and humidity that made him gasp. 'Jeez! It's hotter even than Bangkok, and Bangkok was sweltering,' said Wright. He put down his suitcase and holdall and surveyed the line of gleaming white Toyotas. 'One of them?' he asked.

Bamber rubbed his chin thoughtfully. 'Might be a bit suspicious climbing into a cab here and heading straight out into the country,' he said. 'I reckon we should go to Saigon and switch cars there.'

'Whatever,' said Wright. Bamber seemed to know what he was doing so Wright was happy to let him take charge. Wright was having trouble concentrating – all he could think about was the tunnels.

Hammack kicked his motorcycle into life and blipped the throttle. 'Sounds sweet,' he said.

Hammack was sitting astride a Yamaha trail bike, his kitbag tied to the back. Doc and Ramirez were on fairly new Honda trail bikes, the wheels of which were crusted with mud. All three Americans were wearing jeans and white cotton shirts with the sleeves buttoned at the wrist to provide protection from the sun, and they had rented gloves and full-face helmets with tinted visors from the man who'd supplied the bikes.

Ramirez gave Doc a thumbs-up. 'Rock and roll,' he said.

'Remember, the roads can be dangerous, so we take it slow and watch out for potholes,' said Doc. 'I don't want to have to do any needlework on the way up, okay?'

Hammack and Ramirez nodded.

Doc flicked his visor down and led the way out of the shop, bumping carefully off the pavement and on to the road. Hammack and Ramirez followed. The three motorcyclists headed north, nudging their way through the battalions of cyclists and moped riders.

A red Isuzu turned out of a side street and headed after them.

'Okay, stop here,' said Bamber, tapping the taxi driver on the shoulder. At the roadside was a line of shabby cars, and a group of Vietnamese men stood in the shade of a tree, watching a flickering television fixed to the inside wall of one of the shops that lined the road.

Bamber paid the driver with a handful of Vietnamese currency as Wright climbed out. The two men put their suitcases and holdalls on the pavement and watched their taxi drive away.

'Now what?' asked Wright.

'I'm pretty sure these guys are for hire,' said Bamber.

'They don't have taxi signs,' said Wright.

Two of the men who'd been watching television walked over. 'You want car?' the taller of the two asked.

Bamber winked at Wright. 'Told you.' He nodded at the car at the head of the queue, a Mercedes with rusty wings that must have been at least twenty years old. 'How much for one day?'

The two men spoke to each other in Vietnamese. The shorter one shook his head. 'Where you want to go?'

'North,' said Bamber. 'Past Ben Suc, up by the Thi Tinh River.'

The two men pulled faces and shrugged. 'One hundred and twenty dollars for one day,' said the shorter one.

'Eighty,' said Bamber.

'One hundred,' said the man.

Bamber nodded. 'Okay.' He grinned at Wright. 'What the hell, the Bureau's picking up the check, right?'

Wright picked up his suitcase. The man already had the boot open and he helped Wright heave it in. 'My name Chinh,' he said.

'I'm Nick. He's Jim.'

'Nick. Jim.' The driver said their names several times as if trying to commit them to memory as he loaded Bamber's metal suitcase on top of Wright's. Bamber and Wright got into the back of the car with their holdalls. The driver went into one of the roadside shops and emerged with a carrier bag containing two plastic bottles of mineral water. He handed them to Wright and started the car. Clouds of black smoke billowed from the exhaust and the engine coughed, backfired, then roared. 'Diesel,' said the driver. 'Okay soon. Where we go?'

'Head for Ben Suc, then I'll show you.'

A policeman blew a whistle and held up a white gloved hand to stop the traffic. Chinh braked hard, throwing the Americans forward. 'You want to go down the tunnels?' said Chinh. 'Better you go to Cu Chi. Many tourists go there. Lots of fun.'

'We don't want to go to the Cu Chi tunnels,' said Bamber, as hundreds of bicycles rolled by. 'We want to go further north. And we want you to wait for us.'

'How long?'

'Ten hours. Maybe longer.'

Chinh clicked his tongue. 'Where you go?' he asked.

'That's not your problem,' said Bamber. 'You drop us, you wait for us, you drive us back to Saigon.'

The policeman blew his whistle again and Chinh put the taxi in gear and edged forward.

'Okay,' said Chinh. 'You the boss.'

May Eckhardt drove through a small village where women were using hoes to spread rice along the roadside so that it would dry in the baking hot sun. Several of the women looked up as she went by – it was still unusual to see a woman behind the wheel in Vietnam. May accelerated as she reached the outskirts of the village, veering over to the wrong side of the road to give a wide berth to a cart being pulled by two massive water buffaloes, their spreading horns at least six feet wide. The cart was piled high with sacks of rice, grains of which dribbled from the sides of the cart. Rice splattered against the Isuzu like rain, then she was past the cart and powering down the dusty road. Rice paddies stretched on either side almost to the horizon, lush and green, and young men stood knee deep in the canals that ran around the rice fields, fishing with nets that they threw like lassos.

In the far distance she could just make out the three motorcyclists and she slowed down. There was no need to get too close. She knew exactly where they were going. Her hands were light on the steering wheel, caressing rather than gripping, and she hummed softly to herself.

Jim Bamber unzipped his holdall and took out a green plastic map case. He unfolded it and held it up so that Wright could see it. It was hand drawn in black ink, the paper yellowing at the edges.

'This is a Defense Department map?' asked Wright. 'They let you have the original?'

'Yeah, I was surprised, but I guess they've got copies,' said Bamber.

The map was in five parts, each a sheet about two feet square. The top sheet showed features of the landscape – hills, a river, several small villages – and there were several crosses marked on it. In the top right-hand corner of the map was a compass showing north.

'This area was called the Long Nguyen Secret Zone,' said Bamber. 'It covered both sides of the Thi Tinh River. The Iron Triangle was about fifteen miles south, here.' He pointed at the map.

'And the crosses?'

'Tunnel entrances,' said Bamber.

'I thought there was only one way in?' said Wright.

Chinh pounded on his horn. From the moment he'd left the outskirts of Saigon he'd insisted on using the horn every time he came up behind a cyclist, letting them know that he was about to overtake. The constant noise irritated Wright, but despite several times asking him to stop doing it, Chinh persisted.

'There are entrances all over the area,' said the FBI agent, 'but they're not all connected. That was one of the reasons the army found it so difficult to close them down.'

He flipped over the first sheet, which also had a compass in the top right corner. Written across the top in capital letters was 'FIRST LEVEL'. The map had black crosses that coincided with the crosses on the first sheet.

'This is where the entrances lead to,' said Bamber. 'See what I mean? They're not all connected.'

The various entrances were linked by a network of tunnels. Some of the tunnels simply ran from one entrance to another, apparently connecting firing points, while others ran to larger rooms. Scattered across the map were four red crosses. Wright tapped one of them.

'What do they represent?' he asked.

'Hatches that lead down to the second level,' said Bamber.

He flipped the sheet over. Underneath was a map marked 'SECOND LEVEL', with matching red crosses on it. The second level contained much larger rooms and fewer tunnels. Wright peered at the notes that had been made alongside several of the squares that denoted the different rooms.

'A cinema?' he said in amazement.

'Yeah, they used to show propaganda movies underground. And they had dance troupes that used to tour around giving performances, poetry readings, the works.'

'And this,' said Wright, pointing at the map. 'This is a well?'

'That's right. They could draw their own water without leaving the tunnels. They had water, food stores, supplies of fuel. They could live down there for months.' He turned the sheet. 'This is the third level. They only discovered one way down, so much of the third level is unexplored.' He pointed at a blue cross. 'And this is the only way down to the fourth level.'

'The fourth level? I thought you said there were only three.'

Chinh slammed on the brakes and swerved into the middle of the road. Wright and Bamber were thrown apart and the map tore. Chinh pounded his horn. A flock of more than a hundred white ducks with bright orange bills scattered across the road. Two young Vietnamese boys with long canes jogged after the birds, shouting and waving. Bamber inspected the damaged map. It was only a small rip.

Chinh swung the car back on to the right side of the road. He twisted around in his seat and smiled apologetically. 'Roads bad up country,' he said.

'Sure are,' agreed Bamber. Ahead of them loomed a truck piled high with boxes of fruit. Bamber pointed at the truck and raised his eyebrows. Chinh turned around and narrowly avoided crashing into it. Two women riding bicycles piled high with firewood watched open mouthed as the car flashed by, missing them by inches.

Wright reached over and turned to the last page of the map. There were only two chambers drawn; a large one linked by a short length of tunnel to a second, smaller, room. The only writing on the sheet was the words 'FOURTH LEVEL'.

'That's obviously where they're going,' said Bamber. 'It must have been important to be so far underground.'

'How far below ground is this?' asked Wright, tapping the page.

'Fifty-five feet, I guess.'

Wright sat back and closed his eyes. He rubbed his temples with the palms of his hands. He could feel the pressure building behind his eyes, the prelude to a major headache. 'O'Leary mentioned booby traps,' he said.

Bamber folded up the sheets and slotted them back into the map case. 'Don't worry,' he said. 'I'll be ahead of you. If there are any problems, I'll come across them first.'

Problems sounded innocuous; problems sounded like small obstacles that could easily be overcome. O'Leary hadn't said problems, he'd said booby traps. 'What sort of problems?' asked Wright.

'Punji sticks in pits.'

Wright opened his eyes. 'What?'

Bamber smiled easily. 'Nick, we'll be following Doc and the rest. They've been down there already, they'll have exposed any traps.'

'You can't be sure of that.'

'They're almost fifty years old. You think they'd be putting their lives at risk if they didn't think they could handle it?'

'Maybe,' said Wright, unconvinced. 'Is there anything else I should worry about?'

Bamber put a hand on Wright's shoulder. 'It's going to work out just fine,' he said reassuringly.

Wright looked out of the window. They drove through a small village, on the outskirts of which was a school, little more than a long single-storey building and a dusty playground surrounded by a waist-high metal fence. Groups of young children in blue and white uniforms lined up in front of an open doorway while a teacher carried out a head count. It reminded Wright of the orphanage in Bangkok, and the basement where Eric Horvitz had died. He wondered what it must have been like, dying in a cold dark place, tortured and killed, begging for mercy and receiving none. He shuddered.

Doc pulled in at the side of the road and took a map out of the holdall strapped to his petrol tank. Hammack and Ramirez stopped their bikes either side of him. Doc flipped up his visor and studied the markings on the map. He checked his milometer and ran his finger along the thin line that represented the road they were on. He looked across the rice fields to a lone hill, a bump in the landscape that was much the same shape as the conical hats that the peasants wore.

'Much further?' asked Ramirez, using his sleeve to wipe away the red dust which had coated his visor.

'About an hour,' said Doc. 'Then we leave the road. There's a track that leads to the river. According to the map it's three miles from this road. Once we reach the river, we should be able to find the entrance.'

'You think we'll be able to find it, after twenty-five years?'

'We'll find the rock formation. That won't have changed,' said Doc. 'And then all we've got to do is to find the rock that we put over the hatch. It's not going to be a problem, Sergio.'

Hammack rubbed his arms. 'My arms are going numb,' he complained. 'Makes you miss the old Hueys, doesn't it?'

'You'll be telling us next that you miss the war,' said Doc.

Hammack shook his helmeted head. 'No fucking way,' he said.

Doc put the map away. 'Okay?' His two companions nodded. Doc put the bike in gear and roared off.

W hile Gerry Hunter waited for the woman in the registrar's office to call him back, he went over to make himself a coffee. He picked up the wrong mug by mistake, then realised with a jolt that it was Clive's. He stared at the chipped white mug with its map of Australia on one side and a grinning kangaroo on the other, wondering what to do with it. It was too personal to throw away, but he didn't want anyone else to use it. He took it back to his desk. He still expected Clive to walk into the incident room at any moment, cursing the London traffic or the weather or the canteen food or whatever it was that was annoying him that day.

Hunter picked up his telephone and dialled Anna Littman's number. Even as the phone rang out, Hunter wasn't exactly sure what he was going to say to her, and when she answered the words tumbled out in a rush.

'Anna, look, this is Gerry. I know this is crazy and I know you'll say that I'm clutching at straws and that I'm making something out of nothing, but is it in any way possible that Clive's death wasn't an accident?'

For several seconds she didn't speak. 'Gerry, you know what I'm going to say,' she said, her voice a concerned whisper.

'I know, I know. I want to feel that I'm doing something, I want to have someone to blame, I can't accept that sometimes shit just happens. I know the drill. I get it all the time, Anna, people who've lost their nearest and dearest and who aren't prepared to accept that it was an accident. They're convinced that it was an arsonist and not a faulty electrical heater or that someone tampered with the brakes and it wasn't just carelessness that sent the car off the road. I know, Anna, I'm not stupid.'

'No one said you're stupid, Gerry, but you've just lost a close, personal friend. More than that, a partner, someone who trusted you and relied on you. It's only natural that you're going to feel guilty.'

'I know all about survivor guilt, too, Anna.'

'So what do you want me to tell you? That Clive's death wasn't an accident?'

'Is it possible?'

'God, Gerry, how long have you been in the job? Anything's possible, you know that. But just think what that would mean. Someone would have had to have got into Clive's flat and forced him to drink the best part of a bottle of whisky, then forced him to throw up and choked him to death. Does that sound at all likely to you?'

Hunter put his hand up to his forehead. 'No, of course it's not likely. But is it possible?'

Dr Littman sighed. 'Yes, Gerry. It's possible. It's also possible that I'm really a visitor from another planet and that you're going to win the lottery this weekend. Anything's possible. But do I think that there's any likelihood that Clive was murdered? No, Gerry. I don't. You're going to have to let it go. Grief is all well and good, it's part of the—'

'— healing process, I know. I know. That's not what this is about.'

'What is it about, Gerry?'

Hunter considered her question. He wanted to tell her about Bamber, a man pretending to be an FBI agent. He wanted to tell her about the missing video cassette, about the ace of spades being a death card, but he knew that it wouldn't make any sense to her. It barely made any sense to him. 'I don't know, Anna. It's been a bad week.'

'Do you want to come around and talk about it? I serve an excellent coffee.'

Hunter ran his finger down the kangaroo on Clive's mug. 'Thanks, Anna, but I'll be okay.'

'My door's always open,' she said. 'Hell of a draught, but what can you do?'

Hunter laughed. When he replaced the receiver the phone rang almost immediately. It was the woman in the registrar's office, apologising for the delay in getting back to him.

'May Hampshire graduated in 1986, with first-class Honours,' said the woman.

'Hampshire?' queried Hunter. He'd been expecting an Oriental name.

'She was the only May in Computer Science, and I checked from 1980 right up to last year, just to be sure,' said the woman. 'The date of birth matches so there's no doubt that it's the girl you're looking for. Oh, you're worried about the name? I wondered about that because you said she was Chinese. Her photograph was on file and she's definitely Oriental. Very pretty girl.'

'Do you have her address?'

'I do. It's in Sale, just like you said. Her parents are Peter and Emily Hampshire.' The woman gave Hunter the full address and a telephone number. Hunter thanked her and cut the connection.

He sat staring at Clive's mug, thinking over what Anna Littman had said, wondering if she was right when she suggested he was suffering from survivor's guilt. He shook his head. No, there was a nagging doubt that wouldn't go away, no matter how dispassionately he thought about his partner's death. The missing video couldn't be explained, not unless someone else had been at Clive's flat. Then there was the Vietnam War connection: the movie, Eckhardt's war service, and the ace of spades death card. All were somehow linked, he was sure of that. He needed to talk to May Eckhardt, to find out what she knew of her husband's wartime experiences.

He dialled the number the woman had given him. Emily Hampshire answered the phone, her voice apprehensive as if she didn't get many calls and those that she did get rarely brought good news. Hunter identified himself.

'Mrs Hampshire, I'm actually calling about your daughter . . .'

'May? What's . . . ?'

'Mrs Hampshire, please don't worry. I just need to ask you a few questions, there's nothing for you to be alarmed about, really.' Hunter looked at his watch and came to a sudden decision. He could drive up to Sale in four hours or so, assuming the motorway was clear. 'Mrs Hampshire, will you and your husband be at home this afternoon?'

'Yes, I suppose so,' she said hesitantly.

'I'd like to pop along for a chat,' said Hunter. 'Nothing to worry about, I can assure you. Let's say three o'clock, shall we?'

The handlebars of Doc's motorcycle kicked from side to side and he fought to keep the machine moving in a straight line. Ramirez and Hammack followed in single file. The track was wide enough for a car, but it was uneven and dotted with potholes. They passed a small village, a cluster of houses with corrugated-iron roofs and television aerials on poles more than twenty feet long. A group of small children rushed out to watch the motorcycles drive by. They giggled and waved and Ramirez waved back. In the middle of the village was a large hut, open at the sides. Inside more than a dozen men sat in deckchairs watching an old black and white television set. None of them noticed the Americans ride by.

Beyond the village were acres of rice paddies. Half a dozen farmers in conical hats were burning rice stalks and the grey smoke blew over the track in billowing clouds. The three Americans drove through the smoke. The smell brought back memories for Doc, memories of helicopters hovering above a village, the rattle of AK-47s and the dull crump of mortars exploding in the paddies. Huts were on fire, the thatched roofs crackling and hissing like the burning rice stalks, and from inside the huts came screams and cries for help. Doc shook his head, trying to clear the thoughts from his head. It was no time for flashbacks.

They followed the track to the river, and then headed north. The rice paddies gave way to undergrowth, and then secondary jungle, areas which had been defoliated during the war but which had been reclaimed by trees, shrubs and ground-hugging plants. Doc took a look at his milometer and slowed his bike, looking around for landmarks. Twenty-five years ago the area had been as barren as a lunar landscape.

He saw what he was looking for over to his right, a jagged spar of rock amid the trees, leaning to the side like a massive javelin that had stuck point first in the ground. Next to it was a smaller rock formation, shaped like the comb of a rooster.

Doc stopped and put his feet on the ground. Ramirez and Hammack pulled up either side of him. All three were coated in red dust. Doc flipped up his visor and pointed at the rocks.

Hammack nodded. 'That's it,' he said. 'You did it, Doc. You got us here.'

Ramirez looked around. 'I never thought anything would grow here again, what with all the Agent Orange and shit they dumped and all.'

'Yeah, must have worked its way right through the food chain by now,' said Hammack.

Doc climbed off his bike. 'We won't be here long enough for it to affect us,' he said. 'Tomorrow lunchtime we'll be back in Saigon drinking beer and laughing at this.' He pushed his bike off the track and into the undergrowth.

'Yeah, I sure hope so,' said Hammack. He dismounted and pushed his bike after Doc. Ramirez followed.

All three men were bathed in sweat by the time they reached the sandstone rock formations. They parked their bikes and took off their helmets and gloves. Ramirez wiped his forehead with his sleeve, smearing red dust across his skin.

Doc went over to an anvil-shaped rock that came up to his waist. 'This is it,' he said. Hammack and Ramirez walked over to stand by him. They stood in silence, staring at the rock.

'I can't believe we came back,' said Ramirez.

'Believe it,' said Doc. 'We're here.'

All three men put their shoulders against the rock and pushed. It slid slowly to the side.

'That's enough,' said Doc. He knelt down and began scraping away the red soil with his hands until he found the trapdoor. Ramirez helped him and together they lifted up the wood and bamboo hatch, revealing the hole underneath.

'We know one thing for sure,' said Doc. 'No one came out this way after us. They wouldn't have been able to budge the rock.'

'That doesn't mean anything,' said Ramirez. 'There could be lots of other ways out that we didn't know about.'

'Always looking on the bright side, aren't you, Sergio?' said Doc sarcastically. 'Okay, let's get our gear on.'

They went back to their bikes and untied their kitbags. After stripping off their dusty clothes they changed into T-shirts and jeans and slung their rucksacks on. Doc and Hammack pulled on soft caps made of camouflage material, and Ramirez tied a scarf of green and brown around his head. They put their clothes into the kitbags, along with their helmets and gloves and the keys to the motorcycles.

'Okay?' asked Doc.

The two men nodded. 'Let's do it,' said Ramirez.

'We'll leave the kitbags down in the tunnel,' said Doc.

They carried the bags to the tunnel entrance. All three men were breathing heavily and sweating. Hammack's T-shirt was already soaked. They dropped their bags and stood around the hole, looking down. Doc patted Ramirez on the shoulder. 'Do you wanna lead the way, Sergio?' he said.

'Happy to,' said Ramirez.

He switched on his flashlight and sat down on the ground, swinging his legs into the square of darkness. He took several deep breaths and then crossed himself. He slid down through the hatchway, then dropped into a crouch and shuffled to the side. Doc and Hammack passed the kitbags down. Ramirez stacked them at the far side of the tunnel and then moved away from the hatch.

Hammack eased himself into the hole, his shoulders scraping against the wooden frame. He grunted, then he was through, bending his legs and crawling forward. Doc followed. He switched on his flashlight and then pulled the cover across the entrance.

'Stop here, Chinh,' said Bamber, pointing at a roadside shack. Chinh jammed on his brakes and they shuddered to a halt in a cloud of dust.

Wright opened his eyes. 'Are we there?' he asked.

'Not yet,' said the FBI agent. He opened the door and got out. 'I figured we should get some water.'

Bamber went over to the shack where an old woman in a wide-brimmed hat was hacking away at a coconut with a machete. Wright climbed out of the taxi and joined him. In the back of the shack was a refrigerator full of cans of soft drinks and bottles of water. An old man was sprawled on a sun-lounger, his head turned to a wall.

He was skeletally thin, his ribs clearly outlined through his mahogany skin.

Bamber pointed at the water and held up four fingers. The old woman gave him four bottles. 'Do you want a Coke or something?' Bamber asked Wright.

Wright shook his head. An ancient bus rattled down the road towards Saigon, scattering a group of scrawny chickens that had been pecking at spilled rice grains. He rubbed the back of his neck, trying to loosen the knotted muscles there. The sun was dipping towards the horizon. 'How long until it gets dark?' he asked.

'A couple of hours,' said Bamber. 'Don't worry, we'll be there well before the sun goes down. And once we're underground, it won't matter whether it's night or day.' He handed two of the bottles to Wright. 'You okay?'

Wright smiled tightly. 'Getting a bit of a headache, that's all.'

'It'll all be over in a few hours,' said Bamber, patting him on the back and guiding him towards the taxi where Chinh was gunning the engine impatiently.

M ay Eckhardt climbed out of the Isuzu and stretched lazily. The heat of the afternoon sun had been almost unbearable, even with the pick-up's airconditioning full on, but now it was early evening and there was a soft breeze from the north. She was wearing a faded sweatshirt and blue jeans, which she stripped off and tossed into the back of the pick-up truck. She kicked off her sandals and took off her bra and pants and stood naked, enjoying the feel of warm wind on her skin. She had a sudden urge to run across the sand, to go jumping over the rocks and skipping around the trees as she had done as a child. She smiled to herself. She wasn't a child any more and she had an adult's work to do.

She took the blue and green holdall off the passenger seat and took out a pair of black pyjamas, the sort that peasants still wore when they were tending their fields. She shrugged them on, then tied a black and white checked scarf around her neck. The sandals she put on were old and worn, but comfortable, the soles cut from truck tyres, the strip that ran between her toes made from an old inner tube. She took a leather belt and fastened it around her waist, then attached two metal water canteens, one either side. Also in the bag was a long hunting knife in an oiled leather scabbard, and she clipped that to the back of the belt. Everything else she needed was down in the tunnels already. The only food she was taking was a ball of rice wrapped in a silk handkerchief and placed in a small cloth bag that she tied to the front of the belt. She didn't need food to sustain her. Hate would be more than enough.

May used a rubber band to tie back her hair in a ponytail, locked the doors of the Isuzu and slid the key into the exhaust pipe. From the back of the pick-up she took a long flashlight. She walked confidently through the undergrowth, skirting a bomb crater half filled with green stagnant water.

The three motorbikes were in the shade of the jagged rock. One by one she pushed them to the water-filled crater and rolled them in. When she'd finished she stood at the edge watching the oily bubbles gradually subside until the surface was still once more. She wiped her hands on her trousers and walked over to the anvil-shaped rock.

The hatch covering the tunnel entrance had been pulled back into place but there had been no one to replace its covering of dirt. She pulled it open, and put her head to the opening, listening. There was only silence. She dropped down into the tunnel. Three kitbags lay to one side. Closing her eyes, she breathed in, sniffing like a tracker dog. She smelled sweat, cigarette smoke and beer, and the minty odour of toothpaste.

She pulled the hatch over her head, blocking out the light. It was a perfect fit and the darkness was absolute. May sat for a while, her back pressed against the hard, dry clay, breathing in the smell of the tunnels. The entrails of Mother Earth held no fear for her. They would protect her, as they had done in the past. She twisted around and began to move down the tunnel in a half crouch, still in total darkness because she wanted to use the batteries of her flashlight as little as possible. Besides, there were no traps in the early part of the tunnel. All the dangers lay ahead.

Ramirez played the beam of his torch along the floor of the tunnel. It ran for some fifty feet before it bent to the right. The roof was arched and the tunnel was slightly wider at the base than at the top. It was about three feet tall, so Ramirez could crawl on his hands and knees without banging his head. The Viet Cong, being smaller and slighter, were able to run along in a low crouch, giving them the advantage of speed. Ramirez knew, though, that speed wasn't what counted when exploring the underground labyrinth. Care and caution were the watchwords. The tunnels were a death trap for the unwary.

'How's it going, Sergio?' asked Hammack. The black man was about ten feet behind Ramirez.

'No problem,' said Ramirez. 'Makes all the difference knowing that a VC isn't just around the corner with a loaded AK-47, doesn't it?' Ramirez looked over his shoulder. Sweat was pouring off Hammack's face and he wiped his forehead with his massive forearm. 'Don't forget to drink,' said Ramirez. 'It's easy to get dehydrated down here.'

Hammack grinned and his gold tooth glinted. 'You wanna teach me to suck eggs while you're at it?' he said.

Ramirez smiled. 'Bet you're regretting all that fried chicken now, huh? You must be what, twenty pounds heavier than last time we were down here?'

'At least,' said Hammack. 'You want me to go point, thin man?'

'Hell no,' said Ramirez. 'This is the fun part.'

He turned away from Hammack and began to crawl forward, his flashlight in his left hand, his knife in his right.

'There,' said Bamber, pointing at the jagged rock formation to their right. He grabbed Chinh by the shoulder and told him to stop. He checked the map, looked at the milometer, then rechecked the map. 'Yup, this is it,' he said.

He pointed to the side of the road. 'Can you pull off here?' he asked Chinh.

The driver frowned. 'No road,' he said.

'I know there's no road, but the undergrowth isn't too thick, you can drive through it.'

Chinh pulled a face. He shook his head.

Bamber took a handful of Vietnamese banknotes out of his pocket and thrust them at the driver. 'If it's your paintwork you're worried about . . .'

Whether or not Chinh understood what Bamber had said, he grabbed the money and put the car in gear. He edged the Mercedes off the road and through the vegetation.

'I just want us away from the road,' said Bamber. 'Just in case someone goes by and wonders why Chinh's waiting.'

'Sure,' said Wright. He peered out of the window at the darkening sky. 'We made it just in time.'

'It's perfect,' said Bamber. 'We'll be out again at dawn. And the car's less likely to be spotted at night.'

The Mercedes slowed to a crawl. It had to skirt a bomb crater and then circle around a clump of tall trees covered with vines. Bamber looked over his shoulder. He couldn't see the track they'd left. 'Okay, Chinh, this'll do fine,' he said. Chinh brought the car to a halt.

Bamber opened the door and climbed out. Wright followed him. 'Is it far?' Wright asked.

'Over by the rocks,' said Bamber. 'According to the map, it's by a rock shaped like an anvil.'

He popped open the boot and clicked the combination locks on his suitcase. 'Mickey Mouse or Snoopy?' he asked.

'What?'

'The mouse or the dog? Which do you prefer?' He held up

two knapsacks, the sort children used to carry their books to school. One had a grinning Mickey Mouse on it, the other featured Snoopy lying on his kennel.

'Either,' said Wright.

Bamber tossed him the Mickey Mouse bag. 'You'll need this to carry your stuff,' he said. He handed him one of the infra-red goggle sets, spare batteries, a flashlight, and a large plastic bag.

'What's the plastic bag for?'

'You'll find out,' said Bamber, packing his stuff into the Snoopy knapsack. He took his jacket off and threw it into the boot. 'I suggest you strip down to the basics,' he said.

Wright removed his jacket. He was wearing dark brown Chinos and a fake Lacoste polo shirt that he'd bought for a couple of pounds on Sukhumvit Road. He loosened the straps on the knapsack as far as they'd go and put it on his back. It was a snug fit, but not uncomfortable. He took it off again and filled it with the equipment that Bamber had given him, then put in the two bottles of water.

'Ready?' asked Bamber.

'As I'll ever be,' said Wright.

Chinh got out of the car as Bamber slammed the boot shut. 'Where we go now?'

'You don't go anywhere,' said Bamber. 'You stay here, with the car.' He looked at his wristwatch. 'We'll be back here in twelve hours.'

Chinh looked at the two men, totally confused. 'You go walking at night?' he said.

'Don't worry about what we're doing,' said Bamber. 'Just make sure you're here when we get back.' He took a one-hundred-dollar bill from his pocket, tore it in two and gave one half to Chinh. 'You get the rest tomorrow,' he said.

Chinh nodded enthusiastically. 'No problem,' he said.

Bamber put the map case under one arm. 'Okay, Nick, let's go.' He walked towards the rocks and Wright followed. A bird squawked off to their left, then fell silent. The colour was draining from the trees and bushes, turning them from bright green to a muted grey. Something settled on Bamber's neck and he felt a sharp stabbing pain. He ignored it. He studied the map, and took a bearing with a small compass. 'This way,' he said, pushing through a cluster of broad-leaved bushes. Hundreds of small flies swarmed around them and a large purple dragonfly buzzed over their heads.

They walked through a clearing, then around a clump of tall palm trees. The ground dipped and then they stood in front of the rock formation, weathered from centuries of wind and rain. Bamber looked around. He pointed at the anvil-shaped rock. The wood and bamboo hatchway was clearly visible in the dirt. Bamber went over and pulled it up. He peered inside.

Wright came up behind him. 'That's it?' he said.

'That's it,' said Bamber. 'That's the way in. Doc and the rest are already down there.'

Wright crouched down. 'It looks so small,' he said.

'More than enough room,' said Bamber. He folded the map case. 'Why don't you go down first, just to get a feel for it. I'm going to make sure that Chinh understands he has to wait.'

'Okay,' said Wright.

Bamber walked through the undergrowth, making almost no sound. Crickets clicked all around him, like Geiger counters gone crazy. The sun slipped down below the horizon, leaving behind only a red smear in the sky. Dark clouds scudded overhead and beyond them stars began to become visible, winking into existence one at a time.

Chinh was standing at the back of the car, the boot open. He was fiddling with the catches to the metal suitcase. Bamber crept up behind him. In a smooth, fluid movement he grabbed Chinh's head and twisted it savagely, snapping his neck like a dry twig.

The tunnel dipped down ahead of him and Sergio Ramirez felt his centre of gravity move forward so that more of his weight was on his hands. Grains of dirt sprinkled down from the roof and pitter-pattered on his scarfed head. Behind him he could hear Hammack grunting with exertion. They'd been underground for almost an hour and by Ramirez's reckoning they'd covered about half a mile. The muscles in his shoulders were aching and he'd scuffed his palms in several places. The floor of the tunnel was rock hard, and it was like crawling along a road.

Ramirez stopped and played his flashlight beam along the length of the tunnel. Something moved and Ramirez stiffened.

'What?' asked Hammack, behind him.

'Centipede,' said Ramirez. It was more than six inches long, dark green in colour with countless legs, and it was moving purposefully towards the Americans, its antennae twitching. Ramirez had once been bitten by a similar insect and his arm had swollen up like a football for more than a week.

The centipede seemed oblivious to the flashlight. Ramirez pressed himself against the side of the tunnel and raised his knife.

'Kill it, man,' hissed Hammack.

'Well, Jeez, Bernie, why didn't I think of that?'

'What's the hold-up?' called Doc, from the rear.

'Centipede,' said Hammack.

'Just kill it and let's get moving,' said Doc.

'Yeah, well, if I had a gun, I'd just shoot it, but seeing as I've only got a knife I'm gonna have to wait until it gets close, okay?' said Ramirez. 'Now will you guys just pipe down and let me take care of business?'

Doc and Hammack fell silent, but Ramirez could still hear them breathing. The centipede stopped and its antennae twitched as if probing for vibrations in the air. 'Come on, lovely,' whispered Ramirez. He held the knife in his fist, point downwards. 'Come to Papa.'

The centipede's legs began to ripple again and the insect moved forward. It headed towards the wall and ran along it. Ramirez jabbed the knife at the middle of the insect and impaled it. The centipede reared up and tried to snap at his hand. Ramirez twisted the knife and it made a crunching sound. Still the centipede refused to die. Ramirez scraped it along the tunnel wall but it continued to thrash about. He held it down with the knife and squashed its head with the end of his flashlight, gently so that he wouldn't break the bulb. Green, milky fluid squirted from the insect's body and splashed along Ramirez's hand. Eventually it went still and Ramirez pulled his knife out. He flicked the dead insect out of the way. 'Okay,' he said. 'Let's go.'

Nick Wright sat with his legs down the hatchway, staring into the darkness. Around him insects clicked and whirred and he heard something slithering on the rocks behind him. There'd be snakes, he was sure of that. Snakes and spiders and God knows what else. He shuddered. His mouth had gone dry and he wanted to drink some of the water in his knapsack but knew that he should save it for later. He held the flashlight in both hands. It was made from black rubber and was long enough to hold three batteries. How long would three batteries last? he wondered. Six hours? Twelve?

A figure materialised in the gloom. It was Bamber. 'Okay?' Wright asked.

'Yeah, he knows what he's got to do,' said the FBI agent. He crouched down next to Wright and illuminated the map with his flashlight. 'The first part's a piece of cake,' he said. 'The tunnel runs pretty much north all the way. There'll be kinks and bends but nothing to worry us.'

Wright nodded. He switched on his own flashlight. Bamber's face shone a deathly white in the beam.

'I'll go first,' continued Bamber. 'Stay fairly close. You'll probably find that you don't need to have your flashlight on.'

'What about the goggles?'

'Let's see how you get on with the flashlight first,' said Bamber. 'You'll find the goggles uncomfortable if you wear them for more than an hour or so.' He gestured at the hole. 'Do you wanna go down?'

Wright swallowed. His throat felt as if it had shrunk to half its normal size. 'Okay,' he said. He edged forward and slid his legs into the hole, taking his weight on his arms. For a second his feet swung freely and then his toes scraped on the floor and he dropped down. He scraped his cheek against the side of the tunnel as he wriggled through.

Wright twisted his neck up so that he could see the square of light above his head. Bamber was looking down on him, smiling. Wright flashed him a thumbs-up and tried to grin. He ducked down and examined the tunnel. To the north, it ran off into the distance, then curved to the left. Wright could just about shuffle forwards in a crouch, his knees up against his chest, but it was painful and he knew he wouldn't be able to keep it up for long. He squatted back down. There wasn't enough room to walk bent double, and his only option was to crawl.

'Okay, Nick?' called Bamber.

'Yeah,' replied Wright. He moved back, making room for Bamber to come down. He bumped against something soft. It was a green kitbag, with 'USMC' stencilled on it in white letters. 'There's some stuff down here. It looks like they left it.'

Bamber's feet dropped through the hole. The FBI agent's toes scraped against the side, kicking down a small avalanche of dirt, then he lowered himself down and squatted, facing Wright. The beam of Bamber's flashlight was shining up under his chin and it gave him a ghostly appearance, his eyes transformed into black pits in a stark white face. He reached up to grab hold of the cover.

'Leave it,' said Wright, quickly. Too quickly, he realised. He could hear the panic in his own voice.

'Nick, we're going to be almost two miles away from here,' said Bamber. 'Open or closed, it's not going to make any difference.'

'Humour me,' said Wright.

More grains of soil tumbled down from the hatchway. Wright shone his flashlight along the sides of the tunnel. He patted the tunnel wall with the flat of his hand. The earth was hard, like concrete, reddish in colour.

'It's solid,' said Bamber. 'It's been like this for twenty-five years, it's not going to collapse now.'

Wright rested the back of his head against the clay. 'I know,' he said. He took deep breaths. The air was hot and sticky and it felt as if he had to drag in each lungful. He looked up at the hole and the stars behind. They were maybe four feet underground. Just about the depth a coffin would be. He tried to block the image out of his mind but it kept returning: a black coffin, lowered into the ground, a group of mourners standing on artificial grass as a robed priest muttered Latin, then a handful of wet earth thrown down, thudding against the polished walnut. Wright standing next to his mother, holding her hand and listening to her cry, squeezing her fingers to let her know that he was there, but getting no reaction from her.

'Nick?'

Wright snapped back to reality. 'What?'

'Time to go.'

Wright nodded.

Bamber shuffled around and crawled forward on his hands and knees. The beam of his flashlight danced crazily, throwing eerie shadows against the tunnel walls. Wright tried to clear his throat but almost choked, and he began coughing, the noise echoing around the confined space. Bamber was almost fifteen feet away and the light from his flashlight was already fading. Wright crawled after him, his eyes fixed on the soles of Bamber's training shoes.

R amirez emerged into the chamber and stood up, arching his spine and exhaling deeply. He was drenched and his hair and skin glistened. The chamber was almost twenty paces long and ten wide and about twice the height of a man. Hammack crawled out behind him. He too was soaked to the skin. He stood up and surveyed the room with Ramirez. There were reed mats on the floor, and on the far end of the chamber a sheet that had once been white was pinned to the wall. At the opposite end an old projector sat on a wooden table, covered in cobwebs and dust.

'Wonder what the last feature was?' said Ramirez.

'Probably *A Thousand And One Ways To Kill The White Devil*,' said Doc as he crawled into the chamber. He ran his hand over his face, wiping away the moisture that clung to his skin, then took off his rucksack and shook it. It too was dripping wet. He took a swig from one of his canteens, spat, then drank deeply. He wiped his mouth and offered his canteen to Ramirez.

There was a flurry of movement above their heads and dozens of small black shapes whizzed by, spinning and curving through the air. All three men ducked instinctively.

'What the . . .' said Hammack.

'Bats,' said Doc. 'They're harmless.'

The bats flew around the chamber, their sonic radar allowing them to whiz by the men so closely that they could feel the draught from their wings, then almost as one they flew off down a side tunnel to the left of the makeshift movie screen.

Ramirez handed the canteen back to Doc. Doc had taken a Marlboro pack and his Zippo lighter from a small plastic bag and he lit up.

Ramirez shook his head. 'Can't see why a doctor smokes,' he said.

Doc exhaled and grinned at Ramirez. 'This from a man who snorts heroin?'

'Recreational use, Doc,' said Ramirez.

Hammack was walking around the perimeter of the chamber. Three tunnels led off the room: the one they'd come through, the one the bats had flown down, and another, midway along the wall. In the far corner, to the right of the screen, was a jagged hole in the floor. Hammack went over to it. The hole was about three feet deep and at the bottom were sharpened bamboo spears, pointing up. 'Damn near lost my foot to that thing,' said Hammack.

'Yeah, well, you should know they always put punji traps in the corners,' said Ramirez. 'That's where you hide when you're scared of the dark.'

Hammack sneered. 'Hell, I weren't ever scared of the dark,' he said.

'That's right,' said Ramirez. 'When you closed your eyes and your mouth you were damn near invisible.'

Hammack laughed throatily. He popped a fresh piece of chewing gum into his mouth and went over to the tunnel the bats had flown into. He knelt down and looked inside.

There were fragments of metal embedded in the red clay. Hammack pulled one out and held it in the palm of his hand. Doc peered over Hammack's shoulder.

'Max was lucky,' said Hammack, probing the metal with his finger. 'Got down just in time. Another second and it would have killed him.'

'Shouldn't have gone in without probing for tripwires first,' said Ramirez. 'It was an obvious place.'

'Easy enough to say after the event, Sergio,' said Doc.

'Come on, Doc. He was panicking, he wanted to get out and he took the wrong tunnel. If you hadn't heard the click, if you hadn't shouted . . .'

'Yeah, well, I did and he got away with a backful of shrapnel,' said Doc, crushing his cigarette with his heel. 'Come on, let's go.' He slipped his rucksack on. 'Bernie, are you okay going point for a while?'

'Sure,' said Hammack.

'I can do it,' said Ramirez defensively.

Doc shook his head. 'You've been in front for two hours, Sergio. You need a rest. You take the rear.'

Ramirez looked for a moment as if he was going to argue, but Doc's eyes hardened and Ramirez nodded. Hammack went over to the hole in the middle of the wall. He pointed his flashlight into the darkness, ran the beam over the walls and ceiling, and crawled in. Doc and Ramirez followed.

Nick Wright had no idea how deep he was. The tunnel had been sloping downwards for some time, a gradual incline but a definite one. He wondered how much earth was above his head. If there was a collapse, he'd never be able to claw his way to the surface, of that he was sure. The tunnel sides seemed to be pressing in on him, and the roof seemed to be lower than it had been in the first section. Occasionally his back would bang against it and there'd be a small shower of red dirt. The tunnel had zigzagged left and right until he'd lost all sense of direction, though Bamber had insisted that they were still heading north. Wright wondered what they'd do if the way ahead proved to be blocked. The tunnel was so narrow that he doubted he'd be able to turn around, they'd have to shuffle backwards for upwards of three hundred metres to a small chamber which had apparently been a resting place for VC on their way to the main tunnel complex. The thought brought on feelings of panic and Wright tried to think of relaxing images: trees, fields, beaches. He closed his eyes and tried to imagine he was out in the open, that above his head was clear blue sky and not unyielding clay.

It was bad enough fighting the claustrophobia. Wright couldn't imagine what it must have been like for the Tunnel Rats, knowing that the enemy was waiting for them somewhere underground, an enemy with guns and knives, hiding in the darkness.

His hands and knees were sore and his back and neck ached, and the rough surface kept scuffing and scratching his skin. Gritty dust constantly worked its way into the cuts and abrasions on his hands, stinging and burning.

He opened his eyes. Bamber was ten feet or so in front of him, crawling with slow, regular movements. Wright tried to follow the FBI agent's rhythm, right arm and right leg moving together, then left arm and left leg. It produced a rolling motion that would have been soothing if it wasn't for the friction on his palms and knees.

His shoulders banged against the concrete-hard walls. He'd never be able to dig his way out if anything went wrong. He pictured himself clawing at the impenetrable clay, his fingers bleeding, his nails breaking, screaming for help with no one able to hear him. Wright's chest began to pound. He was underground, he was surrounded by the earth, he was buried deep below the ground and if the roof were to collapse he'd die with his mouth full of soil and clay with no one to help him. He shook his head. Nothing was going to go wrong, he told himself. The tunnels had been there for decades, there was no reason for them to start collapsing now. He took deep breaths, willing the panic to subside.

His hand squashed against something soft and mushy and he jerked it back. He shone his flashlight on to his palm. There were pieces of dead insect on it. Something long and thin with dozens of legs. Wright flinched. His head banged against the roof of the tunnel and he yelped. He frantically wiped his hand on the wall, trying to get the mess off his skin. There was another, longer, piece of centipede on the floor, its legs sticking lifelessly up into the air.

'What's wrong?' asked Bamber. He'd stopped and was looking over his shoulder.

'I put my hand on a centipede,' said Wright. He rubbed his hand on his shirt.

'Did it bite you?'

'I think it was dead already.'

'You okay?'

'I've been better.'

Bamber nodded. 'We're almost at the main complex,' he said. 'Then we go down to the second level.'

Wright nodded. He took deep breaths, fighting to stay calm, knowing that if he did panic there was nowhere to go. He couldn't turn around, and the FBI agent blocked the way forward. He had never felt so trapped and helpless in his life.

D oc leaned back against the wall of the chamber and sighed. 'I'm too old for this,' he said.

'We're all too old for this,' agreed Hammack. He unwrapped a stick of gum and put it in his mouth. He offered the pack to Doc and Ramirez but both men shook their heads.

Doc flipped his Zippo open and lit a cigarette. He looked around. The chamber they were in was conical, like a concrete teepee, with two tunnel entrances. It was big enough to hold four people and Doc knew it had been constructed as an air-raid shelter for Viet Cong cadres. The conical structure was virtually indestructible, even by a direct hit from a 750-pound bomb dropped by a B-52. The shape of the structure amplified sound from above ground so that the cadres would be able to hear the planes long before they arrived over the tunnel complex.

Ramirez drank from his canteen and wiped his mouth with the back of his hand. 'We must be fucking crazy,' he said.

Doc looked at his wristwatch. They'd been underground for four hours. 'If we're crazy now, think how crazy we were twenty-five years ago,' he said.

Hammack nodded. 'We were young. We thought we'd live for ever. I did, anyway. I was fucking invincible. I was the man.'

Doc blew a smoke ring up at the apex of the chamber.

'Secondary smoking kills, Doc,' said Ramirez, grinning.

The three men laughed, but it was an uneasy, disjointed sound and it echoed eerily around the chamber.

'Do you ever think about what happened, last time we were here?' asked Hammack when the last echo had faded.

'About Jumbo?'

'About Jumbo. About what we did.'

Doc rolled his shoulders and twisted his neck from side to side. 'I try not to,' he said.

'I think about it every day,' said Hammack. 'Especially at night.'

Ramirez nodded. 'Yeah. The nights are the worst. Sometimes I wake up and for a moment I forget where I am. It's like I'm back down in the tunnels, in the dark. Then I'll hear a noise and I'm up in a crouch, hands out.' He flashed a humourless smile. 'Scares the shit out of the girls.'

'That's not what I meant,' said Hammack. He interlinked his fingers and cracked his knuckles. 'I get flashbacks and stuff, but anyone who was in 'Nam gets them. I'm talking about guilt.'

Doc and Ramirez exchanged looks, then stared at Hammack. Hammack raised his hands.

'I'm just saying, that's all. I think what we did was wrong.'

Doc stubbed his cigarette out on the floor. 'We were fighting a war, Bernie. They killed Jumbo, slit his throat like they were killing a pig.'

'Yeah, but—'

'There are no buts, it was kill or be killed.'

Hammack shook his head. 'Not at the end it wasn't, Doc. It was murder.'

Doc's eyes hardened. Before he could speak there was a scrabbling noise from one of the tunnels and all the men jumped. A large grey rat rushed out of the hole next to Ramirez, leaped across his outstretched legs, and disappeared through the other hole.

Hammack put his hand on his chest and let out a long sigh. 'I almost had a seizure,' he said. 'That'd be one for the books, wouldn't it? Killed by a rat.'

M ay Eckhardt sat in the darkness, listening to the laughter echoing down the tunnels. She sat cross-legged, her unlit flashlight in her lap. The darkness was total, but her other senses were telling her everything she needed to know. She could hear the men, even though they were more than five hundred feet away. She could smell the cigarette that Doc had smoked and the spearmint gum that Hammack was chewing. On her right cheek she could feel a light breeze, fresh air blowing in through a small ventilation tunnel only a few inches in diameter. She placed the flat of her hand on the floor, feeling the vibrations made by the men as they started to move again.

She knew exactly where they were going, and the route they would take. May had all the time in the world. She knew her way around parts of the tunnel complex that the

Americans didn't even know existed. She took her knife out of its scabbard and used her black and white checked scarf to polish it, smiling to herself as she worked.

Bamber stopped and opened his map case. Wright crawled up behind him. 'What?' he said.

'You'll need to get the plastic bag out,' said the FBI agent.

Wright knelt back, ducking his head so that it wouldn't scrape along the tunnel roof. 'What are you talking about?'

The tunnel had widened a little, giving Bamber enough room to twist around so that he was facing Wright. He kept his flashlight down so as not to dazzle him. 'You remember I told you about the water trap? The U-bend, to stop gas going all the way through the complex.'

Wright realised what Bamber was getting at. He shook his head fiercely. 'No,' he said. 'No way.'

'It's no big deal,' said Bamber. 'Eight feet at most.' He put the map on the ground and pointed at a length of tunnel. 'We go through the water, then we go down to the second level.'

Wright continued to shake his head.

'Nick, we've no choice. It's the only way forward. Doc and the rest have already gone this way.'

Wright felt suddenly light headed. He was hyperventilating. He held his breath for a while, then exhaled. He shone his flashlight over Bamber's shoulder. An oval

pool of water glistened. Beyond it was nothing but red clay.
'Eight feet?' he said.

'Maximum. You hold your breath and you crawl down,
then up. You don't even have to swim.'

'What about the flashlights?'

'What do you mean?'

'Are they waterproof?'

'They're rubber coated, but I wouldn't want to risk
exposing them under water.'

'Jim, you don't know how tough it is for me to be down
here in the first place. It's all I can do to stop myself from
screaming. There's no way I can go underwater in pitch
darkness.'

'You can, and you will.'

'I can't be in the dark. I'll freak out.'

'Because of your claustrophobia?'

Wright nodded.

'Hell, Nick, you're already underground. What is it with
you and dark places?'

Wright put his hands over his face. 'It's a long story,'
he said.

'Give me the short version. We don't have too much
time.'

Wright sighed. 'When I was a kid, my father built me a
train set, a huge one, scenery, stations, points, the works.
He built it and I helped him. It got so big we had to put
it in the basement. When I was ten, he and my mum got
divorced. To this day I don't know why. I don't remember
any rows, it's not as if he used to hit her or anything. But
my mum moved out, and I went to live with her. We didn't
live far away so I used to go around to my dad's house all
the time. I had a key so I could I let myself in.'

Wright went quiet as the memories flooded back. Bamber waited patiently for him to finish.

'I went around one Saturday afternoon. I rang the doorbell but there was no answer. Sometimes he went away, he was a salesman, selling life insurance and stuff, and he often went on sales trips. I let myself in. The light in the basement wasn't working, but there were lights on the train set, for the stations and the houses, and I knew the switch, for that was in the far corner, so I went down in the dark. I got halfway down the stairs and the door closed. I kept on going, figuring I could find the switch in the dark.'

Wright fell silent again as he relived the experience in his mind. Walking slowly through the dark, his hands stretched out in front of him. He shook his head.

'I bumped into something, something hanging from the ceiling. He'd hanged himself. At first I didn't know what it was, then I felt his shoes. They were wet and there was a funny smell. He'd pissed himself. People who hang themselves always do.'

'I know,' said Bamber quietly.

'I turned and ran, slap bang into the table. Knocked myself out. I woke up a couple of hours later, didn't know where I was or what had happened. It was pitch black. I don't know how long it took me to find my way back up the stairs and to open the door, but it seemed like for ever. It still does.' Wright smiled ruefully at Bamber. 'That's the abridged version,' he said. 'But the upshot is, I always leave a light on when I sleep, because if I wake up in the middle of the night and it's dark, I panic.'

Bamber looked at him for several seconds. 'I don't know what to say. You want to go back? You want to quit?'

'No, I don't want to quit,' said Wright quickly. The words

came out without thinking, but he realised that he meant what he said. Just then nothing meant more to him than finding out who had killed Max Eckhardt and Eric Horvitz. He wasn't going to quit, not after he'd come this far. He shrugged off the knapsack and took out the plastic bag. He put the knapsack into the bag, then put his flashlight inside, still switched on, before twisting the neck of the bag to form a seal.

Bamber followed Wright's example. The lights were dimmer, but they still illuminated the tunnel around them. 'I'll go first,' Bamber said. 'Give me thirty seconds, then follow me through. If you can, I'd recommend you keep your eyes closed, there's no telling what shit's in there.'

He turned around, took a deep breath, and plunged head first into the water. His legs kicked, then they disappeared, leaving only ripples in the surface. Water spilled on to the floor of the tunnel, and then ran back into the pool. Wright stared at the water. It was inky black, like oil. He wondered if there were snakes in the water, or worse. They were bound to find their way into the tunnels; what would he do if he got bitten? He imagined himself writhing in agony, already entombed in the earth, dying alone, in the dark. He twisted the plastic bag so that the beam of the flashlight ran along the length of the tunnel behind him. It was clear. How fast could snakes move? he wondered. Would they attack him from behind, or did they only bite if threatened? Wright didn't know, and he didn't want to find out.

He looked back at the pool. Its surface was still once more, a black mirror through which he had to pass. He had no way of knowing if Bamber had got through safely. He could be trapped under the surface, the last breath escaping from his body. Wright shuffled up to the edge of the pool.

His reflection stared back at him. 'Eight feet,' he whispered to himself. 'It's only eight feet.'

He swallowed, then took deep breaths. He said a silent prayer, then dipped the bag into the pool. He took a final breath of air and ducked his head under the surface. He pushed himself forward, his hands and knees scrabbling on the tunnel floor. The water pushed him up and his head banged on the roof and he arched his back and pushed again with his toes. He felt as if he was hardly making any progress. The back of his head scraped the clay again. His natural buoyancy and the air in the plastic bag were pushing him up against the roof. His eyes began to sting and he clamped them shut.

His feet floated up and he kicked them but he was being pushed against the tunnel roof so strongly that he couldn't move forward. Wright's lungs began to burn and he knew he was only seconds away from drowning. He tried to claw his way along the tunnel floor but he couldn't get a grip. His head slammed into the roof again.

He opened his eyes but the water was so dirty that he could only see a few inches in front of his face. He tried kicking again, but his feet had nothing to push against and his heels flailed uselessly against the roof. His chest began to heave and he clamped his jaws shut tight. He hadn't even reached the halfway mark; the roof was still curving down. Wright twisted around so that his face was turned towards the roof. He scrabbled with his hands and feet, the plastic bag banging into the side of his head, but finally he managed to get a grip on the slippery clay and he pulled himself down. The tunnel began to curve up again and his buoyancy pulled him around the bend and he popped up to the surface, crying and gasping for air.

A hand gripped him by the collar and pulled him out of the water. 'What the hell kept you?' asked Bamber. Wright rolled on to his hands and knees and retched. The FBI agent slapped him on the back. 'I'd just about given up on you,' said Bamber.

Wright coughed and spat. 'You and me both,' he gasped. He flicked his wet hair out of his eyes. 'Are you telling me that the VC did that every time they used the tunnel?'

'Sure did. Probably with a bit more finesse than you, though.' He fastened the straps of his knapsack, then took Wright's out of its plastic bag.

Wright put his knapsack on and wiped his face with his hands, then picked up his flashlight. Bamber was already crawling down the tunnel and Wright followed him. The air seemed staler, and it was an effort to breathe. The tunnel bent sharply to the left and for a few seconds Bamber was out of sight. Wright had a sudden feeling of panic and he crawled faster.

Bamber had stopped around the corner and Wright almost bumped into him. The FBI agent was pulling at a hatch in the floor. He tossed the wooden cover to the side and peered down.

'This is where we go down?' asked Wright.

'That's right,' said Bamber. He opened the map case and studied the hand-drawn plan of the second level. 'We've got several chambers to get through, but the tunnels linking them are quite short,' he said.

Wright nodded. 'How does air get down to the lower levels?' he asked.

'Ventilation tunnels,' said Bamber. 'There are a few marked on the map. They're small tunnels that lead up to the surface, usually facing into the wind so that air blows into them.' He slipped the map case underneath his shirt. 'Okay, let's do it,' he said. He lowered his legs through the hatchway and dropped down. Wright took a couple of deep breaths to steady his nerves and then followed him.

P eter and Emily Hampshire's house was a neat mock-Tudor semi-detached in a tree-lined avenue off the main road that cut through Sale, much the same sort of house that Gerry Hunter had lived in as a child. A small patch of grass was surrounded by carefully pruned roses and next to the front door was a wooden sign on which had been painted 'The Hampshires' in white flowery script. Hunter pressed the doorbell and a tune he didn't recognise chimed for a full ten seconds.

The front door opened and a woman in her sixties frowned out at him. Hunter smiled and showed her his warrant card. 'Mrs Hampshire? I'm Detective Inspector Gerry Hunter, I spoke to you this morning.'

The woman peered past him as if fearing he'd parked a squad car with flashing lights in her driveway, but she visibly relaxed when she saw his blue Vauxhall Cavalier. Hunter figured he was probably the first policeman to have called at her house. She opened the door wider and ushered him inside. She was a large woman, only a few inches shorter than Hunter and considerably broader, and he had to squeeze past her in the narrow hallway.

'My husband's in the sitting room,' she said. 'Just to your right.'

The sitting room was feminine and fussy: lace trimmings on the sofa and armchairs, glass display cases filled with pottery figures and glass animals, brass knicknacks on the mantelpiece, ornately framed pictures on the walls. Among the clutter Hunter almost overlooked Mr Hampshire, a small man with bird-like features, perched on the edge of the sofa as if he feared being engulfed by the overstuffed cushions. Hunter shook hands gingerly, his own hand dwarfing the older man's.

'How about a nice cup of tea?' asked Mrs Hampshire. 'I've got the kettle on.' She had a barrel-like figure, the excess weight blurring her breasts, waist and hips into one smooth, featureless body mass. Her face, however, wasn't fat at all and she had strong cheekbones and thin lips. It was a forceful face and Hunter reckoned she had probably been quite attractive when she was younger. She was at least twice the weight of her husband and Hunter couldn't stop himself picturing the couple in bed together. He wondered what positions they favoured, because if she went on top there was a good chance the poor man would be crushed to death.

'Tea would be lovely,' he said, smiling.

He sat down as she left the room and smiled at Mr Hampshire who was wearing a blue blazer with a regimental crest on the pocket and grey slacks.

'How were the roads?' Mr Hampshire asked, peering at the detective over the top of tortoiseshell-framed reading glasses.

'Fine,' said Hunter. He got the feeling that Mrs Hampshire had told her husband not to discuss the reason for his visit while she was out of the room.

'The traffic just gets worse and worse, doesn't it?'

Mr Hampshire pushed his glasses up his nose with his finger. 'Do you collect stamps, by any chance?'

'Afraid not,' said Hunter.

'Ah,' said Mr Hampshire. He looked at the lace curtains around the bay window and raised his eyebrows. The two men sat in silence as a grandfather clock ticked off the seconds.

H ammack used the point of his knife to pry open the hatch. 'I'll take over from here, Bernie,' said Doc.

'I don't mind going first,' said Hammack, putting his knife away.

'No,' said Doc, sharply.

'There's nothing down there, Doc,' said Hammack. Doc stared at Hammack, his jaw set tight. 'Okay,' said Hammack. 'Have it your way.' He crawled over the hatchway and turned around.

Doc shuffled over to the hole, his face impassive. He sat back on his heels and looked down into the dark. Twenty-five years earlier, he'd sat in the same position. Hammack had been there, and Ramirez. Horvitz had been at the rear, with Eckhardt, and Burrow had been just behind Doc, waiting to hear Doc's decision. O'Leary had been marking the hatchway on his map. And Jumbo had been there, looking over Doc's shoulder, saying that it was his turn, that he should go down first.

Doc had thought long and hard, back then. They'd mapped the first and second levels, but this had been the first time they'd found a way down to the third level, so it had meant going into the unknown. Ramirez would usually have been Doc's choice but the Latino had taken the lead for three hours and the strain was starting to tell on him. Horvitz had volunteered but he'd almost fallen into a punji trap earlier in the day and his nerves were still on edge. Hammack was just about the least experienced of the Tunnel Rats, and Burrow, well, Burrow was with Psyops, psychological operations, he wasn't a tunnel specialist. Jumbo had been the obvious choice, and he was so damn keen.

Jumbo had drawn his knife and checked his flashlight, then slowly eased himself through the hatch. He'd reached the bottom, then looked up and grinned at Doc. Doc had wanted to warn him, to tell him not to let down his guard, but before he could open his mouth there had been a flash of steel around Jumbo's neck and a look of terror in his eyes, then the knife had disappeared and the blood had flowed in a scarlet curtain down his chest.

Doc had plunged headfirst through the hatchway and grabbed Jumbo under the arms. Jumbo was gurgling, his legs thudding against the tunnel floor, his eyes wide and imploring as if begging Doc to help him. Burrow had pulled Doc's legs and together they'd dragged Jumbo back up to the second level. Doc had done his best, but the cut was too deep. It had taken Jumbo more than a minute to die, sixty seconds during which Doc had had his hands clamped around Jumbo's throat in a vain attempt to stem the flow of blood, whispering words of encouragement even though he had known it was hopeless.

'Doc?' said Ramirez.

Doc shook his head. 'Okay,' he said. 'I'm going down.'

Ramirez put his hand on Doc's shoulder. 'It was Jumbo's decision,' he said.

'No, Sergio. It was my call. He wanted to go but it was my call.'

Doc's knife was in its scabbard, hanging on his belt. He reached for it but then hesitated. Hammack was right, there was nothing down there. The VC had long gone, taking their place above ground as victors of the war against the Americans. He nodded curtly at Ramirez and Hammack, and lowered himself through the hatchway. The vertical tunnel was three feet deep, so Doc had to bend his knees and duck his head to look around the third level. He turned his body through three hundred and sixty degrees, his heart racing, images of Jumbo flashing through his mind. The tunnel was clear, north and south. He looked up and gave Ramirez a thumbs-up.

Doc crawled a short way down the tunnel so that Ramirez and Hammack could join him. As they dropped down into the tunnel, something bit Doc on the back of his neck and he slapped it with the flat of his hand. It was an ant, half an inch long. He felt another sharp pain, just below his ear, then another, on his ankle. He shone his flashlight along the tunnel wall. There were hundreds of ants scurrying around. He'd been so intent on checking that the tunnel was clear that he hadn't seen the insects. He jerked his hand back as an ant bit him on the thumb. 'Watch it, guys, ants!' he said, as he took off his rucksack.

Ramirez and Hammack scuttled backwards. Hammack began slapping his legs and cursing.

Doc pulled a can of insecticide out of his rucksack and sprayed the sides of the tunnel. The ants shrivelled into black balls and dropped to the floor. The bitter smell made Doc gag and he put his hand over his mouth and nose. Dead ants fell from the tunnel roof and rolled off his cap. Live ants were still biting at his neck and he slapped himself.

'Throw me the spray, Doc!' shouted Hammack, and Doc tossed him the can. Hammack pushed it down the front of his pants and sprayed himself, wriggling his legs so that the insecticide could work its way down. 'The little bastards are biting my nuts!'

Ramirez was laughing at the black man's discomfort, but then he too began to slap himself. 'Fuck, they're everywhere,' he shouted.

Hammack sprayed the inside of his shirt, then the ground on which he was sitting. He passed the can to Ramirez.

More ants ran along the tunnel walls, hundreds and hundreds of them. Doc pulled another can of insecticide out of his rucksack. He took off his cap and used it to cover his mouth as he sprayed the walls and floor. He felt ants wriggling along his back, biting his flesh, but he ignored the discomfort as he crawled down the tunnel, spraying everywhere. Hammack and Ramirez crawled after him.

After fifty feet or so the walls were clear and the floor of the tunnel behind them was littered with dead insects. The three Americans sat down and disposed of the remaining ants on their bodies, with slaps and sprays of insecticide. Doc pulled up the legs of his trousers and inspected his legs. There were dozens of small red bumps where he'd been bitten and they were already starting to itch. Hammack asked Ramirez to clear his back and Ramirez pushed his shirt up and killed them one by one.

May Eckhardt finished attaching the thin metal wire to the bamboo cage and backed away. When she was a safe distance she turned around. In the distance she could hear the Americans talking. When they'd come across the ants she'd heard them from five hundred feet away as she lay in a sleeping chamber in the second level. The sleeping chamber was a safe place to hide: there were four exits and entrances, two of which were booby-trapped. They were careless, the Americans, because they weren't afraid. They thought that there was nothing down the tunnels that could harm them. She smiled to herself. They were so wrong.

She bent double, her spine parallel to the floor of the tunnel. With her head down and her knees slightly bent she could run, moving at a speed that would be beyond the Americans. She ran silently towards the hatchway that led down to the third level. Soon they would realise that the tunnels were now more dangerous than they had ever been.

Wright and Bamber emerged from the tunnel into the chamber. 'My God,' said Wright. 'It's huge.'

Bamber dropped his knapsack on the floor and stretched. 'It's where they used to show movies, hold lectures, stuff like that.' He took a deep breath. 'The air's fresher, too, did you notice?' He pointed at two large holes close to the ceiling. 'It's coming from there.' He held his palms up. 'You can feel the breeze. VC airconditioning, huh?'

Wright took off his knapsack and put it on the floor. He stripped off his shirt and screwed it up to wring out the water, then used it to wipe his face and hands. 'How far underground are we here?' he asked.

'This is still on level two, so about thirty feet, I guess.'

Wright looked around the chamber. 'How the hell did they dig this out?'

'With their hands. Small shovels, maybe. Like I said, during the rainy season the clay is softer.'

'But all the earth must have been carried back along that tunnel. It must have taken for ever.'

'I guess they figured they had for ever,' said Bamber. 'The VC philosophy was that they didn't have to win the war, they just had to make sure they didn't lose.' He knelt down and picked up a squashed cigarette butt. He sniffed it, then dropped it back on to the floor.

Wright went over to the white sheet pinned to the wall. To the right was a hole in the floor. He looked down at the sharpened bamboo stakes that lined the bottom. 'Bloody hell,' he said.

Bamber joined him. 'The VC used to smear them with shit so that any wounds would get infected.' He unfolded his map, looked at it, then nodded at the tunnel that led from the middle of one of the chamber walls. 'This way,' he said. He put his knapsack on and crouched down, using his flashlight to illuminate the tunnel.

Wright looked around the chamber. It was a relief to be in a place where he could stand up and where the walls didn't feel as if they were closing in on him. It was just about bearable. He got down on his hands and knees and crawled across the reed mats to the hole. It was smaller than the tunnel they'd arrived in, so narrow that his shoulders brushed either side as he crawled into it.

The tunnel walls weren't as dry as they had been in the upper level, and the air smelt damp and fetid. The knees of Wright's trousers were frayed and torn and he winced with each movement of his legs. His hands were grazed and bleeding, too, but he gritted his teeth and continued to crawl. He'd come this far, and he was damned if he'd give up now just because of a few cuts and scratches.

The tunnel was thankfully short and opened up into another conical chamber, this one with three exits. Wright looked up at the apex and flinched. The top of the chamber was filled with a mass of white feathery cobwebs, and several dozen large spiders stared down at him. Each spider was about the size of Wright's hand with long, hairy legs.

'Jim,' said Wright. He pointed with his flashlight.

Bamber looked at the spiders and shrugged. 'They won't bite,' he said, unfolding the map.

One of the spiders stepped off the web and moved down the side of the chamber, its beady eyes fixed on Wright. Two black jaws clicked back and forth.

'Come on, Jim, let's get out of here,' said Wright through gritted teeth.

'We have to choose the right exit,' said the FBI agent. 'The wrong one could be rigged with a booby trap.'

The spider stopped. Another, slightly larger, moved off the web and walked slowly down the chamber wall. It raised its two front legs and seemed to be sensing the air with them.

'Jim . . .'

'Hang on,' said Bamber.

The larger spider ran down the chamber towards Wright. Half a dozen more left the web and began moving down the wall in a black, spindly mass.

Wright lashed out with his flashlight and squashed the big spider against the wall. It fell on to Wright's leg and he jerked it out of the way. The spider rolled on to the floor, its legs scrabbling in the air. Wright stamped on it, keeping his head down so that he wouldn't brush against the web.

The rest of the spiders kept coming and Wright hit them with his flashlight. He squashed one, then another, but still they came down the wall towards him.

'Okay, this way,' said Bamber, crawling into the right-hand tunnel.

A spider dropped from the web and landed on Wright's head. He gasped and used his flashlight to knock it from his hair. He knelt down and smashed it with his flashlight. The glass shattered and the bulb went out. He was alone in the dark. For a moment he panicked, forgetting which way Bamber had gone. He groped with his hands, trembling at the thought of touching one of the spiders, then found empty space and knew it was the exit. He ducked down and crawled into it, immediately seeing the yellow glow from Bamber's flashlight. He crawled after the FBI agent, breathing furiously. He glanced over his shoulder, but it was pitch dark behind him and he had no way of knowing if the spiders were pursuing him.

He practically stumbled into the back of Bamber. 'Hey, easy,' said the FBI agent.

'The spiders . . .' gasped Wright.

'They won't bite,' said Bamber. 'And if they did, it

wouldn't be fatal. There isn't a single spider in the world with a fatal bite, unless you're very old or very young.'

'How do you know that?'

'Read it somewhere,' said Bamber. '*National Geographic*, maybe.' He emerged into another chamber and Wright hurried after him.

'My flashlight,' said Wright. 'It's broken.'

Bamber turned around and shone his flashlight on Wright's.

'It's the bulb,' said Wright. 'Have you got a spare?'

'Sorry, no.'

Wright threw his useless flashlight to the ground. 'Shit,' he said. 'I'm going to use the goggles.'

'I'd save them if I were you,' said Bamber. 'You'll need them on the way back.' He illuminated the map. 'We're almost there, Nick. Stick close to me, you'll be all right.'

Bamber shone his flashlight around the chamber. It was huge, twice the size of the one where the VC had showed movies. The walls were covered in a dark green silky fabric. Wright reached out and stroked it. It was soft to the touch.

'Parachute silk,' said Bamber. 'Watch where you put your feet. According to the map they didn't check all the floor area. There could be traps.'

They walked together to the centre of the chamber. 'What is this place?' asked Wright.

'The map says it's an ammunition chamber,' said Bamber. He played his flashlight on the ceiling. It was reinforced with sheets of corrugated iron and thick steel beams that had turned brown with rust. Long-disused oil lamps hung from the beams.

Wright shivered. He was still soaking wet from the water

trap. He stood close to Bamber, not wanting to get too far from the flashlight in the FBI agent's hand. The disc of light travelled along the roof and down one of the walls. It picked out a row of machines, vertical lathes and grinding equipment, covered with dust and cobwebs. Behind the lathes was a stack of wooden boxes. Bamber went over to them and pried off one of the lids.

'Ammunition,' said Bamber, peering into the box. 'For AK-47s by the look of it.' He replaced the lid.

He ran the flashlight along the bottom of one of the walls and picked out a tunnel. 'We go along there for about six hundred feet, through two more chambers, then we should find the way down to the fourth level.'

Wright nodded. His feelings of claustrophobia had lessened, mainly because of the sheer size of the chamber he was in. He wasn't sure how he was going to cope with the fourth level, but if he was ever to get to the bottom of the mystery of the Tunnel Rats, he had no choice but to go deeper.

Mrs Hampshire returned with a tray filled with tea things. She poured weak tea into three delicate cups, handed a cup and saucer to Hunter, then sat down on the overstuffed sofa next to her husband, almost bouncing him into the air. 'Well now, it's about May, is it?' she asked.

Gerry Hunter nodded and pulled out his notebook. 'When was the last time you saw her?' he asked.

'Nineteen eighty-six,' said Mrs Hampshire.

Hunter frowned. 'Nineteen eighty-six?' he repeated. 'That was when she graduated, wasn't it? You haven't seen her since?'

'That's right,' said Mrs Hampshire. 'She didn't even tell us that she was graduating. We weren't invited to the ceremony.'

Mrs Hampshire heaved herself up off the sofa and waddled over to a sideboard that was bedecked with bowls and vases. She bent down, opened a cupboard and took out a framed photograph. She handed it to Hunter without looking at it. It was a family group, an Oriental girl in her teens with a much younger Mr and Mrs Hampshire either side. The girl had a tight, nervous smile as if she didn't like being photographed. Mrs Hampshire was beaming proudly at the camera and Mr Hampshire was looking across at them, adoration in his eyes. Hunter stood up and went to look at the picture. 'When was this taken?' he asked.

'About nineteen seventy-seven, I think.'

'She's a lovely girl,' said Hunter. 'Did something happen?' he asked. 'Is there a reason you haven't kept in touch?'

'You'd have to ask her that,' said Mrs Hampshire, her voice loaded with bitterness. 'We gave her everything: we gave her a home, an education, a good start in life, and how did she thank us? We don't even get Christmas cards from her. It was a mistake, right from the beginning. I said so, but Peter insisted, said that it was a chance for us to have a family. A real family.' She glared across at her husband and he winced from the intensity of the look. 'He can't have children, you see. We've seen specialists.'

Peter Hampshire stared silently out of the window, his hurt and embarrassment making Hunter's stomach churn. Resentment and suppressed anger hung in the air like a storm

411

about to break. Hunter could picture Peter Hampshire taking an axe to his wife one day, then sitting in court and pleading guilty with a satisfied smile on his face. 'So she's adopted?' said Hunter.

'She came to us when she was ten years old,' said Mrs Hampshire.

'From?'

'From Vietnam.'

Hunter stiffened at the mention of Vietnam. 'She was Vietnamese?'

'Didn't you know? She was an orphan. The *Daily Mail* helped rescue her, along with almost a hundred others. Flew them out just before the end of the war. In nineteen seventy-five. She was quite a celebrity for a while; her picture was always in the local paper.'

Hunter picked up his cup and sipped his tea, giving himself time to gather his thoughts. Mrs Hampshire put two heaped teaspoons of sugar into her tea and stirred it slowly.

'A journalist from the *Mail* rang us a few years ago. They were doing an article about what had happened to the orphans, twenty years on. I had to tell the girl that I didn't know where May was. I was so embarrassed, I can tell you.'

Hunter was finding it harder and harder to smile at Mrs Hampshire. He sipped his tea again. Mr Hampshire was still staring at the window. Hunter wondered if he, too, was considering running away and never coming back.

'You never said why you were looking for May,' said Mrs Hampshire. She offered him a plate of custard cream biscuits but Hunter shook his head.

'There's no easy way to say this,' said Hunter. 'I'm afraid her husband was murdered several weeks ago.'

'She was married?' said Mrs Hampshire. She looked sharply across at her husband as if accusing him of keeping secrets from her. 'She didn't even tell us she'd married.' She looked back at Hunter. 'Does she have any children? Do I have grandchildren?'

'Not that I know of,' he said. 'The thing is, Mrs Hampshire, I need to talk to May and I was hoping you might have some idea where she'd be.'

Mrs Hampshire shrugged her large shoulders. 'Now you know different,' she said. She took Hunter's empty cup and put it on the tray with the rest of the tea things. 'She got what she wanted from us and then she made a life of her own. You know what I feel like, Mr Hunter? I feel like I had a cuckoo in my nest. I fed her, nurtured her as if she was my own daughter, but all the time she was just using me, waiting for the opportunity to take wing.' She stood up and dusted her flower-print dress with her hands. 'She was the biggest mistake of my life,' she said, her voice trembling.

She picked up the tray and left the room. Hunter could tell that she was close to tears.

T he three Americans stood in the antechamber, breathing heavily. Doc stood at the threshold, Ramirez and Hammack at either shoulder. They played their flashlights around the main chamber, their beams reflecting off the shiny silk lining that covered the walls. Ramirez took off his headscarf and used it to wipe his face.

The room was about thirty feet square and just over ten

feet high. At the far end was a wooden desk which had once been painted brown but which was now rotting and peppered with white fungus. An oil lamp stood on one end of the desk.

'I remember it being bigger,' said Hammack, his voice a hoarse whisper.

'This is definitely it,' said Doc. He aimed the beam of his flashlight at the far corner of the room.

'I know,' said Hammack. 'I know this is it.'

'Come on, let's get on with it,' said Ramirez. 'The air's bad down here.'

Doc stepped into the main chamber. He walked slowly across the reed mats. There were rusty-coloured patches all over the floor. Old bloodstains. Doc tried to avoid stepping on them, like a child jumping over the cracks between paving stones. There was a rhyme that went with avoiding the cracks, something that Doc had sung as a child, but he couldn't remember the words. Something about breaking a grandmother's back. Hammack and Ramirez followed him into the chamber.

Doc jumped at the sound of water splashing and whirled around, his hand groping for the knife in his belt. Ramirez was holding his water canteen above his head and dousing himself. He grinned sheepishly at Doc.

Doc turned his back on Ramirez and pulled the reed mats away from the corner. He threw them to the side, then took off his rucksack. Ramirez and Hammack stood just inside the entrance as if trying to put as much distance as possible between themselves and what was buried in the chamber. Doc took the folding shovel from his rucksack and straightened it out. He took a deep breath, then began to hack away at the earth, the

414

blows echoing around the chamber like the crunching of a giant's footsteps.

Wright's arms and legs were shaking uncontrollably and he closed his eyes and imagined he was outside, above ground, forcing out the images of being buried alive and replacing them with pictures of Sean: Sean at the zoo, Sean playing football, Sean falling asleep in front of the television. He opened his eyes. The walls and floor of the tunnels were damp and in places pieces of wet clay had fallen from the roof. The tunnel they were in had dipped down and he figured they must be close to the water table. He wondered what would happen if it began to rain, whether the water would rise. He dismissed the idea. The Viet Cong would never have constructed the tunnels so that they'd flood every rainy season.

Bamber was crawling purposefully forward and Wright had to struggle to keep up. The back of Bamber's shirt was caked with wet mud from where the FBI agent had scraped against the tunnel roof. The tunnel forked and Bamber headed down the left-hand section.

'Where does the other one go?' asked Wright, peering into the darkness. The air smelled fresher in the right-hand tunnel.

'The map doesn't say,' said Bamber. 'We'd better keep clear of any areas that aren't mapped.'

'How much further?'

'Fifteen minutes.'

'Feels like the tunnel's getting narrower.'

Bamber chuckled. 'Optical illusion,' he said.

A piece of wet clay fell on to Wright's hair and rolled down his neck. He shivered. Every breath was an effort, as if the fetid air had to be pulled into his lungs. He wondered what it would be like to be buried alive, to have the soil force its way into his mouth and nose, to have the dirt pressed against his face, his eyes, to feel nothing but earth around him. How long would it take to die? he wondered. More than seconds, surely. Minutes, at least. It would depend on how much air was trapped with him. He wondered how he'd face death, whether he'd just lie down and accept it, or if he'd die screaming and futilely trying to claw his way out.

He closed his eyes and concentrated on his movements, keeping his crawl at a steady rhythm. There were tons and tons of earth above his head, but Wright tried not to think about it. A tunnel was a tunnel, he told himself, it didn't matter how deep it was. He tried to convince himself that the tunnel he was in was just below the surface, that if anything went wrong he could just force his way up through a few inches of topsoil and be able to breathe clean, fresh air. He knew it was a lie, but it helped to calm his nerves. He realised that he was panting and he struggled to slow down his breathing.

'Nick!'

Wright opened his eyes. Bamber had stopped a few feet ahead of him. 'What?'

'Don't move.' Bamber's voice was icily cold.

Wright stopped in his tracks.

'There's a snake here.'

'Can you kill it?' asked Wright.

'It's about four feet long,' said the FBI agent, 'and all

I've got is my flashlight. There's a knife in my knapsack, but I don't want to risk reaching for it.'

'What's it doing?'

'It's coiled up in the middle of the tunnel. I think it's asleep. Get my knife out, will you?'

Wright swallowed.

'I'm going to switch the flashlight off in case the light disturbs it.'

'No!' said Wright hurriedly.

The tunnel was plunged into darkness. Wright became suddenly disorientated and his head swam. He felt as if he was falling and he put both hands flat on the tunnel floor, wanting to feel something solid on his skin. He inched forward.

'Come on, Nick. Hurry up. I can hear it moving.'

'Switch the flashlight on,' said Wright.

'Not yet,' said Bamber.

'I thought snakes couldn't see well, anyway. I thought they used their tongues to sense air movements.'

'If you were in front, I'd probably take the risk, but as I'm here, I think I'll stick with the flashlight off. Now get a move on, will you?'

Wright bumped into Bamber's feet. He felt his way up the FBI agent's back and ran his hands over the knapsack. Wright undid the flap and groped inside. It was like a party game he'd played as a child, touching objects under a cloth and trying to recognise them from their shape. He could feel the infra-red goggles, and hard metal cylinders that he assumed were batteries, and the two bottles of water. His fingers touched something plastic, long and thin, with a metal edge. He held it in his palm. It was a Swiss Army knife, he realised. Every Boy Scout's best friend. He pulled it out.

He fumbled with the knife, trying to pry out a blade with his thumbnail. 'Turn the light on, Jim,' he said.

'Have you got the knife?'

'Yeah, but I can't open it, I can't see what I'm doing.'

The light flickered on. Wright looked at the knife in his hand. He'd been trying to pull out a nail file.

'Nick. It's moving.'

The knife slipped from Wright's fingers and he cursed.

'Now what?' hissed Bamber.

'I've dropped it.' The knife was covered with red mud, and so were Wright's hands. He picked up the knife but couldn't get a grip on the blade. 'Where's the snake?' he whispered.

Bamber didn't reply.

'Jim? The snake. Where is it?'

The FBI agent had stiffened. As Wright looked up, he saw why. Two glass-hard eyes were staring at him from a diamond-shaped head. The snake had pushed itself between Bamber's legs and was heading purposefully down the tunnel towards Wright. A shiny black forked tongue flicked out as the snake slid forward.

'Can you see it?' whispered Bamber.

The snake stared at Wright, inches away from his face. The tongue flicked out again. Wright was on his knees, the unopened knife in his hands. His centre of gravity was so far forward that he couldn't shuffle back.

The snake began to move its head from side to side, its eyes still fixed on Wright. He managed to get his thumbnail into the groove on the side of the main blade and he eased it out. The snake stopped moving.

'Nick?' said Bamber.

Wright said nothing. He didn't know if snakes could hear

but he didn't want to risk doing anything that might cause it to bite. He held the knife in his right hand.

The snake started moving again, its red and black striped body slithering silently across the muddy tunnel floor.

Bamber bent his head down and peered back between his legs. The snake's tail brushed against his thigh.

Wright raised the knife slowly. The snake stopped moving forward and lifted its head off the ground. The tongue flicked out and the snake opened its mouth revealing two white fangs. Wright held his breath. He'd only have one chance.

Bamber's left knee cracked, and the snake turned its head towards the sound. Wright brought the knife down, driving the point into the snake's head. It crunched through the bone and then bit into the floor of the tunnel. The snake thrashed around, its tail flailing like a whip. Bamber grabbed the tail with both hands. The knife jerked in Wright's hand and he gripped it tighter, pressing the blade into the ground as hard as he could so that the snake couldn't move its head. With his left hand he pressed down on the snake's body. He could feel the animal's immense strength; even in its death throes he couldn't keep the body still.

The snake's mouth kept opening and closing and its eyes glared at Wright, silently cursing him. Bamber dropped down on the snake, using his bodyweight to keep it from thrashing about.

Wright twisted the knife around, shuddering at the crunching sound it made, but knowing that he'd hasten the snake's death by mashing up its brain. Dark red blood oozed out around the blade and the animal's movements became slower and slower, though it was a full two minutes before the snake was completely still.

Wright pulled out the knife and wiped the blade on his trousers. He refolded the knife and handed it to Bamber.

'Let's go,' said Wright.

The snake's lifeless eyes continued to stare accusingly at Wright as he crawled over it.

'Would you like to see some more pictures of her?' asked Mr Hampshire, his voice a conspiratorial whisper as if the offer was somehow subversive. His wife was in the kitchen, washing the teacups.

'I'd love to,' said Hunter.

Mr Hampshire walked over to the sideboard and knelt down beside it. He pulled out a large green photo album and handed it to Hunter. 'I put this together,' he said. 'Emily keeps saying that I should throw it away, but . . .' He left the sentence unfinished as if he feared retribution for defying his wife. Mr Hampshire leaned forward. 'She loves May, there's nothing she'd like more than for her to walk through that door. You'll never get her to admit it, though. Never in a million years.'

Hunter opened the album. The first page contained a newspaper article about the plight of Vietnamese refugees in Saigon at the end of the Vietnam War. Hunter read it quickly. Just before the North Vietnamese overran Saigon, hundreds of orphan babies and children were stranded and there were fears for their survival. The American government had organised an airlift to America, and as the defences around the city began to crumble, the *Daily*

Mail had joined in the appeal for something to be done about the children. Hunter turned the page. There was a second newspaper cutting, this one detailing a horrific crash in which 189 orphans were killed when a United States Air Force cargo plane crashed on take-off at Saigon airport.

Mr Hampshire sat down on the arm of Hunter's chair. 'She was on that flight,' he said, pointing at the newspaper cutting. 'One of eighty-nine who survived. God, what that little girl went through. To have lived through a war, then be told you were being flown to safety and to see so many die in the crash. Can you imagine what that must have been like, at ten years old?'

Hunter shook his head. 'What about her parents?' he asked. 'What happened to them?'

'We've no idea,' said Mr Hampshire. 'All their records were destroyed when the plane crashed. We don't even know her family name. She didn't speak a word for the first year she was in this country. Post traumatic stress syndrome, the doctors said. Love and affection was what she needed, they said. And we gave her that, Mr Hunter, don't doubt that for one moment. She had more love than any child could ask for. Don't let my wife make you think otherwise. She wasn't always like this. She had so much love to give, to me and to May. She really wanted children of her own.'

'I understand,' said Hunter, and he meant it. He felt a sudden wave of compassion for Emily Hampshire and her bird-like husband.

'It really was a miracle,' said Mr Hampshire. 'It was a miracle that she survived the crash, and it was a miracle that they found a place for her on the *Daily Mail* flight. Turn the page.'

Hunter did as he was asked. There was another cutting, which like the rest had yellowed with age around the edges. It was from the *Daily Mail*, detailing how the editor, David English, had decided that leader articles and calls for action weren't enough, that something had to be done. The newspaper was chartering its own plane, and sending in a team of doctors and nurses to help evacuate as many children as they could.

The next article detailed the mercy flight, how the *Daily Mail*'s Operation Mercy airlift plucked ninety-nine children from the beleaguered city in a Boeing 707 just days before the North Vietnamese stormed into Saigon.

'The Americans got about a thousand children out,' said Mr Hampshire. 'The *Daily Mail* rescued ninety-nine. Most of them were malnourished, and three died within hours of arriving in Britain. Fair broke our hearts, it did, the suffering and everything. We applied to adopt one of them and they gave us May.'

Hunter turned the page. There was only one photograph, black and white, the sort that might have been used in a passport. A young girl stared vacantly at the camera, the face so lifeless that it could have been that of a corpse. On the page opposite was a letter from an adoption agency saying that the Hampshires' application had been approved.

'You should have seen her,' said Mr Hampshire. 'They weren't sure how old she was because all her paperwork was destroyed in the Galaxy crash. She looked like a six-year-old, so thin that her ribs were showing through and her legs were covered with bites and scars. The doctors reckoned she was ten and they gave her a birth date, just made it up because she'd need it for school and passports and so on. We always celebrated it as her birthday, but we knew that it wasn't real.'

Hunter looked at the photograph and wondered what horrors the little girl had seen, an orphan trapped in a war zone. 'She came here? To this house?'

Mr Hampshire nodded. 'We moved in the day after we married and we've been here ever since. I can show you May's bedroom if you want. It's just the same as when she left to go to university.' He leaned forward so that his face was only inches away from Hunter's. 'Emily still hopes . . . you know?'

Hunter smiled thinly. He knew.

'Her husband? What was he like?'

'An American,' said Hunter, his eyes still on the small black and white photograph. 'He was a photographer. They'd only been married for a couple of years.'

'Murdered, you said?'

'I'm afraid so.'

Mr Hampshire took off his spectacles and began polishing them with a white handkerchief. 'How is she?' he asked quietly.

'I really don't know,' admitted Hunter. 'I haven't actually met her. She was interviewed by a colleague.'

'She must be devastated,' said Mr Hampshire softly. 'She must need us.' He looked up and Hunter saw that his eyes were brimming with tears. 'Why hasn't she been in touch with us, Mr Hunter?'

'I don't know,' said Hunter. He averted his eyes, embarrassed by the raw emotion etched on the man's face. 'I'm sorry,' he added.

D oc stopped digging and shouldered his shovel. 'Is it there?' asked Hammack from behind him.

'Come and look for yourself,' said Doc.

Hammack walked slowly across the chamber, the beam of his flashlight dancing crazily across the parachute-silk-lined walls. Ramirez stayed where he was, retying his camouflage scarf around his head.

Doc was looking down into an oblong hole just over five feet long and a couple of feet wide. He'd piled the earth up next to the wall. The surface had been hard and he'd had to chip his way through, but several inches underneath the red clay was damp and pliable. A skull leered up at them, the bone glistening in the damp earth. A worm wriggled from an eye socket and burrowed into the soil. Doc knelt down and used his shovel to scrape away the earth from the skeleton's chest.

'It's definitely him?' asked Hammack.

Doc sighed with exasperation. 'For God's sake, Bernie, how many corpses do you think there are buried down here?'

Hammack flinched as if he'd been slapped across the face.

'I'm sorry,' said Doc.

'No sweat,' said Hammack. 'It was a stupid question.' He rubbed his jaw. 'At least now we know,' he said.

'What do we know?' asked Doc. 'We know he's not the killer, that's all.' He reached down and picked up a piece of card. He wiped it on his trousers. It was a playing card. An ace of spades. He gave it to Hammack who stared at it and then passed it to Ramirez.

Doc straightened up and wiped his hands on his trousers. 'We've wasted our time.'

'What do we do now?' asked Ramirez, throwing the playing card on to the skeleton.

'Bury it again and go home,' said Doc. He picked up the shovel.

'Wait!' said Hammack. 'Max's dogtags. He had Max's dogtags. We should take them with us.'

Doc nodded and knelt down and grabbed the right arm of the skeleton. It made a sucking sound as he pulled it out of the damp earth. The hand was clenched into a fist. Doc used the end of his shovel to pry open the bones, one by one. He looked up at Hammack, deep frown lines furrowed across his brow. He showed him the hand. It was empty.

H unter turned over the page. There were half a dozen colour photographs, three per page, of the ten-year-old May playing in the back garden. May on a red swing. May with a doting Emily Hampshire. May throwing a ball to Peter Hampshire. May sitting on the grass reading a picture book. In none of the photographs was the little girl smiling.

'That was during the first few months,' said Mr Hampshire. 'She was like a little robot. She did as she was told, she played when we asked her to play, ate when we gave her food, slept when we put her to bed. But she never smiled, never looked at us, never showed any emotion at all.'

'Perhaps she didn't speak English,' said Hunter.

'No, she understood. And she was a very quick learner. Very bright.'

Hunter remembered that May had graduated with first-class Honours. He told Mr Hampshire, who smiled proudly. 'I was the one who got her interested in computers,' he said. 'I was cataloguing my stamp collection and putting it all on disc. She used to sit and watch me.'

Hunter turned the page. More photographs. A slightly older May. Occasional smiles. May riding a pony. May holding a bow and arrow.

'She won prizes for archery,' said Mr Hampshire. 'We used to have her trophies in here, but Emily . . .' He looked away, the sentence unfinished. The bow she was holding was almost as tall as she was. In another picture she was taking aim at a distant target, the bow at full stretch.

Hunter looked closely at the photograph. There was something around her neck. A necklace with two oblong objects hanging from it. Hunter frowned. He flicked back several pages and looked at another photograph, May in her school uniform, a brown leather satchel on her back. There was something in her right hand. It looked like the same necklace. He looked across at another of the pictures. May balancing on a bicycle. She was holding something in that picture, too. Hunter flicked back to the previous page. Whatever it was, the girl was holding it in all the photographs.

'What is that?' he asked, pointing at the picture of May throwing a ball. 'In her right hand? She's wearing it in some of the later pictures.'

426

Mr Hampshire finished polishing his spectacles and put them back on. 'They're dogtags,' he said. 'It was the funniest thing. She had them in her right hand when they flew her out of Saigon, and she never once let go of them. All the time she was in the orphanage in Vietnam, all the time she was on the plane, when she was in hospital in the UK, she wouldn't let go of them. The doctors tried but she screamed and screamed until they decided it was better to let her have them. She had the end of the chain wrapped around her wrist and her fingers were clenched as if she was scared that she'd lose them. For the first year she was with us, she never unclasped that hand, even when she was asleep. Eventually she wore them around her neck, and as far as I know she never once took them off. When she was older, we asked her who they belonged to, but she never told us. Emily and I thought that maybe they belonged to an American soldier who'd saved her life, that maybe he'd died and she kept them as a reminder.'

Hunter put his face closer to the photograph. 'Do you have a magnifying glass?' Hunter asked.

'Of course,' said Mr Hampshire. He scurried over to the sideboard and returned with a magnifying glass like an eager-to-please puppy carrying his master's slippers. 'I use them for my stamps.'

Hunter focused the glass on the dogtags. He could just about make out the letters and numbers. The soldier's date of birth. His religion. His blood group. His name. Hunter froze. He felt as if a block of ice was being drawn slowly up his spine. The name on the dogtags was Eckhardt, M.

427

The three Americans stared at the bony fingers of the skeleton's hand. 'They're not there,' said Hammack.

'Maybe the other hand,' said Ramirez. 'Maybe he was left handed.'

Doc prised open the fingers of the skeleton's left hand. It too was empty. He stood up, wiping his hands on his trousers, and took a step back from the open grave.

For several seconds the only sound in the chamber was that of their breathing, then Doc spoke. 'Someone else was here,' he said quietly. 'Someone saw what we did.'

He backed away from the skeleton, his hands twitching. He kept on moving until his shoulders were up against the wall.

'Impossible,' said Ramirez. 'There's only the one way in, through the antechamber, and Eric was standing there. If anyone had been watching, Eric would have seen them.'

Doc turned around and grabbed a piece of the parachute silk that lined the chamber. He ripped it down, revealing the damp clay wall behind it. Dozens of tiny centipedes scuttled away from the flashlight beams.

'What are you doing?' asked Hammack.

Doc ignored him. He reached for another piece of green silk and pulled it away from the wall. At the base of the wall was an arched hole, cut into the clay, just big enough for a man to hide in if he crouched down.

'Shit,' said Ramirez.

'So now we know,' said Doc quietly.

Wright opened his mouth wide and took deep breaths. He squatted back on his knees, his face inches from the damp tunnel floor. The air seemed thick, almost like liquid, and each lungful was an effort.

Ahead of him, Bamber was finding the going equally tough. He was panting and moving one limb at a time. The tunnel had narrowed considerably and Wright couldn't see beyond Bamber's feet and backside. Wright was in almost complete darkness and several times he'd come close to telling the FBI agent that he wanted to put on the infra-red goggles. The only thing that stopped him was the realisation that even with the goggles on he wouldn't be able to see any further forward.

Wright couldn't imagine how the Viet Cong had managed to live underground for years at a time. Even allowing for the fact that they'd have been able to go up for fresh air at night, they'd still have had to cope with the dirt and the bad air, the snakes and insects, and the constant pressure of knowing that at any moment they could be buried alive.

Sweat poured off Wright and his clothes were dripping wet. 'Jim!' he called. 'I've got to have a drink.'

Bamber stopped. 'Okay.'

Wright struggled to remove his knapsack. He had to lean forward and wriggle his shoulders to get the straps off, then push himself against the tunnel wall to drag the bag between his legs.

He took out one of the plastic bottles. The water was

hot but he gulped it down. 'How much further?' he asked Bamber.

'Five minutes, at this rate,' said Bamber.

'Do you want some water?'

'Yeah,' said Bamber. He reached back for the bottle and Wright passed it to him. There were only a couple of mouthfuls in the bottle and Bamber emptied it. He tossed it to the side.

Wright had no idea in which direction they were heading, or how deep they were. Bamber had the compass, and Wright had only glanced briefly at the map.

'Ready to move on?' asked Bamber. His flashlight flickered and he slapped it against his palm. The beam intensified.

'Yeah,' said Wright.

'Not long now, Nick,' said Bamber confidently. 'It'll soon be over.'

Doc, Ramirez and Hammack crouched together under the hatch. Doc wiped his hands on his trousers.

'Who could it be, Doc?' asked Hammack. 'Who could have been there?'

'Let's talk about it when we're up top, Bernie,' said Doc. 'There's nothing we can do down here.'

Hammack nodded. He played his flashlight around the hatchway. 'Yeah, you're right,' he said. 'We can talk it through over a few beers at the Rex. Maybe it won't seem so bad then.'

'Don't count on it,' said Ramirez. He took a drink from his canteen but it only contained one mouthful. He shook his second canteen but that too was empty. 'You got any water?'

Hammack shook his head. Doc handed one of his canteens to Ramirez. 'That's the last of mine,' he said.

'Save it,' said Ramirez.

'Take it,' said Doc. 'Three hours and we'll be back on the surface.' He looked up at the hatch. 'I'll go first.'

Ramirez drained the canteen and handed it back to Doc. 'It's my turn, Doc,' he said.

Doc was about to argue but Ramirez had already got to his feet. Ramirez checked his flashlight and took his knife out of its scabbard. He winked at Doc, then eased himself up through the hatch. 'Last one out's a sissy,' said Ramirez, his voice muffled by the sides of the tunnel.

Doc clipped the empty canteen to his webbing belt. 'Okay, you go next, Bernie,' he said. 'I'll bring up the rear.'

Hammack nodded grimly. He was obviously still troubled by what they'd found in the chamber, but Doc was determined not to discuss it while they were down in the tunnels. Doc put a hand on Hammack's shoulder, just as Ramirez's legs began to kick and judder.

'Stop messing about, Sergio!' Doc shouted.

One of Ramirez's feet smacked into Hammack's head.

'Cut it out, you wop bastard!' shouted Hammack. 'It's not funny!'

Suddenly Ramirez's legs stopped kicking. Doc shone his flashlight up at the hatch. Blood was dripping down between Ramirez's waist and the hatchway. Red spots peppered the lens of Doc's flashlight, turning the beam pink and casting a macabre glow around the tunnel.

Hammack shuffled away from the feet, his eyes wide. Blood plopped down on the tunnel floor.

'Oh Christ,' gasped Hammack. 'What the fuck's happening?'

'Bernie, help me get him down,' said Doc. He grabbed Ramirez's feet and pulled while Hammack took hold of the man's knees. 'Harder,' said Doc. 'Pull harder.'

The two men tugged on Ramirez's legs but they couldn't shift him.

'Something's holding him,' said Hammack.

Rivulets of blood trickled down from the hatchway and smeared Hammack's face. Hammack let go of Ramirez's knees and wiped his face with the bottom of his shirt.

Doc put his hand up between Ramirez's legs and felt for a pulse in the man's groin. He couldn't find one.

'I didn't hear anything, did you?' asked Hammack. 'No gunshot, no explosion, nothing. He didn't make a sound.'

Doc shrugged but said nothing.

'It wasn't a booby trap, was it?' said Hammack, his voice a hoarse whisper. 'If it was a booby trap we'd have seen it coming in. Somebody killed him, Doc. Somebody up there killed Sergio, just like they killed Jumbo.'

'I know,' said Doc, staring up at the blocked hatchway. He shook his head. 'I should have gone first,' he said quietly.

'The killer's down here with us, Doc,' said Hammack, holding his flashlight in front of him as if it were a knife. 'What are we going to do?'

Doc sat back on his heels and stared at the lower half of the lifeless body. 'We're going to have to find another way out,' he said as his flashlight began to flicker. He opened his rucksack, took out three spare batteries, and slotted them in.

'What about Sergio?'

'We can't pull him down. If we can get up to the third level and double back, we'll be able to pull him up.'

Doc got on to his hands and knees and began to crawl back to the main chamber.

'Doc?'

Doc turned to look at Hammack.

'What if there isn't another way up?'

Gerry Hunter could sense Emily Hampshire staring at him through the net curtains so he didn't look around. He drove away from the Hampshires' house, fumbling for the mobile phone in his inside pocket. He'd stored the BTP incident room number on autodial and it was already ringing as he turned the corner and pulled in at the side of the road. Tommy Reid answered.

'Tommy, it's Gerry. Have you heard from Nick yet?' I need to talk to him. About May Eckhardt.' Hunter explained about May Eckhardt's adopted parents, and what he'd seen in the photographs. It was obvious from Reid's silence that the BTP detective hadn't grasped the significance of the discovery.

'A ten-year-old girl is rescued from Vietnam clutching the dog-tags of an American soldier she marries almost twenty years later,' said Hunter. 'Two years after they marry, he's murdered. This isn't a love story, Tommy. It's revenge. I don't know why, but she killed him, I'm sure of it. And now she's bolted.'

'Jesus Christ.'

'Do you know if Nick's uncovered anything about Horvitz over there?'

'Oh Jesus,' said Reid. 'I was supposed to pass the details on to you. Apparently Eckhardt and Horvitz served together in Vietnam in an outfit called the Tunnel Rats. Something happened out there that they're desperate to keep a secret. Jim Bamber's out there with him.'

'Bamber's there? Shit, I need to talk to Nick,' said Hunter. 'Do you know what hotel he's staying at? This is important.'

'You can try his mobile. I got him a few days ago. It's a GSM so it works out there, assuming it's switched on.'

Reid gave Hunter the number and he keyed it in, read it back to Reid, then cut the connection. He pressed the 'send' button and waited impatiently for it to ring, hoping that the BTP detective hadn't got himself into trouble.

Bamber stopped crawling. Wright thought he was about to consult his map again so he waited, concentrating on the FBI agent's back and breathing slowly so as not to hyperventilate in the damp, sour air. Wright had to keep fighting off images of collapsing tunnels: the walls were damp and each time he rubbed against them small avalanches of red dirt spilled on to the floor. Bamber made no move to open his map case.

'What's wrong?' Wright asked.

'We've got a problem,' said Bamber.

'What?'

Bamber rolled to the side and pressed himself against the wall of the tunnel, allowing Wright to see ahead. The beam of Bamber's flashlight illuminated the head and chest of Sergio Ramirez, his eyes closed, his mouth open in a silent scream. A bamboo spear was impaled through his stomach and blood seeped through his mud-stained T-shirt. One end of the spear had been thrust into the tunnel wall, locking the body into position. He had a flashlight in one hand and a knife lay on the floor in front of him.

'Was it a booby trap?' asked Wright.

'No. Somebody did that to him,' said Bamber. He crawled forward and took something that was poking out from Ramirez's T-shirt. He handed it to Wright. It was a playing card, smeared with blood. An ace of spades.

Wright stared at it. 'Oh Christ,' he whispered. 'The killer's down here with us.'

Bamber bared his teeth. 'Of course he is, Nick. What did you expect?'

Wright stared at the FBI agent in horror. 'You knew?'

'What did you think all this was about?' He pulled the playing card from Wright's hand. 'Why do you think he left the cards on the bodies? So that they'd know that he knew their secret. He wanted them to come back here, he wanted them down the tunnels so that he could kill them.'

'Why?' asked Wright. 'Why does he want them dead?'

Bamber threw the card on the ground. 'Come on,' he said, 'we have to get him out of there. It's the only way down.'

'Down? We're going down?'

'We have to follow this through to the end. Doc and Hammack are down there, and the killer will be after them.'

Wright pointed at Ramirez. 'Jim, whoever killed Ramirez is still up here, in the third level.' He felt a presence behind him and jerked around, but there was nobody there.

'You're jumping at shadows,' said Bamber. 'And you're wrong, Nick. My map only shows one way down to the fourth level, but there are bound to be others.' He crawled forward and grabbed Ramirez by the shoulders. He pulled but the bamboo spear was wedged into the damp clay, preventing him from moving the body. He twisted the stick savagely to the side, ripping open the wound in Ramirez's stomach. Greasy grey intestines spilled out.

'Oh Jesus,' whispered Wright, turning his head away.

'He's dead, Nick.'

'I know he's dead,' said Wright. 'That doesn't make it any more pleasant.' Intestinal gas bubbled out of the wound, making Wright gag.

'You're going to have to help me,' said Bamber. 'I can't move him myself.' He yanked at the spear and it snapped.

Wright crawled over to Bamber. Together they heaved Ramirez's body out of the hatchway. Wright prised the flashlight out of the dead man's hand. He reached for the knife but Bamber beat him to it.

'I'll go first,' said Bamber, nodding at the hatch. There was a gleam in his eyes that was almost manic in its intensity. He looked as if he relished the opportunity of meeting the killer face to face.

'Okay,' said Wright. He gripped the flashlight tightly and looked away as Bamber crawled over the body, his knee digging into the stomach wound with a sickening squelching sound.

Bamber put his head down the hatch and slithered down,

opening his legs wide and pressing them against the tunnel walls for leverage. The hairs on the back of Wright's neck stood on end and he whirled around, his flashlight held high like a club. There was nobody there. He forced himself to relax.

Bamber pulled himself back into the tunnel 'It's clear,' he said. 'Wait till I call you.' He slid his feet through the hatchway and dropped down.

Wright edged towards Ramirez. Slippery grey tubes slid snake-like out of the gaping belly wound and pooled in a steaming mass on the damp clay floor. Wright kept as close to the tunnel wall as possible but he couldn't avoid contact with the entrails. He'd seen more than his fair share of bodies and had sat in on several post mortems, but seeing was one thing, physical contact with a corpse was another. He closed his eyes and crawled over it, wrinkling his nose at the smell.

'Okay, Nick,' Bamber called from below.

Wright squatted over the hatch and lowered himself down.

Doc and Hammack ripped the sheets of parachute silk from the walls of the chamber, gathered them up in their arms and dumped them on the floor. 'Come on, there has to be another way out,' muttered Doc.

Hammack tossed a rolled-up piece of silk into the middle of the chamber. 'What if there isn't?' he said.

'This was the command centre,' said Doc. 'They'd have been crazy not to have had an escape route.' He pulled a large sheet away from the wall, revealing damp clay underneath. Three of the walls were now bare. Other than the hiding place, the walls were perfectly flat.

Hammack wiped his forehead with his arm. Suddenly he looked up. 'Did you hear that?' he asked.

Doc stopped peeling away a piece of silk. 'What?'

Hammack held up his hand. 'Listen,' he said.

The two men stood in silence. 'I don't hear anything,' said Doc eventually.

'I thought . . .' Hammack shook his head. 'I don't know. Maybe I imagined it.' He bent down and picked at a section of parachute silk, then slowly pulled at it. It came away with a sound like tearing paper.

Doc cleared the rest of the wall, then stood back with a look of dismay on his face. The wall was flat and featureless. He frowned. 'Impossible,' he said. 'No one would build a command centre with just one way in.' He looked around the chamber. The pile of parachute silk in the centre of the room almost came up to his waist. 'The floor,' he said.

'Give it up, Doc,' said Hammack, squatting down, his back against the wall.

Doc began ripping up the mats that covered the floor. There was damp, hard clay underneath. He tossed two of the mats to the side, then bent down and picked up another. A trapdoor lay underneath, the sides flush with the floor. Doc grinned triumphantly. 'I knew it,' he hissed.

He used his knife to prise the hatch open. Hammack

scrambled to his feet and joined Doc. The two men shone the beams of their flashlight into the darkness.

'Wonder where it leads to?' said Hammack.

'There's only one way to find out,' said Doc, dropping down through the hatch.

M ay played the rope between her fingers until she felt the bucket hit the surface of the water, some twenty feet below where she lay on the floor of the tunnel. She allowed the bucket to sink, then slowly pulled it back up. She sniffed the water cautiously, and then sipped it from the plastic bucket. It tasted fresh and clean but she drank sparingly. The Americans had sprayed tons of Agent Orange on the ground above and it still seeped through the soil into the water. May had been to local hospitals and seen the damage the chemical was still doing to newborn babies more than a quarter of a century later.

She put the bucket on the floor and pressed her ear against the tunnel wall so that she could hear the two Americans moving along the tunnel from the command centre. She smiled to herself. They thought they had found a way out, but they were wrong.

Suddenly May tensed. Her forehead creased into a worried frown. She shuffled over to the other side of the tunnel and put her ear against the clay. There was someone else in the network. She listened intently. Two people. Two men. Moving into the command centre. She could hear the dull murmur of their voices, but couldn't make out what they were saying.

Wright ran his flashlight beam along the floor and up the walls. 'What the hell were they doing?' he asked.

'Looking for a way out, is my guess,' said Bamber. He nodded at the open hatchway in the floor. 'And they found it.'

Wright went over to the fungus-covered desk. He stopped short as he saw the open grave and the skull leering up at him. 'Jim. Come here,' said Wright quietly.

The FBI agent joined Wright and shone his flashlight on the skeleton. Something glinted in the beam.

'What's that?' asked Wright.

'An old playing card,' said Bamber.

Wright knelt down and picked it up. He showed it to Bamber. 'The ace of spades,' he said.

Bamber took the card from Wright and examined it. 'Bicycle brand,' he said. 'Same as in London.'

'And Bangkok,' said Wright. 'Except this one is twenty-five years old. This is what it's all been about,' he said, straightening up. 'They killed this guy. Killed him and buried him here.' He frowned. 'But why? And who killed Eckhardt and Horvitz?'

Bamber went over to the hatch and looked down into the tunnel below. 'Why don't we catch them up and ask them?' he said.

Wright walked around the perimeter of the chamber, examining the walls. He stopped when he got to the alcove cut into the clay. He bent down and examined it,

440

running his fingers along its smooth sides. He wondered what it was. A storage area maybe. He looked at the silk that had once covered the walls. The hole would have been concealed. Perhaps it was a hiding place. But for who?

'Come on,' said Bamber, swinging his legs through the hatch. 'They can't be far away.'

The tunnel was only a few inches wider than Doc's shoulders and he had to haul himself along with his arms, dragging his legs behind him. Behind him, Hammack grunted with each movement.

'Bernie, are you okay?' whispered Doc.

Hammack laughed harshly. 'Let's just say that I know what a fucking sperm feels like,' he said.

The tunnel sloped upwards. Doc put the end of the flashlight between his teeth so that he could grip with both of his hands. He had to stretch his arms out, get as much leverage as he could with his palms and forearms, then pull himself up. The best he could manage was six inches at a time. Every muscle in his body ached and he had to strain to breathe. They'd taken off their rucksacks and tied them to their waists with lengths of string so that they could drag them along behind.

'Doc, have you any idea where this tunnel leads to?' asked Hammack.

Doc stopped where he was and took the flashlight out of his mouth. 'The third level, I guess,' he said. 'We're heading west, so with any luck we'll link up with a passage that we recognise.'

'And if we don't?'

'Then we keep heading north and up.'

Doc put the flashlight back in his mouth. He stretched his arms out and splayed his fingers on the tunnel floor. He gripped with his fingertips, but as he did he felt a sliver of something hard and smooth running perpendicular to the tunnel. He froze.

'What's up?' asked Bernie from behind him.

Doc moved his head, directing the beam of the flashlight at his hands. His neck burned with the effort of keeping his head up. All he could see was the back of his hands and the muddy floor of the tunnel. He moved his left hand slightly. He could just about make out a thin piece of bamboo set into the tunnel floor. He eased his head down and allowed the flashlight to rest on the ground.

'Can you back up, Bernie?'

'Oh shit,' said Hammack. Doc heard him scrabble backwards, breathing heavily.

'Don't be too long about it, Bernie. I'm not sure how long I can keep my hands still.'

'What is it?'

'I can't see. I think I've tripped it already, whatever it is.'

Doc put his forehead on the tunnel floor. His fingers felt as if they were on fire and the muscles in his arms were aching.

Hammack stopped. 'I'm not leaving you,' he said.

'There's no point in both of us getting it,' said Doc.

'I'm staying.'

'Do as you're fucking told, Bernie.'

Doc heard a rustling sound from behind him, then a grunt.

'What are you doing?'

'I'm getting the rope out of my rucksack.'

'We don't have time for this,' said Doc. 'I can't hold my hands steady for much longer.'

Doc felt rope being looped around his ankles, then tied tightly. 'It's about thirty feet back to the hatch,' said Hammack. 'That's about how much rope I've got.'

'Bernie, it's going to take you at least five minutes to get back. The tunnel's too tight.'

'I'll make it. Just hang on.'

'I can't.'

'You can. If I can get to the hatch, I can pull you back. If I can get you away fast enough . . .'

'It won't work, Bernie.'

'It's worth a try.'

Doc heard Hammack back slowly down the tunnel. Doc's fingers were in agony. Sweat was pouring off his hands and he felt them begin to slide off the bamboo. 'I can't hold it,' said Doc, his voice a hoarse whisper. His arms began to tremble and he gritted his teeth, willing the shaking to cease. For a moment he managed to get the trembling under control but then his fingers slipped and the piece of bamboo flicked upwards. He heard a click, then another, and soil cascaded down from the roof.

His first thought was that it was a cave-in and that he'd be buried alive, but then among the soil and mud he saw shiny black creatures with claws and stinging tails. Scorpions, he realised. Deadly scorpions.

'No way,' said Wright. 'There's no way I'm going in there.'

Bamber shone his flashlight down the narrow tunnel, and lowered himself through the hatch. 'It won't be far,' he said.

'You don't know that.'

'It's an escape route, a way to get out if there was a problem with the main entrance.'

'So maybe it's never been used,' said Wright. 'Maybe it's blocked.' He was lying on the floor of the chamber, looking down through the hatch.

'That's the way they went,' said Bamber. 'We have to follow them.'

Wright shook his head. 'It's too narrow.'

'Hammack went that way. Neither of us is bigger than him. If he can squeeze through, so can we.'

Wright shook his head again. He backed away from the hatch. 'I'll go the other way, the way we came in.'

Bamber stood up and poked his head and shoulders up through the hatch. He had his flashlight in his left hand and Ramirez's knife in his right. For several seconds he locked eyes with Wright. 'I don't think that's a good idea, Nick,' he said quietly.

The skin on the back of Wright's neck began to tingle. He got to his feet. Bamber continued to stare at him, and Wright took a step backwards. Bamber put his elbows on either side of the hatch. He pushed himself up, his eyes fixed on Wright. Wright shivered. It reminded him of the dead stare that the snake had given him.

'What's wrong?' Wright asked.

Bamber was halfway out when he cocked his head on one side. He looked at Wright quizzically. 'Did you hear that?' he asked.

Wright's voice caught in his throat. He coughed and shook his head.

Bamber popped back down the hatch. A few seconds later he reappeared. 'They're coming back,' he whispered. He pulled himself up and moved on tiptoe to the side of the chamber. He waved Wright back. Wright flattened himself against the wall. Bamber motioned for Wright to switch off his flashlight. Wright did as he was told. Bamber's flashlight went out a second later.

Wright could hear the FBI agent's shallow breathing from across the chamber, and even though the darkness was absolute he could sense Bamber staring at him. Wright shivered and held the flashlight close to his chest. Wright didn't know what had come over Bamber, but he knew one thing for sure: when the FBI agent had emerged from the hatch with the knife in his hand, there had been murder in his eyes.

His train of thought was interrupted by a scraping noise from the hatch. Wright held his breath. He heard whispering, then the sound of something being dragged across the ground. There was a muffled curse, then more scraping. The hatchway was suddenly filled with a warm glow, then a flashlight beam carved through the darkness of the chamber. Wright ducked as the beam sliced above his head.

Hammack grunted and heaved himself through the hatch, then lay sprawled on the floor, gasping for breath. He rolled on to his back, his chest heaving.

Thirty seconds later Doc's head popped through the hatch. He was also exhausted and it took him several attempts before he managed to claw his way into the chamber. 'Thanks, Bernie,' he groaned. 'If you hadn't pulled me back . . .'

'Forget it,' said Hammack. 'It don't even make us close to even.'

Wright switched his flashlight on. Doc and Hammack jerked as if they'd been stung. Hammack jumped to his feet and pulled a knife from his belt.

'Easy,' said Wright. 'It's me, Nick Wright.'

Doc sat up. His face and hat were smeared with red mud. As Wright walked closer to Doc he realised that there was also blood on his face, from dozens of small scratches that crisscrossed his flesh.

'What the hell are you doing here?' asked Doc.

Hammack lowered his knife. He was staring at Wright in amazement.

Bamber's flashlight came on and Doc and Hammack whirled around to face him.

'What happened down there?' asked Wright.

'There was a booby trap,' said Doc, breathing heavily. 'A cage full of scorpions rigged to open when a bamboo trigger was touched.' He took off his cap and used it to wipe his forehead. 'If Bernie hadn't yanked me away, I'd be dead for sure.'

'Scorpions?' said Wright. 'They can't have been there for long, can they? Days, at most.'

'That's right,' said Doc. 'It was set up by someone who knew we were coming. Someone who knew we'd be using the tunnel.'

Doc sat down with his back to the wall. He shook one

of his water canteens, but it was empty. Wright took his remaining bottle of water from his knapsack and gave it to him. Doc drank gratefully.

'What are you doing here?' Doc asked. He poured water into a cupped hand then splashed it on to his face, wincing as it got into the cuts and scratches.

'Following you,' said Wright.

'You must be mad. Stark raving mad.' Doc handed the bottle to Hammack.

Wright grinned ruefully. 'Yeah, you might be right,' he said. He sat down next to him. 'What's it all about, Doc?' he asked. He gestured at the open grave at the far end of the chamber. 'Who was he?'

Doc shook his head. 'Still asking questions, Detective?'

'Fuck you, Doc!' Wright hissed. 'I'm down here with you, I've earned the right to ask.'

'You've earned nothing,' said Doc.

'We're in this together now,' said Wright. 'Whoever killed Horvitz and Eckhardt killed Ramirez, too. That means he's down here with us.'

'You think I don't know that?'

Hammack gave the bottle of water back to Wright, who put it into his knapsack.

'Think about it for a moment, will you?' said Wright. 'He wants to kill you and Bernie and he's damn well going to want to make sure that there are no witnesses. Jim, am I right?'

Bamber nodded slowly. 'Makes sense to me,' he said.

'And who the fuck are you?' asked Doc.

'He's with the FBI,' said Wright.

Doc stared at Bamber in disbelief. 'The FBI?' he said.

'What happened, Doc?' said Wright quietly. 'What happened all those years ago?'

447

Doc shook his head and looked away. He put his head in his hands.

'Tell him, Doc,' said Hammack. 'If you don't, I will.'

Doc stared at the open grave.

'Doc,' prompted Hammack.

Doc took a deep breath and held it for several seconds, then he sighed and began to speak, hesitantly at first. 'There were eight of us,' he said. 'To start with, anyway. It was my mission, I was the ranking officer. Not that rank meant anything in the Tunnel Rats. Experience was the only thing that mattered. Experience and luck.'

He rested the back of his head against the damp clay wall. 'Bernie, Sergio, Eric, Max and Dennis, you know about. There were two others, a Tunnel Rat we called Jumbo and an intelligence guy called Rabbit. We were down here for three days. Three fucking days.'

Hammack squatted down against the wall facing Doc. He put his massive forearms on his knees and interlinked his fingers.

'We were tracking a VC major, a guy called Vin,' continued Doc. 'Dennis had been mapping the network for months, and he added to his maps as we went deeper and deeper. We used string and compasses, measuring it inch by inch, all the time getting closer and closer to Vin.'

'As part of Operation Phoenix?' asked Bamber.

Doc shook his head. 'We were on some Phoenix operations, but this was something else. Half a dozen bombs had gone off in Saigon, big ones. More than twenty of our boys had been killed, fifty civilians. Vin was behind the bombs and we knew there were more on the way. Cinemas, bars, shops, the VC didn't care who they killed. You know about bombs, don't you, Sergeant

Wright? You're from London, you've seen what terrorists can do.'

Wright nodded. He took off his Mickey Mouse knapsack and placed it on the floor next to him.

'Rabbit was an interrogation expert,' Doc continued. 'Our mission was to get Vin and find out where the next bombs were going to be planted. We knew he had a command centre down in the fourth level, but we'd never been further than the second level before. Three days, can you imagine being down here for three days?'

Wright shuddered, and shook his head.

'We ate cold rations, drank the minimum of fluid, just enough to keep going. We were living on our nerves. They had snakes, you know? Snakes tethered with wires. The VC knew how to pull the wires back so that they could get by, but we shot the snakes, shot them with silenced guns. The VC had trip wires connected to grenades, others that caused cave-ins. Pits with stakes smeared with shit. With shit, Sergeant Wright, so that any wounds would get infected. They were sick bastards. Sick, sick bastards. They weren't soldiers, they were terrorists.' He ran his hands through his hair.

Hammack had rested his forehead on his arms and was breathing heavily.

'On the third day we found the way down to the fourth level. Jumbo went down first and they cut his throat. He died in my arms, begging me to help him. There was so much blood.' He put a hand up to the bridge of his nose. 'So much fucking blood. You wouldn't believe there was so much blood in a man.' He shook his head, then put his cap back on.

'We killed half a dozen VC to get here. Took us three

hours to find Vin.' He gestured at the room. 'We caught up with him in here. Jumbo's blood was still wet. It was dripping off me, like sweat.' He took a deep breath as if gathering his strength for what was to come. 'Vin was a tough motherfucker. Wouldn't talk. Wouldn't say a fucking word. Just stood there with a secret fucking smile on his face like he thought there was nothing we could do to stop him. Rabbit threatened him, offered him bribes to change sides. He tried everything he could to get him to talk. Nothing worked. Then Rabbit hit him. Just a slap, across the face. Wasn't even that hard.'

Doc leaned forward and took off his rucksack. He reached inside and took out a plastic bag containing a pack of Marlboro and his Zippo lighter. He lit a cigarette and blew smoke up to the ceiling.

'Vin just glared back at him, smiling the way they do. Smiling like he didn't give a fuck. So Rabbit hit him again. Harder. Vin's lip started to bleed but he just kept on smiling.'

He took another long pull on his cigarette. 'Max was close to Jumbo, really close. Jumbo had saved Max's life more times than either of them could remember. He started urging Rabbit to hit him harder. And Rabbit did. Punched him in the gut, in the face, in the balls. Vin didn't even flinch. He was like a fucking rock. Like there was nothing Rabbit could do to get to him. He just kept staring at the wall.'

He flicked ash on to the floor, then stared at the alcove that had been carved into the wall of the chamber. His eyes widened. 'He wasn't staring at the wall,' he whispered. 'He was staring at the hiding place. Making sure that whoever was there stayed put.' He closed his eyes and banged the back of his head against the wall. 'I should have guessed,' he whispered. 'That's why he didn't cry out.'

'What do you mean?' asked Wright.

'No matter what we did to him, he didn't say a word. He didn't scream, he didn't cry out, he didn't even beg us to stop. Now I know why.'

Wright looked across at the alcove, then at the pile of parachute silk that had previously lined the walls. 'Someone else was down here?'

Doc nodded. 'Someone was down here and they saw what we did to Vin. And afterwards, after we'd buried the body and gone, whoever it was crawled out and took Max's dogtags.'

'Dogtags?' repeated Wright.

Doc stubbed the butt of his cigarette on the ground. 'When we eventually got out, Max discovered that his dogtags were missing. He remembered that Vin had grabbed them.' He gestured at the open grave. 'They're not there now.'

'So whoever was hiding there knew who Eckhardt was. Are you saying they spent twenty-five years tracking you all down?'

'That's the way it's starting to look,' said Doc.

'That's a hell of a long time to wait for revenge,' said Wright.

'You don't know the Vietnamese,' said Doc. 'They dug most of these tunnels by hand, knowing that it would take years before they were finished. Time doesn't mean the same to them, it's the passing of seasons, that's all. Part of the cycle.'

'What exactly did you do to Vin?' asked Bamber.

Doc looked across at the open grave. He shook his head.

'You butchered him,' said Wright. 'You cut him up. You cut him up and you cut off his dick.'

Doc winced under Wright's verbal attack. 'We lost it,' said Doc. 'We'd been through hell, we'd seen Jumbo die in front of us, and we knew that the bastard was in the process of planting more bombs in Saigon, bombs that would kill our boys. We had to get him to talk.'

Hammack laughed harshly, a guttural roar that made Wright jump. 'Bullshit,' said Hammack. 'It wasn't about getting him to talk. It was murder. Cold-blooded murder.'

'Cold it wasn't,' said Doc, his voice barely a whisper. 'We were angry, we wanted revenge, we wanted to hurt him the way he'd hurt our friends.'

'And you were all involved?' asked Wright. 'You all had a hand in it?'

Doc nodded and lit another cigarette.

'Rabbit and Max started it,' said Hammack. 'Max telling Rabbit to kick the shit out of him. Then Ramirez pulled out his knife and slashed him across the face. Something happened when we saw the blood. It was like we were with Jumbo again, watching him die.' He put his forehead down on his folded arms again.

'After a while we stopped asking questions,' said Doc. 'We just kept cutting him. Cutting and cutting. The little bastard didn't cry out once. That just made us madder. If he'd just said something, if he'd begged us to stop, maybe we'd have realised what we were doing. Maybe we'd have stopped.'

He closed his eyes and banged the back of his head against the wall again. The cigarette smouldered between his fingers.

'It took him hours to die. Fucking hours.'

'Who cut his dick off?'

'Rabbit. He'd lost it by then. He wanted to do more to the body, but Bernie and Eric pulled him off.'

'And the card?'

'That was Rabbit, too. Psyops used to leave them as calling cards.'

He opened his eyes and looked at Wright. 'I'm not trying to pass the buck, we were all to blame. Every one of us.'

'You tried to stop them, Doc,' said Hammack. 'You told them they were going too far.'

'We were a team, Bernie.'

'All for one and one for all?' said Wright. 'Like musketeers?'

Doc gave him a withering look. 'You wouldn't understand,' he said.

'Maybe not. But I understand murder.'

'It was a war,' said Doc.

Wright pushed himself up against the wall, then went over to the grave and looked down at the skeleton.

Doc got to his feet. 'We have to get out of here,' he said.

'How?' asked Hammack. He nodded at the hatch in the floor. 'Scorpions down there.' He gestured at the antechamber with his thumb. 'The killer's up there.'

'Maybe not,' said Wright. 'We got down all right.'

'Once we'd moved Ramirez's body,' said Bamber.

'So what are you saying?' asked Doc, dropping his cigarette on the floor and grinding it into the clay with his heel. 'We go back the same way? Maybe it's a trap, maybe the killer let you down so that he could kill us on the way back up.'

Wright stared at the grinning skull. He'd seen bodies before, but never a skeleton. It made him realise what lay ahead. No matter how he lived his life, no matter what he did, he would end up the same way, bones in the ground. He shuddered and turned away. He nodded at Bamber. 'What about the map, Jim? Does it show any other way out?'

'Map?' said Doc, wiping his hands on his trousers. 'What map?'

'We've got a Defense Department map of the tunnel complex,' said Wright. 'Jim got it from the Pentagon.'

Doc frowned. He looked at Hammack, then back to Wright. 'Impossible,' he said. 'We never gave the map to headquarters. Why would we want anyone else coming down here and seeing what we'd done?' He stared at the map case in Bamber's hand.

Wright reached for the case, but Bamber moved it out of his reach.

'What's going on, Jim?' Wright asked.

Bamber said nothing. He tossed the map case to Doc. Doc opened it and flicked through the maps. He looked across at Wright, his eyes narrowing. 'These belong to Dennis,' he said coldly.

Wright turned to look at Bamber, confusion written all over his face. 'Tell him, Jim.'

The FBI agent ignored him. He was staring at Doc, the knife in his hand twitching from side to side.

G erry Hunter had tried Wright's number more than a dozen times as he drove back to London. It was ringing, but Wright wasn't answering and each time a recorded voice cut in asking if he wanted to leave a message. He had begun to hate the prim, prissy female voice and would cheerfully have strangled the woman if she'd been in the car with him. After trying for more than an hour, he called up the company that had supplied Wright's mobile and asked to speak to somebody on the technical side. A man with a slight stutter explained that the recorded message meant that the phone was responding to the signal sent out over the satellite network. It wasn't a case of the phone being switched off. If the signal had reached the phone and it had been switched off, Hunter would hear a different message.

'I think it's in Bangkok, would that make a difference?' asked Hunter.

'Shouldn't,' said the man. 'We cover most of South-East Asia. Parts of Thailand might be out of our range, but certainly Bangkok is well covered. The person you're calling just isn't answering the phone.'

Hunter thanked the man, though he'd been no more help than the prerecorded message. He punched in Wright's number again and hit the 'send' button.

'Jim, what the hell's going on?' Wright's voice echoed around the chamber.

'I'll tell you what's going on,' said Doc. He pulled his knife from his belt and held it out in front of him. He threw the map at Wright's feet. 'That map belongs to Dennis. I want to hear how he got it.' He took a step towards Bamber.

Bamber stood his ground, his own knife held low, the point aimed at Doc's stomach. He was smiling.

Hammack got to his feet, a puzzled frown on his face. He slid his own knife from its sheath and stood holding it as if unsure what to do next.

'Sergio and Bernie went to get it the day after he was killed,' said Doc. 'If he's got the map, he must have seen Dennis. What I want to know is if Dennis was alive when he went around to the house. And if he was, I want to know how he managed to persuade him to part with it.'

Bamber continued to smile at Doc. He took a step forward, keeping the knife low.

'Come on, Jim, stop this,' said Wright. Bamber ignored him. 'Just tell him how you got the map.'

'Yeah, Jim,' said Hammack. 'Tell us how you got the map.'

'I don't have to tell you anything,' said Bamber. He waved his knife and it glinted in the beam of his flashlight. 'It's been a long time since you used a knife, hasn't it? You're not really sure how to hold it, are you?'

Doc threw Hammack a quick glance and Hammack moved to the side, widening the gap between them.

Bamber moved into the middle of the chamber, closer to the pile of parachute silk. 'You're an old man now, Doc. Your reflexes aren't what they were. Eyesight's going. Muscle tone's deteriorating.' He moved his knife in a slow circle.

Doc looked at Wright and made a small gesture with his chin, telling him to move behind Bamber so that the three men were equally spaced around him. Wright wasn't sure what was going on, but this time there was no mistaking the murderous intent in Bamber's eyes.

'I guess you're feeling pretty happy about the odds right

now,' said Bamber. 'Three against one. I guess you're thinking that three of you can take me. But you're wrong, Doc. Dead wrong. Nick here's a pussycat. You're an old man, and the nigger, well, I've never met a nigger yet that I couldn't fight one handed.'

'Fuck you,' said Hammack. He stepped forward, his knife raised.

'Bernie, no!' hissed Wright. 'He's just trying to rile you.'

'Man's succeeded,' said Hammack, but he lowered his knife.

'Always like to see a nigger kept in his place,' said Bamber.

Hammack roared and lashed out at Bamber. Bamber moved quickly, stepping to the side and drawing his knife across Hammack's chest in a fluid motion. Hammack yelled, but Wright couldn't tell if it was from anger or pain. The black man stabbed at Bamber but Bamber was too quick for him and he spun around like a matador goading a bull before slashing out again, this time to Hammack's upper arm. Blood spurted in a crimson stream and Hammack's knife dropped from his nerveless fingers. Blood was flowing down Hammack's T-shirt in a jagged red curtain and he sank to his knees, a look of despair on his face. Bamber raised his knife once more.

Wright could see that Bamber was going to slash Hammack's throat. He yelled 'No!' and threw his flashlight as hard as he could. It smashed into Bamber's arm and the light winked out. Hammack pitched forward and fell on to the pile of parachute silk, one hand clutching the wound on his chest. Doc dashed forward but Bamber struck out with his knife, hacking at Doc's stomach. Doc moved back.

Bamber bent down and picked up Hammack's flashlight, switched it off and tucked it into his belt. He backed up, his bloodstained knife moving in a lazy figure of eight, alternating between Doc and Wright.

'We can take him, Doc,' said Wright.

'Sure you can, Nick,' said Bamber. 'You can't even handle your own wife, how do you think you're going to be able to stop me?'

Wright didn't reply. He held his arms out to the side, fingers splayed, looking for an opportunity to grab the knife.

'I mean, how much of a man can you be, letting another guy screw your wife in your own bed? You've taken being pussy-whipped to a whole new level.'

Wright felt a surge of anger, but he fought to stay calm. He looked at Doc. Doc made a small gesture with his chin and the two men moved further apart so that Bamber had to turn his head to keep them both in vision.

'Screwed him with your boy in the next room, hey? Do you think he heard them? Rutting like pigs? What if she screamed out his name? How do you think little Sean would feel? His mother screwing another man? And you letting her?'

Hammack groaned. Blood trickled from between his fingers, staining the parachute silk.

Wright's pulse pounded in his ears and he took a step forward.

'Nick . . .' said Doc.

Wright smiled tightly. 'I know, Doc, don't worry.' He glared at Bamber. 'It's not going to work,' he said. 'Sticks and stones.'

A look of uncertainty flashed across Bamber's face, but he quickly regained his composure. 'Remember what it was like when you found your father, Nick? Remember what it was like when you were locked in with his body, in the dark? How alone you felt? How vulnerable?' He grinned evilly. 'Time for a flashback,' he whispered. He switched off the flashlight and the chamber was instantly plunged into darkness.

Wright stepped back, then dropped into a crouch. He heard Bamber move, but couldn't tell in which direction. He had visions of Bamber slashing his knife from side to side like a scythe and his stomach tensed. He took another step back and his foot caught on the pile of parachute silks, sending him tumbling backwards. He gasped as he hit the ground, and immediately rolled over, knowing that Bamber would be able to pinpoint the sound. He kept on rolling, then realised that if he wasn't careful he'd end up in the shallow grave with the skeleton. He stopped moving and listened intently.

'Nick?' hissed Doc. 'You okay?'

'Don't talk,' snapped Wright. He got up but kept low, and took several steps back, skirting the parachute silk. Wright heard a footfall to his right, and he froze. Hammack moaned and the silk rustled as he shifted his position.

Wright's brain, starved of visual stimulation, began to manufacture its own images. He saw whirling circles and multicoloured grids, strange shapes that disappeared when he tried to focus on them but reappeared as soon as he looked away. It was as if he was floating in a universe of computer-generated shapes, and he swayed on his feet as his sense of balance began to desert him. He blinked several times and shook his head, but then felt as if he was falling, so he dropped down into a crouch and put his hands on the floor.

Wright heard more footsteps, fainter this time, then a

scraping sound. He waited several seconds, but heard nothing else. 'Doc?' he said hesitantly.

'Yeah, I think he's gone.'

'Where's your flashlight?' Wright asked.

'In the tunnel. I dropped it when the scorpions fell on me.' Hammack groaned in pain again. 'Bernie, are you okay?' asked Doc.

Hammack muttered something unintelligible.

'Bernie?'

'I'm bleeding bad, Doc.'

'Hang on, we'll get to you.'

'Your Zippo, Doc,' said Wright. 'Where is it?'

'On the floor, where I was sitting.'

'Let's see if we can find it.'

Wright tried to picture the chamber, but he couldn't even recall which direction he was facing. He got down on his hands and knees and groped around. His hand touched the pile of parachute silk torn from the walls. He moved to his left, feeling with his fingertips.

His hands brushed against a mat, then the damp floor. He crept forward. There was a scraping noise from the opposite side of the chamber. Wright knew it was Doc, but he couldn't stop himself thinking of snakes and scorpions and spiders. He crawled slowly, patting the ground with his right hand.

Hammack moaned again. 'Doc . . .' he gasped.

'We're coming, Bernie,' said Doc.

The ground in front of Wright disappeared and he pitched forward, his head slamming into the wooden sides of the trapdoor. He cursed.

'What's wrong?' asked Doc.

'Damn near fell in the hatch,' said Wright, pushing

himself up. He touched his head. His hand came away wet with blood.

'You okay?'

'Yeah.'

Doc had been sitting about six feet from the hatch, so at least Wright now had his bearings. He crawled away from the trapdoor, brushing the ground with his fingertips. He touched something soft and picked it up. It was the Marlboro pack. He put it down and patted the area around his knees. His left hand fell on something metallic. The lighter. He picked it up, pulled open the top and flicked the wheel. There was a shower of sparks and a flickering yellow light.

Wright held up the Zippo. Doc was on his hands and knees, close to the chamber wall. He got to his feet, picked up his rucksack, and ran over to Hammack.

Hammack was lying on his back, his hands clutched to his chest, his eyes closed tight. Doc took his medical kit out and slapped a dressing on Hammack's chest. 'Nick, hold this for me. Keep the pressure on,' he said.

Wright held the burning Zippo in his left hand and clamped the dressing to Hammack's wound with his right. Doc pulled a second dressing out and wrapped it around Hammack's bleeding arm.

'How bad is it?' Hammack asked through gritted teeth.

'Not too bad,' said Doc. He shook four white tablets out of a plastic bottle and held them up to Hammack's mouth. 'Swallow these,' he said. 'They'll help with the pain.'

Hammack opened his mouth and swallowed the tablets one by one.

The Zippo got hotter and hotter until Wright couldn't hold it any longer. He cursed as it fell from his fingers, plunging the chamber into darkness once more. 'Sorry,' he said. He grabbed for the Zippo but it was still too hot to touch. He tossed it from hand to hand and blew on it, then flicked it into life again. Doc handed him another dressing.

'Wrap this around it,' said Doc. 'It'll act as insulation.'

Wright held the Zippo up in the air and watched as Doc applied sticking plaster to the wound on Hammack's arm.

Doc nodded at Wright, who took his hand away. Doc tossed aside the soiled dressing, inspected the wound, then smeared antiseptic ointment across the bloody flesh. He placed a fresh dressing over it and applied strips of sticking plaster to keep it in place.

'Is he going to be okay?' Wright asked.

'Yeah, Doc, will I be able to play the piano again?'

Doc grinned at Wright. 'I think that answers your question, Nick,' he said. 'If he can make jokes, he can walk out of here.' He helped Hammack to sit up.

'Where'd the crazy guy go?' asked Hammack.

Doc gestured at the antechamber. 'Back up to the third level. Who is he, Nick?'

'He's an FBI agent, investigating the two murders.'

'Like hell,' said Doc. 'He's the killer, I'm sure of it.'

'Couldn't be,' said Wright. 'He didn't kill Ramirez. And I know for a fact that he was in the UK when Horvitz was murdered.'

Doc put an arm around Hammack to support him. Hammack was weak, but he could stand.

'He killed Dennis, though. And he would've killed the three of us, given a chance.'

'So that means what? Two killers?'

Doc shrugged. 'I can't think of any other explanation.'

Despite the dressing around the Zippo, Wright could feel the lighter getting uncomfortably hot. 'What are we going to do about a light?' he said. 'This isn't going to last much longer.'

'What about your flashlight?'

'The bulb went when I threw it at Bamber.'

Doc pointed at his rucksack. 'I've got spares in there. See if they'll fit.'

Wright picked up the broken flashlight and went over to the rucksack. He put the burning Zippo on the ground and in its flickering light found and fitted one of the bulbs. To his immense relief, it worked. He flipped the Zippo shut and pocketed the lighter.

'Have you got any weapons?' Wright asked Doc.

'Knives. I've got one, so does Bernie.'

'I don't think I'm gonna be winning any knife fights,' said Hammack.'

Wright went over and retrieved Hammack's knife. He stuck it into his belt, then crouched down next to his knapsack. He pulled out the goggles.

'What the hell are those?' asked Doc.

'Infra-red goggles.'

'They work?'

'I bloody well hope so. We're not going to get anywhere with one flashlight between three of us.'

M ay sat with her ear pressed against the clay wall, listening intently. She'd heard angry voices, then there had been silence, then a man had left the command centre and moved up to the third level. She knew where he was, about three hundred feet west of her position. The three other men were still in the command centre, talking in hushed voices, so she couldn't make out what they were saying.

The chamber she was in had once functioned as a dormitory area for families. There were still sleeping mats on the floor and in one corner stood two large earthenware pots that had once stored water for drinking and washing. So far as May was concerned, the main advantage of the chamber was that it had four exits. From where she was she could easily reach the second level, and get quickly to most parts of the tunnel complex.

She went over to one of the pots. It came up almost to her waist and she leaned into it and pulled out a case. She sat cross-legged on the floor as she opened it. Inside was a crossbow and six bolts. She assembled the weapon with practised ease, then slotted the bolts into a plastic clip that attached to the bottom of the crossbow. May hoped she wouldn't have to use the weapon. She wanted to get close enough to use her knife, to look into their eyes as they died.

'He could be up there,' whispered Doc, looking up at the hatch. Ramirez's blood was still wet on the wooden sides of the hatchway.

'I'll go,' said Wright, fastening the straps on his goggles.

'No!' said Doc sharply. 'I'm leading.'

Wright shook his head. 'You're going to have to take care of Bernie,' he said. He tapped the goggles. 'Besides, I've got these. It's better I go first.'

'You know which way to go?'

'I think so. If I have a problem, I'll shout back to you. Bernie, are you okay?'

Hammack forced a smile. 'I'll make it,' he said.

'Keep your distance,' said Wright. 'There's no telling what's up there now. Don't get too close in case . . .' He left the sentence hanging.

Doc squeezed Wright's shoulder. 'Good luck.'

Wright had a last look around the tunnel, took Hammack's knife from his belt, then edged slowly through the hatch, turning his head from side to side, ready to duck back at the first sign of a threat. Except for Ramirez's corpse, the tunnel above was clear. He pushed himself up, using his elbows for leverage.

He backed away from the hatch, then helped Hammack through. The big man was clearly in pain but fighting not to show it. He was weak, too, and Wright realised there was no way Hammack would have been able to get up without his and Doc's help.

Doc crawled over to Ramirez and felt for a pulse in the man's neck.

'He's dead, Doc,' said Wright quietly, but Doc threw him a warning look. Wright nodded, acknowledging that the two men had a friendship going back more than a quarter of a century and that Doc had the right to check for himself.

Doc made the sign of a cross over Ramirez, and closed his eyes for a few seconds as if in prayer.

Wright looked down the tunnel, wondering where Bamber

was, and what he was doing. He could think of no reason why the FBI agent had acted in the way that he had. Whatever Bamber's motives, his actions suggested that Doc had been right, that Bamber had taken the map from O'Leary. If he'd taken the map, he'd probably killed O'Leary, too. But why? And why had Bamber been so determined to come down the tunnels?

Kruse took the infra-red goggles out of his Snoopy knapsack and slipped them on, adjusting the straps so that they stayed firmly in place. He switched them on. Within seconds they'd warmed up and he turned off his flashlight. He put the flashlight back in the knapsack and eased it over his shoulders.

He was looking forward to the hunt, relishing the opportunity to use his killing skills. For too long he'd been limited by the environment in which he'd operated, where every killing had to be made to look like an accident. Deep underground, there were no restrictions. No limits.

He caressed the knife he'd taken from Ramirez. It was a good weapon, a killing knife, razor sharp with a slightly curved end so that it would slip easily between the ribs. It had sliced cleanly through the black man's chest and arm, and only Wright's thrown flashlight had prevented Kruse from cutting Hammack's throat. Kruse smiled at how easily he'd made Hammack lose his temper. Kruse wasn't a racist, but he'd known instinctively that racial abuse was Hammack's weak spot, in the same way that he'd known that he could get to Wright through the policeman's feelings for his ex-wife. Kruse was as expert at finding weak spots as he was at killing.

Kruse had never intended to kill the three men in the chamber. He'd wanted to weaken them, to injure them if possible, but he wanted them alive. He needed them as bait.

Kruse crawled towards the hatch that led up to the second level. He'd wait there for his victims, assuming that the other killer didn't get to them first. He smiled at the thought of a slogan he'd once seen printed on a T-shirt: 'Yeah, though I walk through the valley of the shadow of death, I fear no evil. Because I am the meanest son of a bitch in the valley.' Kruse's smile widened. Of one thing he was sure: he was the meanest son of a bitch down the tunnels.

W right waited under the hatch that led up to the second level, sitting to one side so that he wasn't exposed from above. The hatch was closed, but he had no way of knowing if Bamber had already gone through or not. He looked back along the tunnel to where Hammack was dragging himself along. The tunnel was narrow, so Wright couldn't see Doc, who was bringing up the rear, but he could hear his whispers of encouragement.

There was nothing either man could do physically to help Hammack, as there wasn't enough room to pull or push him. Hammack grunted with each movement, and he was able to use only his left arm as he crawled. Doc had used Ramirez's headscarf as a sling to support Hammack's injured arm and Hammack kept it close to his chest in an attempt to maintain pressure on the dressings there.

It took Hammack almost twenty minutes to crawl the hundred feet to where Wright was sitting. He grinned ruefully at Wright. 'Sorry 'bout this,' he said.

'Hey, there's no rush,' said Wright. 'I'm tired, too. This pace is fine.'

Hammack lay down on his side and groaned. 'I could sleep for a month,' he said.

'We can rest here for a while,' said Doc.

'How 'bout you call room service and order us all a beer?' said Hammack. He chuckled, but the chuckle swiftly turned into a series of coughs that wracked his chest.

Wright took off his goggles and blinked as his eyes became accustomed to the pale yellow light from Doc's flashlight. 'Have you got spare batteries for that?' asked Wright.

'Three more,' said Doc. 'I figured I'd wait until these fail completely before I put them in.'

Hammack's chest began to rise and fall slowly and he snored quietly.

'Do you think he's going to be okay?' asked Wright.

'He's lost a lot of blood,' said Doc, 'but he's not in shock, not yet, anyway. He's tough. He'll make it.'

'I think it might be better if you went ahead of him,' said Wright. 'Let him bring up the rear.'

'We're not leaving him,' said Doc.

'That's not what I meant,' said Wright.

'What did you mean?'

'If anything did happen, you'd be trapped behind him. If you were in the middle, you could still move.'

'If he dies, you mean?'

Wright sighed. 'Look, don't be so defensive, Doc. I just mean that in the event of there being a problem, there'd be no point in you being stuck behind him. Besides, you've got the flashlight, you should be in front of him, not behind. He can't use the flashlight, not with his injured arm.'

'The man's right, Doc,' said Hammack, his eyes still closed.

'I thought you were asleep,' said Doc, patting him on the leg.

'Too much noise to sleep,' said Hammack. 'Time we started moving, huh? We haven't got all day.'

K ruse crouched down in the conical chamber, his knife in his hand. He switched off his infra-red goggles to get rid of the distracting high-pitched humming noise they made, then took them off and laid them on the floor. There were three exits leading from the chamber, and Kruse knew that his quarry would be coming down the tunnel he was facing. They were making slow and noisy progress, which was just what Kruse wanted. If he could hear them coming, so could the killer. All Kruse had to do was to watch and wait, and when the killer eventually struck, Kruse would be there to take care of the business. He smiled in the darkness.

He stiffened as he heard a scraping sound behind him. He pulled on the goggles and switched them on. They hummed and after a few seconds they flickered into life. He headed towards the source of the sound, his knife poised.

May moved slowly down the tunnel, the crossbow out in front of her. A group of red ants marched purposefully in single file across the floor of the tunnel, out of one tiny hole and into another. She took care not to trample on them as she crossed over their ranks. She squatted down and took a drink from her canteen. A sudden noise made her look back the way she'd come. She grabbed for the crossbow. A bolt was already in place, and she slid her finger over the trigger.

She heard another noise, then the rustle of clothing. She sniffed softly, moving her head back as she inhaled. She could smell a man's sweat.

The tunnel she was in stretched for a hundred and fifty feet behind her. She couldn't risk turning around to get away because she'd have to expose her back. She crouched down. Ahead of her was a thirty-foot length of tunnel, just big enough for her to kneel up in. It met a T-junction, with larger tunnels running east–west. To the east was a conical air-raid chamber; to the west was a hospital chamber. May had set a booby trap at the entrance to the hospital: a cage containing scorpions, similar to the one she'd placed in the escape tunnel leading from the command centre. Whoever it was would probably continue straight ahead; there was no reason to take the smaller tunnel, the one she was in. She switched off her flashlight, put it on the ground, and waited.

She heard the man move slowly forward, then stop. May

frowned in the darkness. She held the crossbow with both hands. There was no glow at the end of the tunnel, no light to show that he was approaching. Could he be moving in the dark? She dismissed the thought immediately. It was impossible. Even she wouldn't move through an unexplored section in total darkness: there were too many dangers for the unwary. Although she knew where all the traps were, there were still the snakes and insects to contend with.

Another sound came from the man's direction – a high-pitched whine, like a mosquito. She put her head on one side, focusing her attention on the sound. There was another rustling noise, like a sleeve brushing against the tunnel wall. He was moving again. Still there was no light.

May took her left hand off the crossbow and picked up her flashlight. The crossbow wavered as she pointed the flashlight down the tunnel and switched it on.

She stifled a scream. Crouched at the T-junction was a monster, a huge insect-like creature with glassy eyes and a bulbous head, looking straight at her. It was holding a knife in its hand. May backed away in horror. She didn't believe in ghosts or demons – all the horrors she'd witnessed in her life were the actions of men – but this, this was something that could only have crawled out of hell. It had the body of a man and the head of a giant locust, and whatever it was, it could see in the dark. The creature moved towards her, its mouth parting to reveal human teeth. Its blank eyes stared at her, and she could see her own reflection in its stare. She saw the look of horror on her own face, the scarf around her neck, and the crossbow shaking in her hand. The crossbow. She'd forgotten about the crossbow. She put the flashlight on the ground, its beam highlighting the monstrous creature, and aimed her crossbow with both hands.

As she sighted along the bolt, she realised it wasn't a monster she was facing, but a man, a man wearing a mask. No, not a mask, something else, something that helped him to see in the dark. She aimed at the man's chest and pulled the trigger. The man was already moving and the bolt hit him in the shoulder. He fell back against the tunnel wall. May fumbled for another bolt.

H ammack groaned and lay down on the tunnel floor. 'Doc, I'm beat,' he gasped.

'It's not much further, Bernie,' said Doc.

'Don't kid a kidder,' whispered Hammack. 'We're not even up to the second level yet. I'm bleeding again. And I need water.'

Doc reached over his back and undid the top of his rucksack. He pulled out his medical kit and passed it back to Hammack. 'Take a dressing out and slap it on the wound,' he said. 'And if the pain gets worse, chew on another tablet.'

Hammack reached for the kit with his good arm.

'I'll go ahead and bring the Brit back,' said Doc.

'Then what?'

'He's got water in his backpack. Enough for you, anyway. He had Dennis's map, maybe he can remember where the well was and we can find water.'

'That's a big maybe, Doc.'

'I'm going to have to leave you in the dark. You okay with that?'

Hammack nodded. He rolled over on to his back, opened the medical kit and took out a dressing. Doc waited until he'd put it over his wound before crawling away.

Hammack rested his head on the floor and sucked in the warm air. Every breath sent stabbing pains through his chest wound. He put his hand up and placed it on the dressings, using pressure to stem the flow of blood. He shivered. He could feel his body temperature dropping, despite the heat of the tunnel. 'Hurry back, Doc,' he whispered.

K ruse gritted his teeth and pulled out the bolt. He probed the wound with his fingers. It was painful but there didn't appear to be too much damage. He flexed his fingers. The bolt seemed to have missed the nerves and the blood flow was far from life threatening. He'd been lucky, if lucky meant reflexes honed almost to perfection by years of training. A woman had been the last thing he'd expected to see down the tunnels, especially a woman dressed in the black pyjamas uniform of a Viet Cong guerrilla. That was what had slowed him down, kept him rooted to the spot while she'd aimed her crossbow. She must have been surprised too, because her aim had been off.

He dropped the bolt on the floor and began crawling again. He had to put as much distance between himself and the woman as he could. She had the advantage of range, so in the long tunnels she'd have the upper hand. To be sure of defeating her he'd have to lie in ambush, wait for her to show herself, using the darkness as a cloak. One of the chambers would be the best bet. He could wait in the dark and the beam of her flashlight would announce her presence. Then he could move in close, with the knife.

Kruse didn't care who the woman was. All he cared about was that he now knew who he was up against. The fact that it was a woman made it a little more interesting, but he gave no thought as to who she was or why she wanted to kill the Tunnel Rats. Jody Meacher could deal with the questions; all Kruse cared about was his mission – to kill everyone who knew the secret that had lain buried in the fourth level for so long.

He moved quickly along the tunnel, through a small resting chamber, not even bothering to consult the map. He ducked into a side tunnel, scampering along on all fours, his knapsack rubbing against the tunnel roof. He stopped suddenly as he heard voices ahead. It was Doc and Hammack, talking in hushed voices.

Kruse crawled forward cautiously. The tunnel he was in merged with another. Doc and Hammack were around the corner. Kruse crept along to the point where the two tunnels intersected, and leaned against the clay wall. He could see along the full length of the tunnel ahead of him, but didn't want to risk looking around to see where the two men were. In the distance he had a back view of Nick Wright about two hundred feet from the intersection. Kruse tightened his grip on his knife. It wouldn't take him long to catch up, then he could plunge his knife into Wright's back without him ever knowing what had happened. He was about to crawl after Wright when he heard someone moving along the tunnel. Kruse backed up, his knife out in front of him. It was Doc.

Kruse moved further back down the tunnel to where

it zigzagged so that Doc wouldn't be able to see him. He waited until he was sure that Doc had passed the intersection before crawling back into the tunnel. He looked after Doc, only thirty feet away and clearly trying to catch up with Wright. Kruse turned to look at Hammack. The black man was lying on his side, his eyes closed. Kruse decided to go after Doc.

Kruse moved quickly and easily gained on Doc. He raised his knife and slashed at Doc's legs. Doc yelped and Kruse stabbed him in the thigh, using the knife as leverage to pull himself up on Doc's legs. Kruse felt like a cheetah bringing down a running antelope; once it had its claws embedded into the animal's flanks, it was all over.

Doc screamed in pain. Kruse saw Wright twist around in the tunnel, and grinned. He grabbed Doc's hair and pulled back the man's head, waited until he was sure that Wright could see what he was doing, then slashed at Doc's throat so savagely that he almost severed the neck. Blood spurted over the sides of the tunnel and Doc's body went into convulsions.

'You're next!' Kruse shouted at Wright. He crawled over Doc's body but Doc's rucksack blocked his way. There wasn't enough room to get by. Kruse pounded the rucksack, trying to flatten it down. It was no good. Kruse clawed at the straps and yanked the bloodstained rucksack off Doc's back. He passed it through his legs then clambered over Doc's body. Wright had already disappeared around a bend in the tunnel. Kruse sped after him, the smell of blood so strong in his nostrils that it made him giddy.

Hammack heard a soft scraping sound and opened his eyes. He had no way of knowing how long he'd been lying in the tunnel as he'd been drifting in and out of consciousness. A flashlight beam illuminated the ceiling and he twisted his head back to see who was coming.

'Doc? That you?'

There was no reply but he could still hear whoever it was crawling towards him. Hammack swallowed.

'Doc?' His voice echoed around the tunnel.

The light wavered, then got stronger. Hammack forced his head back but all he could see was red clay. Something fluttered across his face and he flinched. He spluttered and brushed whatever it was away with his hand, but it wasn't an insect, it was a piece of card. Hammack groped for it and held it in front of his face. It was a playing card and he was looking at the back of it. He knew what it was before he'd even turned it around. An ace of spades. He gave a groan of resignation and closed his eyes.

When he opened them again a face was looking down at him, the face of a woman. A Vietnamese woman. Around her neck was a black and white checked scarf, the sort that the VC used to wear. Hammack wondered if he was having a flashback, if the medication Doc had given him was producing hallucinations. He tried to speak, but his throat was too dry. Even though her face was the wrong way up, Hammack could see that she was pretty, with a small mouth, high cheekbones, and soft, brown eyes. He smiled up at her. She didn't smile back. Something flashed at the periphery of his vision. It was only as it sliced through his throat that he realised it was a knife.

W right crawled out of the tunnel and emerged into a large chamber. He looked around at the lathes and metal-turning machinery and the stacks of boxes. He was in the ammunition chamber. He turned and listened. He could hear Bamber in the tunnel, coming after him. Wright looked around for somewhere to hide. The boxes were the best bet. They gave him a sudden idea. He climbed up on a stack and took down one of the old oil lamps that hung from the overhead metal beams. He shook it. There was still oil inside.

His heart raced as he unscrewed the oil filler cap. He yanked open the box that Bamber had prised off last time they'd passed through the chamber and splashed oil over the cartridges. He trickled oil over the rest of the boxes, then dropped the lamp on to the floor and went back to the tunnel. He bent down and peered inside. Bamber was only twenty feet away, and roared as he saw Wright.

Wright ducked out of the way, then ran to the centre of the chamber and pulled Doc's Zippo out of his pocket. He flicked it, but it stubbornly refused to light. 'Come on,' he hissed, and flicked the metal wheel with his thumb again. There were sparks, but still no light.

Wright shook the Zippo and tried again. This time it burst

into life. He tossed it on to the pile of ammunition boxes and they immediately caught light with a whooshing noise.

Wright ran to the exit. He turned in time to see Bamber stagger out of his tunnel. He ran across the chamber, towards Wright, his knife high in the air. Wright stared in horror, knowing that he was no match for Bamber in a knife fight. Or any sort of fight, for that matter.

The top ammunition box exploded in a series of ear-splitting bangs. Wright ducked instinctively. Dozens of cartridges detonated and bullets thwacked into the parachute silk that lined the chamber.

A pool of flame spread across the floor and the reed mats ignited easily. Plumes of choking black smoke billowed up between Wright and Bamber, and Wright stepped back. There was another explosion as a second crate caught fire.

Wright bent down and scurried into the exit tunnel. He crawled frantically. A few seconds later there was a third, even bigger explosion, that sent a wave of burning hot air down the tunnel. He crawled faster, coughing and spluttering. After fifty feet or so he turned and looked behind him. There was no sign of Bamber.

He lay on his back, gasping for air, but started crawling again as soon as he'd caught his breath. He wasn't sure how much life there was left in the batteries of his goggles.

He crawled along to the conical chamber which had contained the spiders and rushed through it, just in case they bore any grudges from his last visit. He kept his head down and didn't look up as he passed through, not stopping for a rest until he'd reached the cinema. He sat on the floor by the white sheet screen with his back to the parachute-silk-lined wall, fighting off the feelings of nausea that washed over him.

His throat was painfully dry and his nose and lips were coated with thick dust. He took off his goggles and rubbed his face. The rubber seal irritated his skin, but it was still a small price to pay for being able to see.

He put the goggles back on and crawled out of the cinema chamber. All he had to do now was to find the hatch up the first level, and get through the water in the U-bend. Wright laughed harshly. After everything he'd been though, he figured that this time it'd be a breeze.

M ay wrapped her scarf around the lower part of her face and narrowed her eyes against the stinging dust. She had no idea what had caused the explosion in the ammunition chamber, but she could see the after-effects for herself. The tunnel leading to it had collapsed, and the chamber itself had almost certainly caved in. The chambers had been built to withstand bombs falling outside, not explosions from within. She backed away, then twisted around. There were a number of different ways up to the first level and from there she knew of several ventilation tunnels that she could use to get to the surface.

W right knelt down beside the water. He slipped off his goggles, dipped a hand into the water and splashed it over his face, taking care not to get any of it in his mouth. He put the goggles back on and rummaged through his knapsack. The plastic bag wasn't there. He searched again but it had definitely gone. He must have lost it when he'd taken the water bottles out. He cursed. He wasn't sure how the goggles would stand up to being immersed in water. They were rubber coated, but that didn't mean they were waterproof.

He took off the goggles and put them in the knapsack, trying not to think about the dark. He tucked his knife in the back of his belt, all the time keeping his eyes firmly closed, clinging to the illusion that he wasn't in total darkness, that it was something he'd chosen, that at any time he could open his eyes.

He slipped his arms through the straps of the knapsack, and felt for the water. He took two deep breaths, then threw himself headfirst into the pool. He kicked, then immediately turned around so that he could use his hands and feet to propel himself through the U-bend. His fingers dug into the wet clay and he pulled himself down.

The air trapped in his knapsack pushed him up against the tunnel roof and he banged his head, but he kicked with his feet, surged around the bend and popped up to the surface, barely out of breath. He grinned to himself as he climbed out of the water. It had been easy compared with his chaotic first attempt.

He crawled away from the water and knelt on the tunnel floor, flicking his wet hair from his eyes. He shrugged off his knapsack and felt for the goggles. He fitted them, then said a silent prayer as he switched them on. They clicked and hissed, and after a tense five-second delay they flickered into life. Wright sighed with relief and leaned back against the tunnel wall. He was going to make it. All he had to do now was to get up to the first level and then find the trapdoor.

He reached for his knapsack, and as he did, Bamber shot out of the water, his mouth wide open. His shirt was scorched and torn and there were burn marks on his hands and arms. In his left hand he held his flashlight and infra-red goggles wrapped in a plastic bag; in his right hand a wicked hunting knife. Water cascaded from Bamber's body as he surged forward, his knife raised in the air.

Wright screamed, holding his knapsack up for protection. The knife slashed into it, slicing through Mickey Mouse's smiling face. Bamber slashed again and again as he pulled himself out of the water, roaring with each blow. Wright scuttled backwards and kicked out with his feet. He caught Bamber under the chin and the FBI agent fell back.

Wright threw his knapsack at Bamber and it struck him a glancing blow on his cheek. Bamber slashed down with the knife and Wright felt a burning pain in his left calf. He kicked out again and struck Bamber in the chest. Wright groped behind him, trying to find his own knife. It wasn't there. It must have fallen out while he was under water.

Bamber grunted and drew back his knife. It glistened with blood. Wright grunted and drew both his legs up to his chest. Bamber shuffled towards Wright, waving the knife from side to side. Wright lashed out with both feet, catching Bamber in the stomach.

Bamber fell backwards, his head slamming into the roof of the tunnel. Wright scraped his right foot along the tunnel roof, kicking red clay into Bamber's face, then kept up the attack, shuffling forwards on his backside and kicking, forcing Bamber back down the tunnel towards the water.

As Bamber wiped the soil from his eyes, Wright lashed out at the bag in his hand. It fell to the ground and Wright stamped on it, smashing the flashlight with his heel. He kicked it again and heard the lenses of the goggles smash. At last he had the advantage. Bamber couldn't see.

Wright picked up the bag full of broken metal and glass and slammed the end against Bamber's head, again and again, whipping it back and forth.

Bamber tried to stab him with the knife but Wright easily evaded the blows. Bamber cocked his head on one side, listening intently. Wright held his breath so as not to give away his position, but he realised that Bamber was listening for the buzzing of his infra-red goggles.

Wright pulled the flashlight out of the bag and stabbed the end of it into Bamber's face, grinding the broken glass into his cheek. Bamber cried in pain and Wright brought the flashlight down on his nose with a satisfying crack. Bamber put his hands up to his broken nose and fell back into the water. He disappeared under the surface, head first. Wright crouched over the water, the flashlight raised like a club, waiting for Bamber to reappear, but after half a minute the ripples had subsided and the surface was as flat as a mirror. Wright counted a full two minutes in his head before lowering the broken flashlight. He turned and began to crawl along the tunnel, looking over his shoulder every few seconds, just in case. He'd hit Bamber hard, but he was reasonably sure that he hadn't him hit hard enough to kill him.

M ay undid the trip wire. It was connected to a small bamboo cage containing two venomous snakes that she'd bought from a dealer in Saigon. She crept by the cage, which she'd set into the tunnel wall, then retied the trip wire. The three Americans who'd come down the tunnel were all dead. She'd killed Ramirez and Hammack herself, though the man in the strange headset had beaten her to Doc Marshall. Still, she'd managed to place an ace of spades on Marshall's corpse. That had given her no small satisfaction. There were two men still in the tunnels: the man in the goggles and the other man, whom she hadn't yet seen. Neither concerned her. She'd completed her work in the tunnels and was now intent on getting back to the surface and out of Vietnam.

The tunnel she was in was relatively tall and the roof arched, so that she was able to run along it providing she kept her upper body thrust forward and her knees slightly bent. She cradled the crossbow in her hands as she ran, a bolt in place even though she didn't anticipate meeting anyone. The two men were the other side of the collapse, and one had probably died in the explosion.

She reached the end of the tunnel and paused for breath in a resting chamber large enough to hold six men. A slight breeze came from a small hole close to the roof of the chamber. May turned her head towards it and let it play over her face.

As a child she'd crawled through ventilation tunnels, despite her father's warning that it was dangerous, that they weren't built to such a high standard as the chambers and the communication tunnels. She had grown since then, but she knew that she would still be able to crawl up through the ventilation tunnel, all the way to the surface. It would be a tight fit, and she would come out almost half a mile from her pick-up truck, but it was still the quickest route out. She drank the last of her water, then stood up and pushed her crossbow into the hole. She used both hands to get a grip on the hard clay, and heaved herself up.

The green flickering image faded and the buzzing of the infra-red goggles became suddenly fainter. Wright had a sick feeling in the pit of his stomach. The infra-red image had been getting steadily worse over the past few minutes, but he'd tried to convince himself that he was imagining it. Now there was no doubt. He couldn't see more than ten feet ahead of him and his field of vision was fading fast. He crawled faster, wanting to take advantage of what little life remained in the equipment, but he'd barely managed twenty feet before they failed completely. Despair washed over him and he beat his hands on the ground.

He ripped off the goggles and threw them down. He cursed himself, he cursed the tunnels, and he cursed Jim Bamber. He started to hyperventilate and fought to steady his breathing.

'It's okay,' he whispered to himself. 'It's one straight tunnel. A walk in the park.' He started to crawl forward, groping ahead with his fingers, staring ahead with unseeing eyes. 'A walk in the park,' he repeated, though he could hear the uncertainty in his voice.

Gerry Hunter opened the front door. 'Hey!' he called. 'Hiya, honey!' Janie shouted from the kitchen. 'We're in here.'

She was standing by the dishwashing machine. Sean was helping her to load it.

'Hiya, Sean,' said Hunter, dropping his briefcase next to the kitchen table. 'How was school?'

'Okay,' said Sean. He closed the door of the machine and rushed out of the kitchen. Hunter watched him go.

Janie kissed him on the cheek. 'He'll get used to you,' she said, and slipped her arms around his neck. 'I'm pleased to see you.' She kissed him on the lips. 'But you're late.'

'Yeah, Nick's in trouble.'

Janie held up her hands. 'I don't want to hear any more,' she snapped.

'But—'

'No, Gerry. He's out of my house, he's out of my life, I don't want to talk about him.'

'You're over-reacting, Janie.'

'You didn't have to live with the man, Gerry. With his moods, his nightmares, his fixation with work. You didn't get woken up in the middle of the night to find him downstairs playing his bloody mouth organ.' She stamped her foot. 'Damn him, damn him for never leaving me alone.' She turned on her heel and stormed out of the kitchen.

Hunter groaned and took off his coat. He was finding it harder and harder to deal with Janie's mood swings. When he first met her he'd thought that the break-up of her marriage had been Nick Wright's fault, but the longer he spent with her the more he realised that Janie was far from the catch she first appeared. She was moody, spoiled and selfish, and while the sex was terrific, she was impossible to live with. In fact, Hunter had made it a point not to live with her. She'd given him a key, and he often stayed until the early hours, but he was never there in the morning. He always left before first light, partly because he didn't think it fair on Sean, but partly because he didn't want to make a commitment to Janie which he might have to break.

He switched on the kettle, then took his mobile phone out of his briefcase. He tapped out Wright's number. To his surprise, after half a dozen rings, it was answered by a laconic male voice.

'Nick?'

'What?'

'Nick? It's Gerry.'

'Gerry who?'

It wasn't Wright, Hunter realised. He checked the number with the man. He was one digit out. He apologised for bothering the man, and redialled, taking care to press the correct buttons. It rang out for a while, then he got the recording again, asking him to leave a message.

W right probed forward with his fingers, testing the dirt ahead for trip wires. He had no idea what he'd do if he did touch something. What could he possibly do in the dark? He would have no way of knowing what sort of trap it was. Bamber had mentioned snakes, and Doc had said there had been a scorpion trap down in the escape tunnel. What would he do if he touched a snake or a stinging insect? He could feel blood trickling from the wound on his calf each time he moved his left leg but he blanked the pain from his mind, focusing all his attention on the tunnel ahead of him.

He had no sense of time passing, no way of knowing if it was day or night outside. He couldn't see his watch, so for a while he'd tried to mark the passing of time by counting. He'd given up after reaching three thousand. Three thousand seconds was fifty minutes, almost an hour, but he couldn't tell how far he'd crawled during the time he'd been counting. At least his infra-red goggles had held out until he reached the upper level. He would never have been able to get up from the second level without being able to see the trapdoor.

A sudden thought gripped his heart. What if the trapdoor had been replaced? What if Chinh had found the entrance and had put the hatch back? Maybe Wright had already crawled under the trapdoor and was now heading away from it, crawling to oblivion, to a waterless, lightless, lonely death. He shook his head. No, the kitbags were in the tunnel. To miss the hatch he'd have to pass the kitbags the Americans had left. All he had to do was to crawl until he reached the kitbags. Unless Chinh had taken them, figuring he was better off stealing what they contained than waiting for Bamber's half of the hundred-dollar bill. He pushed the thought out of his mind and began counting again, ticking off the seconds as he crawled.

M ay squeezed through the last section of the ventilation tunnel. She could feel the breeze on her face, stronger than before, and hear the sound of birdsong and running water. She pushed the crossbow ahead of herself, then pulled with her arms and wriggled with her legs.

She burst through a veil of spindly white tree roots and hauled herself out into the sunlight. The tunnel opened into the wet clay of a riverbank and some six feet below muddy water rippled past. She slid down towards the river, but grabbed on to a rock and swung her legs to the side until she managed to get a grip on the slippery clay. She dragged herself up and lay on her back on the bank, gulping in lungfuls of clean, fresh air.

W right had counted to two thousand when he saw the patch of light ahead of him. He stopped and stared at the sunbeam that lanced through the dusty air of the tunnel. It looked solid, almost as if it could be sliced with a knife. He started crawling, oblivious to the pain in his leg, all thoughts of booby traps forgotten, his eyes fixed on the small square of light, staring at it as if he feared it would disappear at any moment.

He roared with triumph as he got closer, an animal-like bellow that swelled to fill the tunnel. He'd made it. He'd survived.

He dragged himself up through the opening, and rolled over and over in the sand like a puppy. He stared up at the brilliant blue sky and the white feathery clouds that moved slowly across it, revelling in the fact that he was alive, then rolled on to his front and sat up on his knees, his eyes half closed against the blinding sun. He shaded his eyes with his hand and squinted around, trying to recall where the Mercedes was. If he could find the car, then Chinh, the driver, would help him.

He tried to get to his feet but he had no strength left and fell back on to his hands and knees. He kept his head down and began to crawl, his left leg dragging in the sand. After several minutes he realised he was in the shadow of a rock formation. He clawed himself up the sandstone rock, then twisted around and sat with his back to it, breathing heavily.

He rolled up his trouser leg and examined the wound on his calf. His ripped jeans were stained with blood, but the cut itself wasn't too deep. Wright could see grains of dirt among the cut tissue and he realised there was a good chance of the wound becoming infected if he didn't clean it soon. He didn't have any antiseptic or water, so he put his head close to the cut and spat at it several times, then smeared the saliva around it. He tried to spit again but his mouth was too dry.

'Chinh!' he shouted, but his voice wasn't much more than a hoarse whisper.

The elation that he'd felt as he climbed out into the open began to fade, and Wright's mind started to wander. A series of disjointed images flashed through his mind. Eckhardt's mutilated body in the Battersea tunnel. The blood streaming from Hammack's chest wound. Bamber, the crazed look in his eyes and the knife in his hand. His father, hanging from the beam, his shoes stinking of urine.

Wright's head slumped forward and the jolt woke him up. He slapped his face several times, but barely felt the blows. His whole body seemed to have gone numb. He had to find Chinh. He pushed himself up, using the rock for leverage, and scanned the surrounding vegetation. There were no features that he recognised. He staggered out of the shadow and back into the searing sunlight, shading his eyes with his hands. Once he'd walked some distance from the rocks, he turned to look at them, trying to recall what they'd looked like when he and Bamber had first approached the hatch. He stood staring at the rock formation for almost a minute, then figured that they'd come in from an angle to his left. He looked down to see if there were any footprints, but the wind had obliterated all tracks.

A large black and yellow bird flew overhead and settled in the branches of a spreading tree. Wright staggered towards a gap in the vegetation, wincing each time he put his weight on his left leg. He had to stop after a dozen steps to rest. He wiped his forehead with his hand and it came away sopping wet. Sweat was pouring off him. He put his hands on his hips and took deep breaths, then started walking again.

He heard a noise behind him and whirled around. Bamber was crawling out of the hatch, his knife in his right hand.

'Wright!' he yelled.

Wright felt as if he'd been punched in the solar plexus. Any remaining strength he had seemed to drain away from him and his arms hung uselessly at his sides. He was exhausted. He couldn't run. He couldn't hide. He couldn't fight back. He stood and watched as Bamber hauled himself out of the tunnel.

'It's over, Wright!' shouted Bamber. He walked slowly towards Wright, the knife raised in the air. The steel glinted in the harsh sunlight. The yellow and black bird cawed and took flight.

Wright's heart began to race and he felt a surge of adrenalin. He turned and staggered into the jungle, pushing branches and vines away with his hands, barely managing a fast walk, his left leg dragging, a dead weight. It was like walking through treacle, as if the ground was sucking at his feet, slowing him down so that every step required a superhuman effort. Wright looked over his shoulder. Bamber was gaining. He too was exhausted, but he didn't have an injured leg and he had a knife.

Wright turned and forced himself to jog, though every step was agonising. He could hear Bamber breathing and snorting behind him, and the sound of his feet slapping into the dirt. Wright stumbled over a fallen branch and pitched forward. He fell on to his hands and knees, his chest heaving, tears of frustration and rage stinging his eyes. He pushed himself up. In the distance he could see the Mercedes, its windscreen a mass of reflected sunlight. He got to his feet and staggered towards the car, his arms outstretched as if reaching for it.

His legs became heavier and heavier with each step, but behind him Bamber maintained his pace, breathing like a bull at stud. Wright risked another look over his shoulder. Bamber was only six paces behind him, the knife held high. He was grinning maniacally, his eyes wide and staring, his face smeared with blood and mud like hastily applied warpaint.

Wright fell again. He hit the ground hard and rolled over on to his back, his hands up in front of his chest in an attempt to defend himself against the attack he knew would come. Bamber slowed and stood over Wright, a look of total triumph on his face.

Bamber opened his mouth to speak, but before he could say anything, there was a swooshing sound and something thwacked into his neck, just below his right ear. The look of triumph turned to one of disbelief. His hand clawed up at the object in his neck, but as he touched it his legs folded under him and he fell to his knees. Blood streamed from his neck, and Wright watched in horror as Bamber's mouth worked soundlessly. It was a crossbow bolt, Wright realised. Someone had shot Bamber with a crossbow bolt.

Wright scuttled away on his back like a startled crab, but he couldn't take his eyes off Bamber's face. Bamber reached out a hand as if begging Wright to help him, but then he fell face down into the sand.

Wright rolled on to his front and crawled, head down, towards the car. He had to find Chinh. Blood was pouring from the wound in his leg, but he ignored the pain.

He crawled into a clearing and towards the Mercedes. 'Chinh!' he shouted hoarsely. There was no sign of the driver.

As he got closer to the car, Wright heard a muffled ringing sound. It was his mobile telephone. 'The phone!' he muttered. He could use it to call for help. He struggled to the rear of the car and pulled himself up, grunting with the effort.

He pulled open the boot, then stepped back in horror. Chinh was there, his eyes staring lifelessly up at the sky, dried blood over his chin. The telephone continued to ring. It was inside his suitcase, at the bottom of the boot. Wright grabbed the body by the arms and heaved it out. It dropped on to the dirt with a dull thud. Wright pulled Bamber's metal suitcase out of the boot and placed it next to the body, then opened his own suitcase.

The mobile was under a pair of Levis. He put it to his ear. It was the last person in the world he expected to hear from. Gerry Hunter.

'Nick!' said Hunter. 'Thank God.'

'What the hell do you want, Hunter?' asked Wright.

'The killer,' said Hunter. 'I know who the killer is.'

Wright smiled grimly. He slammed down the boot door. 'Yeah, well, you're about three hours too late,' he said, looking down at Chinh's corpse.

'Nick, shut up and listen, will you?' interrupted Hunter. 'It was Eckhardt's wife. May. She's the killer.'

Wright stiffened. He heard a footfall behind him and turned around, slowly. May Eckhardt was looking at him, a puzzled frown on her face. She was wearing black pyjamas and sandals, and around her neck was a black and white checked scarf. She had her hair tied back and her face was streaked with dirt. In her right hand she carried a loaded crossbow; in her left, the knife that Bamber had been holding.

Gerry Hunter paced up and down the hallway, his mobile phone pressed against his ear. 'Nick? Are you there?' The phone buzzed and clicked. 'Nick?'

'Yes, I'm here.'

'Did you hear what I said? May Eckhardt killed her husband.'

'Are you sure?'

'Positive. She was flown out of Vietnam when she was a kid, holding a set of dogtags. The dogtags belonged to Max Eckhardt.'

There was a longer silence. Then the line went dead.

'Nick? Nick, can you hear me?' There was no reply.

The phone dropped from Wright's hand. 'Why, May?' he asked.

May slung the crossbow on her back and transferred the knife to her right hand.

'He was going to kill you,' she said flatly.

'Not Bamber!' he shouted. 'Your husband. And the rest of them.'

'They killed my father,' she said. 'They tortured him and they cut him to pieces. They deserved to die.'

Wright staggered back against the boot of the Mercedes. 'You were down there? You saw them? You saw what they did?'

'I saw everything,' she said, her voice a dull monotone.

'But you couldn't have been more than . . .'

'I was eight years old,' she said. 'I'd been living down the tunnels with my father for almost a year. My mother had been killed in the fields.' There was a faraway look in her eyes as she relived the memory in her mind. 'I saw her die, too. She was planting rice with a group of women from her village, and a helicopter flew overhead. We were always told to wave at the American helicopters, so that they'd know that we weren't VC.' She put a hand against the black pyjama top. 'The peasants wore tunics like this, but so did the Viet Cong.' She shrugged. 'My mother refused to wave. She stood glaring up at the helicopter, glaring at it as if she wanted it to fall out of the sky. I was at the side of the field, fishing in a canal. The helicopter circled around her, then there were gunshots, lots of gunshots, from the big gun they had inside. There was a black man firing and laughing, and lots of splashes around my mother, like tiny fish jumping, then she fell back and the water became red. The helicopter flew away. They didn't even land to see what they'd done.'

Wright leaned back against the Mercedes and slowly slid to the ground, his legs out in front of him.

'They burned our village a week later, and my father took me down into the tunnels.' She stared at Wright. He expected to see tears, but her eyes were dry. 'You don't want to hear this,' she said.

Wright looked from her face to the knife in her hand, and back to her face. 'I do,' he said.

She swallowed. 'It wasn't so bad down in the tunnels. There were lots of children there. We played games, we had lessons, we helped catch snakes and scorpions for the booby traps. We even helped dig the tunnels. We were small so we could get into difficult places.'

'Weren't you scared?'

She shook her head. 'Never,' she said. 'The tunnels were our homes. We were safe there.'

'Until the Americans came.'

'That's right,' she said. 'Until the Americans came.' The faraway look returned to her eyes and she stared off into the middle distance. Wright wondered if she intended to use the knife in her hand, if she was intent on removing all witnesses to what she'd done. The one thing that gave him hope was that she'd killed Bamber to save his life.

'My father heard them coming, but we didn't have time to use the escape tunnel. He hid me in the wall and told me not to come out, no matter what happened, no matter what I heard. I said I wanted to stay with him but he made me promise. Then he went back to his desk, just as they burst into the chamber. They were like madmen, Nick. Like animals. I could see through a tiny gap in the parachute silk. I saw everything.'

'They said they interrogated your father. That they started out by asking questions.'

She laughed harshly. 'A lie,' she said. 'They had a bloodlust. They just wanted to hurt and to kill. I saw everything they did to him. Everything.'

For the first time she looked as if she was about to cry, but she shook her head, refusing to allow the tears to come. 'Afterwards, they buried him, as if they were finally ashamed of what they'd done. The one called Burrow threw a playing card on my father's body. The ace of spades. Then they left. I waited for hours in the dark, convinced that they would come back for me. Can you imagine what it's like, Nick, to be trapped in a pitch-black room with your dead father, too scared to move?'

She moved closer to Wright. The sun was behind her and Wright had to shade his eyes to look up at her. 'Actually, May, I can,' he said quietly. 'You probably won't believe me, but yes, I can appreciate what you went through.'

She continued to talk as if she hadn't heard what he'd said. 'Eventually I crawled out of my hiding place. I dug the earth away from my father with my bare hands. That's when I found the dogtags. Eckhardt, M. Max Eckhardt. I took the tags and reburied my father.'

'And you waited more than twenty years to find Eckhardt?'

She nodded. 'That's how long it took. And then I had

to get him to tell me who his friends were, who he'd served with in Vietnam.'

'And to do that, you had to marry him?'

'I did what I had to do to avenge my father.'

'How could you do that?'

'How could I do what? Seduce him? Sleep with him? Every time I opened my legs to the man, I thought of what he'd done to my father and what I would one day do to him. The hatred kept me going.'

'For more than two decades?'

She shrugged. 'How long it took didn't matter. All that mattered was that my father's death was avenged. Now it's almost done. Soon I'll be able to rest.'

She knelt down and Wright flinched. She smiled, and used the knife to tear a slit up the leg of his trousers. She put the knife on the ground, then reached behind her back. Her hand reappeared with a green plastic pack. It was Doc's medical kit. She took out a piece of cotton wool and a bottle of iodine and cleaned his wound, smiling again when he winced with pain.

As she placed a dressing on the wound, Wright cleared his throat. 'May Eckhardt, I am placing you under arrest for the murder of Max Eckhardt.' The words sounded oddly stilted and he stumbled over the word 'murder'.

May smiled and brushed a stray lock of muddy hair from her face. She picked up her knife and slid it into its scabbard.

'You are not obliged to say anything, but—'

She placed a hand on his chin and kissed him softly on the cheek. 'Goodbye, Nick,' she said. 'Take care.'

She turned and walked away without a backward look. Wright slumped down against the wheel of the

Mercedes and watched as the jungle swallowed her up.

His mobile phone began to ring again. He groped for it and put it to his ear. It was Tommy Reid. 'Hell's bells, Nick, where've you been?' asked his partner. 'I've been trying to get hold of you for hours. What have you been doing, fooling around with some gorgeous Asian babe?'

Wright's arm fell to the side and the mobile phone knocked against a small rock. He could still hear Reid talking, his voice buzzing like a trapped wasp. Wright threw back his head and began to laugh, louder and louder, until the laughter became an ugly, pain-filled scream that echoed around the jungle, quietening even the insects and birds.

D ean Burrow removed his reading glasses and surveyed the cheering crowd. There were more than five thousand people, and the sound of their clapping and shouting vibrated through his body like an earthquake tremor. He could understand why rock stars became addicted to performing; nothing came close to the sensation of being on the receiving end of the adulation of thousands of people. Placards praising his virtues and huge posters of his face were displayed at strategic intervals, placed to obtain maximum television coverage from the cameras that were scattered around the auditorium.

It had been the best speech Burrow had ever given; modest but farsighted, laying out his vision of a united, prosperous, caring America. Jody Meacher had done him proud. The only minor criticism that Burrow had raised was that the speech seemed more suited to a presidential campaign, but Meacher had just smiled at that. Both men knew that the Vice President's job was just a stepping stone.

Burrow put up a hand to acknowledge the cheers, then turned to look at his wife. She smiled on cue, the pride and admiration pouring out of her, a look as practised as any of Burrow's gestures. Flashes went off as the assembled photographers captured the image. That would be the one splashed across the morning editions of the world's newspapers. That or the picture of the President shaking his hand, congratulating him on becoming the second most powerful man in the world.

The cheering began to die down and Burrow put his glasses on. He had considered wearing contact lenses, but Meacher had disagreed, pointing out that the glasses gave Burrow a more serious air, adding maturity but not detracting from his looks. The time would come when Burrow would want to lose the glasses and some of the grey that was spreading through his hair, but that time was almost a decade away. Burrow had ceded to Meacher, knowing that when it came to image-making, Meacher was second to none.

Burrow looked across at the bank of television cameras that were transmitting the event around the world. It was all about image now. Getting elected was a matter of presentation, of media manipulation, of not making mistakes, and Jody Meacher would be there to guide him every step of the way. Burrow scanned the crowd as the cheering swelled again. Meacher's enthusiastic young team scattered through the audience would keep the applause going for a full two minutes before giving him the chance to continue his speech. Meacher wasn't in the auditorium, he was in an office upstairs watching the television coverage on a bank of monitors.

Burrow held up both hands as if trying to quieten the audience down. He knew it was futile; Meacher had stipulated the two minutes at rehearsal and there was nothing Burrow could do to change the programme. The gesture showed modesty, though, humility, even. Burrow smiled and gave a small shrug as if finally accepting that there was nothing he could do to stop the applause.

He waved at the audience. It was a good mixture: nobody too old, nobody too young, nobody too black, nobody too disabled. A camera-friendly melting pot that showed how all America was behind the new Vice President.

Suddenly Burrow stiffened. An unsmiling face glared at him with undisguised hatred, an Oriental woman with high cheekbones and shoulder-length hair. Her eyes bored into his as if she was staring into his soul. Burrow swallowed. The crowd around the woman cheered and waved, but she sat motionless, her lips set tight, her arms folded across her chest.

Burrow looked around to see if any of his Secret Service agents had noticed her. There were six of them, all in dark suits with radio earpieces and dark glasses, strategically placed around the stage. They were all scanning the audience but none appeared to be looking in the direction of the woman. There was nothing he could do to attract their attention, not with the world's cameras aimed at him.

He forced himself to smile and turned back to face the audience. The woman had gone. He couldn't even find the place in the crowd where she'd been. Burrow's smile widened and he raised both arms in a victory salute. The cheering welled around him. Maybe he'd imagined her. Besides, he had nothing to worry about. He was the Vice President of the United States of America and only one man in the country was better protected. He had nothing to fear from a sullen-faced Oriental woman. Nothing.

STEPHEN LEATHER

THE BOMBMAKER

It wasn't an especially large bomb . . .

Ten years ago, Andrea Hayes was the best master bombmaker in the business. Young, beautiful and deadly, she was the favourite of her Irish republican masters. Then it all went wrong. Five children were killed when disruption was all that was intended. It all became too much, and she turned away from the trade . . .

Now, a new Andrea Hayes lives a safe suburban life, with her loving husband and young daughter, safe in the knowledge that her past is another country. But then her daughter is kidnapped by persons unknown and the past has come knocking.

As Andrea gets blackmailed into returning to her craft and building a bomb that dwarfs any planted by the IRA, a faceless mastermind is working behind the scenes to pull off one of the most daring scams in world history . . .

'The denouement of the novel is as gripping as its beginning . . . This is as hi-tech and as world-class as the thriller genre gets'   *Express on Sunday*

HODDER AND STOUGHTON PAPERBACKS

STEPHEN LEATHER

THE DOUBLE TRAP

Masterly plotting . . . rapid-fire prose' *Sunday Express*

'A fine tale, brilliantly told' *Oxford Times*

The assassin – the world's most successful contract killer – ice-cool, accurate and elusive. An anonymous professional with a unique calling card – one bullet in the head and one in the chest for each of his targets.

The Judas goat – an ex-member of the SAS, Mike Cramer is the perfect sacrificial bait. When the FBI discover the next name on the assassin's hitlist, Cramer is set up to take his place.

The wild card – Cramer's past has caught up with him. Ex-IRA extremist Dermott Lynch blames Cramer for his lover's death and he's out for revenge.

As Cramer trains for the most dangerous mission in his career, Lynch hunts down his sworn enemy. And the unknown assassin silently closes in on his target.

The players are in position for the final deadly game . . .

HODDER AND STOUGHTON PAPERBACKS

STEPHEN LEATHER

HUNGRY GHOST

Ex-SAS hired killing machine Geoff Howells is brought out of retirement and sent to Hong Kong, his brief to assassinate a Chinese mafia leader, Simon Ng. But Howells finds Ng is well guarded, and devises a complicated plan to reach his victim – only to find himself the next target . . .

Hong Kong policeman Patrick Dugan has been held back in his career because of his connections – his sister is married to Simon Ng. When the Ng's daughter Sophie is kidnapped, and Simon herself disappears, Dugan is caught up in a series of violent events and an international spying intrigue that has run out of control . . . .

Tough writing, relentless storytelling and a searingly evocative background of Hong Kong in the aftermath of Tiananmen Square make *Hungry* Ghost a compulsive read.

'The sort of book that could easily take up a complete weekend – and be time really well spent . . . as topical as today's headlines' *Bolton Evening News*

'Very complicated. Fun' *Daily Telegraph*

HODDER AND STOUGHTON PAPERBACKS

STEPHEN LEATHER

THE LONG SHOT

'In the top rank of thriller writers' *Jack Higgins*

The plan is so complex, the target so well protected that the three snipers have to rehearse the killing in the seclusion of the Arizona desert.

Cole Howard of the FBI knows he has only days to prevent the audacious assassination. But he doesn't know who the target is. Or where the crack marksmen will strike.

Former SAS sergeant Mike Cramer is also on the trail, infiltrating the Irish community in New York as he tracks down Mary Hennessy, the ruthless killer who tore his life apart.

Unless Cramer and Howard agree to co-operate, the world will witness the most spectacular terrorist camp of all time . . .

'The Long Shot consolidates Leather's position in the top rank of thriller writers. An ingenious plot, plenty of action and solid, believable characters – wrapped up in taut snappy prose that grabs your attention by the throat . . . A top-notch thriller which whips the reader along at breakneck speed'

Yorkshire Post

HODDER AND STOUGHTON PAPERBACKS